NEW YO... ...RIDE THE STORM

# KAREN
# CHANCE

A CASSIE
PALMER NOVEL

# Brave the
# Tempest

"Chance is a true storyteller." —CHARLAINE HARRIS

**BERKLEY**

S ▷ EAN

ISBN 978-1-101-99000-1

9 781101 990001

5 0 7 9 9

# Brave the Tempest

## A CASSIE PALMER NOVEL

## KAREN CHANCE

BERKLEY
New York

BERKLEY
An imprint of Penguin Random House LLC
1745 Broadway, New York, NY 10019

ISBN: 9781101990001

First Edition: July 2019

Printed in the United States of America
1   3   5   7   9   10   8   6   4   2

Cover design by Adam Auerbach
Cover art by Larry Rostant

# Chapter One

The small pouf was a little overly excited. It was jade green velvet, and a bit worn in the center, where years of feet had left a permanent divot. But the gold silk tassels at the corners were still fat and sassy, and the little round feet were polished to a high shine.

Not to mention the personality, which was, um, happy.

"I think it's trying to hump your leg," Billy told me.

"It is not!"

"Okay," he said, eyeing the little thing warily. It was currently up on its back two feet, jumping up and down like an overly emotional puppy. Probably because nobody used poufs these days and it wanted out of the small shop we were in.

"It's jumping," I told him. "It's excited."

"Oh, it's excited all right."

"Billy!" I whispered, and glanced around. "There are children in here!"

Normally, that wouldn't have mattered, since Billy Joe had been among the life-challenged for something like a century and a half now, and ghosts didn't have to watch what they said. But the children in question were part of the Pythian Court and were all seers of one variety or another. Not that all of them could see Billy—gifts differ—but some could, and more could hear him.

"I'm just saying, maybe a perverted footstool ain't the best thing to have around the palace."

I frowned. Our current living arrangements were a sore spot. "It's not a palace. We don't live in a palace. It's a penthouse—"

"Which covers a whole floor and is full of marble and shit."

"—and I told the girls they could pick out their own stuff."

It was the least I could do, considering that their former furniture had gone up in a fireball, like their former house. Now *that* had been a palace, an old charmer of a mansion in London full of priceless antiques and crystal chandeliers, a fit home for the Pythian Court. Unlike a still mostly empty penthouse in a tacky Vegas hotel.

Some days—all right, most days—I wondered if I'd ever get the hang of this Pythia stuff. "Chief Seer of the supernatural world" sounded like a great title, until you saw the job description. Not that I had.

I think they were afraid to show it to me.

My name is Cassie Palmer, and I'd been Pythia for four months. Four very long months. You'd think by now that I'd have some kind of a grip, and I did—sort of. I was still alive, which lately felt like an accomplishment in itself. But elegant? Imposing? One of the awesome Pythias of legend who decided the fates of kings and never blinked?

I caught sight of myself in a large standing mirror that wasn't standing so much as mincing by, reflecting back a wobbly image of a young blonde with flyaway curls, worried blue eyes, and a T-shirt and jeans combo. The T-shirt was pretty cool, being red with black crossed swords on the front and a caption that read, "As You Can See, the Assassins Failed." But there was a spaghetti sauce stain from lunch on the jeans. I tried to pull down the tee to hide it, but it wasn't long enough and bounced back up.

I sighed. The little pouf humped my leg some more. There was probably a metaphor in there somewhere, but I didn't get a chance to look for it.

Because a small girl of maybe five had come up and started tugging on Billy's jeans.

He jumped—not surprisingly, since the "jeans" were just a projection. It was all Billy, like the red ruffled shirt and the cowboy hat that completed the ensemble, and the cigarettes he smoked because lung cancer wasn't an issue for him anymore. So she'd basically just grabbed part of his spirit and started tugging on it, which, yeah.

I'd probably jump, too.

But Billy was surprisingly good with kids, maybe because he'd come from a large Irish family back in the day. Or maybe because it was fun to have someone to interact with besides me. He went down on one knee to see what the child was trying to show him.

"Emily, right?" Billy said, and she nodded. There were so many kids around these days, I kept getting their names confused, but he always knew.

"For you." She held up a book so big that she needed two hands to lift it.

"For me?" Billy smiled and ruffled her hair. Some of it even moved, so he was exerting some power. "And why would you want me to have that, sweetheart?"

"Look." She tried putting the massive tome down on the pouf, but the little thing was going ballistic. It didn't seem to like the book, maybe because it was a rival in the get-out-of-dodge camp and the pouf was going home with us, goddamn it. Or maybe it was something else, I thought, getting a bad feeling suddenly.

"Uh, Emily—" I began, but it was too late. She must have worked the heavy buckles on the sides open before she came over, so all she had to do was drop the thing on the floor and flip up the cover—

"Oh, shit!" I said, earning me a disapproving glance.

"Rhea says you have to say 'poo,'" Emily told me seriously.

"Oh, poo," I said, and pulled her behind me, because that—

Was a seriously messed-up book.

"Ghost," Emily said happily, peering around my legs.

"Yes, there's a ghost in there," I agreed, looking around for something—anything—to use to shut the damned thing. I couldn't use my hands, because the boiling mass of magic—dark, by the feel of it—swirling around in there was not a good thing to touch. Not for anyone, but especially not for me.

Touch clairvoyance is a bitch, and while I wasn't sensitive enough for everything to trigger it like some poor people, that . . .

Would probably do it.

"Oh, *poo*!" I said, a little more forcefully, because the ghost had just noticed us. What looked like black smoke started to leak out of the book's pages, and Billy predictably freaked. Vengeful ghosts were not something to play around with.

"Shut it! Shut it!"

"With what?" There was nothing within reach.

"With your shoe! Take off your shoe!"

"I'm trying!" And I was. But instead of my usual Keds, I'd decided to be fancy today and was wearing cute little open-toed sandals with a buckled strap. One that was stubbornly not. Coming. Off.

"Just rip it!" Billy yelled.

"It's elastic!" I told him, hopping around on one foot.

"If it's elastic, then just pull it off!"

"It's tough elastic!"

And then somebody slammed the book closed for us.

I looked up, shoe in hand, to see the shop owner holding a heavy wooden walking stick. He had muttonchops; jowls; small, piercing blue eyes; and incongruously pink cheeks that would have been perfect on Santa, only he didn't look like Santa. He looked like what he was: a guy who ran a magical secondhand shop and intended to make a sale.

"Gaylord!" he told me, on a little explosion of air.

"Uh. What?"

"Gaylord. That's what we call him. He's a rotter." He bent over the book and buckled the buckles. "I can show you some much finer tomes, Lady, including several first editions."

"What's wrong with that one?" I asked, because I'd never seen anything like it. I knew ghosts could haunt things as well as places—I was wearing proof of that around my neck—but that . . . hadn't felt like a haunting.

At least, not a normal one.

"Oh, nothing," he said, waving it away. "They get like that when you leave them in too long."

"Leave them in . . . where?"

He looked at me through little half-moon spectacles that, again, would have looked good on Santa. Only the eyes behind them weren't nearly so nice. And neither was the oily smile that he clearly thought was charming.

"Sorcerers sometimes imprison ghosts in books, to use their souls to power an enchantment," he informed me. "They typically let them free after a while, once they no longer need a perfect lock or an unbreakable cypher or what have you. But sometimes they forget."

I swallowed hard and stared at the book. "You're saying that somebody didn't let Gaylord . . . out?"

"No. The mage died, y'see, quite unexpectedly, and his relatives inherited the house. Only they had no use for the contents and sold the lot to me. Some good items—most went fast, as the better sort usually does. But Gaylord here—"

"But if the sorcerer died," I interrupted, because I didn't care about his stock issues. "Shouldn't that have broken the enchantment?"

"For a regular spell, certainly," he agreed. "Once there was no more magic being funneled into it. But Gaylord isn't a spell. He's a power source, bound to the book with no one to set him free, since the only one who could have done it is dead."

I stared. "That's horrible!"

"Yes, indeed," the shop owner agreed. "Ruins the re-sale value."

Billy Joe whispered something rude and stared at the book, probably remembering his time in a necklace at the bottom of the Mississippi.

Even unbound ghosts could only go so far from their resting places. For most, that was a graveyard, where the life energy shed by visitors kept the hungry ghosts going. But for some, like Billy, it was an enchanted item, like a talisman, that collected enough power to let a ghost survive. Although survival kind of loses its luster when you're stuck in the middle of nowhere, buried underneath a river.

Billy had been lucky; some fishermen had trawled up the gaudy ruby necklace he lived in, which had eventually ended up in the magical junk shop where I'd stumbled across it. But what if they hadn't? And what if, instead of being able to explore the area for fifty miles or so around his home—his usual range when I wasn't topping him up—Billy had been trapped inside, all alone, for who knew how long? Only to slowly realize that the person who had put him there was dead, and that he'd never get out?

I felt a hard shiver go down my spine.

I guessed Billy did, too, because he rippled all over, just once, like a gust of wind had blown through him.

"Cassie—"

"I'll take it," I told the salesman, who had started toward a large bookcase, the tome under his arm, but at that he turned around.

And, suddenly, I was looking at Santa Claus after all. The man was positively beaming. "Oh, of course, of course. So useful for . . . any number of things. I'll add it to the pile, shall I?"

He looked at the counter, which a delighted bunch of little girls had already piled high. I nodded, and he started off again, only to have me call him back a second time. Because the pouf was losing its tiny cotton mind.

"And that," I said. What the hell. I'd gift it to one of my bodyguards if it was too much of a nuisance.

"Excellent choice," the salesman said, his eyes gleaming, and hurried off before I changed my mind.

"Thanks," Billy told me quietly.

I nodded and bent down to pat the little hassock, which started running around in circles excitedly, as if it somehow knew it had found a home.

"Lady?" That was Rhea, my acolyte.

Rhea was in jeans today, too, having been persuaded—not that it had taken a lot of talking—to give up the white, Victorian-looking dresses that the Pythian Court had worn for more than a century. I'd been told they were an improvement on what had gone before, but found that hard to believe. The girls were now dressed in shorts, because Vegas in the summer is scorching, and various brightly colored tees with cartoon characters on them, because they were kids.

Rhea, on the other hand, was nineteen, and could choose her own clothes. And, somehow, she'd continued to look serene and otherworldly despite the lack of traditional attire. Her long, dark hair was in a messy chignon today, and her jeans had been paired with a soft blue lace shirt with a high neck.

If you didn't know her, you'd never guess that the neckline was to cover the scars from a recent "accident" in which she'd been held captive while a dark mage tried to blackmail me with her life. So Rhea had taken what she'd thought was her only option. And my timid, soft-voiced, sweet-faced acolyte who wouldn't hurt a fly had *cut her own throat* on his knife blade to ensure that he didn't have anything left to bargain with.

Yeah.

People aren't always what they seem.

Only, at the moment, Rhea was looking a little less timid and a little more outraged, which probably meant that something was up with the kids. She was the type who would never stand up for herself, but was a lioness in defense of the talented tots who made up the court. She had, after all, been one herself once.

"What is—oh." I stopped, after glancing behind her. Because of course. "Hilde?"

Rhea nodded, looking over her shoulder at my not-at-all timid, frequently-made-*other-people*-timid acolyte Hildegarde.

Hilde was . . . something else.

The exact opposite of Rhea's soft motherliness, Hilde could have been a Valkyrie in another existence. Admittedly, the cap of silver white curls and the wrinkles—not many, despite her almost two centuries, because the body was, um, sturdy, and filled them out—might have worked against her, but the 'tude would have gotten her in anyway. Hilde was a force of freaking nature.

She'd joined the Pythian Court only recently, coming out of retirement to return to the organization she'd belonged to many, many years ago, before her sister was chosen as Pythia instead of her. Gertie had gone on to have an illustrious career and to train my predecessor, Agnes. Hilde, on the other hand, had eventually gotten married, popped out a couple of kids, and had several careers of her own. And then retired, never mentioning to a soul along the way, including her three husbands, that she'd never really left the court at all.

She'd become a fail-safe, one of only two currently living, who were former acolytes selected by the Pythias to take over the court in case of emergency. And since an emergency might include an attack on the court and anybody supporting it, the fail-safes' existence had to be kept quiet. Nobody knew who they were or even that they existed at all until needed, and it was up to the fail-safes themselves to decide when that might be.

Since the whole supernatural world was currently at war, and the Pythian Court in London had recently blown up, and the hotel and casino we were currently calling home had been attacked by an army of dark mages, Hildegarde had finally decided—you know, this looks a lot like an emergency.

And unlike Abigail, the other fail-safe appointed by Agnes, Hilde no longer had young kids, or even young grandkids, to go home to when the immediate threat was over. I suspected that she'd been a little bored, messing about with her garden when she'd always led a very busy life. And then we came along, a court, as she saw it, in serious need of straightening out. Hildegarde had found her calling.

I still wasn't sure if I was happy about that or not.

But I was pretty damned sure that Rhea wasn't. I doubted that Hilde had noticed, because Hilde rarely noticed anything less subtle than a bat to the head, but Rhea was not on board with some of the changes she'd been making around the court. Not on board at all.

"What now?" I sighed.

"I am sorry, Lady," Rhea said, dropping a curtsy. And damned if she didn't make it look elegant even in jeans. "But I think you should hear this."

"Hear what?" I asked, only to have Hilde's booming laughter float across the room from where she was holding forth over a display case.

I looked at Billy; he looked back at me. "You're Pythia, kid," he reminded me.

As if I could forget.

I pulled up my big girl panties and went off to see what had Rhea looking flushed and bothered.

"No! You do not age the knife," Hilde was saying to a cluster of the older girls while waving around a wicked-looking weapon. "It is metal. It will take a very long time—and thus a great deal of your energy—to do it any harm."

"Then what do you do?" One of the oldest, who was maybe twelve, asked. Her name was Belvia, because magical families hadn't gotten the memo about modern names, but everybody called her Belle. Some of the other girls looked scared or intimidated, which wasn't surprising considering the array of weapons in front of them and everything they'd been through lately, but she was grimly determined.

I felt my own face fall into a frown.

No kid should have to look like that.

But Hildegarde regarded her approvingly. "You age the hand *holding* the knife." She thought about it. "Unless it's fey, in which case you're probably better off aging the knife. Those bastards live forever."

"Hilde," I said brightly. "Can I see you for a minute?"

Hilde didn't curtsy, but she agreed affably enough. "When I come back, we'll discuss magical restraints and how to get out of them," she promised the girls.

I led her out of the shop, to the cracked sidewalk in front where several of my vamp bodyguards were trying to look unobtrusive. Armani suits and Gucci loafers were working against them, as were the chiseled, model-worthy profiles. Mircea—the master vampire who'd loaned them to me—normally worked in diplomacy, and he'd discovered centuries ago that his own good looks were a useful tool. So, he often Changed handsome men.

I'd once asked him why he bothered, when a glamourie could make anybody look good. He'd just laughed and said yes, but that men who were attractive from birth knew it and had a confidence that was virtually impossible to teach. They also ventured in where angels feared to tread, because they were used to getting away with things.

I'd also asked him why he never Changed women, but

didn't get an answer there. As the one-time diplomat to the North American Vampire Senate, Mircea's secrets had secrets. I'd found out the hard way that I actually preferred when I didn't know what he was up to.

The guards smiled at me, and one stubbed out a cigarette before they disappeared inside. Not that it mattered; they could hear us perfectly well from there or from a couple blocks away. But that sort of thing was intended to put people at ease.

They shouldn't have bothered; Hilde struck me as the type who'd never been ill at ease in her life—and who never let anyone else take the lead.

"You're going to tell me the initiates are too young," she began, before I could get a word out.

"Because they are! And they've just been through a trauma—"

"Exactly so." She looked at me kindly, but with resolve. "It's been made very clear that our enemies will not take their youth into consideration, other than to view them as easy targets. They have to be able to defend themselves."

"*We* have to defend them. It's our job—"

"And what are we to use to accomplish this job, hm?" she demanded, her head tilting. "There's you—and you're always away, battling gods; there's me, and while I am certainly formidable, I'm not as young as I used to be; there's a bunch of vampires, God help us, who're good enough for the simple things, I'll grant you, but—"

"They helped!" I said, remembering the Battle on the Drag, as it had come to be known, the recent assault on our home base by several hundred dark mages.

"Yes, they did," Hilde agreed. "But it was your ability with the Pythian power that saved the day. We must have more adepts."

"We have Rhea—"

Hilde harrumphed. I stared. I'd never heard anyone actually do that before.

"Something might be made of that girl eventually, it's true, if she has anything of her parents in her," Hilde said. "But right now, she's almost as ignorant as the rest of 'em. They need training, not coddling."

She sounded like somebody else I knew. John Pritkin was a war mage who had helped to protect me when I stumbled into this crazy new life—well, eventually. Our first meeting had not gone well, and neither had a bunch of subsequent ones. But when he finally figured out that I was serious—that, untrained as I was, I was trying, god-damn it—he got on board.

And when Pritkin gets on board, he *really* gets on board. The guy doesn't know what half measures are. Which had resulted in me hating my life more than I already did when he put me through a training regimen that would have done a marine proud.

Not everyone had agreed with that approach. Mircea, for one, preferred the wrap-her-in-cotton-balls-and-sit-a-ton-of-vamps-on-her method, which, to be fair, had helped me out more than once. But Pritkin's training had increased my self-esteem and my belief that I could maybe, possibly, eventually, kind of do this, and had al-lowed me to save myself.

So I understood where Hilde was coming from, I really did. But there was one crucial difference. I was an adult and a Pythia, while the girls . . .

I looked back through the shop window and didn't see warriors. I saw kids playing with toys and running around, finding new treasures with which to decorate their currently spartan bedrooms to make them their own. And laughing and talking in spite of everything, es-pecially the little ones, because they were resilient, as children tend to be.

But there was a limit to what anyone could take.

And, suddenly, a huge surge of protectiveness swept over me.

I'd had to be an adult before I was ready, and it had left me with more scars than I could name. I passionately wanted these little girls to be able to be kids, as I never had. To live for just a few years free of worry, to be able to laugh and run and play, instead of looking over their shoulders every few minutes, lying awake at night riddled with fear, and walking on eggshells.

War or no bloody war.

I turned back around and realized that Hilde was

watching me, and that her eyes had softened. "You've a good heart," she told me. "But you can't protect everyone all the time. Neither can I."

"No," I admitted. "I can't. Which is why we need help."

# Chapter Two

"You're sure this is it?" I asked as Hilde paid the cabbie. We were supposed to be here to see about getting some coven girls for the court, but I didn't see any—or much of anything else. Unless you counted miles of unforgiving desert and a merciless sun beating down like it had forgotten summer was over.

"It's here," a pink-haired witch said, and piled out of the front seat of the cab.

Her name was Saffy, short for Saphronia, which she hated, maybe because I'd never seen a name less suited to its owner. There was nothing old-fashioned about her. She had blond roots under short pink hair, a septum ring, and a half sleeve of tats, at least two of which were magical, because I occasionally saw them moving. She'd been inside the shop helping with the kids, instead of outside with the vamps keeping an eye on the local junkies, but that was by choice.

Saffy was a badass.

She'd proven that recently by helping to save the court during the Battle on the Drag. She and a handful of other witches had shown up and taken on a whole army of dark mages, at least long enough for me, Rhea, and some reporters who'd been caught in the cross fire to get out. The local coven leaders had afterward lent her little posse to my court, because, as they put it, I obviously needed some competent help.

That hadn't gone over well with the Silver Circle, the world's leading magical organization, which traditionally guarded the Pythian Court. Or with Mircea's vamps, who had protested both the mage *and* witch additions to the household. But they hadn't protested as loudly as I'd expected.

I think the attack had rattled even them.

Despite her badass demeanor, Saffy had proven really good with the kids. She made their crayon drawings move, delighting the younger girls, and helped some of the older ones put rinses of various colors on their hair. She'd also let Belle wear her punked-out leather vest back to the hotel while we came out here, leaving her in a tank top, jeans, a wrist full of charms, and some biker boots.

And black nail polish on the finger she was currently poking at the air with.

"I can wait," the taxi driver offered, watching her worriedly. And then glancing around at the sparse scrub and some vultures on a hill, looking at us hopefully from atop their latest carcass.

"No, no, that's fine," Hilde assured him. "We're going hiking."

The man took in Hilde's smart crepe de chine flowered dress, sensible low-heeled shoes, and old-lady support hose. She had a purse that matched the shoes, in bright, candy apple pink, and a little pearl brooch that kept the ruffled bosom on the dress properly in place. She did not have a hat, but looked like the kind of woman who should have a hat, or at least an Ascot-worthy fascinator.

"What?" the man said.

Hilde sighed and waved a hand at him, and his concerned eyes went blank. "Go back to work and forget about us," she told him shortly, and the man obligingly drove off, the cab bumping a little on the rocky soil because we'd left the blacktop behind a few minutes ago.

"Is that what everyone does?" I asked, worried about the man's suddenly slack-jawed, bespelled face. If every witch who needed a ride zapped him, I had to wonder what the long-term effects might be. But Saffy didn't seem concerned.

"Most of us don't take taxis," she assured me, still poking at the air.

"What do you take?"

"A portal from town."

"Then why didn't we do that?"

That got me a look I didn't understand from black-rimmed eyes. "Because none of them would recognize you. They're spelled to keep out unknowns. It's a security thing, like changing the location on a regular basis."

"Changing?" I frowned.

Portals had to be licensed out the wazoo, and the license had to include the location, from fixed point A to fixed point B, because allowing people to just appear anywhere they wanted would make law enforcement impossible. And that was even more true since the war. Unless . . .

"Saffy, we are talking about *legal* portals, right?"

" 'Legal' by whose definition?"

*"Saffy—"*

That won me another look. "If you're going to rep the whole magical community, you have to understand that the world doesn't revolve around the Silver Circle," she told me. "No matter what they think!"

"I know that; that's why we're here."

"You think you know, but you were born into a world the Circle controls—"

"I was born into a world the vampires control," I corrected her, because I hadn't been one of the clairvoyants identified early and popped into the Pythian Court for training. Instead, a greedy mob boss of a vampire had co-opted me into his shabby little court and used my gift as a way to make him more of the money he craved.

It hadn't been a fun life for a kid.

Of course, it hadn't been a fun life for anyone else, either.

Tony was a dick.

"That's rather like an agnostic saying they were born into a secular family when they live in the United States," Hilde said, because she'd never met an argument she didn't like. "Perhaps their parents didn't take them to church, but the culture of Christianity pervaded their upbringing whether they realized it or not. Everything from the holidays they celebrate to the curse words they use revolves around the Judeo-Christian religions."

"I'm not sure I get the point," I told her. I also wasn't

sure we'd come to the right place, and sweat was starting to drip down my back.

"The point," she told me, "is that the Circle won their war with the covens centuries ago and have been able to shape the overall magical culture ever since. And while I'm sure the effect was less pervasive at a vampire's court, if it had to do with magic, it was likely still done the Circle's way."

Saffy nodded angrily. "They did their best to erase coven practices, like they tried to erase the covens themselves. But it didn't work!"

"I know that—"

She cut me off. "No, you *think* you know. Now you *really* do."

And before I could ask what she meant, reality bent around us, the desert colors all slurred together, and the heat was replaced by a wash of cool air, deep and dark and mountain-chilled.

Maybe because we were suddenly standing in what looked a lot like the inside of a mountain. A huge, hollowed-out one, leaving a sprawling, cave-like area with dark, reddish brown walls rising up to a massive dome far overhead, like a mighty stone cathedral. It should have been impressive; it should have been breathtaking.

But my breath was already being stolen by something else.

"What . . . *is* this?" I asked, spinning slowly around.

I was looking in all directions, because we'd just materialized inside a huge circle of portals.

Some were on the ground nearby, *thrum thrum thrumming* hard enough to make my whole body shake. Others hovered in midair or overhead, forming a spotted dome half the size of a football field and multiple stories high. One through which people—and things, and things that might be people—were hurrying, and sometimes flying, at an alarming rate.

Something came at me in a rush of huge, bat-like wings, but Saffy jerked me to the side before I saw it clearly. And before I ended up as road kill, although I barely noticed. I was too busy gawping like a tourist, because I'd seen portals before, and even been in a few. But nothing like this.

Nothing even *close* to this.

It was the Grand Central Station of portals, I thought, in awe.

They were all different colors: one electric blue; another neon green; one pink enough to rival Hilde's handbag; another a brilliant, sunny yellow; there was a purple so rich it looked like it was laced with glitter, a white so bright it hurt my eyes, and an ebony so dark that no light seemed to escape it at all, like a black hole had opened up inside the room.

There had to be thirty of them, maybe more. I couldn't tell because, while some were at least two stories tall, others were as small as my doubled fists, just tiny things, and hard to spot in all the moving light. It cascaded down from the largest as if through stained glass, increasing the cathedral-like feel of the place. And throwing a moving, watery rainbow onto the crowd, while the combined energy field vibrated the rock beneath our feet.

But the fact that the portals were literally powerful enough to move a mountain wasn't the most impressive thing about them. That would be the fact that they were fritzing and sparking with tiny, lightning-like filaments, sometimes fighting with each other, and occasionally arcing away to blow off this person's hat or to shock that person's backside. The wind generated by all that energy was also blowing people's hair and stuff around, causing them to clutch their belongings tightly as they plowed ahead.

I could see it all, because the portals were just giant, 2-D, semitransparent circles hanging in the air, instead of being projected against anything. Passengers entered them from the interior of the circle and exited from the opposite side, often at the same time. That sometimes made it appear as if a man went in and a woman came out, causing me to do a few double takes.

And then to do another when a portal—roughly human height and bright green—suddenly winked out, causing a fey-looking woman barreling ahead and carrying a load of packages to hit a large . . . something . . . that had just emerged from the other side.

She went down, her packages scattering everywhere, while the large shaggy something, with a head the size and shape of a buffalo's, turned to regard her in surprise. And then to help her up with a giant paw and assist her in picking up her belongings. She shoved bright purple hair out of her face and thanked him prettily.

I just stood there and blinked at them.

"May I have your attention, please." The announcement cut through the cacophony, loud enough to make me jump. "May I have your attention, please. We are sorry to announce that service to Lalaquaie, Avery, and the Green Mountains has been disrupted. This is due to a roaming party having been sighted in the area. Management apologizes for any inconvenience this may cause."

A groan went through the space, and a bunch of people broke off from the crowd and went grumbling back out of the circle of light, looking like travelers who had just missed their train.

Which is basically what they were, I realized.

It really *was* Grand Central, or at least the magical, highly illegal, the-Circle-would-shit-a-brick-if-they-saw-this equivalent.

"Where are they getting all the power?" I yelled at Saffy, while it blew my hair in my face. "I didn't think there was a ley line sink anywhere near here!"

That was the only thing I knew of that could fuel something like this. The ley lines, usually used for quick transport by people with the stomach for it, were rivers of magical power that flowed around the earth. Their source was debated, but one thing was sure: when a number of them crossed at the same point, they created pools of energy that were a coveted resource in the magical world. But the only place like that nearby was on the other side of Vegas, not to mention being in the Circle's hands.

Saffy said something, but I couldn't hear her. It was deafening this close. She must have thought so, too, because she was already tugging me away, out of the cathedral-like central space, and into . . .

"What is *this*?" I asked, stumbling forward slightly, because the floor was uneven and I was too busy staring around to pay attention. The portal light was still bright here, but no longer blinding. Allowing me to see that the main travel hub bisected a long, rock-cut corridor lined with shops, cafés, restaurants, and—

"What's *that*?" I said. And hurried across the crowded causeway to a shop framed by large, glowing crystal formations in bright pink and yellow, where dwarves were hammering out something on giant anvils.

The anvils were huge, as were the hammers they were using. But scattered around the cave-like shop, behind force fields covering depressions in the rock, were the most exquisite, delicate creations imaginable. Gorgeous necklaces in quivering gold flakes that scintillated fascinatingly when you breathed on them. Daggers of chased silver set with what had to be talisman jewels, because they boiled with enough power to raise the hair on my arms, and I wasn't even that close. Chalices covered with runes that flashed different colors as various sorts of people passed by, one of which had an almost human-looking eye that opened and blinked at me when I accidentally brushed the pedestal it was on.

I reached out, unthinking, to steady it, and Hilde grabbed my arm. "You bond with it, you buy the nasty thing," she warned me, as a dwarf rubbed his hands on his apron and came hurrying over.

But the cup righted itself on its own, and I was already caught in wonder by the next shop in line.

"Oh, wow," I murmured, running over to stare through the huge, force field–like front window, behind which a trio of animated mannequins was slowly turning.

They were interesting enough on their own—with scarlet lips that stretched into smiles when they noticed my interest and bright, jewel-like eyes that completely failed to look human, but I was more captivated by what they were wearing.

"What *is* that?" I breathed, watching as the exquisite evening dress one of them had on, a light, floaty, silken thing, like flower petals made into cloth, suddenly changed—into scale-like armor that cascaded down the full length of it, turning it into a battle dress to match the shield that folded out from the purse she'd been carrying.

Goddamn, I could use one of those!

But I hardly had time to take it in before a little graf-fitied crab was waving its pincers at me from a nearby rock wall. It was bright red and blended in a little too well with the stone. But the movement caught my eye, and its urgency made me follow it from the front of the sushi place it had been decorating, across the bumpy floor, and over to the other side of the huge, mall-like space.

Where I was promptly distracted by a magical tattoo parlor where powerful tats were being applied to several clients. And by a candy store, where a kid had just dropped a package, releasing a cloud of buzzing taffy bees. And by a bookstore full of animated ladders that zipped around overstuffed shelves five stories high and advertised book binding in "properly sourced dragon hide—certificates upon request." And by a florist, where gorgeous flowers spilled out of the shop and into the walkway in colorful profusion.

The scent was almost overpowering this close, because I didn't know these fragrances. And because the baskets of dried herbs inside were adding their perfume to the fresh flowers piled around the door. But despite that, a group of bright pink blooms were so sweet that I couldn't resist moving in for a—

Saffy grabbed my arm. "Don't sniff those. Unless you like fur."

"What?"

But then I noticed that my little red guide was waiting for me, just up ahead, where—

"Oh my God!"

"It's like shopping with a sugared-up toddler," some-one said behind me, but I was already off, heading for a large force field of the kind that subbed for window glass around here, but this wasn't covering a window. It stretched from the bumpy floor to the rocky overhang of a ceiling, several stories up, and curved as if flowing around a corner. Only there was no bend here, just a wedge-shaped protrusion out into the corridor, one that was filled with—

No.

It couldn't be.

I ran up and pushed a finger against the field, which bounced around like jelly. Or like what it was, a huge slab of water jutting out from the stone like an aquarium. But it wasn't an aquarium, because inside weren't fish but—

"*Oh my God!*"

"Can you do something?" somebody asked.

"You're the one who brought her here with no buildup. I told you—"

I wasn't listening. I was pressing my hands and face against the surface of the barrier, passionately wishing the kids were here to see this. We have to bring them, I thought, staring at a bunch of tiny yellow fish—because there *were* fish in there, after all, zipping by in the light of more of those weird crystal formations. The crystals were blue and yellow this time, and spiking out from rocky promontories and occasionally the floor, sending what looked like sunlight filtered through water cascading everywhere. Enough that I could see flickers of silver tails, larger than any fish would have, flashing in and out of stalactite-like formations in front of what appeared to be an extensive cave system.

But I didn't care about the caves. I cared about—

There! Right there!

I leaned in, trying to get a better look, sure I was seeing things. Because it couldn't be what I thought it was. It couldn't—

My face suddenly slipped inside the wedge.

Oh, shit, I thought, and tried to back out. But before I could manage it, the rest of me was sucked in, too. Leaving me stunned from the sudden shock of cold water, like jumping into a November pool.

It was close to freezing, but the lack of air was more of a motivator. I started thrashing against the skin of the force field and panicking when it refused to let me through, before I remembered that I could just shift out. Spatial shifting was a perk of an office that desperately needed a few, and it had gotten me out of sticky situations in the past.

But not this one.

Because my power didn't work.

And, okay, *now* I was panicking. And staring at Hilde's horrified, slightly distorted face outside the force field, only she wasn't looking at me. She was looking at something behind me.

I spun around in the water, almost dropping the damned book I'd been lugging around, because Saffy had said she knew someone who might be able to disenchant it. And then clutching it to my chest, because the whole not-being-able-to-breathe thing had just been complicated by the arrival of—

Well, call them what they are, I thought, staring in awe in spite of everything.

Because they were *mermaids*.

Or mer-something, I corrected, noticing the finely muscled torsos dipping low to thick, scale-covered tails. Even with long, filmy hair that floated out behind them like smoke, huge colorless eyes, and weird, almost transparent filaments wafting from the sides of their necks and faces, they didn't look remotely female. They were also vaguely blue, or maybe that was the light.

I couldn't really tell and didn't care because I was *drowning*, and because they currently had strange-looking spears pointed at me menacingly.

One of them, wearing a neckpiece of glowing crystals in some kind of metal, struck out with his weapon and stabbed violently at my chest. Or, I realized a second later, at the huge bound volume I was holding in front of it. I didn't think he'd missed, since he was all of a few yards away, and then I really didn't when bright, yellow-white glints of light started spearing outward from the book.

I would have dropped it, but I was afraid he'd miss and hit me. Because he was stabbing it again and again, causing cracks like lightning to run all over it and shedding more of that terrible light. To the point that I couldn't look at it anymore, I couldn't look at them, I couldn't look at anything with my eyes scrunched up in pain.

Which is why I didn't see what was coming.

But I heard it when a sound tore through the eerie quiet, like a hundred whales all deciding to signal at once.

And I felt it when something slammed into me, hard as a fist. It was just a current under the water, but it threw me and the book I was still clutching back at the force field, pressing us against it so hard that I opened my mouth to scream before forgetting that I couldn't, sure that every bone in my body was about to break.

But the field broke first.

Suddenly, I was hitting the ground outside along with what felt like half an ocean's worth of water, leaving me gasping and heaving and coughing until I thought my lungs would come up. Which is why it took me a moment to notice several things: the field was back in place, and half a dozen mermen were on the other side, staring at me with their huge, colorless eyes. Hilde and Saffy were standing in front of me, trying to give me a chance to recover while holding back what looked like a mass stampede of people. And the book—

Was going insane.

I finally gasped in some air and scrambled back a few paces, getting my feet under me in the process. And getting away from where the tome was writhing and jumping and spilling a searchlight's worth of radiance everywhere. It was strobing the faces of the panicked people flowing around us, who were running away from—

What the hell were they running away from?

I couldn't see with all that light in my eyes, and with taller people and things flowing around me. And it was so loud in here, with people screaming and the loudspeaker blaring and my ears still half full of water, that I also couldn't hear what Saffy was yelling at me. Until my ears popped and her voice got through.

"—of here! *Did you hear me?*" she screamed, grabbing and shaking me.

"No," I said, and threw up some more water.

But then the light shifted and the crowd parted for a second, and I was able to see past her shoulder. More specifically, I was able to see a bunch of light fey pouring through one of the portals down the hall, a big one. Along with what looked like—

"What the hell is *that*?" I yelled.

"Time to go!" Saffy said, a wand in either fist.

But there was no time to go. No time to process the few dozen impossible things that had just happened and were still happening, because one of said things was about to run us down. The silver-haired light fey soldiers streaming out of the portal were attacking people with the weird spears they liked to use, which could deliver anything from cattle-prod-like encouragement to fry-you-where-you-stand bolts, but that wasn't the main problem.

No, the main problem was the elephant-like thing that a bunch of them were riding, and that had just torn its way through the portal. It was enormous, at least five times the size of the earthly animal, and suddenly made the huge space seem a lot smaller and more claustropho-bic. And when it bellowed, the very air seemed to shake.

Or maybe that was all the screams that suddenly joined in, like a chorus following the lead singer, because the thing was about to charge. Make that *was* charging, right down the rock-cut corridor, giving people very few places to go. Especially us, because the only "shop" within reach was full of mermen, who were still floating there, enjoying the show.

Only they weren't looking at the crazed, mutant ele-phant, I realized. They were looking at—

"You have got to be *kidding* me!" I screamed, as something finished shredding the book and boiled out into the air. And, unlike in evil Santa's shop, I got a good look at it.

"That's not a ghost!" Hilde yelled.

No shit, I thought, staring upward.

At the giant column of black smoke that had already filled the space above us, looking like an oil fire, except oil fires don't have glowing red eyes. Ones that turned on me menacingly a second later, as what I guess was a head stopped churning around the ceiling and dropped down in a sinuous, almost snakelike gesture. Right in my face.

I just stood there, trying to think where my power could send it, assuming I had any right now, which I wasn't sure of, because I couldn't feel it. I couldn't feel anything but stark raving terror. Which wasn't helped by the latest screeching bellow the damned charging ele-phant I'd somehow managed to forget about let out.

I screamed, because that's what you do when you're trapped between a powerful, pissed-off demon and ten tons of charging fury, wondering which will kill you first.

It looked like it was going to be the elephant, which was almost on top of us now, roaring and blowing and slinging people out of the way, left and right, with its huge tusks—

And then trying to stop on a dime when it was suddenly confronted with an even bigger, even madder, even more destructive force that, for some reason, was now grabbing the feys' huge ride and—

"Oh God!" I yelled, right before Saffy tackled me and flung us both back against the merpeople's ward, causing several of them to rear back in alarm.

But this time, we didn't go through. This time, we stayed put, Hilde and Saffy warding like mad, putting a shield in front of us and several other people who had ducked inside that I'd have defied anything to get through.

Including the elephant thing's guts, which were spraying all over the place, like bloody rain. Some people were still screaming, and others were just standing there, covered in blood and watching in shock as not-a-ghost sliced and diced the ride and then started on the fey. And then the whole long concourse of traumatized shoppers gasped when the mighty group of fey warriors turned tail and ran like all the demons of hell were after them.

Or, you know, one really big one.

Only he wasn't giving chase. He was coming back over to me. And bending down to get those freaky eyes on my level. And looking at me expectantly.

"Sh-Sh-Sh-Shadowland?" I finally managed to say, naming the nearest hell region, and the easiest one to shift him to.

The great smoky head inclined.

"You got it," I said.

And the next second, he was gone.

# Chapter Three

Half an hour later, there was still a lot of screaming going on.

Most of it wasn't directed at me, surprisingly, but seemed to be generally spread around the several dozen women crowded into a small space. Coven witches, I'd already figured out, did not have a hierarchal structure to their culture the way the Silver Circle did. There, the Lord Protector, currently a man named Jonas Marsden, called the shots, and while there was a council that he led and had to get approval from for certain actions, everything very much flowed from the top down.

It reminded me of a military, even in the areas that weren't part of the War Mage Corps—the Circle's military/police branch. Everyone seemed to be slotted into a distinct place in the hierarchy, answerable to people above them and ordering about those below. It was all very organized.

This . . . was not the Circle.

Hilde had gone out for tea a while ago without bothering to ask for permission, and nobody had stopped her. Maybe because everybody was too busy making sure they had a say in the general melee that passed for conversation. I'd expected to be a center point in that, considering that I (A) had just brought a demon into the middle of a bunch of women who hated demonkind, (B) had trashed their shopping center, and (C) wasn't supposed to be here anyway.

I'd thought there was an outside chance that maybe, just maybe, I might be thanked for helping out with the invasion thing they'd had going on, although given past experience, I wasn't counting on it.

Probably just as well, I thought, as one of the women broke off her conversation to whirl about and face me.

"You expect to be *thanked*?" she bellowed, loudly enough to make me twitch. Of course, her appearance was already doing that.

I was getting the impression that the covens intermarried with the fey more than the Circle-led magical community. There were people in here with skin the color of peonies and fresh-cut rosebuds; there was a woman with antlers coming out of her head, which she'd draped with little bows and bells; there was a man with a human face but a cat's eyes. But, somehow, this woman was the most impressive of all.

I wasn't sure why. She looked pretty human, compared to some of the others. She had hair the same silver white as Hilde's, only it wasn't cut in a cute little permed bob. Instead, it flowed like a mane over her shoulders before cascading almost to the floor. It also seemed to have a life of its own, churning around her on currents of magical power like the mermen's had on currents of water. It was mesmerizing.

Or it would have been, had it framed any other face. This one, however, was up to the competition. It wasn't exactly beautiful, being old and weathered and bronzed, but it was arresting, captivating, and hard to look away from. Especially the eyes, which were literally the color of sapphires.

I had blue eyes, too, but mine had never looked like that. No human's did. I knew without being told that the woman was part fey, like the little fiefdom she oversaw. Or maybe oversaw. She'd been bellowing the loudest, but I wasn't sure if that meant anything or not. Nobody had actually bothered to introduce themselves, and the few coven leaders I knew weren't in the room.

And unlike her, I wasn't a mind reader.

"No," I said, trying for a calmer tone than I was feeling. "I didn't come to cause trouble—"

"Too late," the witch with the antlers said.

"Then why did you come?" the impressive woman demanded, and then her eyes grew round before I could answer. "You want us to do *what*?"

"What does she want?" the rosebud woman asked, peering over her shoulder.

"She expects—she actually believes—"

"She wants us to fight with the Circle in the war, doesn't she?" This came from a tiny lavender-colored woman with pixie-like features. "I told you this was going to happen. Didn't I tell you? Just the other day—"

"Damned Evelyn!" someone said. "She never should have sent her help—"

"Yes, that's right, that's perfect!" Saffy said, butting in. "Let's do what we always do and retreat from everything. It's not our problem—"

"Everyone already knows how you feel," a human-looking woman told her. "We've heard it often enough."

"And you'll hear it again! Until it gets through your thick skulls! This war concerns all of us!"

"This is your doing," the impressive woman said, looking at her angrily. "You brought her here—"

"Damned straight. Should have done it before—"

"—knowing full well what she is, what she'll do!"

"You don't know anything about her!"

"I know she has no business here! She's no coven witch—"

*"She's as coven as any of you!"*

There was a sudden, stunned silence. Maybe because of the decibel level; if I hadn't known better, I'd have thought Saffy had used a spell to enhance her voice. But she hadn't so much as made a move toward the wands sticking out of the tops of her boots.

I guess growing up in the covens, you learned to project.

I looked around, the absence of yelling making my ears ring, and met maybe three dozen pairs of eyes. Because more people had been pouring in all the time, and now they were all looking at me. "Uh," I said brilliantly.

"Well?" A grandmotherly type poked the impressive looking woman. "Is she? Is it true?"

"Beatrice said it, too," somebody offered.

"Well, where is she, then? She ought to be here, along with Zara and that damned Evelyn—"

"Oh, please, not Evelyn!" someone said. "Hasn't my day been bad enough?"

"It's true," the impressive woman suddenly said. She'd been staring at me intently, ever since Saffy's declaration. But since I hadn't felt anything, I wasn't sure if she was attempting to mind read or just had a headache.

If it was the latter, I could relate.

"What?" That was the grandmotherly type. "What's true?"

"She passed the Gauntlet. She won her coven—"

Conversation suddenly exploded again.

"It doesn't mean anything!" the impressive woman yelled. "It doesn't mean anything!"

"Like hell," Saffy said, from next to me. "Don't let them get to you," she added.

But then, before I could say anything, or ask what the heck was going on, she was swept away on the tide of conversation. I didn't follow, because I didn't know how to navigate these waters. I didn't know anything.

Except that my towel was clammy and no longer helping.

It had been nice when I first got here, but it had absorbed all the water it was going to, and it was getting uncomfortable. I pulled it off my shoulders and dropped it onto a nearby "sofa," if that was the right name for something that grew up out of the floor and was made solely out of wood. But it had little butt-like indentations in the seat, so I guessed you were supposed to fill them, only I wasn't sure.

I wasn't sure of much, because I was standing in a tree.

It was another thing besides the people that kept throwing me off balance. Because it wasn't a tree so much as a *tree*. Huge and leafy and taking up pride of place at the end of the concourse with the portals. It was hollowed out near the top, creating a cozy room with none of the saw or chisel marks you might have expected. Instead, it looked as if it had simply grown this way, with a satiny, slightly uneven floor, where occasional knots in the wood poked up as if defying whatever spell had been used to make it, like the way a few tiny branches popped out here and there from the otherwise smooth walls.

And from the sofa, I noticed. All around where I'd just dropped my towel. I picked it up, and sure enough, one little butt depression now looked like a Chia Pet, with the indentations full of tiny oak trees.

I swallowed and glanced around, but everybody was too busy yelling at each other to notice. I put the towel back down and edged away, only to realize that that hadn't really helped any. Because the same thing was happening wherever I stood.

My jeans had soaked up a lot of water, and gravity had carried it down my legs into my equally soaked shoes. And now it was growing a tiny garden wherever I stepped. I danced back a couple of paces, but that only made it worse; small green footsteps followed me everywhere I went, and oh God, now I was trashing their living room, too!

I bumped into somebody, and thankfully, it was Saffy. I guess she'd gone off to fetch another towel, which she handed to me. "You okay?" she asked, seeing my worried face and bitten lip.

"I think I did something," I whispered, and nodded at the sofa, which was now more like a forested lump in the middle of the room as the greenery spread across the seat. I could just imagine some of the ladies deciding to sit down and getting saplings up the bum.

"What?" She looked confused. And then she seemed to get it. "Oh, don't worry. Happens a lot," she told me. "It's how they tell the tree what to make."

"What?"

"Water. You put it wherever you want something, and it grows up to meet it. Like that." She nodded outside the window, at the staircase we'd climbed up on.

It was a beautiful thing, winding around the outside of the trunk, with steps and banister flowing seamlessly out of the wood. If you climbed as far as you could, as we had at the invitation of a group of wand-wielding witches, it left you six or seven stories above the concourse. Which kept drawing the eye.

At least, it drew mine.

For my whole life, magic was something you had to hide, something done in secret behind closed doors and warded windows. Something that human society could never be allowed to see, or at least to remember, because they outnumbered us so greatly that exposing ourselves would be a disaster. Magic or no, we'd be on slabs getting dissected in a matter of days, and probably wiped out shortly thereafter, like every other humanoid type who'd ever tried to inhabit this planet alongside the dominant species.

*Homo sapiens sapiens* didn't share well, and they bred like rabbits.

But we didn't, so we had to be careful. Only this wasn't careful. This was magic in all of its colorful, glittery, in-your-face glory.

"Cool, huh?" Saffy asked. She pulled out a wand and murmured a spell, and the saplings retreated back into the wood again, but she didn't move off. She seemed to be enjoying my reaction.

"I don't get it," I whispered. "How is this *here*? The portals alone—"

"Are routed through Faerie. That way, the Circle has no way to detect them, because the power isn't coming from here, or even from a source they understand."

"They go to Faerie?" I asked, because I didn't see how that helped.

"They're routed *through* Faerie," she corrected. "Some do stop there; others just use it as an anchor for the line and whizz on by."

"What?"

"It's clever, really," she said patiently. "The covens discovered that they could anchor a portal in Faerie, then use it to spawn multiple portals elsewhere. They're all connected, like a train on the subway that uses a single track. But there's many stations on the line, and only one of them has to be in Faerie in order to use its energy."

"Its energy?"

"Elemental magic. The covens use a bastardized version of fey magic, you know?"

I nodded. That much I did know. Mainly because Rhea had been raised partly by the covens before joining the Pythian Court. I'd seen her fish for elemental magic the fey way, using a wand with a tiny blob of her own power at the end, like a lure, which the natural magic of earth glommed onto like a trout taking bait. In that case, it had been lightning from a storm outside, which she had been able to control and direct like a weapon against some very powerful magic users.

Very powerful magic users who had subsequently been blown through a wall.

The Circle's form of magic also involved capturing the magical energy of the earth, to supplement what their bodies made naturally. But they did it slowly, over time, using talismans like the jewel in Billy's necklace, which collected magical power and stored it like a battery. They viewed their method as sensible, safe, and responsible, and saw the covens' use of wild magic as unstable and dangerous—rather like they viewed the covens themselves.

But I had to admit, the covens' version was more exiting, latching onto the wild magic of the world and taking it for a ride instead of waiting for it to build up in some battery. It also allowed the covens to outlast the average war mage in battle, formidable though the Circle's mages could be, because they were mostly using wild magic against them. They only needed to expend a small portion of their own power with each spell, to give the wild magic something to hold on to.

It had always seemed strange to me that the Circle had won the war anyway, but then, I didn't claim to be an expert on magical history.

"But aren't portals just doorways cut into a ley line?" I asked. "And there aren't any ley lines over this far." At least, I didn't think so.

"Oh, there are ways to extend them," Saffy said, without explaining what those were. "And since the portals make a stop in Faerie, some of the fey come here to trade," she added, nodding at the concourse. And at the large green creature heading our way. I stared some more, because that seemed to be all I was doing today.

But he was worth it.

He was only vaguely humanoid, and huge—maybe

twelve feet tall, maybe more; it was hard to tell from this angle. He had tiny ears that stuck out from his head, a big forehead, and enough muscles to make a professional powerlifter weep with envy. He was wearing a loincloth and had a normal-sized backpack as a wristlet. He also had a bunch of full-size, loaded pallets in tow, on levitation charms floating through the air behind him, and chained together to form a train of what I guessed was his shopping.

"—of the other towns," Saffy was saying.

I refocused enough to blink at her. "What? You mean there's more like this?"

She grinned.

"How many more?"

She started to answer, and then stopped. "You know, Hilde was right earlier. We might want to take this slow."

Someone called her name, and she started to move away, but I grabbed her arm. "But . . . there are covens all over the world. Are you telling me there's places like this everywhere, too?"

"I'm not telling you anything right now."

"Saffy!"

"Look, you've had a shock," she said, not unkindly. "I should have thought. But you needed to see this. We need you to see this. We've stayed apart from the world for so long, but we can't keep doing it. Not and win the war, which looks like it's headed to Faerie, which we know better than anyone!"

I glanced around the room. "I can see that," I said, my mind going a hundred miles a minute.

"But the Mothers *don't* see that," she said. "They won't have anything to do with the Circle, much less fight alongside it, not even with the world at stake! I've talked till I'm blue in the face, and when you asked to see them . . . well, I may have rushed things a bit. I'm sorry."

I wasn't. I was flabbergasted. And still way, way behind.

I also wasn't exactly sure what she was telling me. But it sounded like there were little towns like this scattered all over the world where humans and fey mingled like it was no big thing. Like there was this whole underground community that no one knew about if they weren't a member, one that defied pretty much every magical law there was.

"Saffy! You can't just hide a whole community from the rest of the world!" I told her. "It's nuts!"

One blond eyebrow went up. "Really? We've been doing it to the humans for years."

And then someone called her name again, and she was off, disappearing into the steadily growing crowd. I just stayed there, caught flat-footed like I'd been all day, and resenting it. Because every time I thought I had a grip on the magical world, it did something like this.

No, it did something like *that*, I thought, staring out the window some more, at the bustling crowd below.

In less than a minute, I counted humans; dwarves; trolls; satyrs; a werewolf in full transformation, prowling along with its fur gleaming with reflected colors; several members of the light fey, standing a foot or more above the rest of the crowd and faintly glowing; and a flock of tiny pixies, who zoomed around shoppers' heads before flying into a row of exquisite little stores set into the rock above a tea shop.

There are pixie-sized shops, I thought.

Of course there are.

It was enough to make me dizzy. Literally. I'd sat on the floor by the window, because it was easier to see down that way, and now I rested my head on the smooth wood of the wall for extra support, feeling like I might pass out.

Because it just kept coming.

Like the magical 3-D graffiti gleaming over and around the shops in ever-changing enticements. A tea shop, which I guessed was where Hilde had gone, had a pot that tipped over every so often, sending a flood of steaming liquid down onto the crowd that dissipated in the air above their heads before it scalded anybody. A sewing shop, likewise, had a needle that embroidered the rock face in beautiful patterns, creating rolling hills and 3-D flowers out of magical thread, which disappeared after a few moments to leave a blank canvas for new creations. A bakery was positively ringed by graffitied pastries of all kinds, topped off by a grandmotherly figure that kept throwing dirty looks and napkins at the passionately embracing couple above an erotic bookstore next door.

And then there was the cleanup crew.

I got back on my hands and knees to see them better. But, no, I wasn't imagining things. A squad of animated mops was weaving through the crowd, attempting to clear up the alarming amount of elephant guts, or at least to corral it into a pile. There had to be fifty of them. It looked like *The Sorcerer's Apprentice* down there.

You know, except for all the blood.

I'd seen magic before, even magical creatures. But that was in a world where the different species stayed apart, in their own little enclaves. The vamps had their courts, where they occasionally brought in a mage or two to help with warding, or a handful of weres for daytime muscle. Likewise, the mages stayed mostly to themselves, occasionally mixing with a few fey, although nothing like this.

Nothing close to this!

"Did you hear me?" someone demanded.

I looked up to see the impressive-looking woman again. She appeared even more incensed than before, although I had no idea why. It was all over now.

Well, except for the mopping up.

"I need some of those," I told her.

"What?"

"The mops." I turned to look at them again in fascination. My bodyguards thought that cleaning was beneath them, but they were also seriously suspicious of any hotel personnel they didn't know. Things got a little odorous on the days that their approved cleaners were off.

But the mops seemed to know what to do on their own, with no custodian in sight. They were currently trying to chase off some fey—little dark things in robes that seemed to disappear when I looked directly at them— who were attempting to carve a slab off the fallen beast's giant haunch.

There followed a tussle between the mops, who clearly had orders to get the concourse back to normal, and the tiny robed guys, who didn't see any reason why they couldn't have the meat. It resulted in mop handles battering small robed heads and little spell bolts being thrown around, setting a couple of the mops on fire. I laughed.

"I'm glad you think this is funny!"

I looked up at her.

"I think it's awesome," I said, because she seemed to be waiting for something.

Her face scrunched up, maybe trying to read my thoughts, but if so, let her. I was honestly enchanted. "Is she all right?" she finally asked someone.

"Of course she's all right!" That was Hilde, who I guessed had gotten back at some point. "She's just had a shock, that's all."

"*She's* had a shock?" The woman sounded furious. "She isn't even supposed to *be* here—"

"It seems to have been a good thing that she was."

"—much less with a demonic monster in tow!"

"One who saved your collective arses."

"As if we couldn't have handled the Svarestri!" the woman snapped.

"Are you in the habit of having to?" Hilde inquired sharply.

The woman's face flushed red. "That's none of your business! None of this is any of your business! You have no right—"

"I have every right. The last time I checked, I was a witch, just like you."

"You're nothing like us. *She* is nothing like us!" An arm protruded from the flowing gray robes she wore. "The Pythias have never been witches!"

"I beg your pardon?"

"They're pawns of the Circle—"

"Or of the vampires," someone else added.

"—everybody knows that! And now that you've brought her here, what do you think she's going to do? She'll run straight back to the Circle—"

"That's a lie!"

"—and we'll have to fight them off or have them crawling all over everything! Dealing with the fey would have been easier!"

"If you'd listen for a moment, instead of shouting," Hilde shouted, "perhaps you would learn something—"

"Oh, yes. Another Circle-trained witch about to instruct me!"

"Not if I can't get a word in edgewise!"

"I think we should hear from the Pythia," someone said, and for the second time, everybody paused to look at me.

I looked back, too bewildered to feel intimidated this time. "I'm not a pawn of anyone," I told them.

"Then you'd be the first Pythia I ever heard of who wasn't!" That was from the imposing woman again.

Hilde started to blow up, probably because her sister had just been insulted as much as me, but she was cut off.

"Jury's still out," a familiar voice said, and I looked up to see the only three coven leaders I did know making their way through the crowd.

"Heard you were here," Evelyn, the imposing one in front, told me. "You have some lady balls, to try this."

"She has big, fat lady balls!" Hilde said staunchly.

"I was looking for you," I told her.

"Well, you've found me. Let's talk."

# Chapter Four

I finally got some tea. A sylphlike figure with a pair of small, glittery wings that couldn't possibly have supported her weight brought around a tray. It took me a moment to notice that both her hands were busy preparing my cup over the top of it, leading to the obvious question of how it was staying in the air like that. The easy answer was a levitation spell, or some kind of charm; but there was also another possibility.

I eyed the wings and wondered exactly how many arms she had.

She started to hand me a cup, hesitated, then pulled it back and added something out of a bunch of little vials in a wooden stand. "Flavoring?" I asked.

"Courage," she answered, and moved on to a group of witches behind me.

I eyed my cup unhappily.

I'd really wanted some tea.

"It's okay," Saffy said, sitting beside me. "I got Restraint. See?"

I peered into her cup and found that it was faintly pink and somewhat floral. Mine, on the other hand, was dark brown, with a woodsy, almost earthy scent. I cautiously took a sip. I didn't feel more courageous, that I could tell, but it was good tea.

"They're giving some of the more combative ones Calm," Saffy said.

"Think it'll help?"

She shrugged. "Can't hurt."

I glanced at the brouhaha going on behind us and hoped some of them had gotten a double.

Zara, the youngest of the coven leaders who I knew, came over and pulled up a hassock. Not by grabbing one and dragging it over, you understand, but by holding out a hand and literally pulling it up from the floor. It was shaped vaguely like a mushroom, with a fat base and a round, slightly-indented-for-comfort top, and she settled onto it with a small sigh. I didn't even blink at this point, even though I hadn't seen her drop any water. But then, as powerful as she was, the tree probably figured it shouldn't piss her off.

Not that she was looking particularly upset at the moment.

I glanced in her cup. "Calm?" I guessed.

"Peppermint," she informed me, and took a sip.

I was actually kind of relieved that it was Zara who'd come to talk. I'd nicknamed her Jasmine when we first met, because she looked like a beautiful Middle Eastern princess, with sloe dark eyes and golden skin. And black hair with a sheen to it that was looking faintly purple at the moment, because a giant graffitied purple dragon had just stuck its glowing nose in the window and was looking around curiously.

A couple of the witches shooed it off, after which it went back to preening over a nearby smoke shop and Zara's hair returned to normal. Which, unlike the real Jasmine's huge, bouncy ponytail, was a shorter, swingy style that matched her modern suit and bright blue blouse. She drank tea at me for a while.

"You read the leaves?" she finally asked, and I realized that she'd finished her cup.

"Um, no. Sorry."

She shrugged. "Worth a shot."

I pulled a soggy pack of tarot cards out of my purse, because making a friend never hurt, but unlike normal, they weren't talking. My old governess had had them enchanted for me when I was young, to give the overall aura of a situation, and I'd found them to be eerily accurate at times. But not today. Today, the cards, which were usually fighting, arguing, and trying to speak over each other, were a block of muttering, soggy paper, their voices so muddled that no one stuck out above the others.

Maybe that was the message, I thought, glancing at the quarreling witches behind me.

I put them back.

"Perhaps another time," Zara said wryly. Right before a graffitied bat flew through the window and fluttered around everyone's hair, causing another disruption. She sighed. "Annoying, isn't it?"

"Cassie likes it here," Saffy said staunchly.

"It gets irritating after a while," Zara told me, taking out a small cigarette case. "That's why I live in town."

"Then why have it like this?"

She shrugged. "Makes the fey feel more at home, so they come more readily. And we have to get potion supplies from somewhere."

"You can't just get them at the usual places?" I asked, because there were potion shops all over Vegas. Just on the street with the used furniture shop, I'd seen no less than three—four, if you counted a charm store that also stocked a few ingredients behind the counter.

To human eyes, they'd appeared to be closed and boarded-up storefronts, their interiors full of nothing but dust. But to anyone with magic in their veins, they looked like what they were: stores humming with shoppers and stuffed full of potion supplies, everything from the mundane stuff needed for cleaning and warding your house to stronger things used in medicine or pest control. Or the little beauty tricks that didn't count as glamouries but still took ten years off your face.

There was even a Rothgay's, the Circle-owned potion shop that had its towering main store in London. I'd never been there, but everyone had heard stories of its pristine interior, gleaming old-world fixtures, and knowledgeable staff, any of whom could have headed up a store of his or her own, but who preferred to stay and learn from the truly brilliant alchemists in back. They experimented on new potions and elixirs all the time, the best of which quickly made their way to Rothgay's many branches worldwide.

Of course, there'd been a couple of derelict types lounging around outside the famous store, looking like panhandlers but in reality serving as guards, because

Rothgay's carried the kind of stuff you needed a license for. I wasn't sure a coven witch would get a license, considering it was the Circle that issued them. But even if not, there were plenty of alternatives. The presence of a large supernatural community and a sizable contingent of the War Mage Corps ensured that you couldn't swing a dead cat in Vegas without it coming back smelling like wormwood.

Yet the covens needed more?

"We don't like the Circle to know what we're buying," Zara said, lighting a small herbal cigarette. She smiled.

I smiled back—before I realized the implication.

"Jas—uh, Zara," I said, trying not to look as freaked-out as I was. "It would be a really bad idea to attack the Circle when they're in the middle of a war."

"Is that what you meant?" Saffy asked, sitting forward.

Zara blew some fragrant smoke at her. "It's been mentioned."

"Really, *really* bad," I added.

"Why would anybody even *think* of such a thing?" Saffy demanded. "What good would it do to beat the Circle only to have the gods come back and destroy us all? Besides, you know why we can't attack them, even in peacetime—"

"I know," Zara agreed lightly. "I'm not the one suggesting it."

And before I could ask what Saffy meant, she was telling me. "The Circle's power supports a spell, one laid thousands of years ago, to keep out the gods. Without them, it would fall, and those bastards would be back and we'd all be screwed! Like we are if anyone actually goes through with this!"

I nodded, because for once, I probably knew more than she did. She was talking about the ouroboros spell, one cast by the goddess Artemis to protect the world after she kicked all the other godly butts to the curb, with "the curb" being their own dimension. There was some debate as to why she'd done this, but none whatsoever about its usefulness.

Of course, I could be wrong about that, I thought, seeing Zara's expression.

"The spell does exist," I told her.

"Perhaps—"

"No perhaps. It *does*."

"Perhaps," she repeated, showing teeth this time. "But it was very . . . convenient . . . that we only learned of this during our war with the Circle. We had a truce once, to fight a more pressing enemy. They broke it, attacked us when we were at our most vulnerable, and then, when our leaders vowed to fight on nonetheless, told us this story. And, somehow, persuaded the Mothers to believe it! As a result, while we never accepted the yoke they call their rule, we also did not continue to fight back."

She looked at me soberly. "And now, there is another war."

"Yes, one we have to win."

"Perhaps." It seemed to be her favorite word. "Or perhaps the Circle want an excuse to finish us off."

"You don't believe that!" Saffy said, looking shocked.

"I'm merely telling you what's been said," Zara replied innocently. "The Circle has viewed the covens as a thorn in its side for centuries. What if they see this war—whether needed or not—as a way to persuade us to ally with them as they did once before? And to complete the betrayal they started then?"

I was the one sitting forward this time. "You know who I am; who my mother was."

"I know what they say." Zara's beautiful eyes narrowed. "Daughter of the virgin goddess, one of the only true demigods left on earth."

"But you don't believe it."

"Frankly, I don't know what to believe."

"I saw it!" Saffy said, breaking in, and almost vibrating at my side. That tea was apparently really overrated. "You weren't there, at the Battle on the Drag. She took on a whole dark mage army—"

"Yes, so you've told me. A number of times."

"—and won! All by herself—"

"I wasn't by myself," I corrected quietly. "And if it hadn't been for you, I'd have died there."

Zara raised a perfect eyebrow at me. I guess she hadn't expected candor. Unfortunately, it was all I had to work with, as I'd never been particularly good with diplomacy. But, for once, it seemed to be an asset.

From what I'd seen of the covens, they didn't do diplomacy all that well, either.

"The stories are true," I told her. "Artemis was my mother. But she was greatly diminished when she had me, and died shortly thereafter. And in any case, demigods have varied skill sets. I don't claim to be all-powerful, or anything close to it. That's why I came. I need help."

"Really? And here I thought you came to argue the Circle's case."

I frowned. "No."

"Oh, then you're not trying to recruit us? To persuade us to fight alongside the people who butchered our ancestors and would do the same to us if they thought they could get away with it? Who restrict our travel?—or try to," she said, with a satisfied little glance back down the mall, to where the distant glow of the portals could still be seen. "And who attempt to monitor our every movement?"

"No," I said again. "I'm not going to lie, it would be a huge asset to have the covens on board for the war, but I'm not a fool. I know the odds on that."

"Then why risk this? Do you know what usually happens to interlopers here?"

"She isn't an interloper," Saffy said. "She's a coven leader—"

"An unaffiliated one. It amounts to the same thing."

"It isn't the same thing! And she's willing to work with us! Do you know how long it's been since *anybody*—"

"Willing to work with us how?" Zara asked, looking at me. "If you don't expect us to help in the war, then what do you want?"

I glanced behind me at my other two acquaintances among the coven leaders. One of them, Evelyn, was another Valkyrie type, albeit younger than Hilde, with steel gray hair cut short and a matching business suit. She was recounting how we first met, and what had followed: my battle to save my court from some rogue acolytes and their dark mage allies. She and her two friends had played a big part in that, not to mention that it had involved some time travel, so she had a fairly rapt audience.

The other was named Beatrice, a mahogany-skinned disco-granny type who stood maybe four-foot-seven without the giant afro she was known for. She was not in a business suit, something I'd never seen her wear, but rather a bright crimson caftan that highlighted the fortune in fine gold chains around her neck and the matching rings and bracelets on her expressive hands. Her long nails were also bright gold, like the eye shadow that highlighted her intelligent dark eyes. They were snapping at the moment, because she was scooping up any stragglers by deliberately starting arguments with them—never too hard around here. Together, they were doing a good job of holding the conversation away from us.

So Zara could pump me for info, maybe?

Not that she had to work too hard.

"I need coven witches," I said, turning back to her. "For my court."

"You have them." An elegant hand indicated Saffy.

"Yes, and they've been wonderful, and very much appreciated."

"But?" The dark eyes gleamed.

"But I wasn't talking about guards."

It took her a moment, and then her eyes widened. "You can't be serious."

"She's serious," Saffy said, and would have said more, knowing her, but Zara quieted her.

"I need adepts," I said bluntly. "And we both know you have them. Coven girls used to come to the court, powerful seers who—"

"Who are needed to guard our enclaves from the damned Circle! Not to mention that none of the girls we sent ever had a chance of becoming Pythia! Not with the Circle's influence pervading every inch of that place!"

I blinked at her, because for the first time, Zara had lost her famous cool. Her golden cheeks were flushed pink, and her dark eyes were giving Beatrice's a run for their money. And that . . . wasn't a great sign.

Zara was the most even tempered of the coven leaders I'd met so far. If she was this appalled by my request—

Well, at least I'd enjoyed the tea, I thought grimly.

But as long as I was here, I was having my say. I gulped the rest of my drink, just in case it helped, and sat the cup down with a thunk. "I'm sorry for the way you've been treated—"

"It's a little late for that!"

"—but that was by my predecessors, not me. I can assure you that any girls you send me will be treated with the same respect as any other acolytes. They'll be housed the same; they'll be trained the same. And they'll have the same chance at succeeding me—"

"Oh, please." Zara looked at me for the first time with dislike. "I thought you might at least be honest with us."

"And I'm not?"

"Hardly. You know as well as we do who will succeed you. Everyone does."

"Maybe you'll enlighten me?"

"Drop the act. We know who Rhea Silvanus' true parents are. She was raised by a coven, remember? The Silver Circle has been influencing the Pythias for years, and now their leader is to have his daughter on the throne? If there was ever any question who runs things—"

"The power chooses the Pythia," I told her. "Rhea is Jonas' daughter, it's true, and her mother was the former Pythia Agnes—"

"Then you admit it!"

"Didn't I just say so?"

I glanced around because the distraction technique suddenly wasn't working so well anymore. Our little group was starting to be hedged by unhappy faces, with enough passive power coming off them to send my hair crackling around my face. Damn, I could use another cup of tea!

But I didn't have any, so I soldiered on regardless.

"So, yes, Rhea has a strong pedigree. But so did Myra, Agnes' former heir, yet the power came to me—"

"Considering who your mother was?" Someone laughed. "I'd damned well hope so!"

A murmur went around the group. It seemed that some hadn't been reading the papers, because there were a few gasps as questions were asked and answered, and a few audible snorts of derision. Yeah, I thought, that's why I didn't go around name-dropping.

"And," I said, raising my voice, since that seemed to be considered normal around here, "there's the fact that Agnes never wanted Rhea to follow in her footsteps, something she made quite clear to her daughter, who was never trained. She can't even shift—"

The murmuring got louder.

"—and may never do so. But either way, the power chooses the Pythia—"

"Then why does it always go to a Circle girl, hm? Explain that," someone else said.

"Because they're the ones who are trained!" I looked around the ring of faces in exasperation. "The power chooses the best candidate possible. Are you surprised that is usually someone with the right training?"

"And you expect us to believe that there's no politics, no Circle intervention, involved in that selection?" That was Zara again.

"No, I'm not saying that," I told her. "Quite the contrary."

"See! See!" Someone said.

"The Circle has exerted a great deal of influence for some time on which initiates are selected as acolytes," I said, because it was true. "They want to give the old Circle families, the ones they feel they can trust, the best chance to get one of their daughters on the throne. A lot of arm-twisting is done to get those girls into position, and then it's usually a cutthroat scrabble between them for the top spot."

"And yet you wish us to send you girls." That was Evelyn. She'd stopped trying to distract anyone, since they were all over here anyway.

"Yes, I do."

I looked around at them and tried not to let the various expressions get to me. Other than from Saffy, I didn't see any encouragement in the room. Hilde was frowning along with the rest, or maybe *at* the rest—I wasn't sure.

She was in the back, and it was hard to tell. But a party this wasn't.

"I'm sorry for how you've been treated in the past," I repeated. "It was unfair—"

I heard somebody snort again.

"—but some of that—a lot of it—was on you."

That earned me a few gasps. Damned if you do; damned if you don't, I thought. And carried on anyway.

"When you withdrew your girls from the court, you also greatly lowered the chance of ever having a coven Pythia. Rhea was partly raised by the covens, as you know. If she does end up with the top spot, maybe she'll be sympathetic to your issues, maybe she won't. But that's as close as you're likely to get if you don't send anybody to be trained. The power isn't likely to go to someone who doesn't know how to use it, and you're making sure they don't.

"And by doing that, you're willfully conceding yet another area of the magical world to the Circle's control. It's like expecting to win a game when you refuse to play, even though"—I raised my voice again, because the room had just exploded—"even though you have a Pythia right here, right now, willing to give your girls an equal shot! If you don't take it, don't blame the Circle. If you don't have an advocate, it's because you don't want one! If you don't have equality, it's because you'd rather blame someone else for your problems than take it when it's offered!"

"Damn," Saffy muttered, looking into my cup. "What the hell was in here?"

"You wanted the truth," I told Zara. "That's the truth."

"It's also dangerous," she said, glancing around.

Saffy jumped to her feet at that, although nobody had made a move—yet. But I didn't need her. "It's all right," I said.

"You sure about that?"

"Yes," I answered, but I wasn't talking to her. "I can shift us all out of here at a moment's notice, although I don't need to. I can turn back time to before we even arrived and erase all this from everyone's memories. I can make this as though it never happened, because for all of you, it won't have. Even more, I can freeze you where you stand and do whatever I like, up to and including slaughtering everyone in the room, because that is the power of the Pythian office! *That* is the power you forfeited for your pride!"

No one was talking now. They were all staring at me, some calculating, some angry, most shocked. But they were looking, and for once, they were listening.

"You talk about war with the Circle?" I said. "War leaves many dead on both sides, and as you discovered, to your cost, it often achieves little. There are other ways to wield power, safer ways, *better* ways, and more of it than you could ever dream! But it requires taking a risk and reentering the world in order to claim it."

"And if we take this risk," the impressive-looking woman said, her white mane of hair floating about her as if electrified, "what guarantee do we have that you're not another Agnes? Lady Phemonoe had relatives in one of our covens, and distant though they were, they took in her child, raised her up, gave her a new name to hide her identity until she could safely return to court as just another initiate. And what did that win us? *Nothing!*"

"Because she was dating Marsden, damn his eyes!" another woman said, and there was loud agreement everywhere.

"Yes, she was dating Jonas Marsden," I cut in. "And she let that influence her when she shouldn't have. But I'm not Agnes, and the Circle doesn't rule me. No one does."

"So you say," the impressive woman spat.

"Read my mind, if you doubt me. Isn't that your gift?" I challenged her. "It isn't mine, so I don't know how much you can see. But if you have the skill, do it, and tell them what you find."

The room went quiet.

"I haven't forgotten that it was the covens who went with me, to save my court," I said, my voice trembling a little in memory. "I wouldn't have it now without Zara and Evelyn and Beatrice. And if your witches hadn't arrived in the middle of that terrible Battle on the Drag, I might not be here, either. I owe you a debt, and I will not forget that. But I will not be ruled by you. I will not be ruled by anyone. I am Pythia, and I am asking if you want to work with me."

I stood up.

"Let me know what you decide."

# Chapter Five

Three hours later, I shifted into the foyer of my penthouse, along with Saffy, Hildegarde, and about a hundred packages. Only to have one of my own bodyguards pull a gun on me. "Hey!" I said, startled. "Put that down!"

He did not put it down.

"Show yourself!" he demanded, the gun trembling a little, because he was new. And thus wasn't used to three overburdened women appearing out of nowhere almost in his face. Of course, I wouldn't have been in his face if he'd been over by the door where he should have been, instead of prowling around the large interior space.

"You're supposed to be by the door," I told him helpfully. "This is the landing strip."

"Wh-what?" He stared at me. Or, rather, he stared at my right eye, which is all he could see through the tower of packages I was carrying.

"By the *door*," I repeated, and started for the item in question.

Only to have the gun shoved back at me again.

"Hold up, or I'll shoot!" he shrieked—right before he disappeared.

I blinked for a moment at the space where he'd been, and then my packages and I turned so I could see Hilde. Or at least the mountain of stuff in front of her. "Where'd you send him?"

"To the lobby."

"He's not going to like that."

"As if I give a damn," she said, trying to maneuver over to the door, but not being able to see made it difficult. She ended up moseying around the foyer. "He should go back where he came from. The boy is obviously unstable."

"He's new," I told her, zeroing in on the door via the sliver of space between two of the biggest boxes. I remembered the troll, or whatever he'd been, on the mall. I could have really used his floating setup right now.

But I didn't have it, so I made do. And kicked the door with my shoe. And almost fell over in the process, because that put me off balance, and I'd never counted gracefulness as one of my attributes.

"Careful," Saffy said, steadying me. With a *hand*.

How the hell did she have one free?

I couldn't tell because I couldn't see. And then the vamp was back, even though elevators don't work nearly that fast, but then, he hadn't taken one. He'd taken the stairs.

And even for a vamp, running up twenty-something flights will piss you off.

"All right, listen up!" he began shrilly.

Then he was gone again.

"Hilde!" I said.

"What?" she demanded, from the other side of the foyer.

"First of all, don't do that, and second of all, the door's over here."

"Where?" she asked, and then she cursed. Probably because she'd just run into a potted plant. "All right, I've had enough!" she said.

And the next thing I knew, my tower of packages was levitating into the air to join the multitude that were already floating overhead, studding the high, domed ceiling like brightly colored birds let loose from their cages.

Exactly like, I thought, looking up. The ceiling was white with gold ribs every four feet or so, giving it a cage-like look, and the packages had been wrapped in a rainbow of different-colored papers. It was all very pretty.

It was also well above my reach.

"Okay," I said, admiring the view. "But how do we get them *down*?"

"She has a point," Saffy said. "Some of that's breakable. We can't just drop the spell, or—"

The vamp was back.

And this time, he came in shooting.

"Son of a *bitch*!" I heard someone say, I think it was Saffy. I wasn't sure, because the door behind me burst open at almost the same moment, and a bunch of people ran out. And one of them tackled me to the floor.

Make that several of them, I thought, as someone else opened fire.

Fortunately, it didn't last long.

"*That's enough!*" a familiar voice bellowed, loud enough to threaten my ear drums. The gunfire abruptly stopped. I looked up, trying to see past whoever was on top of me, but it was at least two and possibly three guys, so all I saw was expensive couture.

Even worse, I couldn't *breathe*.

I decided to do a Hilde and say to hell with it, and shifted out from under the little mountain of vamps, who hit the floor with an *oof*. I looked up from my own bit of floor, winded and pissed off and seriously worried that one of those bullets had connected with somebody. But all I saw was legs.

I hauled myself back to my feet in time to see Saffy—with a wand out and glaring—and Hilde having a stand-off with Marco, my lead bodyguard. Marco is six-foot-five in his stocking feet, and probably six-foot-six or so in the expensive Italian loafers he favors. Which is why the gun-happy vamp's toes weren't even touching the floor. Marco had him in one hand and was shaking him like a maraca, even while he informed Saffy that this was his vamp and—

"Your idiot, you mean!" Hilde was red-faced and *pissed*, probably because the shield she'd erected in front of her was riddled with bullets.

She dropped it a second later and they rattled to the floor, rolling around underfoot and threatening to trip people up. Meanwhile, the overflow from her magic, which had been a little sloppy due to speed, was sending sparks pinging off the marble, shocking some of the vamps who had poured into the room and were standing too close to the sides. A few of them jumped like they'd been bit, while others stared upward at the slowly rotating packages, some of which now had holes in them.

"What . . . the hell . . . just happened?" I wheezed, trying to get my breath back.

"Somebody earned himself a one-way ticket back home," Roy snapped. He was a red-haired charmer—a broad-shouldered Southern vamp who liked checkered suits and inventing new cocktails to get us all plastered on a regular basis. Although he wasn't looking so charming at the moment.

Maybe because the idiot in question was his.

"Who did we lose this time?" I asked, because the new guy had to be a replacement for someone.

"Paulie," Marco said, his eyes still on Hildegarde. "Mircea pulled him back two days ago."

Damn.

I'd liked Paulie.

"This has to stop," I told Marco.

"That it does," he said, looking pointedly at me. Because this wasn't a problem he could fix. I sighed and went indoors, snagging a low-hanging package on the way in.

"Get Mircea on the phone," I told one of the boys, who was so new that I didn't even know his name yet. But he looked slightly more with-it than the maraca outside. He nodded and pulled out a phone, while I dealt with problem number two.

"It's okay," I said, grabbing a friend's arm as she headed past.

A hundred tiny beads on a hundred tiny braids clacked together as her head spun to look at me. "One rule," she said, her voice trembling. "I have *one* rule—"

"I know. It won't happen again."

"That's what you said the last time! Why are there *idiots* running around—"

"Tami—"

"—with guns where there are *children* playing?"

She gestured across the living room to where a bunch of kids were gathered around a tall, exquisite creature, whose long arms were holding them protectively against his body. I blinked, because I'd never seen Augustine, couturier to the stars, give a damn about anybody but himself. It was almost . . . wholesome.

"It's okay," I told them. "There was just an, uh, accident."

"The last one," Tami said flatly. "I've had enough. I'm taking their guns."

On the surface, it seemed like a ridiculous statement. My bodyguards were mostly massive vamps, master-level rank for the most part, and armed to the teeth, not that they needed to be, considering the teeth in question. They sent most people into cardiac arrest with barely a glance.

Tami wasn't most people.

On the surface, she was a delicate beauty with café au lait skin, bright hazel eyes, and, currently, a head of Cleopatra braids. She looked like she should be walking a runway somewhere instead of trying to corral the crazy I lived with. But she was fully capable of taking on the job, and of enforcing exactly what she said.

Because Tami was a null witch.

It was a relatively rare ability that allowed her to pull magic off of anybody who had it, meaning pretty much anyone within these walls. That would include my new witch bodyguards, courtesy of the covens, and the lone Circle mage, who we'd all agreed to tolerate because he was mostly okay and it kept Jonas off my back. Even the vampires, who didn't do magic, were nonetheless magical creatures.

I didn't know what would happen if Tami decided to try her talents on one of them, but I doubted he'd enjoy the experience.

The new vamp handed me a phone, which didn't help, because Augustine had gotten his voice back and was using it to scream. That started some of the kids crying, because they had no idea what was going on, and they were somewhat sensitive at the moment. And that brought Rhea running from somewhere inside the sprawling suite, which took up an entire floor in one of the towers at Dante's, the casino I currently called home.

I put a finger in my ear, and tried to hear what Mircea was saying, only he wasn't saying anything. It was someone else's voice, but I couldn't tell whose: "—until four o'clock. I can pencil you . . . a call . . . if you'd like."

"What?" I said.

There was a pause on the other end of the line, which was probably space for a silent sigh, because Mircea's people would never utter such a thing out loud. They were far too polite. Well, except for the ones he'd sent me, probably because they were less diplomatic and therefore less useful in his former profession.

But Mircea was no longer the chief diplomat of the North American Vampire Senate. He was the Enforcer now, of the newly combined übersenate that had recently been made from select members of the world's six vampire governments. They'd come together to fight the war and had appointed him their general, something that had entirely changed his view of his family members' usefulness.

After all, we didn't intend to negotiate with the gods.

"Tell him he can't keep taking my guards," I yelled, because the noise level in here had just gone up again, thanks to everybody pouring back in from the foyer. "I need the people I have. They're trained how to handle this place—"

"—dinner, although there is a . . . tomorrow, after—"

"What? Hold on," I yelled, and pushed my way through the crowd. I went back out to the foyer, but several vamps were still there, jumping around and trying to grab the floating packages, so I reversed course. Through the living room, across a large open space with a couple of half-moon couches, where some of the older girls had been having a lesson, judging by all the books and papers scattered about, and into the butler's pantry next to the formal dining room, which was currently empty. Thank God!

"Are you there?" a polite voice asked.

It sounded like Mircea's new personal assistant, who'd been brought on to help with all the extra work connected with the war, only they didn't call him that. They called him some weird military name out of another time. "Are you Batman?" I asked, and forgot not to yell.

"Gerald, Lady," I was informed, in a pained-sounding voice. "Please call me Gerald."

"You know," I told him, "if I had a job that allowed me to go by Batman, I don't think I'd ever use any other name."

The sigh actually got through that time.

"Do you wish me to pencil you in for tomorrow?" he asked. "Otherwise, I'm afraid the first available appointment is—"

"I don't want an appointment. I just want to talk to Mircea."

"I understand, but the master is—"

"Busy, yes, I know. Taking all my bodyguards for colonels or whatever in his new army. Look, he sent them to me because he said he didn't need them. I get that times have changed, but you can't expect Joe Vampire to handle things around here. We just had an incident with another new arrival that could have been bad—very bad—over nothing. Literally nothing! I can't—"

Marco came in. He was still dragging the gun-happy vamp, but almost absently, like he'd forgotten that he had the guy's throat in one catcher's mitt–sized paw. "What. The. Hell?" he demanded.

"I'm trying to get through to Mircea now," I told him.

"Not that."

"Then what?"

Tami came in, her arms full of firepower, her face thunderous.

Well, shit.

"She wants our guns," Marco said accusingly. "She said you authorized it."

"*You* authorized it," I reminded him. "You said if there was another incident—"

"From one of my guys. This wasn't one of my guys!"

"Then what would you call him? I thought Roy—"

"Exactly! He's one of Roy's guys—"

"I cannot work in these conditions!" The door blew open again and Augustine was there, in all his glittery, insect-like glory. He was blond, fashionably thin—which allowed him to squeeze past Tami—and easily as tall as Marco. Only instead of the linebacker type, he was the praying mantis type, with an elongated body draped in couture bodysuits that he designed himself and stick-thin arms and legs.

And fingers, I thought, as one was waved in my face.

"You promised me peace and quiet! You also promised me some sort of guidelines, of which I've received exactly nothing! You promised me—"

"Here." I cut him off, because I didn't have time for this, and thrust the box I'd grabbed into his arms. "That's what I want."

"What?" He looked at it like it was something I'd dragged in on the bottom of my shoe, despite the slick gold wrapping paper the shop had swathed it in. "What is this?"

"Open it and see."

"Cassie—" That was Tami, giving me The Look. I'd known it since childhood, and it had never boded well.

"One second," I told the guy on the phone, who was trying to pass me off to a subordinate.

"—my assistant will set up a time—"

"I don't want Robin, I want you!" I snarled. "Don't you dare go anywhere!"

"Who is that?" Marco demanded.

"Batman."

"Very funny."

"Mircea's batman."

"Oh, that prick."

"He can probably hear you—"

"Then he's doing better than I am," Marco said sardonically, probably because Augustine had started screaming. Again.

"What the hell is wrong with you?" I asked, because the man had opened the package and was now standing there shrieking at the contents, I didn't know why. It was the gorgeous battle dress I'd seen in the mall, which was currently in its metallic silver state, the tiny, delicate-looking scales flowing like water over Augustine's long fingers.

"Where did you get this?" he screeched. "*Where?* You tell me *right now*—"

"I'm not telling you anything until you stop screaming," I said. "And anyway, you don't need to know that. Just tell me you can duplicate it."

"Auggghhhh!"

I stared at him. Genius and insanity, I thought. Augustine had finally lost it.

"Would you get him out of here?" Marco snapped at the vamp who'd just come in. "And find me that idiot of Roy's, what's his name?"

"D-Daniel," croaked Daniel—I presumed—since he was still hanging from Marco's fist.

"This is high court work," Augustine shrieked in my face, his blue eyes wild. "Do you understand what that means?"

"No," I said, and looked at Tami. "Listen—"

"We talked about this." It was flat. "We all agreed—"

"That was before Mircea started poaching my guys—"

"Oh, like the old ones are any better!"

"Hey!" Marco said.

"They're master vampires!" Tami said. "They don't need guns!"

"It's a point," I told Marco.

"Bullshit it's a point!" he told me back. "They need guns *because* they're masters! You know how fast a master, even one like that loser—and why aren't you going after him?" he demanded, looking at the new vamp. He was the one who'd given me the phone.

"I . . . think you're holding him, sir," the new guy said.

"What?" Black eyes focused on Daniel, who fortunately didn't need to breathe. "Yeah, this guy," Marco said, and slammed him down on the prep table. "Pathetic as he is, he could drain you in a matter of seconds. That's why we give 'em guns. As a deterrent, sure, 'cause most civilians suddenly get accommodating when you start flashing hardware around. But also as a safeguard—"

"A *safeguard*?" Tami was furious.

"If they're reaching for a gun, they aren't draining you," Marco said. "And most bullet wounds aren't fatal, despite what you might have seen on TV. But losing all the blood in your body? Yeah. The docs aren't putting that back."

"I can't believe we're debating which means of deadly force to use in a suite full of children!"

"They're not meant for the kids, but for anybody who might wanna harm the kids—"

"Really, I must go," Batman told me.

"I will make your life a living hell," I promised.

He shut up.

"*Cassie* didn't want to harm anybody," Tami yelled. "Yet he pulled a gun on an unarmed woman—"

"She's Pythia. She ain't unarmed," Marco said dryly.

"Oh my God, nobody cares!" Augustine shrieked.

Everybody paused to look at him, because he both looked and sounded like somebody seconds away from a massive heart attack. He grabbed me, and those sticklike fingers were surprisingly strong. "What is wrong with you?" I demanded.

"You! You are what is wrong with me! This is *high court work*. You drag it in here like it's nothing—nothing!" He looked outraged. *"Where did you find it?"*

"In a store window. There were others—"

"Auggghhhh!"

"Okay, that's enough," Marco said, and let go of the traumatized vamp long enough to grab Augustine and put his glittery self outside the door. "He gets back in, you go home, too," he told the other newbie.

"That . . . might not be the best incentive right now," I pointed out.

"Hey. They should be honored to be here, all right?" Marco said, looking pointedly at the guy on the table, who hadn't dared move. "It's the fucking Pythian Court—"

"Language," Tami snapped.

Marco got out his wallet and handed her a twenty. "They get to be around all the big shots—assuming you ever start seeing any," he added.

"The waiting list is getting a little long," Tami confirmed, adding the twenty to a jar full of them in a nearby cabinet.

"I'm doing what I can," I told her, which was true. It felt like I hit the ground running every day, yet never caught up. And now I was supposed to sit in our big audience chamber solving other people's problems when I couldn't even fix all of my own?

"Rhea says there's usually a grace period after a new Pythia comes on board," Tami added. "To let her get things sorted out. But it's normally only a couple of weeks. It's been months now—"

"There's also a war!" I said, wondering why I was holding a phone.

"Yes, and that's bought us some time, but it's also brought up a lot of new issues that people want addressed. You're going to have to start seeing at least a few of the big names on the list—"

"Soon," I promised.

"You said that last week," Marco said. And then he and Tami both crossed their arms and looked at me.

"Aren't you supposed to be fighting?" I said, glancing pointedly at the guns Tami had heaped on a counter.

"No. We're explaining the issue and waiting on a ruling from our Pythia," Tami said.

Great.

Somebody was squawking something out of the phone, so I put it to my ear. "Hello?"

The squawking stopped. "Hello?" It sounded tentative.

"Who is speaking, please?" I asked impatiently.

"G-Gerald?"

He sounded like he wasn't sure, which made two of us. "Who?"

A long sigh came through the line. "Batman."

Oh, right. "I want to speak to Mircea," I told him.

There was a pause.

"You know," he gritted out. "I'm not supposed to do this, but I can tell you that they're about to take a break. If you get here in an hour or so, you might be able to catch him—"

"Where's 'here'?"

"The new senate hall, at the consul's home in New York—"

"Thanks, I'll be there."

"Cassie!" That was Tami.

"All right, this one goes home," I said, patting Daniel

on the shoulder and receiving a grateful look in return. "Guns are permitted only for the original group under Marco's control. Newbies have to earn the right to carry, and they are only assigned outside work—in the hotel and casino, but *not* in the court itself—for at least a month after arrival. You guys need to work together to come up with a training regimen for them so they don't freak out at the kind of stuff that goes on around here."

"And what are you going to do?" Marco asked.

"Get a bath."

# Chapter Six

I was glad I had an hour, and not only because I was pooped. But because of that thing everyone does when they're going to see an ex. You know the one I mean. Even if it's over and you know it's over and you don't even want it to *not* be over, you're not going to show up looking less than your best.

Like in spaghetti-stained jeans, washed-off makeup, and hair that had dried on its own after being electrocuted by a merman.

Okay, that last part was more my life than most people's, but you get the idea. It was gild-the-lily time. And I had one hell of a place to do it in.

My old digs were downstairs, serving as housing for some of my bodyguards, because they liked being close and didn't mind the bullet holes in the walls. I'd lived there when it was just me, but with the whole Pythian Court showing up, I'd needed more space. Something I suspected had been anticipated by a mind far older and sneakier than mine.

Strongly suspected, I thought, eyeing the Greek key designs on the tiles in my huge, basin-like tub as I drew a bath.

They matched the blue border on the white tiled floor and the mosaics of fish and weird-looking dolphins around the sink area. There were more dolphins in the mural in the attached dressing room, frolicking in a crystal blue sea visible through ivy-covered, painted columns, which looked like it had been taken from a postcard of Santorini. It hadn't. I knew that because I knew who'd commissioned it. So it was probably the view off Alexandria or something, the way it had been two thousand years ago.

Because the mind behind my luxurious new bathroom, and the rest of this place, was no less than the consul of the North American Vampire Senate. She looked like Cleopatra if she'd had a modern makeover, maybe because she was Cleopatra with a modern makeover. Some vamps' histories could really play with your head.

But she was still around and more powerful than ever, and sometime after I ended up Pythia against everybody's expectations, and then further surprised them by managing not to die, she'd realized that one of two things was going to happen. I was going to end up back in Britain, where the Pythian Court had resided for a while—and thus back under the thumb of the Circle, who had their main base of operations there. Or . . . she needed to get busy.

So she had, booting me out of my old penthouse, which had stood in a fraction of this huge new space, and then gutting it along with the rest of the floor. The reason given was that her former local abode—at MAGIC, the supernatural version of a United Nations—had been an early casualty in the war. She'd therefore had no choice but to move in here and create a mansion for herself and the army of servants she supposedly needed.

But despite my blond hair, I'm not completely dumb. And I'd noticed that, once she'd finished the place, she and the rest of the crew had flitted off back to New York, where she had a truly palatial estate near the Catskills, and where she'd remained. I'd be surprised if she'd spent more than a week rattling around in here.

So why go to all the trouble?

Call me evil-minded—comes from spending too much time around vamps—but it had occurred to me that maybe, just maybe, my ending up here had been the idea all along.

I wasn't from Britain; I didn't know anybody there. But I *was* fond of Vegas. I liked the gorgeous desert sunsets I saw from my windows at night, the palette of soft reds and dark purples, and of orange, yellow, and flashes of jade that painted the skies every evening, only to come back for an even more spectacular show in the morning.

I liked the people, everybody from the native Nevadans, with their rugged individualism and practicality, to the crazy transplants from all over, to the always surprising denizens of Dante's, the hotel and casino I called home. It was a vamp-owned property with the best wards around, so it had become the senate's local outpost after MAGIC ended up a glass slick in the desert. Back in the bad old days, when I was hiding out here, pretending to be a casino employee while it felt like everybody in the world was gunning for my head, I'd spent hours listening to the stories they told.

I'd met a woman who'd had a little bar in El Paso where she'd served the likes of Billy the Kid, Wild Bill Hickok, and the assassin Jim Miller—and seen the steel plate he wore, like an early version of Kevlar, under his famous black coat.

I'd met the Mad Monk, one of the first Jesuits to arrive in California, who was hanged by his order for babbling about fanged demons in the desert and trying to bite the brothers. He could still show you the rope marks. They'd never faded, because the hanging had taken place during his Change.

I'd met a Native American bootlegger and stagecoach robber named Sadie Skull, after the tattoo that covered her entire face. She usually hid it with a glamourie these days, but could drop it in an instant and scare the everloving crap out of you. And then laugh and laugh and buy you a beer.

I'd met a pair of Chinese Siamese twins who'd run a successful chain of laundries back in the day—bought with profits from a series of train robberies that they'd somehow convinced the authorities had been done by some *other* pair of Siamese twins.

I even liked the city itself, in all its glitz and glamour and tacky wonderfulness, which shouldn't even be here because this was the middle of the desert, where nothing was supposed live except for some desert hares and parched-looking bushes. It had no business being where it was or doing what it was doing. Yet it was here anyway, just like I was. We fit.

And the consul knew that.

Which is why I found it suspicious that the perfect Pythian Court, complete with plenty of rooms for the girls, a formal audience chamber, a ballroom, a library, a massive dining room and kitchen, a huge master suite, big open common rooms, and a large outdoor garden and pool area—which, until Tami got hold of it, had featured actual Greek statuary—just happened to be left empty *right freaking above me.*

Of course, the consul hadn't invited us to occupy it, oh, my, no. Vampires, especially vampires as old as her, never did anything so obvious, and if they did, you'd better run. No, she just vacated it once the reno was complete, leaving it for my very competent housemother/majordomo/I-am-the-captain-now Tami to notice.

Which she shortly had, and moved us in while I was away.

Tami was so proud of her find that I hadn't had the heart to tell her that she'd been manipulated. It wasn't a problem in itself; I liked the place overall, and was glad to have it. But it didn't bode well for the future.

It didn't bode well at all.

Someone tapped on the partly open door from the bedroom while I was trying to decide between mango madness and papaya passion bath bombs. I said to heck with it, chucked in both, and stuck my head out the door. And found Rhea standing there with a tray.

"Tami thought you might like lunch," she told me. "Hilde said you didn't have any."

"No, we were afraid we'd get kicked out if we stopped moving." I lifted up the fancy cover. Tami had found the dinner service of the gods when we moved in and had fallen in love with the antique Victorian food domes. She put them on everything now, even when the tray wasn't going far enough to need one. But it did a wonder for capturing aromas.

Like off the homemade cassoulet that I guess everybody had had for lunch.

My stomach grumbled plaintively. "Hot damn."

Rhea laughed. I used to shock her with my occasional colorful language, but after being around the guys for weeks now, she was immune. "I'll put it on the table, shall I?"

I nodded. "I'll be out in a few."

I shucked my clothes and eased into the bath, which was too hot but felt amazing on my tired muscles. And tried to just zone out for a few minutes, because this was the best part of my day. The tub was huge and had more tech in it than the space station. I'd spent half an hour when I first moved in playing with the water jets and the different-colored lights. I'd finally settled on blue, because it was soothing, and it matched the décor.

That tub almost made me forgive the senate for everything.

Almost.

But it was a little hard to forgive when the manipulation was ongoing. I scowled and lathered up my hair, because I didn't want to think about that right now. Or, you know, at all. But my brain had different ideas.

The vamps had wanted my power under their control ever since they knew there was a potential Pythia who hadn't been raised by the Circle. That wouldn't have bothered me so much; it was politics 101, and the senate was just better at it than most people. If, that is, their brilliant plan hadn't involved having Mircea get me to fall in love with him.

That hadn't been too hard, since I'd already been halfway there. I'd had a crush on him ever since I was a kid, when he'd visited Tony's terrible court. And had left quite an impression.

The warm, dark eyes were the first I'd ever dreamed about. The mahogany hair, long enough to flow over my hands like silk, had probably given me a lifelong fetish. But it was the humor that really got to me, the way the handsome face could light up, and the sensual mouth could quirk at the corners with an appreciation for the absurd that someone like him wasn't supposed to have— senate member, master vampire, dangerous über Alpha of dangerous über Alphas . . .

And yet he did. He always had. It was the thing I'd

loved best about him, although, let's be honest, I'd loved practically everything.

And he'd loved me, at least for a little while, even though he wasn't supposed to. He was supposed to be the manipulator, the one who kept me enthralled while staying well out of harm's way himself. It must have seemed easy, to anyone looking at us from the outside. After all, what did I have to attract him, other than my position? What did he need with a screwball blonde with too-skinny legs, too-plump cheeks, and freckles on her nose?

But then, Mircea had always had quirky tastes. His many residences were known for their designer opulence in the public areas, meant to overawe his guests. But his private rooms were full of unusual little touches, like carved wardrobes from Maramures, the woodworking heart of the old country, or a tubby porcelain tambourine player from his stint as the consul's ambassador at the East Asian Court, or some old wooden spoons. They'd cost practically nothing, they wouldn't cause awe in anybody, anywhere, and they were frankly kind of tacky. But he liked them.

Like he'd liked me?

Cut it out, I told myself, angrily scrubbing my scalp. You know damned well what happened there, and it had nothing to do with your dubious charms. The senate's happy little plan to get themselves a Pythia had been messed up by the *geis*, a spell gone wrong that had caused Mircea and I to genuinely fall in love with each other. And that was a no-no.

The consul had started to get nervous about what might happen when an already too powerful senator with huge wealth, a winning personality, and an extensive family behind him also acquired a Pythia. Not wanting to get hoisted by her own petard and end up having him use me against her, she'd started working to muddy the waters in paradise.

Of course, she'd had some help with that.

Mircea had failed to mention that he had a daughter, a crazy dhampir who'd been sired during the short period between when he was cursed with vampirism—because he was one of the rare type of vamps who hadn't been bitten—and when the Change finished taking effect.

That in itself was a problem, since we were basically married under vampire law, thanks to an incident that took place when the geis was screwing with his head. And you'd think a daughter was something a person might mention to his wife. Like he might take her to see his main court, or introduce her to his family, or actually put a ring on it—things that also had not happened.

Of course, I couldn't complain too much, since I'd stubbornly refused to recognize the marriage, which I'd never agreed to in the first place. And since recent events had called into question our compatibility when a spell wasn't controlling us. And because Pythias weren't supposed to get married anyway. But Mircea kept insisting that it was a done deal, so why not tell me about his daughter?

Probably because that might have brought up questions about the mother, too.

Mircea had also failed to mention anything about his first wife, Elena, a human woman he'd married before the Change who had died centuries ago. And that should have been that, because death tended to be pretty final, right? Only no. Not when he'd spent months trying to figure out how to ask me to use the Pythian power to go back in time and prevent her demise.

Yes, you heard that right. He wanted his current "wife" to save his former one, risking the timeline in the process, and bring her to this century, where, I guess, we were all supposed to live happily ever after? It was *insane*.

At least, it was for a human. For a master vampire, it was Tuesday, since most of them had harems anyway. The Change tended to cause a surge of devotion that felt a lot like love, from what I'd been told, and one thing tended to lead to another. Maybe that was why Mircea had never Changed a woman.

He'd had lovers through the years since Elena's death, but they'd been temporary flings. An immortal paramour, on the other hand, one bound to you by blood, was something else again. That might have felt like he was cheating on his dead wife, who he was so devoted to that he'd been romancing Pythias for the last five hundred years, trying to find one who could go back and rewrite time for him!

Of course, *I* was bound to him by blood. He bit me, half-crazed and ridden hard by the geis, but he *bit me* nonetheless. And not any normal old bite, either. But one that bound the recipient to a vampire family for all eternity, the one considered the same as a marriage in their culture, the one I still carried the memory of in two little bumps on my neck. He'd taken me when he felt like it, and thrown me away when he felt like it, and that was just—

Oh, but I forgot.

He hadn't.

His and Elena's marriage had ended with his death, he'd said. I was his true love now, he just felt an obligation to Elena, he'd said. This didn't have to change anything, Cassie, why are you getting so upset, you're still my second favorite wife, he'd said!

Okay, he hadn't actually said that last one, but it had been heavily implied. For someone who was usually highly intuitive to human emotions, Mircea was surprisingly tone-deaf on this subject. There was, of course, a reason for that.

Just like the geis had played with his head, causing him to fall in love with the boring little Pythia who he was supposed to be manipulating, another factor—not a spell, but a syndrome—was screwing with him now.

Mircea was currently suffering from a condition common among ancient vamps, one that explained why there weren't many ancient vamps. The consul was older than dirt, and many members of the senate had five or six hundred years under their belts, but they were the exception, not the rule. "Older" for vamps usually meant a couple of centuries, not a couple of millennia, which was weird, when you stopped to think about it.

New vamps were created all the time. And while many never managed to make it beyond a normal human life span, getting killed in duels or on errands for their masters or from "greeting the sun," as they called it when one decided to suicide by waiting for the dawn, many others did just fine. So where were they?

All those millennia of vamps, and yet so few survived. Maybe because of the same thing that had started happening to Mircea. They began to obsess over something in their human lives that hadn't gone according to plan, or that had been left unresolved when they Changed. And by "obsess," I mean fixate on to the point that they couldn't see anything else.

Including the assassins sneaking up behind them.

It reminded me of the way some ghosts hung around after death, trying to put right events that had taken place, in some cases, hundreds of years before. Of course, for the ghosts, that was usually impossible, both because of how hard it was for them to actually interact with the world and because the people who had wronged them were often long dead themselves. That was not always true for vampires, however.

Especially not for vampires who knew a Pythia.

I'd found out about all this—what had happened to Elena, Mircea's plan for me, and his growing obsession— not by Mircea telling me about it, *as he should have done*, but in an explosive confrontation with said crazy dhampir. Who had almost killed me, assuming me to be a threat to her beloved father. Who had then, and only then, spilled the beans. Because the consul had already let part of the story "slip" anyway, and because he was shortly going into Faerie at the head of our army and wanted to make sure that Elena was taken care of in case he didn't come back.

Out of obligation, of course.

So yeah. I'd been shocked and horrified and heartbroken and a bunch of other things, and to a degree, I still was. But I got it, okay? I wasn't completely heartless; I understood why you'd want to save someone whom you'd loved enough to marry, and who had given birth to your only flesh and blood child.

I even understood why it must have seemed like a godsend to Mircea when he'd discovered that there were people who could actually *travel in time*. And could undo the terrible travesty of justice that had ended with his wife writhing out her final hours on a sharpened stake set up by his own brother. Anyone would understand that.

But anyone wasn't a Pythia, and responsible for guarding the timeline. Like from interference that might end up with a lot of other people dead who weren't supposed to be! Of course, Mircea wasn't in love with them—and he *was* in love with Elena, whether he realized it or not. It had been in his face that night, when he finally told me everything, even while he was vehemently declaring otherwise. It had been in the flashes of images I'd caught of his past, either through my seer abilities or because his mental powers were projecting them unknowingly in his distress. It had been clear as anything.

He still loved her, and he hadn't needed a geis for that.

So how was I supposed to tell him no?

But that was the job, and something every other Pythia had managed for five hundred years. And I probably would have, too, but before I could he'd struck preemptively, sending me a gorgeous copy of *Le Morte d'Arthur* as a gift. I still had it in the library. It was a beautiful thing, gilt edged and leather bound, with full-color illustrations scattered throughout.

It was lovely . . .

It was also a threat. A handsome, classy threat, because Mircea was a handsome, classy guy. But a threat nonetheless.

Because if I didn't do what he wanted, he was going to release to the public a secret he'd discovered about the other man in my life, John Pritkin.

My one-time bodyguard and partner in crime, Pritkin had been by my side almost since I'd stumbled into this crazy new life. We'd started out hating each other, had slowly learned to tolerate and then to respect each other, and had finally ended up in love almost without realizing it, even though we hadn't had a geis. But Pritkin wasn't his real name—at least, not the one he'd been born with—and Mircea knew it.

And soon, so would everybody else, if I didn't pony up.

Dating Merlin, it seemed, had its downsides.

Not that we *were* dating. I'd barely seen him since a demon curse had left him more or less dead for two weeks and sent me on a crazy race through time after his disembodied soul. I'd gotten him back, and had foolishly thought he'd stay put for a while. Ha!

Something weird had happened in Hong Kong recently, and Pritkin had gotten up—*off his literal deathbed*—to go deal with it. Of course he had. Without so much as telling me a word about it, because I might have had an objection to his getting himself killed just after getting himself killed!

Honestly, was it any wonder that, sometimes, I just wanted to stay in a bubble bath and never get out?

A bubble bath in a vamp-built penthouse in a hotel that Mircea owned, I thought evilly. One I was taking while he and the senate battled it out for who got to pull my strings this week. I was supposed to be an independent entity, able to arbitrate between the various supernatural groups because I wasn't beholden to one side over another. Could I do that here? Could I do that *anywhere*?

I'd told the covens that I could—that I *would*—and had somehow sounded confident doing it. But if Agnes hadn't managed it, what shot did I have? I couldn't even keep Mircea from taking my goddamned bodyguards! It was maddening!

Like my loofah brush suddenly deciding to break. I guess I'd been scrubbing a little too hard, and it snapped, causing me to spear my damned leg with a splinter. Damn it!

I threw it across the room, which was childish, but I was stressed. And was even more so when it hit not the smirking dolphins on the far wall but something in between. Something that wasn't there, because nothing was, but that gave a yelp anyway.

And then rushed at me, an invisible terror except for the suds now streaming down its chest.

# Chapter Seven

I should have shifted out and let my bodyguards deal with it, but it happened so fast that I reacted instead, sending a time wave that froze whatever it was in its tracks.

Or, to be more precise, in midair.

As far as I could tell, it had been halfway through a leap and now was stuck there as time literally stopped all around it. Except for me. I was left panting and slumped against the side of the tub, because time stoppages might not work on me, but they were still a bitch! And then slowly climbing to my feet and wading over to a towel rack, grabbing one, and wrapping it around me.

And going to see what this latest threat was.

I still wasn't sure. It was frozen solid, I could tell that much from the power loss alone, as well as the line of suds, hovering like a small cloud in the middle of the room. I tried throwing some more up there, but they didn't help all that much. I got a watery, soapy outline that was vaguely humanoid, but that was it.

So I went and got some body powder instead.

Halfway through shooting bursts of talcum everywhere, I started frowning. An expression that was a full-on scowl by the time I finished plastering what looked like a human-shaped statue, if a lumpy and rather streaky one. Not to mention wobbly, as my spell started to unravel.

My hands were shaking from the power loss by then, so I fished a little potion bottle out of my makeup bag, downed about a third of it, and felt ease and calm flood back through my system. And herbs scrape my tongue, because the stuff was nasty. I returned the bottle and brushed my teeth to get the taste out of my mouth, and because some people around here were nosy. Then came back over, sat on the edge of the tub, and waited.

It didn't take long.

The long legs started flailing, the equally elongated arms started windmilling, and the momentum the body had had before time literally stopped around it suddenly carried it forward—straight into the tub.

It—or rather, he—hit down, half-in and half-out of the large basin, with his head underneath the water. He came up, gasping and shrieking, and then choking, because I guess something went down the wrong way. Until one of the long legs scrabbling for purchase on the water-slick floor slipped, and he ended up getting dunked again.

He finally got two hands on the side of the tub and pushed up, popping his head out. Or I guess he did. The water had washed off the powder, making him invisible again from the chest up.

But I still had enough indicators to get the broken end of the bath brush under what I guessed was a chin. And it must have been close enough. Because the invisible man suddenly decided to become visible again.

Leaving me looking into the bug-eyed, terrified face of—

*"Augustine?"* I'd strongly suspected it was him, but I was still pissed.

"Aughhh!"

"Augustine!"

"Aughhh!"

"Stop shrieking!"

"Well, stop . . . *wheeze* . . . threatening me . . . *wheeze* . . . you psycho!"

I stared at him. *I* was the psycho? "What are you *doing* in here?"

He looked cross-eyed at the loofah stick and seemed to be having trouble breathing. Probably because his solar plexis had taken a hit when he slammed into the tub. "I had . . . to talk . . . to you—"

"Right *now*?"

"Yes, now! Now! It's important." He grabbed his chest. "What did you . . . *wheeze* . . . do to me?"

"Nothing permanent, although you're lucky I didn't kill you! What the hell were you jumping at me for?"

"I was afraid . . . that you were about . . . to scream. I didn't want . . . to have to deal . . . with that overgrown gorilla." He looked around, I guess noticing the fact that we were alone. "Where is he, anyway?"

"If you mean Marco, probably in the common rooms somewhere. The consul had a silence spell woven around the bedroom."

"Gods be praised!" Augustine tried getting up, only to slide back down onto his ass again.

I grabbed his arm, pulled him up, and slapped a towel onto his chest. "What did you do? And why didn't they see you sneaking in here?"

He rolled his eyes and disappeared again. For a second, I thought that was partly due to my stinging, blurry eyesight, because some soap had dripped from my hair into my face and screwed with my vision. And because no glamourie was that good. I was at point-blank range, and I still couldn't see him. But when I reached out a hand—

He was standing there, solid under my palm.

Son of a bitch.

"Move around," I ordered, because one of the things camo spells had trouble with was movement.

Nothing.

"Are you moving?"

"Yes! And stop feeling me up!"

"Well, I can't see you," I pointed out.

"That's the idea!" He slowly came back into view. First a shining blond head with a sharp, razor cut hairstyle that was now a dripping mess; then a lean, angular face with slightly crazed, pale blue eyes; and finally a shimmery jumpsuit that looked like a Buck Rogers costume from the eighties, with an opalescent white background that flashed prismatic colors whenever he moved.

"How are you doing that?" I asked, genuinely impressed.

He brushed it away. "It's something . . . I'm working on . . . for the Circle. For the war, you know?"

"Yeah." Augustine had been approached to help design some items for the invasion. It wasn't as weird as it sounds. He was part fey, and his designs had showed a tendency for creativity in the past. And, frankly, we could use all the help we could get.

"We're getting an invisible army?" My mood suddenly improved.

Augustine snorted. "They wish."

"It looks like it works to me!"

"Oh, it does. For about ninety seconds. Best-case scenario, it'll help some of our spies. But it takes too much power for general use."

Figured.

"Now listen," he said, toweling off. "What I need from you is—"

"What *I* need is a rinse off," I told him, turning on the shower because I had soap in my hair, and everywhere else. "Go wait in the dressing room."

"But I—"

"Out!" I said, massaging my stinging eyes. "Or I'll call Marco, I swear."

"Damn it, Cassie—"

"*And* I'll mention that gorilla comment."

He went.

I de-soaped, except for my eyes, which required some eye drops before I stopped looking tragic. I took my time, blowing out my hair and doing the mousse, curling iron, and round brush thing that made my tight little angry curls into big, soft bouncy ones that looked happy to be there. I even curled my eyelashes, because what the hell, and put on extra liner and mascara.

I thought about the fey woman's vivid blue eye color and added some shadow. It didn't really make mine much bluer, but it countered a bit of the lingering redness. So, score?

Finally, I traded my towel for a big terry cloth bathrobe and went into the dressing room. And immediately wished I'd arrived sooner. Because Augustine wasn't sitting at my dressing table, ankles primly crossed, waiting for me. He wasn't even sitting at all. His weird, too-skinny bod was in my walk-in closet, which had already

looked a little bare and was now being completely de-
nuded.

"Crap, crap, *unbelievable* crap!" He looked at me in
outrage, brandishing a shirt. "Have you been shopping at
thrift stores?"

"Hey!" I snatched my property back. It was one of my
favorites, a plain white tee with a bowl of leaves on the
front and "Salad, the Taste of Sadness" underneath. He'd
just ripped it off a hanger and was in the process of tossing it on a pile he was making in the corner. "Don't disre-
spect thrift stores. Half of my wardrobe used to come
from there."

"Used to?"

"Augustine—"

"You're right," he agreed. "I was being rude."

"That's better."

"You've clearly been mugging hobos." And he upturned an entire drawer.

"What are you *doing*?"

"Crap, crap—that's nice. Oh, it's mine. I should have—"

"Cut it out!"

"You need to come see me, darling," he said seriously.
"This is excrement, all of it. Except for my pieces, of
course."

"See you where? Your place burned down!" Along
with the rest of the main drag of the hotel. Which was
how the Battle on the Drag had gotten its name.

Dante's was currently undergoing renovations due to
the attack and was closed to the public, which was why
Augustine was staying here. His shop was barely an outline on the floor at the moment, so the builders had an
idea of where everything was supposed to go. And he had
flatly refused to return to his apartment, being sure that
the dark mages who'd attacked us were out to get him.
Since he'd helped in the fight, I'd offered him a place with
us—temporarily.

Why did I do these things?

"I'm doing a trunk show next week in the gold ballroom," he informed me. "Only for preferred clients, of
course. A sneak preview of my new, war-themed line. It's
*exquisite*."

Considering that the last time I'd heard him say that, it had been about a pith helmet that projected scenes out of *Lawrence of Arabia* into the air—complete with spitting camel—I had my doubts.

Like I doubted I'd have anything left to wear if he didn't stop already!

I grabbed the latest item destined for the pile, a nice black pencil skirt that I'd planned to pair with . . . something . . . for my trip, only Augustine wasn't letting go.

"I need this!"

The thin lips sneered. "For what? Your new secretarial position? Your job as a paralegal? Your upcoming debut as the Pythia with the worst fashion sense in the history of—"

"All right! Then what would you suggest I wear? I have to go to the senate—"

Augustine's blue eyes narrowed.

"What?" I said warily.

"I have the perfect thing," he told me. "Absolutely ravishing. The kind of ensemble, I daresay, that might make even a . . . consul . . . jealous?"

I licked my lips. And thought of Cleo and her outrageous fashion sense. She only did it for the shock value, no longer needing to play the power games that most vamps did. They sometimes wore outfits out of their pasts as an intimidation tactic, to show how old and therefore how strong they were. It made any gathering of venerable vamps look like a costume party and any human, aka me, who stumbled into their midst feel even more insignificant than normal.

Not that I planned to *be* in their midst. I needed to catch Mircea alone, where I could actually get a word in, not surrounded by a crowd like he usually was these days. But still . . . it would be nice to wear something impressive for a change.

"How much?" I asked apprehensively. Because Augustine didn't come cheap.

"It's not for sale," he told me. "I'll gift it to you."

I felt my own eyes narrow.

"Why?"

"You're going to do me a favor."

The eye-narrowing intensified. "What kind of favor?"

"You know very well what kind! I want to know where you found that dress—"

"What dress?"

*"What dre—"*

I clapped a hand over his mouth, because I wasn't sure if the soundproofing worked if you were already inside the suite, and Rhea might still be out there. "Hush!" I hissed. "Or do you want everybody to find out how easily you run around, spying on everyone?"

"Hn bmph mph anmph!"

"What?"

He removed the hand. "I don't spy on anyone!"

He was still yelling, but he was whisper yelling, so I guessed that was an improvement.

"Anyone but me," I pointed out.

"I wasn't spying! You jump around like a manic chicken; no one can get a word in—"

"That's not true!"

"It's entirely true! You're never here, and when you are, you're closeted away somewhere—"

"I am not!" I thought about it. "All right, maybe I am, but when I'm not, I'm *mobbed.* I have to go to the bathroom to get some peace and quiet anymore, and when I do, I *still* don't. I have the right to some privacy!"

"Yes, you do," said the man who'd just ruined it. "But your court also needs to see you occasionally. Do you even know all their names yet?"

"I was with them just this morning," I pointed out.

"Yes, guarding them. But not *interacting* with them. I'd be willing to bet that more of them are afraid of you than of Marco—"

"That's absurd!"

"—who at least gets down on all fours and plays with them, looking like some kind of huge bear—"

"First a gorilla, and now a bear. You really have a death wish, don't you?"

"—whereas you do what, exactly? When was the last time you spent quality time with them? Have you *ever?*"

He stood there, hands on skinny hips, looking at me accusingly.

I stared back, completely flat-footed. Where had this come from? And what the hell was his problem? My court was fine. No, my court was *better* than fine! And where did Augustine, who wasn't even part of it, get the right to tell me off? I was about to return the favor, but he didn't give me a chance.

"Your own court doesn't even know you yet," he said reproachfully. "They speak of you in hushed whispers or in awed little voices—or maybe fearful ones—"

"They're not afraid of me!"

"How would you know? I spend more time with them than you do!"

*"I have a war to fight!"*

A long-fingered hand clapped over my mouth. "Careful," he said nastily. "They'll hear you."

I pulled it off and glared at him. "Is that why you're here? To lecture me about my court?"

"No, I told you why I'm here. But apparently everyone else is too in awe of the great demigoddess to point out that her court still doesn't have a Pythia. You'd think you were afraid of them, or maybe it's just disdain. Like all those snooty women who buy my clothes and spend hours debating with me—as if they know anything—about button types, while the nannies raise the kids—hey!" He grabbed my arm. "Where are you going?"

"Out! I don't need to listen to this!"

"Ah, so it's fear, then."

I rounded on him, unexpectedly furious. "You know exactly nothing about me! You don't get to come in here—"

"And who else is going to?" he demanded. "Meek little Rhea, who worships the ground you walk on? The damned vampires, who don't care what you do as long as it doesn't cause the roof to cave in? Hildegarde, who might actually tell you the truth about some things, but who grew up in a time when children were best seen and not heard?"

"There's Tami," I said defensively, while wondering why I was arguing with a madman.

"Who is run off her feet and who isn't *you*."

He stopped the tirade as suddenly as it had begun and dropped onto the little pale blue velvet chair in front of my dressing table, although he was too tall for it and it left his knees poking up awkwardly. He ran a hand through his wet blond hair, making it stick up in little Pritkin spikes. And I felt a sudden pang of longing.

The war was playing havoc with my personal life, not that I had much of one anymore. I had to make an appointment to see my ex-"husband"; my supposed lover—who wasn't one, since we'd never had a spare moment to define our relationship—was off trying to get himself killed; and now I was being told that I was managing to screw up my court.

Great.

I flopped onto another chair opposite Augustine and fiddled with my robe ties. "Maybe I'm better off at war," I finally admitted. "I'm learning how to deal with that. I'm . . . not so great with the personal stuff."

Augustine chuffed out a laugh and let his head fall back, exposing the long line of his throat. "Neither am I."

We sat in silence for a moment.

"All I know," he finally said, "all I can tell you, is what it's like growing up in an environment where nobody cares. Or where it seems that way."

I thought of Tony's court, and my heart seized a little. I thought of Eugenie, my one-time governess, and it got worse. I'd clung to her because she was one of the only people who seemed to give the slightest of damns about me. But she'd been like Hilde—stiff upper lip, mind your manners, emotions are bad m'kay?—and I'd always, always, ended up feeling like I was starving, subsisting on crumbs of affection when I needed a full meal.

I didn't want to be Eugenie. I didn't want my girls growing up in a court that was physically safe but emotionally barren. But what was I supposed to do about it? They already had what I could give them: security, a nice place to live, other people to meet their emotional needs. I couldn't do that. I *literally* couldn't do that.

You learn to love by being loved. You learn to nurture

by being nurtured. You learn to meet other people's emotional needs by having your own met, and I never had.

Even at Tami's, where I'd found a home after running away from Tony, I'd been one of twenty, maybe thirty kids at any given time, all of us strays that she'd taken in and worked to house and clothe and feed. Some women are crazy cat ladies; Tami had been the crazy orphan lady, picking up kids off the streets or breaking them out of the Circle's special "schools"—basically just detention centers for children with unapproved types of magic. And many of the kids she picked up had had far worse emotional problems than me.

Or maybe they'd just been louder, I thought now.

Because I hadn't been okay, either.

I'd grown up feeling stunted, like a part of me was missing or just really, really underdeveloped. Augustine wasn't asking for much, I knew that. Just that I open up a bit more, let a few people in, be a little more approachable—

And make myself vulnerable, leave myself unprotected, start to care, only to have it all ripped away again! He was right, it *was* fear—or, rather, stark raving terror. Of a bunch of little girls!

Or, no, not of *them* so much, but of what they *represented*. Another Eugenie, dead on the floor after Tony ripped her to pieces; another Mac, a war mage—a decent man—who had given his life for mine; another Raphael, my substitute father growing up, burnt to a crisp in the desert trying to help me; another Mircea—

Goddamn it! Didn't Augustine *get* it? I didn't *want* to get to know them! I didn't want to care more than I already did!

Superficial stuff was fine; superficial I could do. Like taking them shopping or . . . or watching them eat breakfast—I'd done that a couple of times. But anything more left me feeling like I wanted to run in the opposite direction. Or hide out in my luxurious new suite within a suite, letting other people manage my court while I took care of business with a few trusted confidants, emerging when there was a threat to be dealt with or some problem to be managed. *That* was how a real court worked, I thought; less like a family and more like a business. One that was streamlined and efficient, and where everyone knew their place. One like the court I'd grown up in, where—

Oh God.

# Chapter Eight

"What is it?" Augustine asked, and I realized that I'd closed myself up at some point, physically as well as every other way, pulling my knees to my chest and wrapping my arms around them. If I'd been a hedgehog, I would have been in a tiny ball by now. If I'd been a porcupine, I would have been bristling.

As it was, I just sat there, fear clogging my throat, for a long moment. I didn't want to give voice to my little epiphany, in case it made it real. But it already was real, wasn't it?

I'd made sure of that.

"Tony," I finally croaked. "He was the vampire who ran the court I grew up in. I hated him. He was vicious and vile and cruel, and the only thing he loved was money."

Augustine looked confused. "So?"

"So I never saw him if I could avoid it, and I usually could. He didn't seem to actually like his own court very much. He stayed in his private apartments, locked away with a few trusted people—or as trusted as they got. Tony was paranoid, he never let anybody get too close . . ."

Like somebody else I knew.

Because it hadn't been Eugenie who'd run things at Tony's, had it? She'd just been a servant, like all the rest of us. There'd been only one person in that court with real power, only one who decided life or death, only one who . . .

Who a young, impressionable girl might have imprinted on.

Oh *God*.

"Hey." Long fingers wrapped around my hands, which I realized had the terry cloth in a death grip, probably to keep from shaking. I looked up to find Augustine's face a few inches from mine. He looked angry, for some reason. "You are *not* Tony."

"And you'd know? You never even met him!"

I didn't know why I was suddenly angry. Maybe because I didn't like talking about this stuff, not with anyone. And especially not with Augustine! I barely even knew him!

"I met him!" he said, that hair-trigger temper firing again and overriding my own. "Or ones just like him! Where the hell do you think I grew up, hm?"

"I—I don't—"

"No, you don't! I don't talk about it; I never talk about it," he snapped. And then he proceeded to talk about it. "You may not know this, but I have fey ancestry."

I blinked at him, from the too tall, too thin body, to the overlarge eyes, to the perfect, if haughty, features. "I . . . wouldn't have guessed."

"Yes, well, it's true. It wasn't recent, but I was a throwback—or my magic was. It was both the best and worst thing that ever happened to me." He got up, looming over me, and then sat back down discontentedly, because there wasn't really anywhere to go. "They came for me one night—"

"The fey?"

"No, not the fey!" he sneered. "They're supposed to come back for their children, but that's a lie. They come back for you, but only if you have some ability they want. My magic is unusual here, but back home—" He laughed suddenly. "Home! As if I had one of those! No, my magic is . . . common. Unremarkable. Unworthy of chasing down, especially if the fey blood is Svarestri, who hate humans and don't want their precious bloodlines tainted!"

He got up again.

"Then . . . who came?"

"Who do you think?" The blue eyes blazed down at me. "The Circle! Locked me up in one of those "schools" of theirs. And there was no Tami to come break me out.

Yes, we talked about that. I can't believe she dared—but then daring doesn't seem to be a problem for her."

"It's not," I swallowed. "It never was."

"Well, I wish I'd known her, or someone like her. As it was, I sat there, rotting, for sixteen years! Until they finally decided that maybe I wasn't the monster my parents had made me out to be, and let me out—"

"Your parents?"

He nodded fiercely. "I was a throwback, remember? A genetic joke. They didn't want anyone to know about me, didn't want the stares and pointed fingers, didn't even want me to bear their so-illustrious name. So I don't," he added proudly. "I am Augustine, just Augustine, and they can go fuck themselves!"

I looked up at him, blinking some more, because I'd never seen him like this. Of course, I'd never seen him much, period. He made pretty dresses that I occasionally bought, that was all—until the battle threw us together.

He suddenly crouched down, his height still leaving us mostly on a level, and looked at me. It was the most earnest expression I'd ever seen on the self-important face. "I overstepped my bounds earlier," he said. "I'm sorry for that. But I grew up in a place where I was a number, nothing more. They fed me. They clothed me. They gave me a basic education. That was all.

"I never felt for one minute like anyone there knew me, or that anyone cared. Perhaps because no one did. I was merely a number, an annoyance, a duty. Don't let these girls be numbers, Cassie, *please*."

I sat there, staring at him, because I didn't want that, either. But I also didn't know what to do about it. I'd rescued my court because they'd been in danger. I hadn't really thought about what came after that. And now that I did—

It was frankly terrifying.

"You're afraid of losing them, aren't you?" Augustine said, watching my face. "Of all this falling apart. It's understandable—"

I shook my head. "No, that's—it's not that."

"Then what is it?"

I stared into those suddenly kind blue eyes and wondered how to explain it to him. I wasn't sure I could, because I wasn't sure I could explain it to myself. It came out haltingly, slowly, as I tried to find words for something I'd never had to voice.

Usually, when I got to the Tony part, my brain flipped a switch, changing the subject. Going with something less painful, less raw. Because I could. It was my life and I could do what I damned well wanted!

But it was different now, wasn't it?

And I didn't know what to do with that.

"It's . . . off script," I finally said. "All of it."

"What is?"

"This." I gestured around at the pretty room. "The job. The kids. This *place*. I never had a home—"

"I understand—"

"No, you don't!" I stopped, struggling to figure out how to say it so that he would understand. "You were there, at that school, as they called it. And it was terrible and lonely—Tami's told me some things, how they practically brainwashed people to think that their abilities were bad, something to be repressed, to be ashamed of. How they made them feel that *they* were bad, without ever actually saying it, that they were dirty—"

A flash of remembered pain resculpted Augustine's face, and his eyes went distant. For a second, I could almost see the boy he'd been, so shining with talent, with hope, with life. And then slowly changing, drawing inward, shutting down.

I'd never done that.

I hadn't had any optimism to begin with.

"You didn't start out believing it," he told me. "You just . . . ended up that way. After a while, without hearing any other voices, their lies started to sound like the truth. Although there were always us defiant ones. We practiced our gifts in private, rebelling in the only way we knew how. It was shocking how much illegal magic went on behind the Circle's perfect walls!"

He laughed suddenly, and then cocked his head, his eyes refocusing on me. "Was that you at this vampire's court?"

"No." I hugged my knees. "Tony wanted me to use my

gift. It made him money. He would have liked me to have had more visions, not less. The Circle was trying to make you guys fit in to magical society, to force a square peg into a round hole, no matter how much they had to beat on it to make it go. Tony didn't care if I fit in anywhere—and that was the problem! I never did! I couldn't, even after I left him. I—"

I stopped, because I'd gone from halting and slow to a torrent of words and I didn't know where they'd come from. I didn't talk about this stuff. That had been one of the first lessons I'd learned. You never talked about anything but superficial stuff, because the deeper things . . .

Would be used against you.

But those days were over, I told myself harshly. Augustine wasn't going to use anything against me, and anyway, what I had to tell him couldn't be turned into a weapon. And for some reason, I wanted to tell him. I wanted to tell *somebody*.

"I never had a home," I repeated. "Even at Tami's, among the other Misfits—that's what we called ourselves, because none of us fit in. But we were . . ." I searched for the right words. "We were all different pegs, you know?"

"And none of the rest were vampire shaped," he guessed.

Augustine could be pretty astute sometimes.

"No. Some had come out of pretty terrible places—worse than I had, at times. But they were different. They didn't understand. We formed a group, learned to rely on each other, tried to make a family. But I couldn't stay still. I couldn't just let it be. I'd learned that Tony had ordered the hit on my parents, and I had to make him pay for that. I went back to him for three years, to try to set him up, and when I ran away again, I couldn't find them. Tami and the rest had already moved on."

And part of me had been relieved about that. Even as I searched everywhere for them, part of me had been relieved. I'd felt guilty about it at the time, even though I hadn't really understood it because I'd cared about them. I'd told myself that it was because Tony was after me and

I didn't want to endanger them, which had been true. But there'd also been something else.

Something I was just beginning to see.

"And Tony was looking for you," Augustine said, bringing me back to the point.

I nodded absently. "I'd run away from him twice at that point, made him look bad, made him look weak. He had to find me or maybe someone would start to believe he *was* weak, and that . . . doesn't work too well in their society."

"So you couldn't stay in one place for too long."

"I had to stay ahead of him, changing my looks, my name, my location, every little while. Because he'd find me otherwise. I became new people all the time, and every time I did, all the old stuff went away, and I started fresh. Every little while . . ."

"But that's all behind you now, don't you see?" Augustine took my hands. "Cassie, this isn't going to fade away. This is *permanent*."

Yeah, I thought. Permanent.

"I remember when I finally got out," he told me, his eyes shining. "It felt like a whole new life—and it was! It was hard at first, with no support, no contacts. My parents had them, of course, but that didn't matter. The fact that I'd been exonerated didn't matter. But after a while, I realized that—"

"Lady?"

The call came from the outer room, causing both of us to jerk our heads up. I grabbed Augustine, preparing to shift him . . . somewhere. But it was only Rhea, thank God. Augustine would be down for an ass kicking if the boys found out he'd snuck in here, but Rhea knew how to keep a secret.

Not that it mattered, since he'd just disappeared again.

"Lady, your food is getting cold," she informed me, from a respectful distance outside the door.

"Go," the invisible man whispered. "We'll talk later."

I went.

I didn't have anything constructive to say anyway.

Rhea had put my lunch on the sitting room table, a

gleaming beauty that could have held a family of eight with room left over. Maybe because, as Hilde had told me, it was customary for Pythias to use their private rooms for small meetings instead of the formal audience chamber, which I guess made sense. That place was so big it echoed.

This one didn't, not because it was smaller but because of all the luxurious soft furnishings everywhere. Like the large area rug over the dark hardwood floors that shaded from cream and sand on one end through all colors of blue on the other, like the tide hitting a beach. Or the huge, round bed, with its dark blue velvet coverlet, which had curtains that swooped closed at the press of a button, giving more privacy. Or the sand-colored couches in front of the big, widescreen TV in the sitting area across from the dining table. It was usually masked by a painting of sea nymphs, but it slid open at the touch of another button.

There was a fireplace underneath, in case I wanted to roast marshmallows, I guessed, because this was *Vegas*. And a private balcony where I could roast myself in the sun, buck naked if I wanted, because the only thing that might be higher than us was a helicopter. The balcony— excuse me, the outdoor terrace—was already my favorite part, and was bigger than the main one in my old suite. In fact, I wasn't sure that my old suite wouldn't have fit into just the master bedroom here.

You had to give the consul that much, I thought.

When she threw you a bribe, she did it right.

It was the perfect retreat, calm, serene, an oasis in the crazy. It was bigger than my whole apartment back in Atlanta, and way more comfortable. I could hunker down in here and just never leave . . .

"Lady?" Rhea said, sounding a little worried. Possibly because I was just standing in the middle of the room, staring blankly. "Is anything wrong?"

"No." I cleared my throat, because that had come out a little hoarse. "No, everything's fine."

I walked over to the table, and it took a while, because the sitting room was on the other side of the large space. I stood looking down on the neat place setting Rhea had laid out: heavy, genuine silverware; pristine white linen napkin; and bone china dishes. There was even a rose in a silver fluted vase. It was all very pretty.

And very lonely.

Of course, there were worse things. Because Augustine didn't get it. There was a power in starting over, a freedom, a *relief*. Yes, you paid a price for it, and that price was high: no permanent friends, no family, no roots. And I'd wanted those things; I'd wanted them badly. But, I was starting to realize, I'd feared them, too.

Permanence was scary.

There were no do-overs anymore. No way to erase old mistakes just by picking up and starting a new life in a new place. And there were people here, so many and so small, who depended on me. What if I got it wrong this time? What if I screwed up all of their lives as well as my own? Because I did that, I did that a lot, only I couldn't now and—

I bit my lip, trying not to panic, wondering why I was like this. And if I was ever going to get my stupid head sorted out. If I was ever going to stop wanting to *run*.

This was why I never wanted to think about this stuff, why I pushed it aside and pretended everything was fine, fine, we're all fine here. Because it wasn't a single problem but dozens, most of which were contradictions. Wanting a home and not wanting one. Wanting to be accepted and wanting to escape. Wanting love and friendship and yet pushing people away.

I didn't know what was wrong with me or what to do about it. Which is why it was really funny that other people wanted my advice so badly. I couldn't even figure myself out! Because it didn't just happen, did it? You didn't just wake up one day and suddenly decide to be normal, did you?

Or maybe that was exactly what you had to do.

Pritkin's father and I had gotten to know each other a little recently, and Rosier was . . . different. A selfish asshole most of the time, he had these weird flashes of decency, like glimpses of what he might have been had his life gone differently. For a demon lord, he'd had a pretty rough time of it, a lot of which had stemmed from his own father's early demise at the hands of my mother.

She'd hunted him down, killed and eaten him, or at least his energy.

It had made the partnership a little . . . tense.

But he'd given me one piece of good advice, at least: "fake it till you make it" wasn't just a human thing.

I hesitated for another moment, because I was a mess. And then I piled everything back on the tray and picked it up. "Lady?" Rhea said, coming up behind me. "Did you want me to have it reheated?"

"No, it's fine," I said. "I just, uh, think I'll eat outside today," I told her casually. And walked out, past a very surprised-looking acolyte.

# Chapter Nine

The main outdoor terrace of the suite branched off the salon and was truly huge, with part of it having been reclaimed from the old living room. It had a forest of plants, a curving glass solarium-style roof, a large pool, some lounge chairs, and a table with a happy-looking blue and white umbrella over it. The sun was shining, and some of the smaller girls were splashing around in the pool wearing water wings.

A swimsuit-clad Tami was sitting on the side, watching them with eagle eyes. She spotted me as soon as I emerged from the hallway with all the bedrooms, and waved me over. But some of the girls were coloring at the umbrella table, and I didn't want to disturb them. I opted for the big, sand-colored sectional and coffee table in the salon instead.

And finally got to enjoy my cassoulet. It was warm and filling and the definition of comfort food. I hadn't realized how hungry I was until I took the cover off and that fragrance hit my nose again. I ended up eating two portions, along with some fresh baked bread and a hoppy beer that my waistline didn't need but that went perfectly with the meal—until I noticed that I had an observer.

A small dark-haired girl had sidled up to the sofa unnoticed in my food haze. She jumped a little when my eyes focused on her, dropped something, and fled. I picked it up.

It was a picture of a tall woman with flowing blond hair, a goddess-type dress, and hands that appeared to be doing something, but I couldn't tell what, because the artist didn't really do hands. More like circles with lines in them. But the circles appeared to be conjuring something up. There was a lot of golden light being thrown around anyway, or golden something.

The yellow crayon was probably a nub by now.

I looked up at Fred, my shortest, portliest, and most food-obsessed bodyguard, who had also sidled over, in order to steal the rest of my bread. He had slathered it with butter and was currently making little orgasmic noises while he stuffed it in, which would have been creepy except that I did the same thing when eating Tami's bread. Everybody did. You want magic? That stuff was magic.

"Ha!" Fred said, sitting down and pulling my tray over so he could get better access.

"Ha, what?" I asked, and stole back the end piece of the bread.

"That's the best part," he protested, around a mouthful of stolen food.

"I know." I buttered it up and savored the way the crust crackled on my tongue. Just yum. "It's still warm," I informed him.

"You're evil. She should have used black."

"What?"

"Black vibes, like black magic, you know?" He nodded at the picture.

I picked it up again. "This isn't me."

Fred frowned around some of my cassoulet. His little fangs were out, probably to help him strip the flesh off one of the tiny chicken legs. Tami used small chickens, because she said the sauce penetrated better, and they were more tender.

Couldn't argue with that.

"Of course it's you," Fred said. "Who else would it be?"

I looked at it again. "I don't know, but I'm not that tall."

"You are if the artist is five," he pointed out.

"And that's not my hair."

Fred considered it for a minute. "You got a point there. She's got better hair."

He could talk, Mr. What-Comb-Over-I-Don't-Have-a-

Comb-Over. As a master vamp, he could have easily looked however he wanted to other people. Yet he continued to be the pudgy guy in the button-up shirts that strained slightly across the middle, showing a gap filled with white undershirt. And ties, when he remembered to wear them, that invariably ended up under one ear. And ill-fitting, off-the-rack suits, when even newbies to the family wore Armani.

Yet Fred was probably the easiest to relate to of all my guards. Except for right now. "I don't look like that."

"The kid's *five*," he repeated. "What do you expect?"

I didn't know, but that wasn't me. That woman was tall and strong and glowed with power. Circle hands and lopsided eyes and all, she was someone who looked forceful and imposing, surrounded by a halo of golden light. She looked like a goddess.

I put the picture down, and some of the warm feeling from lunch faded.

Fred was eyeing me up while scarfing down the rest of my meal. "It's like Picasso, you know?"

"Why, because the eyes are off center?"

"No, because it's not about the surface." He picked it up. "Come on," he said suddenly, getting to his feet.

"What?"

"I got something to show you. You can take your pie." He looked enviously at the thick slice of lemon meringue waiting for me on my tray.

I took the pie.

Around here, you guarded your desserts or you didn't have them for long.

Fred led the way out of the main lounge and through the secondary one with the moon-shaped couches, which provided a sort of hub where various wide hallways met. But he didn't go down any of them. He veered off into the formal dining room, where I'd rarely been. But that obviously wasn't true for the girls, and they'd made it their own.

The consul hadn't been able to decide what era or style she wanted, and had kept changing her mind between rooms. This was British colonial, with dark wood everywhere, which Tami fussed about because it showed dust so easily; genuine Persian rugs on the floor, complete with frayed spots for authenticity; and paintings showing bewildered Englishmen in exotic settings. Or, at least, they had, until somebody'd covered them with drawings.

I guessed when you had a couple dozen kids, a fridge just didn't cut it. So somebody had started scotch-taping the girls' drawings up in here. Like, *all* the drawings. Some were quite good and I guess done by the older initiates, while others were just cheerful squiggles done by the youngest, which Tami—at a guess—had nonetheless proudly displayed alongside all the rest. Including some that . . .

Oh.

That looked like me.

My attention had been caught by a Cassie with a *lot* of blond curls and a massive head—seriously, I had more head than body—who was lurching around, chasing what I assumed were tiny dark mages in black trench coats. They were moving because the drawing had been animated—it looked like Saffy had been in here—and because the creature chasing them was terrifying. The neck supporting the giant head was just two tiny marks and totally insufficient. Meaning that it flopped about as I ran, with a large, grinning rictus of a mouth that never changed expression and little stick arms that swatted at the mages, who were running for their lives, their mouths open and screaming in silent horror.

Which, yeah.

I'd be running if that thing was after me, too.

There was another one nearby, this time featuring a slightly less wild-haired Cassie sprinting through a forest, dodging painted bombs that exploded and set painted trees on fire. And then another who was busy bopping a giant red dude who I guessed was meant to be Ares on the head with a wand I don't have. And another . . .

They were almost all me, I realized. I found myself looking at a cartoon version of my life of the last summer. It was surreal.

"Hilde's been telling them stories," Fred said.

Yeah, I guessed, I thought, looking at another girl's efforts. Judging by the level of the artwork, I was assuming that she was one of the younger initiates, although she'd unknowingly re-created one of the great master-pieces of the nineteenth century: *Saturn Devouring His Son*. Only I was Saturn. And was busy stuffing down my enemies, my working cheeks distended by tiny flailing arms and legs, but an otherwise cheerful expression on my face as I chewed.

I stared at it for a while, and then at some of the others, which were mostly more pics of me raining down my wrath in various ways. Was that how they saw me? As some kind of monster?

No wonder Augustine thought they feared me!

I must have said that last bit aloud, because Fred turned from taping up the latest masterpiece, which in retrospect was one of the least disturbing, and looked at me. "Is that what he said?"

I nodded, still a little stunned.

Fred snorted. "Augustine should stick to designing dresses. He'd make a lousy shrink."

"It doesn't look that way to me."

Fred scowled and gestured at the latest glowing god-dess. "Then you're not looking at it right. It's all about inner emotions, see? That's how Rita feels when she looks at you, like she has a guardian angel or something. What could possibly hurt her with someone like that in the way?" He chuckled. "All you need is a flaming sword."

Yeah, and a lot more power.

Fred was helping my anxiety exactly none at all.

*This* was why I didn't want to get to know my court, I thought, biting my lip. *This* was why I hid away in my room. Because all those little girls who were idolizing me as their protector hadn't seen just how close some of those events had been. I hadn't been striding across the landscape, throwing thunderbolts amid cheerful slaughter. I'd been running on fumes, trusting to luck and perseverance and a shitload of other people's help to survive, and had somehow come out on top, maybe because people kept underestimating me. But that sort of thing didn't last forever, and the biggest challenges lay ahead.

"You're still looking at it wrong," Fred said, eyeing me.

"How am I supposed to look at it? I'm not that person—"

"Aren't you?" He examined the wall and selected another picture of me torturing poor Ares, which seemed to be a theme. This one had me stabbing him in the face repeatedly. The artist had really gotten into it. There was a massive spurt of blood that momentarily obscured the image after every strike.

"That wasn't you?"

"No!"

"Oh, Ares is still alive, then?"

"You know damned well he isn't! But that—"

"Then that was you." He looked at it in satisfaction. A vamp would like that much blood, I thought crossly.

"I did not stab Ares in the face!"

Fred waved it away. "Artistic license."

He tapped another, which looked more like my mother than me. It was of the other main grouping, the goddess-y line, showing flowy dresses and flowers and castles, which I guessed the blood-crazed demon went back to when she was tired of face stabbing. "That's not you?"

"Fred—"

"'Cause it kinda looks like you. Better hair, of course—"

"I did my hair today!" I said, snatching it away from him.

He eyed me doubtfully. "Maybe it needs a cut. You know, the salon downstairs is still open—"

"Fred!"

"Just saying. Like I'm saying that you need to look closer." He flicked the page with a nail. "That's this place. This is their safe space, their castle. You gave them that, and you stand guard over it, making sure nothing can hurt them. *Look*."

I looked. Back across the row of pictures, some in crayon, some in colored pencil, a few in vigorous pastel. But Fred was right, they all had a theme. And it fucking broke me.

I already had a home, I realized, a castle in the clouds as some of them had drawn it, safe and secure from all attackers. And if it wasn't, well there was a guardian, wasn't there? Not a dragon, but a Pythia, fierce and capable and—

"You're not gonna cry, are you?" Fred asked, looking at me worriedly.

"No."

"Liar."

He put an arm around me while I shivered through a second epiphany in the space of an hour.

We stood like that for a long time, staring at the pictures. I couldn't take it all in; I just couldn't. Not right now. But it felt like something had changed in that moment. Something big.

"Cassie?"

"Hm?" I looked at Fred, who was looking back earnestly.

"You've had an emotional day, I can tell—"

"Yeah."

"—so I'm gonna do you a solid—"

"Yeah?"

"—and eat your pie."

He grabbed it.

"What?"

"Well, you're obviously too upset to enjoy it—"

"Fred!"

"I'm only trying to help!" he said, sprinting for the door.

"Come back here!"

"Gonna have to catch me!"

Son of a bitch!

Fred did not eat my pie. Of course, I didn't, either, at least not right away. By the time I'd hunted him down and made it back to the living room, the coffee table was already in use—by my tarot cards.

I'd taken the soaked pack out of my purse, but had only tossed it on the counter in the kitchen. I'd meant to get to it later, but someone had beaten me to it, laying them out in neat little rows to dry. Not that it seemed to be helping.

"I think they may be broken," Rhea said. She was sitting on the sofa, poking at them and looking worried.

I put the pie I'd retrieved from Fred on a side table,

where I could keep an eye on it, and bent closer. Weird little sounds were coming from some of the cards: discontented mutterings, some stuff that sounded like sneezes or hiccups, and one little trooper that was just managing to get some words out, although I could barely hear what it was saying. Until I held it to my ear, where it sounded like it had a run-down battery.

"Streeeeeennnnnnnthhhhh," it moaned at me. "Streeeeeennnnnnnthhhhh."

"Okay, that's not creepy at all," I said, putting it back down.

But I'd forgotten that showing interest in one of the cards tended to cause it to rev up. "Streeeeeennnnnnnthhhhh," it said, suddenly louder. "Streeeeeennnnnnnthhhhh!"

"Will it . . . stop that . . . eventually?" Rhea asked.

"No." I glanced around. "The only thing that shuts them up is being put back in the pack. Have you seen it?"

"I left it in the kitchen. I'll go get it." She ran off, looking relieved.

I hoped she'd hurry. The voice kept getting louder and louder, but it seemed stuck on that one word. Until it was practically screaming it at me: "Streeeeeennnnnnnthhhhh! Streeeeeennnnnnnthhhhh! Streeeeeennnnnnnthhhhh!"

"Shut up!" I snapped, but it didn't shut up.

So I slammed Tami's food dome over top of it, which helped a little.

"Streeeeeennnnnnnthhhhh!" it said peevishly, the word still coming through fairly audibly. "Streeeeeennnnnnnthhhhh!"

I regarded the dome for a moment, then went back to my bathroom, picked up my hair dryer, and came back in.

"Streeeeeennnnnnnthhhhh!" it yelled at me, as I lifted up the cover again. "Streeeeeee—EEEEEEEEEEEEEEE!"

The last was because I'd grabbed the card and turned the dryer on, and the little thing was flapping in the breeze.

"Stren-stren-stren-stren—" it said, as I rotated it this way and that. Rhea came back in, saw what I was doing, and left again.

"Stren-stren-stren-stren—"

"I have an idea," she said, running back in, holding one of the extra pillowcases that had come with my gigantic bed.

"Good idea!" It was easily twice the size of a regular pillowcase, because the pillows were twice the size of regular pillows. They had to be, or they'd have looked ridiculous on that thing.

I glanced back at the bedroom worriedly. Under the assumption that the consul had prepped this place for me, what, exactly, had she thought a hundred-and-fifteen-pound woman needed with a bed that big? Was it a status thing? Was it done to fit the size of the room? Was I supposed to be holding orgies? What?

"Lady?" Rhea said, and I turned to find her holding up the case, now full of waterlogged cards.

"Stren-stren-stren-stren—"

I tossed my card in with the others. And then blasted the lot of them on high, while Rhea held the other end of the case and fluffed it around so that the hot air would reach them all equally.

"We could use the clothes dryer!" she yelled, because more of them were talking now.

"But it wouldn't be as much fun!" I yelled back, laughing.

Because it was. And I guess Rhea thought so, too. Because for a minute, she looked like the kid she'd never gotten to be.

All this talk about childhood made me wonder how it had been for her, growing up at that other Pythian Court. Because it hadn't seemed all that much fun to me. Prim, proper, and beautiful, yes; fun, no.

And while the other girls had been able to flaunt their family names and the age-old pedigrees that went with them, Rhea had had to be a nobody, just a coven girl that someone had been dumb enough to let in and who never fit in with the cool kids. The ones who'd acceded to acolyte status almost as a matter of course, as if it had been ordained from the time they exited the womb. And who had received all the training that was denied to her, because she supposedly wasn't talented enough.

Hilde was right; Rhea was probably super talented, considering who her parents were. But she didn't believe it, because she'd always been told otherwise. She couldn't see her own worth, because no one else had ever seen it, except for her mother. And Agnes hadn't wanted her daughter following in her footsteps because she had thought she'd be happier elsewhere. But shouldn't that have been Rhea's decision?

I thought about Jo, another outsider in the court, although for a different reason. Jo had made acolyte, as Rhea had not, because she belonged to an old magical family who had pulled the usual strings. But she hadn't been part of the cool girls' clique, either, although not because of a lack of talent. Because her talent had gone down an unauthorized path.

Jo had been a necromancer, a magic worker with power over the dead, one of the most reviled of magical gifts.

During the wars between vamps and mages hundreds of years ago, necros had served both sides, wherever they could get a patron who would protect them. Low-level necromancers had been prized by vamps as field medics, with their ability to manipulate dead flesh allowing them to greatly speed up the healing process. Mages had likewise employed them as spies, since their ability to see what their creatures were seeing gave them eyes in an enemy camp that were virtually impossible to detect.

But as soon as the wars were over, all of that changed. Necromancers went from being a tolerated asset to a feared danger almost overnight. Vampires hated them because they could influence and sometimes even control baby vamps. Mages mistrusted them because they could create unkillable creatures to do their bidding and steal information from dead minds. Which was why one of the first stipulations of the treaty that had ended the long conflict had been to put considerable restrictions on what they were allowed to do.

And serving on the Pythian Court was definitely not allowed.

Jo had been forced to hide her gift, and to use conventional magic—her secondary skill—against the other girls' primary ones. So, of course, she'd made a poor showing. They'd resented her as a political appointment who they didn't think deserved the honor and treated her as deadweight that would soon be winnowed out.

And, oh, how she'd resented it!

Over time, Jo had turned from an angry, narcissistic young woman into what I have no reservations at all about calling a monster. She'd joined the other side in the war, not in hopes of wealth or honor or position, but simply out of revenge. She'd worked to bring the god Ares back to earth specifically because she knew what kind of destruction he'd wreak. She planned to use him, as she'd triumphantly told me, to utterly destroy the magical world that had marginalized and rejected her.

She hadn't succeeded, but she'd come awfully close. I still had nightmares about how close. I could still see the glee in those bright green eyes at the death and destruction she was causing, and the stretch of that wide, red mouth while watching others' pain.

I guess some girls really did just want to watch the world burn.

Which is what made it all the more amazing that Rhea had gone down an entirely different path.

And that was despite being in a worse position than Jo ever was. As an older initiate without acolyte status, she'd been left in limbo, not fitting in with either the younger girls or the older adepts. She'd ended up as little more than a servant, helping out in the nursery where the youngest initiates were kept until they were old enough to move into shared rooms.

She'd nursed their colds and held their hands at night when they cried because they missed their families. She'd read them stories, taught them their ABC's, and helped the older girls with their homework. She'd been a constant prop to her mother, especially in the final days of her life, when Agnes was so ill. And, as far as I could tell, she'd never uttered a single complaint.

Or, you know, tried to burn the world down.

She'd even helped a bumbling, clueless Pythia, the woman who had gotten the position that another girl might have thought she deserved. But instead of sulking in a corner or trying to sabotage me, Rhea had fiercely defended me and my office. She'd taught me things I'd never known about the Pythian Court, she'd gone into a firefight with me and some crazy coven witches to rescue that court, and she'd *slit her own throat* later on to protect it.

I didn't deserve her.

I knew I didn't.

But I was selfish enough to be grateful that she was here anyway.

"What is it?" she asked me now, probably because I was tearing up like an idiot.

"Thank you," I told her, which made her look confused, because all she was doing at the moment was holding a pillowcase.

"You're welcome?" She peered inside. "I think they're dry," she said, as the newly fluffed cards babbled away happily.

"Finally!" I started fishing them out and shoving them back into their case, before they could talk my ear off.

"Lady . . . I was wondering . . ."

"It's Cassie," I said absently, for the eight hundredth time.

Rhea was a big one for protecting the dignity of the court, and had been appalled at the thought of calling me by my first name in public. She didn't even do it much when we were alone, as we basically were now, since the only others in sight were out on the terrace. I guess she was afraid it might cause her to slip up later.

"Cassie," she said, lowering her voice. "I thought perhaps—"

"Strength!" the first little card interrupted smartly, as I picked it up from the pile.

It was sadly rumpled and slightly fuzzy, and looked like it needed a good ironing. But the picture on the front was clear enough, showing a large, muscular lion being hugged gently by a woman with golden hair that almost matched his fur. She showed no sign of fear; in fact, she seemed almost peaceful.

Which was a weird way to look when you're hugging a lion.

"The lion on our card symbolizes raw passions and desires," the card informed me. "Which can be expressed positively or negatively. But for the former to manifest, the lion needs a trainer. The woman on our card has begun to tame this wild beast, not through painful coercion but through kindness and love. If she can complete the training, she will have the beast's strength to use on her behalf. If not . . ."

"If not?" I prompted.

"Well, at least the lion will have a tasty snack."

I frowned, and shoved the cheeky little thing back into the pack.

"Lady? I mean Cassie?"

I looked up.

"I'm sorry," I told Rhea. "I'm spacing out today. What did you want?"

"Permission to go with Saffy tomorrow night. There's to be a meeting of the covens—we had a call a little while ago. I'm not specifically invited—"

"And neither am I," I guessed, because I was pretty sure what the meeting was about.

"Er, no," she agreed. "But I could go and tell you what was said. It's to be in the same market where you went shopping today. They have a meeting hall there, so it's not far. I could—"

"Do what?" I asked curiously. "Saffy can tell me what they say."

"Yes, but . . ." Rhea bit her lip, but probably not for the same reason I would have. I tended to be overly blunt, and have to remind myself that a Pythia was supposed to be a diplomat. Rhea, on the other hand, hated saying anything that might be construed as criticism of another person.

"But?" I asked.

"Saffy can be . . . passionate . . . about her beliefs," she said carefully. "That is admirable, but since she works here now, whatever she says might be misconstrued as, well—"

"As coming from me?"

She nodded. "I can't vote, as I'm not an active member of my old coven. But I have speaking rights, and can make clear what is and is not our position. If you would like?"

I thought about it. Knowing Saffy—and the covens' preferred debating method—a cool head might not be a bad idea. And neither would something else.

"Give me a minute," I told her, and ran back into the dressing room. "Augustine!" I whispered.

There was no answer.

"Augustine. I'm willing to make that deal!"

Still nothing.

Even more telling, the pile of rejected clothes in the corner hadn't gotten any bigger. It looked like he'd gotten bored and decided not to wait for me. Which was weird, considering how urgent he'd been.

*Geniuses*, I thought.

And then I saw it, gleaming on the surface of my dressing table: a little silver key.

All right! I thought, and grabbed it. Now *that* was a score.

# Chapter Ten

I finally got my pie, sitting in the sunshine out by the pool, where the little girls had abandoned their crayons to join the party in the water and the older ones were giving me a fashion show. Including Rhea and Saffy, who were trying to decide what to wear to impress the covens. Considering everything I'd seen this morning, I didn't think that was too likely, no matter what they chose.

But if anybody could do it, it was Augustine.

"I'm thinking dom," Saffy said, turning around in front of me. She had on a Vivienne Westwood–inspired number in dark purple, almost black—what Augustine probably called aubergine. But there were iridescent swirls of paler hues in the fabric when the sun hit it just right. It had a low-cut, skintight bustier; ruched leggings; thigh-high suede boots of the same color; and a fitted jacket with huge lapels that spread out over the shoulders and came up around the head, forming a hood.

She was right; she looked like a really well-dressed dominatrix sans the whip, although the handles of two wands were sticking up out of the high tops of the boots. I saw several of the guys eyeing her appreciatively, and Saffy obviously liked her choice. I wasn't sure that was quite the message we wanted to be sending, but what did I know? Maybe glam dom was in with the covens.

I hadn't noticed any shrinking violets in their number.

"If Rhea's coming along, we can do good cop, bad cop, you know?" she added.

"And which are you going to be?" Rico asked, his dark eyes gleaming.

But not at her.

The bad boy among my bodyguards was a soft-spoken Italian who tended to let his weapons talk for him—unless, of course, he was sitting with Rhea. He'd guarded her fiercely while she'd been bedridden, barely even letting the healers get anywhere near her, and although he'd backed off a bit once she was on her feet again, I'd noticed the dark eyes following her around the suite more than once. And if I'd noticed, so had everyone else, although nobody but Marco had had the cojones to tease him about it.

My guys weren't stupid.

"What?" Saffy said, before glancing behind her. And doing a double take along with the rest of us. Because it seemed that Rhea had chosen something from Augustine's stash as well, although not what anyone could have expected.

Because my sweet-faced acolyte had found the black leather, and damned if it didn't look good on her.

There was none of Saffy's glamour here. In fact, I wasn't even sure what Rhea's getup had been doing among Augustine's usual society butterfly chic, unless it was part of the new war line he'd mentioned. Because that's what it looked like: something a ninja assassin might have worn, if she was a little better-heeled than average.

Make that a lot better, I thought, as Rhea slowly rotated. And the black, asymmetrical, ribbed leather tunic she was wearing over skintight leggings fell off her shoulders all at once, in a burst of Augustine's signature origami, unfolding like a flower to become a gauzy ball gown with a poufy skirt and strapless bodice. The skirt was black tulle over a taupe underskirt and studded with what looked like black diamonds that glimmered darkly against the mesh-like fabric.

Her arms were covered with high black leather gloves, which the now missing sleeves had peeled away to reveal, and which gave even the dressier version of the outfit an edge. And the skirt wasn't full-length, giving a clear view of the high-heeled black boots she wore, still covered in buckles and straps. I hadn't noticed in the wonder of the transformation, but part of the tunic had become a cool, biker-type jacket, which she effortlessly slung over her shoulder but which would look equally good on.

"It folds back up again just as fast," she told us eagerly. "Do you want to see?"

"I want to switch outfits," Saffy said enviously.

Rico didn't say anything. But something in his eyes made even me blush. Rhea didn't notice, being too busy fluffing out a couple of folds in the skirt. But then she looked up and caught his eyes.

And smiled at him. "Do you like it?"

"Yes." The voice was rough. "I like it."

The implication was clear as crystal to everybody but Rhea: he'd like it better on the floor.

"Down, boy," Marco said, putting a hand on Rico's shoulder as he passed by.

Rico didn't respond, still staring at Rhea.

And I suddenly wondered if I was going to have a problem there. And then I wondered if it was any of my business. Normally, the answer would have been no. Rhea was nineteen, and despite the fact that she'd been pretty darned sheltered at the Pythian Court, she had a right to make her own decisions—and her own mistakes. Not that I necessarily thought Rico would be one, but still. It wasn't up to me.

Except that, in this case, it kinda was.

Because Rhea was in running for the top spot in the court, aka my heir. In fact, right now, considering my complete lack of other young acolytes, she was the only contender. And while I might live to be an old woman—unlikely—and while she might not want it now, after years of her mother's indoctrination—more likely—she might change her mind later.

And that . . . created a problem.

Or maybe not. Because I didn't know what the rules were anymore—nobody did. For thousands of years, the Pythian power went to a new Pythia in a very specific ceremony, one involving the marriage of the selected girl to the god Apollo. That made sense, since he had originally gifted the power to his priestesses at Delphi. But Apollo was dead, and good riddance, so what happened now?

The power seemed to be functioning fine so far, having taken on a life of its own after it broke away from its master. But then, nobody had tried to pass it on since his death. An avatar had been needed for the original ceremony, as a stand-in for the absent god. When the avatar and the selected priestess got busy, the power transferred over. And because it was considered a marriage and the old-timey Greeks were sexist as hell, the selected girl was expected to come to the ceremony a virgin.

Was she still?

It probably depended on whether that had been one of the original requirements woven into the spell when it was laid, or whether it had just been a cultural thing. Agnes had said something once that had made it sound like the latter, but I wasn't sure. Agnes had said a lot of things.

But until I found out, Rhea—assuming she wanted to keep her options open—needed to play it cool.

And so did Rico.

Well, shit.

I really wanted to postpone this, but I'd finished my pie, and Saffy had just dragged Rhea off to help her find a new outfit, and . . .

And I was out of excuses.

I leaned over. "Can I talk to you?" I asked Rico, and had to repeat the question twice.

He finally glanced at me, blinked a couple of times, and nodded.

We got up and moved inside, at least far enough to put us out of hearing range of the kids. The younger ones were making a racket, splashing about in water wings or clinging to noodles, because the London court hadn't had a pool and half of them didn't know how to swim. The older girls were helping Tami lifeguard, or trying on outfits, even though the ones Augustine had promised to design for them weren't ready yet.

That was another reason he was staying with us. Everybody needed new formal attire, because the old lacy dresses the court had once worn were seriously outdated, and because they'd mostly burned up in the bombing anyway. Silver linings, I thought, and watched the older girls pirouette in front of Tami.

"They think you're going to let them choose their own outfits," Rico told me, in an undertone.

"Yeah, no," I said, watching two of the older girls, Belvia and Lettuce—and yes, her name was actually Lettuce—strut around in leather and lace. But mostly leather. It was couture biker chic, including, in Belvia's case, an entire arm of colorful, real-looking tats.

"They come off with the outfit," Rico informed me, smiling slightly at my expression.

"I hope so!" How had I ever thought that running a court full of little girls—and soon to be hormonal teens— was going to be easy? Speaking of which—

"Rico, we need to have an understanding about something."

"Not someone?" he asked, because he wasn't stupid.

"Okay, someone," I agreed.

"I know the rules," he told me tersely. "Marco made them clear."

"Really." I hadn't known we'd established any rules for the court yet, much less that Marco was enforcing them. "What did he say?"

"Leaving off the more graphic details, if any of us get any ideas about the girls, we should, er, geld ourselves, before he does it for us."

"That was leaving off the graphic stuff?"

Rico smiled again and lit up a cigarette. "He likes to be clear," he repeated.

I guessed.

I watched the end of his smoke flare, and doubted that Tami would approve, but she was out of eyesight. And anyway, he looked like he needed it. Not that the bad boy vibe was in any way lacking. The dark hair that wanted so badly to curl, but that he ruthlessly kept tamed, was the same as ever, as was the strong, tanned throat; the liquid dark eyes; and the set of tats he sported—which didn't come off—on one T-shirt-clad shoulder, because I'd never seen him in a suit. But there was something sad about his expression.

Sad or hungry? I wondered, and sighed.

"Then let me be even clearer," I said, "because I don't know if he explained why."

"I know why." It was harsh.

I frowned. Because that reaction seemed a little . . . odd. "You do?"

"I know who I am, and I know who she is, all right?" he said, in an undertone.

I frowned some more, because I was getting confused. "Who you are?"

"I know my place!" he told me, and stubbed out the barely smoked cigarette on the bottom of his boot. "Now, if that's all?"

"Yeah, not quite," I said, grabbing his bicep when he started to leave.

Rico gave me a less-than-fond look, which was not normal, but he followed me out into the foyer when I tugged on him. "Take a break," I told Simon, the vamp on duty.

The tall Nigerian with the normally quick smile nodded solemnly and went inside. It looked like he thought Rico was about to get a chewing out. Rico obviously did, too, because his jaw was clenched and he looked like he wished he had that cigarette back.

It was weird, because I didn't know why he'd be worried about anything I might say, unless he was afraid of being sent back home. As if. He was one of my most competent guys; nothing rattled him, at least not in combat.

Relationships, however, seemed to be another story.

"Look," I told him. "I normally wouldn't get involved, but—" I broke off, because Rico had suddenly jumped up, higher than my head, and grabbed something.

It was a little package, one of the ones Hilde had enchanted. It had been overlooked because it had been rotating behind one of the ribbed columns and was tricked out in white and gold like the ceiling. But he'd seen it. Rico's eyes didn't miss much.

Like my frown when he handed it over.

"I'm not stalling," he told me. "Say what you have to say."

"I will." But I didn't really want to do this, so I took a moment to open the package. A perfume bottle fell out into my hand. Lucky thing he'd caught it. The wrapping paper was wafting around on currents from the air-conditioning, but the magic was mostly spent. It would have been on the ground soon.

"What is that?" he asked, as if he cared.

"Perfume—or cologne. It works on both sexes, because it smells differently on every wearer. It's supposed to tell you something about your true self."

I eyed him up, which got me a raised eyebrow. "Are you going to try it?" he asked.

"I've already tried it."

"Well, don't douse me with it," he said, leaning against the wall and lighting up again. "Unless you like the smell of fish."

"Fish?"

"If it works." He breathed deep and then let it out. The smoke was nothing special. Marco liked expensive Cuban cigars, and Mircea smoked little imported cigarettes with brown wrappers and an exotic, sweet scent. But Rico just used the usual stuff.

His cigarettes were like him: simple, straightforward, no-nonsense. It reminded me of what he'd told me when I first met him and had asked what he did: "I see trouble and I shoot it." That was Rico in a nutshell.

Or maybe not.

I didn't really know that much about him.

"Why fish?" I asked, and leaned against the wall, mirroring his stance.

"That's what I used to do, growing up. I was a fisherman, in Napoli."

"What's wrong with that?"

"Nothing," he said, while his face argued with him.

I crossed my ankles and waited.

He eyed me without favor. "You have princes all but begging to get in here. All day, we get the calls. Marco tried to make a special phone number with an answering machine, but it filled up the first day. It has a generic message now, telling them to wait."

"And your point is?"

"They all want to talk to you, yet here you are."

"With someone who doesn't?" It wasn't a guess. I'd

never seen Rico so uncomfortable before. Despite the casual pose, his shoulders were tense, and the cigarette ash was going everywhere, because he couldn't keep his hands still.

"Okay," I said. "Don't tell me about the fish—"

"What is there to tell? They were fish!"

I waited some more.

"One of the men who lived with my mother for a while had a little boat," he said, staring up at where the package had been. "It leaked and it had no motor. There were no motors then."

I nodded, even though he wasn't looking at me.

"He took me along to row and to bail. I asked him one day, why don't we patch the boat? Then it won't leak. He said, if we patch it, somebody maybe thinks it worth stealing. As it is, nobody wants a leaky boat."

There was another awkward silence.

He turned to look at me suddenly. "You have the . . ." He tapped the side of his head. "The sight, yes? You see things?"

"Sometimes." Not often anymore, thank God. The Pythian power was doing joyrides with my abilities most of the time, using them to help it guard the timeline, which was fine by me. I'd never had a good vision in my life.

"Then can you see it?" he asked. "Where we lived? *How* we lived?"

"No. At least, I might someday, but I don't just order things up."

He looked vaguely disappointed. "If you could, we wouldn't be having this conversation," he told me.

I wasn't aware that we were having one, anyway. "Rico, could you possibly—"

"Eleven children, in two rooms," he interrupted. "Mother used to laugh and say there was no room for the mice. But there was. There was just no room for me. As soon as I was old enough, I was on the streets. The fisherman was gone, and anyway, there were younger boys to bail by then."

"How old was old enough?" I asked quietly.

"Fourteen. I think. I don't know when my birthday was."

"You weren't baptized?"

He laughed suddenly, a short, quick bark. "Mother wasn't often in church."

He smoked for a while.

"It was just as well," he finally said. "In those days, if you were *non legittimo*, they wanted everyone to know it. If I had been baptized, they would have called me Proietti, the Cast Out; or D'Ignoti, the Unknown; or Esposito, the Exposed."

"The Exposed?" I got the others, but that one seemed strange.

"They used to expose unwanted babies on the hillsides, so that they died." He shrugged.

I felt a shiver go down my arms.

This wasn't . . . I hadn't actually expected things to get this dark.

"I named myself Marino—of the sea," he added. "I thought to be a fisherman. It was all I knew, and there were plenty of boats in Napoli. But one of the men knew my mother, and said stupid things." He shrugged again. "I put a scaling knife in his eye."

"Rico," I said, not even knowing what I was going to say. But feeling like I ought to say something.

"I ended up a mercenary after that," he continued, his voice low. "I did things, not so good things, you understand? If you could see them, you would know . . ."

"Know what?"

He looked away, back at that oh-so-interesting spot on the ceiling. "Her father is Jonas Marsden, yes? And her mother is—was—Agnes Wee-thcr-by. That is right?"

He'd stumbled a little over the pronunciation of Weatherby, the harsher English syllables sounding strange on a tongue that, even now, was more used to lyrical Italian. Rico was the only one of my guards with a noticeable accent, unless they chose to have one. Or unless you counted Roy's slight Southern drawl.

"Close enough," I agreed.

He looked satisfied. "So. You see."

I didn't see a damned thing.

I said as much, and Rico looked at me like I was slow. But instead of trying to explain, he took the perfume bottle from my hands and frowned at it, as if trying to figure out the little bulb-like sprayer. Then he turned it on himself.

"You see?" he asked. "Or, rather, do you smell?"

I didn't, actually. Until I leaned closer. I closed my eyes and filled my lungs, but it wasn't the smell of fish, even newly caught ones, that met my nose. It wasn't anything I could name exactly. If I'd had to describe it, it would have sounded like the cover of a romance novel: a dark night, a full moon, a highwayman galloping past a field of lavender, a girl waiting in a tall tower by the sea, plaiting roses in her hair—

I broke away, laughing at myself.

God, I needed to get laid!

"What is it?" Rico asked, trying to sniff himself. I guess I didn't look like a woman who'd just been breathing fish guts.

"You can't smell it yourself. You have to have someone tell you," I said. Or so the fey shopkeeper had insisted.

"Then what do you smell?"

"Not fish."

The door to the suite opened before I could say anything else, and Saffy's pink head poked out. "Hey! We found it!"

"Found what?"

"An outfit for you."

Okay, now I was legitimately afraid. "Um, Saffy—"

"No, really. You'll love it!"

She started tugging me inside.

"Cassie—" That was Rico, looking strangely desperate, all of a sudden.

"It's hard to describe," I said. "But you keep it. It smells better on you."

"Better?" He looked at the little bottle in confusion. "What did it smell like on you?"

But Saffy had already pulled me inside.

Just as well.

Hilde had only smelled ozone.

# Chapter Eleven

I didn't wear the ridiculously elaborate outfit the girls had found for me, although I did keep it, because Augustine had been right—it was perfect for a Pythia. Or, at least, a Pythia going to a ball, which I wasn't. I put on my sensible black skirt instead, with a cute blue blouse that was silky and ruffly and matched my eyes, and dressed the ensemble up nicely, thank you very much.

Then I went looking for Mircea.

He wasn't in his office, where I scared a maid half to death by popping in just as she turned away from cleaning the desk. When the screaming died down, I tried his private rooms, but he wasn't in there, either. I poked my head out of the door to the hallway, wondering where else to look, only to freak out the two huge senate guards who'd been posted there for some reason.

I frowned at them, but not because of the shiny-tipped spears they'd thrust in my face, which was par for the course around here. But because they shouldn't have been there at all. Mircea had had guards when he was injured, the day the senate was attacked a month ago, but he'd long since healed. And of all people, he was able to take care of himself. Unless something else had happened—

My heart leapt to my throat, and I grabbed one of the spear shafts without thinking. "Is Mircea all right? Has he been hurt? Where is he?"

Instead of being upset—or worse—that I'd grabbed his weapon, the beefy-looking blond visibly relaxed. It looked like he'd been startled, but had belatedly recognized me. The same wasn't true in reverse, but there were so damned many people around anymore, that wasn't surprising.

"He's fine," he assured me. "Or he was last I saw him, earlier today."

"Then what are you two doing here?" I demanded, letting him go, although my pulse was still pounding in my ears.

"We could ask the same of you!" The speaker was a tall brunet—because the consul had a height fetish where her guards were concerned—and good-looking if you liked the bruiser type. I didn't, and I didn't care for his tone, either.

"I'm supposed to be here," I snapped. "But if Mircea isn't injured, he doesn't need guards."

"Consul's orders," the blond told me.

"Why? Have there been problems?"

He sighed and rolled his eyes. "Just all the time—"

"Don't answer her! Why are you answering her?" the brunet demanded, thrusting his spear a little closer to my nose.

"He is smarter than you," someone said from behind me.

I turned to find that the corridor, which was wide and marble-bright, was looking smaller and darker suddenly. Because a glowing golden demigod was striding down it. Now there was someone who didn't need a calling card, I thought enviously.

"Lord Caedmon," the brunet said, quickly lowering his spear and bowing. "My apologies. I didn't mean to harass your secretary."

I scowled down at my serviceable black skirt, Augustine's laughter ringing in my ears. And then back up at Caedmon, one of the kings of the light fey. Whose lips were twitching.

"What a pleasure to see you again, Lady Cassandra," he said, bowing, and kissing my hand with exaggerated gallantry.

It was weird, to put it mildly. Not the kiss, but running into him like this. The last time I'd seen him had been on a battlefield in Wales, fifteen hundred years ago. Or, rather, fifteen hundred for him. It had been about two weeks for me, because time travel.

Yet here he was, acting as if we'd just seen each other yesterday.

It was bizarre.

Like his slight smile that said he was putting on a show for the ill-mannered help, and inviting me to go along with it. While his lips on my skin, lingering a little too long, said something else. Something that might have gotten more of a response if I didn't already have two men in my life, and no idea what to do with either one of them.

But damned if he wasn't amazing to look at.

At least seven feet tall, with blond hair spilling over broad shoulders and piercing green eyes, he also had the perfect face. Like, literally perfect—I couldn't find a flaw. With strong, aristocratic features paired with eyelashes longer than a Hollywood starlet's and a fuller, more sensual mouth than any man had a right to, he would have been stunning in a cardboard box.

But he wasn't wearing a box. He was wearing golden armor with thin traceries of vines and leaves and winged animals all over it, slightly raised from the rest of the metal and blackened, so that the designs stood out. And, as if that wasn't enough, among the greenery were sapphires, some around the neckline as big as my thumb, others tiny, almost bead-like, in the eyes of the strange animals peering out of the foliage.

"Gryphons," Caedmon said, seeing the direction of my gaze. "The sigil of my house."

"There are gryphons?" I'd always thought those were a myth.

But then, I'd thought the same about the fey, not so long ago.

"In the mountain fastnesses of my realm," he told me. "They build their nests on the very highest peaks. Some of our more courageous—or more foolhardy—warriors occasionally climb up in an attempt to steal an egg."

He smiled. "Sometimes, they even come back."

I swallowed. "How, uh, how interesting."

"Visit my realm, princess, and I'll take you for a ride."

"I'm not a princess," I told him, before what he'd said registered. "You *ride gryphons*?"

I couldn't quite keep the excitement out of my voice.

His smile widened. "Your mother was Queen of Heaven; I believe you deserve the title. As to the other, you shall have to visit and find out."

Caedmon tucked my hand under his arm and pulled me away from the stunned-looking guards and down the hall. "I—I'm looking for Mircea," I told him, wondering why I was walking away from anywhere Mircea was likely to be.

But I kept on doing it anyway.

Caedmon was a little overwhelming.

"As am I. Let's find him together, shall we?"

It sounded like a plan, but it quickly became obvious that it was going to be tougher than I'd thought. The consul's palace had been damaged in the attack, and rebuilding had been going on ever since. But it looked like she'd decided to throw some renovations in there, too, while she was at it.

Big ones.

Caedmon and I passed through a wall that used to indicate the end of the passage, but which now opened onto a massive new wing. Workmen were running everywhere, down a corridor the length of a football field and at least half as wide. One which I knew, I *knew*, hadn't been there a month ago.

"Impressive, isn't it?" Caedmon asked. "I'm told that they are working around the clock: vampires at night and human servants during the day." He leaned closer and dropped his voice. "I've also heard that the consul visits daily, to check on their progress. I believe that may have helped to expedite matters."

I flashed to an image of Darth Vader visiting the Death Star, only with more snakes. I'd seen her send vampires hundreds of years old running for cover with barely a flash from those dark eyes. I was surprised the workmen weren't pissing themselves.

What they *were* doing was moving mountains, or at least sizable hills, considering the countryside around here. Which I guess I should have expected. The consul had recently found herself with a distinct lack of living space.

The world's six vampire senates had joined forces for the war, something that had never been done before, or even attempted, because they mostly hated each other. Fortunately, they hated the gods more. But they still needed to govern their own territories, something that war-related issues might have interfered with.

So they'd decided to have some of their senior members become part of a new governing body to deal exclusively with the conflict. Mircea, for instance, used to be the consul's go-to diplomat, but was now her general. His official title was Chief Enforcer of the Vampire World Senate, because Enforcer was the senatorial position that did a consul's dirty work—but in wartime, it amounted to the same thing.

Of course, he'd needed a new staff to help with all the extra responsibilities, hence Batman and a couple hundred others. And so did everybody else who'd snagged a seat. Our senate had expected that, and had somehow figured out places to stow them all when they weren't working.

What they hadn't expected was everyone else who kept turning up.

There were senate members from foreign courts who were not on the new body, but who had finagled positions assisting those who were. There were functionaries out the wazoo, because everybody seemed to need a phalanx of aides for everything from taking notes to running back and forth with trays of booze, because the new arrivals drank like fish, from what I'd heard. Then there was the army, with troops pouring in from all over, accompanied by commanders who seemed more worried about the style of their armor than the discipline of their men. And finally, there were the hangers-on, vampires itching to move up the usually rigid hierarchy and seeing the war as an opportunity.

The result was thousands of vamps showing up all the time, and while the majority were not being housed here or even let in the door, there were plenty of sufficient rank that somewhere had to be found for them. I'd heard that from my bodyguards, who'd heard it from others in the family who'd been assigned here. Vampires gossiped like magpies, being constantly in each other's heads, and nothing stayed secret for long.

Yet I hadn't heard about *this*.

Caedmon and I swanned down the huge corridor, and I decided that I'd been wrong. It was longer than a football field. Above our heads, the ceiling arched high enough that I was surprised I didn't see clouds floating around, and was inset with panels of what looked like hammered gold. They covered the interior of the arch, while more gold coated the finials on huge marble columns supporting the roof. Even more gold covered what looked like massive picture frames on the walls between the columns, inside of which was—

What the *hell*?

I stopped dead in front of the nearest one.

There was a mural on the wall inside the frame, giving it the look of a gigantic painting. It wasn't completed; a third of the space was still smooth white plaster with a few pale sketch marks on it. But what it did show—

"That's not how it happened!" I said. The painter looked down from his ladder—a vamp, despite it being the middle of the day, so not low-ranking. Still, he got down swiftly and bowed to Caedmon. But he was looking at me, and seemed concerned by what I'd said.

"I was instructed to show the grandeur of battle—"

"Grandeur?" I stared at him. "There was no grandeur! It was mud and blood and fear and—"

I stopped, because I got hit with a flashback hard enough to stagger me. For a second, I was back in that hell of butchered men and dying horses. Thunder boomed in my ears, loud as cannon fire; lightning flashed overhead like nuclear blasts; rain hit me in the face, all but blinding me; while blood and panicked sweat and the metallic taste of spent magic clogged my throat, threatening to choke me.

The little scene cut out as abruptly as it had come, leaving me clinging to Caedmon, who had put a hand under my arm, and staring instead at the heroic scene on the wall, which showed the final battle with Ares. The one I'd been refighting in my head ever since it happened. Only, no, that was what it *should have* shown. But what the artist had actually painted was . . . it was . . .

I didn't have words, but it felt like a violation.

A golden warrior—Caedmon, I guessed, since he was glowing like a lantern—stood on a hill, lightning wreathing his head and a staff in his hand that more lightning was spilling out of in all directions. It would have been laughable if I'd been in a different mood, because he hadn't looked anything like that. He'd been down in the mud with the rest of us, dirty and bloody and soaking wet from the storm raging overhead—which hadn't made the cut for the painting, either.

But at least there was some truth there, just greatly exaggerated. The real lie wasn't Caedmon—or the too perfect battlefield, with no panicked men or blood or entrails or feces. Or Caedmon's blackened and smoking arm after Ares destroyed his staff with barely a glance.

No, the real lie was me.

Because, instead of being huddled in a washerman's tent, dirty, wet and frightened out of my mind, I was on another hill, opposite Caedmon. I had something in my hand, too, but I wasn't sure what it was supposed to be. It was bright green and shaped like another lightning bolt, and I was doing something with it—

Oh.

I was ripping open the sky, I realized, like I'd taken a knife to its belly. Only instead of blood and guts spilling out, there was only a cascade of pale white light, illuminating half of the battle going on below. Which I suppose was meant to stand in for the ghost of Apollo.

He'd been stuck in a spirit realm known as the Badlands after a previous encounter with Pritkin and me left him mostly dead and without the power to leave it. Yet as soon as I released him, he hadn't gone after me as I'd half expected. Instead, he'd flown straight at Ares, the most potent source of godly power around.

He'd been trying to absorb enough energy to live again, and then to battle Ares for control of the world they both coveted. He hadn't succeeded, but the threat of another god on the battlefield had done what nothing else could. It had pulled Ares' attention away from our side at a crucial moment, giving us a chance to kill them both.

So the painting told the truth, but embellished it so much that it almost didn't matter. Instead of two gods battling it out in the sky while the rest of us scurried around like frightened ants, we had . . . this. Whatever the hell this was!

The figure who was supposed to be me had a banner of blond hair streaming out behind her almost as long as she was tall, mirroring Caedmon's heroic cape on the other side of the painting. She had a fierce, proud expression that I had worn exactly never, and certainly not that night! And, for the final insult, she was wearing a flowy gown that made me look like my mother, instead of the filthy dancer's outfit I'd actually been running around in, torn and tawdry and not at all camera ready.

It was Hollywood's version of war, and so wrong it left me breathless, far more so than the children's innocent drawings back at Dante's had done. Those had been weirdly cute, if gruesomely bloody, and an understandable reaction to the months of fear and confusion they'd recently experienced. I'd felt proud and not a little awed that they saw me as their protector, and determined to live up to their expectations. But this . . .

This just made me *furious*.

It made it look so easy, when it had been nothing of the kind! We'd pulled out a victory through a lucky break and because all of us had given everything we had down in the trenches. We hadn't been lording it up on a hill somewhere, looking faintly bored! We'd been screaming and crying and praying and cursing and—

"It's a lie!" I said, rounding on the man.

The artist looked taken aback; I guess because he'd expected praise. "I was assured that the main events of the battle are correct—" he began stiffly.

"You were assured wrong!"

"—by a number of people who have studied the old sources—"

"They weren't there!"

"—and as for the minor details, well. The artistic mind

fills in the gaps," I was told loftily, with more than a hint of a sneer, because all artists are gods in their own minds.

Of course, some of them actually deserve the title, I thought, catching sight of a familiar figure coming down the hall.

"Rafe!"

I suddenly forgot all about my quarrel with the would-be artist and ran to meet one worthy of the term—and then some. To the rest of the world, the man with the head of dark curls now hurrying down the hall to meet me was the great Renaissance master Raphael. To me, he was the closest thing I'd had to a father growing up.

I could see his handsome, laughing face as he painted the ceiling of my bedroom with cerulean skies and fat winged cherubs. And little birds on their delicate limbs and bowers, so real that I'd sometimes thought they'd stop pretending one day and just fly away. Rafe had been one of the few bright spots at Tony's, although he'd often been gone. Tony had used him as an errand boy, never appreciating his gift. But when he was there, he'd defended me fiercely, even taking a beating once in my place.

He'd taken another blow for me recently, although not from a fist. But from something far more dangerous for a vampire. Although there were no signs of it now.

He picked me up and whirled me around, laughing, because laughter came easily to Rafe. And I realized that I'd been wrong: there *were* signs. But so subtle that I could barely make them out, even at this distance.

"Rafe." I put a hand on his cheek, when he finally set me down, and I could feel them, too. Tiny scarification lines, in the places where his skin had cracked and split and bled from exposure to the sun. They were healed now, but had left a subtle pattern behind that was invisible from any distance, but up close, was almost beautiful.

Or maybe that was just me, because Rafe would always be beautiful to me.

"*Mia stella*," he said, and hugged me again.

"How long have you been back?" Rafe had been away, recovering from his burns, for most of the summer.

"Almost two weeks. They have me directing all this." He gestured around.

And I belatedly noticed that the interiors of other frames were also being worked on, although most of them were still in the sketch phase. There was one exception, however, directly across from us. And, like the one behind me, it was also a complete fabrication.

"That's not how it happened," I said, looking at an image of the very house we were standing in. Only the painted version was shown surrounded by a massive fey army, while devilish-looking things poured forth from the mouths of a couple dozen portals dotting the night sky.

The attack on the consul's home a month ago *had* involved portals, but they'd opened up inside the walls, not in the sky and hills surrounding it. And the creatures that had been sent through hadn't been demons. They'd been some weird experiments that the fey had been doing.

Really weird.

Our enemies had been trying to create hybrids between dark fey—whom they regarded as little more than animals—and humans. They'd wanted to create troops that could fight on earth, because fey magic didn't work any better here than ours did there. So far, their efforts had failed, and the creatures they'd thrown at us had been rejects that they'd used as cannon fodder.

But that's not what the scene showed. It had fearsome beasts leaping forth from the portals, maws open and claws reaching. Only to be held off by the valiant efforts of the consul, who stood atop her house holding a flaming sword.

No, seriously.

She had a *flaming sword.*

A *vampire.*

They burn like gasoline-soaked tinder, but sure. Why not? And I couldn't exactly talk, since I'd ended up a freaking goddess!

Rafe looked behind him. And then turned back around, a mischievous little grin on his face. "Oh, don't you like it?"

"As art, sure. But it didn't happen like that!"

It was Rafe's turn to take my arm, while Caedmon

walked beside us. "*Mia stella*, have you learned nothing from all your years with us? Reality is . . . malleable. And in time of war, even more so."

"That's not malleable," I said, craning my neck to look behind me. "That's *Gumby*."

He laughed. "Perhaps. But it is also useful, no?"

"Very much so," Caedmon said.

He was looking at a knot of people—judging by their outfits, they were from the East Asian Court—who were standing in front of one of Rafe's sketches down the hall. I wasn't close enough to see what it depicted; the outlines he'd done for the artists were deliberately light, so they'd be easier to cover up with paint. But the viewers seemed strangely intent.

Until they caught sight of us, and began whispering behind their hands.

"But did you get my chin all right?" Caedmon asked, suddenly turning to Raphael.

Rafe regarded him seriously for a moment, then dropped my arm to grasp his chin, moving it this way and that, the dark eyes narrowed. Caedmon put up with it, because genius trumps titles, and because he was probably vain as shit. Anyone who looked like that had to be.

"Hm, perhaps not. I will see to it," Rafe promised.

Caedmon smiled winningly, and I swear, it was like the sun coming out. "Excellent! And once you're done here, perhaps you might visit my palace. I have a wall in my solarium simply calling out for—"

"Stop trying to poach Rafe!" I said, taking his arm again, before I remembered who I was talking to. But Caedmon only laughed.

"That is exactly what I am doing," he admitted. "I would steal him away permanently if I could."

"I prefer it here," Rafe told him dryly. "But we can talk about a painting—although not in a solarium. The sun would fade it."

"Which would be a shame," Caedmon agreed. "Perhaps you could—"

I stopped listening. There was a strange undercurrent in this new palace that I didn't like. Not between the two men, who appeared to be getting along famously, but with the little knots of people here and there. The gallery, which is what I guessed the huge corridor was going to be, wasn't even finished, yet there were people everywhere. And most of them seemed a little intense for art lovers.

And now most of them were looking at us.

"What's going on?" I asked Rafe, who was one of the only vamps I knew who might tell me the truth.

And, yes, something weird was happening, because he glanced around first instead of just answering. "Come," he said. "Let me show you my current project—and my personal favorite. It's this way."

And before I could stop him, he'd taken off down the hall, leaving two clueless demigods looking at each other. And then hurrying to catch up when Rafe turned around and snapped his fingers impatiently. Because I don't care who you are, you don't argue with genius.

# Chapter Twelve

A hundred corridors seemed to branch off the main hall, although a lot of them were still under construction. I passed one covered by a tarp that had come loose and was blowing in the wind, showing only open air outside— and a huge tent city crowding the house and dotting the nearby hillsides. It looked like thousands of people were sheltering out there.

"The army," Caedmon told me, as we hurried past, because the Rafe train wasn't stopping. "The invasion is imminent."

"How imminent?" Because I hadn't heard anything.

"That is still being determined. There are a few impediments."

I wanted to ask what kind, but didn't get a chance. A bunch of workmen zoomed by with vampire speed and almost took me along with them, but Caedmon twirled me out of the way at the last second. It looked like a dance move and felt like one, too, as the corridor swirled around me. Then we were off again, a little farther up the hall, through a massive set of doors and into what I guessed was a waiting room.

It was a large space, but there had to be a few hundred people piled on sofas and propping up walls, or gazing at the room's centerpiece, a gorgeous, golden . . . thing . . . that I didn't even have a name for.

It sort of looked like an astrolabe, one of those old-fashioned devices that people once used to determine eclipses, with rings within rings. But it was huge, easily filling a quarter of the extended ceiling, maybe a couple of stories high at the top. And there was no sun at the center.

In fact, there was no sun at all. Just two planets whirling around each other in a crazy dance like the one Caedmon and I had just executed. Sometimes closer, sometimes farther away, but always turning, turning, turning.

And every time they did, every rotation they made, other things turned with them. The most eye-catching were the thousand or so golden strands, like threads on a loom, that moved over and beside and underneath the planets. How they didn't get caught up in snarls and knots, I didn't know, because they were crossing and crisscrossing all the time, in no discernible pattern that I could see. But they were beautiful, nonetheless: a woven metallic cat's cradle dancing around and between the two worlds like—

Like ley lines, I thought, finally realizing what I was looking at.

"That's earth and Faerie, isn't it?" I asked Caedmon, who was looking at it, too.

"Indeed. And that is time, you see?"

He pointed to a silver ring encircling the planet that was meant to be earth, judging by the continents standing out in vague relief. Although it kind of looked like a fat kid with a hula hoop, because the metal ring wasn't stationary. It was slinging about erratically, first to one side of the planet and then to the other. And all the while, it was expanding and contracting, sometimes almost touching the surface of the world, while at others flaring so far out that I was sure it would collide with a similar ring around Faerie.

The whole thing was a beautiful, kinetic sculpture, almost dizzying to watch. But kind of mesmerizing, too. Like the workings of a particularly complex watch.

"It's only a representation, of course," Caedmon murmured, when I said so. "But then, a clock is also only a representation of time, yet it serves."

"Then that's Faerie's timeline?" I asked, pointing at the silver ring around the other planet, and he nodded.

"My artisans made this as a gift for your consul. Your people lacked an understanding of how time flows differently in our two realms. That gap in knowledge allowed Aeslinn to plan attacks seemingly back to back, knowing when time would be flowing faster in our world relative to yours. You and your people had scarce time to catch your breath from one battle before another was upon you, while he had months to plan in between."

I nodded, remembering Mircea telling me something similar not long ago. Not that I'd needed it. The attacks from the other side had been like a barrage, falling fast and furious, leaving me not knowing what to do or where to run.

But they'd still lost, I thought, flashing back once more to that muddy battlefield. And no, it hadn't been pretty, and it sure as hell hadn't been the walk in the park the artist had made it seem. A lot of good people had gone into that mud and had never come out again.

But we'd *won*.

And for a moment, I felt some pride in that stupid painting, after all.

"But the tide turns," Caedmon whispered, bending down to me. "As it always does. Soon, time will begin to run slower in Faerie than here, and for a good span. We must be ready to take advantage of it, for such an opportunity will not come again for a decade."

"So that's when we invade."

He inclined his head. "It is . . . less than optimal," he admitted. "The slowdown has already begun, and will reach full effect by the end of this week—"

"This *week*?"

He nodded. "We could wish for more time to prepare."

"How long will it last?"

"Here? A few months. There, several days."

I licked my lips. A few months. We were invading another world in the next few months. It didn't seem real.

Which was good, because if it had, it would have been terrifying.

Caedmon was watching me, but he didn't have time to say anything before Rafe appeared on the other side of the universe. "What are you two doing out here?" the annoyed genius demanded. Hands were on slim hips, and his face had *that* look.

"Sorry!" I said, and scurried to catch up. Caedmon followed, looking slightly bemused—at what, I didn't know. "Hurry," I told him when he lagged behind, and grabbed his hand. He laughed then, and ran along with me, heedless of his dignity.

There were more guards on the other side of the room, near the entrance to yet another corridor. But they only straightened up a little as we went past into something more normal-sized for a hallway. There was some lovely honey-colored stone under our feet now instead of marble, an only slightly taller than normal ceiling, and a bunch of rooms with arched doorways but no actual doors yet. A lot of artistic types were visible inside the rooms, hunched over workstations, painting, carving, or arguing about what I assumed were more parts to the consul's great puzzle.

One of them called out to Rafe in what sounded like serious distress, and Rafe sighed and looked at me. "Would you mind? My office is just down there. I'll be with you in a moment."

I nodded, and he went off to help the hapless soul. Caedmon and I walked to the end of the hall, and found a room that simply had to be Rafe's. For one thing, it had a door—made of heavy old planks and banded with iron, like somebody had looted a castle—that was half-open, allowing us to push our way inside. For another, it was just *him*.

Stuccoed walls with rounded corners, like in an old monastery, rose up to a point in the center of the ceiling, where a decorative finial dropped down, capping it off. Elsewhere, there were scarred wooden tables littered with reference books and loose papers, old crockery full of paintbrushes and knives, and jars of the paints Rafe mixed himself, out of ocher and cinnabar, lapis and pearls, gold and silver. And it smelled just like I remembered: of turpentine and linseed oil, charcoal and wine—because who can paint without a glass of wine?

But there were no sketchbooks, or rather, there were, but they were all around us, the clean white stucco being offensive to an artist's eye. Not that it was clean anymore: everywhere I looked were faces, hands, and profiles. Here a guy with a pert backside, looking at me coquettishly over his shoulder; there a mother with a baby at her breast, serenity radiating from her face; here a rearing horse, its mane flowing majestically in the breeze; there a beautifully rendered snake head, its scales like perfect little jewels—

And me, I realized, staring at the drawings above a cluttered workbench.

Some of them were me as a child, my pudgy cheeks and big eyes and bouncy ponytails making me look vaguely like an anime character. Others showed me with the long hair I used to have as a teen, before I cut it off while on the run, because hip-length red-gold hair is damned hard to hide. Others looked to be more recent, although there was something off about them.

It wasn't the facial features, which were accurate, because Rafe was always accurate. It wasn't the hair, which for once was my current curly bob. It wasn't the clothes, not that many were shown because the portraits were mostly from the neck up.

I didn't know what it was.

And then I realized: it looked like my skin but with somebody else inside.

Like the painting outside in the corridor, that wasn't me. The proud lift to the chin, the resolute gaze, the confidence that that woman wore like a cloak—all were things I wished I had, but that wasn't what I saw in the mirror every morning. And it suddenly hit me, like a pang under the breast.

Was this how he saw me?

It should have been flattering—that woman looked better than I ever had—but it wasn't. I thought Rafe knew me better than this. I thought that he, of all people, liked *me*, not whatever everyone kept trying to make out of me.

It seemed like I wasn't enough for him, either.

And then I saw Caedmon, or rather, his hand clutching the now destroyed staff. And a fallen horse, its eye round and frightened. And Mircea—only the upper half of the face, but I'd know that hawklike gaze anywhere. And the consul—

"These must have been practice for the paintings," I said, relief obvious in my voice.

Until I turned around to see Caedmon pulling a sheet off of something on a central worktable.

"Not just for the paintings," he told me gently.

For a moment, I just blinked at what he'd revealed, unable to process it. I felt like my brain had taken a vacation and was refusing to acknowledge what my eyes were seeing, although my body seemed to understand. Because my pulse was suddenly hammering in my throat, goose bumps had broken out on my arms, and there was a roaring in my ears.

And then I turned around and left the room.

Caedmon caught up with me almost before I got out the door. "People need heroes, Cassie, in war even more than in peace."

"So go be a hero!"

A hand caught my bicep as I started to move away. "A hero they can understand, one they can identify with. The ancient Greeks knew that. Why do you think the stories of Hercules outnumber those of any other god? He was half-human—"

"I'm not Hercules!"

"Perhaps. But you are a target, whether you like it or not. You are a leader in this war, whether you like it or not. You are already involved, as are we all. What harm does that do?"

He gestured back at the monstrosity on the table.

And it *was* a monstrosity. In fact, that was being kind. It was a bunch of small, individual statues: me, the consul, Mircea, Caedmon, and a headless guy I thought might be Marlowe, given the Elizabethan outfit, only he wasn't finished yet. We were standing in the middle of the table, chins and even a few arms raised, Caedmon's cloak flying out dramatically behind him.

We looked like crappy superheroes. We looked like we'd just dropped our first mixtape. We looked like we were posing for the world's cheesiest album cover.

It was *awful*.

Even worse, these weren't the finished versions. They'd been made on a wire base—a little loop of it stuck out of Marlowe's neck, for the head, I supposed. Another protruded from under the sleeve of the consul's flowing robe, waiting for a hand and probably a snake to be put in it. But the rest were covered with some sort of polymer clay, in sculpted, flowing lines that mimicked the brush strokes Rafe had put on paper.

He'd drawn them; somebody else was sculpting them. But not here. Maybe because they wouldn't fit?

I had a sudden, horrible thought. There'd been niches for statuary outside, in the big main corridor, between every two or three paintings. Empty niches. I hadn't thought much about them at the time, but now . . .

"Those are mock-ups," I said, my lips going numb.

"Yeeees," Caedmon admitted. "That was my understanding."

"How big is the final version?"

He hesitated, but finally came out with it. "Sixteen feet?"

I turned around and walked away.

He jogged up alongside. "Cassie, wars need heroes. People need to *believe* they can win. That is why the kinetic sculpture is outside. Made in fey workshops, beyond human skill, to show everyone that you have allies among my people as well as enemies—"

"That's not the sculpture I'm upset about!"

Instead of another goddess gown, my little mock-up had been wearing a breastplate over some kind of leather getup. Huntress garb, I thought, my blood boiling. I didn't know why Rafe hadn't just given me a bow and quiver and been done with it!

Of course, maybe he had. Maybe they were off getting sculpted, along with Marlowe's head and the consul's damned snakes! And *screw* this!

Caedmon caught my arm again, halfway down a side corridor, and damn it, that was getting old! I whirled on him. "What do you *want*?"

"To understand."

"You want to understand? Understand *this*. I am not your chosen one. I'm not Hercules; I'm not my mother; I'm not some savior come to make everything okay again! I'm just me, and I can't have any more people depending on me! I can't have them looking to me to save them when I can barely save myself!"

"I understand—"

"Do you? I already have a court I don't know if I can protect, a bunch of little kids who will *die* if I screw up! Do you understand *that*? Do you have *any* idea—"

But of course he didn't. What the hell was I thinking? Caedmon looked like some kind of god himself, which he sort of was, because god + fey is a hell of a lot less diluted than god + Roger freaking Palmer! And, of course, I'd taken after my father, who was good at running scams— and running, period, when those scams blew up in his face—but not much else.

Which was why he and Mom were dead and I was here, and probably about to screw up massively because I was *due*, and—

I felt when it hit, an incipient panic attack boiling under my breastbone, tightening my chest, threatening my breathing. My head went swimmy, and I simultaneously wanted to throw up and start laughing hysterically. There might be something wrong with me, I thought, as the corridor started closing in.

And then snapped back to normal when a fussy-looking little guy burst out of a door just up the hall. He looked spooked, like a mouse with a hawk after him. Which wasn't far from the truth, I thought, as Mircea's voice followed him through the opening.

"—constantly undermining my authority. I won't have it!"

"*You* won't have it?" The consul's usually honeyed tones sounded more like the lashes of a whip. "Parendra is a consul; you are not. You would do well to remember that."

"I am head of this army. He would do well to remember *that*!"

Caedmon and I looked at each other, and he made little hand motions that somehow managed both to be comical and to convey "let's tiptoe on by this mess, shall we" at the same time. I bit my lip. Because, yeah, normally that would have been my go-to as well, but Mircea had sounded a little . . . tense. And for him, that was basically the same thing as anyone else having a meltdown.

Maybe an interruption wouldn't be a bad thing.

I tried to head down the hall, but found a damned demigod in the way. And then the door the little man had come through closed and the sound cut out, so completely that it probably indicated a ward over the entrance. Not a problem, I thought, and started to shift—

But Caedmon grasped my arm again, preventing it. And he *did* prevent it. My magic swirled around us and then paused, as if waiting for him to release it or for me to push it. My eyes narrowed, and he nodded abruptly.

"There you are," he said. "I knew you were in there somewhere."

"What are you talking about?"

"The goddess. I saw her on the battlefield; I haven't seen her since."

"You haven't seen me at all since!"

"Oh, but I hear things," he said, bending closer. And suddenly the whimsical joker was gone, and the king was looking at me. "I hear you have a number of talents: seer, necromancer, opener of ways—"

"What's that to you?"

"A great deal. I have talents, too. We need to spend some time together, Cassie Palmer, and find out how our gifts can complement each other. Make sure that we know them all—and that we're not afraid to use them."

"I'm not afraid," I said, and meant it. I should have been; Caedmon had just proven that his power could at least impede if not stop mine. But not overcome it. I could feel it, waiting, surging at my fingertips. I could push *back* if I wanted, it whispered, and right then, I damned well wanted!

"Yes, there she is," he smiled, but it was a different one this time. I couldn't name it, exactly, like I couldn't name the expression in his eyes. But it made my power surge. I wanted to push it, to find out what he could do, to force him to show himself.

To see which one of us was best.

"It's your mother's blood you feel," he told me. "Our people's blood. It sings in my veins as well. Did you think it was only the Pythian power that made you strong?"

I just stared at him, trying to will myself calm when my every instinct said *go*.

"As I said, I have talents," he added. "But I have had thousands of years to learn them, their gifts and their limitations. If we are to win, you must learn yours. And accept the role you were born to play."

I wanted to ask him what the hell that meant, but I didn't get the chance. He finally let go, and not just physically. My power surged, my interrupted shift grabbed me, and the next thing I knew—

I was back on that damned battlefield.

# Chapter Thirteen

For a moment, I was sliding in gore and stumbling across bodies. I smelled the sharp, metallic stench, felt viscera slipping beneath my shoes, tasted blood in my mouth. And then I snapped back in time to see it all again, spread out on the floor all around me.

And being dragged through a set of double doors in front of me.

It took me a confused few seconds to realize that I was where I'd expected to be—in some kind of office next to the hallway—and not back in time. Only nobody had noticed my arrival, because I'd shown up at the same moment as something else. Something that was still being carried in from the waiting area through doors I hadn't seen when we came in, because I'd been following Rafe through a side entrance.

But I could see a few hints of gold from the kinetic statue in the lobby, so I knew where I was. Along with part of the bored crowd, who weren't looking so bored right now. Some of them were crowding the doors, getting an eyeful, and getting shoved back by the soldiers bringing in more bodies.

Most of which were in pieces.

I stumbled back, sliding on blood, and staring at maybe a couple dozen men—or what was left of them. In some cases, the only thing holding them together appeared to be their armor. And that didn't work too well where the heads were concerned.

One had been hanging by a bit of skin, which I guessed had been stretched to the limit. Because it gave way, allowing the severed thing to bounce, bounce, bounce, on the tiles of the floor before coming to rest at my feet.

I fought a serious urge to retch.

Glassy blue eyes stared up at me out of an unknown face. The tongue lolled out of the mouth in a way that would have been comical under very different circumstances. Fangs glistened in the overhead lighting.

I swallowed and swayed slightly, but stayed on my feet. You'll sit down in blood, I told myself sternly. You'll sit down in—

"Cassie!" That was Mircea; I could tell by the voice, although the room had begun to fade out. He caught my arm—just my arm—because the office was filling with other vamps and we couldn't afford to look weak.

Stay up, I told myself sternly, as someone put a glass of water in my hand.

A chair appeared a moment later as if by magic, but it was probably just that Mircea had navigated us a path back to a large walnut desk sitting in the middle of the room. I clutched the glass gratefully and stared at my feet until the nausea started to recede and my eyesight improved. And then I looked up.

Only to notice the trail of bloody footprints we'd left all the way here.

They were bright against the white marble floor, because the golden tile hadn't made it this far. Nor had much of anything else. There was a lot of echoing stone, some niches with nothing in them, a large chandelier glittering overhead rather sheepishly, as if it didn't know what it was doing there, either, and a few chairs. That was it, unless you counted some maps tacked up on the walls near the desk.

And the bodies and parts of bodies on the floor, leaking all over everything. What had happened to them? Why had they been brought in here? And in that condition?

Shouldn't they be . . . somewhere . . .

"Cassie? Are you all right?"

That was Caedmon. Guess he found a way past the ward, I thought blankly. I swallowed and nodded, but didn't say anything. I probably wouldn't have been heard anyway, over the shouting.

"—damned bokor in here!" That was Marlowe, reminding me of Raphael with his dark eyes and head of brown curls. And in no other way.

"Belay that." That was Mircea.

"With respect, my lord, we have but a small window!" another dark-haired man said.

He was a vamp, too, but unlike most, he hadn't bothered with a glamourie to make himself more attractive. Instead, he had a rather jowly face, a shock of grizzled black hair, a wide nose, and a slight double chin. Small brown eyes peered out of bags of wrinkled flesh, which was a few shades too light to be ebony, looking angry but controlled. His outfit was like him—blunt and unadorned—being a set of old-fashioned armor made from plain, unpolished steel, with grass clippings and mud adhering to the dented shin guards.

This wasn't parade armor like Caedmon's; it wasn't meant to impress. This armor had been used. And then kept for some reason—probably sentiment, because when would you ever wear something like that again?

When you were about to battle foes who still made war the old-fashioned way, I thought. The way humans had for most of our history. Except that the fey combined it with magic we didn't fully understand, but which was as bad as any modern weapon.

I'd want armor, too.

"I want to know what happened to my men!" the old soldier told Mircea. It was respectful, but the brown eyes caught and held the hawklike gaze, and they didn't falter.

"I understand," Mircea said. "But we've had leaks, and have reason to suspect some of the humans on staff. I don't want to risk a bokor until—"

"Why do you need a bokor?" Caedmon broke in.

Mircea looked irritated—unusual for him. Not that he'd feel it, but that he would show it. But he didn't say anything, because Marlowe answered for him. "It's another word for a necromancer," he informed the fey king. "A low-level one. We keep them on staff for—"

"Yes, I know that," Caedmon interrupted, with the casual rudeness of someone used to being catered to. "But that doesn't answer my question."

"And what question would that be?" Mircea asked, his voice a little clipped for someone addressing a king.

But Caedmon only smiled at him.

"Why you need a bokor when Lady Cassandra is already here?"

I looked up at him, startled, and still half–zoned out. "What?"

A big, handsome smile beamed down at me out of the big, handsome face. "You are a necromancer, are you not?"

I stared at him, because that wasn't the sort of thing I wanted to have get around! Yeah, the Pythian Court had ended up with a necromancer for a Pythia, after all, thanks to my father's abilities, some of which had passed down to me. Although it was doubtful that many people knew that, since he'd specialized in ghosts, which are a lot less visible than shambling bodies.

Only I guess the secret was out now—thanks, Caedmon. I guess he'd heard rumors about some stuff that had happened on that battlefield. And now, so had everyone else.

"I—my father was," I hedged, because everybody was looking at me.

"Lady Cassandra has many gifts," Mircea began. "However—"

"Oh, good, it's settled, then," Caedmon said, looking pleased.

"Nothing is settled!"

"You are Lady Cassandra?" the military guy cut in. He looked surprised, eyeing up my pencil skirt and cute ruffly blouse.

All right, Augustine, I thought evilly. You win. I'm dumping this thing as soon as I get home.

"Yeah," I told him, and then *I* got a surprise.

The old soldier limped over. He was a vamp, so he must have been injured sometime before the change. It made him strangely relatable somehow, as did the way he let out a slight grunt as he went down on one knee to look me in the eyes.

"A Pythia saved my life once, long ago," he told me. "I've never forgotten."

I blinked. Despite ample evidence to the contrary, I

tended to think of Pythias as sitting around their throne rooms all day, listening to petitioners' BS. It was nice to know that that wasn't always the case.

"Which one?" I asked, wondering if she was somebody I knew.

"The last of the great Byzantine Pythias. I believe her given name was—"

"Berenice." I nodded. "I heard she was formidable."

He grinned, showing slightly yellow old man's teeth. "That she was. Knocked me on my, er, behind with a bloody great stick she had. I was unhappy about it until I saw the knife sticking out of the thing. Would have taken me right between the eyes if she hadn't acted. Still don't know what that was all about."

Someone was messing with the timeline and you got killed in the process, I didn't say, because that sort of thing rarely went down well.

"She knew you had more to do," I said instead.

The old knight nodded. "Was Changed barely a month later, so I suppose she was right." He looked behind him, at the bodies on the floor, and his jaw tightened. His face turned back to me, and it was sorrowful and angry and sad, all at the same time. "Can you help me as well? Can you tell me what happened to my men?"

"You're asking for a vision?" I said, confused.

"Nothing so difficult," Caedmon said cheerfully. "Merely a look inside the mind."

For a moment, I didn't get it. And then I did, and thought about retching again. Instead, I glared at the fey king and wondered why I'd ever thought him attractive.

"I deal with ghosts, not . . . flesh," I said curtly.

"New experiences often teach us things about ourselves we didn't know," was the bland reply.

I upped the oomph on my glare, but couldn't do much else. And that included refusing, unless I wanted to look weak in front of a room full of vamps. All of whom, except for a few soldiers who'd acted as litter bearers, looked important.

And I wasn't the only one who thought so.

The snake queen was living up to her rep today in a full-length sheath of the little monsters, bright yellow in this case, with subtle markings in black and gray. From a distance, it might look like a patterned dress, if you ignored the way the "pattern" slithered and writhed. From up close, it was frankly horrific.

It was also strange. Not that I hadn't seen the consul wear similar things before, but usually only in a full senate meeting or when she needed to impress—aka intimidate the crap out of someone. Otherwise, she usually opted for more normal clothing, albeit with a snake or two as accessories.

But today we were getting the full treatment, including matching bright yellow nails tipped in black. I wondered if there was a reason for that. And then I wondered what was wrong with me, because of course there was a reason! A few thousand of them—vampires from all over the world, many of whom rivaled her in power—who were crawling all over this place.

Not that she was showing the strain. We were about to invade another world, while every enemy she had in this one was probably somewhere on the grounds, plotting. Yet she looked as cool and calm as always. But her little pets had started to slither a bit faster, and her eyes were a tad too intense.

She thought I was about to make her look bad, I realized.

Somewhere, some poor bastard was chiseling out a sixteen-foot example of my supposed power, but that was just propaganda, wasn't it? Like that damned painting. She and Mircea had sold the rest of the vampire world on her leadership of the coalition partly on the basis of my supposed power.

What would happen, I wondered, if everyone realized it was a lie?

I licked my lips and looked up at Mircea, whose jaw was tight. "The Pythia has had a long day," he said. "I can call one of my own bokors. He'll be here in less than an hour."

"That will be too long," the old knight said, taking away my only lifeline without realizing it. "I saw a necromancer at work once, after a battle. I admonished him to wait until the wounded had been carried off the field, but he said that he could not. The memories fade after more than an hour, and sometimes less. We must act now!"

I swallowed and looked about, but didn't see any way out of this. Well, except for maybe one. I got up and walked over to the bodies, as if to pick out the best candidate, but in reality I barely saw them. I was too busy giving Billy Joe a mental poke.

I could feel him resting comfortably in the necklace nestled between my breasts. His talisman was old and ugly, but also invisible to human eyes—and hopefully vampire ones—thanks to a little chameleon ward that an old friend had given me. It hid any magical devices or weapons I wore, to keep them from being taken whenever I landed in trouble. Some of the fey had been able to see through the disguise, if they were making an effort, although if Caedmon could, he gave no sign.

If he wanted to see what I could do, there were better ways, I thought, sending him a look.

He just smiled back encouragingly, which enraged me even more for some reason. Maybe because the asshole didn't get what was at stake here. He could ruin the whole damned alliance with his little joke!

I saw his eyes flash as if he'd heard the insult. I didn't know if he had; who the hell knew what he could do? But just in case, I sent him a few more.

His eyes might have widened a little, but I wasn't sure. I wasn't sure about anything except that Billy wasn't waking up, damn him! Which was a problem, since the only person in our family who had ever picked up anything from a brain was him!

"Damn it! Quit poking me in the ass," he grumped, finally bothering to roust himself. A moment later, a surly head poked out of my torso to glare at me.

Technically, it was sticking out of his necklace, but it was at a weird angle, making it look like I'd grown another head. The visual and the abruptness almost made me lose my balance—damned high heels! But I recovered and crouched down in front of a pile of limbs and broken bodies, none of which seemed to go together, as if I was studying them.

And then realized that I couldn't talk to him like this.

"Well, what is it?" he demanded.

I looked at him numbly.

"Cat got your tongue?"

Get inside, get inside, get inside, I thought at him, which of course didn't help. I am not a telepath, and neither is Billy. We have a weird sort of connection that neither of us understands, but it doesn't stretch to sharing a brain—thank God. I'd hate to see what was in Billy's head, although I was pretty sure it would be prettier than what I was looking at right now.

Beer and boobies, I thought randomly, and heard Caedmon turn a laugh into a sneeze.

"Sorry," he told everyone. "Is it drafty in here?"

"Holy shit!" Billy said, suddenly noticing the seven-foot-tall, glowing fey. And then the snake-draped queen. And the seriously tense master vamp—a number of them. And they didn't all belong to the consul, or she wouldn't be this worried.

I was running out of time.

And then Billy noticed the bodies.

"What the actual *fuck*?"

Get inside, get inside, get inside, get inside, I thought, but couldn't say. Or even whisper, with vamp hearing all around. Damn it, Billy! Get a clue!

But, of course, he was going to bitch first. "Why do you always do this to me?" he complained. "There I was, having a perfectly nice dream about a brew and a busty lass—"

Caedmon burst out laughing.

"Sorry," he told everyone, from behind his hanky. "I'm just excited."

I glared at him some more, and he waved the hanky at me for some reason. Like saying go ahead, get on with it. Yeah, I thought back, that would be nice!

"—and what do I wake up to? Bodies!" Billy looked about in disgust. "Why is it always bodies?"

Get inside, get inside, get inside, get *inside*.

"You could wake me up for a party sometime," he pointed out. "Or a nice card game, or a chat, or a barbecue. I mean, I couldn't eat the food, but it's the thought that—" He stopped. "Why aren't you saying anything?"

Get inside, get inside, get inside, get *inside, you son of a—*

Billy slipped inside my skin.

*"—bitch!"*

"Oh, that's nice," he said, and it echoed in my head. Because there was one way we could silently communicate, but it required sharing a body. Something I had no problem with, since we'd only done it about a thousand times now, and because I needed help!

*"Help!"* I almost shrieked, and mentally grabbed him.

*"Oof! What the—let go of me!"*

*"You have to help me! They want me to read these guys' minds and they're dead and I don't know how and they're* dead*!"*

*"Okay, okay, wait,"* Billy said, extricating himself from the death grip I had on his spirit. *"They want you to do what now?"*

I explained. *"So you have to help me!"* I said when I finished. Because people were starting to shift position impatiently. It was put up or shut up time, only I didn't have anything to put up!

Billy looked around again. *"But . . . they're dead."*

*"I know they're dead!"*

*"Don't yell. I'm already in your head."*

*"Fine, just tell me what to do."*

*"About what?"*

*"What do you mean about what? You've done this before—"*

*"What? When?"*

*"You do it all the time! You drift through people's heads, picking up on their thoughts—"*

*"Yeah,* live *people. Which these ain't, in case you missed it. They're not even whole anymore."*

And the next thing I knew, I was picking up the severed head, or rather, Billy was. The dishwater blond hair was wet against my hands, although not with blood. It felt like water.

"Beer," Billy and I said aloud, and the officer nodded.

"He was drinking with some of these others. Or perhaps just fell into a puddle of it. We found an overturned table and spilled tankards among the bodies. But they

were in one of the large dorm tents. Nobody saw what
happened."

I didn't answer. I was trying, really hard, not to notice
that I was holding a man's head in my hands, but it wasn't
working. The blue eyes were fixed and staring, and had
started to dry out. I suddenly understood why they always
closed corpses' eyes in the movies, even weighting them
down with something. That blank, lifeless stare was—

I shuddered; I couldn't help it.

It was *horrible.*

"Cassandra—" Mircea began, and then cut off when
the consul put a hand on his arm, the bright yellow talons
looking like they were sinking into the skin. She glared at
me; she could afford to, since the other vamps were behind her. I gave her blank face back. This is partly your
fault, bitch, I thought, and didn't care if Caedmon heard.

Frankly, right then, I wouldn't have cared if *she* had.

"Sinking into another mind is awkward," I said curtly.
"There may be some physical reactions."

"Aye," the officer said. "The bokor I knew fair shit
himself."

*"Oh, that's great,"* Billy said. *"I'm really enthused now."*

*"Just do it,"* I told him.

*"Yeah, about that. Like I said, I know the basics for
scanning living minds. But I'm not the necromancer
here. Dead bodies are just dead bodies to me. Closed off.
Silent."*

*"What are you saying?"* I asked, my gorge rising. Because I was afraid I already knew.

*"I'm saying we do this together. Or not at all."*

# Chapter Fourteen

*Everything was blurry, with almost an underwater feel. I was walking through the tent city outside, or rather, he was. And the dead vamp was walking fast.*

*I saw a banner flutter overhead like a piece of seaweed caught in a gentle tide. I saw a piece of trash blow by in ultra-slow motion. I saw several human servants chatting over the top of a garbage can on wheels. They looked almost like they were frozen in time.*

*They weren't; the vamp was just sped up, darting around the camp with liquid speed. He didn't like to be out in the sun like this. They'd laced the shield that was protecting the camp—or so they claimed—with spells to shade everyone and given them all something called Night's Ease as an extra precaution.*

*Night's Ease. Ha! It sounded like a laxative and tasted vile, and he still had little red spots on the skin he hadn't kept covered up well enough!*

*He scratched at them worriedly. He looked like he'd been sleeping in a patch of poison ivy, and that was despite layering up like it was winter in the Arctic. They said the fey sun wouldn't burn them, but did they know? What if everyone popped out of the portal only to promptly go up like a bunch of Roman candles? What about that?*

*Thankfully, some friends had invited him to play cards, to take his mind off things. He just hoped he wasn't late. He didn't want to lose his place, since there was nothing else to do here. Except sit around, exhausted and itchy, working himself into knots.*

*It was better to stay busy. Kept the mind off things. Kept him out of trouble, too.*

He scowled at some other vampires lounging by a tent, one of them in a wife-beater. Show-offs. He changed his course to avoid them. What else could you expect from Zakhar's creatures, little better than animals. They'd have weres here next!

Or worse, demons.

He felt sick suddenly. They couldn't make him take one, could they? Everyone said not, but he wasn't sure. It wasn't right, taking one of those things inside you. It was dirty, wrong! His skin crawled at the very thought.

Of course, it also did at the thought of what his master would do to him if he was sent back. That's what happened if you couldn't or wouldn't work with the creatures: they sent you back to your master, and somebody else had to come in your place. And with war looming, his master wasn't going to be pleased at having to send one of his best fighters, which he might need to guard his ancient ass!

Instead, he'd sent three musicians and a damned librarian. If any of them were sent back, his master had joked that he was sending the pool boy. Of course, it wasn't supposed to matter who filled the levy. They were just housing, after all, just flesh that some thing could use.

He thought of what he'd seen a week ago, when he'd first arrived, and shivered. The four of them had stood around, clutching their luggage—a single knapsack only, they'd been told, so no instruments to play to make themselves feel better, not unless they wanted to go without underwear in the damned apocalypse! They'd felt horribly out of place, and probably looked it, too, and then the shouting had started.

We should have just found our tent, he thought now. But he'd been hungry and cold, not having had a chance to eat for over a day. Masters were like camels—they could seemingly go forever without food—but he wasn't one. He hurt. But when he tried getting a fast meal off some flunky, shortly after they were dropped off, he'd been pulled away by a guard and threatened with bodily harm! For trying to feed!

It was insanity, and no one was telling them anything, and they were hungry and bored. So, of course, they'd gone to see what all the ruckus was about. There had been a huge throng around a makeshift arena—humans as well as vamps—yelling and drinking and placing bets. He didn't know about the others, but he'd just hoped to get a taste while everybody was too distracted to notice. But then he'd been distracted.

By somebody throwing a giant at his head!

He'd just stood there, watching it come, frozen in disbelief. And would have been flattened if Lucas hadn't jerked him aside at the last minute. He and the lute player had lain there in the mud, shaken and wide-eyed, the lights all but blinding them, the cheers deafening them, watching the great creature lumber back to its feet, a cudgel the size of a car in its massive fist—

And saw it get picked up by a mage's spell and thrown at another part of the crowd.

Only they said it wasn't a mage. They said it was a vampire—demon-possessed and magic-wielding. They said that he and the others would soon be able to do as much or more.

They could go fuck themselves.

He wasn't that stupid—vampires didn't use magic; everybody knew that! But even if it were true, he didn't care! Like he didn't care about the power boost they'd promised from the union, which might push him toward master status.

Great. So he could get a court of his own, and a bunch of scheming followers just waiting to stake him in the back and take over. No! He didn't want any of it! He wanted to go home, back to his beautiful, messy practice room, with sheaves of old sheet music going golden from age and polished instruments smelling of beeswax and lemon oil, and the scent of flowers drifting in from the garden.

He didn't want to be here, scrabbling about in the mud with a bunch of savages!

We're supposed to be above such things, he thought angrily. He was supposed to be. Spend a century becoming an expert musician, a talent to rival Mozart himself, and what did it buy you? A possession and a trip to Faerie, where some damned fey could . . . cut your . . . head off . . .

*It happened so fast that he never even felt it. One second, he was throwing open the flap to his friend's tent, and the next the world was skewing wildly around him. He didn't know what had happened until his vision stopped spinning and his cheek came to rest on some wet grass, just in time to see—*

"No!" *he screamed*—we screamed—*and scrambled back—*

Into Mircea, who grabbed us—me—us—whoever the hell! I didn't know anymore! And Billy was yelling and Mircea was talking and people were staring, and my damned skirt had a huge blood splatter on it from where I'd dropped the head when I—

*"Aughhh!" I screamed again, seeing the vamp's now headless body being forced to its knees, before a stake descended and—*

"No!" I shrieked, grabbing my breast, trying to run. But I'd lost a shoe and somebody's arms were around me. I fought, but couldn't go anywhere, and then Billy was hovering in front of me. Ghostly hands cupped my cheeks, ghostly coolness suffused me, soothing, calming, quiet. Another scream died in my throat.

"It's okay. Cas—it's okay. You're out now, we're both out. Are you hearing me?"

I nodded, but didn't look at him. I was too busy looking at the head, still rotating slightly on the floor where I'd dropped it. Thankfully when it stopped, it was facing the other way. I didn't know what I'd have done if it hadn't. Coming out of there had been—

I hadn't liked coming out of there.

Better than staying in, I thought, or maybe that was somebody else. I'd turned my head into Mircea's chest, but the weird, almost foreign thought made me look up at Caedmon. But he was looking as concerned as the rest; guess he'd lost his sense of humor.

So had I.

" 'm out," I said thickly, and I didn't mean just of the guy's head. I meant this whole thing! But no way could I shift like this, with my brain feeling strange, almost sticky. Like parts of that other mind had clung to it when we pulled away. God, that had been horrible, horrible! And *fuck* this!

I tried to get up, but the lost shoe and a foot smeared with blood prevented it.

"Shh, take a moment," Mircea murmured.

I didn't want a moment. I wanted to get out of here! But maybe I need it, I thought, feeling sick.

"What did you see?" the consul asked, squatting in front of me, and somehow making the movement elegant despite wearing a dress made out of live snakes.

I didn't immediately answer, and the bright yellow nails raised, as if she planned to grasp my chin. But something in my face stopped her. "Don't," I forced out. I wasn't going to be responsible for what I did if she touched me.

She didn't.

A moment later, somebody else was crouching there.

"I'm sorry. Was it so bad?" the old soldier asked gruffly.

I just stared at him.

"Take a moment, lass," he said, and a callused old hand covered mine.

I took a moment. I'd had to leave my body in order to drift through the dead vamp's, and it felt like I'd been away a little too long. Which was any time at all, because no soul in residence = dying! And while necromancers' souls are a little more flexible than most, that universal law doesn't change.

"Water," I said hoarsely.

Mircea helped me up, and they gave me a glass. It was the same one I'd had before, and it was still chilled. So not away so long, after all.

I drank it down, almost finishing it before wiping a hand across my mouth.

"He didn't want to be here," I said, remembering that old wood-paneled music room, the one I'd never been in. But it had been lovely: faded carpets on polished wood floors, beautiful antique instruments, lovingly cared for, the smell of flowers . . .

He should have been back there, composing some pretentious new composition. He should have been nibbling on his pens—he'd liked to chew on his pens, he'd had a cup of the mangled things on a table. He should have been—

Somewhere else.

"None of us wants to be here, Lady," the old soldier told me. "War is a terrible thing, and anybody thinks otherwise was never in one."

"Hey, Cass!" Billy called, before I could respond. "Check it out!"

He was hovering over another corpse, which had landed on its stomach, but the head was to the side, so I guess he could see the face.

"Is it him?" I asked, and I said it out loud, because fuck it, that's why. Billy nodded, and I walked over. The face was dead now, and mushed strangely against the floor, almost like it was trying to form a puddle. A puddle of flesh, I thought, and shuddered.

But he was right; it was the same guy.

"That's the one," I said, to whoever happened to be listening.

I guess it was the old soldier, because he came over and turned the body on its back. That wasn't a great move, because the man who everyone crowded around to see appeared to have been split in half—at least the upper body had been. The face had separated into two parts, which explained why he'd looked like he was melting into the floor. And because there didn't seem to be much in there to hold him together anymore.

The chest had been vacated, too, with a bunch of raw, red flesh visible through a half-shredded breastplate, along with the insides of some ribs. But the sides of the armor were still kind of keeping it intact. The head didn't have that advantage, and it was just . . . floppy.

I should have been losing my lunch, or running off somewhere, possibly screaming. But my brain seemed to have switched off my emotions, and a weird sort of numbness had overtaken me. Or maybe that was Mircea. He had a lot of mental gifts, and he had a hand on my shoulder that felt unusually weighty.

Anyway, I didn't react, even when the old soldier literally pulled the man's face back together.

Whatever glamourie the vamp had been using had gone with death, so he was pale as milk, although he'd probably been that way in life, too. He had a patchy red beard but no mustache, a mop of red hair, and a mole on his temple like a very misplaced beauty mark. I focused on it because it was easier, and because that was how I knew we'd found our man.

"He killed the other one," I said, gesturing at the head. "Decapitated him when he was entering the tent, out of nowhere."

"For what reason?" the consul asked.

I shook my head, but stopped because it made me feel dizzy. I drank more water. "No idea."

"No idea?" It was sharp. "What did you see?"

I opened my mouth, and Mircea's hand tightened. Okay, yeah. We had company.

"The ground," I rasped. "As his head bounced across it."

"And what else?"

"Nothing else. That's all he saw. Then that guy"— I pointed at the redhead—"staked him through the heart, and that was it. He didn't know why he died, so I can't tell you."

"Can you tell us anything else, any detail?"

That was Mircea. He sounded tense, because yeah. Somebody was slaughtering his army before it even went to war. And his boss was glaring at him like this was all his fault.

It looked like he wasn't having any better of a day than I was.

"He was surprised," I said, remembering that brief surge of shock, and not just the physical kind. "They knew each other."

"They all knew each other," the officer told me. "They're part of the same squad!"

"I think . . . I think that guy"—I indicated the redhead again—"was the one who invited him to play cards. He invited other people, too."

"He invited them so he could kill them?" the consul asked. "It was premeditated, then."

I nodded.

Looked pretty premeditated to me.

"Tensions have been running high," the old officer said, his face troubled. "Many of the families here have long-standing grudges, as do some of the senates. Add that to what we're asking them to do—"

"There has been violence on a daily basis," one of the other vamps said. "Although nothing this . . . extreme."

"Yes, but that's not what happened here." Mircea knelt by the ravaged man.

"And how do you know that?" the vamp asked. His tone wasn't exactly a sneer, but it wasn't one I'd have expected from someone addressing his general. I didn't know him: a generic blond in a uniform that was more braid and medals than cloth. He obviously thought well of himself.

Mircea looked up, the dark eyes sardonic. "He killed all these others, then, in your view?"

The vamp nodded. "Likely was unstable before he came. That, or the pressure—"

"Did nothing! Are ye blind, man?" the old soldier demanded.

The officer drew himself up. "I simply pointed out that we have our killer. The Pythia even thinks so!"

"Perhaps," Mircea said gently. "But then who killed him?"

Everybody looked at the blond idiot for a moment, who flushed with embarrassment.

And then everybody looked at me.

I stared back for a second, and then started shaking my head. Vigorously. Dizziness be damned!

"Cassie—"

"Not only no, but *hell* no!"

"We're not asking—"

"Like hell you're not! I am not going back in there! Forget it, I'm done!"

"That is your prerogative, of course."

"Damn straight it is! There's nothing to go *into* anyway, even if I wanted! His head is . . . is like that!" I gestured at the flattened cranium, which looked like one of those full-size head masks they sell for Halloween, only with nothing inside. I didn't know what had happened to the guy's brain, but it wasn't in there anymore.

Most of it wasn't, anyway.

"Yeah," Billy agreed. "Ain't nobody getting anything out of that."

"Especially if it's me!" I didn't care if it looked like I was talking to myself. I didn't care if I looked unstable in front of the consul's new friends. I didn't care about anything but getting out!

And now everybody was looking at Mircea, because of course they were. He was supposed to control the crazy Pythia, right? Only not this time.

He pulled me away from the rest—why, I didn't know. It wasn't like they couldn't hear us anyway. Although I was frankly past caring.

"You don't have to do this," he told me, and sounded like he meant it.

"Damn straight!" I repeated, and then I shuddered, and felt his arms go around me. I was supposed to be mad at him—furious, even. And I was. But I couldn't deny that, right then, those arms felt good. I shuddered again, and they tightened.

"I'm sorry," Mircea whispered. "We shouldn't have put you through that."

I looked up and met dark, velvety eyes that looked absolutely sincere. Of course, his usually did, no matter the truth level involved. But still . . .

It was nice to have someone at least pretend to give a damn.

"Thank you," I said, and meant it.

And then I waited, because of course he was going to attempt to talk me into it anyway. That's what Mircea did: bring people around to the consul's point of view. And right now, she didn't care what price I paid for her information, she just wanted it.

Which was stupid, because it wouldn't even help!

"What do they expect me to do?" I asked when he just stood there, giving me body heat but no arguments. "Go mind to mind, watching him slaughter the rest of them?"

"No," someone said, but it wasn't Mircea.

I looked up to see that Marlowe had walked over to join us, in the silent way vamps have, Mircea excepted. He always made his footsteps audible, even to human ears, maybe because he knew that anything else freaked me out. Kind of like Marlowe was doing now, although for a different reason.

Because he was talking to me, but looking at Mircea.

He didn't seem too happy.

"We need you to try with that one," Marlowe said, jerking his chin at a corpse—an intact one, for a change—that was being dragged forward—

By its feet.

"Stop!" I yelled, because the soldiers were smearing a broad swath of red and brown across the floor behind the corpse. They stopped, looking confused. And then just stood there while a widening stain spread across the tile.

Billy whistled, while I tried not to gag. "Gutted," he said, speaking the obvious. "Somebody unzipped him from neck to nuts."

"Put him down!" I told them, furious. That had been a person, a few minutes ago, and now they were dragging him around like—

Like a sack of potatoes, I thought, when they abruptly dropped him on the floor.

The old soldier wasn't any happier. "Have a care!" He knocked one of the men's hands away. "Or would ye want someone doing the same t'you?"

The vamp blinked at him, like the subject of his own possible mortality had never crossed his mind.

"Who is—was—he?" I asked, my hand in front of my face.

"Not one of mine, Lady, but no soldier should be handled like that!"

"Agreed," Mircea said, and the look he turned on the two hapless soldiers was hot enough to burn. "It is time you started acting like an army, not a collection of individual squads. The other soldiers you see here are the only backup you are shortly going to have. Show them respect—all of them. They may save your life one day."

He smiled slightly, and it was a little scary. "Or not."

"Go wait outside," the old soldier told them curtly. "We'll call you when we need you!"

They fled, while I stared down at the crumpled remains of another life. He looked like a Spaniard or an

Italian, or possibly from somewhere in the Middle East. He had olive skin and dark hair. I honestly couldn't tell much more than that, because he also had a couple gallons of blood splattered all over him.

Unlike the others, who'd been killed in more usual ways, he looked like a wild animal had gotten to him.

Marlowe appeared in front of my vision. "He was on patrol, trying to cut down on the stupidity out there. He heard something, possibly saw something. Something he fought for a moment—long enough to draw attention to the area, anyway. But when my people arrived, they found him like this."

Dark eyes met mine steadily. "Did he die for nothing?"

I felt my throat go tight. I knew what he was doing, and it was a dirty trick. Particularly now, with us standing over the damned body. But that didn't make him wrong. This man had given his life trying to do his duty, while all I was being asked for was a little discomfort.

Okay, a lot of discomfort, because I really didn't want to go in there!

But we were running out of time. If we were going to get anything at all, it had to be now. "Billy," I said thickly, and felt him slip inside.

"Who is Billy?" I heard somebody ask, as I knelt by the side of the dead man. And then I didn't hear anything. No wonder they call it diving, I thought, as what felt like water closed over my head.

# Chapter Fifteen

There was no tent city this time.

"*Okaaaay,*" Billy said, looking around. "*Are we too late?*"

*It kind of felt like it. Kind of looked like it, too. Darkness, deep and dark and cold, spread out all around us. It was quiet, but it echoed. Like we were in some vast underground cistern instead of somebody's head. And every time I moved, every time I breathed, it came back to me, only magnified and louder.*

*It sounded like a whole army was breathing in here.*

"*Okay, that's creepy as shit,*" Billy whispered, because it was. And then we both paused, waiting for the inevitable return.

*But there wasn't one.*

"*Hey, why didn't that echo?*" he asked. "*Hellllloooooo!*" he added, and we waited some more, but there was nothing. "*What's the deal?*"

"*I don't know—*" I began, and stopped, because it was suddenly like being inside a kettle drum.

"*Don't know. DOn't KNow. don'T knoW,*" echoed from a hundred different directions.

"*Okay, weirded out now,*" Billy said unevenly.

*Yeah, that made two of us.*

"*Look, Cass, there's nothing to see. We got here too late. Let's just call it a—*"

*A light came on in the distance.*

"*—day?*"

*It was dim, almost indistinguishable against all the darkness, except it was the only light around. It was also distant, flickering somewhere off in the gloom, almost like—like a candle about to go out, I thought, as it was suddenly extinguished. I blinked in the dark, wondering if I'd imagined the whole thing.*

*"I vote we pretend that didn't happen," Billy said.*

*And then it happened again.*

*"Well, shit."*

*"Come on," I told him, and started forward—only to almost bean myself on something hidden in the darkness. I felt around, and it was sort of like a cave wall, if it had been buffed by water for years. Smooth and undulating, but weirdly spongy. "What the hell?"*

*"I don't know, but it's like a maze in here," Billy said.*

*"Ghost light," I told him, and winced as it came echoing back to me. He sighed.*

*"That's gonna get old fast," he said, and then light was spilling out all around us, green-tinged and bright, almost blinding.*

*"Tone it down," I whispered, and then, when a thousand voices whispered "DOwn, down, doWN," back at me, vowed not to do that anymore.*

*Billy toned it down.*

*We crept forward into darkness.*

*It was a maze, I discovered, filled with barriers I couldn't pass, forcing me to find my way through channels I couldn't see. That would have been bad enough on its own, but it was also a graveyard. Ghostly images flickered here and there for an instant, echoes in a dying brain. They were pale, translucent, but vivid against the gloom.*

*A little girl in an old-fashioned frock darted out in front of us, running after an equally ghostly cat, only to disappear a moment later. An old woman picked grapes in a vineyard high overhead, spilling pale light down on us for a moment, before she, too, winked out. And then a massive cavalry charge almost ran us down.*

*I screamed as what appeared to be every horse on the planet thundered at us out of nowhere. They should have been silent, but the echoes of my own voice pounded against us so hard that they almost had tangible weight. For a moment, it actually felt like we were being trampled under a thousand flailing hooves.*

*And then they cut out, disappearing like the ghosts*

*they weren't. Leaving me panting on all fours with my arms over my head. And gazing into blackness so deep it boiled at the corners of my vision, while my heartbeat sounded in my ears like another charge.*

Billy pulled himself off the floor, crawled over beside one of the "walls," and just sat there, shivering and staring at me. "Is that . . . going to keep . . . happening?"

I don't know, *I mouthed.*

"Well, that's not very helpful, is it?" he snapped.

I crawled over beside him. "I think it's just the last few synapses flaring," I said softly. Synapses, synapSes, synapSES. "The longer we're here," here, hERe, here, "the fewer there should be." Be, BE, be.

"That does not make me want to stick around," Billy snarled.

"Me, neither." NEIther, neiTHer, neither.

"Oh, for the love of—let's get this crap over with!"

I couldn't agree more.

*We headed for the little light again, which I eventually figured out wasn't flickering. It was passing behind the strange shapes that clogged the darkness here, misshapen pillars and half walls, and sudden dips or rises that left us scrambling across a landscape filled with pitfalls. But Billy's light helped, once we figured out how to direct it, and we slowly started gaining.*

*Ghostly images continued to be a problem, although we learned to ignore them. The echoes became eerie background noises, but they weren't really an issue, either, because we weren't chasing whatever was ahead of us by sound. And the weird protrusions and undulating floor got easier to navigate after a while.*

*Until the latter dropped out from under me a moment later, like I'd hit a fun house slide.*

*I didn't scream that time; I was learning.*

*But I did bounce around, hitting walls, or something like them, while scrabbling for purchase with hands and feet and not finding any. And then having the floor completely disappear for a second, leaving me with the horrible sensation of falling through open air. Before I hit a hard surface, what felt like stories below where we'd started, with a* whummp.

*I just lay there for a moment, dizzy and freaked-out and very, very, quiet.*

*And not just because the echoes of my landing were shivering the air all around me, sounding like a thousand lumberjacks chopping a thousand trees.*

*But because there was something else down here.*

*I didn't know how I knew. There was no sound, once the echoes faded, except for Billy's cursing, somewhere up above. He seemed to have avoided whatever pitfall had caught me, and was calling my name, sounding increasingly worried.*

*I didn't call back.*

*For a long moment, I just stayed where I was, not moving, barely even breathing. Just staring into utter darkness, because I didn't have Billy's light anymore. And the strange illumination we'd been following was no longer in sight, either.*

*That left me with taste, smell, touch, and sound, none of which were helping. All my senses felt like they'd gone hyperacute, yet all of them told me the same thing: there was nothing here. I was imagining things. Everything was fine.*

*Everything was not fine.*

*And maybe Caedmon, the asshole, had had a point after all, I thought, because deprivation of the other senses seemed to have opened up a new one. One that I decided to call weight, although it wasn't really related to touch. The air just seemed heavier in some places, more meaningful, like gravity bending around a star.*

*Only it wasn't a star that was huddled in a corner, under a jutting shelf of the cave material.*

*And, once I identified it, it was impossible to miss. Something small, something weak, something frightened. Especially when it realized that I could detect it.*

*It let out a small noise that sounded thunderous to my straining ears, and took off—to the left. I knew because I could track it. Not with my eyes, but with the sense of weight that pulled at me, like I was holding a wildly careening kite caught in a gale.*

*I scrambled to my feet and followed the crazed little thing, which was bouncing off walls and breathing heavily in rapid little puffs. I was frightening it, even though I wasn't trying to. I wanted to call out, to reassure it, but the scary echoes might make things worse instead of better. I didn't know what to do, and I was getting farther away from anywhere Billy might look for me.*

*I should turn back, I thought.*

*But if I did, that was it. I wouldn't know anything more than I already did, and I didn't know anything! Not what this thing was, why it was inhabiting a dead brain, or—*

*Or why it was flying at my face! The small creature suddenly reversed course, coming back at a run and slamming straight into me. "Kulullû," it whispered in a panicked voice. "Kulullû, Kulullû!"*

*"No, Cassie," I said—to no one. Because it was already tearing back the way we'd come, like a literal bat out of hell. Which wouldn't have been so bad, except that it was dragging me along with it!*

*We'd gotten tangled up, but I couldn't see how and didn't have time to ask. I was jerked along behind it and then under another overhang I also couldn't see but felt pressing down on top of me. The creature was at my side, quivering in fear, but not of me, I realized. I might have startled it before, but now it was huddled up against me as if I could somehow save it from . . . what, exactly?*

*"Kulullû," it whispered. And if that meant "fuck," I agreed, I thought, as light started to push elongated fingers into the darkness.*

*It was the same light I'd seen up top, or at least, it looked that way. But I wasn't real interested in seeing what was shedding it, suddenly. I was beginning to think that maybe it had been hunter, not prey, and that it was looking for us.*

*And it was getting close.*

*We stayed there, me and the small thing, soundless, breathless, huddled together in fear of whatever was slouching this way. Or squelching, I thought, because that was what it sounded like. Not footsteps or even hooves striking down, just . . . squelching. With a weird sucking sound at the end of every step that made me think of a formless ball of phlegm—and wasn't that just all I needed?*

*No, I thought.*

*What I needed was Billy Joe, because without him, I didn't know how to leave this place!*

*And then I realized that no, no I didn't need him, at least not now, when a familiar voice called out: "Cass! Cassie! Damn it, where did you go?"*

*Billy, I thought, my heart in my throat.*

*The squelching stopped.*

*I couldn't see what was happening, because we were too far under the ledge. A green haze had started to filter down from above, almost too thin to see. But any light was bright down here. And then something pale, with a glistening skin that shed some kind of viscous ooze, paused outside the opening of the overhang—for an instant.*

*Before scrabbling up what appeared to be some kind of cliff face, almost too fast to see.*

*It was headed straight for my oldest friend, the one who had come in here with me when he didn't have to, the one who'd saved my life more times than I could count, the one who would never see it coming.*

*I didn't think; I didn't even hesitate. I burst out of our hiding place and screamed: "Billy!* Run!"

*There was no time to see if he did or not. There was no time for anything. The creature turned on a dime, lightning fast, and flung itself back down at me.*

*All I saw was a pale white underbelly, blotting out the sky. I tried a time spell, but it didn't work—maybe because this was a spirit battle, where time didn't have the same effect, or maybe because I was pissing myself; I didn't know. And then it was on me.*

*I felt claws rake me, the pain of a power loss stagger me, a weight far heavier than anything my human body could have withstood flatten me.*

*"Kill it!" I screamed mentally, letting loose the only weapons I had left, a pair of ghostly looking knives that reside in the bracelet I had stolen off a dark mage months ago. They were horribly unreliable, and as often ignored me as not, not to mention the fact that I didn't even know if they'd work in—*

*Here. I finished the thought while being deluged in*

*what smelled like fish guts. My knives had taken my attacker right through what I guess was its belly.*

That was both good and bad, because it reared up over top of me, releasing the pressure but also giving me my first good look at it. And it was horrifying. Like something out of Escher's worst nightmare, it kept changing, but none of its forms were good. An eldritch horror of a thing, one second it was a large, lumpy undersea monster filling the narrow corridor and thrashing around with a dozen tentacles; the next it was half-man, half-fish, only nothing like the merpeople I'd seen. They had been beautiful, graceful—and terrible, yes, but in the way a summer storm is terrible, flashing across the sky, filling you with awe and wonder.

There was neither of those things here. It had a face that would have turned Medusa to stone, with slitted, pale eyes and more slits for a nose, and a huge mouth filled with long, superthin, razor sharp teeth. The backbone was humpbacked and misshapen, halfway between fin and bone, and the hugely muscled arms ended in incredibly elongated webbed fingers, like king crab legs if they commonly came with spiked talons on the ends.

It also didn't seem to bleed blood. My knives were flying around, stabbing and stabbing at it, but the only thing that bubbled up to the surface of the skin was some kind of strange, translucent jelly. I knew that because it spat a lump of it at me, and it burned—God, it burned!

I screamed, because it didn't matter now, and the thing roared back, a stuttering, nails-on-a-chalkboard-times-one-thousand sort of sound that had my skin crawling and my own scream turning into more of a shriek, and then it brought one of those huge arms down.

Another scream died in my throat, or maybe in my chest, which those wicked-looking claws had just stabbed all the way through. It was a stunning blow, one that left wild, windblown echoes swirling around us. And me trapped against the ground, my mouth open but unable to speak, my body writhing like a bug on a pin—on four of them.

"Hey!" someone yelled, and the creature's head turned. "Hey, big and ugly!"

Billy, I thought. Run!

*He wasn't running. He was waving his arms, trying to get the creature to let go of me and chase him. And that was so stupid I didn't even have words.*

*Didn't he get it? In a spirit battle he'd go down before I would! I had the strength of my body to draw on; he had nothing, no protection at all!*

*So I did the only thing I could think of and grabbed one of my knives as it passed. I couldn't normally touch them, unless you counted the tiny, interlocking daggers on my bracelet. But that wasn't true in the spirit realm, where the hilt felt cool and solid against my palm when I closed my hand on it.*

*And used it to slash at the creature's claws.*

*It cut them clean through, leaking more of that burning jelly, but the rest were still buried in the ground—and in me! I wasn't any better off, I realized, as the monster looked down, as if surprised that his prey would fight back. But it wasn't alarmed—not until my second knife slapped into my palm, and the two of them together lunged upward, pulling me up and off the terrible, bony protrusions.*

*Power flooded out into the air, my spiritual substitute for blood. I was hemorrhaging and wouldn't last long, not bleeding life energy like a geyser. Which is why I dove underneath the claws and started digging a trench in the creature's side.*

*But although the knives worked a lot better with some guidance, it didn't seem to matter. The wound closed up almost as soon as I carved it out, the mucus solidifying and then repairing the damage. I was irritating him; I wasn't killing him, I realized.*

*And then he threw me at the wall and surged after Billy.*

*I hit with a sickening squelch of my own, bleeding from half a dozen wounds. A positive flood of power cascaded into the air around me, and a sickening lurch told me I didn't have much time left. But Billy had even less. I staggered off the wall; I had to get to him before that thing did. I had to find him, somehow . . .*

*And then a new light appeared, shining in the darkness.*

"I hope you don't mind," someone said, and I looked up to see Caedmon standing there, brilliant as the sun, almost too bright to look at. Just as he had been once before, when I had been stuck in a dark place, all alone. "I followed your trail."

I had no idea what that meant, and right then, I didn't care.

"I'm sorry . . . I called you . . . an asshole," I whispered, as the creature turned away from Billy once more.

Caedmon laughed, a strange, joyous sound in this terrible place. "I will allow you to make it up to me," he said, bowing gallantly and unsheathing a brilliant sword that lit up the darkness.

And then flying into a thousand meaty chunks as the creature boiled right through him with the power of a cyclone.

"Caedmon!" I screamed, and it echoed in the air, like the horrible sounds being reflected back, over and over: bones breaking, skin ripping, flesh splattering on floor and ceiling and walls. And then a rain of what looked like sunlight shimmering through the air and pattering down all around us.

Caedmon's light nullified by the power of the dark.

But the dark wasn't having so much fun, either. The light, so dazzling next to anything down here, seemed to hurt it. It writhed, slashing its talons against the walls, and gave off that stuttering scream again, the echoes loud and deafening.

But not so loud that I couldn't hear Billy.

"Cassie!" he yelled. "Where the hell are you?"

Because, yeah. We had exactly as long as it took the light to fade before we were toast. Not to mention that I'd been away for too long. I was getting dizzy, and not just from the power loss. It was a sure sign that I had to get back to my body—

I stopped.

Body.

"Cassie!" Billy was sounding increasingly desperate, and I didn't blame him. The light was starting to dim.

"Billy! I need you to find me the location of its body!"

"What?"

"The creature's body. I need you to show me where it is!"

"Are you nuts? Let's just go!"

Normally, I'd have agreed. But I was after a murderer, and it looked like I'd found him. And then all those faces came back to me: the thin blond who had just wanted to go home; the redhead whose body had been used to kill two dozen of his friends; the brunet who had just been doing his job and had died for it.

Caedmon, who had come to rescue me . . .

And, suddenly, a wave of emotion swamped me. I didn't know where it came from; I didn't know what it was. I just knew I was roaring in something beyond rage and jumping toward the creature, with no knives, no Pythian power, no weapons of any kind. Just fury so deep I could taste it.

Like I could taste its blood a second later. Because my hands did what the knives could not. They found the nearly closed wound in its side, and I followed, plunging elbows-deep in biting, stinging poison. I didn't care, like I didn't care about the creature's talons spearing into me, over and over, or its great maw snapping at the air, trying to bite. It still couldn't see worth a damn, but it could feel, and it wanted to tear, to rend me, as it had Caedmon. But he had been a child of the light, whereas I—

Was the firstborn and only child of Hel, goddess of death, which had been the Norse name for Artemis, and a powerful necromancer. I wasn't of the light any more than it was. Time to prove it.

I clawed my way inside the creature, cracking bones and tearing viscera. And what my hands took, it did not heal. It did run, though, a slashing, slithering motion as it transformed yet again, into something like a giant eel, if eels had intelligent eyes. It tore through the passages with me clinging to its side, screaming in rage as it repeatedly slammed me into the wall, trying to scrape me off.

It didn't succeed, but I could feel myself growing weaker, power sheering away with every blow. I had my mother's wrath, but not her power. I wasn't going to be enough—

But, then, I didn't have to be.

*Because I had help.*

*I'd barely had the thought when Billy was there, cursing louder and more profanely than I'd ever heard him, and I'd heard a lot. But he had it. Somehow, he'd gotten into the creature's mind and he had it.*

*Please, I thought, my power searching for the body the thing had left behind. Just give me this. Give me strength enough for one. Great. Shift.*

"Cassie! Cassie!" Light burst over me, so bright it seared my eyes and made me cover them protectively with my arm. And when I looked again, the dark, cave-like interior was gone and I was back in a room full of blood—

And a huge, writhing monster out of a nightmare, its physical body dwarfing the large space, rising up, up, up, until it filled the three-story-high ceiling above me.

# Chapter Sixteen

"What the *fuck*?" Marlowe rasped, being the first to break the silence.

"That's it!" I panted, clinging to consciousness. "That's what killed your men!"

The creature had been staring around, its strange, blunt, eel-like face with the terrible human eyes seeming confused by what had just happened. But at the sound of my voice, it refocused downward to where us tiny human types were staring up in shock. And a split second later, it was back in half-man form again and screaming in rage.

If I'd thought that sound was awful in the spirit realm, it was nothing compared to hearing it in person. Or of watching its physical form morph as easily as its soul had, with one long finger suddenly pushing out, elongating even more, becoming a bony spear. One he used to slash down at me—

Only to be met by a glowing, golden sword, wielded by a seriously pissed-off demigod.

"Let's try that again," Caedmon said, with blood on his mouth.

I didn't see what happened next, not because my vision cut out on me, but because it was just that fast. I'd seen vampires look like blurs before, but this wasn't that. I couldn't track the two of them at all when they moved; I could only see them when they didn't, suddenly appearing here, there, and everywhere when they paused for a split second.

But I saw when that golden blade saved me half a dozen times, because the monster seemed to have a serious hard-on for ending my life. I saw when Mircea grabbed the thing's elongated tail, pulling the huge body away from me and sending it crashing through the doors to the waiting room. I saw when the old knight pulled a sword of his own, as venerable as his armor, but oiled and sharp and deadly.

And, with a yell, jumped onto the monster's back.

His courage seemed to finally break the shock that had held the rest of the officers in place, their mouths open. They got a clue and tried to emulate him, only to be slammed through the wall and then several others by that massive tail. A bunch of palace guards—no light-weights themselves—came running down the hall and were treated likewise, although they might have been the lucky ones. Because the next group was impaled, armor and all, by those terrible, bony claws, all of which were far beyond spear length now.

We need the army, I thought desperately. Specifically, we needed the demon-possessed force that was spear-heading the assault on Faerie. We needed them *now*.

Because things were already going to hell. People were running and screaming, walls were being blown out, and huge pillars were falling. One of them struck the giant golden orb off its plinth and sent it rolling heavily down the great hall.

We had the numbers, but I wasn't at all sure that we had the advantage.

Until I heard a great HISSSSSSSSSS coming from somewhere in the air, high above me.

All the skin at the base of my neck ruffled up, my eyes got big, and I swallowed convulsively. Please let that be on our side, I thought, clinging to the floor. Please . . .

It was on our side.

Or should I say, *she* was.

Because a midnight viper longer than a couple of buses and thicker around than a great oak tree suddenly tore past me, almost too fast to see. Which was fine; I was completely fine with that. But fish man clearly felt other-wise. He turned from smashing the skewered vamps against the wall in time for those slitted eyes to blow wide, and then she was on him.

And I might have been wrong about the viper thing, I thought, staring. Because a second later—like a literal second—she'd wrapped him up in those giant coils and *squeezed*. And she squeezed hard.

His eyes bulged, his face darkened, and he thrashed hard enough to knock a hole through another wall and into what looked like a ballroom. But the consul held on, even when he morphed back into an eel, thinning and elongating his body and almost slipping out of her grasp. But Mircea, Marlowe, and Caedmon had grabbed spears off the fallen, and now they stabbed them through the beast's tail and into the floor, pinning it in place.

Or they tried. But it thrashed so hard that it shot the weapons back out as huge, flying projectiles that turned the nearby walls—and some of the guards who had been unfortunate enough to be standing in front of them—into porcupines. One swipe of that great tail also sent Marlowe, who was both a master vamp and a senate member, slamming back through the ruined waiting room and into the office as if he were nothing.

He flew by me and crashed into the far wall, although he didn't go through it. But he hit hard enough to shake the whole room and to send the chandelier swinging wildly overhead. But a second later he was up and snarling, his fangs out, his eyes glowing.

And a second after that, the wall behind the great beast was being riddled with holes as large as cannonballs. The blasts—from Marlowe's master power, at a guess—blew plaster and brick and marble sheeting everywhere, causing the screams from the fleeing people to reach a crescendo. But they didn't blow through the creature, who dodged them easily.

It really *was* faster than a vamp, I thought, barely believing my own eyes. And I wasn't the only one who thought so. I saw guards and even senators looking around in confusion, the way humans usually did when they saw vamps move. The only ones who seemed able to keep up with it were the consul and Caedmon, and they clearly weren't going to be taking it down alone.

What *was* this thing?

I didn't know, but a second later Marlowe was back in

the fray, where Mircea had commandeered a forest of spears from arriving soldiers. And it seemed they'd learned from last time, driving them almost up to their hilts in the stone floor. The creature didn't seem to have so easy a time throwing them off after that, any more than it did the old soldier, who had been stabbing and slicing and riding it like a bucking bronco this whole time. Or the consul, who just tightened her grip no matter what it did, matching it move for move.

It looked like a stalemate, with neither of them able to get an advantage over the other. But that was good enough, I realized, relief flooding me. All she had to do was hold it there while her men finished it off!

Only I guess the creature had figured that out, too. Because it abruptly changed form again, this time into a giant squid, with seemingly a tentacle for every attacker. They were huge, each of them almost as big around as the consul's alter ego, but they looked like water—almost clear except for sickly pink suckers on the undersides— and flowed like it, too.

They contracted back through her coils like deflated balloons, only to expand again once free, at which point they tried to wrap *her* up.

The two of them fought the big battle, writhing together in a constant, mind-bending coil that felt like it was turning my brain inside out. While new, weirdly fluid arms just poured around the spears that had been pinning it down, and then slid off, leaving the vamps looking like they were trying to stab water. The latest version of the creature had also finally neutralized the old soldier, sucking him in and leaving him floating in the gelatinous mass of its body, unable to fight or even to move.

We were losing, I realized in shock. Two demigods, a consul, and a small army of senior vampires, and we were *losing*. How was this *possible*?

But it was, and I'd brought that thing here; this was *my* fault. I had to help, but I was out of power, to the point that I couldn't even stand. I tried anyway, but only flopped back down, sliding in blood when my legs gave out from underneath me.

Billy popped up beside me as I stared at the battle helplessly. "Cass! What are you doing? They need you!"

I just looked at him numbly. "I don't . . . have anything . . . left."

"But I do!" he snarled, also staring at that thing. "Use it well, 'cause it's all I got." And the next second, I felt it—something like the outpouring of power that took place whenever I fed him to increase his stamina or range. But this time it was pouring back into me, a rush of strength, of life, that practically pulled me off the floor and onto my feet.

I felt Billy flow into his necklace to keep from fading, while I staggered and almost fell, my body trying to adjust to the sudden, dizzying return of power.

But not much of it. Billy was a ghost, not a god; he only had so much to give. But it was something, maybe enough for a single spell. Not a time stoppage; no way could I manage that. But maybe one of the easier ones—

My thoughts cut out and I hit the ground again as a blast of blood and body parts exploded through the air above me. The latest group of guards, I realized, as legs and arms and other things began raining down everywhere, battering me like fleshy hail. And then scrabbling around and kicking out after they hit the floor in a hundred squirming pieces, because they were *vampire* body parts, and they weren't dead.

Not yet, I thought sickly.

But we were all going to be pretty soon, because this latest incarnation of the creature was laying *waste*.

Rafe's beautiful sketches were splattered with gore as another wave of guards arrived—just grist for the mill. The guards couldn't handle this any more than the regular soldiers could. Call the army, I tried to scream, but there was blood in my mouth, a great gout of it sliding down my throat, threatening to choke me.

I spat it out, but before I could try again, I saw Mircea yelling something at the remaining troops. I couldn't hear him, but I didn't have to. The gestures were eloquent.

And I suddenly realized that we had a bigger problem than I'd thought.

The tent city was just outside, filled with soldiers who not only didn't have a demon partner yet, but in many cases weren't even really soldiers. The blond musician whose thoughts I'd drifted through had been right. Many masters weren't sending their best; they were sending those they considered expendable, the ones they didn't care much if they never saw again.

And if that thing broke through a few more walls, they wouldn't.

There was a good chance that the only reason the creature hadn't gone after them yet was because it didn't know where it was. It had been outside before, in the tent city, when it was possessing the redhead. It hadn't been in here, and shifts tended to be disorienting anyway. It might not know how close it was to its former prey.

But any minute now, it was going to find out.

And then it did, because a bunch of soldiers decided to take a shortcut, tearing open a tarp rather than finding a door. I saw Mircea curse, and he must have sent a mental command—a harsh one, judging by how fast they tried to correct their mistake. But it was too late.

The creature turned, and for a second, I could see it clearly as it paused in shock at the sight of the flapping tarp and open air. And all those tents, arrayed in neat, orderly rows, just outside. Rows where an army of mostly non-masters were sleeping or playing cards, huddled out of the sun, groggy during the day, if they were conscious at all.

They wouldn't even know what hit them.

I got up and started wading through the carnage for the hall.

Mircea had stopped yelling and was standing instead, his eyes glowing amber bright and focused on the creature. He was trying to get a mental lock, I realized, because Mircea's master powers were of the mind. And he must have done something, because a huge tentacle suddenly speared out and slammed him in the chest, knocking him back down the corridor by what had to be a hundred yards.

I screamed, because that blow would have killed a mortal man, and for a terrible second, I thought it had killed *him*.

But a moment later, he was back on his feet, shaking it off. And then running back this way, yelling something I couldn't hear. It was probably a call for the demon-possessed, elite troops, if he hadn't done that already, but I didn't know where they were, and all this was happening at vampire speed or faster. The cavalry might be coming over the hill, but they wouldn't be in time.

Not unless time got an assist.

I'd hit the waiting room, which was a mess of rubble-strewn floors, squirming body parts, and fallen walls, with rebar twisting upward out of some of the latter, in strange, modern art–style flourishes. I used the wreckage for cover, getting as close to the hall as I dared. I wouldn't get another shot at this, so I couldn't miss. I looked up through the plaster dust swirling around the great hall and put out a hand, feeling like an idiot, because that was almost the same pose as on that stupid statue.

Only I wasn't reaching for a bow.

Time slid across my fingers like silk, as slippery and as hard to hold. But unlike the weapons I'd never been comfortable with, the guns and knives that had always felt alien in my hands no matter how much I practiced with them, this was different. It was familiar, comforting, known. It flowed and embraced, soothed and calmed, like a mother's touch, like Billy's ghostly caress, like the Pythian power sparkling around me, whispering a strange language in my ear that I didn't understand.

But I understood *this*, I thought, and closed my fist. And felt the flow of time slow down, down, down around the creature. It wasn't a time stoppage; not even close. A human observer wouldn't have thought I'd done anything at all.

But there weren't a lot of humans around here.

And the vampires sure as hell knew what had just happened—and so did the creature.

It didn't roar again—I wasn't sure it could in this form—but it twisted the huge, bulbous head around to stare at me instead of the tents. Because I guess with me, it was personal. And then the vamps jumped it—not some of them, but *all* of them—as it lunged for me. But it was still lightning fast, barely visible to my human eyes, until I *pulled*, tightening my grip on time around it, almost screaming in effort.

And watched the creature slow to the speed of a human run.

But that only helped so much. The vampires were savaging it, but it didn't seem to care. It just kept coming, and I knew I should shift away, that I *had* to. But if I did, it would just go back for the tents again, and I couldn't let it go for the tents!

So I threw everything I had left into slowing it as much as I could, to the point that the room started to spin around me, that my legs felt like jelly, that my vision narrowed and darkened worryingly at the corners.

Yet it hardly seemed to matter. Mircea was yelling something from the other side of the creature, his horrified face visible through that terrible, gelatinous body. Marlowe was running for me, only to get slammed aside again, beyond my field of vision. And while the consul was still holding on, she was just getting carried along for the ride at this point, because I'd accidentally slowed her down, too.

I might have just made a mistake, I thought.

And then it was there, right there, close enough that I could feel the rush of strangely cold air in front of it, could smell the rotten fish stench coming off it, could see myself in the huge, glistening eyes—

Before I was knocked aside, my spell shattering, as a bunch of new arrivals surged all around me.

I was thrown to the ground, dizzy and exhausted and scared half out of my mind. But I landed on my back in time to see fifty or sixty vampires leaping on the thing all at once, like a hurricane. I didn't have to ask who they were; I *knew*.

They tore into it as it loomed above me, literally right over top. I stared up at the massive body, rising three, four, maybe five stories high, because there was nothing constraining it now, and watched as our best troops carved huge pieces off of it even as it tried to fall on me. Even as it writhed and twisted and did its best to take me with it. Even as it was dissected where it stood, carved up and separated out so it couldn't form back up.

Because if our guys couldn't kill it outright, they'd take it in pieces.

And then it morphed again, but this time, I wasn't sure it had been on purpose. The thing was suddenly going through a series of changes, almost too fast to see. The body changed and twisted, bulged and shrank and then bulged again, as I scrambled back, trying to get out of the way. I hit what remained of the wall between the waiting room and the office just as it settled into a massive, full-on fish thing with a protruding eye—

Which the consul put out with fangs longer than my arms.

And, finally, *finally*, that turned the tide. The whole concourse of us watched in total silence as she savaged the thing that had assaulted her army and killed her men. Blood splattered the crowd, thick and black and steaming. And burning, containing flecks of that pale, poisonous fat, which seemed to have aerosolized, because I could feel it burning in my lungs. But nobody moved until the thing lay dead on the ground, the consul's fangs buried deep in its throat, a huge pool of ugly blood spreading over and staining the pretty new mosaic.

For a second, there was only more stunned, echoing silence.

And then the screaming started, and the cheering and the crying, along with sounds I couldn't even name from the throats of what looked like thousands of people who'd taken refuge here, there, and everywhere. They were emerging from hallways and rubble-filled rooms, and they were running all around us now, their cries hammering against me like a tide, their hands reaching out to touch, even as I tried to get up and failed and sat down hard on my ass.

Well, I thought dizzily.

Looked like we were going to need another painting now.

# Chapter Seventeen

I shifted into the foyer of my suite a couple hours later, and for a wonder, nobody tried to shoot me. One of my guys—a sweet-faced Cuban named Emilio—was on guard, and he even smiled in welcome. "Heard you had some fun."

Vampires. Honestly, they really did gossip worse than old women. "I had something."

"Hey, did you ask about, you know?" He looked at me expectantly.

I blinked tiredly back.

I didn't know.

"The thing about Lord Mircea not pulling us back?"

Oh, yeah. Only the whole reason why I'd gone. "It, uh, didn't come up. Yet," I added when his face fell.

The perpetual smile reemerged, and it was blinding. "Maybe tomorrow."

Yeah, maybe a phone call tomorrow. I was really starting to hate going to the consul's. "Yeah."

I put my hand on the doorknob, but he shook his head. "They're having a thing on the terrace. Maybe you oughta, you know." He looked at my destroyed outfit and then did the *Bewitched* thing with his nose. Only he couldn't twitch it independently and had to use a finger. It was so goddamn adorable that I actually smiled, and I'd thought I was out of those.

It was good to be home.

"Thanks," I said, and shifted.

Annnnd immediately regretted it. I reappeared in my bathroom, my second-favorite landing pad, because nobody was supposed to be in there but me. Which was

extra fortunate tonight, since I collapsed to my knees
from the power loss, biting my lip on a scream. And then
wondering why I bothered; this place was soundproofed,
right?

I let out a heartfelt groan, and immediately there was
a knock on the door.

*That* was why, I told myself. You didn't take chances,
because there was always. Somebody. Listening!

This time it was Marco. "Cassie? You all right in
there?"

Why does everybody keep asking me that? I thought,
and then I giggled.

This did not appear to be the appropriate response.

"Cassie!"

"I'm fine," I gasped out, because if I didn't, I was going
to need another door, and I was trying to go a whole
month without trashing my suite. It would be a new record. I was gonna get ice cream.

I unclenched my body and crawled over to the sink.

"You don't sound fine," Marco said, and his tone informed me that my door was still in jeopardy.

"We had a thing—"

"So I heard."

Of course he had, I thought, while trying and failing
to get my fumbling fingers to open my damned makeup
bag. Vamps communicated mentally. He'd probably seen
it in 3-D, surround sound, 4K, or whatever the hell. Damn
it, I didn't care, I just wanted—

There!

A little triangular bottle fell out in my hand, strangely
and wonderfully heavy for its size. But I couldn't use it
yet. Marco would smell it through the door.

"I'm fine," I told him again, trying to sound a little
more convincing.

"Prove it."

"What?" I blinked at the door in confusion.

"I said, if you're all right, prove it."

"How? By letting you in?"

Because I didn't think that would be such a good idea.
I'd washed my hands and face at the consul's, but there
was dried blood and God knew what else all over me—

including on my bare legs, I noticed with some horror. Splotches of something had dried white and crusty, like I'd had a sudden onset of leprosy. I let my head fall back against the cabinet.

I wasn't all right.

"No, by joining us," Marco said. "We're having dinner on the terrace."

I swallowed and tried not to stare at the stuff on my legs. I didn't want dinner. I might never want dinner again.

But I did want Marco to go away.

"Okay. But I have to clean up first."

I almost saw the big head nod. "Don't take too long. There's somebody here to see you."

Great. That was all I needed. Somebody else who wanted something.

But Marco finally left, and I had the cork out of the bottle as soon as I heard the outer door shut.

I shuddered through half of what was left and did some more head-resting. A thousand questions were whirling around in my mind, but I was too tired to think straight. And smarter heads than mine hadn't done much better.

What the hell had we just fought? Why had it possessed the redheaded soldier when it could have just laid waste in its real form? What was the small dark thing I'd encountered and hidden out with for a while, and why had the monster been searching for it in somebody else's head?

Nobody knew. The best guesses were some kind of demon—because of the possession—although the demons on hand had never seen anything like it and had seemed as weirded out as the rest of us. And that it had taken control of the redheaded soldier to get past the shield protecting the camp, which . . . all I could say was, that must be one hell of a shield. And nobody had any idea about the little dark thing at all.

Marlowe had suggested that the idea behind the possession might have been to cause a revolt among the troops by causing them to blame each other for the deaths. The invasion was being rushed to take advantage of the slow time period coming up in Faerie; the last thing anybody needed right now was dissent in the ranks. But that seemed a little far-fetched, too.

These weren't normal soldiers; these were *vamps*. They might get pissed off, even lash out at each other occasionally. But they weren't high-level masters who could make their own decisions. If their masters wanted them somewhere, they'd stay there, and they'd toe the line, no matter how much some of them might grumble about it.

And most of their masters *did* want them there. They might not like that a levy had been placed on their households, but let's face it, they weren't sending their best guys. If they didn't get them back, they could always make more, and maybe they'd get luckier next time. And if they *did* get them back, they'd likely be far more powerful than when they left, due to some of the demons' power leaking over.

That had been the big selling point to get people to join the elite force. Because no matter what the blond musician thought, he wouldn't have been forced. The demons couldn't work effectively in an unwilling host, so he'd have likely been sent back or—more probably—given some kind of support position if he declined. Maybe he'd have even ended up entertaining the troops!

But not now.

I thought again about his little rash, his chewed-up pens, and his general prissiness. I'd liked him, in the few minutes I'd had to get to know him, and now he was dead. I wondered how many more would be dead if I couldn't figure this out?

I pulled my legs up and let my head drop onto my knees. I could feel the blood vessels at my temples *throb, throb, throbbing* out a beat. I could smell the thing's blood on me, a weird, peppery, fishy smell. It was gross and I was gross and I needed a bath, but it had been a very long day, and even with a shot of liquid strength, I didn't want to move.

What *was* that thing?

I sat there for a while longer, until the potion did its magic and I started to feel more or less human again. A very old and creaky human, I thought, finally getting up. And catching sight of myself in the mirror.

Dear God.

I took a shower. It took a while, because there was a lot of scrubbing that needed to happen. Dried ancient demigod guts do not come off easily. Not that I knew for sure that they were from an ancient demigod, but that was my personal theory.

Everybody else seemed obsessed with what the monster had been doing there, if there were any more, how to detect them, etc., which were all good questions. But they seemed to me to be missing the point. We couldn't fight something we couldn't even identify. Like the Spartoi, I thought, remembering Ares' disgusting children.

Nobody had realized that they were still in the world, either. Had this been another demigod, some long-forgotten spawn of an elder deity sent to screw with us? It seemed at least possible, especially now. If the invasion had to be delayed and we missed the upcoming window, it would certainly help the other side. Caedmon had said there wouldn't be another opportunity like this for a decade, forcing us to fight on a more or less even playing field thereafter.

I didn't want an even playing field! I wanted a damned advantage for a change! I was tired of this war; I wanted a chance to finish it quickly—and so did everybody else.

Denying us that . . . yeah.

Maybe it would be worth burning a demigod.

I rubbed the back of my neck. I actually kind of hoped that was the answer. Because that would mean this was a one-off. Otherwise . . .

I didn't want to think about "otherwise."

The fish guts finally came out of my hair, which I didn't bother blowing dry. I also didn't bother getting dressed, unless you counted panties, an oversized T-shirt, and my big, fluffy pink bathrobe. I was being petty, I knew that, but damn it, this wasn't just my office, it was my *home*. If petitioners didn't like how I looked, maybe they ought to make a goddamned appointment!

I didn't want to see anybody anyway, I thought sulkily while running a comb through my wet hair. I wanted to go to bed, pull the covers over my head, and forget today ever happened. I wanted a bolt-hole like Billy had, where

I could just disappear and lick some wounds. I wanted to be left alone!

But I knew how likely that was.

I finally left my bedroom and walked down the hall, still fuming, only to run into Fred, coming from the direction of the kitchen and almost weighted down with trays. "Here, hold this," he told me, shoving one of them into my hands.

"Are you . . . feeling okay?" I asked after getting a look at the contents. Because the silver serving dish appeared to contain cooked broccoli, mushrooms, and asparagus, which was absurd. Fred considered vegetables and arsenic to be essentially the same thing.

"Yeah, the smell was making me nauseous, too," he said, agreeing with the point I hadn't been making. "But don't worry; I got the good stuff."

"What good stuff?" I asked, trailing behind as he headed for the terrace.

"All sorts!" He grinned at me over his shoulder. "We're having s'mores!"

Broccoli s'mores? I thought, but followed him out anyway. And then stopped dead, and almost dropped the tray, because we did not have a visitor. We had—

*"Pritkin!"*

A blond head looked up, and for a long moment, I just stared. Not only because he looked good, although he did—he really did. The green eyes were bright and lacking the bloodshot quality they'd had lately; the face had filled out slightly, back to its usual square-jawed stubbornness instead of being gaunt and full of unfamiliar shadows; and the hair . . . well, the hair was a disaster, but I probably wouldn't have recognized him otherwise. In short, he looked fully healed instead of like the hollow-eyed, half-dead man I'd been visiting when he stayed put long enough.

But that wasn't why I was staring.

I was staring because he was sitting on an armchair that looked like the one from Rhea's room, helping a tiny child put something on a skewer almost as long as she was.

I think my brain broke. People were moving about,

putting things on various tables and rearranging the chairs, stools, and ottomans that had been dragged out of the suite and clustered around a firepit, while I just stood there, holding broccoli. And staring at Pritkin, the big bad muscle-y war mage, and the teeny tiny tot.

She had a head full of red curls and big gray eyes, and despite the fact that she couldn't have been more than three, she already boasted a face full of freckles. It was a very serious face, though, because there was serious stuff happening. Stuff involving what appeared to be every ingredient on earth.

"What is all this?" I asked Rhea, who came over to take the veggie platter.

She sighed and shook her head.

"Victory!" Fred crowed from behind a table crowded with ham and sausages and various meats on platters and what looked like every cheese on earth.

"And that means?"

"S'mores for dinner!"

I raised an eyebrow, or at least I tried to. "S'mores are a dessert." I looked at Rhea. "We're having dessert for dinner?"

She sighed again. "It's complicated."

"It's nothing of the kind," Fred said, and the next thing I knew, he'd bustled over with something that he popped into my mouth before I could protest.

It wasn't dessert. I wasn't sure what it was. But my stomach suddenly woke up to express vigorous approval.

"Huh? Huh?" Fred asked. "What about that?"

I swallowed. "What was it?"

"S'mores!"

"We're stretching the term," Pritkin informed me, green eyes amused, as he steadied the marshmallow on a stick that the little girl was holding.

It went over the fire, and I watched it slowly brown. There were other sticks with other offerings already there: cubes of cheese getting goopy and melty, cherry tomatoes with their little bottoms turning fatter and redder, pieces of bread getting toasty, tiny party sausages bursting with juices that sizzled and popped over the open flames, and chunks of blackened red pepper starting to smoke. And laid out on the tables was an amazing assortment of other ingredients for the truly crazy concoctions that I guessed were passing for dinner.

There were a lot of them.

"Are you in on this?" I asked Tami, who'd just come out of the suite with a platter of gingerbread, homemade chocolate chip cookies, and graham crackers.

She rolled her eyes. "I was outvoted."

I know the feeling, I thought, when I suddenly found myself plopped down onto a hassock with a stick and a plate and told to get creative. So I did. Hot honey, brie, thin-cut figs, and prosciutto on a toasted baguette was nice. Salami, tapenade, mozzarella, and roasted tomato on an herbed cracker was better. And mushroom, blue cheese, and bacon in a potato skin was to die for.

Of course, things got a little crazy when the guys got involved, with Marco pretending to be mortally afraid of the fire, which resulted in him lounging on a chaise and being fed a steady stream of marshmallows by concerned little girls. Roy was trying to mix the adults cocktails to go with their crazy creations, and doing surprisingly well at it. Ophélie and Anaïs, the two French girls, were wafting around looking very sophisticated with the Shirley Temples he'd concocted for them. While Tami's son, Jesse, and Jiao—one of the kids who had come with Tami's group—were attempting to outdo each other with the weirdest combinations possible: chicken, dark chocolate, and hot sauce on a waffle, anyone?

And then came the guess-the-recipe game.

Fred was obviously going to win. Fred always won any game that involved food. But tonight, he had some competition.

The setting sun had been turning the balcony orange and gilding the undersides of the clouds when I'd first come out, but it was full-on dark now, and the vamps were feeling frisky. The flames of the firepit were splashing everyone's faces with light, from the excited, overly stuffed children still staring at the barely diminished treasure trove on the tables—because when Fred put out a spread, he did it right—to the indulgent faces of my guards. Which was why I wasn't too surprised when Rico plopped down on one of the straight-backed chairs being dragged into a line for the game.

And so did Saffy, who ended up being paired with Roy. And then another witch joined in, who went by Vi— probably because her given name was Violet and I'd never seen anyone who looked less like a Violet. I was starting to wonder if witches deliberately chose baby names that played against type, or if kids saddled with girlie monikers just tended to rebel. But Vi was . . . not exactly a shrinking violet.

Covered in tats and piercings, she was taller than some of the guys and looked like she ate nails for breakfast. Of course, she also had beautiful olive skin, big, warm brown eyes, and a booming laugh that tended to be infectious. But it usually took people a while to notice the latter, considering that, like most witches I'd met, she also had an in-your-face attitude on first acquaintance.

And second acquaintance.

And very often third.

She was paired with Reggie. He was a skinny, jug-eared, sandy blond with a buzz cut who looked perpetually startled and unsure of himself. But he'd nonetheless ended up the lone Circle mage assigned to my court, since the others had been dicks.

He was currently looking less than enthusiastic about all this, maybe because Vi had just grabbed his shirt in a fist and jerked him up from the chair. "We're gonna win. Right, war mage?"

He nodded, his prominent Adam's apple bobbing worriedly. "S-sure."

"You don't sound sure."

"I'm positive!"

"Make me believe it."

"We're going to win, sir! I mean, ma'am. I mean Vi!"

She grinned, showing a lot of large, healthy teeth, and let him go.

Then Pritkin sat down next to Fred, who'd claimed the fourth seat, prompting me to do a double take. And to wonder if he *was* feeling all right after all. Joining in wasn't really his thing. He gave me inscrutable-war-mage face back. And then me, Rhea, and Tami were volunteered to be the remaining chefs.

"Okay, okay. This is sudden death, all right? You guess wrong, you're out," Fred said, tying on a flimsy blindfold. It looked like he'd borrowed a scarf from one of the girls—a suspiciously see-through one.

"Oh, I don't think so." Marco, who was somehow still mobile after eating maybe fifty marshmallows, draped a thick woolen number over top of that one, and handed me a second. I guessed for Pritkin, since he was closest.

I got behind him and wrapped it around his eyes. "Never knew you were a foodie," I said softly into his ear.

He tilted his head back, exposing a strong, tanned throat. "I'm not."

"You're going to lose, then. Fred's practically an Iron Chef."

He gave me a strange, slow smile. "We'll see."

I didn't know what to say to that, so I went over to the chef's table, where the guys were laying out a cornucopia of ingredients. I laughed suddenly, I didn't know why, maybe at the sheer abundance, and Tami shot me a look. "That's better."

"What is?"

She lowered her voice. "You go away to that damned court, and you always come back the same way: exhausted, pale-faced, and traumatized."

"We had a . . . problem . . . today," I said, because I didn't want to discuss it in front of the kids. Or at all. But she just frowned.

"There's always a problem. This damned world's full of them, and they don't stop coming."

"I noticed." I'd spent all summer climbing one mountain after the other, only to find a vista of bigger peaks waiting on the other side. "It never ends."

"Which is why you can't let it get to you. That way lies the men in the white coats, you hear me?"

"I hear you."

A hand with a sparkly pink manicure—the girls had been at her again—suddenly grasped my arm. "Do you?"

I looked at her in surprise. The dark eyes were reflecting the flames from the nearby firepit, and her cheeks were flushed and rosy. But it was the concern on the familiar face that truly warmed it. "Yes. But I can't stop shi—stuff—from happening."

"No, you can't. None of us can." She put a glass of beer in my hand. "So here's to the times in between."

I clinked glasses with her, and stupidly felt myself tearing up. "To the times in between."

"Are we going to start or what?" Fred said impatiently. "I'm starving!"

"I'm not sure how this works. Are we supposed to try to fool you?" Rhea asked, looking a little concerned to find herself in front of Rico.

"You're supposed to feed us!"

"I'm beginning to suspect this was just a way to get us to do the hard work for them," Tami told her.

Rhea frowned, and a glint of steely determination flashed in her eyes. "Then I say we fool them."

I grinned. "Game on."

# Chapter Eighteen

"Pecans, bacon, and brie on a stroopwafel. Seriously, are you even trying?" Fred demanded.

"I didn't think you'd know the brie," Tami said, scowling.

"Not know brie?" The part of his face I could see looked confused. "How does a person not know brie?"

"It's one of those weird French cheeses," she said, reading the label on the little round box.

"It's not weird, it's *brie*."

"Not all of us grew up in a la-di-da mansion, all right?" There was a hint of irritation in her voice.

"But brie isn't—that's not—no, no, no," Fred said, waving his hands around in a way that successfully conveyed impatience, embarrassment, and something that I guess was passion, because if there was anything Fred loved, it was food. "Brie isn't la-di-da. Brie is . . ." He searched for the right words. "It's sunlight on a pretty girl's face while she stomps grapes with legs purple up to the knees. It's bells clinking around cows' necks as milkmaids drive them home beside golden wheat fields. It's an old man playing sad songs on a ragged accordion to a long-lost love. It's—"

Tami smacked him on the head with a roll of paper towels. "It's *cheese*."

"You have no poetry in your soul."

"But I got cheese on my cracker," she said, and took a bite. "Hm. It's okay."

"I'm judging you right now, so hard, if you could only see my eyes."

"Rhea's turn," I said, grinning. Because she'd asked to

be skipped over as she finished up something a little different.

Rico opened his mouth, and she popped a bite-size piece inside, blushing a little for some reason. He chewed thoughtfully. "I call it the Elvis," she told him, and Fred freaked out.

"What?" He pointed wildly in her general direction. "That's cheating! What do you call it? That's *cheating*!"

"I wasn't!" Rhea looked appalled. "I wouldn't!"

"Banana, peanut butter, and bacon," Rico said. "On a graham cracker."

"Oh, brilliant work," Fred told him sourly. "I could have told you that, and I didn't even taste it."

"My turn," I said, and fed Pritkin my offering. His tongue grazed my fingers for a moment, almost as if he was trying to taste *them*, and a little shiver went through me. I snatched my hand back, and caught Tami watching me.

I hoped I wasn't blushing as much as Rhea.

"Strawberry, steak, and balsamic on a baguette," Pritkin said, as if nothing had happened.

"Um, yes. Right."

"No, no, no," Fred said, "not right. These are *s'mores*. If you're not gonna have marshmallow, then you have to have something ooey gooey that subs for it. Cheese or jam or dulce de leche—"

"Hear that? You owe me some ooey gooey," Pritkin said, and I stared at him in disbelief.

I must be more tired than I'd thought.

"—or *something*, or else it's just an appetizer. You made an appetizer."

"I'll, uh, I'll keep it in mind," I said, staring at Pritkin's blindfolded face.

I suddenly really wished I could see his eyes. And then I thought, No, no, I don't wish that at all. I swallowed and turned around and started making up the next bite—with plenty of ooey gooey.

Three more rounds took place, with Rico finally missing cinnamon, cayenne, and dark chocolate on a potato chip, and going out to the sound of Rhea's apologies. He laughed and kissed her hand, and told her he'd liked it. She offered to make him another.

Two more rounds and Saffy bit the dust, or rather the cheese, on an avocado, sriracha, and fontina offering that she mistook for provolone. And then, in the very next round, Vi missed the boat on a combo of crab, cream cheese, artichoke, and capers.

"What the hell's a caper?" she demanded.

Reggie swallowed and held out a handful. "Um. These?"

She picked one up, looking at it suspiciously. "I still don't know what the fu—funny thing that is."

"Ooh, close one," Marco said, grinning.

"You got me twice yesterday, fat boy," she told him. "I've donated enough to the cause."

Marco patted his belly. "This isn't fat, it's muscle."

"You ate like a hundred damned marshmallows!" And then she realized what she'd said. "Son of a—"

She cut herself off, pulled a wallet out of the back of her jeans, and handed over a twenty.

"It's fat," she told him sourly.

"Cop a feel and find out, sweetheart."

"You'd like that too much."

"And I wouldn't," Saffy said, draping an arm around her girlfriend's waist.

"What I'd like," Tami said loudly, "is to finish up sometime tonight."

"You're gonna be next," Fred told Pritkin, who turned his blindfolded face to look at him.

"You do realize that potions are my specialty?" he asked.

"What does that have to do with anything?"

"To properly mix a potion, even a simple one, you have to have what they call a potion maker's nose. I'll put it up against a foodie's palate any day."

Fred started to look worried.

And, sure enough, Pritkin kept up with him, bite for bite, through cherries, Nutella, and marshmallow on cinnamon bread; cheesecake, dark chocolate, and raspberries on a graham cracker; broccoli, melted cheddar, and chili on bacon—"almost made broccoli palatable," according to Fred; peaches, honey, and brie on a crostini; asparagus, ricotta, and caramelized onions on phyllo; ricotta, honey, figs, and crushed pistachios on a chocolate wafer—"the pistachios almost got me," Fred said, looking panicked; and white chocolate, pineapple, and marshmallow on a graham cracker.

"All right, it's getting late," Tami finally announced. "Last round."

"No, wait! What if he gets it?" Fred demanded. Because his title was on the line.

"Then it's a tie."

"A *tie*? I can't go down in a tie to a war mage! I'll never hear the end of it!"

"Got that right," one of the guys said.

"Better get it right, then," Tami warned.

"Shit! I mean poo!"

"Don't try to save it now," Marco said, snapping his fingers.

Fred sighed but ponied up a twenty.

At this rate, we were going to be able to buy the court a limo just from the swear jar, I thought, and then I noticed Pritkin looking smug.

"Don't expect me to go easy on you," I warned him.

The blindfolded face turned unerringly up to mine. "Actually, I prefer it rough."

I dropped a spoon.

And came up scowling. So that's how it was, huh? Because the first time might have been an accident, but that . . . that had been deliberate.

Okeydokey, then.

I went to the bar.

While I was gone, Fred correctly guessed blackberry, lemon curd, and white chocolate on shortbread and looked like he was making a mental note for future reference. I grabbed a toasted marshmallow from one of the guys, put a naked knee on the seat of Pritkin's chair, between his legs, dipped the ooey gooey item in Baileys, almost burning my fingers, and fed it to him. Slowly.

"All right, that's my idea of a s'more," somebody said.

I didn't see who. The balcony abruptly receded—the kids talking and laughing, Rhea and Hilde coming and going, taking the smaller ones to bed, and the vamps drinking and clandestinely smoking, because Tami was distracted and the firepit covered the smell. For a moment, there were only Pritkin's lips, wet and shining from the alcohol, the warmth of his mouth, closing around my fingers, and the feel of his tongue, working the last remaining sticky marshmallow off my skin, making sure to get every . . . last . . . bit.

"Okay," Tami said dryly, shocking me back into myself. "Time for bed."

Couldn't agree more, I thought dizzily.

"Wait—we're not done!" Fred said, looking at Pritkin. "You didn't guess that last one; what was that last one?"

"I have no idea." It was rough.

"Woo-hoo, I won!"

"I think *he* won," somebody said.

And then dinner was over.

But, unfortunately, my responsibilities weren't. Because Augustine, who'd come in late, wanted to bitch about the mess we'd supposedly made in his workroom and get his key back. And Rhea cornered me to talk about one of the girls, who was acting out by stealing everybody's stuff, which had been found under her bed. And then Hilde followed me in my room to talk about Rhea—and she wasn't taking any hints.

"I don't understand it," she said, striding back in forth in front of my bed. "The girl has the talent—I know she does—but there's some mental block in the way."

"I'm sure she'll, uh, deal with it eventually," I said, pondering my sleepwear.

It consisted of old T-shirts and a pair of flannel pj's I'd bought in anticipation of cold winter nights. I picked them up. They had little moose on them—mooses? Meece? And were about as unsexy as it was possible to get.

I'd had some nicer stuff, but it had all been bought for me by Sal, one of Tony's vamps, who'd been trying to refine my look in order to butter up Mircea. She'd hoped that he'd take her on since her boss had gone screwy and joined the other side in the war. Mircea was Tony's master, so technically he could appropriate any of his vassal's vamps if he wanted, although since Tony was emancipated, that was seen as bad form. But then, so was turning traitor.

But the changeover had never happened. Sal had ended up being used against us by her master, and I had been left with a bunch of slutty nightwear I couldn't have used in this case anyway, for obvious reasons. Not that it mattered. It had been tossed, along with everything else that reminded me of Mircea, in the post-breakup fury. Leaving me with . . . this.

I sighed.

"That's the point!" Hilde said sternly. "She isn't dealing with it. With her background, and having grown up at the Pythian Court, seeing the power being used on a daily basis—"

"But not trained in it," I pointed out. "Agnes didn't allow that."

"Not formerly trained, perhaps. But she *saw* it, and as you know perfectly well, a good deal of the Pythian power is instinctive. At the very least, she should be picking up some of the simpler spells, refining her spatial shifts, perhaps even attempting a short time hop by now. But instead—"

"She isn't even trying?" I guessed.

"It's ludicrous!" Hilde plopped down into a chair with the air of someone who planned to be there awhile. "It isn't as if she's a lightweight magically. She can switch between normal magic and the coven variety with ease, and has enough power for a war mage! But ask her to do the simplest of time spells and she falls apart!"

I frowned, and then remembered Rhea's panic when I had first made her an acolyte. I'd expected her to be pleased, intending it as a reward for all the help she'd given me, and as a way of making up for the fact that the position had been unfairly denied her in the past. But instead, she'd looked like someone headed for the gallows with a noose around her neck. She'd calmed down after a while, and I hadn't thought about it again, but now . . .

"What's wrong with her?" I asked, and Hilde threw her hands up.

"Who knows? She won't talk to me. Acts evasive, sometimes even snappy or annoyed."

"Rhea?" I frowned some more. "That doesn't sound like her."

"She doesn't like me," Hilde said flatly. "Thinks I'm pushing too hard—and not only her. She wants to wrap the girls in cotton wool instead of teaching them self-defense. That would be dangerous at the best of times, but in the middle of a war—"

"Most of them aren't old enough to learn that much anyway," I pointed out. "And they've been through a lot of trauma lately."

"They'll be through a good deal more if our enemies get to them!"

"They're not going to get to them."

"Of course not." Hilde's shrewd old-lady eyes met mine. "You're going to be here every moment of every day."

I crossed my arms at her. "We're not doing this again."

"Oh, but we are. We have to. The covens are obviously not giving us any girls, and even if they did, it would take ages to train them properly—"

"Whereas the old acolytes are already trained. Yes, so you've said. Many times."

"And am saying again! You have to face facts, Cassie! We need competent help—"

I slammed the drawer. "And I need to know that I'm not bringing more Jo's in here! Or Lizzie's, or any of the rest of them!"

"Cassie—"

"Every single one," I said, stalking over to her. "Every. Single. One. Of Agnes' acolytes went bad—"

"Every one of the current crop," Hilde said stubbornly. "The ones the gods were targeting. She had plenty of other acolytes through the years, sturdy, well-trained girls—well, women now—not to mention a few of us old bats from my sister's court—"

"And how do we know they haven't been turned as well?" I demanded. "Or that they'd even want to join a wartime court in the first place?"

Hilde brightened. "I'm glad you asked."

"Oh God."

"I've been in touch with a few old friends—"

"Hilde!"

"—who I have since spoken to some more. So far, I

have three from Gertie's court and two from Lady Phemonoe's—we'd have more there, but many of them are married now and—"

"I didn't tell you to speak to anybody!"

"You also didn't tell me not to. And in any case, we need them—"

"We need to be safe!"

"And here we are, back to it again," Hilde said.

"Back to what again?"

"The same argument I've been having with Rhea. As counterintuitive as it may seem, sometimes the only path to safety is to take a risk. Otherwise, one day, you are going to be away on Circle business, or helping those vampires, or tracking some miscreant through time. And I am going to be here, alone—"

I started to interrupt, but she just raised her voice.

"—except for those guards of yours, who are good for many things, but who can't handle some of the challenges we face. And what do you think is going to happen then, hm?"

I started to respond, and then I saw that . . . thing . . . that had been at the consul's again. I'd had plenty of help there, and it almost hadn't been enough. What if something similar was sent against my court? Against my girls?

The very idea made my stomach clench painfully. No! That couldn't happen!

But it could. That thing had walked right into the middle of a vampire army, right through every checkpoint and security measure put in place to keep something like that from happening. And it had just started slaughtering people. It had killed over a hundred in its assault on the consul's home: a quarter in the initial attack and three times that many in the battle in the hallway.

Maybe more, since they'd still been trying to pick up the pieces when I left.

Literally, I thought, remembering a servant hurrying by with a basket of squirming body parts.

I sat down on my bed, my legs like jelly.

It could happen here, and I couldn't stop it. I'd barely stopped it there, and only because I'd had some of the most powerful creatures on earth battling alongside me. My guys were good, and against any normal danger, they'd be deadly. But today?

They would have been shredded right alongside everyone else.

But what was the alternative?

"I still see Jo sometimes," I told Hilde. "Her eyes, the way she looked at the battle, the way she *enjoyed* it. We don't even know if she's really gone, and—"

"All the more reason to be prepared."

Hilde was relentless; like a river running over stone, wearing it down. She'd been after me for two weeks to bring in some of the retired acolytes, and I'd been refusing, because I hadn't wanted to bring a potential viper into the nest. But a viper had saved my life today, had saved all our lives. I didn't like the consul, but when push came to shove, she'd put her life on the line and bled alongside the rest of us. That's what a leader did.

And if I'd been wrong about her, was I wrong again now?

"I don't blame you for being cautious," Hilde said. "But there's such a thing as being too careful. We have a war to fight, and we need soldiers." A veined and age-spotted hand covered mine. "And you've fought alone long enough. Time to accept some help."

I thought about Jo again, that lovely, hateful face. And then I thought about the other acolytes I'd seen with Gertie, like a flock of delicate, white-clad birds. What would it be like to have my own team behind me, strong, capable, loyal? What would it have been like today, had there been others who could wield the Pythian power, besides just me?

The tarot card had screamed "strength" at me for a good five minutes—was this what it had meant? Because strength was usually found in numbers. . . . Goddamn it.

"They'd need to interview with you, of course," Hilde said. "And any you didn't like, well, that would be that."

I narrowed my eyes at her. How had we gotten from the question of whether to consider the old acolytes at all to discussing interviews? And why couldn't I do shit like that? Talk about magic.

"Have them come by," I said sourly. "But not here. I'll talk to them downstairs."

"They voluntarily gave up the Pythian power when they left the court," Hilde pointed out. "The only ones allowed to retain it were the fail-safes. Even if they had another Jo among their number, they'd be no threat to us."

"Even so—"

"And there's not a downstairs so much anymore. Are you going to interview them in a construction zone?"

"Fine! I'll talk to them here!" I got up. "Now, if there's nothing else?"

"Other than you having a chat with Rhea? No, I believe that covers it."

I hung my head. Why did people want to be Pythia again? I honestly didn't know.

I sighed. "Where is she?"

# Chapter Nineteen

I found Rhea in the kitchen, helping Tami and a bunch of the guys and gals clean up. Of course, that was a relative term, considering that there was more than one sink, and they each came equipped with spray hoses. Neither of which was being used on the food.

"I'm breaking out the mops! You think I won't?" Tami yelled before she saw me. "What are you doing here?"

"I—why shouldn't I be here?"

She rolled her eyes. "Seriously?"

And then a spray of lukewarm water hit us both, prompting me to duck behind the counter and Tami to charge.

"Mops!" she yelled, while Rico came in the door, loaded down with dirty dishes, all of which got a presoak a second later.

"You will pay for that," he told Saffy, who was on the other end of the hose. And then he saw me. "What are you doing here?"

"Why does everyone keep asking me that?"

"Mage Pritkin left half an hour ago," he noted.

"What does that have to do with anything?"

Rico just looked at me. And then he did that thing, that damned annoying, almost sociopathic thing that all Mircea's vamps could do except for Fred. I swear it had been part of their training or something.

"Don't give me the eyebrow!"

Rico started to say something, but then Rhea came in, and he pulled her down out of harm's way just before a spray of water sailed overhead.

"What's happening?" she asked as somebody squealed

and somebody laughed, and Tami yelled, "I've got 'em. And you're all getting one!" from what sounded like the walk-in pantry.

"They are playing their little games," Emilio said, passing by with some clean dishes.

He paused and blinked at me. "Hey. What are you—"

"Never mind!" I told him, and looked at Rhea. "I need to talk to you."

We ended up in her room a few minutes later, which got us both out of mop duty. We'd even managed to snag some tea on the way, because it was in the butler's pantry, where the chaos had yet to spread. Sometimes, things worked out.

Like the living quarters for the court, which were even more spacious than those at the old Pythian Court, where everybody except the acolytes had had to double up.

These bedrooms had been designed for the consul's servants—ostensibly—so of course they were nice. Most of the girls had a decent-sized bedroom and an attached bath of their own. Rhea's was bigger still, and also boasted a small sitting area. We sat there, in front of a dark fireplace over which a mantle was strewn with pics of the girls and one of Agnes in a garden, laughing over some roses. And I guess she wasn't the only one who liked flowers, because Rhea had added some watercolor prints to the walls, and a vase of preserved, pale pink specimens, the old ruffly kind, sat on a side table. They looked like the ones as in the photo, but I couldn't be sure.

Otherwise, it was the same tasteful beige and white room it had been when we moved in, either because she liked it that way or because none of us had had much time for decoration.

Well, with one exception.

I'd brought a mug of tea along, and almost spilled it all over me when my feet abruptly went up. "What the—" I said, staring down in the darkness between the chair and the coffee table. And saw not someone but something. The little hassock from this morning.

"Oh, how cu—" I began, when something wonderful happened. "Oh my God. Oh, oh, oh my *God*."

"What is it?" Rhea asked, sitting forward and looking

concerned. Probably because I sounded like a dying water buffalo.

I didn't even care. Because the small thing was massaging my feet. How, I didn't know, since it didn't have hands, and I didn't care. I lay back against the cushions of the overstuffed wing chair and decided I'd died and gone to heaven.

Best. Purchase. *Ever.*

"It was running around all over the place, tripping people up, so I shut it in here," Rhea said. "I hope you don't mind."

"Ngghhhh."

We sat there in silence for a moment, Rhea drinking tea and trying to hide a smile, and me thinking about just sleeping here. My libido was battling a full stomach and a seriously fine foot massage. My libido was losing.

But I had a job to do, and after a while, I managed to woman up. "Rhea—" And then I stopped again, because I didn't have Hilde's gift of the gab and wasn't sure how to phrase things.

And because we had more than a training issue to discuss.

I hadn't said anything before, because Rhea had had a pretty hard recovery from her injury, having lost a lot of blood, and like the rest of the girls from Agnes' old court, she'd been thoroughly traumatized lately. I hadn't wanted to add to it, but at the same time, there were things I needed her to understand.

I sighed.

I hated this kind of thing.

"Lady?" Rhea had started looking a little concerned.

"You know I'm not good with diplomacy, right?" I said.

It was why Mircea's vamps and I got along okay. He'd sent me his blunt, hopeless causes, the kind who sucked at tact on their best day, but who could still handle themselves in a fight. It had been good for them, giving them a renewed sense of purpose after feeling like the odd men out in his otherwise suave, urbane family. And after a lifetime of vampire misdirection and out-and-out lies, I'd found them oddly . . . refreshing.

And maybe because I was kind of like them.

"I don't like to hurt anybody's feelings," I said now.
"But—"

"You won't," she told me, setting down her teacup.

Welp, I guess we were doing this.

"Okay, here's the deal," I told her. "I want you to know
that I'm very happy with you and extremely pleased that
you are a part of this court—"

"But?" She smiled gently.

"But. We need to talk about what happened on the
drag."

I thought back to how I'd felt, seeing her trapped
against that dark mage's chest. It reminded me of how I'd
felt tonight, when I'd thought that creature had killed
Caedmon—only worse. I wasn't responsible for Caedmon.

Some dark mages had lured Rhea outside by pretending to be from her old coven, who had some girls who
wanted to join my court. The ruse was one of the things
that had prompted my visit today; I'd been thinking about
it ever since. But, unfortunately, it hadn't been a bunch of
little girls waiting for Rhea. The Black Knights, as they
liked to style themselves, had grabbed her to force me to
give up a prisoner they wanted.

Elizabeth Warrender, or Lizzie, as she was better
known, was the last of Agnes' rogue acolytes left alive. I'd
taken her captive after she tried to kill me, but I hadn't
kept her. I'd turned her over to the Circle's hands for safe-
keeping, so I couldn't have given the dark mages Lizzie
even if I'd wanted to.

But they hadn't known that, and wouldn't have believed me if I'd told them. They'd been hopped up on stolen magic, almost drunk with it, manic and fuzzy-brained
and eager to use the power buzzing in their veins. I wasn't
even sure that they wanted me to agree; they wanted a
fight, and if I didn't give them what they wanted, the first
casualty was going to be Rhea.

I'd stood there, trying to formulate a plan to save her
while battling a tide of unusually strong emotions. The tie
between a Pythia and her court is strong, and right then,
I'd wanted to rip the leader's freaking head off. I'd wanted
to feel his blood on my hands. I'd wanted to hear him
scream in anguish as I—

"Cassie?" Rhea was looking seriously freaked-out now, so I made an effort to moderate whatever was on my face.

"I wanted to kill him," I told her honestly. "That dark knight who grabbed you. I wanted to do a vamp thing and pull his heart out of his chest, or at least shift it out and watch him twitch and jerk and die. But he had you, and a couple hundred guys to back him up, and I was running on empty. I had to think it out, not fight, but I wanted him dead so damned bad."

"You're Pythia," she told me, a little hoarsely. "You're the head of your own coven. That's what the Pythian Court *is*, whatever some may say. And a coven leader . . ." She stopped, swallowing. "The old title was Great Mother. It's still used sometimes. It came into being as a result of the bond between coven members and their leader. At its best, it is like a family, and you feel that here." She touched her breast.

And yes, I did. I had ever since they first came to me, all those bewildered, frightened little girls. They'd already lost one family when their gift caused them to be sent away from their homes for training, and then they'd lost another with Agnes' death and the subsequent chaos it had brought to the court. They hadn't known what to do or where to go, and bad men had been trying to kill them, and the very people supposed to be protecting them—the acolytes—had sided with their enemies!

The acolytes had fallen, one by one, as the gods used threats and promises of power and immortality to lure them away, while their Pythia lay dying, too weak to oppose them. The war had started a long time before the first shot had been fired, inside the Pythian Court itself. And Agnes had fought it, all alone.

Yet while she couldn't save her acolytes, she had saved the court by locating me, a new successor far from the gods' influence. One whose mother had been one of them, and who was therefore not so susceptible to their lies. She had thereafter died defending her court, as a Pythia should, her last act being to get rid of Myra, her former heir, buying me some much-needed time to grow into my office.

She'd been my hero for a long time, the shining example of what a Pythia should be. But, as I'd recently learned, she'd also been a flawed human woman who'd made mistakes. Maybe that was why I liked her so much: I could relate.

But Rhea didn't seem to see it that way.

"My mother did not complete that bond," she said quietly, looking at the picture on the mantel. "She wasn't a coven witch, but it wouldn't have mattered if she had been. She didn't win her court as you did; it was gifted to her. A true coven bond requires blood, not that of others but of *yours*. Or at least the willingness to spill yours, to sacrifice everything, for the coven you represent. You did that! Not her!"

"Rhea—"

"I saw you that night," she said, looking back at me, her voice shaking. "The night they came for the court, for the *children*. You held them off while we escaped. You had nothing left; you *knew* you didn't. You'd die if you stayed, yet you stayed anyway! While I ran with the others, while I *ran*—"

"I told you to," I said, because I didn't know where all this had come from. "You couldn't have helped me—"

She laughed suddenly, and it was bitter. "Oh, I know that! I knew it then. Like my mother, I could never—" She broke off, biting her lip, and then looked at me seriously. "I'm sorry for what happened on the drag. Another battle, and I was as useless as before—worse, because I didn't listen to you. You told me not to do anything, to let you handle it, but I was so afraid—"

"It's all right—"

"It's not all right! I should have listened. You're my Pythia, and I should have listened! Like I should have stayed with you in London; I should have stayed to help you get out."

"There was nothing you could have done. And the demon council pulled me out."

As much as they'd hated and feared my mother, who had decimated their population, hunting them for sport and for the power boost they gave her, they'd also realized that a new war was coming, and that I was the closest thing to a goddess they had left. And while that wasn't really all that close at all, they'd proven to be remarkably pragmatic beings who would take what they could get.

So I'd been rescued at the last second, with a burning bolt of magical energy literally inches away from my face.

"But you didn't know they would," Rhea said vehemently. "You didn't know they'd been watching you, and neither did I! Yet I ran . . ."

I stared at her. I'd never known that Rhea had been this bothered about that night in London. We'd won; the kids had gotten away, with the coven leaders and Rhea hurrying them from the building while I used what power I had left to slow down our attackers. It had been a close shave, but it had worked. I counted that as a victory.

But clearly, Rhea didn't.

She'd also said something else I didn't understand, something about Agnes. "What did you mean, you're like your mother?" I asked now, even while worrying that maybe I didn't have the right. But it had almost sounded like Rhea blamed her mother for the situation we were in, only that couldn't be correct.

But I guess it was, because her face crumpled. "She wasn't strong enough. She knew how to use the power, but she was blind to what was happening all around her. She let this happen—"

"Rhea, no—"

"She did! She and my father both did! They were too wrapped up in each other to see the growing threat before it was too late. They let people find out about their affair—not many, but enough for it to undermine the neutrality of the court. And if that wasn't enough, she couldn't even tell that one of her own acolytes was poisoning her until—"

She broke off and jumped up, her face anguished and turned away from me. "And what did it get them? What was the result of all that? Me—and I'm even weaker than she was! I can't use the power at all, and I shouldn't! I'd just screw it up, just like she did, and—"

I got up and put my arms around her, because she looked like she needed a hug.

"If it hadn't been for you—" she began, but I cut her off.

"If it hadn't been for your mother, I wouldn't be here," I told her firmly. "She saved my life, warned me about an assassination that would have succeeded without her. She brought me back a copy of my own obituary to prove it. I didn't know anything about this world then, but that got me to run, and saved my life."

"I . . . didn't know that."

"We should have talked about your mother before," I admitted. "But there never seemed to be enough time. I sent you to Françoise, but I should have explained myself—"

"She wouldn't talk to me," Rhea said.

"What?"

Rhea shook her head. The neat chignon she was wearing had partly come down, and that finished the job, causing her hair to fall messily around her tear-stained face. "I tried to talk to her, as you suggested, but she wouldn't. She said she couldn't say anything good about my mother, but she wouldn't say anything bad, either, to a grieving daughter. She wouldn't say anything at all."

I stared at her, hearing a record scratch in my head.

She didn't know, I realized. She didn't know the truth about Agnes' death, or the crazy, brilliant, and dangerous game she'd played, and played alone, to help me. For a moment, I just stood there, frowning in shock.

And remembering a woman who looked so like Rhea that it broke my heart every time I saw her. I remembered how Agnes had used the last of her power to shift back to me in time, to a grubby old dungeon in Carcassonne, France. How she'd given me what information she could, while she could, even knowing that she wouldn't have the power left to shift back, that she would likely die there.

Only, no. Someone *else* would have died there. But Agnes was cleverer than that, and she had one last errand to do, and one more trick up her sleeve to allow her to do it. Her rogue heir Myra, with more power than all the acolytes combined, was still on the loose, and she had years of training I lacked. Someone had to help me deal with her, and Agnes knew it.

A young French witch named Françoise had been about to get kidnapped and dragged off to Faerie, just another missing person in the long-running fey slave trade. That would have happened regardless; Agnes didn't change anything there. She just hitched a ride.

She'd shifted to me in spirit form, an old Pythian trick to preserve energy by possessing someone in another time. She'd had no choice, as she hadn't had enough strength to bring her dying body along, which wouldn't have allowed her to do what was needed anyway. I could still close my eyes and see her, a ghostly presence pirouetting in the dark, looking for a brief moment like the dark-haired girl she'd once been.

And being there in spirit form had given her more than just freedom; it had allowed her to possess Françoise and wait out the centuries in Faerie, where time flows so differently than here. After what seemed like only a few years, she helped Françoise engineer an escape from the fey and return to earth. Where she possessed another body, Myra's body, using all her power for one last burst of strength.

And slit her throat.

I could still see her falling gracefully to the floor, the white flutter of her Pythian gown like angel's wings around her, the brilliant crimson of her blood a spill of rubies. I could see their two spirits, rising up together, because Agnes had known that Myra would try the same trick she had. But she'd denied her that. She had fought her to the very end, grabbing hold and dragging her spirit away with her, to wherever we go after death.

No one had bled more for the Pythian Court than Agnes, no one at all.

I thought her daughter had a right to know that.

"Sit down," I told her hoarsely. "It's time I told you about your mother."

# Chapter Twenty

I schlepped back to my room some time later, leaving Rhea looking shocked and thoughtful behind me, but not teary eyed. Hell, I'd cried more than she had. Maybe I'd explained it wrong? I didn't know how I could have explained it wrong. There were only so many ways to—to—to—

A huge yawn almost cracked my skull.

Damn, I was tired! And no longer remotely in the mood for . . . anything . . . even assuming Pritkin was up for that. He'd seemed pretty interested earlier, but maybe I'd read him wrong. I seemed to be doing that a lot lately.

But I needed to explain what had happened, not to mention that I just wanted to talk to him, damn it! I hadn't seen him much at all these last few weeks, and while tonight had been fun, it was just like it had been all those days visiting his sickroom. Half the time he'd been sleeping, and the rest there'd been other people milling around, usually war mages, because he kept having these weird dreams.

And conjuring stuff out of them.

Like a bunch of little fire sprites that had poured out of a portal he'd called into being from some hell dimension. They hadn't been as bad as you might expect, but there'd been about a thousand of them, and everything they touched went up in flames. And, of course, that meant the vamps couldn't round them up, so the mages had had their hands full.

That had been fun.

The casino manager had loved that.

Although it hadn't been as bad as the huge fireball Pritkin had thrown at somebody in a dream—and in real life, because his magic hadn't seemed to know the difference. Magical types were supposed to have a mental lock on their gifts at night, like humans did on their movements, so they weren't constantly throwing spells in their sleep. But like with sleepwalking people, something in Pritkin's brain seemed to have been off, and it wasn't applying the brakes hard enough.

Anyway, he'd needed babysitting while he recovered, and that had meant no alone time. Or, at least, very little alone time—and his brain had been foggy through most of that. And then he'd run off on some errand for Jonas, and I hadn't seen him at all!

But things had seemed better tonight. Not normal, exactly; Pritkin didn't flirt, so I didn't know what the hell had gotten into him there, but at least he'd seemed healthy. So maybe his babysitters weren't around anymore? I bit my lip. I should go say good night, at least. It was the polite thing to do. And find out what the heck he'd been doing in Britain for a week, or Hong Kong before that, or . . . or just talk a little. I'd missed him so damned much. Why was I even debating this? Just go say good night, Cassie, God!

I shifted, and for a moment, I wasn't sure I was in the right room. It was a generic hotel suite, nicer than the tiny bolt-hole he'd had before, because these days, there were plenty to choose from. The hotel was closed for renovations following the recent attack, and while there were still members of the local supernatural community milling around, waiting for the new MAGIC—their version of the UN—to be completed out in the desert, there was plenty of extra space.

Which meant that Pritkin might have decided he preferred another room?

Because there was no messy potion's bench stuck in a corner, strewn with horrible-smelling ingredients and little bottles. There was no clothing cheerfully flung about, as if hangers had never been invented. There was no trunk full o' weapons overflowing onto the floor, or combat boots peeking out from under the bed.

Pritkin might be a war mage, but he'd somehow missed the whole military-precision thing.

Shit, I thought; I bet I had the wrong room! And worse, the current resident was in the shower. I prepared to shift away, to go find out where Pritkin had moved to, when the bathroom door opened and somebody came out.

He had a towel around his waist and another was covering his head, which he was using to scrub his wet hair. But that didn't matter. I'd know those abs anywhere.

There were some new scars, I noticed, and a bruise on his side as big as my fist, causing the tat of a sharp-edged sword to bulge oddly in the middle, because the swelling hadn't gone down yet. But the lightly furred chest was unmarked, and the scars over one bicep and at his rib cage were well on their way to being healed. They weren't even discolored anymore, although I could still feel the raised ridges under my fingertips.

I realized that I'd crossed the room and started feeling him up without saying a word, which was weird, but I didn't stop there. The body under my hands was hard and solid and warm and *alive*, and that libido thing? Yeah, that was back.

With a vengeance.

"I thought you weren't coming," he said as I slid my arms around his neck and then hopped, wrapping my legs around him, too.

"Got caught up," I murmured, my teeth on his bottom lip, which was plumper than I remembered. Of course, I didn't have a lot of experience trying to eat Pritkin. Need to change that, I decided, and tightened my legs.

I could feel him respond, in more ways than one, and I laughed and mangled that delicious lip some more. And then went on to nibble along the jawline. And to worry his earlobe, and God, I *would* eat him if I could, a raging hunger suddenly ripping through me.

I landed on the bed a moment later, with him on top of me, and that was even better, that was perfect. I rubbed up against him, found his lips, drank him down. Much better, but not enough. The hunger seemed to grow with every movement instead of satiating, my tongue in his mouth, his in mine, warm, sweet, stroking, no! Not what I wanted!

"Thought you liked it rough," I growled, and saw his eyes catch fire.

What followed was not a sweet kiss. It was not gentle and romantic. It was almost a fight in kiss form, and if that didn't say everything about the man, I thought, and rolled over, getting on top, using a move he'd taught me.

I was vaguely surprised that it had worked, but he was distracted. Or maybe he let me win. He didn't look upset, despite the small "oof" he let out before I kissed him back.

Mine wasn't gentle, either. It was full of weeks of terror and worry that I'd lost him, that I'd never see him again. Other than as an empty shell of a body, with the soul it should have housed having been cursed and sent tumbling back through time to his birth, in order to snuff it out.

That had been a gift from the demon high council, who viewed Pritkin as a dangerous renegade, a stubborn son of a bitch with a temper and more magic than was good for him, who they couldn't control. And they were right; nobody had ever been able to control him. Of course, the same could be said of me, which is why I'd immediately taken off after him.

And found him—just. And brought him back. And gotten less time with him than anyone!

"I was going to go slow," he told me, his hands expertly working me out of the damned robe. "Take you to dinner; buy you flowers . . ."

"I already ate, and I have flowers upstairs," I panted, ripping off the T-shirt.

"Then what can I do for you?"

"I can only think of a couple hundred things," I said, and pounced.

And promptly found myself on my back, a war mage between my legs, sliding my panties down. "No," he said, pointing a finger at me as I tried to move.

"What?"

"Stay there."

"No, I can't! I don't need foreplay, damn it!"

"Well, that's unfortunate," the impossible man said. "Because I do."

Liar, I thought, catching sight of a healthy bulge. At least somebody looked happy to see me. But it was covered by damned terry cloth and wasn't getting any closer. In fact, the opposite was true, as Pritkin slid down my body.

Damn it, I was Pythia! Why did nobody do what I told them? Wasn't I supposed to be in charge? Wasn't I supposed to be—

Uhgnnn!

My brain broke, descending into garbled, incoherent thoughts, because Pritkin wasn't as blasé as he seemed. Instead of kissing his way up my thighs, torturing me as I'd feared, he'd decided to torture me in another way. A far more direct one.

I almost came off the bed when his mouth closed over me, and I did arch up and make a sound that I probably would have been embarrassed about another time. Right then, I didn't care. Right then, I just wanted him to—

Uhgnnn! "Yes, there. Right there!" Pritkin looked up at me and laughed, the bastard, the utter, utter bastard. "What are you doing?" I panted. "Go back to work. Go back!"

"I love an appreciative audience," he said, letting me wait until I was throwing pillows at his head.

And then he went back to work.

And God, the man missed his calling, I thought. No way should he have been a war mage. No way in hell. He had a goddamned *gift*, and I was so ready anyway that every stroke felt like literal magic. They shuddered through me like a possession, like sparkling rivers of sensation, like bright fingers of sunlight illuminating the darkest corners of me, filling me up with—with—with—

UHGNNN!

Brilliance burst over me, through me, like a star suddenly going supernova, sending me shuddering and then thrashing and then screaming. And it just went on and on. It was like riding a rushing river that kept swelling and swelling. Whenever I thought it was done, that it had to be, it climbed higher still, until I wasn't sure if I was going to come apart at the seams or just explode.

And then I did both.

The river ended in a waterfall of sensation, not the swift dive over the edge but the churning, crazy, jumbled-up stuff at the bottom of the falls, where everything seems to hit you at once. There was joy there, oh, yes, a sparkling world of it, and passion, and the warm, all-encompassing hug of a feeling that I'd started to label "love." But there was pain, too, and the desperate fear of the chase, of almost losing him; there were the nights of exhaustion and crippling anxiety, when I cried myself to sleep, sure I'd never be enough, that I couldn't do this; there was guilt and pain and fury over Mircea, because I loved him, too, I loved him still, but the betrayal cut so fucking deep; and there was worry over the future, of where this was going, of if it would just crash and burn, too.

I didn't know where it was all coming from, or why it was coming out now. But it was, and suddenly I was sobbing gut-wrenching, body-shaking sobs in the arms of a man who was probably really fucking confused, but who was holding me anyway. Letting me get it out, letting my nails cut into him as I held him so tight, too tight, but I couldn't seem to let go. Afraid that, if I did, he'd disappear on me again, and I couldn't go through that, I couldn't!

It finally stopped, the shaking reduced to slight shivers, my body exhausted and warm and safe in what felt like the first time in forever.

I yawned, right in his face, and was mortified, but he only laughed and kissed the top of my head. "Go to sleep, Cassie."

"I can't. I haven't—we aren't—don't you want—"

"I want you to sleep. You're exhausted."

"'m not exhausted. That's ridiculous," I said, and then spoiled it by yawning again.

"Then let's just lie here a moment," he said, tucking my head against his chest. "All right?"

I nodded, because it felt so good. He pulled the covers

up over us, and it was like being in a warm cocoon, one that smelled of soap and clean sweat and sex, which was not at all a bad combination. And him; it smelled like him, a scent I'd never thought I'd encounter again, like I'd never thought I'd have him so close, hard and warm and undeniably *there*.

There was this weird sensation in my chest as my breathing slowed down. I didn't know what it was at first, but then I realized: it was lightness. The heavy ball of anxiety and dread I'd carried about for so long that it had become almost normal had just gone. Untangling and smoothing out somewhere in all that, until it just wasn't there anymore.

I felt almost weightless suddenly, which was stupid. I had a thousand problems, most of which I had no idea what to do about, and those were just the ones I knew of. I needed to . . . I needed to . . .

I yawned again, and a hand smoothed my hair. "Sleep," someone said. "I'm not going anywhere."

And then the tide was carrying me under.

I awoke to sunlight flooding over an unfamiliar bed, in an unfamiliar room, with an unfamiliar guy bending over me.

Because it was Pritkin, but it wasn't.

I blinked up at him, sleep blurring my vision, pretty sure I was still half-under. Because the man I knew was starched, buttoned-down, and as proper as it was possible to be in his usual uniform of a T-shirt and jeans. He wasn't stiff exactly, or stuck-up. But he was . . . careful. Guarded. Watchful.

He didn't smile easily, or at all most of the time. He didn't trust. He didn't volunteer. Getting personal information out of him was like trying to break into Fort Knox. It had come as a surprise that he was half-demon. It had come as a surprise that he was highly ranked in the Corps. Hell, if it hadn't been for the accent, it would have come as a surprise that he was *British*.

And then there were our interactions, where he went out of his way not to touch me, not to notice me, not to even look at me some days. For a long time, I'd just thought I wasn't his type. There was a chance I'd been wrong about that, I thought dizzily, as his eyes swept over me.

They were different eyes than I was used to: hot, possessive, and more black than green. He moved differently, too, more unconsciously graceful, more fluid, almost predatory. And he *felt* different in some way I couldn't quite define. I knew what my Pritkin would do, at least in most circumstances.

I wasn't so sure about this one.

But that bottom lip was too tempting to resist. I arched up, taking it between mine, felt it give between my teeth, a swollen heat. My body reacted, but the desperate, almost painful desire of last night was gone. In its place was a languid heat, a dreamy sort of craving, a lazy, satiated kind of feeling, like staring at a dessert cart after a generous meal. You're no longer hungry, but still . . .

You could eat.

"I've had fantasies that began this way," he told me, smoothing a callused hand over a breast, watching the nipple peak excitedly under his touch. A liquid pulse went through me.

"What way?"

"You. Sprawled in my bed. Of course, you were wearing the slave girl costume at the time."

It took me a moment, and then I remembered that awful *I Dream of Jeannie* ensemble I'd worn when Caleb, a war mage friend of Pritkin's, and I had gone on a rescue mission into hell. Not one of the nastier hells, but the desert world where Rosier had his main court.

"Is that what it was?" I asked, trying to keep my voice steady. Because that damned callused thumb was stroking, stroking, stroking, even though my nipple was already as hard as it was going to get. Leaving the other feeling strangely cold and neglected—until a warm mouth closed over it. "It was . . . the only thing . . . they had in my size."

He raised his head for a moment, the green eyes halfdrunk, half-sardonic. "It was not in your size. It was not close to your size."

"Are you complaining?"

"No." He went back to his former occupation, feasting

on my breasts until I swear he'd mapped, licked, and sucked every inch of them. Until I was squirming underneath him, and panting slightly, failing the half-hearted attempt I'd been making to act cool and collected.

I wasn't cool. I was definitely not collected. Especially not when he moved over top of me with obvious intent.

But then he just stayed there, motionless except for the faster rise and fall of his chest. Letting me look, letting me touch. Letting me run my hands over hard muscles and soft hair until they grew a little rough, stroking possessively over the big, firm body as I'd never been able to do before.

Pritkin didn't check me out, so I'd never been able to do it to him. Well, not often. We'd even switched bodies once, through the kind of universal joke that only seems to happen to me, and I'd *still* behaved. Partly because I was too freaked-out to take liberties, but still. That's the kind of opportunity that only comes around once . . .

Kind of like this, I realized.

And I wasn't going to waste it.

"Did you touch me?" I asked, pushing him over and climbing on top.

An eyebrow arched.

"When we switched bodies that time. Did you . . . do anything?"

"Did I take advantage of a metaphysical accident to molest the woman I was sworn to protect?" he asked, rephrasing in that annoying way of his.

I sighed. "That sounds like a no."

"And that sounds like disappointment."

"Hm. You could have looked."

"I didn't say I didn't look." Hands found my hips, steadying me, if clenching on my ass counted.

"You did?"

"I had to get dressed. That is difficult on an unfamiliar body if the eyes are closed." His head tilted. "Why do you look absurdly pleased about this?"

"I'm not." It would have been more convincing if I could have stopped grinning.

"It sounds as if you want exculpation."

"What?"

"Did *you* do anything?"

"No. But I'm about to make up for it now," I warned him.

"You're not."

I tried to arch an eyebrow, but as usual, they both went up. "And why is that?"

"It's my turn," he growled, and rolled us again.

# Chapter Twenty-one

And, just like that, the atmosphere changed. From light banter and slowly awakening arousal to . . . whatever this was, I thought, staring up at him. Suddenly, it was all very real: I was on my back, and Pritkin was braced over me with one arm, the muscles standing out from the strain. He used the other to position me, his eyes holding mine as he moved, slowly and deliberately, letting me know what was coming.

Yet I still didn't believe it until I felt him at the entrance of my body, warm and hard and thick and heavy. Until he bent his head to mine and whispered, "Say yes," against my skin.

"Yes."

He closed his eyes, but did nothing else for a long moment. It was like he wanted to prolong this, too, like he wanted to remember every whisper, every sigh. Every shiver that broke over my body, every small movement that I made because I just couldn't stay still, every breath against his lips that had turned into something closer to gasps when he just stayed there, immobile, with almost inhuman control.

And when he did move, it wasn't what I'd expected at all. The kiss he pressed against my lips was sweet and gentle, almost chaste. Until I opened beneath him with a faint whimper of need and it turned into fire, the heat of it sinking into my bones and setting me alight.

I arched up and he deepened the kiss, taking my lips in a long, slow, lingering exploration, before taking everything else. He pushed inside, filling me up until I thought I would burst, until I thought I would die from the perfection of it, the warmth of the heavily muscled body over mine, the hot, thick glide of him inside me, the knowledge that he was back, that he was safe, that we were together and nothing was going to change that. *Finally, finally, finally.*

It resonated like the beat of my heart, like the shout of victory I wanted to give, like the laughter that bubbled up to my lips and came out as a groan instead. I put a hand behind his head and pulled him farther down, farther into me, as our tongues dueled, as our bodies intertwined, as the scent of our arousal flooded the air around us. Until his heartbeat pulsed at the core of my being.

It was perfect—it was absolutely perfect.

For a moment.

And then my own heart was threatening to beat out of my chest, sweat was slicking my skin, and my breath was coming quick and ragged in my throat. This wasn't the first time we'd done this, but it *felt* like the first time. Because the other time had been on a battlefield while an angry god tried to kill us along with the rest of the world!

Wales had been colors and sights and sensations, but not the right ones. Passion had been mixed with pain, desire with desperation, and pleasure with the certainty that the world was about to end. To say that I'd been distracted was to put it mildly.

But I wasn't distracted now, and it was almost *too* much. Too much sensation, too much emotion, too much everything. I'd waited so long, anticipated this so much, and now that it was here . . .

I was panicking, for no reason at all.

Goddamn it, what was *wrong* with me?

I didn't want to dissolve into tears again. Pritkin was going to think I had some kind of sex phobia! I didn't; I wanted him, like I wanted to relax and enjoy this, but I didn't know how. It felt like it had last night, with so many emotions suddenly bubbling up that I didn't know what to do with any of them.

And then it hit me, and I really freaked out: this was Pritkin's first time in more than a century, and I was screwing it up!

When we had first met, he'd been that strangest of

strange things, a celibate incubus. Or half of one, with the half in question thanks to an overbearing demon lord of a father with ambitions he'd expected Pritkin to help him fulfill. Specifically, by having sex with other formidable demons, an act that allowed members of the incubus royal line to create a feedback loop that magnified power, giving both parties more than they'd started out with—a lot more. Power Pritkin had been expected to use to secure his father's delusions of grandeur.

Imagine Rosier's pique when his son decided that he didn't want to be a glorified prostitute and told the old man no. I assume that had something to do with why Rosier never bothered to warn Pritkin that his pretty fiancée was a power-hungry demon in her own right, and planned to gain what birth had denied her by instigating the feedback loop on their wedding night. Something that . . . hadn't gone well.

Pritkin had never had sex with a fellow demon before and didn't know how to stop the spell once it had begun. And Ruth, his fiancée, didn't get the chance, not being strong enough to participate in a loop in the first place, something that Rosier should have known. The result had been Pritkin draining her dry before she ever got anything back, leaving the horrified bridegroom with a dried-up husk in his arms instead of a warm, living woman.

At least, it did until he got up, strapped on his weapons, and went to find daddy.

That hadn't gone well, either, since the demon council takes a dim view of those who attempt to slaughter one of its members. Pritkin had been sentenced to death, something that Rosier—who'd realized he'd screwed up—managed to get commuted to banishment on earth. That had suited Pritkin, since he hated the hell regions anyway. What didn't suit him was the other part of the deal: no sex. Of any kind.

I wasn't sure if Rosier had been the one to include that, but I was suspicious. He had hoped that Ruth, who had loved the hell regions as much as Pritkin had hated them, might be good for his son. Or, at least, that she might be good for *him* by persuading Pritkin to give his father's realm another try. And when that blew up in his face, he'd gone with plan B.

He'd assumed that his son would come running back in no time, desperate for the very position he'd once refused. Because, for an incubus, no sex equaled starvation, pain, and a slow, lingering death. But Pritkin was only half incubus, the other half being an amalgamation of human and fey, and stubborn as all hell, so he survived.

But freedom had come at a price, including the loss of all the power he'd once gained from his incubus nature, which was slowly starving. Not to mention the lack of any kind of a normal life—no wife, no kids, no close friends who might notice that he just never aged. It was a lonely and bitter existence, and one that left him with no chance to grow or escape, or do anything except endure.

But now he could. Now, he could finally have a normal life again, except he was with me and I was a mess who'd repressed my feelings for so long that I didn't know what to do with them now that I couldn't. And I *couldn't*.

I stared up at him, my breath coming faster, tears filling my eyes. This was important, and I was screwing it up. This was *important*—

Pritkin took my face between his hands and regarded me soberly for a moment. His palms were big and warm and rough, and the green eyes were steady and calming. He'd showered, but not shaved, and at least a day's worth of stubble clung to the cheeks and jawline. Along with the serious case of bedhead he was currently sporting, it made him look rumpled and real and young, like the much younger version of him that I'd encountered on my search. And fallen in love with, because apparently, my heart knew Pritkin no matter the time or incarnation.

And just like that, I felt my pulse settle down a little.

Then I saw it again: the mischievous grin of that boy I'd met in Wales. "It's all right," he told me. "I understand."

"You do?"

"Of course. Many have found it to be somewhat . . . intimidating."

"Intimidating?"

"My size."

I stared at him, caught completely off guard. "I—what?" And then I realized what he'd said, and I felt my cheeks flush. "*How* many?"

The grin tilted toward smug. "I'll give you a moment to adjust, shall I?"

"I don't need a moment!"

"You know, there's no shame in admitting—oof," he said, as I rolled us, while kissing him furiously to shut him up, because it was either that or beat him to death. And I discovered that anger and passion weren't a bad combination.

Not a bad combination at all, I thought, sitting up and finding my seat. And proving my point by getting used to the feel of him, stretching me, filling me from a new angle. My breath caught a little, but it was a good ache, and I slapped at his hands when he looked concerned and moved to reposition me.

"Not a chance," I told him, and inwardly grinned at his surprise when I started to move, biting my lip a little because he *was* big, not that I'd ever admit it, and it had been a while. But the burn felt good, too, a strange mixture of pain and pleasure, like the look on Pritkin's face as he stared up at me.

I held his eyes as I rode him, feeling self-conscious at first, although that didn't last long. Callused hands came up again, but only to my hips to steady me and help me find a rhythm. Until I pushed them down to the bed and put my knees on top of them.

"No touching until I say."

The lips quirked slightly, but he stayed where I'd put him. He was obviously humoring me. Yeah, keep thinking that, big boy, I thought, and got to work.

I don't know where the idea came from. Maybe the hot green gaze that followed my every movement but couldn't actually touch me. Only it *felt* like a touch; I swear it had both weight and heat. And I suddenly thought, why not do the touching for him?

So everywhere he looked, my hands followed. He caught on to the game fast; I guess there's not many that an incubus doesn't know. But it seemed that I'd picked one he liked, because his gaze fairly sizzled over my skin.

Here a finger followed a collarbone, causing me to remember how he'd once traced it with his tongue. There a bead of sweat rolled down the valley of my sternum, only to get trapped by my naval as I undulated above him. Here I steadied myself with hands on his chest, stroking hard pecs and straining abs for a moment before removing them again, because I never said *I* couldn't touch. There I cupped my breasts—

And Pritkin's eyes flashed purely black for a second.

Ahh, I thought so. He'd always liked my breasts, even when we were pretending to hate each other. I'd had to quit wearing a certain tank top, which was cut slightly lower and was slightly thinner than my other ones, because he'd stop interacting with me at all when I had it on. Other times he'd made comments I'd brushed off at the time, but seeing the heat in that gaze, I was pretty sure they'd been deliberate.

Let's test a theory, I thought, and brushed my nipples playfully with my thumbs. He made a noise from somewhere lower than his chest that resonated through me, making me bite my lip. And tighten around him for a moment, before remembering who was supposed to be in charge here. And then I did it again, and again, until I was straight up playing with them, until they were rosy pink and fully erect and I was pulling sound after sound out of him, until he was trying to come off the bed and I was having to grind my knees down to keep him in place.

Until the game had turned into something else entirely.

I stared down at him, quietly amazed by the look in his eyes, the one I'd never thought I'd see. The naked hunger, the raw desire, and something else that made my stomach twist and my heart clench. And my body flash hot and liquid and strangely bold.

I finished off with a butterfly brush of fingertips, like lips on my skin, down, down, down to where our bodies met and merged. But I wasn't watching me; I was watching him. And the fascinating way his eyes got darker and darker, until I wasn't sure if they were deep jade or pure black.

They stared at me as if he wasn't sure he knew me anymore, and maybe he was right. I felt different, bolder, exhilarated, a little crazy. Maybe because I was moving easily now, riding him hard, sending pulses of pleasure through me and wringing out more of those sounds he kept making.

It was like the reverse of the touching game, like he was vocalizing for me. A shudder tore through me, but came out of his lips. A pulse of pleasure almost threw me off my rhythm, and he groaned in sympathy. My breath started coming faster, shallower, but he was the one panting.

A girl could get addicted to this, I thought dizzily.

"Cassie—" he finally gasped.

I tossed my hair saucily, and didn't answer.

"Cassie." It had been pleading a moment ago. Now it was an order.

I grinned; too bad I don't take orders.

"Cassie—" It was desperate, hoarse and strained, and cords were standing out on the heavily muscled arms, as if he was having to grip the bed to stay still.

"One more minute," I told him, and watched him shiver.

And defy me, although I'm not sure he knew it. The eyes were a little crazed, and he'd started bucking up to meet me, making me feel like I was an actual cowgirl, riding a barely controlled beast. A big one, with rough hands that freed themselves and then slid up my sides to grip bouncing softness, gently at first and then hard enough to bruise, although I was past caring.

Way past.

All I needed was a hat to wave around, I thought, feeling a strange urge to laugh.

Until I looked down at Pritkin's face. He'd been laughing, too, a few moments ago, or as close to it as he ever got, joking and playful, almost like the boy he'd once been. But now, there was something leaking through the cracks, something he couldn't seem to control. Something raw and real and—I didn't know.

I wanted to see more of that look, wanted to see how far it went, wanted to know what he might be hiding in there. I wanted to see that perfect stoicism ruined and smoking on the ground. I wanted to see him laid bare as I was, as I had been when I sobbed in his arms. Not to hurt him but to heal.

Because whatever I had pent up inside me, Pritkin had far, far more.

But this wasn't the time. Today wasn't about reliving trauma, even to ease it. Today wasn't about lessons to be learned or trials to be overcome. Today was about rediscovering pleasure, about ending a century-old fast, about the end of a very long road.

Today was about love.

"Now," I said softly, bending over him—

And was on my back before I could blink, momentarily breathless from a move he made that shot sparks straight up my spine.

A purely wicked face looked down at me, flushed and panting and sweaty and strained, but wearing the tiniest of evil grins.

Uh-oh, I thought.

And uh-oh it was, because oh, how he made me pay!

He proved, really freaking fast, that he understood how to play this game better than I did. Way better. Oh God, so much better!

Every time my body started to shiver, every time I began to gasp with every stroke, every time I felt myself tightening helplessly around him, oh God, so good, *so good, oh God*—

The.

Bastard.

Eased.

Off.

Just as he knew how to drive me crazy, he knew how to make me wait for it, beg for it, demand it with flashing eyes and snarled speech, while he denied me again and again. Until I couldn't think at all, except for oh and ahh and help and *please*. Until I was grabbing the bedsheets, gripping them in knotted fists, and thrashing and squirming and trying to hold on, because Pritkin hadn't lied—he liked it rough. And so did I, judging from the way my body bucked and flailed and gripped and hung on.

And then practically convulsed when he finally whispered: "Now."

I came screaming and crying and laughing and cursing. I came so hard I almost passed out. I came with his name on my lips and his body spilling into mine, his own cry of mingled pain and bliss and strange catharsis echoing my own.

Totally . . . wasted . . . in the Corps, I thought, clinging to him when he finally collapsed on top of me, panting and sweaty and tired and limp.

And asleep, I realized, a moment later, hearing a gentle snore against my neck. I wore him out, I thought proudly, clutching him against me. I completely wore him out.

I was totally going to buy a hat, I decided, and slipped back into sleep.

# Chapter Twenty-two

*Wub, wub, wub.*

I frowned, and stirred in my sleep.

*Wub, wub, wub.*

Damn it, I hated having an apartment right over top of a Laundromat. The machines could shake the walls and wake the dead. Especially on Saturday morning, when everybody and their dog decided to—

*Wub, wub, wub.*

That wasn't a washing machine, I thought blearily, and then someone was yelling: "Cassie! *Shift!*"

I came awake instantly, because that was Pritkin's oh-shit voice, and he didn't use it lightly. I opened my eyes to the red and black swirl of a hellmouth at the foot of the bed, and a crowd of huge metallic creatures flooding into the room. Allû, I thought, recognizing the demon high council's hideous guards.

Pritkin was fighting them, and doing a damned good job, considering that he was naked and his potion belt was nowhere to be seen. But one of the Allû went flying anyway, virtue of a roundhouse kick, back into the portal behind him. And backup was already pound, pound, pounding on the door.

Not the door to the hallway, as might have been expected, but the *closet* door. Because Pritkin's weapons didn't need a hand on the trigger to be deadly. But they did need a hand on the door, or at least the doorknob, in order to get out, and they didn't have one. So they shot their way out, in a hail of bullets that were absorbed by Pritkin's shields but that blew various-sized holes in two more of the creatures.

Not that it mattered. The Allû were spirits in armor-like suits, to give their attacks more oomph, I supposed, or maybe just to be more intimidating. Which worked really well, since they looked like a cross between Cylons and Iron Man, with huge, burnished bronze bodies that didn't feel pain because they were basically tanks that the spirits inside drove around in—and drove over people who pissed off the demon council.

Not to mention that even the Cylons had eyes, but the Allû didn't.

Just blank bronze faceplates that lacked even the outlines of features the Allû didn't need, since they used demon senses to get around. Like they couldn't be harmed by the bullets tearing through them, although they could be inconvenienced by having their metallic skins destroyed. Which was happening everywhere now, because Pritkin's arsenal was speeding into the room, but also because—

"Pritkin!" I yelled. "They're not fighting back!"

He looked up from literally ripping the head off an Allû, but I don't think he heard me. He just knew that I'd called out, and he launched himself at me—and was almost taken out by his own weapons. Because, instead of helping him, the majority had sped through the line of creatures to create a floating barrier in front of the bed. One I didn't need, because the only person going ham right now was my defender.

The Allû were just standing there, or what remained of them, since Pritkin had managed to dispose of three, and his weapons had taken out three more. But that still left a good half dozen just hanging around, looking so out of place in a Vegas hotel room that it hurt my brain.

Like the idea that this was starting all over again.

"You're not taking him," I told them flatly.

The metallic mountains didn't move.

"What do you want?" Pritkin snarled, finally understanding that the ones he hadn't attacked weren't fighting him.

And, finally, that got a response. A bunch of spears raised, not to attack, but to point. And I suddenly realized that maybe they weren't there for Pritkin after all.

Because they were pointing at me.

And that . . . didn't go down well. Not with me so much, since I was still trying to figure out what I'd done to piss off the demon council. But with Pritkin, who had already been looking surprisingly feral, and not at all like the super-controlled man I knew.

Of course, the nudity had something to do with that, with the hard-muscled body bare and reflected a bunch of times in the Allûs' shiny suits. But it had more to do with the expression in the wild green eyes, which appeared even brighter than usual, and the vicious look on his face. And the way he jumped one of the Allû with a roar.

I'd stood up, in order to see over the floating weapons, but now I sat back down, feeling more than a little nonplussed. And then I lay down abruptly, when a bunch of small bottles came speeding through the air by my nose. It looked like Pritkin had been brewing potions in the bathroom again, judging by the army flying out of the partly open door as if on a mission, said mission being to melt a bunch of demons' faces off.

Pritkin still had a workout disposing of the rest of them, because they seemed insistent on not leaving without me. He was just as clear on the idea that they would. And he was winning, which was a surprise, because the demon council's guards weren't lightweights. Of course, neither was Pritkin, but the numbers were against him, and most of his arsenal was still protecting me.

Not to mention that the guards, once their metallic suits failed, were perfectly capable of attacking in their spirit forms, which had me trying to crawl under the floating arsenal to shift us both out of there and tell the council to go hang itself!

But a gun butt kept bumping my nose, and when I didn't take the hint, a couple others, along with the hilts of half a dozen floating knives, combined into a wedge to poke me back into place.

I stared at them, nonplussed again, and then angry. I didn't need the help, damn it! But Pritkin did. A spirit had just leapt out of a bullet-riddled suit and twined itself around his forearm, getting metaphysical fangs in and attempting to drain him. I stood back up on the bed, trying to get a clear view to shift him out—only to see his eyes suddenly flash super bright, almost like they were glowing, and for him to flick the incorporeal mass into the portal like an annoying insect.

Okay, I thought, a little stunned.

That was new.

I stood there for a second, watching what looked like a street brawl between the Hulk and a bunch of Keystone Cops. Only they weren't. They were ten-foot-tall, burnished bronze, demon-possessed suits of armor that he was *obliterating*.

And then I started looking for my bathrobe, because I'd learned a few things about demons.

Like the fact that he wasn't the only stubborn one.

And, sure enough, he'd no sooner tossed the last guard down the portal's gullet than they were back. Only this time, it wasn't a dozen, or even two. It was a whole damned army, and Pritkin was yelling at me to shift away and I was now trying to locate his jeans, because I'd found my robe, but he never put anything away properly, damn it!

I finally grabbed a pair right before something grabbed me.

And a moment later, I was standing in hell.

There was asphalt under my feet and a streetlight nearby, so I was pretty sure that this was the realm known as the Shadowland. But, honestly, I couldn't have guessed otherwise. For the first time ever, it actually looked like the conventional version of hell.

Because it was on fire.

The streetlight was burning, the asphalt was threatening to melt under my feet, and a nearby building was writhing in the middle of a conflagration—literally. It looked tortured and off center, and had strange bulges poking out here and there. Even worse, it couldn't decide what it wanted to be.

For a second there, just after the portal coughed us up, it was a stately Victorian, the brickwork a little grimy from coal dust, but the front stoop newly painted and pristine. Then I blinked and it was a modern skyscraper, maybe twenty stories tall, with the flames that were eating up one side reflected in acres' worth of glass. And a moment after that, it was a beautiful old Spanish mission with a bell that was *clang, clang, clanging* out a distress call because its tower was going up in flames.

This . . . was not normal, even for hell. Especially this little hell. The Shadowland was the demon realm that the other demon worlds used as a meeting place, market, and neutral zone for resolving disputes that had gotten out of hand. That's why the demon council met here, where violence was supposed to be outlawed, and why it regularly received a steady stream of visitors from all over.

To accommodate the many different races, each of which had their own idea of what constituted comfortable surroundings, the city had long ago devised a spell that took images out of its visitors' minds to project over whatever constituted reality around here. They didn't bother with the area beyond the city, which just looked like a twilit desert, with long blue shadows even at midday—hence the name—and a lot of rocks. But the city itself . . .

Well, it looked like whatever you wanted it to.

Except for tonight, I thought, watching the fiery building change once again. Only this time, it didn't resemble much of anything, or maybe I should say, it resembled *everything*. A Chinese upturned roof poked out over a sweet old Southern porch meant for moonlight and magnolias; a rustic log cabin was perched on top of that, with what looked like dung mortar peeking out from between newly stripped logs; and a precarious third story of Georgian red bricks teetered over it all, while beautiful Middle Eastern tile kept breaking out in patches, here and there, like the house had a rash.

A second later, the flames spread across the roof, and the building really lost it, morphing faster than I could blink into things I was pretty sure hadn't come out of my brain, since it couldn't even comprehend most of them.

And then it started shaking.

"Get down!" Pritkin yelled, knocking me to the ground and covering me with his body. But that wasn't necessary. The guards made a shaking motion with their arms, all at once, and formed a wall from the huge shields that popped out of their armor, which must have been twelve feet tall.

We needed every inch of them. A second later, the house exploded, sending a powerful rush of magic and strange fiery sludge shooting over us, hard enough to knock some of the guards off their feet. But the ones in front of us held the line, the bottoms of their shields buried in asphalt—which was now cobblestones, I noticed, since my nose was all of an inch away from them—while their bodies braced above.

I stared up at the lines of fire painted on the bronze armor the Allû wore and finally realized that they weren't there to hurt us. They were there to *protect* us. Because it looked like the whole city was going up.

Buildings were writhing and morphing on every side, the usually twilit sky was burning with a reddish haze, and the spell that covered this place was getting rents in it, allowing me to glimpse mind-altering things beyond it. Meanwhile, the guards were straightening up again, ripping their shields out of the ground, and hedging us around. And, as soon as we scrambled back to our feet, starting a quick march forward.

"Here," Pritkin told me, handing me a pair of boots. His boots. Or, at least, they were the same big, black combat variety he often wore.

"You grabbed boots?" I asked, hurrying along. And wondering how I was supposed to get them on.

"Always protect your feet."

"And other things?" I asked, because other things were hanging out right now.

"Priorities. If you can't move you can't fight."

"Well, you'll fight better in these," I said, and handed over the jeans.

He pulled them on, then took back the boots and put those on, too. Because no amount of tight lacing was going to keep them on my feet. And then he picked me and my fluffy bathrobe up, because the street ahead was actually smoking. But the area to either side was even worse, so we soldiered on, all but blind once we descended from the hill we'd appeared on into a valley where the guards' huge bodies blocked most of the view. But I didn't feel like complaining, because they blocked other things as well. Including a vending machine that came running down the street, screaming.

The spell was definitely getting screwy and assigning completely wrong images to things. Normally, the other people here looked like the somewhat harried city types you could see anywhere from New York to Bangkok. That wasn't true in all cases; there were things the spell didn't seem to work on, or that maybe my seer's eyes occasionally saw through. But for the most part, the denizens of the Shadowland looked like regular Joes, just as I was pretty sure I looked like whatever bug-eyed, tentacle-draped, horn-wearing thing they considered everyday and boring.

But not now. Now the spell was losing it and was just slapping any old images onto the backdrop, like it was pulling stuff randomly from my mind but couldn't be bothered to make sure that it fit or not. Hence the flailing snack machine. And the potted people outside the entrance to a building, waving back and forth in the breeze off the fires, with creepy, fixed smiles on their faces. And the bicycle and taxicab, the latter full of what looked like looted merchandise, throwing down in the middle of the street. I also saw a sapling just uproot itself and walk off, apparently getting tired of the bullshit, and found myself in full solidarity with the tree.

What the literal hell was going on?

"Some kind of attack," Pritkin said, when I asked. "Although I can't imagine who would be this foolish. The entire council will come down on whoever broke the peace."

"Wouldn't want to be him," I said, gazing around.

Pritkin started looking worried for some reason.

"You haven't been . . . up to anything . . . while I was away?" he asked.

"What does that mean?"

He shot me a look. "You know perfectly well what it means. Marco informed me that you went shopping yesterday and then to a meeting with the senate."

"Um. More or less." Now I was starting to get worried, too.

"Well?"

"Well, what?"

"Did anything unusual happen on either of those two occasions?"

". . . Define 'unusual.'"

Pritkin's frown tipped over into a scowl.

But he didn't get a chance to reply, because we were being quick-marched into a familiar building. I don't know what the demon council's meeting hall actually looked like, but my mind had assigned it the facade of a drab, slightly shabby-looking hotel with the most boring lobby imaginable. And, thankfully, it was still as boring as ever, because whatever was happening outside hadn't made it this far.

The beige carpet that met my bare toes when Pritkin sat me down was still beige and still in need of cleaning. The potted plants were still just plants, ones that looked like they'd seen better days. The reception desk was still a cheap wood laminate that had a few chips in the surface, and a fat little demon on the other side who looked relieved to see us. He waved us on back.

Only back to where, I wasn't sure. The only place I knew in here was through the big double doors opposite the entrance, which led down a hall to the dark amphitheater where the council met. But I didn't put up a fuss, because anything was better than hanging around the lobby.

I looked at Pritkin, who was staring at a spot near the doors, which looked as nondescript as everything else. It wasn't. It was where he'd fallen, the spot where he'd been cursed, the place where he'd died. The demon spell that had sent his soul careening back through time and me on my epic journey to try to save him had all started here.

Right here.

I took Pritkin's hand and squeezed it. "You all right?"

He didn't say anything for a moment, just stared at the spot some more. And then he nodded, a quick up-and-down movement of the chin that said as loud as anything that no, he was not all right. But I didn't know what to do about it, except to keep hold of his hand as we were guided down a hall.

It was on the opposite side of the lobby from the one

that held the bathrooms and the ratty old sofa where Caleb, Casanova, and I had sat while Pritkin's trial went on. As bad as this was, it was better than having to sit around for hours waiting on what we all knew was a kangaroo court. The council hadn't wanted justice; they'd wanted him dead, although I'd never understood why.

Yes, he was powerful, and that had been before his incubus abilities came back online, so to speak. Based on what I'd just seen I'd say he'd gotten an upgrade, but even so, he was *one man*. It didn't make sense to me that a council of superpowerful, ancient beings would be so concerned over the fate of any single individual— especially one who hated the hells and never came here anyway—when they presumably had legions of soldiers under their command.

But they had been, and they'd killed him. And even though they'd reconsidered later, when they decided it might be useful to have a friendly Pythia on their side, and had given me the counterspell, I still wasn't okay with it. We needed them for the war, so I was playing nice, but that did not remotely mean I was okay.

They had better *hope* this is about me, I thought, as we turned into a small office. Because if they decided to go after Pritkin again, whatever had happened outside would be the least of their worries. And then the heavy door snicked closed behind us.

# Chapter Twenty-three

The man who rose to meet us was not any more prepossessing than his office, which matched the rest of the hotel. There was a desk that looked like it ought to be in a high school classroom facing a couple of hard wooden chairs. There were carpet tiles on the floor under my feet, the industrial kind with no padding, one of which was missing and showing a patch of plain, concrete subfloor. And, strangely, there was an aquarium, small and dingy, bubbling against one wall, complete with a small scuba diver in an old-fashioned wet suit, endlessly waving.

And then there was Adra.

Adra, aka Adramelech, was a trans-dimensional being of immense power and, presumably, wealth. Yet his go-to disguise was a discount glamourie that looked like it had been picked up at the magical equivalent of a convenience store, crammed in between the five-hour energy potions and the Slim Jims. It was not exactly high-end, is what I'm saying.

It left him looking like he belonged with the desk: a slightly portly, middle-aged high school teacher, with a pleasant, round face that managed to be slightly creepy because of its complete lack of identifying features. Most people have something at least slightly unusual about them: acne scars, buck teeth, a bump on their nose, freckled lips. *Something.*

But not Adra. He'd tried out a few accessories in the past, to dress up the face, like a kid with a Mr. Potato Head doll—a cleft chin, a mustache, some truly scary bushy eyebrows—but none of them had really helped. And I guess he'd been too busy to bother today. Because this version had perfectly smooth baby skin; pale, almost colorless eyes; completely average features; and short blond hair cut in the most boring style possible.

A police sketch artist would have had a fit.

I, for one, was grateful for the normalcy. And then, when Pritkin almost squeezed my hand in two, I realized that this wasn't really normal at all. Because that spot outside? Yeah, that wasn't nearly as big of a deal as suddenly coming face-to-face with his murderer.

Because guess who had thrown that damned spell?

But if Adra felt awkward, he didn't show it. "Ah, Mage Pritkin. Kind of you to come along as the Pythia's . . . pit bull?"

"Partner," I said sharply, and sat down without being asked.

Pritkin took the other chair, and thankfully the aggressive energy he'd shown with the Allû was no longer in evidence. And neither was anything else. The vibrant man I'd been with all night was shut down and closed off, with only the single vein beating at his temple giving any indication of his feelings.

'Cause, yeah. He had always hated this place. And, I assumed, even more now.

But he'd come with me, nonetheless.

I promised myself to make it up to him, and looked at Adra. "You wanted something?"

"Indeed, yes," he said simply, and casually lit a cigarette.

Most of the demons I knew smoked; I wasn't sure why. Pritkin always said it was because it reminded them of home, all smoke and brimstone, but I'd learned not to listen to Pritkin about the hells. My current theory was that the smoke helped to obscure less-than-perfect glamouries, and the actions of fishing out a cigarette, lighting, and then smoking it gave them a set rota of things to do with their hands. That was helpful, because some of them who visited earth didn't have the usual number, or understand what passed for normal human motions.

Smoking gave them an out.

Or, at least, it used to.

"That's going out of style," I told him, to give Pritkin a minute. "People don't smoke so much anymore."

Adra sighed in what sounded like annoyance. "Humans live on fast-forward," he told me. "It's quite distressing."

"Is it?"

"Terribly. I adopt a habit to help me fit in, and the next time I visit, it's doing precisely the opposite. Snuff, you know."

"Snuff?"

He nodded solemnly. "Your people used to have these pretty little jeweled or carved boxes—I had one of elephant ivory—at the European courts. All the nobility carried them, even the women. They went around sniffing and sneezing all day long." His nose twitched, and something about the combo of the round face and the wide eyes and the rapidly twitching nose reminded me of a rabbit. It made me want to laugh, in spite of everything.

I wondered if that had been the point.

"But the next time I visited," he continued, "just a few hundred years later, and took out my box, everyone looked at me as if I was mad!"

"It . . . must be frustrating," I said, because what do you say to that?

"You have no idea. And now you tell me that these"—he regarded his cigarette sadly—"are on their way out, too?"

"They're bad for your health," I said, and received an eye roll in return.

"As if humans ever cared about that." He put it out in an ashtray he conjured up—at least, I was pretty sure that it hadn't been there a second ago—and looked at me pleasantly. "I was wondering if perhaps there was a reason you sicced an Ancient Horror on us?"

I blinked at him for a second, having been caught off guard by the question, which had been asked in the same genial tone as everything else. "What?"

He regarded me for a moment, and then he nodded. "As I thought. You didn't know."

"Know . . . what?"

"That yesterday morning, you shifted an ancient demon into the Shadowland, right in the middle of the marketplace."

"What?" Pritkin said, suddenly coming back to life.

Adra stopped and considered. "What *was* the marketplace," he amended. "As you may have noticed, the damned thing destroyed most of it."

I looked back and forth between the two men, feeling seriously confused. "Adra, I don't know what you're—"

And then I did.

It said something for the way my life worked lately that I'd actually forgotten all about that.

"Oh, shit."

"Yes," he agreed. "That's what we said. Among other things."

"And how do you know Cassie had anything to do with this?" Pritkin asked harshly.

"Ah, yes, that's right, isn't it?" Adra asked him. "Unlike most heirs apparent, you never bothered to attend the meetings."

"Adra," I said, but he held up a hand.

"There are safeguards to protect the city. They were needed in the dark times, and were never dismantled afterward due to the number of delicate issues regularly discussed here. Among other things, they do not allow one of the Great Dangers to simply transition in." He'd been looking at Pritkin, but now he glanced at me. "At least, not without help."

"How . . ."

I stopped and swallowed, feeling sick. I'd shifted away the creature at the coven's version of Grand Central Station to protect the people there, without bothering to consider the ones here. I'd been attempting to help, but instead, I'd just passed the buck. How many had paid for it?

"Were there many casualties?" I asked, because I had to know.

"None, as far as I know."

"*None?* But how—"

"It was targeting merchandise, not people. The creature appears to have had a disagreement with the family who used to control this world, long ago, before the council settled here. They also had a market, and it seemed to believe that if it destroyed enough of their wares, it would draw them out. However, the council was drawn out instead." He lit another cigarette. "It was an . . . interesting . . . fight."

I swallowed some more and decided I didn't feel well. Relief was warring with guilt, and they were both being put in overdrive by a rush of adrenaline. It was making me want to bolt out of my chair and pass out at the same time, and the combo was making me nauseous.

I settled for sitting there miserably instead.

"I'm . . . really sorry," I said, because Adra was looking at me, and tried not to wince at how inadequate that sounded.

But he shook his head. "I am less concerned with apologies than with where you found it. We thought we had the Ancient Horrors safely locked away."

"In a book," I said, and told them about my shopping trip, which felt like a hundred years ago now.

"A fey released it?" Adra asked when I'd finished. "You are sure?"

"Pretty sure," I said, remembering the merperson's otherworldly appearance. He'd been amazing, mesmerizing— like he'd been formed out of the water itself. As if the currents had decided to sculpt something, but couldn't decide whether to make a man or a fish. He'd been beautiful . . . in a murderous sort of way.

And didn't that just sum up Faerie perfectly?

"Make that absolutely sure," I said, in case Adra didn't get sarcasm.

"This is troubling," he said, but his face didn't reflect it. It had fallen into the blank, almost dead look he got when he was too busy to remember to animate it. So instead of a bad glamourie, it looked like what it really was: a mask hiding a terribly old, terribly powerful, terribly intelligent being.

Who suddenly snapped out of it and smiled charmingly at me. "Could I see this book?"

"You could, if I hadn't left it behind," I admitted. "The covens have it now, if they haven't destroyed it. Which they might have. They don't like demons, and right now, I'm not much more pop—hey!" I said, because he'd reached out a hand, only to have Pritkin jerk me away.

He'd pulled me completely out of my chair before I realized what was happening, and got between me and Adra. And he didn't look so closed off now. He looked furious.

"You don't touch her!"

"Ah," Adra said, studying him, maybe because the green eyes were definitely glowing now. I'd thought that might have been a trick of the light back in his room, but in the dim little office, there was no question. He suddenly looked like what he was: a powerful demon lord in his own right.

One who was ready to throw down.

I caught his arm, because no, no, no, not again! We didn't need a replay of last time, and I was pretty sure that that's what we were about to have. Because Pritkin might have gotten an upgrade, but Adra wasn't head of the demon high council for nothing. And this was *his* turf.

Unlike us, he had plenty of backup.

But Adra wasn't looking angry. If anything, he looked the opposite, with a strange little smile flirting with his face. "Pit bull, indeed," he murmured, and then glanced at me. "With your permission, of course."

"Permission for what?"

"A different way to see." He looked at Pritkin, who hadn't moved, and sighed. "Sit down and stop acting like the maniac everyone believes you to be."

Pritkin did not sit down. "I've been called worse than maniac through the years. But hurt her and find out how true it is!"

Adra started to look annoyed. "If I wanted to hurt you—either of you—you would be hurt. If I wanted to kill you, you would be dead. I clearly want to talk, which we cannot do if we have nothing to talk about!"

The not-sitting-down thing did not change.

Adra sighed again. "I am using the—" he began, and then went on to utter a stream of syllables that made my inner ears want to turn inside out and crawl off somewhere. Preferably somewhere that wasn't using whatever language that was. It sounded the way the things I'd seen outside had looked, the ones I'd glimpsed behind the failing cloaking spell. My brain hadn't been able to handle them, either, giving me a scrambled egg feeling up there, and this wasn't helping. I was about to have to ask him to stop when he finally did anyway.

"That is all?" Pritkin demanded, having apparently been able to follow all that. "You will swear to it?"

"I assume you mean formally?" And before I could ask what that meant, a series of what sounded like bells rang out, loud enough to make me jump.

I just . . . really want to go home now, I thought, clinging to Pritkin.

"He swore a formal oath. He can't hurt you," Pritkin told me. "He will be using an ancient spell to allow us to see what you saw. If you agree?"

I nodded.

I wanted to get this over with.

We all sat back down. Adra reached over the desk again, to hover a finger above my right temple. "Concentrate on this book," he told me. "See it clearly in your mind."

And the next thing I knew, there it was, sitting in the middle of the desk, as perfect as when I first saw it, the black cover shining in the low lighting. Only that wasn't right, was it? There should be—

Six or seven large ruptures, I thought, jumping a little as they suddenly appeared in the surface, almost before I'd finished the thought. They exploded out of the leather like someone had shot it. Only they weren't from a gun.

Damage from the fey's spear, I realized.

Man, he'd really done a number on it.

And then the cover grew swimmy and faint, almost blurry.

"Concentrate," Adra told me. "See it as you first did, when it was whole."

I tried, I really did, but I hadn't been paying much attention. I hadn't been interested in the book, but in what it contained. Which was nothing, I realized, as Adra began flipping through the pages.

All of which were blank.

"You didn't open it, I take it?" he asked.

"No. I mean, I saw inside the front cover, but I wasn't paying attention . . ."

Which was probably why, although the first page had color and some faint lines on it, none of them were readable.

Adra closed the cover again and looked at it instead. It was beautiful in a Goth-y, I-am-probably-evil sort of way. A little scuffed up, and one of the buckles on the straps was missing. But there was about an acre of beautifully tooled black leather; a ring of shiny black jewels, each as big as my thumb; and the other straps, all of which were undone at the moment, I guess because that was how I first saw them.

There was also a title in faded gold, but I couldn't read it, either. Every time I tried, it writhed and morphed, showing different things that might be letters, although not in English, or sometimes just squiggles that weren't letters at all. I tried to focus, to recall whatever it had been, but I couldn't. The words simply hadn't registered.

"It's all right," Adra said. "You've done well."

Funny; it didn't feel that way. And what was so important that it needed an Ancient Horror to guard it anyway? And how had somebody trapped one of them? From what I understood, even the demons themselves were scared of those things.

"I thought the Ancient Horrors were superpowerful old demons that scared the bejeezus out of everybody, so you locked them all away," I said.

"That is . . . a strangely accurate assessment," Adra agreed, smiling slightly.

"Then how could one have been in there? The shop owner—"

I stopped, because Evil Santa had just materialized, too, along with his oily smile and be-ringed hands. I hadn't realized I'd even noticed those. It was like my brain was more observant than I was.

Adra sized the man up, and then he waved a hand, and the weird little guy dissipated like smoke. "My people shall see him presently," he said. "After they have spoken with these witches of yours."

"The shop owner," I continued stubbornly, "said that the Ancient Horror was imprisoned by some mage in order to secure the book. To create an unbreakable lock or a cypher that nobody could decrypt." Adra nodded. "But how could a human mage have done something like that?"

"They trap our people occasionally for such uses, or to create golems," he murmured, his hands ghosting over the surface of the book. It felt solid and real under my fingertips, when I dared to touch it, too, just at the edge. But like this morning, I didn't get anything from it. Maybe I would have if the cover had been opened, but with the lock spell in place, I'd felt nothing.

And it didn't seem to be doing much for Adra, either.

"But they don't trap Ancient Horrors," I pointed out. "The amount of power it would take to do something like that—" I stopped, because I didn't know. But I didn't think it was something the average mage would have lying around.

"Magic is about knowledge as much as power. It may be that the mage knew something that our friend from the market did not." He looked at Pritkin. "And that I do not."

He didn't ask for help, but he didn't have to. Pritkin was already bent over the desk, examining the book, his legendary curiosity getting the better even of his suspicious nature. A finger traced the intricate designs in the cover.

"This is fey work," he told me. "But old. It's not in any of the styles currently in use by the major houses. But you can see bits of them here and there, such as the shape of this leaf, like those on the Alorestri royal seal. Or that curlicue, like one the Svarestri use on their elite armor. And that flourish was designed after the shape of the Eirental, one of the main rivers that flows through the south. It's the one House Veyris has above their—"

"But it is fey," Adra broke in. "You are sure?"

Pritkin looked up. "Yes. I don't need a title to tell me that."

"No, you wouldn't, would you?"

"So maybe that was why a fey could break it?" I asked,

because the two men were sparking off of each other again.

Pritkin looked back at me and nodded. "And these stones—they are in the form of a faerie ring, a common pattern used to build a ward around an area to keep something inside safe—or in this case, to trap it."

I frowned. "So the mage knew fey magic?"

"Or was fey himself."

"But why would that matter?"

"Magic is about knowledge, Cassie," he said, repeating Adra's words. "Knowledge that the Ancient Horror didn't have."

"Yes, but—"

"Think of it like a Chinese finger trap. You've seen them before? They're common as party favors."

"The kind you stick your fingers in the ends of, and then can't pull them out?"

He nodded. "You are far more powerful than the trap, which is usually made of flimsy bamboo. But unless you know the secret—to push inward instead of the natural instinct to pull your fingers apart—it can hold you for a very long time."

"Then you're saying the demon was tricked?"

"Not . . . precisely. I can't imagine a scenario in which a mage—any mage—summoned an Ancient Horror on purpose. Even if he was mad enough to try, most of their names have been lost to time. More likely, he called it up by accident."

"A syllable off, you know," Adra agreed, taking some snuff. "It happened to me once."

"A mage summoned you by accident?" I said.

He nodded. "Well, I assume it was by accident. He seemed quite surprised." He sneezed prettily. "For a moment."

I didn't ask him to elaborate.

"But the mage in this case was lucky," Pritkin continued. "The monster he summoned had no familiarity with the kind of magic he was using."

Adra ignored the implied insult, maybe because Pritkin had actually helped out, and sat back in his chair. He looked thoughtful. "The Ancient Horrors were imprisoned millennia ago, in some cases before we encountered the fey, and thus know little about them. This one doubtless tried to escape using every means at his disposal—ones that would have worked easily against human or demonic magic—but which left the fey spells untouched."

We sat in silence for a minute, thinking—or at least I was—about the awfulness of being trapped for so long, when he had the power to escape all the time. He just hadn't known it. And then I thought of something else.

"I wonder if that's what happened to the other one?"

# Chapter Twenty-four

I shifted back into my suite at Dante's an hour later, walked out onto my balcony, stripped off my robe, and face-planted onto my nice, soft chaise.

I just stayed there for a while, breathing and feeling the sun sink into my skin. I needed to get up and get some sunscreen, or I was going to burn. But right then, I didn't care. Right then, I had bigger things to worry about.

*Pritkin looked at me, and then he licked his lips. "What . . ." He stopped for a moment, and the vein was back, I noticed, pound, pound, pounding away at his temple. He tried again. "What other one?"*

*"Uh," I said.*

*"The one she helped to slaughter yesterday at the consul's home," Adra said helpfully, because I guess there wasn't much he didn't know.*

*Pritkin looked at me some more.*

*"I didn't know it was an Ancient Horror!" I told him. "I don't even know it now!"*

*"Oh, it was," Adra put in helpfully, as the book disappeared. And in its place—*

*Goddamn, it was ugly! I'd been so terrified that I hadn't had a chance to fully take it in before, but it really was a horror. Half of its head seemed to be razor sharp teeth, like some anime villain come to life, and the slitted eyes, slitted nostrils, and misshapen, bony claws didn't help.*

*"You fought that?" Pritkin asked, staring at the model Adra had conjured up.*

*I was just glad the creature didn't have anything*

*beside it to show scale. It was bad enough as it was. If
he saw it next to a person—*

*Like that, I thought, as a tiny man appeared, look-
ing around the desk in confusion. Before stopping,
like somebody in a horror flick, and slowly, slowly,
slowly . . . looking up. Right before being impaled on
one of those huge claws.*

*Well, shit.*

*"Kulullû!" somebody screamed, accompanied by
a lot of splashing. "Kulullû! Kulullû!"*

*I jumped and looked over at the aquarium, only
to see that the water was sloshing over the sides and
tiny scuba guy had gotten a friend. I couldn't tell much
about it; just that it looked small and dark, more like
an eel than a fish. But it didn't matter.*

*I'd heard that voice before.*

*"He was in the dead vamp's head," I said, and Adra
nodded.*

*"Yes. And is one of the reasons you are not cur-
rently facing the Council. He credits you with his
survival—"*

*"What dead vamp?" Pritkin interrupted, still star-
ing at the thing on the desk.*

*"The one whose head she invaded to retrieve the
Ancient Horror, so that she and the senate could kill
it," Adra said placidly.*

Yeah, that had gone over well. Like trying to explain that
it wasn't such a terribly dangerous Ancient Horror really,
while the damned model was busily devouring its kill.
Pritkin had been . . . well, let's just say that his temper
seemed to have gotten an upgrade, too.

*"How, in the course of one. Fucking. Day—"*

*"—did you meet up with two Ancient Horrors?"
Adra finished for him. "That is what I was going
to ask."*

*"I . . . don't know," I said, looking back and forth
between the two of them. "The book I found—well, it
looked like there was a ghost in there, and I couldn't
just leave it—"*

"You could damned well just leave it!" Pritkin snarled.

"I couldn't!" I stared at him. "The shopkeeper said the mage who had trapped it was dead; it could have been stuck in there for—"

Pritkin grabbed my shoulders. "And you could have been killed! If that damned thing hadn't decided to be grateful, it could have done to you what it did out there!" He flung an arm in the direction of the burning city.

"I was just trying to help!"

"And I'm just trying to keep you alive!" he rasped. "But that's a little difficult when you insist on—"

"I can take care of myself!" I said heatedly, wishing I hadn't downplayed everything quite so much. Not that it should have mattered; he'd seen me take on worse things. "You've seen me take on worse things!"

"And I've seen you almost die to them! I can't—" Pritkin suddenly pulled me out of my chair and up against him. My face was mushed flat against his chest, his hand was on my head and gripping really hard, and overall, it was just seriously uncomfortable. But I didn't pull away, because he was shaking. He was actually really upset.

"I'm okay," I said, my voice muffled. "I'm all right."

"And you're damned well going to stay that way!"

I pulled back enough to look at him. "What does that mean?"

"It means you're Pythia, not a damned foot soldier! You shouldn't have even been there, battling that thing—"

"If she hadn't been, the senate would have lost," Adra said mildly.

"Stay out of this!" Pritkin hissed, and Adra raised a brow. He used to have trouble with that. He must be getting better with the glamourie, I thought, before Pritkin started shaking me. "Listen to me! These insane risks you've been taking have to stop, do you understand?"

My forehead wrinkled, because it wasn't like I had asked for any of this. "We're at war—"

"*This wasn't about the war! Any more than risking your neck to save me was!*"

*I stared at him.* "That wasn't about the war? Did you somehow miss the huge freaking god—"

"Who you didn't know would be there when you went after me! You had no business going after me—"

"*I beg your pardon?*"

"—like you had no business doing what you did today! Leave dangerous magical artifacts alone! Let the damned vampires fight their own battles! None of that is your job!"

"*I'm Pythia—*"

"Yes! You are! And did you see Lady Phemonoe running about, taking on monsters? She stayed in her goddamned *court!*"

Annnnnd that was about the time I got pissed, because Pritkin didn't know Lady Phemonoe. He'd met her, and clearly had respect for her, but he didn't *know* her. Any more than Rhea had seemed to.

Agnes didn't stay home and knit, or whatever the hell they thought she was doing with her time. She was a warrior—they all were—all those crazy, quirky, powerful Pythias I'd recently met, ironically enough, on the search for Pritkin. But he didn't know that, he didn't know *them*, any more than the rest of the Circle did.

They saw the parties and the receptions, the formalities and the audiences, maybe even some of the training. But they didn't see what *really* went on, because Agnes had usually left her guards behind when she shifted, and I was betting the others had done the same. That was probably why the Corpsmen thought she was in her court so much. She wasn't; she just didn't want them causing even more trouble by shooting up the timeline!

"Hey, girl, are you—oops, sorry!" Tami said, coming in the door, and probably seeing the pale moons rising over the balcony.

I raised my head. "It's okay. I needed some sun. You wanna join me?"

She brightened, and then her face fell. "I have to start

dinner, and there's some laundry on, and the accounts have to be brought up to date—"

"Serve leftovers, the hotel has a laundry, and tell Fred to do the books. That's what he used to be—an accountant."

"Is that what he told you?" She laughed. "He can't even add in his head. He had to ask me what to tip the pizza guy the other day."

"Well, maybe he was head of the accounting department or something."

She shook her head in disbelief. "He still can't add!" And then she left, I assumed to get a suit.

I got up and put on a bikini, in case anybody else popped in, fished out an old tube of sunscreen and slathered it on, and went back to slow roasting. The sun was better than a masseuse, and I gradually began to feel some of the stress of the day fall away, despite having no reason for it. Like, none at all.

*"The Ancient Horrors were locked away for thousands of years, and yet two show up in one day?" Pritkin said, finally resuming his seat.*

*"They do get loose from time to time," Adra conceded. "However, two at once is cause for concern. Particularly the second."*

*"Kulullû," the creature in the fish tank cried. It seemed to be all it could say.*

*"What do we know about it?" Pritkin asked, and Adra did the eyebrow thing again, probably because of the "we." But he didn't comment.*

*He sat back in his chair and steepled his fingers, as if he'd been watching old Sherlock Holmes movies. Only he had more of an air of Mycroft about him: pudgy, unassuming, easily overlooked. But with a devastating intellect behind the facade.*

*Not to mention that Mycroft didn't have who knew how many thousands of years of experience on his side.*

*"There is a legend," we were told, "from long before even my time—and not only among the demons. Greek, Roman, Scandinavian, and Babylonian mythology all tell a similar tale. A group of elder gods*

*and a group of younger ones fought a war for dominance, and the younger gods won."*

"The Titans and the Olympians," Pritkin said.

*The blond head inclined. "In one version of the story. The Vanir and the Æsir would be another. In any case, during this titanic struggle, if you will, both sides attempted to gain an advantage. But there were only so many gods to go around. Where was one to find extra troops?"*

"The fey," I said, because this was finally a question I could answer. "There are stories that say that's how the Dark Fey came into being: the gods tinkering with fey genetics."

*"Yes," Adra agreed. "Although not just with the dark. The one who calls himself Caedmon, for instance, the king you fought alongside yesterday, is believed to be the result of a pairing between a fey princess and one of the sky gods, although we have not been able to determine which one."*

I didn't say anything, but I was pretty sure I knew which one.

Those streaks of lightning on the painting hadn't been artistic license.

*"That was often their way," Adra continued. "The gods scattered children everywhere, then took any who showed promise into their service while discarding the rest."*

Yeah, it was something the fey had emulated, I thought, thinking of the part-fey children I'd seen in old Wales, on the search for Pritkin. Because the stories of changelings weren't just a myth. The fey took human children—mostly girls, to use as breeding stock—since human fertility was legendary in their world. And because, sometimes, those half-fey kids ended up inheriting their fathers' abilities and could be useful as frontline troops, to spare the full-fey children that their families actually valued.

But those who took after their mothers . . . well, their fate was even worse. They had been tossed back onto earth as rejects, so-called half-breeds who often looked like monsters to the human population, who

*shunned and, in some cases, hunted them. While even
those who could pass for human never really fit in.
Like Pritkin . . .*

*And then it hit me: I suddenly realized that I'd
never told him about his mother! It had been more
than two weeks since I'd found out about her, and I
hadn't told him. I'd meant to, but we never got any
time alone anymore, and it wasn't something you
brought up in front of a crowd.*

*Of course, he knew part of the story already: that
she had been a part-fey, part-human woman who
Rosier seduced, hoping for a child. Demon birth rates
were even worse than those of the fey, so he'd been
trying to have a child with human women for a while.
But the half-incubus fetuses had drained them all dry
before they could give birth, resulting in the deaths of
both mother and child. So he'd opted for a hybrid instead, hoping that fey heartiness coupled with human
fertility would finally be the winning combination.*

*And he'd been right.*

*What Pritkin hadn't known was his mother's name
or much about his true heritage. Rosier had carefully
kept that from him, wanting his son in hell with him,
not roaming about Faerie. So Pritkin had only discovered her identity right before the last, crazy battle
against Ares, and I didn't know how well his memory
was after that and a mindwipe and fifteen hundred
years! But I'd actually met her, and—God! I had so
much to tell him!*

*But Adra wasn't done.*

*He did something that caused the bloody monster
to disappear and to be replaced by a pretty Greek vase.
It was black and orange and painted with a lounging
woman on the side. She was pretty, too, in a jaded,
seen-it-all sort of way.*

"This is the goddess Tethys, as she was known to
the Greeks," he informed us. "She is shown here
alongside her fish-tailed husband, Okeanos—"

"Fish-tailed?" I asked worriedly.

*And, sure enough, as the vase rotated, here he
came. I braced myself, but he looked more like a con-*

*ventional image of a merman. Not the beautiful, ethe-
real creatures I'd seen in the coven's version of a train
station, but also not the hideous, misshapen thing
we'd fought at the consul's. Basically, just a guy with
a fish tail instead of legs.*

*It was a serious relief.*

*Adra nodded. "Our research indicates that Tethys
was among the gods who believed that the path to
victory was through sourcing additional troops from
among the supposedly lesser species. We believe her
to be directly responsible for the creation of the merpeople who still live in Faerie, for instance."*

*"Like the one who opened my book."*

*He nodded. "Exactly so. But her experiments
there did not prove powerful enough for her needs,
and the war was trending against the elder gods. She
therefore chose to . . . broaden her horizons."*

*I sat there, waiting for the punch line, but it seemed
that Pritkin already had it. Because he was back on
his feet again, his face furious. "That's absurd!"*

*Adra looked up at him blandly. "Is it?"*

*"The gods killed demonkind! They wouldn't
have—they didn't—it's absurd!"*

*"War makes strange bedfellows," Adra murmured.*

*"Wait," I said, finally catching a clue. "She married
a demon?"*

*"It would be more accurate to say that she experi-
mented with a demon," Adra qualified. "With a number of them, in fact, although some exchange of genetic
material does seem to have occurred." He glanced at
the tank, but the small creature was currently silent.*

*"She started with the Apkallu, like our friend over
there, a race inhabiting one of our water worlds, but
she did not end with them. Tethys was known as Tiamat to the Babylonians, who told stories of the many
fearsome children she birthed."*

*The scene changed again, and now it showed a
whole grouping of creatures, some so hideous that I
could hardly bear to look at them.*

*"Eleven children, from four different demonic
races, each more powerful than the last," Adra said.*

*"We believe that some of the other gods followed her
example, although it is possible that the other Ancient
Horrors could be children of the original eleven."*

*Pritkin just stared at them, looking gobsmacked.
Because yeah. Goddess + anything = demigod, didn't
it? And goddess + powerful demon lords . . . well,
what the hell was that?*

*I felt sick, suddenly, and the room seemed to close
in, until all I could see were Tiamat's little horrors on
the table.*

*"How many in all?" I finally asked, my lips numb.*

*Adra looked up, the bland face as expressionless
as always. Like the voice when he said, "Hundreds."*

"Look who I found," Tami said, breaking into my thoughts.

"And look who we found," Saffy and Vi said, pushing
Rhea through the door. She was clutching her blouse as
if she was afraid they'd rip it off her.

"I—I don't have a suit," she stammered, looking at me
for rescue.

She didn't find it. I was still back in that room, staring
at a desk full of monsters, as evidenced by the chills
flooding my arms despite the sun's heat. I wasn't in any
mood to rescue anybody.

"I have one that ought to fit you, in the top drawer of
the dresser," I told her.

"See?" Saffy said, and went to locate it. It was just a
plain red maillot, not a bikini, but Rhea looked at it like
it might have been a snake.

"Go on," Saffy said, giving her a little push toward the
bathroom. "Go change."

"I—but the children—"

"Are fine with the boys for a while," Tami said. "I already told them, this is big girl time."

"But . . . but *you* need a suit," Rhea told Saffy. "And I
don't mind if—"

"Suit?" Vi said, putting down the collapsed chaises
she'd brought in with her and starting to strip off. "Who
the hell needs one of those? You'll just get tan lines."

"Okay," Saffy said, smiling at Rhea's horrified expression. "I mean, if you want to go commando—"

Rhea stared at her blankly for a second, and then snatched the suit and fled.

Vi laughed. "I'm too much woman for her."

Saffy grinned and slapped her ass. "You're almost too much for me!"

They proceeded to lather up, and the smell of coconut butter drifted over the balcony. It smelled good. I turned over before my buns burned, and put a hat over my face because I didn't need any more freckles.

Of course, cutting out distractions was a mistake.

*"Hundreds?"* Pritkin was still on his feet. *"We have one demigod, in case you haven't noticed! The fey also have one, if your information is accurate. Perhaps my math is faulty, but is that not two? Against hundreds?"*

*"Oh, we have at least one more than that," Adra murmured. "If the rumors are true."*

*"What rumors?" I asked.*

*"Those that speak of Lady Nimue, of the fey. They say she also had a goddess for a mother." He had been tracing something on his desk blotter with a finger, but at that he looked up at me.*

*I looked back.*

*And, suddenly, everything made a lot more sense.*

*"I need to talk to Pritkin," I whispered, but Adra shook his head.*

*"I have need of him."*

*"For what?"*

*The eyebrow quirked again. "What do you think? It could be mere coincidence that two of our ancient enemies return on the same day. And if they were both like the creature you released from that book, I would tend to think so. But this Kulullû disturbs me—"*

*"Why? Because he decided to attack the consul's?" I said, wanting another answer, any other answer! We'd barely overcome one of those things; what the hell were we supposed to do against hundreds?*

*"Maybe . . . maybe he had a grudge like the first one. Maybe he just got loose—"*

*"Maybe. And maybe not. We must find out." He looked at Pritkin. "If you will accompany me?"*

And Pritkin nodded.

I stared at him, an even more horrible feeling coming over me. "What—this has nothing—you're not going anywhere!"

"It makes sense, Cassie," Pritkin said, because apparently, he was insane.

"How does this make sense? How does any of this—"

"We must investigate. If there is even a chance that our enemies are attempting the same thing that the gods once did, and looking for extra troops among the demons—"

I stared from him to Adra, who was sitting there with that same little non-expression on his fake face. "Then take someone else!"

"Jonas won't believe someone else." That was Pritkin. He pulled me off a little way, like Mircea had in his office, and why people kept doing that, I didn't know. I didn't need privacy! I was perfectly happy to say everything to Adra's face!

"Cassie," he said softly. "Try to understand. The Circle was not pleased about the bargain the demon council struck with the senate. They fear that a demon/vampire force may give the vampires an advantage over them after the war is over. In fact, they are not pleased about working with the demons at all—"

"Strange bedfellows," Adra repeated, not even trying to pretend he couldn't hear.

Pritkin shot him a purely evil glance. "—and would never trust their word on something like this."

"Then he can take another war mage, someone Jonas will believe—"

"Such as?"

"Such as anyone! Anyone else!"

"Anyone else would be virtually defenseless here. My magic works in the hells; theirs does not. Remember Caleb?"

And for a second there, I did. I'd brought Caleb with me to rescue Pritkin from his father's court, and it had worked—barely. Because as formidable of a mage as Caleb was, his magic had run out quickly in

the hells, where his body could process no more. And
even what he had brought with him had been muted,
inefficient.

And I didn't care!

I threw out an arm at Adra. "He just tried to kill
you—he did kill you!"

"And he gave you the counterspell, or I wouldn't
be here now—"

"Yes, and have you wondered why that is?" I
clung to his shoulders. "They killed you in front of
me, then decided, hey, you know what? Maybe we
could use a Pythia in the war, after all, and gave me a
counterspell they didn't think I'd be able to use! They
thought I wouldn't get to you in time; Adra even said
so! They used that particular spell because it was supposed to be foolproof! And now that I got you back
anyway—"

"Cassie—"

"—they've come up with a new way to kill you!
Somewhere far away, where I'll think it was an accident, only I won't!" I said loudly, glaring at Adra. "I
won't!"

"Cassie," Pritkin told me gently. "I promise you,
I will be fine."

And that was just so typical of the man, so infuri-
atingly, glaringly typical, that I just . . . I couldn't . . .
words, all the torrent of words jumbling around in
my head, couldn't seem to make it out of my mouth.
I stood there, speechless for a moment, still staring at
Adra. Staring hard.

He looked back for a moment, and then made a
small gesture to the fat little demon who had come in
without me even noticing. "My assistant has some
clothes and weapons for you," he told Pritkin. "If you
will follow him?"

# Chapter Twenty-five

"You look like my mother," Rhea said softly. I'd gotten up to get myself a drink at the bar cart the guys had set up for me.

"Really? I don't think I look anything like her," I said absently, and took the glass Tami held out, to get her a refill.

Tami adjusted her shades and sighed. "I could get used to this."

"You need to hire in some help," I told her. "You're not a housekeeper. Half of what you've been doing around here isn't even your job."

"Yeah, but her cookies are bitchin'," Vi said, grinning.

"I'm making snickerdoodles tonight," Tami promised.

"I bow down." And then she did, actually genuflecting.

I was glad to see them getting on so well. There'd been some tension when the coven women first arrived, which had included Tami draining the crap out of Vi and a war mage after the two started threatening each other. For a while there, I'd been worried that our little blended family was going to rip itself apart.

Fortunately, the sole war mages currently on staff were Reggie, aka Jug Ears, who was pretty laid-back for the breed, and an old guy named Stimson who didn't live in and who mostly showed up once a week or so, probably to debrief Reggie. Meanwhile, the coven girls—Saffy, Vi, and a redhead named Ferne who was off for the weekend—appeared to have been won over by Tami's cooking. That wasn't surprising; even Fred couldn't find anything to complain about there, and was frequently seen going back for seconds.

"Yeah, but who else is gonna do it?" Tami asked. "The guys make more mess than the kids, and the hotel's staff—" She shook her head in disgust.

"The old Pythian Court must have had help," I pointed out.

"Sure. I tried them. But they all have families in Britain. They don't want to come out here."

"Maybe if we sweetened the deal? At least for the tutors and such?"

She rolled her eyes; I could see them past the shades. "Cassie. Their old house *blew up*. If the Circle hadn't been paranoid and refused to allow live-in staff, they'd have gone with it. A lot of them decided they could find safer positions elsewhere."

Point. But we still needed more people. There were two dozen little girls who had to be fed, played with, listened to, nursed when sick, and taught their ABC's. There was a vastly bigger suite that needed to be cleaned, and Tami was right: the hotel's staff did the bare minimum, when the guys would even let them in here. Plus, I needed an appointment secretary like yesterday. If I didn't start seeing people soon, we were going to have them beating down the door.

War or no war, we needed staff.

"There have to be people in Vegas," I said. "There's a whole supernatural community out here. And with MAGIC out of the picture—"

"But that's just it," Tami said. "MAGIC's being rebuilt. They're mostly expecting to get their old jobs back. And the ones who aren't don't pass the Marco test."

"I know I'm going to regret this, but what's the Marco test?"

She sighed, and lifted her braids off her neck, because it was hot. And then decided to twist them up into a bun. "He used to do background checks for Mircea before he got assigned here. And I don't mean just credit checks, but real PI-type stuff. It was his job to make sure that anybody employed by the family was completely legit. I think he also checked on anyone the family was doing business with."

"But that's a good thing, right?"

She grinned ruefully. "Sure, it's a good thing. Until it

gets ramped up to an eleven on a ten-point scale 'cause he's not letting anybody suspicious near his girls. Got a traffic ticket when you were sixteen? Next! Ever late on a credit card bill? Later! Got a hangnail—"

"I'll talk to him," I promised.

She rolled her eyes again. "Good luck."

"Oh my God, we've got tequila!" Saffy said. She'd been rooting through the small bar cart, and now she pulled out a bottle that had been hiding behind the rest. She took Tami's beer glass, which I'd just filled up, away from me. "Forget that. I'm making margaritas!"

I looked at Tami, who grinned. "I'm not turning down a margarita."

"Have both," I told her.

"Now, there's an idea!" Saffy said.

"I'm gonna be putting sugar in the meatloaf again," Tami said obscurely.

I decided not to ask, and went over to the railing with my beer. I didn't want a margarita. I wanted not to think for a while.

It didn't work.

*I whirled on Adra as soon as the door closed. "If he dies—"*

*"I assure you, that will not happen."*

*There were times when I wished for Mircea's glibness of tongue, his pretty turn of phrase, his honeyed words. This wasn't one of them. "Bullshit! You already tried to kill him once—"*

*"And now you know why."*

*I stared at him in disbelief. "He isn't one of those . . . those things! Even if the rumors are true, Nimue was his great-grandmother. At most, he's a sixteenth god—"*

*"And his father was a powerful demon lord of the type Tethys and her sort targeted. They were trying to make super soldiers; they didn't go after the weak. And with the fey blood added in—"*

*"Then you admit it," I said, my body going cold. "You think Rosier accidentally re-created the gods' experiments. You think—"*

"Accidentally?" Adra's brows grew together. "Yes, that is what he claimed. But he needed power to help him hold on to that rickety throne of his. He could have gone after any of the half-breeds in Wales, hundreds, perhaps thousands of them. Instead, he chose her—"

"That's not Pritkin's fault!"

"No, it wasn't," he agreed, surprising me. "And killing the heir to one of the great thrones is no small thing. Which is why we watched and waited—until he killed one of us in a duel, showing his strength at a time when he was barely an infant to our eyes! Many wanted him dead then, and more agreed when he returned to the hells, searching for his father, determined to take the life of yet another member of council—"

"He paid for that!" My voice was breathy, even a little squeaky. I didn't care. "He was exiled, almost powerless, for a century—"

"Yes, he was exiled. To earth. Where he met the daughter of Artemis."

His eyes met mine steadily, and I stared back, feeling like I'd just been turned into a block of ice. And, suddenly, my harried, frantic, desperate thoughts slowed way, way down. Some part of me that I barely recognized, some more logical, unemotional part took over. Because if I got this wrong . . .

I didn't think it would be a good idea to get this wrong.

"The very idea of a daughter of the Great Huntress," Adra continued, "she who had hounded some of my people to near extinction—that was bad enough. But the thought of you with the scion of the incubi, whose abilities magnify power—"

"We're not a threat to you," I said, almost eerily calm.

Adra's sharp eyes narrowed. "You can generate the energy of a god between you—"

"But not hold on to it. It almost burned both of us up before I used it to help slay Ares. The gods could channel that kind of power multiple times in battle; we barely managed it once. We are not a threat."

"Perhaps," he murmured, the near colorless eyes still narrowed and thoughtful. "Perhaps not. But I admit, I acted rashly—"

"Rashly." I stared at him, but didn't see him. I was seeing Pritkin instead, suspended in midair, the light of Adra's spell limning his body, his eyes shocked and pained and terrified—

And then blank.

Just blank, as he crashed lifeless to the floor.

And, as suddenly as they'd gone, all of my emotions came flooding back. "You killed him!"

"And you brought him back. You are your mother's daughter, Cassie Palmer, but our ally. Your strength is now our strength. I would not deprive you of any part of that." He glanced at the door that Pritkin had just passed through. "Whatever form it may take."

"I hope not," I said viciously—foolishly—but at that moment, I didn't care. "I consider you an ally as well. I would hate to have to kill you!"

He smiled faintly, but for the first time, it looked genuine.

"More like her every day . . ."

"I wasn't talking about appearance," Rhea said, pulling me back to the present.

I'd been staring sightlessly over the rail, down to where the usual Vegas traffic was snarling the street, but at that I turned to look at her. "What?"

"When I said that you reminded me of my mother— I didn't mean physically. But that look, the one that says you're carrying the weight of the world on your shoulders. I've seen it before, and I—" She stopped, biting her lip. "If I can help . . ."

I hesitated, because Rhea had enough on her plate. But she was right; I didn't have anybody to talk to, not anyone who would get it. I had Pritkin back, but while he understood a lot of things, he didn't understand how it was to be Pythia. And I didn't know how to get through to him.

He'd railed at me for taking chances, yet there he was, off in who knew what kind of black hell, with a creature who had killed him the last time they met, and that was somehow perfectly all right. I was supposed to be fine with that. Because to Pritkin, his life didn't matter, only mine did, and that made me so furious that honestly—

Beer spurted everywhere, and I realized that I'd crushed the can.

"Crap!"

"I'll get some napkins," Rhea said, and rushed off to fetch them. She got me another beer, too, bless her. I preferred bottles, but they didn't fit as nicely in the little fridge under the cart. Just as well. I'd have probably sliced my hand open.

I cleaned up and we popped the tops and got to drinking. It had come as a surprise that Rhea could drink. I guess it was the British in her. Didn't they start them over there at five or six or something?

She laughed when I asked, and a little beer might have come out of her nose. "I think that's the Germans," she said, grinning.

"Ah. Good to know."

We stood there with the sun on our faces for a while, and I slowly began to feel better. Not good—I wouldn't be good until Pritkin was back in one piece. But better.

Which I guess was why I decided to unburden myself on poor Rhea. Not the part about Pritkin; I couldn't afford for anyone to know about that, not after what had just happened at the consul's. He wasn't one of those terrible things, but the senate was no more trusting than the council, so they could stay in the damned dark. It was none of their business anyway!

But other things . . . maybe she would understand those.

"It feels like nobody sees me," I blurted out. "Not like I really am."

"Sees you?"

I searched for words, because it was hard to explain. "When I started this job, people mostly saw me as either evil or a complete idiot who was going to doom us all. When in reality, I was just bumbling around, trying to figure things out and not get killed. I didn't have any train-

ing, I didn't know anything about the Pythian Court—
hell, for a while, I didn't even know there *was* one! Not to
mention that I'd landed in the middle of a war—"

"You've done a brilliant job," Rhea told me fervently.
"Absolutely brilliant—"

I shook my head at her, because Rhea had a habit of
only seeing the good in people. It was nice, but it wasn't
true. Not this time.

"I haven't, though. I've made mistakes—a lot of them.
But I thought . . . I guess I thought people would understand, that they'd realize it would take anyone time to
find her feet. But instead . . . they saw what they wanted
to see."

Rhea frowned. "They usually do."

"But that's just it—they *still* do! I thought that, eventually, everyone would figure out who they were working
with and things would calm down a little. And in some
ways, I guess they have. The Circle's old leadership was
trying to kill me, while Jonas has just been trying to manipulate the shit out of—" I caught myself, but not soon
enough. "I'm sorry," I told her, slightly appalled. "I didn't
mean—"

"Why shouldn't you have meant it?" she asked evenly.
"It's true. Everyone is always trying to manipulate the
Pythia. The Circle has merely proven particularly adept
at it."

There was some bite to that comment; I guess she and
Jonas hadn't had a chance to mend fences yet, assuming
he'd even tried. I knew he was busy, but he hadn't stepped
so much as a foot in here since he visited her—once—
while she was recuperating. And that had been partly
because he had war business to discuss with me!

But then, Rhea hadn't gone to visit him, either, so . . .
I didn't know.

"We made up recently," I told her. "Jonas said he realized that he hadn't been treating me fairly—"

"Good of him to acknowledge that."

Only the tone didn't match the words. The tone said,
"He's a bastard, and you're crazy if you ever forget it,"
which . . . fair enough. Jonas *was* kind of an old bastard,

but he was also head of the Silver Circle and one of my chief allies. And when he wasn't trying to maneuver me into being his little puppet, he was a damned good one.

It was kind of the same deal I had with Mircea. We'd been allies, then lovers, and now . . . I wasn't sure what we were now. But whatever was going on in our personal lives, we still needed each other.

Life was complicated.

Which sucked, because I wasn't. I'd grown up in a vampire's court, in the middle of constant intrigue, so you'd think I'd be better at it. And I was—sometimes—when I had to be. But I'd never learned to like it.

I didn't want to manipulate anybody. I just wanted all the people I cared about to be safe and come hang out and drink margaritas. Seriously, that was everything I wanted in life right now. Was that too much to ask?

Guess so.

I drank beer, and wondered if having a margarita on top of it would get me smashed. Considering that I hadn't eaten all day? Probably.

I sighed.

"You said that people don't really see you?" Rhea prompted, because, yeah. We'd gotten off the subject.

"No. I mean, there's one who does, but his frame of reference is a little out of date. Hopefully, he'll come around. But the rest . . ." I'd been looking at traffic again, but now I turned to look at her. "They're making *statues*, did you know? At the consul's house. These huge, sixteen-foot-tall marble things—one of which is of *me*. And I know it's just propaganda, all right? I *know* that. But—"

"But?"

"But it's not *only* propaganda. People keep expecting things of me." I thought back to what Adra had said, which had so thrown me that I hadn't even had a reply. Because he was wrong. I had my mother's abilities, but not her power, and that wasn't going to change.

I'd told him the truth about what had happened on that battlefield. Together, Pritkin and I had made one big, godlike move—and that had been it. I'd used everything I had, plus everything he'd been able to give me, to rip open a path between realities and let loose a god. Who, even drained almost dry, even basically a ghost, had still been more of a threat than me!

Ares hadn't been looking for me that night; Ares could have given a crap about me. But as soon as Apollo showed up, *he'd* been seen as a threat. And Ares had been right.

Because I wasn't my mother. But if everybody kept expecting that, and worse, if they made actual war plans based on that—well, then I *was* going to freaking doom us all, and I didn't know how to get them to see it.

I also didn't know how to explain all that to Rhea, or want to give her a burden that wasn't hers to bear. "They think I'm more than I am," I finally said.

She didn't say anything, but I saw her biting her lip again.

"It's okay," I told her. "You can say whatever you want."

She hesitated, and then came out with it in a rush. "Is it possible that it's you who doesn't see?"

"What?"

She immediately looked horrified. "I'm sorry! It—it wasn't my place—"

"It's all right. If not yours, then whose?"

But she just shook her head. "Mother used to tell me things sometimes, and I—I wanted to help her, *so much*, but I didn't know what to say—"

"You didn't need to say anything. You being there was enough."

"Was it?" She had on sunglasses, too, but hers were darker than Tami's, so I couldn't see her eyes. But her voice sounded so hopeful that I couldn't do anything but smile.

"She was your mother. I'm sure that having you there was a big help—"

"And am I a help to you?" she asked, grabbing onto my forearm, almost making me spill my drink. "Even a little?"

I looked at her in surprise. "Of course. The kids—"

"But that's not—that's a help to the *court*, yes. But an

acolyte's job is to help the *Pythia*, and I can't—" She broke off again, and even though I could see only half her face, it suddenly looked chagrined. "And here I am, laying my problems on your shoulders as well. I'm making things worse!"

"You're not making things worse," I told her. "You never—"

And then somebody started yelling.

"I'm not looking! I'm not looking! Don't freaking hex me, all right? I'm blind—I'm totally, completely blind!"

"That better not be that flimsy-ass scarf you were trying to cheat with last night," Tami said—to Fred, since that was his voice. Like it was his curses after a *bump*, which sounded like somebody running headfirst into a bedpost.

I couldn't see him, since Rhea and I had ended up behind a potted palm. But when I looked around, there he was, blindfolded and clutching his forehead. "Damn it, are you convinced now?" he demanded.

"Twenty bucks," Tami said, and Fred's scowl grew worse.

"Don't give me that! There's no kids in here!"

"But some of us have delicate sensibilities," Vi said, prompting him to laugh even while still wincing.

"You're about as sensitive as Marco," he told her, or rather the bed, because he was still facing the wrong way. He course-corrected, hands out in front of him this time, although there was nothing to run into. "Speaking of which, I need to talk to Cassie."

"She's not here," Saffy said, licking salt off the rim of her glass and grinning at me. "She took the afternoon off."

"Well, shit," Fred said. "That's great. That's just perfect!"

"Looks like you're gonna have to deal with whatever it is yourself," Tami agreed, putting a hand on my arm when I started forward.

"I can't deal with it myself, and he's already packing! The only person who can maybe do anything is Cassie, and if he's gone by the time she gets back—"

"Packing?" I said. "Who's packing?"

"Cassie?" Fred's head came up. "That you?"

"Can't you tell?" Tami asked. "I thought you guys were like bloodhounds."

"That's only some of us, and it was never my gift. All I can smell is coconut oil and booze and—hey, are those margaritas?"

"Concentrate," I said, throwing the nudists a couple of towels and going to take the blindfold off Fred.

"Thanks," he said, blinking. "The call just came through. I said he was packing, but it's more like trashing his room. The guys are downstairs with him, but I came up here because—look, I know things aren't great between you and Mircea right now, but you're still Pythia, so I thought maybe—"

"Fred, what are you saying?"

"Sorry. I'm just kinda emotional. It's weird, you know? None of us were exactly thrilled to get this assignment, but now we're almost like a family. And to just lose somebody—"

"Fred! Lose *who*?"

He took a breath. "Marco. He's been recalled, like Paulie and the others. We were told that Mircea needs him for the war and we're not getting him back."

"*What?*"

Fred nodded. "It's not fair. He's what keeps this whole group together. With him gone, I don't know who's supposed to make everybody toe the line. Because I'm telling you, it's, uh, it's, uh, um."

He trailed off, at whatever was on my face I guess, because I was momentarily speechless. And then I felt my cheeks start to burn. "You're telling me that they're taking *Marco*?"

"That's what I'm telling you."

"Oh, *hell* no."

# Chapter Twenty-six

The new senate chamber was really something, even for vamps, whose motto was go big or go bigger. The floor was brand-new and shining, with a gorgeous sunburst mosaic that covered most of the huge space. The yellows, oranges, and whites, with little flecks of gold here and there, faded to blue near the edges under a marble colonnade. The color bled upward, blurring the lines where floor met walls and walls met ceiling: first a pale cerulean, then azure, and finally cobalt. The ombre ended in midnight high overhead, on a cavernous vault where a million little stars glimmered across the sky.

Taken as a whole, it looked like the huge sun was floating in space, as if I'd shifted into the middle of the void. The illusion was so good that it left me feeling a little unsteady on my feet. I stared dizzily up at the stars for a moment, wondering how they did that. Maybe lights? Maybe tiny mirrors that caught the diffuse lighting from under the colonnade? Maybe—

Maybe I should be thinking about something else right now, I thought, because everybody was staring at me.

It looked like Batman had been wrong this time.

The latest senate meeting didn't appear to be over yet, after all.

I was suddenly grateful for the people I had backing me up these days. Like Tami, who'd forced me to eat some toast with peanut butter before I left, because I hadn't had anything but a beer all day. And Fred, who'd given me some arguments to use on Mircea instead of grabbing him by the collar—still the current favorite choice. And the girls, who'd done my hair and dressed me in the gown they'd picked out the day before, when they were raiding Augustine's.

I was pretty sure it was the one he'd meant for me, because it practically screamed "modern Pythia." It was a pale blue chiffon with a flowy skirt and gathered sleeves, but with a bodice that would have done Boudicca proud. Silver metallic strips molded to my torso, forming an armor-like creation that stood out from the soft material underneath, like I was about to go into battle and hadn't finished getting dressed yet. It was over the top, it was in your face, it was full-on goddess-y, and it had made me feel more than a little self-conscious.

Or it had, until now.

Because now, there were at least a hundred equally overdressed people staring at me from around a slab of mahogany that looked like it had taken a whole forest to build.

The huge length of dark, shiny wood was covered in papers and report folders, and a hazy, hologram-type map hovered in the air above it. The map was oversize and 3-D, with what looked like a mountain range poking upward into the air. It was also partly see-through, allowing me to note the surprise, annoyance, and—in a few cases—fear on the faces of the powerful creatures sitting around it.

Daniel-the-Ditsy vampire wasn't the only one to find the Pythian power a little disturbing.

What I found disturbing was that, once again, I hadn't been invited to an obviously important meeting. From what I could tell, every mover and shaker in the supernatural community was there—except for the covens, of course. And except for the Pythia, who had yet to attend a single discussion about the war, probably because I hadn't been told they were happening!

I don't know why I reacted the way I did. Possibly the fact that I was already pissed off about Marco. Or worried about Pritkin. Or that I was just over. It. Plenty of people in this room were fast enough to remember my existence when they wanted something, but could give a damn otherwise.

And there was only one way to fix that.

"Cas— Lady Cassandra," Mircea said. He was on his feet, as if he'd been speaking before I popped in, so he didn't rise. But he did smile at me. "What a pleasure."

"I'm sure."

I looked around for a spare seat, but didn't find one. So, I shifted one from beside the wall, where a bunch of extras were lined up. And where several guards had been standing, although they were halfway here now, looking grimly determined. Until I did a Hilde and shifted them, too—about five miles away.

"Sorry I'm late," I said, shoving the chair toward the table. It was an ornate thing of gilded wood that made a loud *screech, scratch, squaaaawk* on the pretty new mosaic. But I finally got it wedged into a too small spot between a guy in a burnoose and a woman in a business suit. "I don't have a secretary yet," I said, climbing over burnoose guy. "And my bodyguards are terrible about reminding me of appointments. What were we talking about?"

I sat down and looked around brightly.

All that had taken only a few seconds, but everyone's expressions had already shifted back to neutrality. Except for the consul, who looked like she'd been sucking on a lemon. And Caedmon, who was grinning openly. And Mircea, his dark good looks on display in a suit so finely cut that it would have made Augustine weep with envy if he wasn't already having a breakdown.

Strangely enough, Mircea had looked almost relieved for a second, when I first arrived, or maybe I'd imagined it. The expression had vanished so fast that I couldn't be sure. And I didn't have time to wonder about it, because another vamp—a woman—hit the table hard enough to cause all the papers to jump.

"Finally! Maybe we can get some answers around here!"

I didn't recognize her, but I suspected who she was, and not only because of the ebony beauty on display in a low-cut, stark white gown. But because of the broad gold necklace she wore that matched the armbands hugging her biceps and the golden net around her hair. The neck-

lace looked like something an old-fashioned knight
would have worn to protect his throat, yet it didn't quite
manage to hide the jagged red line that appeared sometimes when she moved, an ugly reminder that the lovely
head with the Nefertiti profile had once been completely
severed from her body.

Ismitta, I'd been told, had been ambushed right before the war began, presumably to get her out of the
way. Our enemies had been right to fear her: attacked
by overwhelming odds and decapitated, she had nonetheless risen up, tucked her head under her arm, and
fought her assailants to a standstill. "Badass" didn't quite
cover it.

She'd been away for a while, recuperating, but I
guessed it was all hands on deck these days. I briefly wondered why she hadn't used a glamourie on her terrible
wound. There were plenty that would have covered it
without any slipups. But then, maybe she wanted people
to see.

Maybe she wanted her enemies to see.

I felt a shiver go across my arms, which wasn't helped
when she leaned over the table, glaring at me. "Well? Did
you talk to the demons or not?"

"Demons?" It caught me off guard. "How did you
know I was talking to demons?"

Mircea swiftly cut in. "I did not expect you to be back
so soon," he said smoothly. "It was a constructive meeting, I take it?"

It took me a second, because I was having a small fit at
the thought of being spied on. But I didn't think that was
it. There was a small muscle twitching at the edge of his
jaw, the tiniest of tells that he was hoping I'd pick up
on . . . what, exactly? Some kind of bluff? How bad had
the reaction been to what had happened yesterday, anyway?

I didn't know, since I'd cut out early, but it didn't look
like it had been fun. So he'd told them I was checking
on it, probably to calm everybody down. And, in usual
Mircea fashion, he'd gotten lucky, because the demon
high council had decided to kidnap me!

I wondered why he hadn't just talked to the council

himself, but couldn't very well ask under the circumstances. I stood up, since that seemed to be what people did when they wanted to talk. And because the ones down the table wouldn't have been able to see me otherwise.

"Uh, yes. Sort of—"

"Sort of?" Possible-Ismitta asked. "What does that mean?"

"It means they're checking on it—"

"On what? What the hell is there to check on? It was either demonic or it wasn't!"

I just stood there, reflecting on the fact that four months ago, having a senior vamp yelling in my face would have had me peeing myself. Right now, it was just really annoying. And I was annoyed enough already.

"*Well?*" she demanded. "Lord Mircea assured us that you would have some answers about that thing we fought yesterday—"

"We? I don't remember you being at the fight," I said.

There was a sudden, stunned silence around the table.

"What Lady Cassandra means is—" Mircea began, but Ismitta held up a hand. There was no smile twitching at the corners of her mouth, or any other indication I could see, but she somehow gave the impression of mild amusement anyway. As if somebody's pet dog had just done a cute trick.

"No offense taken," she said condescendingly—to Mircea. Because he was the dog owner. At least as far as another first-level master was concerned.

But Mircea knew better. Specifically, he knew *me* better, and probably read something on my face. Because his eyes widened slightly, and he opened his mouth, probably to say something to calm me down.

Too late.

"It was sort of a demon to the demons," I told her flatly. "Called Kulullû. One of the Ancient Horrors, as they're known, because they terrify even the demonic peoples. They're old, they're many times more powerful than most demons, and they're usually insane. The demon high council trapped and imprisoned them millennia ago, but occasionally one gets loose and goes berserk. As I said, Adra—the head of the council—is checking on it."

I sat down.

Mircea had a strange look on his face, part amused, part horrified, and part something I couldn't name but that weirdly looked like pride. Ismitta and the rest of the table just stared at me. They appeared nonplussed rather than angry, like the cute dog had just taken a shit in the middle of the senate chamber and nobody knew what to do about it.

It didn't look like they were used to being spoken to quite that abruptly, and by a lowly human, of all things, but to give Ismitta her due, she recovered quickly. And, this time, she addressed me. "You're saying this wasn't about the war, then?"

"Adra doesn't know. That's why he's checking," I added kindly.

She stared at me some more.

She looked like she was trying to decide what to do with that—not the information so much, but the tone, which had matched hers to me almost perfectly. A master vamp addressing her like that might have been taken as a challenge, but I wasn't one. I was just Mircea's little pet Pythia, so was she supposed to respond to Mircea?

I saw her flick a glance his way, but Mircea had gotten himself under control and was just standing there, trying to look like this was all perfectly normal. He was doing a pretty good job. He appeared calm, polite, and inoffensive, which seemed to confuse her even more.

*What the hell is this?* I could almost see her wondering. *Was he trying to undermine her? Because if so, why?* They were on the same senate, even in the same clique, from what I'd heard. Ismitta's absence had deprived the consul, who had formed a cabal with her, Mircea, and Marlowe, of an important vote. So Mircea was Ismitta's ally, and not someone she'd expect to be angling for . . . what? Some kind of public showdown?

She glanced back at me, and I gave her my best blank-eyed stare back. It didn't help that Mircea was across the table from me, on the same side as her, and down a bit, so she couldn't watch us both at the same time. It seemed to be freaking her out slightly, but I didn't help her.

Because it hadn't occurred to Ismitta that she was undermining *me*. That she was essentially challenging me by speaking to me like that, something she would never have done to anyone else at this table. But I was human, and the Pythias were just tools to be used by the Circle or the senate, depending on who managed to grab us first. Not equals to be spoken to politely, or risk a challenge she might not be able to handle!

Calm down, I told myself. You're angry, but not really at her. How is this different from the way the senate has always treated you? Unless they need propaganda for their war, that is.

Annnnnd now I was mad all over again.

Mircea noticed and moved to distract me, or maybe he was just doing his job. "Did Adramelech happen to mention any reason why the creature should have come here?" he asked, and maybe it was my imagination, but his voice seemed extra polite.

A small frown appeared on Ismitta's beautiful forehead.

I shook my head. "No. But the last time one of them got loose, it trashed the Shadowland, looking for an old enemy."

I decided not to mention that "the last time" was yesterday morning. Things were tense enough in here as it was, and that wasn't all on me. It had been that way when I arrived, with little bursts of power being thrown around the table, which felt like invisible comets sailing past and sometimes colliding with my skin. They weren't attacks; it was just hard to have this much energy in one place without it spilling over.

Especially when people were agitated.

"Possibly this one was doing the same thing, and was after one of the demons assigned to the army," I added.

"Could that have been the small creature you encountered in the dead soldier's brain?" Marlowe asked, and then winced. "That sounds insane to even say," he muttered. But he looked hopeful anyway.

'Cause, yeah.

We'd all be happier if this was just some ancient vendetta.

"Possibly," I said again. "He managed to escape back into the demon world while we were battling Kulullû. But he was traumatized to the point that even Adra wasn't able to get much out of him. Just that there was a chance he was able to recognize Kulullû even in its possessed form, since they originate from the same world."

"Which could also explain why this Kulullû was hunting him," Mircea said. "It knew he could alert the council to the fact that it had escaped—"

"Escaped how?" Marlowe interjected. "And is there a chance that more of those things are on the loose? If our enemies manage to free them, they could use the resulting chaos to preoccupy the demon council—and us, if any more make it to earth—"

There was a general murmuring around the table.

"—and delay the invasion—"

"I don't know yet," I said, because I didn't. And because, until Adra found out something, there was no reason for everybody to freak out.

Especially the way master vamps tended to interpret that term.

"Adra's away right now," I continued. "Looking into it personally. As soon as he tells me anything, I'll pass it on."

Marlowe nodded and sat back against his chair, apparently satisfied. Unlike Ismitta. The frown had been growing as Marlowe and I spoke, maybe because he hadn't acted like he was speaking to an inferior. He'd asked a couple of questions and I'd answered them, something that would have been a normal enough exchange in the human world, if you ignored the subject matter. But in the vampire . . .

Well, it just didn't work like that. Humans were servants or prey, nothing more. And Ismitta had clearly had enough of everyone acting like it was perfectly fine that the family dog had been allowed a seat at the dinner table.

Especially *this* dinner table.

It suddenly occurred to me that part of the weird tension in here might be down to something besides concern over the invasion. Vamps got together all the time in small groups, and every couple of years, the leading masters in a senate's territory assembled for something called Convocation. Which, instead of diplomas and speeches, mostly involved posturing and scheming.

But nobody did *this*. Never before, until the current war, had all six senates met up and tried to talk about anything. Sure, they exchanged ambassadors at times, and discussed conflicts or the sharing of resources between two or three of them. But they didn't all come together to decide on anything, and I wasn't sure they even knew how.

A world senate sounded good in theory, but in practice . . . I wondered how it was going in practice? I didn't know. But Ismitta clearly thought I was embarrassing them all by having opinions and presuming to share them.

She hadn't been here for the last four months while the senate and I struggled to figure out where I belonged. It had been one long power play, with each of us winning part of the time. We'd finally reached a delicate sort of equilibrium, with them mostly acting like I was another master vamp, although never acknowledging that that's what they were doing, and me trying not to yell at them half as much as I wanted.

Yet they still hadn't learned anything! Or they wouldn't have commissioned a massive statue of "Goddess Cassie" and not bothered to tell me about it! Or called a meeting about the war—one I'd been fighting more than any of them—and not thought to invite me! Or let Ismitta get back to her feet with another little smile, preparing to send me out of the room.

Yeah, I thought, back on my feet, too, almost before I realized it.

Let's see how well that goes for you!

I had a chance to see her eyes widen slightly, to watch Mircea say something I couldn't hear because of the heartbeat pounding in my ears, to witness Marlowe jumping up and gesturing and the consul looking pissed. I didn't care. When vamps pushed you, you pushed back, or you were a servant forever. And I was done being a servant!

But the showdown never happened.

Because someone else was angry, too, and he was a lot more vocal about it—and a lot more insane.

# Chapter Twenty-seven

A man, or possibly a fey—it was hard to tell, since he was sitting beside Caedmon and all covered up—suddenly leaned forward and slapped the table.

"Can we get back to the point?" he snarled. "I'm telling you, invasion is impossible!"

I started slightly and then stared at him. I couldn't help it, but not because of the almost palpable anger radiating off him. But because he was wearing what looked like actual dragon hide.

This wasn't the knobby skin of legend, scarred and battle worn, but more like the liquid scales on the dress I'd bought from the coven, although these weren't metal. They looked like flakes of precious stone or fossilized feathers, in a vibrant iridescent green that shone with a prism of other colors whenever he moved: sapphire, ruby, amethyst, and opal. They were like a carpet of jewels, and were beautiful—simply beautiful.

They were also disturbing.

Because the priceless, elegant, floor-length coat with the huge bell sleeves, the kind of thing that would have been the finale piece in any designer's collection, turned into a farce above the neck. Where it was topped by what appeared to be an actual dragon's head. The hollowed-out skull formed a hood—or maybe a helmet, because it was said that nothing could penetrate dragon hide—while the snout pushed out like an extra-long bill on a baseball cap. The creature's eyes had been removed and exchanged for some sort of green stones that glowed yellow when the light hit them, flashing almost like it was still alive.

It was bizarre and freakish even among the glitterati

of the supernatural world, and would have looked ridiculous anywhere else, like an over-the-top Halloween costume. Instead, it sent a shiver up my spine, although I wasn't sure why. And then I realized why.

Dragons were the fey version of shifters, like our weres. They were called two-natured due to having both a human and a dragon form, which they switched between on a regular basis. So he was basically wearing the skin of a *person*—probably a very young person, because the skull was just big enough for his own head to fit inside.

He was wearing the skin of a dragon child, I realized, in creeping horror. And, sure, maybe it had been bought from the family of the deceased, because according to Saffy, dragonkind had very different attitudes toward dead bodies than humans did. But a *child*? Would anybody really sell their child's body? Especially if they knew that someone else was going to wear it like a trophy?

I abruptly sat back down, feeling queasy.

"Yes, thank you, Mage Talbert," Mircea said. "As we were saying before, the geography is certainly a challenge—"

"It isn't a challenge! It's impossible! Even the fey can't get in there anymore!"

I could only see the lower part of the man's face, thanks to the shadow from the snout. But the skin on his chin, underneath some grizzled stubble, looked like tanned leather, and the teeth were gray and black and broken. The face didn't go with the beautiful coat.

"It's true," Caedmon said, looking at me for some reason, maybe because I'd missed the first part of this. "My son barely escaped from a recent scouting trip alive."

"I told you he was a fool to try it," Talbert said. "Svarestri are crawling all over that region, and not small parties, neither. They've shut down all the portals, moved two whole villages out of the area—villages where I had my contacts, at that! And put those giant bloody sentries everywhere—"

"You rule the skies, do you not?" a man asked lazily, from farther down the table. "I fail to see what a mere sentry can do."

I recognized Anthony, the European consul, with his handsome, going-to-seed-and-enjoying-it face and crisp white toga. I thought it was a shame he had missed the toga party era; he'd have made a great frat boy. And then I wondered what was wrong with me.

Anthony had practically invented the thing.

"You haven't seen these sentries!" Talbert snapped, only to be brought down by a slight gesture from Caedmon.

"We've tried," the king told Anthony mildly. "On gryphons and, more recently, on dragonkind, thanks to the auspices of our new dark fey allies. But Mage Talbert is correct; the net my counterpart has thrown over his lands is virtually impenetrable. I won't risk more lives on a fool's errand."

"We'll risk the whole army if we don't know what's waiting for us," Anthony replied.

"Well, I'd like to know how you expect us to find out!" Talbert snapped.

Like me, he apparently hadn't gotten the memo on how to address his betters, although nobody seemed to be taking offense at him. Maybe because he came with Caedmon, who everybody seemed to treat with kid gloves. Or maybe because he creeped them out, too.

"I've been all over those mountains," Talbert added. "Spent half a lifetime crawling through cracks and crannies, losing toes to frostbite and almost getting myself killed, trying to see what that old bastard's doing! And I'm telling you—"

"And we appreciate your input," Mircea broke in smoothly. "We will discuss this in detail at a later time."

"A later time? *A later time?* We're out of time, man! We can't move the army until we know what's waiting on the other side of that pass, and we can't do that until—"

"Tristram," Caedmon said briefly.

Tristram shut up.

"As mentioned before," Mircea continued, after a pause, "the invasion faces several hurdles, with the second no less challenging than the first." The mountain range flickered out to be replaced by the head of a man. One with pale gray eyes, white blond hair, and a manic expression.

I suddenly sat up a little straighter in my chair.

The face wasn't all that remarkable, except that it looked like it should be snapping at the air. There was something feral about it, inhuman, but not in the way that weres were. There were a few of them here now, clustered together at the far end of the table, around a tall, dark-haired man with a handsome face and inhumanly bright blue eyes. When he moved, there was almost a lag effect sometimes, like a double exposure, as if two people changed position at once with a tiny pause in between.

I'd seen that occasionally with his kind before, which was how I'd spotted him, but the effect had never been so pronounced. I wondered if that meant that he was stronger or weaker than the others. Either way, he was a bit uncanny, although there was nothing of the beast about him. And even in his altered state, I doubted he'd look anything like *that*.

I stared at the slowly rotating head and remembered the last time I'd seen it: on a dark mage trying to recruit me in a casino parking lot to what I now knew was the Black Circle.

Unless you were talking to the covens, the Silver Circle was usually viewed as the good guys. They kept order in the supernatural community, served as its police, fought its wars, and held people, including themselves, to some kind of standard. As usual with police forces, it was a thankless task, and people frequently complained about this law or that restriction. But there was little doubt that there would have been chaos without them.

The Black Circle, on the other hand, *was* that chaos.

A group of powerful dark mages, they were the elite of the magical underworld. There were always small-time operators, planning heists or running scams, but the big jobs were almost always Black Circle ops. They probably would have been a far greater threat even than they were, but most suffered from a major addiction—to magic, which they stole to increase their abilities and to get really, really high.

And, fortunately, really, really high people don't plan too well.

Unfortunately, the leadership seemed to be in better

shape. Although how much better, nobody knew, because nobody knew much about them. On the outer edges of the Circle were groups of mages who acted almost independently, running their own criminal enterprises. They paid a percentage to their contacts on the next layer inward, who in turn provided them with tips on jobs. But they rarely knew anybody but their contact, who rarely knew anybody but his contact, and so on.

Each layer in seemed to have a better quality of mage who ran progressively bigger and better cons, as well as reaping rewards from mentoring their contacts on the outer edges. Only those who overperformed in a major way were able to move up—or inward, in this case—and get closer to the center of the organization. My father had been one of them.

He'd scammed the scammers, promising to get his ghosts to spy on the Silver Circle for them, something they'd had little success with themselves. He told them that he was creating a ghost army and needed magic to feed it—a *lot* of magic—only to take it and run when they started getting suspicious. But few people ever got close enough to try something like that, including the Silver Circle itself, which regularly busted dark mages, but had never managed to reach the core.

"This is the dark mage currently known as Jonathan," Mircea said. "Some of you have heard of him; others have not. To sum him up, he is a leading member of the Black Circle who has been assisting our enemies in the war. However, he has been a problem for much longer than the current conflict."

He looked pointedly down the table, where an elderly man rose to his feet.

He was wearing a slightly old-fashioned, dark gray, three-piece suit, nothing special, and although I couldn't see his feet, I was pretty sure he had on the same pair of scuffed brown brogues he always wore, because they were comfy and he could give a crap about fashion. The only impressive thing about him was the halo of white hair, which was the male version of the coven leader's mane I'd seen back in the witches' enclave. It wasn't floor-length, but it *was* electric, wafting about his head as if a sea anemone had decided to perch there for a moment.

He looked like an irascible professor, or maybe a slightly loony librarian.

He wasn't.

He was Jonas Marsden, acting head of the Silver Circle. And as leader of the largest and most powerful magical organization on earth, *he* got respect. It was subtle; thanks to their mental abilities, vamps didn't need to disrupt a meeting to chat. But you could tell when they were in someone else's head: their eyes got a little distant, and their faces tended to sag.

There weren't any saggers in the room right now.

"As Lord Mircea has said, the necromancer goes by Jonathan," Jonas said. "Although whether that is his true name or not is a matter of some debate, as are most other facts about him. We don't know how old he is, where he originally came from, or what training he received. We do know that we have been hunting him for over four hundred years."

And, okay, *that* got an audible reaction.

And then Marlowe made it worse.

"He's far older than that. We have it on good authority that he was alive in the twelfth century, making him at least nine hundred—"

"That's impossible! He's human!" That was Ismitta again, who'd also resumed her seat at some point, but who was now leaning across the table.

"He is using magic to extend his life," Jonas told her. "Something that occurs naturally for mages, who feed off food as ordinary humans do, but also off the magic our bodies process from the world around us. We are essentially fleshy talismans, which is why we live roughly twice as long as other humans, and some more than that, depending on how powerful they are—"

"Everybody knows that!" Ismitta interrupted, her dark eyes flashing scarlet for an instant. "But that means two hundred years, maybe a bit more. Not almost a thousand!"

"It depends on how much magic you are able to acquire," Jonas said mildly. "Jonathan wormed his way into the Dark Circle hierarchy, giving himself access to their sizable stockpiles. Considering his age, I doubt he produces any of his own magic anymore, but he has been artificially prolonging his life with huge quantities of stolen power and now lives mostly or completely off the energy it provides."

"We think that is what allows him to find magical resources that others overlook," Mircea added. "He specializes in locating magically creative individuals and bending their discoveries to the use of his Circle—and lately, to that of our enemies."

But that answer didn't seem to satisfy Ismitta—or a Russian countess I'd met once, at Mircea's main court.

She was a good distance down the table, but impossible to miss, swathed in enough white sable to send PETA into paroxysms and an acre or so of diamonds glittering on a ball gown that some unknown designer had made to look like falling snow, with constantly changing snowflake patterns on black velvet. With her mane of bright red hair and impressive bosom, she was already striking enough, but the booming voice with the thick Russian accent ensured that she drew all eyes.

"Meercha! Are you telling us dere are *hundreds* of dese ancient dark mages running about?"

She made little running man motions with her fingers inside of opera-length gloves, in case anybody had missed her point. But she needn't have worried. Another murmur ran around the table at her words, which Jonas quickly moved to dispel.

"Not hundreds. Probably not even dozens. The process of ingesting magic that is not your own is . . . dangerous."

"Dangerous how?" Ismitta demanded.

Jonas pursed his lips, and he and another mage, almost old enough to be his contemporary, exchanged a glance. They didn't seem to like being interrogated about their specialty, which was the main thing keeping the vamps from taking over the supernatural world. There was peace between the Circle and the senate at the moment, but as Pritkin had noted, that hadn't always been the case, and the mages guarded their knowledge carefully.

But I guess Jonas decided that this wasn't a state secret, because after a pause, he answered.

Or he started to.

"He sources it from us," someone said hoarsely, from the other way down the table.

I craned my neck and recognized another vamp I knew, although I hadn't seen him for a while. Louis-Cesare, a powerful member of the European Senate, had come over to fight a duel for the consul near the beginning of summer. And it looked like he hadn't left yet. Or maybe he was back—everyone else seemed to be.

He looked a little different from the last time I saw him. The thick auburn hair was the same, pulled back from his face with a subtle clip, and the strong jaw, piercing blue eyes, and aristocratic features hadn't changed. But the expression . . .

He hadn't been having a nice time when we met, but he looked worse now. Not physically, not exactly, but the handsome face was haunted. He was speaking to the table, but his gaze never left Jonathan's slowly revolving head.

"He took me," he said, his voice expressionless except for a slight crackle around the edges. "Drained me of magic, of life, brought me to the brink again and again. I died every night and was reborn every morning, only for him to do it all over again. But it was never enough."

He stopped speaking, but nobody said anything. The monotone voice, contrasted with the pain on his face, was chilling. We just sat there, for maybe thirty seconds, until he spoke again.

"My family suffered as much as I did. They became little more than a battery, struggling to source enough energy to keep me alive through the bond. But they weren't feeding me; they were feeding *him*. The only satisfaction I had was knowing that the very power that sustained him was perverting him at the same time. Humans aren't like us; they don't feed the way we do. And when one tries it . . ."

He trailed off, and something about the distance in his eyes told me that he wouldn't speak again.

But that wasn't true for someone else.

A new hand hit the table, and this time the blow was hard enough to vibrate the heavy wood all the way over here. "You find him—any of you—you keep him alive for me, you understand? I want him *alive*."

The speaker was a stunning short-haired brunette with liquid dark eyes and sensual red lips who would have been arresting anyway, but the passion in her face and voice took it to a whole other level. She was stunning, almost literally, to the point that it took me a second to recognize her. And then I slowly sank back against my seat.

She was Mircea's daughter, Dorina, with vampire fangs and the family's trademark glowing golden eyes when their power was up. But she wasn't a vampire; she was something scarier. She was dhampir.

And completely freaking nuts.

The last time we met, she'd tried to kill me. And despite the Pythian power, despite one hell of a lot of backup, despite it being right here, in this house, where that sort of thing wasn't tolerated—at least not without permission—she'd damned near succeeded.

I was beginning to understand why I hadn't been invited to this meeting.

# Chapter Twenty-eight

"Yes, quite," Jonas said, in the silence that followed. And with what, under the circumstances, was an almost eerie little chuckle. "Mixing in the blood of nonhumans can cause a bit of bother."

Everyone stared at him. Anyone else would have been in trouble, maybe even in danger, for that comment, considering the tension in the room. And the unspoken thought on everyone's minds: if such a thing could happen to Louis-Cesare, the famed dueling champion of the European Senate, it could happen to them.

And that . . . wasn't likely to go down well.

Vamps, especially old ones, got out of the habit of fear. Like Adra, they'd been so strong for so long that they began to think themselves impregnable. Untouchable. Over time, they forgot the breath-stealing, spine-tingling, horror-inducing fear that the rest of us weaker creatures have to live with on a daily basis.

Or, at least, that I had lately.

But they didn't. The apex predator wasn't used to being hunted, or to feeling that sense of dread. And when he was suddenly reminded, when a wave of that long-forgotten panic slammed into place, widening the eyes, clenching the hands, making the neck jerk with the desire to stare in all directions at once . . .

Well, most people wouldn't have taken that moment to make a joke.

Most people, but not Jonas.

Because he had a secret weapon, and it was a good one. When I'd first met him, I hadn't been sure if he was crazy, senile, or just really, really weird. But he'd gone around saying outrageous things like "let's have a coup" when talking about overthrowing the Silver Circle's formidable old leadership and installing himself as the new Lord Protector.

Even stranger, it had actually worked.

Because Jonas wasn't crazy. Or the doddering, forgetful old man that he played with the consummate ease of a Shakespearean actor whenever he thought it would help. He was sharp as a whip and one of the most powerful mages alive, not to mention the most cunning.

But I swear to God, watching him now, even I half believed the act.

And then he *kept talking*, I guess giving everyone a moment to calm down.

"For another, it can be adulterated. Magic, that is. The excess energy that some of our people sell—because they must, you know, or it builds up in their systems and can cause all sorts of trouble—is often lumped together by the purchasing agent, and can even be combined with the wild magic of the earth, the kind collected by regular old talismans or recycled from charms."

"Yes, thank you, Jonas," Mircea said.

"That is a perfectly acceptable practice, of course," Jonas added. "Since the magic in question is meant to be used for making wards and such, not for ingesting. But when these shops are raided, and the bulk magic *is* ingested, by the junkies that make up the rank and file of our dark counterpart, it can have an . . . erm . . . deleterious effect."

"Thank you, Lord Protector—"

"Oh, no trouble, no trouble at all," Jonas said, beaming at him, his anemone hair wafting about in the absence of any kind of breeze. "The result, of course, after centuries of taking who knows what kind of magic into his body, is that Jonathan is quite, quite mad. And now, it seems, he has devoted himself to helping our opponents, no doubt in return for a promise of all the magic he can ever use."

Mircea didn't interrupt him this time; I think he'd given up.

"From his perspective," Jonas added, "he is being offered virtual immortality. From ours . . . well, magic or no, the human body has its limits. Sooner or later, he *will* die, but in his madness, it is doubtful that he sees that. Meanwhile, his hunger grows every day, making him incredibly dangerous."

He looked around at us, over the thick glasses that he used as part of his act, and the blue eyes were suddenly sober. "Nine hundred years is a long time. One can absorb a great deal of knowledge in nine hundred years. And he has put it all in the hands of our enemies. He *must* be stopped."

Jonas finally sat back down.

"Yes, but is this really something we need to talk about right now?" a Mayan-looking woman asked from the middle of what looked like an explosion of feathers. "However old he may be, he's just a man—"

"A man who was behind the unfortunate events in Hong Kong last week," Mircea interrupted, causing another murmur to go around the table. "We have a positive ID, provided by the Lord Protector from one of his trusted agents, who was on the scene."

Bet I know which one, I thought grimly.

"The events also bore the hallmarks of Jonathan's MO," Mircea continued. "As I said previously, his acute sensitivity to magic has made him a sort of divining rod for magical oddities. In this case, he discovered a fey flower, known as Dragon's Claw, that, under certain conditions, can cause the attributes of one item or creature to manifest in another—"

"Meaning what?" Ismitta demanded impatiently.

"Meaning these." Mircea opened a fist, and a bunch of little metal pieces hit the tabletop with a clatter.

"And those are?"

"Spent bullets—slugs, as they're called. They were extracted from the corpses of a number of dead vampires after the Battle for Hong Kong. Dragon's Claw had been used to give the lead in the bullets the attributes of wood—"

"What?"

"—allowing them to serve the same purpose as stakes—"

*"What?"*

"—turning simple guns into vampire-killing devices capable of—"

Mircea kept talking, but he was drowned out by a sudden furor. Ancient vampires were on their feet, shouting; other people, who had been quiet until now, were busy talking over each other; and Ismitta was pounding on the table again. It was strange, because she looked like she'd be the serene and calculating type, like the consul, who matched her classic beauty but who hadn't so much as blinked. Probably because the startling news was neither to her, since she'd no doubt been informed ahead of time.

But Ismitta hadn't, and she was *pissed*.

And it looked like a lot of other people agreed with her.

There was a sudden lull in the din, and I looked up to see Ming-de, the diminutive East Asian consul, commanding attention, although not in the normal ways. She wasn't on her feet, since that might have left her peering over the tabletop, because she was tiny. And she wasn't saying anything, because she spoke only Mandarin—or pretended to, for whatever damned reason ancient vamps have for being mysterious.

It also wasn't because of her outfit, although it was gorgeous: bright yellow silk, thick and creamy and covered with embroidered dragons that gamboled about, ducking under sleeves, peering out of the thick sash around her waist, or chasing each other across her bodice. Having dealt with Augustine for a while now, that didn't surprise me, although Ming-de's magical creations were particularly lovely, with precious stones for eyes and the tiny claws on their diminutive paws. However, plenty of other people were dressed to the nines.

But nobody else had her special accessory.

The shrunken head of an unfortunate East India Company officer resided like a handle on the end of her walking stick, and it wasn't just a macabre decoration. Something had been done in the treatment stage to preserve him, and I don't mean merely the withered flesh. He could still talk, and since at some point in life he'd learned

Mandarin, he served as her translator when she wanted to say something.

Which I guess she did, because she'd just thrust the horrible device out over the table, causing everyone in the area to draw back a bit.

"Let's just assume I went through all her titles, shall we?" the little thing rasped. "We've heard them enough, God knows."

"Then get on with it," Ismitta said, looking as disgusted as we all felt.

"Don't get haughty with me," the little thing told her, eyeing her scar with his dried-up raisin eyes. "Or next time you lose your head, maybe they'll put you on a stick!"

Ming-de said something, and then whacked him on the table, like a malfunctioning remote.

He sighed. "Her Serene Highness would like you to know that the matter has been contained."

"How?" Ismitta demanded.

The small thing eyed her without favor. "How do you think? We politely asked them to stop."

*Whack.*

"We butchered everyone involved," he said spitefully. "Of course."

"Including Jonathan?"

"No," Mircea said. "Not including Jonathan."

All eyes swiveled back to him. Mircea didn't have any gruesome accessories, but he didn't need any. He was in his element, the dark gaze sharp and gleaming, the voice clear and commanding, the aura of power easily reclaiming everyone's attention.

Including that of his boss, who was sitting at his side.

That was not a normal occurrence when she was in a room. An ancient queen, burning with power and clothed in her favorite slithering pets—black ones today, their scales glittering like dark sequins—she usually held all eyes. And that was especially true lately. The new wartime senate had needed a leader, and Mircea, in his former job as her chief diplomat, had managed to convince the other five senates that it should be her.

You'd have thought that would have won him some major brownie points, but her gaze wasn't that of a proud mentor. It wasn't that of a jealous rival, either, because the consul was too good to show everything she felt, and because he wasn't one—yet. But if even I could see the way he easily commanded the room—*her* room—so could she.

I glanced around the large space, wondering if the guards I'd been promised were here or not. I'd recently made a deal with Adra for bodyguards for Mircea, the kind that even the consul couldn't see. But the problem with invisible guards is, how do you know if they're slacking off? I sure as hell hadn't seen them in action yesterday, when we were all fighting for our lives!

And she wouldn't need long.

I caught her eyes for a moment, and they narrowed slightly. She glanced around at the same areas I had, the dark gaze opaque and inscrutable. I wondered if mine and Mircea's recent breakup had given her reassurance about our combined power, or if she thought it some kind of mind game—the kind that came before an attack, perhaps?

She needed him, I reminded myself, at least for now.

And when she didn't?

I forced a neutral expression onto my face and resisted the urge to chew on my bottom lip. This was why I hated intrigue. Vamps lived for this stuff, but I always felt like I had too much to watch and not enough eyes. Tami needed staff to help with the kids, but I needed a damned spymaster, like the consul had in Marlowe. I also needed to talk to Adra again—preferably when I wasn't half-asleep and scared out of my mind.

I needed to be sure those damned guards were here.

"Not Jonathan," Mircea repeated, unaware of the drama. "He remains on the loose, which is why we need your help to locate him. We destroyed the flowers and equipped our army with shields—"

"I would damned well hope so!" someone said.

"—but there is every chance that more of those bullets exist. Even worse, it seems that they were merely a lure to bring our senators to Hong Kong on an investigation. The idea seems to have been to destroy the city and take as many of us as possible along with it."

Mircea made no indication that I could see, but Jonathan's disturbing face suddenly changed into an image of a city, sleek and modern and lying above something that looked like . . . well, that had to be a ley line vortex—a massive one. Most vortexes were tiny things, small puddles of power where a couple of lines crossed. But this one was being fed by dozens, maybe hundreds, some so large that they looked like major arteries leading into a pulsing heart of power.

I'd never seen anything like it.

The resulting sea of magical energy shone like a star, or like a supernova when the city suddenly tilted, going from horizontal to vertical like a sinking ship, upending and plowing right into the middle of it. The resulting explosion flashed bright enough to cause some of the people around the table to shield their eyes, including me. And when I looked again—

The city was gone. Just gone, without even any debris to mark where it had been. And pulsing outward from the boiling center of the vortex were rivers of magical power, thrown up by the crash and flooding the ley line system like a tsunami. One that was rapidly spreading outward—

"Oh God," someone said, loud in the silence. While we watched three of the major centers of vampire power on earth be wiped away, like sandcastles when the tide comes in. Because the Chinese, European, and the South Asian senates were situated on the ley lines, for ease of transport.

Might want to do something about that, I thought dizzily.

"As you know," Mircea said, his voice echoing in the stunned silence, "the city of Hong Kong is really two cities in one: the human and the supernatural, the latter of which exists in a phased state slightly outside this dimension, thanks to the magnificent engineering job done during the early years of her highness's reign."

Ming-de graciously inclined her head, making the tassels on her elaborate headdress swing slightly.

"This allows both cities to occupy essentially the same space at the same time, creating a truly supernatural enclave that does not have to rely on subterfuges, such as wards, to hide its existence. It can do this thanks to the enormous energy of the ley line sink that lies beneath it. However, this also left it vulnerable.

"Jonathan's plan seems to have been to knock the supernatural city out of phase, which would send it crashing into the human one with enough force to rupture the ley line sink. All that energy would then overflow its bounds and be pushed through the ley line system, destroying three of our senates and as many members of this one as he had been able to lure into his trap.

"Fortunately, he was stopped in time, by the combined efforts of two operatives, one of ours and one of the Circle's."

"*Just* in time," Jonas muttered, looking disturbed.

No shit, I thought, staring at the pulsing map and thinking of Pritkin. No wonder he hadn't been around! He was supposed to be resting, and *this* was what he got up to?

As he would say, bloody hell.

"Efforts are being made to improve security on the pillars that support the phase, along with moving the vulnerable courts," Mircea added. "But all of this is useless if we do not find Jonathan."

The image changed again to a much less disturbing one of three white pills.

"We first became aware of him in the nineteen eighties. A mage in New Orleans stumbled across a formula that caused the majority of the magic in a person's body to concentrate in a single area. He was selling it to locals who wished to appear more talented than they were in a particular skill set—to cheat on a test, or to win a fight. The pills couldn't give them more magic, but by concentrating everything they had in one area, they could make them appear much more powerful than they actually were."

"Something that would have been nice to know," a mage said nastily, from down the table. "We had people trying to pass the Corps' entrance exam, only to discover later that they were far less able than they seemed!"

Mircea ignored him.

"Jonathan, however, saw more potential in the product, realizing that vampires are magical creatures, too. We do not use magic, as the mages do, but we *are* magic. He utilized the mage's formula to essentially quarantine our power, locking it away from us by redirecting it to a single ability—such as hearing—thus leaving the vampire in question vulnerable."

"Vulnerable how?" a man in a turban demanded. Most people were still looking stunned from watching a city be vaporized, but he appeared to have recovered faster. He looked South Asian, with a handsome thirtyish face and a gold tunic draped in enough jewels to rival a prince.

Of course, maybe he was one.

"Vulnerable in that a vampire's body, without its magic, is simply . . . a corpse," Mircea said.

The vamp just looked at him.

"The kind that necromancers are able to control?"

There was an uncomfortable silence around the table, maybe because most of those present were vampires.

"And?" the prince demanded. "Necromancers have always been able to influence, even briefly control, low-level vampires. It's one reason we regulate the damned things—"

"I wasn't talking about low-level vampires," Mircea told him steadily. "Or even masters—"

"I should hope not!"

"—I was talking about us."

"Us?" The man looked confused. "What do you mean, 'us'?"

"I mean senate members. The pills—"

But that was as far as he got. Mircea broke off, because there was no point even trying to finish that sentence. If I'd thought the former uproar was something, it was nothing to this.

In a matter of minutes, the most powerful vampires on earth had learned about bullets that could mow them down as easily as hot lead could do to a human; they'd seen a city almost destroyed and three of the bastions of vampire power on earth taken out with it; and now they were being told that Jonathan had discovered a way to hijack even their own bodies?

It was pandemonium.

"You're telling us that one man is responsible for this?" the prince yelled, somehow managing to make himself heard above the din. "And that he's *still out there*? What the hell have you been *doing*?"

"Looking for him," was the bland reply. The small muscle in Mircea's jaw was jumping again, but otherwise, you'd never know he was stressed. "We next came across him in Paris, this past summer—"

"This *summer*? You lost him for *decades*?"

"He does not have the recipe for the pills," Mircea assured him. "The bokor who developed it, and who is now deceased, was savvy enough not to give it to him, afraid that he would be double-crossed in their arrangement—"

"And if he *lied*?"

"Then it would stand to reason, would it not, that Jonathan might have used it before now?"

"And how do we know he hasn't?" the prince demanded. "He could have been controlling people for decades! He could be controlling one of us now!"

Annnnnd that tore it. The fizzy comets of power that were being flung around the table were more like fists now, a couple of which sent me reeling, while the pressure in the room, maybe a couple extra atmospheres' worth, was threatening to stop my breathing. It wasn't doing anybody else any good, either.

I saw one of the mages abruptly stand up and move a step or two away from the table, to give himself room to maneuver. I saw a door blow open and additional vamps run in, guards to various senators, judging by their clothes. I saw one of the weres spontaneously change, going from a young brunette to a dark, sleekly dangerous wolf with bright yellow eyes, snarling at a table that didn't even notice her.

Because something bigger was going on.

"Explain yourself!" the princely guy told Mircea,

causing the ever-increasing tension in the room to ratchet up another few notches, although I wouldn't have said that was possible a moment ago. It felt like it had at Tony's when things were really getting serious, like being in a pressure cooker that was about to blow.

Until Mircea did the last thing that I—or anyone else, apparently—had expected.

He laughed.

# Chapter Twenty-nine

The loud, disorderly room abruptly went quiet.

Yet the laughter continued, not a chortle or a guffaw, which might have been put down to stress and would have been over in a moment. But loud, sustained, apparently genuine laughter, that came up from the belly and spilled out of Mircea's mouth, shockingly loud in the silence. Until people started glancing sideways at each other, their confused faces making it clear that they had no idea what to do with *this*.

Neither did I.

Mircea had been under a lot of stress lately—hell, we both had. That was the thing about war. It didn't wait until you were ready, or rested, or in the right frame of mind—if there was one for dealing with the kind of crap this conflict had thrown up. It just came on and on, fast and furious and unrelenting, and you had to either meet it or die.

So we'd met it, time and again, somehow. But everyone had limits, right? I knew I did; I'd felt the strain every second of this last month or so. And I knew that Mircea had, too, despite the immense power he wore like armor, as if it could shield him from all dangers.

But that doesn't work when everyone else is as powerful as you, does it?

Or more so.

"Are you in the habit of laughing at a consul, *Senator*?" the prince snapped, his voice echoing around the room.

And, suddenly, it clicked: I *did* know him. The handsome maybe prince was Parendra, consul of the South Asian Durbar, the Indian version of a senate. I'd seen him once before at an auction, the same one where I'd encountered Ming-de and her little pet, but it had been a while. I hadn't immediately recognized him, since we'd never actually spoken, but I would have now even if he hadn't said anything.

The power pouring off him was enough to lift the hair on my arms, even this far away.

"My apologies," Mircea said, still looking amused. And unafraid, despite the fact that he was probably seconds away from a formal challenge.

What the *hell*?

"Not good enough!" Parendra snarled, getting to his feet so abruptly that the heavy chair he'd been using went flying.

It crashed down, making me and half a dozen other people flinch. But not Mircea. "I thought you were joking," he said, not looking particularly concerned. "I also thought we were all equals here."

"Equal—what? Are you *mad*?" Parendra looked like he thought Mircea might genuinely be losing his mind. Marlowe apparently shared that view, because he was gripping the table edge hard enough to indent the surface around his fingers.

"No. But since it has arisen as a discussion point, let us discuss it," Mircea said calmly. "It has come to my notice that some of my orders pertaining to troop allocations have been ignored or countermanded by some of the people in this room."

"What of it? I need my people—"

"I wasn't finished yet."

It was said quietly, but the effect was electrifying. If I'd thought the room was quiet before, it was nothing to this. Vampires didn't need to breathe, but I didn't think even the humans and weres were doing so at the moment.

"Shit," I heard someone say, very quietly, but couldn't seem to turn my head to see who. It felt like I was riveted in place, wondering if I was supposed to do something, and if so, what? Because, yes, the Pythia was expected to help keep the peace between leaders in the supernatural community, but I suddenly realized that no one had ever bothered to mention how.

I suddenly realized that very clearly.

"This body voted to put me in charge of this war," Mircea continued.

"Of the *army*—"

"And is that not what is going to be fighting the war? But it can't if my orders are overridden or ignored. Or if I am treated as someone of a lesser rank than you, so that your people are constantly torn between whether to listen to my commands or yours. In battle, that can cost lives, even lead to defeat. The rest of the time, it undermines authority and eats away at morale. This must stop."

"How?" Parendra sneered. "By putting you on the level of a consul?"

"Or you on a level of a senator. It matters not to me—"

"You dare!" I thought Parendra was going to go over the table.

I think Marlowe did, too, because he was on his feet suddenly, but Mircea cut him off with a gesture that clearly said, "I don't need the help."

"Yes, I dare," Mircea said evenly. "It is either that or lead this army to destruction, and that I will not do. Once this war is over, I will resume my former rank, and be grateful to be alive to do so. But for now, and for the duration of the conflict, I rank on a level with the rest of this new senate of ours. And where the army is concerned, I rank above it.

"Or you can get yourself another general."

"You son of a *bitch*!"

Marlowe was incandescent. The dark eyes were fire, the dark curls looked like they'd had hands running through them, and the skin was dead white from fear or shock or God knows what. He looked like he would have slammed the door behind him, or possibly ripped it off its hinges and thrown it at Mircea's head, only there wasn't any door. I'd wondered why there was a colonnade inside a building, especially since it wasn't holding up the roof, and now I knew.

Each large segment between giant marble pillars was closed off by an invisible ward, creating a bunch of quiet rooms where different groups could hold discussions in private. I knew that, not because anybody had told me, since nobody was in a mood to tell me anything. But because all sound from outside had cut off as soon as I followed Mircea and Marlowe through two of the pillars.

Which, all things considered, was just as well.

"What the hell were you thinking?" Marlowe demanded, as his friend—usually—turned around.

"I was thinking that a few things needed to be made clear."

Mircea looked eerily calm, and as perfect as always, except for a lock of hair that had escaped from the tight confinement it was usually kept in. Mircea's hair was longer than modern styles permitted, at least for guys who wore Armani suits, meaning a little below shoulder length. Rather than cut it to comply with social expectations, he'd compromised by pulling it back into a discreet clip at the base of his neck.

From a distance, or even up close if you weren't paying attention, his hair looked short, since he frequently wore dark colors that the "ponytail" blended into. But not now. He pulled the clip off and tossed it aside, the tortoiseshell rattling on the stone of the floor because he hadn't bothered to put it in a pocket.

Without it, mahogany waves fell onto broad shoulders, giving him the distinct air of a barbarian prince; he just needed a circlet. Which he was entitled to, although his family had never been ones to lounge around comfy palaces, listening to music while servants peeled them a grape. Mircea looked like what he was: a scion of a line that had battled its way to power on the very disputed borders of a war zone, and then battled both in that war zone and at home to keep what they'd taken.

Wheeling and dealing with dangerous people, or strapping on a sword and going to crack open a few stubborn skulls, was bred in the bone. He just didn't usually look like it. He was kind of looking like it now, but the chief spy was too angry to notice.

"Made clear, he says!" Marlowe snarled. "If you want to make a play like that, you let me know in advance! I didn't have most of my men here. I didn't have *anything*—"

"I didn't plan this," Mircea said. "I merely—"

"Bollocks!" Marlowe snapped. "That was deliberate—"

"Yes, it was deliberate, but it wasn't planned."

And neither was Marlowe's heart attack, I thought, although it looked like one was imminent.

I glanced behind me. Getting a dressing-down from your coworker could be interpreted as weakness, but nobody could see us right now. At least I was pretty sure. The ward had darkened after we came in, enough that it looked like I'd put on shades whenever I looked outside.

Which I probably shouldn't be doing, because it wasn't helping my mood.

That break Batman had told me about had finally been called, and the room had flooded with people. We were supposed to be one big, happy family, but the divisions were only too obvious. The mages were congregated together in a huddle beside Jonas, their long leather coats wafting about as if in a gale because of the magic pouring off them. The fey—including the disturbing dragon-headed guy, were clustered around Caedmon, who for some weird reason was looking pretty upbeat. The weres were in a knot covering the transformed girl, whether trying to calm her down or to shield her while she got redressed, I wasn't sure, but that lag in their movements was extra obvious suddenly. And the vamps . . .

Well, the vamps were everywhere.

It looked like a lot of people had used the excuse the break had provided to call in their family members—all of them. The big space looked like a ballroom suddenly, one filled with high-level vamps who were way twitchier than usual, maybe because of what they'd just heard. Or because there were so many of them that their power streams kept tangling up and ricocheting off. I felt some of them buzzing across my skin even this far away.

It would be a miracle if there was no violence before this was over.

In here as well as outside, I thought, glancing at Marlowe, who was still yelling.

"—extremely ill-advised! What if he'd challenged you—which he almost damned well did! What if it went

badly and you ended up dead? What if it went badly and
*he* did? Because there was no upside here, you understand? Tell me you fucking understand that!"

I just stared. I'd never seen Marlowe this intense. He
was usually the slick charmer with the sharp brown eyes
and the ready smile, but with an edge to it. Just enough
to let you know that maybe, just maybe, there was more
to him than there seemed.

But I rarely saw that other side. I saw a man who was
charming and handsome and occasionally silly. To the
point that, as far as I'd been able to tell, being the consul's
chief spy involved telling the Pythia gruesome stories
about Tudor life, or giving her such extravagant compli-
ments that they seemed designed to make her laugh.

I wasn't laughing now, and neither was Mircea.

"It is not always possible to know the exact moment
for such a ploy," Mircea informed him tightly. "You have
to strike when the moment is right—"

"And you thought *that* was the right damned moment?"

"Yes. You weren't prepared to deal with a challenge
today, but neither was Parendra. Most of his men aren't
here, and those who are tend to the political side of things,
advisers and aides, not warriors. His second wasn't even
in attendance. He couldn't afford to risk it—"

"And if he forgot that? You know his temper! And you
were deliberately trying to humiliate him—"

"Hardly." Mircea's voice went cold. "If anything, it
was the opposite."

"Explain."

I jumped slightly and whirled around, having turned
toward Mircea during the conversation and away from
the nonexistent door. Which was how the consul had
come in without my noticing. Not that that was unusual;
she was a vampire, after all, and could move with the
same silence that they all did. But the two senators hadn't
noticed her, either, judging by their slightly appalled expressions.

Or maybe that was down to the outfit.

I'd been admiring clothes all day, because the senate
always put on a show, especially when they had guests.

But this was next-level, even for her. Because she wasn't just wearing snakes, as I'd originally thought.

She was wearing cobras.

I stumbled back a few paces to get away from the three curious, flat-headed horrors who had just detached from the living sheath covering her from breast to groin and flicked their tongues out at me. Others twined around her arms like living bracelets and climbed up her legs like the straps on gladiator sandals, only she wasn't wearing any. She'd finished the ensemble off with black snakeskin pumps so high that I didn't know how she walked in them and black pearls so lustrous and scattered so thickly through her long, dark hair, that I couldn't tell what was a jewel and what was the gleaming black eyes on another of her creatures.

Taken all together, the ensemble was stunning and eye-catching and horrifying and weirdly beautiful, just like its owner. Especially now, with her color high and her dark eyes flashing. It didn't look like she'd been warned about Mircea's little show, either.

"Of course," he said smoothly. "But perhaps Cassie should—"

"Stay," the consul snapped. "You used her as a strong-arm tactic; she has the right to know why."

"I did not," Mircea said stiffly. "I didn't know she planned to be here."

"Then you took advantage of the opportunity. Or perhaps this was your idea?"

And, suddenly, those flashing eyes were on me.

"What? I—no," I said, stumbling back a bit when one of the damned snakes lunged at me. I didn't know if they responded to their mistress's temper, but it kind of looked like it, with more and more of them peeling off to stretch deadly, snub-nosed heads in my direction.

"Then what are you doing here?"

"I'm supposed to be here! I'm Pythia—"

"Lady Phemonoe did not attend our meetings," she pointed out.

"Well, did you invite her? Because mine got lost in the mail!" I said, trying to recover. "And anyway, we weren't at war then! And this new senate of yours has every other damned head of—of anything—on it, and it didn't even exist in her time!"

I was practically babbling, but damn, it was hard to think with those things reaching, reaching, reaching—

"Shit!" I said, and shifted the closest fanged horror with no destination in mind, just "away." Which I guess my power interpreted as the other side of the senate chamber, because a tray suddenly clattered to the floor and somebody screamed. Although maybe that was down to something else.

Around here, who the hell knew?

"If your invitation was lost, as you say, then why are you here?" the consul persisted.

"I came to see Mircea!"

"About?"

I really considered telling her to go to hell. Or perhaps sending her there. And for some reason, even the thought made me feel better, because I *could* do it. I wouldn't— I wasn't that stupid—because no way would the fallout be worth it.

Besides, she'd probably enjoy it.

I turned to Mircea, since he was the one I'd come to see. "You need to stop poaching my guys," I told him. "It's becoming a problem."

"Poaching?" He actually looked confused. I guess Batman hadn't had a chance to warn him.

"You keep taking my guys," I clarified. "The masters you sent me? My bodyguards?"

Mircea finally looked like he'd caught a clue. "Yes, there has been some necessary reshuffling—"

"No, not necessary! I need my men!"

"Cassie," he said, in his patient voice. "Some of the men I sent you are experts at the kind of warfare considered antiquated on earth, but which is still practiced among the fey. I need their expertise. Marco, for instance—"

I felt my blood run cold all over again. "You are *not* taking Marco!"

Mircea blinked at me. He almost looked taken aback, maybe because I'd shouted it. "I beg your pardon?"

"You can't have him! He's mine!"

An eyebrow arched. Goddamn, he knew I hated that. "On the contrary, I believe that he is mine."

It hit like a punch to the gut, and not just because I'd come to depend on my chief bodyguard. He was scary as hell to almost everyone, a six-foot-five-inch hunk of solid muscle with terrible taste in golf shirts and awful, smelly cigars. But to the little girls of my court, he was a giant teddy bear who let them crawl all over him, who cooked them cartoon character pancakes for breakfast, and who let them paint his fingernails. And when a couple of the other guards made the mistake of laughing at Marco's new, dark blue manicure, he'd sat them down so that the delighted tots could give them a whole makeover.

But it wasn't just the kids who had benefited.

Marco had lost his daughter and wife to bandits while he was away fighting one of the Roman Empire's ceaseless wars. He'd come home, bruised and battered and hurting, only to find his farm burned to the ground and their decomposing bodies flung in a ditch. And even now, two thousand years later, he wasn't over it.

People who say that time heals all wounds have never met a vampire.

Worse still, Marco had passed through the hands of a number of masters in his long life, ones who'd liked his fighting ability and imposing stature, but who had never seen the pain eating him away inside. And who probably wouldn't have cared if they had. But then fate, and Marco's incredibly undiplomatic manner, had landed him with me, and what a change that had made! Particularly after I got my court.

Marco now had dozens of "daughters," who might not be the real thing, but who seemed to have finally eased that terrible pain. Keeping us safe—because I was in no way blind to the fact that, Pythia or no, I fit into the small-thing-that-must-be-protected category in his head—had also saved him. Marco was finally home.

And he was damned well going to stay there!

But the consul was bored now, because she didn't care about my staffing problems. "Explain," she told Mircea again.

"Parendra has been late sending the men he promised," Mircea said. "And when he does, he frequently takes them back again."

"And you cannot merely substitute others? We have more arriving every day. Why risk so much for an inconvenience?"

"It isn't an inconvenience—"

"Then what is it?"

Mircea's eyes flashed gold for a second, but he reined it in.

"Ours is a hybrid army," he said stiffly. "But that depends on a decent pairing, which we don't always have. Not every vampire can handle the idea of possession, and even fewer can learn to work with their partner in harmony. If they are constantly fighting each other, they cannot fight our enemies. But after we go through the long and sometimes very frustrating process of finding good matches, they are being jerked away. If I didn't know better, I would say that Parendra is deliberately trying to sabotage us."

"Is he?" she asked Marlowe. Because it was his job to know these things.

"If so, there's been no other indication," he said. "It could be nerves. After this place was hit a month ago, every senate has been worried about security, afraid they'll be next. And this damned mess in Hong Kong doesn't help. He may not like his best people being pulled away when he thinks he needs them most."

"He'll need them more if we lose," she said dryly.

"Yes, but they're not used to thinking as a group," Marlowe reminded her. "None of us are. Everyone's wondering what happens when this is over, what the fallout will be. They're afraid you won't want to relinquish power, that they may have to fight for it. We ask for their best to help us win; what if those best are then turned back on them?"

"That would be impossible unless the demons stayed in residence," she pointed out. "And perhaps not even then. And the demons go home when the threat is eliminated."

"Do they?" Marlowe persisted. He sounded eager, like someone who has been trying to make a point for a while, but not getting a hearing. But he had one now, and he was taking full advantage. "The other senates only know what we've told them: that the demons are on loan, and the possessions are temporary, lasting solely for the duration of the war."

"But that's true," I said. "That's the deal I made with Adra—"

"Yes, the deal *you* made," Marlowe said. "Exactly."

I frowned. "Meaning?"

"That the demon alliance is with you, not us. Adramelech is your ally; we only receive the benefit of it because you are allied with us."

I frowned some more, because I wasn't getting this. "So?"

The vamps exchanged glances.

"So, Cassie," Mircea said gently, "what if you lied?"

# Chapter Thirty

I started to protest, to tell them I hadn't, before I realized: it didn't matter. Vampires lied all the time, to humans, to each other, even to themselves. It was their favorite pastime. Of course they'd assume I'd lie if Mircea asked me to.

Of course they would.

"So what am I supposed to do?" I asked. "Get Adra to come talk to them?"

Another exchange of glances, this time surprised.

"Would he . . . do that?" Marlowe asked.

"Well, why not?"

Marlowe looked at Mircea, who licked his lips. Which, for him, in a situation like this, where he needed to control his face, was tantamount to anybody else having a freak-out. I stared at him.

"Cassie, I don't think you understand how . . . unusual . . . it is to merely . . . waltz into hell whenever you like and talk to the head of the demon high council."

"I don't waltz."

"But you do go."

"When I have to. It's not exactly my idea of a fun afternoon!"

"You misunderstand," Mircea said. "Anyone can go. The mages go to the nearest hell—the Shadowland, I believe?" I nodded. "The more powerful of them, who can protect themselves, travel there to obtain potion ingredients not often found on earth. But they do not go to see Adramelech." His lips twisted. "Or Adra, as you call him."

"They don't have reason to," I pointed out.

"They wouldn't be let in even if they did!" Marlowe exploded.

I blinked at him, because I was tired and over this and wanted to go home—with a damned assurance about Marco!

"Your point is?" I said—to Mircea, because Marlowe was looking stressed.

"That you have a relationship with these creatures that the rest of us do not and cannot duplicate. Even were you to bring them here, that would only demonstrate your power over them, that you can summon the council at will—"

"I can't summon anyone!"

"But it would look that way," Mircea told me patiently. "And thus put anything they said into question."

I pinched the bridge of my nose. "Then what are we supposed to do?"

"Nothing," the consul said. "Parendra backed down. Fortunately."

The last word had a sting in the tail.

"It was a spur-of-the-moment decision," Mircea told her, and he looked completely sincere.

Only it hadn't been. I remembered that brief flash of relief I'd seen on his face when I'd arrived. Relief he'd had no reason to feel unless he *had* planned this. Probably for the reasons he'd given Marlowe: Parendra wouldn't be expecting it, and wouldn't want to risk a confrontation in an unfamiliar court with no backup.

Vamps dueled all the time, but spur-of-the-moment stuff was for lower-level types with less to lose. When senate members threw down, it was usually after weeks if not months of preparation, with everything from intel gathering on an opponent's weak spots, to ways to make sure they couldn't cheat, to ways to try to cheat yourself, to backup plans for every possible outcome. Mircea had assumed that Parendra wouldn't risk a confrontation with exactly none of that in place, and he'd been right.

And the fact that the Pythian powers would allow cheating without anybody ever being aware didn't hurt, did it?

I narrowed my eyes at Mircea, but didn't say anything,

because I didn't owe the consul shit. I didn't owe him shit, either, especially lately, but he had me over a barrel. A big one.

And he knew it.

Our eyes locked, and I didn't need mental communication to get the message. Mircea knew Pritkin's identity, and until we came to an agreement over what to trade for that, my hands were tied. It was freaking infuriating, but sometimes, the only way to win is to fold.

Especially when you're up against a guy who had just played Parendra, Marlowe, the consul, me, and who knew how many other people in a single afternoon!

"I'll fight you over Marco," I said, and meant it.

I didn't get an answer, because Marlowe suddenly clamped a hand on Mircea's arm, his face going tight. And I turned to see Parendra headed our way, surrounded by a crowd of white-garbed attendants carrying wicked-looking spears. It appears that I'm not such a deterrent after all, I thought, my throat clenching. Or else he'd decided that he had to risk it, because that sort of humiliation could very well cost him his throne.

Why the hell had Mircea pushed it? I thought furiously. Why hadn't he taken the man aside and applied some of that famous charm? Or maybe he had; it sounded like he might have been trying for a while, and not just with Parendra. Maybe that challenge today had been to all of them, all at once, to try to shore up his position before he was forced to invade with a seriously divided army.

But if so, it seemed to have backfired.

In more ways than one. Because, while Marlowe looked like he was about to lose his lunch, Mircea was . . . calm. Too calm. He looked more annoyed than anything else, like he'd expected Parendra to be smarter than this, not like a man who was facing a duel with someone who was supposed to be a far stronger opponent.

And I wasn't the only one who noticed.

"Can you take him?" the consul demanded harshly.

"Yes."

And *shit*, I thought, because there had been no hesitation in that answer, no shred of doubt. Mircea's eyes were focused on Parendra, his target, probably trying to get a mental lock. But mine were on the consul. And she hadn't liked the speed of that answer.

Marlowe noticed, too, and his gaze met mine. For a moment, it felt like we were the only two sane ones in the bunch—and maybe we were. Because this was exactly what Rian, one of Rosier's people, had warned me about. She was old enough and had been on earth long enough to see a lot of vampires go down the road to crazy town, aka give in to the intense obsession that often overtook older vamps concerning something that had gone wrong in their lives.

Maybe that was why Marco had fit in so well in Mircea's house, I thought now: they both had had the same fixation, namely on family members who they hadn't been able to save. But while Marco had finally seemed to deal with his problem, Mircea's was growing in front of my eyes. Rian had said to watch out for signs of carelessness, of preoccupation overriding good sense, of his obsession distracting an otherwise strong intellect until he couldn't see anything else.

Like his boss glaring daggers in his direction?

*Damn it!*

Marlowe flicked his eyes at Mircea and back at me, and the implication was obvious. Could I get him out of here? And, of course, the answer was yes, but how would that help? A challenge was a challenge; it would still be there tomorrow, not to mention the hit that Mircea would take for looking like he'd fled the field.

And what was Marlowe planning to do after we left? Because if he was going to try to talk Parendra down from issuing a challenge in the first place, I'd love to know how. From what I'd seen lately, Marlowe was even less diplomatic than me!

But he was glaring daggers at me currently. And jerking his neck in Mircea's direction, like an epileptic having a seizure. And yes, I *got* it already, but—

But then it didn't matter anyway. Because something else was happening. Something that had papers swirling off the whole length of the giant table and people's gorgeous outfits flapping against their legs. Including Parendra's, causing him to look around sharply, and then to glare back at us, like he thought we were causing it.

But we weren't.

We didn't even know what was going on, at least I didn't, and it looked like the consul felt the same. She transferred her less-than-happy look to Marlowe. "What is this?" she demanded.

He didn't answer, but his face was working again, although differently this time. He was changing expressions three and four times a second in a way that would have gotten anyone else committed—or a call put in for a young priest and an old priest. But he wasn't possessed; he was mentally communicating with his men—all of them, by the look of it, at least the ones spread throughout the house and grounds.

But they didn't seem to know anything, either.

"Nothing is happening," he told us. "Not anywhere else."

"I'm more interested in what is happening in here!" the consul snapped.

And then someone told us.

*"Portal!"* The cry tore through the room just as the wind intensity jumped from that of a summer storm to a hurricane.

Someone screamed, a lot of other someones went running for the exits, and a giant black maw clawed open the air, ripping a hole through reality right in the middle of the room.

It sent a lot of people sliding across the floor or stumbling against the walls—

Including ours, when a man in a business suit skidded helplessly over the slick stone floor and into a ward that someone had erected in front of our conference room. I hadn't seen who did it, but it held, leaving him stuck there like a bug on a fly strip. He flailed around, trying to find purchase, but the ward wouldn't let him in and the wind wouldn't let him move away.

And he wasn't the only one in trouble.

One of the servants had a tray of drinks thrown back in his face. Another went staggering into the clump of weres, causing two more to spontaneously change and one of those to go for his throat, only to be pulled back at the last second by the dark-haired man. I saw the woman with all the feathers resemble a bird for more than one reason when she literally went flying, being picked up off her feet and slammed into a column. Where she stayed, splayed flat, until she managed to roll off into the relative safety of a conference room.

But most of the others weren't trying for temporary safety.

Most of the others were trying to get *out*.

"Nobody leaves!" the consul snapped at Marlowe. "Seal it off!"

He looked at her wildly for a second, but did as he was told. Everywhere, the senate's guards started pushing people back, which was easier than you might expect, because the winds weren't acting normal. They were coming out of the portal in mad gusts, but in all different directions. And then hitting the walls and circling back around from still more.

The result was people being propelled toward the doorways one minute and shoved away from them the next. Or ending up caught in the middle, like one of the servants, who had abandoned his post in an attempt to flee, only to find himself running in place when two strong gusts hit him from opposite directions. And to be flipped on his face when one cut out sooner than the other.

And then the pressure abruptly got worse.

I made a sound of pain, because it felt like someone was stabbing a knife into my eardrums, or like I was on a plane that had decided to head for the stratosphere with no warning. Mircea pulled me against him, while Marlowe started screaming instructions to his men, who had arrived in force to help with the doors, where fights had broken out between those trying to get out and those attempting to keep them in. And I still didn't know why.

"We're in this together," the consul told me viciously, I guess reading the confusion on my face. "If one of us goes, so do the rest. Best they understand that now."

"You think someone in here is to blame?" I asked.

"We're not on a ley line!" Marlowe yelled, as if in answer, although I doubted he'd heard. He was too busy listening to his men. "And we half buried this place in anti-portal charms! How are they *doing* this?"

"Someone is acting as a locus," the consul snarled. Her tone said that it was the last thing they'd ever do.

"A *what*?" I asked, yelling now, too, because the wind was *insane*.

"A spell designed to override the charms," Mircea explained. "It is possible to extend a portal's gate, elongating it to reach from a ley line into an area where you wish it to manifest, if that location is relatively nearby. However, charms can be set up to deny that and reflect it back again. After the last attack, we put a large number of them in place—"

"But a locus could override them if powerful enough," Marlowe shouted. "And if performed by someone inside the charmed space—"

"In other words, we've been betrayed," the consul spat.

But Marlowe wasn't having it. "We've received no warning from the Circle!" he yelled, one hand to his ear, trying to block out the noise so he could hear the voices in his head. "They monitor the portal system. A spike this big should have set off every alarm they had. There's no way in this world to hide that much power!"

In this world? I thought, a weird feeling coming over me. Oh, shit.

"What is it?" Mircea asked, but I didn't get a chance to answer.

Because the people who were close enough had started diving into the conference rooms for protection, and that included Parendra. Who threw the splayed-limbed guy off the front of ours, sending him tumbling into the wind, and somehow pushed inside. The ward crackled and spit around him, but it parted, and a second later he had Mircea by the collar. And was immediately knocked back into Marlowe, who had the presence of mind to hold on to him—also for about a second.

Parendra broke away with a savage gesture and rounded on the consul. Only to get caught again from behind, and Marlowe wasn't playing this time. His face was vicious and his fangs were out and completely extended. In that moment, he looked like a killer.

I stared at him.

I didn't think I'd ever be able to see the laughing charmer again.

But he somehow held on, even as Parendra struggled. I assumed that wouldn't last for long; a consul could destroy Marlowe, but he wasn't giving it his all. He was too busy staring down Marlowe's master, who was regarding him with a sneer on her lovely features.

"You said this couldn't happen again!" he snarled. "You said another attack was impossible! You assured us—"

"And you assured me that you were going to leave the bully boys at home," she said, her voice like a whip. "Yet here we are." She gestured at the small army of tunic-clad men who had taken up positions around the conference room. They were facing out, not in, and had gone to one knee, probably to help stabilize themselves in the wind. But they were holding firm; the only thing moving was the tops of the glittering spears they had simultaneously slammed against the floor.

She was right; they weren't secretaries.

"And now I know why you demanded it! To leave me open to challenge!"

"Damn it, man! That wasn't planned," Marlowe breathed, but those few words seemed to enrage Parendra. He turned on the chief spy, threw him off, and struck him across the face before anyone could intervene. Worse, it was a contemptuous, backhanded slap, the kind you'd give a slave—or a dog.

And the next second, Marlowe was face-to-face and toe-to-toe with a consul, only, judging from his expression, I wasn't sure he remembered that.

I felt my stomach fall, like gravity had just given out. Because a challenge, once given and accepted, couldn't be rescinded. And while it was at least possible that Mircea, a master mentalist, could take Parendra, I had serious doubts about Marlowe.

And it looked like Mircea agreed with me.

"Kit," he said harshly. "Step back."

Kit did not step back. And there was an expression in

his eyes that that—well, I didn't know what it was. It wasn't rage, it wasn't hysteria, and it sure as hell wasn't fear. But if he'd been looking at me like that, I'd have probably passed out.

Even Parendra looked slightly taken aback, as if he hadn't expected that response, either. Or maybe he'd suddenly remembered that he was surrounded by a consul, two senators, and a Pythia. But to give the man his due, he didn't back down.

Unfortunately, neither did Marlowe.

"Hold," the consul said quickly, and Marlowe held—on to the front of Parendra's tunic, which he'd just grabbed a fistful of.

The surprise in Parendra's eyes abruptly changed to something else.

"I see now why they call you her hound," he told Marlowe. "Be a good dog and step back, would you? Or I may have to slap you again."

And then something happened too fast for me to see, but Mircea was somehow hanging off one of Kit's arms and the consul's hand was around his other wrist—the one with a stake in it. But she wasn't looking at her heaving Child, who was, okay, yeah, absolutely going to kill Parendra if he could. She was looking at me.

"Send him out!"

I blinked at her. The whole thing had been a little quick for me. "Send him . . . where?"

"Anywhere!"

I sent him out. It was tricky without sending her and Mircea along, too, since they were still holding on to him. But I managed, more or less. The stake—a weird thing that I guess doubled as a knife, since it had a metal tip on the wooden shaft—stayed behind, quivering out of the floor where it had landed when Marlowe disappeared, in a bit of mortar between two tiles. I watched it vibrate while the three remaining vamps stared at each other in that peculiar way that meant they were mentally talking— or yelling.

For once, I didn't care. It usually annoyed the hell out of me when they did that, which was the same level of rudeness as people speaking a foreign language in front of someone who doesn't understand it. But right now? Yeah, it was fine.

What wasn't fine was this . . . whatever this was. And I didn't just mean the storm, which, if it planned to kill us, was taking its own sweet time. But it was a good reflection of our chaotic group of "allies," every one of which seemed to distrust the other, and none of whom were working together.

I was finally understanding why Mircea had felt it necessary to take that stand today. But it hadn't worked, and I frankly didn't know what the hell would. But we couldn't go into Faerie like this!

"Liar!" Parendra said suddenly, making me jump. "It's not enough to have the wartime senate under your control; you'll have our thrones, too! If you think you're going to get away with this—"

"If we were trying to get away with anything, we wouldn't be destroying our own court!" Mircea snapped.

"Is it?" the consul demanded sharply, staying on point despite the colleague raging in her face.

"No, it's only in here," Mircea said, his eyes going vague, because I guessed he was taking over Marlowe's job. "So far, there are no portals opening anywhere else."

"If they send through a bomb, they don't need to be anywhere else," I pointed out.

"A bomb would be caught by our wards."

"The same ones that were supposed to prevent the opening of portals?"

Mircea cursed and made a sudden move toward the consul, I suppose so I could shift us all out, but Parendra pushed between them. "You bring us here to destroy us, and now you think to leave? You'll die along with us!"

"I'm not doing this!" the consul snapped. "My people are not doing this!"

*"Liar!"*

"Would you two shut up!" I yelled, and they both turned to stare at me. Which would normally have been terrifying, only my terror quotient had just been met by something else.

The wind died down abruptly, leaving some people smacking into the ground and formerly suspended glassware shattering against the floor. I barely noticed. I was too busy pushing my way out of the conference room and past Parendra's men in order to get a better view.

Because the portal wasn't an attack on the senate after all.

It was an attack on me.

Or, to be more precise, on my court, two members of which had just been thrown onto the stones in the middle of the room, their hair wild, their beautiful couture in tatters.

It seemed that the covens had arrived.

# Chapter Thirty-one

The portal had let out at one end of the conference table, and I was standing at the other. The gleaming surface, now unimpeded by paperwork, was reflecting back the stars overhead, the staring faces of the people who had taken refuge underneath and were starting to emerge, and a bunch of wild-haired figures who'd just stepped out of the portal's great maw. It was still churning away behind them, creating a swirling black and gray background that, coincidentally, also perfectly reflected my mood.

Only no. You'd need some red mixed in there for that, like the splatter covering Saffy's face. Or the red line of Rhea's still angry wound, which a glamourie had been hiding.

It had been stripped away now, leaving her looking almost like Ismitta, who was watching the tableau from beside a wall. But she wasn't saying anything. Nobody was saying anything.

Until Saffy let out what sounded like a cross between a sob and a shriek, grabbed Rhea off the floor, and they ran straight for me. A spell tore through the air after them, red and violent and angry. And then shuddered and almost stopped, before proceeding along at a far more leisurely pace.

Because my reflexes might not be as good as a vampire's, but they're not complete shit, either.

My slow time spell turned the slash of crimson into an elongated line that Saffy easily dodged, and the girls reached me a moment later. There hadn't been another blast, although there'd been time. And the shooter had plenty of backup. A large group of dark-clad women had left the portal and arrayed themselves along the far side of the room, but there was no doubt who the leader was. A middle-aged witch with a half-gray, half-red mane of hair stepped forward at the same time that a group of Marlowe's men ran in.

And ended up being thrown against the wall by a spell that also held them there, squirming and fighting, but going nowhere.

"Our quarrel is not with you," the woman told them. "But interfere again and we will defend ourselves!"

"What is the meaning of this?" Jonas demanded. He was on the opposite side of the room from the squirming men, but closer to what looked like a coven out of Macbeth. Like the war mages, their clothes moved about on their own from the power spilling off them. The same power that wafted their mostly long hair around their faces. There was a variety of skin tones, but the same expression.

It wasn't a nice one.

And then Rhea gasped out a warning to her father. "No! They want you to interfere!"

"That's what this is all about," Saffy agreed, staring at the red-haired woman with hate. "They goaded Rhea into challenging and then—"

"You challenged?" I asked, and saw Rhea's eyes fall. "Why?"

"They were talking about you—saying terrible things!" Saffy said. "They want to provoke a war, but not to start it. They want—"

She suddenly choked and went dumb, probably from some kind of gag spell. And I guess it was a good one, because she couldn't seem to break it. It infuriated her to the point that her mouth was writhing around, probably screaming, but nothing was coming out. Rhea looked up at me, equally mute, but her eyes were eloquent—and furious.

So much for sending her along as a peacekeeper, I thought. I'd forgotten that Rhea had a bit of a split personality, probably from years of having to bite her tongue at the Pythian Court. She seemed so meek most of the time that I forgot how quickly she could turn fierce if someone she cared about was attacked.

And someone had used that.

"Your acolyte challenged on your behalf. Do you accept?" the redhead demanded, her voice ringing about the chamber.

And, suddenly, everybody was back, all those who had managed to get past the blockade at the doors, and who had taken refuge in the conference rooms. Vamps love nothing better than a challenge, and the meeting had been long and, by their standards, awfully dull. Some blood would spice things up nicely.

And if it happened to come from Mircea's pet Pythia, so much the better.

Only he didn't seem to think so.

"This is a violation—" he began angrily.

"Of nothing," the redhead told him. "We have no agreements with your senate to violate. And we will leave—as soon as this is done."

"You will do no such thing," Jonas snapped. "The Pythia is under the Circle's protection—"

Rhea and Saffy began gesturing desperately.

"—and she *will be* protected—"

"By the senate," Mircea finished for him, "as they have chosen to attack her here! You are right," he told the redhead, "you have no agreement with us—and therefore no guarantee of safety. You have violated—"

"Violated? But we were invited," she said, and then she laughed. "By the Lord Protector's own daughter."

That sent a murmur around the room. I guess it wasn't universally known who Rhea was outside of the covens. Well, until now.

"The Lord Protector does not have jurisdiction here," the consul said. "I do."

"Then give us the woman and we'll go," the redhead said. "But challenge has been issued and accepted. This will be fought somewhere . . . unless you choose to repudiate?" she asked me slyly.

"And if she does?" Mircea asked, before I could.

"If challenge was made without her authorization, and she is willing to state as much"—the woman's eyes slid to Jonas—"then we will take the girl instead."

And, suddenly, I and everyone else got a very good

demonstration of exactly how powerful Jonas Marsden was. Because the torrent of power that suddenly spilled off him felt like it gave me a sunburn even this far away. And the usually vague and myopic blue eyes were sharp and steady.

"I think not." It was final.

It was also welcomed. Because Saffy was right; the redhead wanted a fight, but not with me. I remembered what Zara had said yesterday. There were covens who hated the Circle, wanted a renewed war, and saw this as their chance. But there were others that did not, and there appeared to have been a quarrel going on between them, one that I'd stumbled into the middle of.

It looked like my offer to Zara had given an excuse for the covens to get together, and the war party had taken the chance to force the issue, goading Rhea into a challenge that they'd deliberately misinterpreted as coming from me.

So now either I fought or they would try to take her, Jonas would resist, and we would get World War III.

"And if the Pythia accepts?" the consul asked, apparently following this at least as well as me. "Who does she duel?"

"Why, all of us," the redhead said, faking surprise. "Rhea challenged the coven—"

"That's a lie!" The voice spoke from behind the other witches, probably because a new arrival had just come through the portal. Evelyn, I thought. I couldn't see her face past the others, but the towering height and head of steel gray curls were unmistakable. And then she pushed through the throng. "Ingaret! Have you gone mad?"

"Quite the contrary." The redhead spread her arms. "I am clearer-headed than I have ever been, and I am tired of waiting. Five hundred years we have hidden, cowering in the shadows—no more! If you don't have the guts to do what must be done, then get out of the way!"

"I won't let you do this! You can't—"

"I can and I have. Challenge was freely made—"

"To *you*. You can't expect—"

"Ah, but she was a bit careless in her wording, was she not?" She looked around at the other women, who I guessed were members of her coven. Or perhaps of several like-minded ones, because there were a lot of witches. "You all heard her. There was no mention of my name—"

"Because she didn't know it!"

"—just a challenge issued on behalf of her Pythia, whom she was there to represent, to my coven—"

"You know damned well that wasn't what she meant—"

"I don't care what she *meant*," Ingaret snapped. "I care what she *said*. And what she said—"

"I accept."

My voice hadn't been loud, but the acoustics in here were excellent. The words echoed off the walls and seemed to fill the whole space, loud as clashing cymbals; or maybe that was my ears ringing. Because I wasn't up to this. Not after shifting here, shifting two guards and Marlowe, and then slowing Ingaret's spell.

The Pythian power was inexhaustible, but it had to be processed through weak human flesh, and when my stamina gave out, so did my power.

Unlike my mother, I didn't own it, I just borrowed it, and I wasn't going to be borrowing much more today. But I couldn't afford to show that. Or to so much as glance at Mircea, whom I'd had problems with in the past and likely would in the future, but who had had a genuine teachable moment earlier. As, weirdly enough, had Rosier.

Fake it till you make it, I reminded myself, and grabbed hold of the table.

It was even bigger than I'd realized. The slab must have been six inches thick and long enough to hold a couple hundred people easily. The huge, shiny surface looked back at me, as if it were challenging me, too.

"What?" Ingaret looked more surprised than anything.

"Yes, I know," I said, as I got an assist from someone else who wasn't here, namely Augustine. Because the metallic bodice of my dress began to glow as my power rose. "That wasn't the plan, was it? You expected me to decline, forcing Jonas to fight you for his daughter's life—"

"Cassie," the man himself said, from somewhere in the darkness. I couldn't see him too well at the moment, because my dress was now shining with power. I could see it in the highly polished surface of the table, reflecting light shadows on my face and body, making me look like an angel—

Or like a Christmas tree topper, some cynical voice in my head said, because it was a little over the top.

But around here, that just made for good theater.

"Rhea is talented," I said, raising my voice to be sure that everyone heard. "But she can't take on a whole coven. So you thought that you'd have your war either way: she'd die and Jonas would retaliate, or he'd wrest her away, but you could still spin the attack and any spilt blood into propaganda to sell to the other covens. To back up the idea that you've already been circulating, that this war is just a way for the Circle to destroy you—"

"As they almost did before!" I couldn't see much, but Ingaret was clearly visible, being surrounded by the boiling heart of the portal, like she'd stepped straight out of hell.

But I knew hell a little these days, and there was nothing there that was any worse than what we made for ourselves right here on earth. In her hatred and jealousy, she'd derail the war, maybe even ensure that we lost it. She'd literally rather die than work together, and there were many who obviously agreed with her.

But there were others—a lot of others, suddenly—who did not.

It looked like Evelyn had brought friends, I thought, seeing vague shadows pushing past the other witches. But instead of lowering the danger in the room, their presence seemed to heighten it. Especially when several dozen wands were drawn, their tips glowing red.

They flashed off Ingaret's eyes and, for a second, she really did look demonic. But she wasn't. She was just a woman—a scared one, currently—because this was not going according to plan.

And it was going to go a lot less well if she and her coven lost it and started attacking people.

"Ingaret!" I yelled, snapping her attention back to me. "Enough of this! You want to duel, let's duel—"

"So be it!" she hissed, and pulled a wand.

"—after these others are evacuated. They have no part in this, and I will not have them injured." I glanced around the room, and weirdly, the same hush had fallen over it that had preceded Jonas speaking earlier. Of course it had, I thought cynically. For all their centuries of experience, the senate only really respected one thing, and that was power.

I wondered if the covens were the same.

"They can take care of themselves!" Ingaret said, a red stream flooding out of her wand. But not at me—not yet. It crawled up into the air like a bloody snake and hung there, I didn't know why. And then I did, when maybe a dozen more witches pulled their own wands, adding their strength to it.

One of them was the impressive woman from yesterday morning, at the coven's version of a train station, although she didn't look too happy to be here. And neither did some of the others. Time to make them unhappier, I thought, and gripped the table harder.

"They can't, actually," I said, pulling attention back to me. "If I have to fight all of you at once, I will not be able to precisely control the area of the effect. Not while channeling that much power." I looked at the consul. "Evacuate this place—and not just this room. Empty the house, and to be on the safe side, get everyone a good half mile away."

"A half mile!" Ingaret sneered. "You should make your lies more believable!" She looked around at her supporters, who had started glancing at each other. "She lies!"

"I wish I did," I told her sadly. "But that's the problem with being only a demigod; there are . . . restrictions. Mine have always been with control. I can channel as much power as my mother ever did—for a short time—but I can't control it nearly so well. In fact, I'm not even as good at that as Agnes was. She had such fine-tuned control; it was a beautiful thing. Like a dagger between the ribs. While I—"

I looked down at the table under my hands, where the beautiful, shiny wood had started to gray and crack and splinter. It was only a puddle now, maybe a couple of feet square; I doubted Ingaret could even see it. And if I wanted this to work, she needed to.

"I've always been more of a hammer," I told her, and *pushed*.

The effect tore down the table, giving me more than I'd expected. A lot more, I thought in surprise, watching not only the table but the gilded chairs around it spontaneously age. And while the slab of thick, dark wood grayed in an instant, fissures forming in the surface and running toward Ingaret's group like claws, it was the chairs that did me proudest. They exploded away from the table like popcorn, causing people to flinch and step back, before hitting the floor with a clatter.

I wasn't exactly sure why they were doing that; maybe some buildup of gases under the gilding as the wood decayed? But I'd take it, because more and more of Ingaret's people were looking like they were having second thoughts. And no more had joined the scarlet thread now wending its way up to the ceiling.

But nobody was leaving, either, and my power was almost spent barely halfway down the table.

"Hurry," I said breathlessly to the consul. "I'm trying to hold it back, but I don't know how long I can! I don't usually summon so much at once!"

"Begin evacuation," she told Mircea, her dark eyes on mine. "Make sure everyone gets out."

"And away," I reminded her, groaning as if trying desperately to hold my power back.

In reality I was pushing forward with everything I had left. The effect continued down the wood, slower now, but almost creepier for it. Little fingers of rot and decay—of death—crept across the mighty slab, as if reaching for the women at the end. And the chairs, formerly exploding, were now collapsing inside their golden sheaths, leaving puddles of gilt behind on the floor, like dropped robes.

Or shed skins.

"You won't look that good," I told the women, who were staring at them. "There won't be anything left of you at all, except possibly for bones. They tend to be more resilient."

"She's bluffing!" Ingaret said again. "No one can channel that much power!"

"No human," I repeated. "I'm not one." And I gave it everything I had, everything I had left, until it felt like I'd hollowed out my bones, stripped my veins, bled out. Until I would have screamed, but I didn't have the strength left, because I'd just poured it all into that last, final PUSH.

I groaned and the mighty table cracked and broke and splintered. It sounded like a hundred guns going off as the great slab cleaved straight down the middle, falling into two distinct halves that hit the ground and all but disintegrated. The remaining chairs exploded in fantastic showers of gold, like brilliant fireworks in the gloom. And Ingaret's own spell finally hit the back wall of the senate chamber and detonated, shaking the room and sending a red glow sifting through the air.

And reflecting in my eyes, or so I was told later, making me look half-angel, half-demon as I shouted: *"Run!"*

They ran.

# Chapter Thirty-two

I woke up to the feeling of somebody watching me.

I didn't open my eyes, having learned a few things in my time as Pythia, and let myself finish waking up first. This didn't feel like my room at Dante's, with the bedclothes under my hands silky rather than velvet, and it didn't smell like it, either. More of a piney sort of musk—

This was Mircea's room. I'd know that scent anywhere, as dark and subtle as the man himself. And suddenly it all came flooding back. Including a memory of me somehow walking out of the echoingly quiet senate chamber, Mircea on one side and the consul on the other. We cleared the heavy doors that swung shut behind us before I collapsed to my knees. And looked up at Mircea desperately.

"Can I pass out now?"

"Yes," he'd told me, his throat working. "Yes, you're safe now."

That was the last thing I remembered.

But it wasn't Mircea in the room with me. The scent of him was distant, muted. He'd been here, but he wasn't here now, and I wasn't a vampire. I couldn't use my nose as another pair of eyes.

So I opened the real thing and almost jumped out of my skin, because that damned dhampir was almost on top of me!

"I knew you were bluffing," she said, as I scrambled back and almost brained myself on the headboard.

Luckily, it was padded.

Unluckily, there didn't seem to be anybody else in here, and shifting was . . . God, so out. My whole body felt like a sprained muscle, weak and sore and hurting, with the very idea of accessing the Pythian power ridiculous. I was on my own.

The dark eyes flashed gold for an instant, then went back to brown again. She tilted her head to look at me, and somehow, she'd moved without my seeing her, because she was once again invading my space. Although, frankly, anything within five miles would have qualified.

But even I had to admit that the lovely face was breathtaking, especially this close: the eyes with amber light boiling just beneath the brown, her power kept on a tight leash; the thick, dark lashes that were so like her father's and didn't require so much as a hint of mascara; the red lips that were likewise natural—or had the best, most perfect lipstick I'd ever seen. The damned woman was stunning, and it pissed me off, because I knew how I probably looked. And it wasn't pretty.

I felt like I'd been on a ten-day bender on the cheap stuff, with my head pounding, my eyes gunky, and my vision blurry, or maybe that last one was down to the room. The bedrooms at the consul's house didn't have windows, for obvious reasons. And the lighting in here was even worse than it had been in the senate chamber.

A single lamp glowed on a table by the wall, just enough to highlight the crimson bedclothes and fine, dark wood furniture of the bedroom Mircea used when he was in residence. It wasn't something he made a habit of, which probably explained why the only touch of the man was a priceless Chagall on the wall, the bright golds, reds, and blues glowing softly through the gloom. Well, almost the only thing, I thought, looking back at the woman.

"What do you want?" I asked, because if she was going to kill me, I kind of thought she'd have done it already.

I didn't get an answer. The examination of my face continued, despite the fact that it couldn't have been pleasant. "Good camouflage," was the final verdict. "You could pass for completely human, except for the eyes."

"What's wrong with my eyes?"

"Nothing—for a seer."

She sat back against the footboard, finally giving me

some space, and lit up a blunt. The strange, sweet odor flooded the air around the bed, despite the fact that I hadn't given her permission to smoke. Not that she'd asked.

I sat up some more and drew the covers farther around me. It was cold in here, more so than I remembered. Considering the size of this pile and the heat outside, the consul's air-conditioning bill had to be really something.

"And what does that mean?" I finally asked, because she seemed content to sprawl there and smoke at me.

"Pale blue, eerily so, and distant, like they look right through you. Worked a trick in the senate chamber, though. You had those witches pissing themselves."

"There's no such thing as seer's eyes," I told her irritably. "They look just like everybody else's."

"Then I guess your mother did you a solid."

"I take after my father, and did you want something?" I snapped, my temper unraveling. "Because I want a bath."

A really hot one. Preferably back in my big, sauna-sized tub in Vegas. Although how I was supposed to get there, I didn't know.

"There's a change of clothes in the bathroom," Dorina told me. "Your acolyte brought them earlier."

"Acolyte?"

"Formidable old gal with a foul mouth and an attitude? I liked her." She blew smoke at me.

Hilde. Bet she's pissed, I thought darkly. God knew what kind of shit I'd just stirred up with the covens.

"There were some witches who tried to follow you out; said they knew you. They were still around, arguing with people, when she showed up." Dorina grinned past the smoke. "Might be one of the top ten dressing-downs I've ever heard in my life—possibly top five. It was a thing of beauty."

Great.

Way to make things worse, I thought, because that was probably Evelyn and company that she'd just told off, and they were the nice witches!

Or they used to be.

"The girls?" I asked hoarsely. "Are they—"

"They're fine—or they were last time I saw them. One tried to follow the covens through the portal, and had to be wrestled down by Pink Hair—"

"Other way around."

"What?"

"Saffy, the one with the pink hair, is the firebrand."

Dorina raised an eyebrow at me, in a way that eerily reminded me of her father. "Yeah, not so much. The dark-haired chick was going *off*. Her father—Marsden?" I nodded. "Yeah, he had to spell her with something to calm her down, *after* the remaining witches tackled her to the ground to keep her from taking on a whole coven. Only it didn't look like it worked so well, because she was still screaming mad when your acolyte showed up and dragged both girls off by the ear."

Holy shit.

"Don't know what happened after that," she added, grinning.

Neither did I, and I didn't want to. What the hell was wrong with Rhea, and how was I supposed to fix it? How was I supposed to fix *any* of this?

I momentarily thought about burying my head under the covers, but I doubted it would help. I knew what *would* help, but that was back home, too. I settled for sitting there miserably, cold chills climbing over my body, my head pounding and my stomach growling. And scowled at the fearsome creature of legend sitting on my bed.

"Great, thanks for telling me. And you're still here because?"

She grinned. And then flopped onto the bed like she owned the place, which, considering that she was blood, was probably fair. "God, I'm glad you're an asshole!"

"I'm not," I snapped.

"Then you're giving a really good impression, but don't take it the wrong way." She rolled her head over to look at me. "I vastly prefer assholes to the slick, smarmy, too-diplomatic-to-ever-say-one-true-thing types around here. At least with assholes, you know where you stand."

"And where do I stand with you?"

She just smiled. "I want to make sure we have an agreement."

"About what?"

"What I said in the senate chamber. Jonathan is going to poke his creepy head out, sooner or later, and I want him alive."

"Fine. Got it." I threw back the bedclothes and started to get up, only to have a deceptively small hand latch onto my arm with the speed of a striking snake and the strength of a bodybuilder.

Make that ten bodybuilders, I thought, because I struggled for a minute and went exactly nowhere. It might as well have been a statue that had latched onto me. God, I didn't need this!

"What do you *want*?"

"Assurance. Jonathan lives off magic; he's drawn to it like a fly to light. And you're the brightest spark around."

I frowned at her. "What do you mean?"

"I mean, that little show you put on in there? That was life magic. I can't feed from it, like the family does, but I've learned to recognize it when I see it."

"So?"

"So, didn't you hear them in there, droning on and on about magical types? I thought I was going to stab myself in the eye. But there is a difference. Wild magic is like electricity; you can do things with it, but you can't feed from it, or trust me, the vamps would be sucking on a ley line's teat twenty-four-seven."

I blinked but didn't reply, trying to get that image out of my head.

"But what you have, that's the good stuff. The rare stuff. The kind only found in *bodies*."

"Like the ones everyone has?"

"But everyone else doesn't have *magical* life energy, the wild magic of the world processed through the body of a mage. Regular old mages don't have enough for Jonathan anymore, and the adulterated piss the Black Circle regularly rips off does almost as much harm as good. But you . . . my God, you're the mother lode!"

I pulled away, and this time, she let me go. I stood by the side of the bed, Augustine's dress feeling ridiculously silky and inadequate, especially without the armor-like breastplate. Somebody had taken that off, and I didn't see where they'd put it, not that it mattered. It wouldn't have provided much heat anyway.

I crossed my arms and scowled at her. "What are you saying?"

"What does it sound like? He's going to come after you, sooner or later—and probably sooner."

"Why sooner?"

"Because he's getting desperate."

She scooted over to the side of the bed, causing me to step back a pace. She noticed, and for the first time, she dropped the insouciant smile. "Sorry, by the way."

"About what?"

"The whole trying-to-kill-you thing? If it helps, it wasn't me."

"I'm . . . pretty sure it was you."

The grin was back, just a flash this time. "The other me. There's two of us in here. It gets crowded sometimes."

"Uh-huh." Mircea had said something of the kind, although I hadn't understood it any better then. It sounded like she had a split personality, with the split being between a mad dog killer and a raging psychopath.

"What exactly do you want me to do?" I asked.

"Hold him for me. He'll come for you, and likely soon. He's getting desperate. He used to pop up every two or three decades, but lately, it's like he's everywhere. He was in New York a month ago, masterminding an attack on the senate's HQ, then in Paris a couple weeks after that, then in Hong Kong just a few days ago. He's probably working on another plan right now, desperate to get the gods back and gain the immortality or whatever the fuck they've offered him. But he's also running out of gas."

"And I'm the gas station."

She nodded. "Now you're getting it. He thought he hit the lottery when he took Louis-Caesar, but the power of a god is even better. The Pythian power would sustain him for, well, maybe ever. With it to draw from, he might not even need the gods."

"Then why hasn't he been after it before?" I demanded, before remembering—he had been. Before I became Pythia in full, when I was just in the running, Jonathan had found me in that parking lot.

Thankfully, so had a lot of other people. A lot of very scary people. He'd been forced to flee, and I hadn't seen him since, maybe because, once I became Pythia, I was a much less easy target. But in the street that night . . .

What had been the plan? I wondered. Kidnap me like Louis-Cesare? Wait to see if the power came to me, then drain me every day, almost to death, sucking down as much of it as possible until my body couldn't channel any more?

A shudder went through me, and Dorina saw it.

"I get it," she said, and her voice this time was softer, sweeter. And the face was just a face—lovely still, but with none of the uncanniness of a minute ago. I couldn't even see her fangs. Just dark eyes full of sympathy for another human being.

I wasn't the only one with good camouflage.

"What do you get?" I asked harshly.

"Jonathan legitimately scares even me, and I don't scare easy."

"Then why do you want him? Is the kill so important to you?"

"It's not about me. I'd gut him and be done with it, or watch you dust him to powder—nice, by the way. As long as he's dead, I wouldn't care."

"Then what—" I began, and then I got it, too. I remembered her passion after Louis-Cesare's impromptu confession, and understood.

"Yeah, we are," she said, answering my unasked question, because she was as quick as her father. She held out a hand. "He got me this. I told him I can't wear it most of the time. In battle, a ring can catch the edge of a knife, and then there goes a finger. But I wear it when I can." She shrugged. "It makes him happy."

I took a look at her ring, and then whistled. I couldn't help it. "Dear God."

She dimpled at me. The feared creature of legend *dimpled*. "Nice, huh?"

"It's gorgeous," I said honestly. Because it was. It had two stones, a huge diamond and a gorgeous cabochon sapphire that looked like it should be the eye in a pagan statue.

A really big pagan statue.

"It's called a *toi et moi* ring," she told me happily. "You and me, because of the two stones, you know?"

I nodded.

She grinned. "He was worried that I'd be disappointed that it wasn't a bigger diamond, but I like colored stones—"

Any bigger, I thought, and how would you lift your hand?

"—and diamonds are only a recent thing for weddings anyway."

"Weddings?" I looked up. "Then you're already married?"

"Yep. A couple weeks ago."

"But . . . you're not marked." Her long neck, visible under the simple V-neck top she wore, was clean and unblemished. I resisted an urge to feel my own throat, where Mircea's marks stood out clearly from the skin.

"I bit him." She saw my surprise. "He never really had a family, at least not the way he looked at it. It's a long story, but basically, he wanted to feel like he finally belonged somewhere . . ." She shrugged again.

And I felt a sudden surge of pure, unadulterated dislike. Not because of the trying-to-kill-me thing, but because of this. This . . . joy . . . radiating off her. She was utterly, blissfully happy with her relationship, and I was a horrible person, because I savagely envied her that.

You suck, I told myself.

You really, seriously suck.

And I did, I knew I did, but goddamn it! After everything I'd gone through lately, my own love life was as screwed up as ever, maybe even worse than usual. I'd broken up with Mircea, something that had absolutely been the right thing to do but that had left an ache in my heart that I couldn't deny. I missed him, more than I'd expected. And the only other man in my life—damn it!

I'd spent weeks scared out of my mind, running after Pritkin, trying to get him back from Adra's freaking spell and all the while being sure I never would. And then, once I somehow *did*, once that whole epic clusterfuck was finally over, what happened? I got one night with him and he disappeared with the guy who killed him!

Not to mention the fact that while I'd told Pritkin I loved him, he'd never said it back. Not once. And yes, he'd been busy battling crazy dark mages in supernatural Hong Kong while recovering from actually being dead for two weeks, but goddamn it!

I stared at Dorina's ring, and it was lovely, but I couldn't see myself wearing one like it. Couldn't imagine a fairy-tale ending to my story. The far more likely scenario, assuming Pritkin didn't manage to get himself killed—*again*—was that I was going to screw this up royally. And end up with nothing, nothing at all.

Of course, considering how Pythias' love lives usually went, maybe that was for the best, I thought darkly.

"Are you okay?" Dorina asked.

"Yeah." It was hoarse.

She looked concerned and went to get me a glass of water, which made it worse. I wanted to hold on to that flash of dislike, because she was prettier than me and she was happier than me and she was living proof of Mircea's ability to get women to fall head over heels for him in whatever era he happened to be in at the moment. He probably didn't even miss me.

And that was fine, okay? I didn't need him or Pritkin or big-ass flashy rings that didn't look flashy on her slender hand, just elegant. She could probably make a croker sack look elegant, I thought evilly, and then I felt bad some more.

Why was I like this? I thought, for what had to be the hundredth time.

As usual, I didn't get an answer.

I did get some water, though. "Look," Dorina said, crouching in front of me, because I'd sat back down on the bed at some point. "I get that you've had a bad day, but I need confirmation on this."

"Why? So you can tie Jonathan up with a bow and give him to your husband as a belated wedding gift?"

"Yes."

I just looked at her.

"Maybe without the bow," she conceded.

"And you think that will help?" Because Louis-Cesare hadn't struck me as the vengeful type.

Admittedly, I didn't know him very well, but he'd seemed strangely . . . normal . . . for a vampire, from what I remembered. And while it sounded crazy to say about a dueling champion, he hadn't actually seemed to like violence. I was sure he was capable of it, but the relish a lot of vamps took in their enemies' pain . . . no. Not so much.

"I think that will end it," she said viciously, and there came the baby fangs. As a hybrid between vamps and humans, I guess it only made sense that she'd have half-sized fangs. But like with everything else about her, they'd ended up cute.

Goddamn it.

"He can't get past it," she told me now, her eyes dark. "I want to help him, but I don't know how. He seems fine, and then I see it—a shadow crossing his face. And he has nightmares. Have you ever known a vampire to have nightmares?"

"Uh, no."

"Well, he does. And it's always the same thing. I don't know everything that went on there, when he was with that monster, but he'd already had some abuse in the past that—"

She broke off abruptly, her jaw clenching. And, suddenly, I wasn't seeing the beautiful woman with the gorgeous husband and the ring of the gods. I was seeing someone suffering from the same uncertainty I felt most of the time, desperately wanting to help but not knowing how. And not knowing if anything she did would be enough.

I really doubted that ripping Jonathan to shreds was going to solve Louis-Cesare's problem, but what did I know? He was a vampire, after all. Maybe it was their version of therapy. Or maybe just knowing that the son of a bitch was dead would be enough.

"I'll do what I can," I told her. "But if it's him or me—"

"Then do your worst," she agreed. "But try to get a picture."

And then she was gone, leaving me sitting on the edge of the bed, clutching my water glass and wondering if I'd imagined the feel of a soft kiss on my cheek.

# Chapter Thirty-three

I got a shower in Mircea's bathroom, although it didn't seem to warm me up any. But something else did. I'd been rummaging through the stuff Hilde had left, which included clothes, shoes, toiletries, even a new toothbrush—

And my makeup bag.

I grabbed it, my hands actually shaking in relief. And sure enough, there it was, hiding under a powder puff: a partly empty bottle of a potion called the Tears of Apollo. Which was completely empty a few seconds later.

My hand caught the edge of the sink, my body shuddering through the feeling of that substance coursing through me, like liquid power. It wasn't, but it *was* liquid stamina, designed to allow a Pythia to access more of the Pythian energy. I'd discovered just how much more on the search for Pritkin, and ever since, it had been my best friend.

It wasn't enough these days; nothing was enough.

But it was close.

And it didn't take long. In seconds, everything became easier. The shaking I'd started doing stopped. My temperature normalized. Even the hunger I'd been feeling went down to I-missed-dinner levels, instead of a burning, gnawing ache. Damn, this stuff was good!

After a few moments, I brushed my teeth, because the Tears was definitely not a taste sensation, and ran a brush through my hair. It was finally long enough to put up in a ponytail, so I did. And then pulled on a pair of jeans and a simple tee.

It was plain, without any cutesy sayings, and technically meant to be worn under another shirt, which I didn't have. There was also no jewelry in what Hilde had provided, or smart pantsuits, or casual little dresses, or anything that might work for further meetings. The implication was clear: get your ass home. Which I planned to do, just as soon as I got a debrief. And some of whatever delicious scent was wafting through the louvers on the door.

I stuck my head out. Mircea was there, tie and jacket off and shoes somewhere other than on his feet. He was putting the contents of a tray on a little table under the Chagall, and there were two place settings. Since I didn't see anybody else around, I wandered over to take a look.

Damn.

Lasagna.

Well, I *had* to stay now.

"Where are you finding cooks?" I asked. "I thought you took them all for soldiers."

"Practice soldiers," he corrected, adding a basket of breadsticks. "Although some turned out to be quite apt. Some of those decided to stay and chance their luck. I believe the consul pulled the rest of her staff out of Dante's to make up the deficiency."

He gestured at the table, and I sat down. And discovered that there was also salad, wine, and sadly thin slices of cheesecake to go along with the meal. I dug in.

Mircea joined me, to my surprise. Vamps don't have to eat, although some seemed to enjoy it anyway. He was off and on. Tonight—and it *was* night; it felt like I'd slept for hours—I guess he wanted to be sociable.

Although, for the next ten minutes, that mostly involved watching me shovel it in. And, seriously, it would have been a shame for whoever made this to end up as a soldier. He—or she—had a gift, one that stretched to homemade noodles, fresh San Marzano tomato sauce, real ricotta, plump creminis—

Damn, I was hungry!

I finally looked up, at the mopping-up-the-plate-with-bread phase, to find Mircea watching me. "What?" I asked, around a mouthful of garlicky goodness that rivaled even Tami's.

"Nothing," he said, smiling, and refilled my glass. "I enjoy watching you eat."

I didn't know how to take that, so I concentrated on the wine. It was red, of course, and dark as blood, but tasted of Tuscany: soft, mellow, and meltingly sweet, almost a dessert wine, but with a bit of a bite to it. It reminded me of the man pouring it, although Mircea was only soft and sweet when he wanted something.

But I was too mellow to even bother narrowing my eyes. I just waited for it. And pulled over the cheesecake.

Mircea did not offer me his, which was a pity, but I couldn't have held it anyway. I finally sat back with the rest of my wine and regarded him through the golden glow of a serious food haze. He knew how to mellow me out.

The bastard.

"To what do I owe this bounty?" I finally asked, because eating had made me sleepy again, and I wanted my bed.

"It was the least we could do."

I tried raising an eyebrow as Dorina had done, but both went up instead. I sighed. Mircea grinned; he seemed much more relaxed tonight for some reason.

"You may have saved the alliance this afternoon," he explained. "I do not think that most of the people there realized that you were bluffing."

"And they needed the lesson because?"

He sat back with his own wine. "It has been a struggle, getting the other senates in line," he admitted. "There's constant resistance, more than I anticipated—and I anticipated a good deal."

"Why?" I looked at him in disbelief. "Don't they *get* it? This isn't a freaking drill! The senate's been attacked—more than once—two gods have almost come back and stomped us out of existence, and now this Jonathan character nearly blew up a city! What does it take?"

"But they did not see any of that, Cassie. Well, except for the assault on this senate a month ago. An assault during which they sat by—quite literally in some cases—while we fought, not willing to risk their people in what might be a charade."

"A charade? But the gods—Apollo, *Ares*—"

"You dealt with the gods," he reminded me. "In one case, far out in the desert; and in the other, far back in time. No one saw you, at least no one whose word they would take. To many, this looks less like a war and more like a power grab on behalf of the consul."

"They can't honestly believe that!" I said, and then I thought of the covens. If they believed something similar, then their attack made a lot more sense. Maybe they weren't willing to die in a worldwide conflagration just to spite the Circle. They just didn't believe there was going to be one.

"Oh, they can," Mircea assured me. "Some suppose this to be a made-up war—or a greatly exaggerated one—meant to put the consul in power. To create a single vampire government for the first time in history, with her at its head. That is what Parendra suspects, and he is not alone."

"That's why you went through all that today," I realized. "Telling them what Jonathan has been up to. You were trying to scare them."

Mircea sat forward suddenly. "I was trying to give them some concrete examples of the seriousness of the threat we face, something they *could* independently verify. They may not believe that ancient gods are trying to return, but vampire-killing bullets and crashing cities will destroy them just as easily. They *must* face reality."

"And if they don't?"

He sat back again and drank wine. "Then I am about to invade Faerie, something that has never been successfully done, with a divided army, a shaky alliance, and a consul who is possibly planning to murder me."

He said it so matter-of-factly that it took a moment to register. "You noticed that."

He smiled slightly, his lips redder than normal from the wine. "It is becoming less subtle by the day."

"And I didn't help," I guessed. If she'd bought that little farce, then I looked powerful and like even more of a threat than before. If she didn't—the more likely scenario, considering that she'd been there when I fell on my face—then I looked weak, which meant she might not have to worry so much about my wrath if she took out Mircea.

I honestly didn't know what I was supposed to do!

"I never know what she thinks," Mircea said, agreeing with me. "No one does; it's part of the reason she's stayed in power for so long. But you helped greatly with the alliance. The consul has had an apology from Parendra for misinterpreting the situation, and I have his men under my direct control for the first time—along with those of several other holdouts."

I frowned around my fork. "But you just said he thinks this is a power grab."

"Oh, he does. That was the most grudging apology I've ever heard."

"Then why give it?"

Mircea looked at me, the dark eyes gleaming. "You, Cassie. The other consuls know you are on our side, and while some of them suspect me of manipulating you into supporting the consul's power play, they aren't sure. Pythian involvement introduces an element of doubt, and your power worries them. They had a demonstration of it the night the alliance was first signed, if you recall, and another tonight."

I stared at him, hoping I was hearing wrong. "So I need to almost die every month to keep them in line?"

The eyebrow was back, along with a slight quirk of the lips. "Once every two months should suffice."

"Gee. Thanks."

Mircea laughed and leaned over to wipe some strawberry jam off my cheek. He hesitated, and then put the finger in his mouth, licking it clean. And I felt an unexpected pulse of pure lust tear through me.

Damn it!

Just when I'd thought he was going to behave himself!

Who was I kidding? This was Mircea. That *was* behaving.

"I don't think I've ever seen anyone appreciate their food so much," he told me, as if nothing had happened.

"You ought to spend more time with Fred," I said sourly.

"I beg your pardon?"

I drank wine resentfully. "Your vampire Fred? You ought to see him over a dish of—"

I stopped, because Mircea was suddenly looking at me strangely. And then continued to do so without commenting, without moving, without even breathing, for a long moment. He looked like a film that had been paused, or a man frozen in time. It was eerie.

Especially since he wasn't one of the vamps who went out of their way to emphasize the difference between themselves and humans. Some made a point of never breathing, rarely blinking, and not bothering to turn their skin anything other than dead white. They moved with a boneless, silent grace that sent the hair ruffling at the back of your neck, because humans didn't walk like that. Some of the most extreme had fingernails they allowed to grow into long, gnarled talons, bodies that were sometimes morphed in weird ways by their master powers, and eyes that glowed inhuman colors all of the time, not just when their power was up.

Or when they were too distracted to mask it.

I studied Mircea's face, but there was none of that in evidence. I'd seen him once without the constant glamourie he wore, but he had been strangely beautiful, not hideous. Terrible, but in an awe-inspiring, otherworldly kind of way: glowing, alabaster skin; inch-long fangs; and eyes of flaming, molten lava.

They weren't lava right now. They weren't even the glowing cinnamon amber that he usually let people see when his power was rising. They were their normal brown velvet, like his skin had its usual golden sheen and his hair—still down around his shoulders—was the characteristic rich mahogany.

Yet there was something different about him.

I'd no sooner had the thought than he abruptly got up and left the table, and then the room, still without a word.

I just sat there for a moment, nonplussed.

Then I followed him.

Mircea's suite at the consul's wasn't anywhere near as large as his old rooms at MAGIC. Maybe because he had an apartment in New York and usually stayed there when he was on this coast—and considering what went on around here normally, I didn't blame him. Or maybe because the consul's sprawling court was seriously overcrowded these days, hosting a ton of senators and their retinues from around the world, all of whom thought they deserved a palace of their own.

So instead of a multi-roomed, self-contained mansion filled with servants and retainers, he had what amounted to a regular one-bedroom apartment, although it looked like he needed more space. Because the living room was full of . . . I had no idea. It looked like Augustine's shop had exploded in here.

There were gorgeous bolts of material everywhere, gleaming or glittering in the ambient lighting. There were soft furs flung over couches and couture hanging from racks. There were boxes of every shape and size piled almost as tall as me in perilous towers, some with more expensive stuff spilling out of the sides.

But none of it said "Augustine."

"Who's Claude?" I asked, checking out a little label. It was on a jungle-print dress covered in elaborate embroidered birds, toucans and macaws, one of which flew off and perched on my shoulder. It had weight like a real bird, but was only two dimensional, which is probably why it kept cocking its head at me, trying to get a better view.

Until it flew off to perch on a lampshade instead and sat there preening its sequined feathers.

Mircea looked up from rummaging in a box. "A French designer. We raided his shop recently."

I looked around. Augustine would be pleased to hear it, no doubt, but why did the senate need to steal their couture? I asked Mircea as much, and received a cocked eyebrow in return.

"We didn't steal it. We confiscated it, with proper remuneration, of course. Claude now has the distinction of being the only designer in the world to sell out a collection before it was even shown."

"That doesn't explain why you wanted it," I pointed out, although some of it was pretty impressive.

And pretty sneaky, I realized, as a beaded monkey leapt off a nearby coat and grabbed my bracelet—

And made off with it!

"Hey!" I said, staring. Because that wasn't an ordinary bracelet. "Give that back!"

But the only response was some chittering from atop a curtain rod over some fake windows and a flash of scary-looking teeth.

"That is why," Mircea told me. "Claude put too much magic into it—of the wrong kind."

"The wrong kind?"

"That is what I want to show you," he said, as I ran around, trying to catch the little thief. Which stayed just ahead of me, only occasionally pausing to look back over its shoulder with beady little eyes.

But it was paying too much attention to me, and not enough to Mircea. Who snatched it out of the air as it leapt past, going from side table to sofa. A moment later, I had my bracelet back, and Mr. Handsy had been dumped onto his jacket again, where he continued to watch me malevolently from underneath a banana leaf.

"Great for kleptomaniacs!" I said, scowling.

"It's a bit more troublesome than that," Mircea said, looking down at his desk.

He'd spread out a cloak on it, a pretty standard thing in black, with a high neck and a white satin lining. It looked like the sort of thing you'd wear to the opera, or to a costume party if you wanted to do a high-end version of Dracula. But I was guessing that it was more important than that, because Mircea was gazing at it like it was a sacred relic.

"Stay here and watch this," he told me.

"Watch what?" I asked, as he took another cloak, a ladies' one this time, and walked back into the bedroom with it.

He didn't answer, and I wasn't sure what it was in the jungle of items spread around that I was supposed to be watching. A bear with real fur and little beads for eyes watched me with distrust from a painted forest and sent three adorable cubs scrambling up a tree for protection. A school of dolphins chased each other around a dress that shimmered like sunlight on water and splashed what felt like real droplets at me as the pod raced by. Another dress boiled red and gold and black, like lava, with the "crust" on top making ever-changing patterns on the mesmerizing surface.

And then I felt something crawling up my hand.

I shook it instinctively and stumbled back, but the small creatures running up my arm didn't come off. Which was alarming, because they looked like small golden beetles. Exactly like.

Crap!

I danced around some more, but it didn't help. And now they were *inside my tee* and *scurrying over my skin*, and I got a sudden flashback to *The Mummy* and freaked the hell out. But they weren't trying to eat me, I realized a moment later. They were trying to—

"Oh," I said, catching a brief glimpse of myself in a mirror. But not of my messy hair. I walked over to the wall to get a better look, and yeah, that's what I'd thought. They were *styling it*.

I stared at them as they scurried over my head, tossing aside my scrunchy disdainfully and working quickly to form an elaborately braided hairstyle. It was sort of a twenties bob crossed with Heidi, which they formed and then clamped off, using their bodies like jeweled hair pins to keep it all in place. It was a gorgeous updo, the sort of thing I'd never worn, and I suddenly wished I had someplace to show it off. I turned this way and that, watching the "pins" glitter and gleam. It was beautiful!

"Cassie?"

"What?"

"Do you see it?" Mircea asked, from the next room.

"See what?"

"See me," he answered strangely—or maybe not. Because when I glanced around again, the interior of the cloak was no longer white, but looked like a TV screen, if TV screens could drape over a desk.

I moved closer and found myself looking down into a dizzying view of the bedroom. It was skewed because Mircea was holding something up at an angle—presumably the other cloak, since the view had folds in it. He threw it over the bed after a moment, and the room skewed even more, showing me a flash of the open bathroom door, the wall, and, finally, the ceiling.

"Do you see?" he asked again.

"I see the bedroom," I said, and saw part of his head nod.

A moment later he came back into the living room, and strode across to join me. "That's the problem," he told me.

"The problem is that I can see the bedroom?"

"No, the problem is why you can."

He indicated a chair, so I took it, and he did a double take at my hair. His lips quirked. "What?" I said defensively, my hand going automatically to my new do.

Only to be slapped away by a tiny claw, because they were damned if I was going to mess up their handiwork. I looked up, going a little cross-eyed, and bit my lip. I wondered how, exactly, you got them out? I mean, I liked the style and all, but I was going to need to wash my hair sometime—

"Cassie."

I looked down to see Mircea leaning over the desk to do something to my hair. Suddenly, my curls were falling around my face again, and the little golden creatures were on the move, trailing back down my neck and arm. And into a black case that I must have accidentally brushed with my hand at some point without realizing it.

I barely realized it now. Because Mircea hadn't moved, putting him close enough that I could see that I'd been wrong. His eyes when his power wasn't up weren't brown. They were cappuccino and cinnamon and gold, with a few flecks of deep green, hedged by thick black lashes any girl would have envied.

And plenty probably had, I reminded myself harshly. Because my body was already responding to his nearness, his scent, his breath on my face. He hadn't come any closer, but he hadn't sat back down again, either, and for a moment we just stayed like that, unmoving.

And then his lips touched mine and I jerked back, furious with him, and even more so with myself. Damn it all, what did it *take*? I meant *nothing* to him—

"You mean everything to me."

"Stop reading my mind!"

"You're projecting—"

"I'm doing no such thing!" Or maybe I was; I didn't care. "Cut it out!"

"I'll try. It's not easy to block someone with whom I share blood."

"I am not your blood," I snapped, even as the two little marks on my neck pulsed in time with my heart. Among other things.

Damn it, sometimes I could just—

"Cassie, please sit down. I brought you here to talk, not for . . . anything else."

I didn't sit down. I couldn't. I just wanted to get out of there before I did something stupid, because my brain was mad at him—no, my brain was *furious*—but my body hadn't gotten the memo. My body didn't want the memo. My body was busy remembering the feel of those hands and the taste of those lips and the strength of him pressing me down into—

*Goddamn it!*

"Say what you have to say," I told him shortly, hugging myself. "It's been a long night."

Mircea sat back, and dropped the hand he'd been holding out to me, I don't know why. He looked like he didn't, suddenly, either. He decided to use it to run through his hair instead.

His expression was that of a man who'd had a long day, too. Someone who had had too much put on him for too long, and who badly needed a break. Everybody went to Mircea, and everything somehow ended up being his responsibility. I didn't know how he did it, honestly.

I went to the bar and got us both a drink.

Mircea looked at it ruefully as I carried it back over. "Do I look that bad?"

"We both look that bad."

"You don't," he told me, his fingers brushing mine as he took the heavy glass.

"Mircea—"

"We have to do this sometime," he said, referring to God knew what. We had about a million things we needed to talk about, because we couldn't before. For so long, for *months*, we'd had so many secrets—his wife and Dorina's existence on his side and Pritkin's true identity on mine—that we hadn't been able to say much of anything. We'd had to tiptoe around each other, like two people on a minefield, so scared of putting a foot wrong that we barely moved at all.

And relationships don't work like that.

"They stagnate like that," Mircea agreed, reading my mind.

"Stop it," I told him, but there was no heat behind it this time.

"I'm trying, Cassie," he told me. "As I tried with us. And I *did* try—just not enough. I should have told you everything earlier, much earlier. But I was too afraid you'd say no."

"I haven't said yes," I reminded him.

"I know." He leaned back in the chair with his whiskey.

We drank in silence for a while. There'd been a lot of silences between us, but this one felt different. Better. We hadn't talked much out in these past weeks, unless you counted a memorable screaming match. Well, screaming on my part and stubborn insistence—he'd probably call it "manful restraint"—on his. We'd both been exhausted, run off our feet, and in no state of mind to discuss anything.

And now that we were . . .

God, I just didn't want to! I liked this peaceful quiet, this knowledge that I *could* talk if I wanted, that I could tell him anything, and that I wouldn't have to bite my tongue or patrol my own thoughts so he wouldn't pick them up. Because everything was finally out in the open.

It was nice.

It wasn't going to stay that way.

And not just because I knew Mircea but because of this infernal, never-ending war! He couldn't just let it all go for a while, let old wounds heal or even become old wounds. He had to press it, because circumstances were pressing him. The only way to end this thing was to kill all the gods—and considering how much trouble we'd had offing two, I wasn't liking our odds there. Or to invade Faerie and take out the bastards running this show before they could let them in.

And no way was Mircea going into Faerie without some kind of assurance about his wife.

No way in hell.

I threw back my whiskey, sat down the glass, and looked at him.

"All right," I said. "Let's talk."

# Chapter Thirty-four

Mircea tilted his head, but when he spoke, it wasn't what I'd expected. "It's strange," he said. "Before everything was revealed, all I could think about was how to tell you. What phrasing to use, how to approach the subject, counterargument after counterargument for anything you might say. And now . . ."

"Now?"

"I don't want to discuss it at all." He looked tired, stressed, and completely believable. But then, that was the problem. He always did. I thought back to how perfectly he'd lied to the consul, without a tick or a tell. He could be lying to me now, and I'd never know—

"I'm not!" He stared at me, and the dark eyes were haunted and pained and utterly, utterly sincere. "I know how badly I fucked up; I've thought of little else. How I should have trusted you, how I could have told you at any time and at least received a hearing, how my cowardice almost got you killed, all of it! How all I want, all I think about anymore, is a way to get you back."

"You're not getting me back," I said, and, for the most part, managed to keep my voice steady. It wasn't easy. Mircea rarely swore, and when he did, it was usually in some long-dead language, leaving me to guess from his tone what he meant. He also never looked like this—tired, desperate, almost . . . frightened? It was insane! Nothing frightened Mircea.

It was also really, really effective.

It made me want to go to him, to comfort, to console. It made me want to drop my guard, which was the last thing I could afford. Mircea the bastard I could handle. Mircea the tired, overworked, and vulnerable?

Not so much.

"Cut it out!" I said again, to myself as much as to him. "You want to talk about your wife, let's talk."

"I want to talk about us—"

"Well, I don't! And there is no us—"

"That has to be your decision, of course," he said, but his eyes said something else. His eyes said, "You are mine and you always will be." His eyes said, "This isn't over." His eyes—

Could go to hell, along with the rest of him!

"Damn it, Mircea!"

"But perhaps I can at least regain some of your trust."

"What?" The sudden course correction caught me off guard. "How?"

"By telling you about this." His hand clenched in the soft fabric of the cape, causing the picture of the bedroom ceiling to scrunch up and wobble around.

I frowned at it. "And that is?"

"The reason we raided Claude's Paris showroom. And his factory floor. And everything in between, including tracking down samples of his new line that he gave to friends."

I looked at the cloak some more. I didn't get it. "Why? There's plenty of spells that can do that, or something like it. If you're talking about espionage—"

"That was the original idea, yes. Anthony feared that certain members of his senate were conspiring against him, and wanted to find out if it was true. But the usual surveillance spells can be counteracted, which people planning to overthrow their consul would certainly take care to do. He needed something new."

"This?" It still looked like a wearable TV to me.

But Mircea nodded. "Claude is Anthony's couturier, and he is known for using old—in some cases very old—spells as inspiration for his collections. In this case, he came across one not seen in five centuries: *Nodo D'Amore*."

"Lover's Knot," I translated.

Another nod. "It was used during the Renaissance, in

the wars that took place between vampire factions following the consul's accession. Some masters did not like the new laws and tighter oversight that she was putting in place, and wanted to overthrow her, or at least to carve out independent fiefdoms for themselves. She . . . demurred."

I bet. The consul didn't share power. Some things never changed.

"Claude came across an old spell book from that time," Mircea continued. "One we missed when Lover's Knot was outlawed, and fell in love with its complexity—"

"Outlawed? But why was it—"

"I'm getting there," he promised. "Claude broke the spell into its component parts, using one strand in his fashion. It caused an item of clothing—the receiver—to reflect an image of whatever another item—the sender—had in front of it. Claude was even planning to add sound, giving Anthony eyes and ears that looked like nothing more than a handkerchief or a forgotten jacket. Anthony intended to leave pieces of the spelled clothing at the homes of the suspected conspirators, in an attempt to discover their plans."

"But wouldn't the counterspells stop that?"

He shook his head. "The spell in question was so old, and so long forgotten, that the newer counterspells had no defense against it. Anthony thought he had found his perfect spy device." Mircea smiled slightly. "But someone else had found it, too."

It took me a moment; it really *had* been a long day. "Jonathan."

"Yes. As usual with him, he had seen something in Claude's work that the man himself had not. You see, the original use for *Nodo D'Amore* was in battle."

"In battle?" I didn't see how that worked.

But Mircea nodded. "When I was a newly turned vampire living in Venice, I encountered a group of kidnapped witches. They were being transported through the port, but their real destination was the war raging in what is now Romania. They were to be used by the consul's enemies to give magical abilities to vampires in the field—"

"What?" My confusion was growing. "But vampires

can't perform human magic. Once a magic worker is Changed, he loses the ability."

That was why masters employed mages instead of simply Changing them and adding them to the family that way. They'd have preferred the latter, since a Child would be much more reliable and much longer-lived than a human, whom vampires always viewed with suspicion. Free will meant possible spies or turncoats, but a vampire, especially a newly Changed one, would do whatever he or she was asked without question.

They wouldn't have a choice.

But Mircea didn't seem to agree. "Not entirely."

"What do you mean, not entirely? Because I've never heard—"

"It's not common knowledge," he agreed. "The first instance I know of was in fifteenth-century Genoa. There was a master in the city in those days, very old and very powerful. And very paranoid."

"Aren't they all."

He smiled slightly. "With reason in his case. He called himself Roberto, but the rumor was that his real name was Riacus, and that he had originally been brought to Rome as a slave after the empire conquered Gaul. In any case, he practically ran Genoa, which was one of the premier seaports in Italy at the time. He was hugely rich—"

"And rich men have enemies."

"As you say. There were two factions fighting for control of the city, and Roberto's was winning. His opponents knew that the only way to change that was to assassinate him, but they couldn't get anywhere near him. His family was huge and his human servants were utterly loyal, not that he had many of them. He had so many masters that he did not need anyone to help guard his sanctum during the day. It seemed impregnable."

"I'm guessing it wasn't."

"Nothing is truly impregnable, as we discovered today," Mircea said dryly. "But attempt after attempt merely resulted in the would-be assassins meeting a gruesome end. Until a group of Roberto's enemies sent in a baby vampire with terms for a truce."

"Wasn't that considered an insult?" I asked, frowning. "To send a baby vamp—"

"Normally, yes, but Roberto was known for his temper. 'Kill the messenger' wasn't merely a euphemism with him."

I winced.

"As a result, people had become accustomed to sending messages through . . . expendable sources. Roberto's people therefore thought nothing of the powerless messenger, but the fact that he *was* so powerless made them careless. They checked him for weapons, but it never once occurred to them that he might be one himself."

"But . . . he wasn't, right?" I said, confused again. "To a human, a baby vamp would be a problem. But to a room full of masters—"

"Ah, but that was the point," Mircea said, his eyes gleaming. He enjoyed telling a story, and he was good at it. "A strong master vampire would never have been allowed in that room. It was so well protected that even a squad of masters had failed at an assault. But the baby vampire was ushered right in."

"But he couldn't do anything!"

"That's what everyone thought. But some time before this, one of Roberto's enemies had found himself in a quarrel with a talented mage. He ended up Changing the man in revenge, thinking that it would be amusing to have the once haughty mage running his errands and filling his cup for the next few centuries. But instead, shortly after rising and realizing what had happened to him, the furious former mage threw a spell—with all the magic left in his body from before his death—and incinerated his foe. The same tactic was used by the conspirators to kill Roberto."

"But the baby vamp couldn't throw a spell!" I said, wondering what I was missing. "No vamp can! And he wasn't a mage anymore—"

"But he wasn't truly a vampire yet, either." Mircea cocked his head. "Have you ever wondered why baby vampires are kept so close to home, and watched so carefully? Indeed, why they are called 'babies' at all?"

"They're young. And they stumble around, running

into things, and looking at you weird because their eye-sight keeps telescoping in and out," I said, thinking of some of the poor bastards at Tony's.

"Yes. Their new vampire eyesight doesn't work prop-erly because it isn't fully developed yet," Mircea said. "And neither are they. They need time to mature."

"But they're *dead*—"

"Yes, which rather puts paid to human development. But not to our kind. Vampires continue to change over most of our lives. Becoming stronger, gaining more powers—including master powers, if the process contin-ues long enough."

"I guess," I said. "But if baby vamps can throw spells, I don't see why adult ones can't. If it's just a lack of magic, they could go buy some—or steal it, like the dark mages do."

"It isn't merely that," Mircea replied. "They run out of leftover magic very soon, of course, but the bigger issue is that they lose their ability to channel it. The more they mature as vampires, the less they resemble their former selves, until they cannot manipulate it any more than non-magical humans can. But that process takes a little time, a fact that the vampires exploited to kill Roberto."

"Okay." I guessed I could see that. "But I don't see what any of this has to do with the Lover's Knot spell. Or what that has to do with us."

Mircea got up to get a refill. He offered me one, but I declined. I had to shift back tonight, and I didn't want to end up stuck somewhere out in the desert because I couldn't see straight.

Or worse, be spliced halfway through a wall.

"You could always stay the night," Mircea told me ca-sually.

"You could always stop reading my mind, before I get pissed off and leave."

He leaned against the edge of the desk, a little too close for comfort, and drank whiskey at me. "You're a hard woman, Cassie Palmer."

I wished. Like I wished I didn't notice the fondness in his eyes, or the way they crinkled up at the corners when he smiled. Or the strong throat revealed by the open collar of his shirt. Or the way the muscles in his thigh bulged under the fine fabric of his trousers when he rested it against the side of the desk.

Or a hundred other things I wasn't cataloging, because none of them had anything to do with me anymore!

"Where is he, by the way?" Mircea asked abruptly.

"What?"

"This war mage of yours. Pritkin, as he calls himself now. Shouldn't he be here?"

"Here?"

"Or in Las Vegas, at least?"

"I—" I paused, seriously confused now, because Pritkin had just spent an evening drinking, eating, and talking with my bodyguards. Hadn't he? For a weird, mind-altering moment, I actually wondered if I'd imagined all that, because otherwise . . . something very weird was going on.

As Mircea had said earlier, my guys weren't really my guys. He'd loaned them to me, back when the Circle had been gunning for my head, in the pre-Jonas days. I'd needed bodyguards, and Mircea had needed to off-load some of the less diplomatic members of his house. It had seemed an obvious solution for both of us.

And, of course, it had helped him to keep tabs on me— or so I assumed. Because, sure, many of the boys were actually centuries-old masters themselves, and long since emancipated, so they could basically do what they chose, but . . . Well, I'd just assumed they kept him up to speed.

Didn't they?

I tested a theory, and made my thoughts as opaque as possible. "He's been in London, debriefing with Jonas—"

"But Jonas was here today, wasn't he?" Mircea lit up one of his little cigarettes. "I should have thought Mage Pritkin would be with him."

"He's . . . they're probably done by now."

"Probably? Then he hasn't called?"

I narrowed my eyes, because that had been feigned surprise if I'd ever heard it. What was this? Some kind of test? Because I really wasn't in the mood.

"We're not doing this," I told him.

"Doing what?" The innocent look was fake as shit, too. "I am merely expressing surprise that a man whom you chased across time, at considerable risk to yourself, can't take a moment to pick up a phone. That is all."

I had to bite my lip on about a hundred comments, any one of which would just prolong this. I was already tired. And I didn't stand a chance against Mircea in a contest of wits even when I was rested.

But then one slipped out anyway.

"Forgive me, but weren't we talking about retrieving your *wife*?"

"Rescuing. And ex-wife."

"She isn't your ex-wife if she doesn't die, Mircea!"

"But I did," he pointed out. "And like those transformed mages, I started a new life as someone very different. I honestly do not know if she'll even recognize me."

I rolled my eyes hard enough that I think I saw my brain. "She'll recognize you," I said sourly, and went to get that refill.

"I'm leaving when I finish this," I told him. "So say what you want to say."

"What I want to say would take all night."

I took a deep breath, because arguing with Mircea never worked. He could steer a conversation with the adroit ease of a pilot navigating a harbor he'd sailed all his life. He could run you ashore or turn you around until you didn't know where you were, until you ended up agreeing with him without even being sure what the hell had been said!

He'd done it to me a hundred times, but not tonight. I took a big drink of whiskey—too much. "Almost done now," I said, and tried not to wheeze.

"Another time," he promised, although it sounded more like a threat. "In any case, the successful assassination of Roberto may have been the catalyst for the development of Lover's Knot. Or perhaps it was an accident—half of what the mages come up with falls into that category, although they'll never admit it."

"A spell to let vampires use magic?" I didn't bother to keep the skepticism out of my voice.

"A spell to let them share it," Mircea corrected. "The Roberto incident showed that it was technically possible for vampires to manipulate magic, but they had simply lost the ability. But what if they could borrow that ability from someone who still had it? That is what Lover's Knot does—it permits two people, as long as they are in a romantic relationship, to share magical gifts. The witches I told you about were headed for the war, but not to fight. They were to be mentally manipulated into believing themselves in love with vampires belonging to the consul's enemies, after which the spell would be cast, allowing their lovers to borrow the witches' magic in battle."

I thought about that. "Why lovers? Why couldn't the spell just bind anybody?"

"It's based on incubus magic," Mircea said, his lip lifting a little in what could have been a smile or a snarl. "There had to be a conduit between the two people involved in the spell, to allow the vampires to access the women's power. Which happens to be exactly what incubi do when they feed: they use emotion to create a channel through which they can connect to their partner's energy. The spell merely coopted the same dynamic for a new purpose.

"The only downside was that the lovers also shared their fates. In other words, if a spelled vampire fell in battle, the witch died as well. Eventually, the witches began to be targeted as a way of taking down powerful masters. The spell was outlawed for that reason, as well as the fact that kidnapping magic workers was threatening to engulf the entire supernatural community in war. We thought all vestiges of it had been destroyed, until Claude found a single reference and brought it back to life. And Jonathan somehow stumbled across it."

"To do what?" I asked, because I couldn't image what a powerful dark mage wanted with a spell that gave *vampires* magic. But then, I've never been half as devious as the people I deal with all the time. It scares the hell out of me.

"He kidnapped Anthony," Mircea said, his eyes strangely intense. "Jonathan intended to place the spell on him and then kill him, thereby taking out his lover, the consul, as well. Fortunately, we found out in time, rescued Anthony, and confiscated all elements of the spell in Claude's possession. We wiped the memory of it from his mind, ensuring that he cannot reproduce it in the future, although he will also be watched, of course."

"Of course." This was all fairly interesting, not to mention scary, but I still didn't get what this had to do with—

And then I did, and felt the world tilt around me.

# Chapter Thirty-five

My whiskey glass hit the floor with a thud, but the thick, leaded crystal didn't shatter. Unlike me, because it felt like my whole world had just come apart. I stumbled back, hit a table, and would have hit the floor, but Mircea caught me.

He was saying something, right in my ear, but I couldn't process it. Not with what sounded like a hurricane roaring in my head. What have you done? I thought in horror. Mircea, what have you *done*?

"Cassie! Cassie!" He was yelling but I still couldn't hear him, could barely even see him. I was too busy seeing something else: the malevolent eyes of Agnes' old acolytes. Because Jo hadn't been the only one to join the other side. They'd all fallen, one by one, as the gods used fear and intimidation, and the promise of power and immortality, to lure them away, while their Pythia lay dying, too weak to oppose them.

They were dead now, except for a little idiot who lay in the Circle's custody, drugged half out of her mind. And Jo herself, whose necromancer abilities had allowed her spirit to evade the fate of her body. The last time I saw her, she'd been animating corpses with her remaining magic, to stave off the inevitable.

I didn't know if she still was. My power had been silent on the subject, not dragging me away to some other time to finish her off. Because that's what a Pythia had to do to rogue acolytes. That's what I'd had to do to the others, the ones who hadn't ended up savaging each other. That's what I had to do to anyone threatening the timeline, anyone at all.

Didn't Mircea *understand that*?

And then I was screaming at him, grabbing hold of his shirt and shaking and yelling. "What did you do? *What did you do?*"

"Nothing! Cassie, listen to me! I've done nothing; I'm not going to do anything!"

I stared at him, my hair in my face, because that had finally gotten through. "You didn't cast it? You didn't steal my power to go back?"

I looked around, half expecting to see Elena, Mircea's dead wife, come walking through a door.

But she wouldn't; she *couldn't*. If he really had used Lover's Knot to take my power, to treat me like those vampires had those witches, I would have received a warning. The Pythian power couldn't stop itself from being used by those with access, but it *always* knew when it was happening. And it had never minded throwing me through history to deal with an heir gone wrong or a dangerous acolyte.

How much more would it have freaked out at a master vampire on a joyride?

I collapsed against Mircea's chest, my hands spreading over his warmth, feeling that he was solid, that he was okay. And then my nails were digging into his flesh, even through the material, bright moons of blood welling up, shock in his eyes. Because he didn't get it, even now, he didn't.

"I have to kill those who misuse the Pythian power, Mircea. I have to kill *all* of them, do you understand?"

"Cassie—"

"No. You've been talking for half the night, now you *listen*. I threw a young woman through a third story window, saw the fear and panic in her eyes as she fell onto cobblestones that left her looking like a broken doll. I dueled another through this building—the night of the attack, *that's* what I was doing. We fought through time, darting around frozen combatants, all while I was sure I was going to die. But she did instead, when I shifted her into the midst of another person's spell."

"Cassie, please—"

"No, you *listen*! You don't know me. You know who I

was, not who I am! Not who I've had to be. I pushed Jo—Jo Zirimis, the best of Agnes' acolytes, although nobody knew it—into a puddle of magical ice, flash freezing her body, if not her soul. I then pursued that soul through half a dozen bodies, both living and dead, fighting her every inch of the way, countering her tricks, leeching her power, until she fled before me. Until she ran for her life, because that was what was at stake, and she knew it!"

I stared at him, my eyes full of everything I was feeling: pain, horror, shock, disbelief. "Don't you realize, I'd do the same to you?"

He just looked at me.

And, no, he didn't realize it. Or, more likely, he didn't *believe* it. And that was so dangerous that I didn't have words, or even a place for it in my head.

I let him go, got up, and went to the phone on a table.

It wasn't on speaker, but it didn't need to be. Mircea could hear every word. I picked it up and dialed a number that few people had.

"Lord Mircea?" Jonas sounded pissed. "I demand—"

"It's not Mircea," I said roughly. "It's me."

The tirade cut off. "Cassie?"

"Yes, I'm in Mircea's rooms, I'm using his phone—"

"Are you all right? They wouldn't let me see you! I threatened to burn this place to the ground and they *still*—"

"I'm fine. I'm ready to deal with Lizzie."

There was a sudden silence on the other end of the phone, one that dragged out for a long moment.

"Are you sure?" Jonas finally said, and his voice was different. Rougher. He didn't like this any better than I did, but unlike Mircea, he understood.

"Yes, wake her up."

"Do you want to see her?"

No, but I didn't have a choice.

There are some things you don't do over the phone.

"Yes."

"Ask Lord Mircea to link up from his end," Jonas said, his voice going clipped.

"Cassie, what is going on?" Mircea asked, and his voice had changed, too.

It saddened me to hear it. All night, he had used what I thought of as our private voice, because I rarely heard it when we weren't alone. It was lighter, less guarded, full of laughter. Mircea laughed in front of others, too, as he had in the senate chamber, to make a point. But that was different, less genuine. Just another tool. But with me . . .

He was different with me.

Or maybe I just wanted him to be.

It didn't matter now, because he was back to his formal voice, the careful, weigh-every-word one he used around court, because you were a fool if you didn't. It cut me to hear it here, but it would cut a lot more if he didn't get this. "Can you link up?" I asked, because he was just standing there.

Mircea walked over to a mirror, the same one I'd used to admire my silly hairstyle, and touched the surface. Immediately it changed to something I'd seen before, so much so that it felt like déjà vu: a sleepy young woman with matted blond hair, a cot, a cell, plain concrete walls.

"Elizabeth Warrender," I told Mircea. "The last acolyte."

As before, she didn't seem happy to see me. "What do you want?" Lizzie demanded. "And why do you always call me in the middle of the damned night?"

"It's not night where you are, Lizzie."

She glanced around. "How the hell would I know? This place doesn't even have windows."

"Makes it harder for you to shift out," I heard someone say from out of frame.

"Shut the hell up!" Lizzie snapped. "How dare you even speak to me? Do you have any idea—"

"Lizzie."

My voice was quiet, but it turned her glare back to me. "They're all idiots here," she snapped. "Sooner or later, they're going to forget a dose, or be a little late, and then I'm gone. If you had any sense, you'd move me—"

"You know I can't do that."

The usual prison for time travelers was in a place known as the Badlands. I'd been there several times, but I still wasn't sure exactly what it was. Another dimension? A fold in this one? The space between universes where time couldn't reach? Nobody seemed to know, even Hilde. All I knew was that the Pythian power didn't work there, making it an ideal cage for time travelers who the court needed to stash for a while.

Of course, most of those were people who had used other methods to travel through time. There were extremely dangerous spells that could manage it, if you were willing to be blown into a thousand pieces if they failed. Or, worse, to be detached from time completely, forever falling through the centuries, unable to gain a foothold ever again.

Those sorts of prisoners were given a time-out—literally. Until the huge amount of magic that they'd somehow acquired to attempt such a thing dissipated. They were then turned over to the Circle for more commonplace punishments.

But the Pythian power didn't run out. And no one could take access back once it was given. It had to be freely surrendered, and Lizzie hadn't surrendered it.

And she was right; this couldn't go on forever.

"I thought she was dead," Lizzie said, talking about Jo. Because she was the reason Lizzie was stuck in limbo. "They told me you killed her."

"I killed her body. But we both know that doesn't end it."

"So go chase her! What the hell do you want with me? I've told you everything I know!"

Lizzie shoved limp, blond, unwashed hair out of her face. She'd had a common sort of prettiness once, but it didn't look like she'd enjoyed her time with the Circle. Dark shadows ringed bloodshot blue eyes, like maybe the drugs they kept her on to keep her from accessing her power didn't allow proper sleep. Her face was also gaunter than I remembered, and her shoulder blades, always prominent, looked like they were trying to tear through her too pale skin.

I felt a stab of pity. Because awful as she was, she hadn't gotten there on her own. In another time, in a different court, without the gods interfering and the other acolytes egging her on, Lizzie would have been . . .

A loser. A not very bright, easily led, vindictive little loser, but a more or less harmless one. She never would have been Pythia, but she probably wouldn't be in there, either. Shivering in a thin nightdress on a hard cot, wondering about her fate.

Which a smarter woman would already have known.

"Jo doesn't give a shit about me," Lizzie said, after a moment. When she remembered that she was supposed to be trying to manipulate me. "She wouldn't risk a trip to the Badlands to rescue me, not when I'd only be competition anyway. And at least I wouldn't have these bastards staring at me all day."

She glared at someone out of view, probably one of her guards. Because the Circle was being very careful with her. Having protected the Pythian Court for centuries, they knew exactly what a trained acolyte could do. Her dosage of the drugs they were using to fuzz her mind would never be late.

But what did that leave? Lizzie was a young woman, probably not even as old as me. Was she supposed to just stay in there, indefinitely, a drugged-out prisoner?

I wouldn't want that.

I would prefer almost anything to that.

But this wasn't about me.

"Cat got your tongue?" Lizzie sneered. "Did you come to talk about moving me, or what? Because I have nothing left to tell—"

"I'm not moving you," I told her flatly. "I can't take that risk."

Lizzie's face changed—not to shock or sadness, as I'd expected. But to rage. She'd obviously been putting all her hopes on that idea, and the fact that a new, clueless Pythia might be stupid enough to make that mistake.

Not stupid enough, Lizzie, I thought, as she called me every name in the book.

I almost wished I was.

Because I didn't want to deal with this. I desperately didn't. But even a not-so-bright Pythian acolyte was a terrible threat to the timeline, especially when she had nothing left to lose.

"So that's it?" she yelled. "You're just going to leave me here, with *them*? Do you know who I am, who my family is? Do you know what they'll do—"

"They won't do anything. We already contacted them," I said, which finally shut her up.

"You did?" The face was still red, but the small blue eyes had suddenly gone huge. She sprang off the bed, before remembering that she couldn't go anywhere without permission.

The Circle had her shackled in place.

"Let her go," I told one of the guards, who put an old-fashioned key in an old-fashioned lock. A moment later, Lizzie was off the bed and practically pressing her nose against the mirror on her side.

"Who did you talk to? When did you—"

"Your father, a week ago."

"A week? What did he say? Why didn't you tell me?"

Because I didn't want to face this, I thought.

"He said . . ." I swallowed and remembered the hard-faced man in the plush green study. It had been very old-world, very rich, very pompous—like its owner. He'd been a paunchy, middle-aged windbag who thought the world revolved around him because his family had been a leading voice in the Circle for centuries. He'd actually thought his daughter was going to be Pythia one day. He hadn't been pleased to learn that he was wrong.

"He said you became part of the Pythian Court when he sent you there," I told her. "He said that you're our problem now."

Lizzie didn't immediately say anything, but her face was eloquent. And this time, there was sadness there, and pain, and something of the little girl she must have been, who was sent away from everything she knew and everything she loved to a cold, foreign place with huge ceilings and echoing marble halls and cutthroat politics. I felt tears well up in my eyes.

"Lizzie. *Please*—"

"You know what he told me, when I left?" she said, not even looking at me. But off into space, her eyes unfocused, her face blank. Like she was also seeing that little girl again. "I was seven, but I remember. My power came late, you know. Other girls were having visions and chatting away to spirits when they were barely old enough to talk, but mine . . ."

She laughed. "I woke up screaming one night; everyone thought it was a nightmare. But it wasn't. And then someone remembered Great-Aunt Agatha, who had the sight . . ."

"Lizzie—"

"They had me tested, and it was wonderful," she told me, her eyes shining. They finally met mine, but I still didn't think she was seeing me. She was seeing something else, something that lit up her face like a child looking at a present-laden tree on Christmas morning. "Everything changed in that moment.

"I'd never been anything. No one had ever wanted me. I had two brothers and two older sisters, and I was just in the way. The stupid one, the plain one, the talentless—but not then. And they were so relieved!"

Her eyes finally focused. "Father paid a witch," she told me, the words pouring out of her now. "One of those coven creatures, old and hideous, but powerful, too. He and mother couldn't have children, like so many of us, but she said she knew a spell. But there was a price: some of the children would be born . . . wrong. Substandard. Even monstrous. But some would be the opposite: strong and smart and talented. Father made the deal."

I bet he did, I thought, remembering that study. And the family photos that had been so prominently displayed all over it. Lizzie hadn't been in any of them, and neither had one of the boys I'd heard about. I'd seen a son and two daughters, arrayed around their proudly beaming parents, because what magical family had so many?

But of the others, there was no sign.

"My eldest brother was wrong," Lizzie said, seeing my face. "I don't know how; we never talked about him. But the others were fine—better than fine! Tall and strong and smart, and their magic came easy. For a while, everyone thought I was another of the wrong kind. They whispered that mother should have quit while she was ahead. That she'd pushed her luck one time too many, and I was the result."

"Lizzie—"

"They watched me all the time. They talked about my brother, how he'd changed as he grew. I think they were waiting for it to happen to me. They spoke about him in whispers, but they never used his name. I asked one of the servants about it once, but she wouldn't tell me. I was spanked for even asking. He didn't exist anymore, you know?"

"I know."

"I was afraid that that would be me. That one day, I'd look in the mirror and see a monster staring back. They wouldn't tell me what had happened to him, so I didn't know what to look for." She laughed suddenly, and it was a little manic. "I got a pimple once, my first one ever, and freaked out. I thought that was it, that I was changing. I started screaming and screaming, and everyone came.

"I never would tell them why."

"Lizzie," I said. "You have a choice—"

"I don't!" She stared at me, the blue eyes wide. "That's what I'm telling you! I had *one* chance, when they realized I wasn't a monster, that I wasn't going to be one. And, even more, that I might have the family gift! And it was glorious! My sisters, so used to ignoring me, to putting me down, to going shopping with mother while I was left behind—well, all of a sudden, *they* were being left! I got all sorts of pretty things, they did my hair, had me sit for pictures. I almost didn't mind the things I saw at night, when the visions came."

"I know how that feels," I told her, remembering. "It's terrifying—"

"No! It was worth it! I was somebody, for the first time. For the only time! I remember when father came to tell me that I had been selected for the Pythian Court. Some acolytes had come a few days before, although I hadn't known who they were then. I just thought they looked like angels, all in white.

"They talked to me for a while, asked about my visions. And then one of them did something that caused me to have one. It was one of the bad ones; I ended up cowering behind the sofa, shivering in fear. I thought they'd hate me then, that they'd think me some kind of idiot. But they just thanked me and left, like nothing had happened! And then, a few days later, father called me to his study."

"He told you that you'd been selected."

She laughed a little then. "It was the happiest day of my life! Everyone had been so weird for those few days—jumpy, nervous, but excited, too. And always watching me, I didn't know why. Until he called for me. You've seen that study, right?"

I nodded.

"I'd never been in there. None of us kids had, except for my eldest brother. My next eldest," she corrected herself. "That's where father did business, where important things happened. That's where he told me I was going to be Pythia someday."

"He couldn't tell you that," I said. "It wasn't his to give."

She brushed it away. "He thought he controlled everything. And in the family, he did. Even beyond it . . ." Her eyes had gone distant again, but now they snapped back to mine. "Do you know what he told me, when I left? That the only thing we'd never had was a Pythia. Every other major office, even Lord Protector, had been ours at one time or another, but not that. Not until me.

"He told me to come back as Pythia, or not at all."

I swallowed. "Lizzie, you're a powerful clairvoyant. You could be rich. Important people would want to see you, important jobs would be open to you—"

"And all I have to do is give back the power, right?" she sneered. "I tried to bring back *gods*. They'll let me rot in here."

"I could talk to Jonas. You could get out—"

"When I'm middle-aged! Or older. And what would I have then? Who would be waiting for me? My name stricken from the roster, debased, demoted, scorned. My family never had an acolyte, either, and they were so proud, you understand? My father was *proud*!"

"Lizzie—"

She shook her head. "It doesn't matter. This isn't just about them, it's about *me*. It was the only thing I ever had that made me special. And I was, you understand? I *am*!

I've done things, seen things, that they never will! Not with all their money, and I—"

She cut off, and this time, when she met my eyes, there was no anger in them. Just utter resolve. "I won't ever be Pythia," she told me. "But I won't go back in shame, either. I'll die as I've lived. As an acolyte."

I bowed my head. I could argue with her all night, but she'd had weeks to make up her mind, and anyway, what could I say? I would have done the same.

"So be it."

One of the previously unseen guards moved forward, into the picture, and looked at me, uncertainty on his face. But she only laughed at him. "That's not how it's done," she said, with a trace of her old haughtiness.

And no, it wasn't. Despite what the Circle seemed to think, they didn't run the Pythian Court. Her death wasn't theirs to give.

A moment later, the guard was joined by another. Both of them senior war mages, both of them frantically looking around the tiny room. But their captive wasn't there.

Blue eyes met mine, in person this time. My hand clenched around her throat—a spasm, not a threat. I'd threatened her with this fate once before, but it wasn't like that now. Now, it was a choice on her part, and a duty on mine.

But it was still so fucking hard.

She saw, and her lips quirked. "You're Pythia," she told me. "It's part of the job."

I swallowed, and nodded.

"And you are an acolyte," I whispered.

A young throat under my hand, a proud tilt of the chin, a glint in the eyes.

And a moment later, I discovered that I'd lied to the witches.

There weren't even any bones.

# Chapter Thirty-six

I flashed back into the foyer of my suite a couple of hours later. Emilio was on guard again, and he smiled in welcome. "Heard we're keeping Marco."

"Yeah."

"Anybody else coming back?"

"No. But we're not losing anyone else, either."

He grinned wider and threw open the door. "Then you won."

"No," I told him quietly. "Nobody won."

I went in.

It was dark and quiet, even though it was the middle of the night. That was usually high noon as far as vampires were concerned, but only Marco's hulking shape was visible, outlined against the slightly less dark of the terrace. His cigar end flared bright red against the night, reminding me of the bonfire I'd just left.

Claude's couture, and the remnants of the ancient spell it contained, had gone up in flames. I wasn't sure if it was the quantity, because they'd cleaned out his warehouse as well as his shop, or if it was the magic imbued within the clothes, but it had turned into a raging inferno. Brilliant red, orange, and green flames had shot up three stories high, sending leaping fingers scratching at the star-strewn sky. Occasionally something would pop, and there would be a sizzle of silver or a flash of blue or purple, to join the other colors. Or a comet-like burst of gold would suddenly shoot out of the heart of the flame, heading for the heavens.

We'd had to stay well back from the event to avoid being skewered, although I still smelled like smoke and the acrid tinge of spent magic. I supposed it should have concerned me that they'd had a special pit on a hill in back of the consul's, where it looked like large fires were regularly held, but it hadn't. I'd had a little too much else on my mind.

"Heard you had a day," Marco said, exhaling a plume that drifted skyward.

I joined him on the terrace. The night air had a bite to it—the only way you could tell that summer had finally passed us by. I briefly wondered if I'd see another, and then told myself to stop being maudlin.

"Yeah," I said, dropping onto a seat at the table. "I had a day."

The consul found us a short time after the fire started, bringing the off-putting man in the dragon-hide coat with her. The wind had been up and the coat had billowed out more like a cloak as they climbed toward us, the shiny surface of the scales catching and reflecting the flames. Of course, she'd wanted something.

"Also heard you got me in the divorce," Marco said, bringing my attention back to the present.

I frowned. "There was no divorce, you know that."

"Heard you got me in whatever there was," he agreed easily, because you don't play word games after two thousand years.

I'd been looking up at the stars, visible through the clear glass roof of the terrace. The light pollution wasn't so bad up here, although it was nothing like at the consul's, where the bonfire had been backlit by the glittering arc of the Milky Way. With the awe-inspiring sky and the barren hillside and the forest crowding the slope, dark and mysterious, it had looked like we were performing some kind of pagan ritual.

And maybe we had been. I felt different somehow, changed. Only not in a good way.

My heart hurt.

"You wanna talk about it?" Marco said, and I suddenly understood why everyone else was missing. Then I wondered if it had been Mircea who was so thoughtful, or if it was Marco's idea. My heart clenched, and I found it hard to breathe.

"You all right?" Marco asked, looking up from tapping some ashes into a mug. Tami didn't allow smoking around the girls and had gotten rid of all the ashtrays, so Marco and the others who enjoyed a smoke had repurposed some old coffee mugs.

"Better remember to wash that out before Tami sees," I told him.

A flash of white teeth in the dark. "Always do." He glanced around. "You want some light?"

"No."

The darkness felt good.

The darkness made it easier.

I don't know how long we sat there, but it was a while. My thoughts were drifting to a dozen places, but not lighting on any of them. But Marco didn't hurry me. Marco never hurried. He had a stillness about him, but not like a person. More like a mountain that had always been there and always would be, ageless, eternal. Mountains didn't hurry.

I wondered how the hell I'd ever gotten along without him.

"Lizzie died tonight," I finally said, but no, that wasn't right. That was a lie. "I killed her."

Better, but still wrong.

"I executed her."

Marco exhaled. "That's it, then. Mircea didn't say."

So, it *had* been him. Or maybe a combination of them both. Or did I just not want to give Mircea credit where it was due?

I ran a hand through my hair and thought about pulling it out.

"You aren't going to say anything?" I asked, after a moment.

"I could," Marco agreed. "But you wouldn't like it."

I frowned at him. "What?"

"I used to be a soldier, Cassie. You know that. If you want comfort, I can give it, but . . ."

"But?"

Marco settled back against his chair, causing the plastic bands to groan. Not that he was fat. I'd guess his weight at between 250 and 260, although I might be off slightly, I didn't know. But the composition I was pretty sure of.

Hugging Marco was like hugging a granite boulder.

"I was fifteen," he told me. "New recruit, green as they come. But big. I grew up fast, which is why the army took me. They usually made you wait until you were sixteen before gaining the privilege of dying for the empire." His mouth twitched. "Anyway, after four months of the hell they called training, I was put into a *contubernium*—a tent group of eight guys, kind of like a squad."

I just looked at him. I didn't know why he was telling me this.

"We slept together, cooked together, fought together. They were your squad, and you were almost treated like one person, which is how you were supposed to behave. But there was one guy—there's always one guy."

Marco sighed.

"His name was Decimus, 'cause he was the tenth child in his family, which was probably why they'd shuffled him off to war—one less mouth to feed. Or maybe because he was shit at everything. How he made it through training I'll never know. But every day, it was the same thing: his feet hurt, he was too hot, the barley soup he'd had for dinner had given him the shits, he was too cold—you get the idea."

I nodded dumbly.

"Anyway, we shoulda seen it coming, but we were young and dumb and more interested in impressing the local girls with our manly physiques than with what Decimus was up to. Until, one day, we woke up and he wasn't there. I'd have just thought that he went out to take an early piss, but his pack was gone, too. He'd up and deserted in the middle of the night, which would have been bad enough, but we'd just got our marching orders and were headed off to war, so it made it look like cowardice.

"I don't think it was; I think he just wanted to go home to mama. He was her youngest, and I kinda got the impression that she'd babied him—and well. He couldn't take army life, or he didn't want to take it, I don't know. But we fucking panicked."

"You panicked? Why? You didn't leave—"

"Yeah, but I *did*. He was part of our squad, and we were one person, right? What one of you did, all of you did. You can damned well better believe we moved heaven and earth to find him. But we were only seven guys, and it was a big camp, plus there was the city nearby and a bunch of open land . . . he could have been anywhere."

"So what happened?"

Marco shrugged. "What happened was that we finally had to tell the *optio*—like a sergeant—that he'd done a runner. He ordered a search, but before it really got started, here came Decimus, with a black eye and a split lip, being dragged between two of the biggest sailors you ever saw. He'd tried to get a ship back home, but they'd realized what was going on and dragged him back to us, hoping for a reward. He looked like a child between them, a really scared child."

"He should have been afraid.

"The punishment for desertion was death."

"Death? But it was his first time!"

"Didn't matter. Well, that's not entirely true," Marco corrected himself. "If he'd been one of the recruits from upper-class families, he might have gotten exile, if his old man greased the right palms. Or a nice, clean decapitation if he didn't. But for us common sons of bitches it was either crucifixion, being burned alive, being beaten to death, being drowned in a sack, or being thrown to the beasts in the arena. As long as you ended up a corpse, the army wasn't real particular about how."

I swallowed. "I don't want to talk about this anymore."

"He ended up being sentenced to be beaten to death," Marco said, ignoring me. And then grabbing my wrist when I tried to get up. "And those of us in his squad had to carry it out. It sucked; like I said, he wasn't a bad kid, just soft and spoiled. None of us wanted to do it, but if we hadn't, the same thing would have happened to us."

I sat back down. "It's not the same."

"It's exactly the same. We were at war. He signed up knowing the deal, the good and the bad. You made it to the end of service, you had a nice, fat payday waiting for you and some land. You rose in the ranks, made it to centurion, and you didn't even have to wait for retirement. You could get married, buy a little farm, have—" Marco stopped, and his expression didn't change, but there was tension in the air suddenly. "Have a life," he finished harshly, after a moment. "But if you screwed it up, you knew the rules then, too. And so did she."

"Lizzie didn't sign up," I rasped.

"Didn't sign up for the court, maybe. She sure as hell signed up to betray it—and the rest of us!"

Couldn't argue with that.

But that wasn't the point.

"I'm upset about Lizzie's death," I told him. "But I expected it. She refused to give up the power, and she was too big of a threat as long as she had it. Not just because of herself but because of Jo, if she's still out there. Another Pythian acolyte would have made a perfect replacement body, and I don't know that Lizzie could have or would have fought her off."

"Then you did what you had to do, like I said."

I shook my head. "It's not what I did. It's when."

I wanted a drink, but I didn't need another one. I wanted some Tears even more, but I only had one bottle left, and I didn't want to waste it. Besides, Jonas was going to want to know why I needed more so soon, when he'd just delivered three bottles a week ago. I didn't know what to tell him.

I leaned on my knees and rested my cheeks on my hands. I tried to avoid that pose because it made me look like a kid, pushing my already less-than-defined cheeks into cherub territory. But right then, I didn't care.

"You've been putting it off for weeks," Marco pointed out. "It had to be done sooner or later. Why not now?"

"Because I didn't do it because it needed to be done. I did it . . ." I stopped, wondering if I wanted to admit it, even to Marco. He never judged me. I guess in a couple millennia you've seen it all, and I didn't think I'd ever managed to truly shock him.

I wondered if I might now.

"I did it because I wanted to make a point to Mircea," I finally said. "I wanted something he'd remember. I used her death as . . . as a kind of lesson. I needed him to understand . . . something . . . and I didn't know how else to get the point across. I was scared and I wasn't thinking clearly, but I knew what I was doing. Do you understand? I knew and I did it anyway!"

I looked up finally, but I couldn't see his face. The cigar was resting on the ashtray, sending a tiny trail of smoke skyward, and without its glow, his face was only shadow. But I thought I caught a liquid gleam in the approximate place of his eyes.

He didn't say anything, though.

"Who *does* that?" I blurted out, after a moment, because maybe I *had* shocked him. I wouldn't blame him; I'd shocked myself.

Marco picked up his cigar again and took a long draw. But the face was the same as always: big, bluff, and calm. He didn't look shocked—or repulsed or disgusted. He just looked like Marco.

He sounded like him, too, when he said: "Me."

"What?"

"Or Mircea. Or Marlowe—especially Marlowe. Or the consul, or any master, for that matter. We'd have all done the same."

"I'm not a vampire!"

"I didn't say a vampire. I said a master. You've been acting like one more and more lately; it's good to see."

"Good?" I stared at him, and some of what I was feeling must have shown on my face, because he frowned slightly.

"You know how we are, Cassie. We push and push—it's in the culture, but more than that, it's in our nature. We're constantly jockeying for position, seeing who's top dog, and it's not always the bigger dog. Sometimes it's about who is willing to step up, to go toe-to-toe, to push *back*. To prove who's a leader and who's a follower. And it's not always who you'd think."

The big head fell back; this time, it was his turn to look at the stars. "You know, when I first met you, I gave you some bad advice."

"What?" I frowned, because the advice I'd gotten from Marco had kept me sane, more often than not.

"Not intentionally," he said. "I thought I was doing

you a favor, telling you like it is, helping you fit in to the nice little servant's position I assumed was to be yours. You were Mircea's woman—that's how you were first introduced to me, and that's how I thought of you. This whole Pythia thing." He shrugged. "I didn't understand it. And when I did think about it, I just thought: good. Another weapon in the family arsenal."

"I'm not a weapon," I said, wrapping my arms around myself because it was cold. And because it was a thought I'd had more than once myself.

"No, you're not," he agreed. "A weapon is a tool somebody else uses, with a power under his control. You're not a weapon, you're a Pythia, and your power is your own—"

I laughed, a bitter little burst. I couldn't help it. And then I saw Marco's face. "I don't have power," I told him. "Not enough, anyway."

"Nobody feels like they got enough these days. But there's lots of types of power, and lots of types of strength. That advice I gave you was that everybody serves somebody—best to realize it early and get in line. But I was wrong. There are leaders in our world, and you're ramping up to be one of them. I think a lot of people realized that today. You've started pushing back, and while they may not like it, they respect it."

"And if I don't respect myself?" I burst out. "When I hate myself because I did something tonight that was *exactly* what Tony would have done? Things started getting out of hand at court, and his answer was always the same: somebody has to bleed, somebody has to die—"

"That's enough!"

It wasn't loud, but it was sharp enough to knock my head back. I blinked at Marco in confusion. Even more so because he was sitting up again, and he looked pissed. He suddenly looked like the centurion he'd once been.

"You're nothing like that fat piece of shit, and I don't want to hear that from you ever again, do you understand?"

I sat there, wondering what had just happened.

*"Do you?"*

My immediate response was sir, yes, sir! But that wasn't true. And I was tired of taking orders, even well-meant ones. "I acted like him, Marco—"

"Bullshit! You let a necessity do double duty, that's all. You didn't go looking for someone to bleed for you, you didn't take joy in what had to be done. You're sitting here beating yourself up over it—do you think Tony ever did that?"

"Maybe he did, in the beginning—"

"Like hell!" Marco chewed angrily on his cigar. "I've known that fat prick for centuries, even before I came to Mircea's, and he was always the same. The Change doesn't change who you are, it just gives losers like him more power than they know how to handle. Mircea should have put him down years ago. But he's the sentimental type, too, at least when it comes to family—"

"I'm not sentimental!"

"Sure." Marco leaned forward, and a shaft of moonlight lit the big, handsome face. "That's why you're sitting out here, shivering and tearing yourself up, instead of going to bed like you ought to, because you're fine with it."

"I'm not fine with it! I just—" I stopped, because I wasn't sure what I felt anymore. "You don't use someone's death like that. You just don't."

"Maybe if you're human, you don't," he agreed. "But you're not one, and you're dealing with some next-level badasses. Sometimes, you gotta give 'em a slap. That's true of the master as much as anyone. He's a good guy, but if you give him an inch, he'll take the whole fucking continent. You don't realize it yet, because you're tired and cold and hurting, but you made a smart play tonight."

I looked at him, and knew there were tears in my eyes, but I couldn't help it. "Then why do I feel like this?"

Marco got up and folded me into a hug, and as always, it was like hugging Gibraltar. But it felt good. " 'Cause you're not Tony," he told me softly. "Now go to bed before I carry you there."

It wasn't an empty threat; he'd done it before, with no more difficulty than anyone else picking up a wayward kitten. "I can't," I said. "I need to talk to the guys first."

"Which ones?"

"All of them."

# Chapter Thirty-seven

Marco didn't ask why. Maybe he already knew. He just went to collect the boys, after tossing me a throw from off the back of the sofa, although he could have summoned them mentally just as easily. But maybe he thought I needed a moment.

He wasn't wrong.

Talking with Marco usually helped me sort out my thoughts. He might not always be right, because nobody was always right, and he was rarely diplomatic. But I didn't need diplomacy; I needed honesty, and he always gave me that.

But sometimes, I couldn't give it back.

There were things I couldn't tell Marco, things I had to sort out for myself.

Like Mircea saying passionately that I'd misunderstood, that he'd told me about Lover's Knot to prove that he *wouldn't* go behind my back.

"I've known about this for weeks," he'd said, the dark eyes urgent, willing me to understand. "And I've done nothing other than confiscate all traces of the spell! I won't do anything—"

"And the others?" I'd asked roughly. "Who else knows?"

"No one. The spell is truly lost this time. Even Claude doesn't have it—"

"And who took it out of his mind? Was it you?"

I'd seen the answer on his face before he'd replied. Of course it had been him. He'd trust no one else with something like that.

So there was someone who still knew it, then.

"I'm not going to use it, Cassie!" he'd said, frustration in his voice as well as his face. He hadn't understood how I would take this. He really, really hadn't. "No one will hear about it from me, no matter what you decide."

"This isn't more blackmail, then?" I'd asked steadily.

Mircea had started to reply, something sharp, judging by his expression, but he caught himself. I always got under his skin somehow, and I wasn't even trying. I didn't want him angry; I just wanted the truth. I needed it, because this was so much bigger than he seemed to think.

"I can hardly blame you for assuming that," he'd said, after a moment. "But no. I was desperate before. I knew how badly our conversation had gone, when I told you about Elena. I thought I'd lost my last chance—"

"And if you get desperate again?"

"I won't. You must believe me!"

And the thing was, I *did* believe Mircea. Or, rather, I believed that Mircea believed Mircea. Maybe I was hopelessly naive, but he was right: he hadn't had to tell me about that spell. He had plenty of mages under his control. He could have had any one of them cast it on him, which would have also put it on me, through the link between us.

And we did have a link. Our recent breakup had made no difference, magically speaking, not with the marks I still bore on my neck. He might have put them there when he was out of his head, but they had still created a bond that nothing could undo. Under vampire law, I was his.

Whether that would be good enough for this particular spell no one knew, because Mircea hadn't tried it. He'd said that he wouldn't risk destroying time for a single woman's life, and right now, I believed him. But next week? Next month? Next year?

Rian had told me about the insidious nature of the obsession that plagued older vamps, how it crept up on them. How it grew over time, little by little, because of course it did. No master would have been caught out if it was obvious. But if the changes were slight, building up slowly, would Mircea notice? Would anyone?

And when the obsession took him, and he couldn't see anything but her, what would he do then?

I sat forward and put my elbows back on my knees and my head in my hands, because I didn't need to ask that question. I already knew. Mircea hadn't been called Mircea the Bold when he was alive for nothing.

He could say whatever he liked, and even mean it. But when push came to shove, when he didn't think he had another choice, he would act. That was just who he was: the daring leader of men, not the diplomat standing on the sidelines, as he'd been pretending. And I wasn't the only one who thought so.

The consul knew him, too, and arguably better than me. She'd certainly known him longer, and she was worried. I'd thought she was just being paranoid—it's a popular vampire pastime, and she had more reason than most. But now I wondered: what if she'd seen something I hadn't?

At least, that I hadn't before today. There had definitely been a different Mircea in that senate chamber. The diplomat act had been wearing thin, maybe because it had never been more than a veneer anyway. Mircea had told me so himself, how carefully he'd cultivated it over many years, learning how to smile, to dissemble, to persuade. He'd done it because he had to—it had literally been his job with the senate—and because he'd wanted to talk some Pythia into breaking every rule there was.

He hadn't succeeded with the latter, but he'd had spectacular success with the former, adroitly navigating centuries of vampire infighting and political maneuvering and a whole flurry of knives headed straight for his back. He'd done it through charm, cunning, and occasional dirty dealing, if some of the rumors I'd heard were true. But he'd always, always, done it subtly. It was practically his trademark.

Until today.

Suddenly, all that had been thrown out the window, cast aside like that hair clip. I didn't know why, but that one small detail kept coming back to me, maybe because I'd always been slightly obsessed with Mircea's hair. In fairness, it was goddamned beautiful hair. And now it was free, no longer confined or restrained in any way.

Like the man himself, staring down a consul.

What was it Marco had said? "Sometimes it's about who is willing to step up, to go toe-to-toe, to push *back*." Mircea had certainly done that, and unlike me, I didn't think he'd been bluffing. He'd made it sound that way to Marlowe, but I'd seen his face when Parendra was approaching our room.

Maybe the consul had something to worry about after all.

And so did I. Because Mircea the Bold wasn't the patient man I knew. The one who had spent an entire year at Tony's crappy court, making friends with a kid on the off chance that she might become Pythia someday. That man would wait to see what I'd do about the blackmail, because I hadn't made a decision yet. But this man?

He'd immediately pushed on to another source of pressure—and a far better one. I hated the idea of Pritkin's real identity getting out, because I knew *he'd* hate it. An intensely private man, he would find it incredibly galling to be mobbed wherever he went and have his privacy permanently invaded. But while I'd been upset on his behalf, I hadn't been afraid.

I was now.

This Mircea wasn't going to wait around forever. Not when he had the means to get what he'd wanted for five hundred years actually in his hands—or in that clever, twisty brain of his. The one that ran circles around me without even trying.

Or maybe I'd been wrong before; maybe he was trying. Because even after I'd made my position plain, even after *Lizzie*, he just kept right on making the same point: he wasn't going to do anything, he wasn't going to risk it. Not that he *couldn't*; that he *wouldn't*. Until he changed his mind, because it was entirely in his hands, wasn't it? It was all down to his choice now.

And mine.

A shudder took me, because the thin cotton throw was doing nothing. I fought with it, trying to get more coverage, and then someone touched my arm. I looked up to see that Marco was back and gazing down at me in concern.

"Hey. You okay?"

I nodded, but couldn't speak.

"You don't have to do this now," he told me, crouching down. And looking at the skin under his palm with a frown. "You're ice-cold. You need to be in bed."

"In a minute," I said, and to my surprise, it sounded fairly normal. Like I wasn't just sitting here, thinking about killing his boss.

Only that was the problem: I wasn't. I should be; as Lizzie had said, it was part of the job. But that . . . I couldn't do that. I *knew* I couldn't. I didn't think I could ever do it to anyone again, after tonight. That had been horrible, horrible! And Mircea—

I shuddered again, and Marco frowned harder.

"Okay, that's it. It's time for beddy-bye. Meeting's canceled," he added, looking past me. I had been facing outward, toward the garden that had been made out of lush pots of flowers and raised boxes filled with greenery. But now I turned around.

And saw a crowd of dark shapes standing just inside the entrance to the suite, their faces in shadow but their eyes glinting gold in the night. They looked like they had when I first saw them, what felt like ages ago now, and had thought them bizarre, disturbing, mysterious. Like dozens of cats staring at me out of the darkness. But I wasn't disturbed any longer, because these were men I knew, men I *trusted*.

Most of them, anyway.

"I talked with Mircea tonight," I said abruptly. "We reached a deal. I do a favor for the war council and he—"

"What's a war council?" That was Lorenzo, from somewhere in the middle of the pack. I couldn't see him, because he was only a few inches taller than me, having been born in an era when food wasn't plentiful. But I recognized the Brooklyn accent he'd picked up in the last century or so.

I guessed I wasn't the only one being kept out of the loop.

"What they're calling the leaders of the Circle and senate these days, and anyone else helping out in the war. I stumbled into one of their meetings—"

"Stumbled? Why weren't you invited?"

That was Santiago, one of Mircea's Spanish masters. About half of Mircea's guys, and as many as two thirds of his masters, were Italian, picked up during his extensive stay in that part of the world after he was cursed. But he had gone other places, too, including making the pilgrimage to Santiago de Compostela back in the sixteenth century, where he'd ended up with a runt-of-the-litter vamp named after the city.

The trip had not been out of religious fervor, although Mircea still considered himself to be one of the faithful—it was yet another way he differed from most vamps. But because a prominent priest had started a vamp-killing brigade. He had been telling the many pilgrims who came to the city every year that there was an evil spreading across Europe like a stain, and that they were the only ones who could wipe it out.

That was a problem, because people came from all over Europe to get the blessing of Saint James, who was supposed to have been buried there. What they mostly received instead was a cheap tin pin to wear on their cloaks, a quick blessing, and an empty purse. And, for a while, a vamp-killing kit, complete with instructions from the priest.

They were pretty good instructions. And the potions included with the kits—which the pilgrims were assured were different kinds of holy water—were pretty effective, too. There was only one requirement in return: ship all the bones back to Compostela.

The priest said it was to allow him to cleanse them of their evil, so that they would not curse the town or city with their presence. But in reality, he was selling them. Vampire bones were worth a fortune to potion sellers, since they greatly increased the effectiveness of any potion they were mixed with. But after the current consul came to power, the trade had suffered a serious blow, in part thanks to Mircea.

One of the first things he did for the senate was to help shut down the trade in Venice, and later to negotiate a pact with the mages regulating it throughout Europe.

He'd thereafter been deputed to find the priest and end the con at Santiago, along with the help of some local vamps, one of whom was killed in the resulting fight. Since he'd died saving Mircea's life, Mircea had absorbed some of his boys, who couldn't find refuge elsewhere, into the family. That had included Santiago, who had been fiercely loyal ever since.

I had a feeling I wasn't going to be seeing him much after this. Or probably most of the rest of them. Mircea was famously loyal to family, and from everything I'd seen, they felt the same way about him. Many of my guys especially, who had been kept on despite proving to be absolute shit with diplomacy, because letting them go to other families, where they might be mistreated, had been unthinkable.

Why on earth would they even consider leaving him now?

"I will be on the war council from now on," I said, trying to keep my voice steady and normal when I wasn't sure I remembered what that was anymore.

"Damned straight," somebody else said. "Imagine not inviting the Pythia!"

There was a general murmur of agreement that almost made me tear up again. I remembered when I'd first arrived, and Mircea's guys had alternated between fear of my power and annoyance at my person. They'd called this place Australia, because they'd felt like they'd been exiled from the seat of power. Meanwhile, I'd resented the hell out of them, viewing them as a cross between babysitters and jailers. I'd badly wanted them gone.

Irony was kind of a running theme in my life lately.

I cleared my throat. "Anyway, they have a problem they don't know how to fix. I make it go away and I get to keep you—all of you."

"Must be some problem," Roy said, coming forward. He had a glass in hand with little floating bits in it. Probably a mint julep; he loved playing to the stereotype. "You sure we're worth it?"

"You're worth it." It came out hoarsely, embarrassingly so, but my nerves were raw. Marco was right; I ought to be in bed. But I had to do this first.

I stood up, because it seemed like the kind of thing you stand up for. And because, considering how things were going with the boss, I needed to be sure they understood. I needed to be damned sure!

"From tonight on, you're free agents," I said. "Mircea left your situation in my hands, but I'm putting it back in yours."

"Meaning?" Roy asked, frowning.

"That if you would prefer to go back to Mircea, you can. I know this wasn't a posting that a lot of you wanted, and all of you are masters, many with courts of your own. I'm sure you've found it boring compared with what you were doing before—"

Somebody burst out laughing. "Sorry," a voice floated in from the back. "Just, uh, not really bored."

"—or terrifying, at times," I continued, because that's how this place was. Quiet until it wasn't, and then it *really* wasn't. "Honestly, that's not likely to get any better. If anything, the opposite is true."

"And what does that mean?" That was Rico, pushing forward from the back, where, knowing him, he'd been standing and smoking, observing everything with those sharp, dark eyes. But now I'd gotten his interest, probably at the thought of a threat to Rhea.

And I wasn't going to sugarcoat it.

"We're at war. More than that, the court itself has enemies, and they seem to grow every day. Right now, the covens are angry—"

"Yeah, we heard!" someone else said eagerly.

"—and so are plenty of others. Including a nine-centuries-old, probably insane dark mage who just came very close to destroying a city and may be targeting us next."

There was silence for a moment after that. "Like I said," the voice from the back came again, sounding a little hollower this time. "Not bored."

"You might be safer with Mircea," I told them. "Even in Faerie."

Roy finished his drink, his strong throat working. He put the glass down on the table and sighed with satisfaction. "Yeah, but you can't get decent whiskey in Faerie, or so I'm told. Think I'll stay here."

"Think carefully," I told him. "All of you. And there's one more thing."

I hesitated, but there was no way to phrase this that was going to make it any better. They were going to be okay with it or they weren't, and there wasn't much I could do about it. Except to make my position clear.

"There are likely going to be times when I tell you one thing and Mircea tells you another. He understands the senate's side of things in ways I can't and never will, but I understand—I have to understand—more than that. I'm supposed to be bringing together the supernatural community, not just being an extra weapon for the senate. That means that sometimes Mircea and I will be on the same team, fighting side by side, and sometimes . . . we won't.

"Some of you are emancipated; all of you are strong enough to decide which commands you follow and which you don't. The question is, when push comes to shove, who are you going to listen to? Because as much as I value each and every one of you, I can't have people guarding my court who I can't absolutely rely on—"

"You're saying you don't trust us?"

That was Lorenzo again, from somewhere in the middle of the pack. He sounded hurt. It caused a pang right under the breastbone, because this wasn't anything I wanted, either. But it had to be done.

"I'm saying the opposite," I told him. "I *do* trust you, which is why I'm telling you this, and giving you the chance to opt out. I won't think worse of you; I understand how a vampire family works, and that what I'm asking is . . . difficult. Some of you may find it impossible. That's okay. What isn't okay is staying here and allowing someone else to countermand my orders when he doesn't have all the facts. Or even if he does.

"This is my court, and you are my men." I saw Fred standing in the doorway to the lounge and caught his eye. "Or else you won't be here at all."

# Chapter Thirty-eight

I still didn't go to bed, although I tried. After the guys filed out, I went to the kitchen to see if we had any hot chocolate. I badly wanted something warm and comforting, but coffee would leave me wired, and I needed to rest. I settled on chocolate as a decent alternative.

But, of course, it wasn't that easy.

The place was massive, a gleaming ode to the nineteen twenties for some reason, with tiny black-and-white tiles in art deco patterns all over the floor, a tin ceiling, and old-fashioned-looking white porcelain appliances with shiny brass fixtures. It even had twenties-era framed paintings on the walls, mostly black-and-white as well, all showing beautiful people with impossibly elongated bodies lounging around not doing much. It did not have a map, which is what I needed to find anything in what looked like a thousand cabinets.

I finally gave up, washed an ashtray mug somebody had left in one of the sinks, and headed for bed.

I almost made it that time.

When I was halfway there, a small creature ran up and started circling my legs, threatening to trip me up. I was tired enough that it took me a moment to recognize it as the velvet pouf I'd bought yesterday morning and that Rhea had had in her room. I'd thought it had just been acting that way to get purchased, but apparently it was pretty hyper all the time.

And then it ran off again, as energetically as it had come, down one of the hallways. I looked after it for a moment, a little nonplussed, because I wasn't used to mobile furniture. Then I continued on toward bed.

Only no.

Because it was back. And even more of a tripping hazard than before. I almost landed on my ass that time, and frowned downward as it encircled my legs, wondering what now? Especially when it started pushing at me. And then bumping my shins when I gingerly tried to move away again. Circle, bump, circle, bump.

It turned around and scampered away a couple feet.

I just stood there, regarding it sleepily.

Circle, bump, circle, bump. Circle, bump, bump, BUMP. And all right, that was enough!

Only it didn't seem to think so, running off again and then stopping, its fat little tassels swinging impatiently, as if it wanted me to—

Oh.

I sighed deeply, because I didn't want to follow it anywhere, but I also didn't want it bumping my door all night. Did it have an off switch? I walked over to see, but before I could grab it, it took off, scampering down the hall like a mad thing.

Only to stop in front of a door and swing its tassels at me pointedly.

It was Augustine's temporary studio, I realized as I approached.

There was a light on under the door, so someone was inside, but that didn't mean he wanted to be disturbed. I wanted to thank him for the outfit, which had really come in handy, but that could wait for morning. Everything could wait for morning, I thought, as a huge yawn threatened to split my head in half.

*BUMP!*

The crazed little pouf was now throwing itself at the closed door, as if it could batter it down. I knew I should have asked for a warranty, I thought, right before the door opened and Augustine's head poked out. "Goddamn it!" he said, catching sight of me, and slammed the door in my face.

*BUMP! BUMP! BUMP!*

The door was flung open again, and then just as quickly closed, except for enough space for an angry blue eye to glare at me. "It's the middle of the night!"

"Tell me about it."

"What do you *want*?"

"My bed."

"Then go to bed!"

"Okay," I agreed, and turned to do just that, but the pouf was in my way.

It was small but determined, and I was sleepy and unsteady. This time, it succeeded in knocking me down. And back into Augustine. And through the door, because I don't think he'd expected a sudden assault of Pythia any more than I had. Given that he screeched and jumped back, stumbled into some clothing racks, and went down.

Leaving me looking up at—

"What the hell is that?" I asked, trying to get my eyes to focus on something that was upside down and freaky and way too close.

"No, no, no, get back!" Augustine was yelling from inside a tumbled mass of couture. "Don't approach!"

"I didn't," I told him.

"I wasn't talking to you!" he snarled, flailing around. Only to have the rack collapse onto his head.

That caused some more drama, but I barely noticed because I was looking at—

I didn't know what I was looking at.

It was small, somewhat shriveled, and mostly bald. There were a few silky strands of long, white hair here and there, blowing in the draft from a vent. Most of them were sprouting out of a lumpy little head, but a few were coming from a small, wizened face. So I supposed I was looking at a male, but couldn't really be sure.

The face wasn't particularly prepossessing, with a cute little button nose but odd bumps under the skin, like it was thinking about growing warts but hadn't made up its mind. And a mouth of mostly missing teeth, although the few that were left were white and shiny. But I barely noticed all that, because the eyes—the eyes were lovely, I thought, staring into huge, purplish orbs with golden striations radiating through them. They looked like twin stars set in a violet sky, like sunrise and sunset all in one, and were glowing so brightly out of the little face that I could barely see it anymore.

"Beautiful," I murmured, because they were.

The tiny creature smiled gently at me.

And then he clocked me over the head with a broom handle, and the world went swimmy.

"Son of a bitch!" I said, holding my now throbbing head and trying to ward off subsequent blows, only there weren't any. Probably because my hassock with the soul of a Doberman had knocked whatever-it-was to the floor and was trying to savage it, only it didn't have any teeth. It did have a good bit of heft and hard little feet and swinging tassels that kept hitting its prey in the face, however, obscuring its view.

Which is why the batty little thing didn't see me roll to my feet and snatch away the broom. Of course, I didn't use it. I didn't do anything at all except spare myself future head trauma, but you'd never know it. The creature stopped wrestling the furniture and huddled before me in fear, old, age-spotted hands curled over its misshapen noggin.

I stared from it to the broom, which I wasn't even brandishing menacingly, wondering *what the hell*, before Augustine jerked it away from me.

And then tossed it aside, booted away my tasseled defender, and gathered up the tiny old whatever-it-was gently into his arms. And stood there glaring at me from over top of its head, like I was the aggressor! I just stood there for a moment, swaying, my head throbbing, and finally reached tilt.

I turned around and started out the door, when a long-fingered hand grabbed my arm. "You don't want to know what's going on?"

"No."

So, of course, he proceeded to tell me.

"They were imprisoning him! I didn't have a choice!"

I sighed, knowing I'd regret this, and turned back around.

"Who were?"

"The damned witches!"

I swear my heart iced over. "What. Witches?"

"Don't look at me like that! This is your fault! You wouldn't tell me, or I wouldn't have had to eavesdrop—"

Fuck.

"—and follow the girls back to where you bought that dress in the first place—"

*Fuck.*

"—and find him laboring in some kind of third-world sweatshop—"

FUCK.

"—so, of course, I had to get him out—"

"You *stole him from the covens*? No wonder they came after me!"

Augustine brushed it away. "They were doing that anyway, that's how I got him out—in the ruckus your representatives were throwing up. I got away clean," he assured me, like that made it better. "Nobody saw me—"

"Put. Him. Back!"

"Not. A. Chance!"

"Augustine!"

"You don't even know who he is yet!"

"I don't want to know!"

"Well, you're going to. This is—"

I held up a finger. "First: is it dangerous?"

"*He*," Augustine snapped, "and no. You scared him!"

"My apologies." My head throbbed some more. "Second: is it something I need to deal with?"

"*He*, and no! This has nothing to do with you!"

"Great. Third: get it—him—out of here before Marco finds out. And don't let the witches know you took him, that you live here, or that you have anything to do with me!"

I shook off his grip and shut the door.

For a moment, I just stayed there, hoping he wouldn't follow me. For a wonder, he didn't. After another moment, I let out a sigh and allowed my head to fall back against the wood.

That had been cowardly, I knew it, but right then, I didn't care. I didn't care about much of anything except sleep, and that chocolate I wasn't going to get. If it had been just me, I'd have gone to bed and not worried about four-foot-nothing, broom-handle-wielding sweatshop workers with crazy eyes.

But it wasn't just me.

Rico, I thought. He was laid-back enough not to make a fuss, but diligent enough to watch the situation and make sure this little guy was as harmless as Augustine claimed. But where was he?

Where were any of them?

I had a sudden vision of my whole bodyguard corps just up and leaving, gleefully running off into the night like they'd finally been paroled from hell. Because I'd given them that choice, hadn't I? Why had I done that? Was I stupid?

The evidence was kind of pointing to stupid.

I rubbed my throbbing temple.

Of course, Jonas would be happy to supply me with any number of war mages, as soon as I picked up a phone. And wouldn't *that* be fun? I had a sudden vision of the stern, competent, but judgmental faces of most of the war mages I'd met.

And then I saw Roy from a couple days ago, freckles over his nose, red hair shining in the sunlight. He'd been laughing about this smoker he was going to get with all the swear jar money—which was apparently approaching epic levels—and telling Fred how he was going to smoke us a whole pig. They'd been positively gleeful about it, debating the virtues of mustard- versus tomato-based sauces for what had to be an hour.

Fred.

My heart hurt.

And then my head came up at some weird noises echoing down one of the halls.

There were three that met nearby, in the lounge with the half-moon couches. I wandered back out there, because I couldn't tell where the sounds were coming from. It wasn't the hall to the bedrooms, which I'd have understood, or to the library and classroom wing, where somebody might have been getting a late-night read. It was the one leading to the offices that we had no one to fill at the moment, and to the formal audience chamber, which was weird, because nobody ever went down there—including me.

Except for tonight.

Because tonight, the big, echoing room had been repurposed—as a training salle.

Or maybe not training, I thought, as a blast of spell fire hit the wall beside me as soon as I walked through the door. It was hot enough to sear the air, but didn't leave so much as a mark on the plaster, being absorbed by something I couldn't see, but which was probably a ward. That was good, because a dozen more bolts were right behind it.

I instinctively ducked, trying to get an assessment of the situation, but they weren't all hitting the same place. They were ricocheting everywhere, because Saffy had some sort of shield in front of her—also invisible, but she was holding her arm up like there was something there. And I guess there was, because the bursts of power were hitting a couple of feet in front of her and leaving red or orange glows hovering in the air until the shield absorbed them.

The remaining energy bounced off in different directions, except for what was causing her to slowly back up. Or, to be more accurate, what was pushing her back, sliding her feet across the highly polished floor despite her best efforts to hold position. And then one great big burst decided to top that, slamming into her with the strength of a giant's sledgehammer.

Saffy flipped in midair, but instead of hitting down face-first, as I probably would have, she somehow came down on one knee. For about half a second. Before jumping back to her feet and pulling out her own wand.

"All right, that's it!"

"Defend yourself!" That was Rhea, her long dark hair down around her face, which was twisted in anger.

"The next thing I throw won't be defense!" Saffy snapped, and Rhea's eyes flashed like the lightning sprawling across the sky outside.

"Go ahead!"

"You think I won't?"

"I said *go ahead*!" And outside, thunder boomed, although from where I couldn't tell.

There wasn't a cloud in the sky.

"What is going on?" I asked, standing up. Both girls started, as if I'd been somehow invisible up until then.

Of course, maybe I had—or as good as. Like the rest

of the suite, the throne room, as the guys had taken to calling it, had been designed by a megalomaniac with an unlimited budget and questionable taste. However, for once, she'd restrained herself. Instead of strange décor choices just to show off how wealthy she was, she'd let the natural beauty of the landscape outside do the work for her. It would have been hard to top the spectacular dawns and sunsets that daily bathed the room in rose and gold, made even more impressive by the huge swath of floor-to-ceiling windows all along the side opposite the door.

However, the glittering cityscape at night, mirrored in the sky by a haze of stars, wasn't too shabby, either. I couldn't really compete. Although I seemed to have gotten the girls' attention now.

"What's going on?" I repeated, because they were both just standing there. Saffy looked defiant and guilty and seriously pissed-off, while Rhea . . .

Rhea looked a little crazed.

"They have been like this for hours," Rico said, coming in behind me. He had a tray in his hands, with steaming mugs of cocoa on it. Because Rico is a *god*.

"How did you know that's what I wanted?" I asked, taking one.

"You were muttering about it in the kitchen."

"Was I?" Entirely possible. "I can't find anything in there."

"It is too large," he agreed. "I am still learning it myself."

"I'm never here long enough to learn it," I said, taking a sip. It scalded my tongue, but I didn't care. Heat and comfort and chocolate to boot. Why did anybody ever drink coffee?

"It's good?" he asked, watching me.

I nodded, unable to answer because my nose was already back in the mug. It was one of the big ones Tami had found on arrival, heavy stoneware things that held way more than a cup. They were better than a hand warmer.

"Did you make this with cream?" I asked, because it was luscious.

"Um," Saffy said.

"Half and half," Rico informed me. "Cream is too heavy on its own. It is too rich, yes?"

"I don't think it's possible to be too rich if you're talking about chocolate," I said honestly.

"Uh, hello?" That was Saffy again.

"There's a little . . . guy . . . in Augustine's room," I told Rico. "I think he's harmless, but if you're still on board—"

"I am still on board," he told me firmly, and I couldn't help a stupid smile from spreading over my face.

"That's . . . good," I said, and suspected that my eyes were wet.

"The others are meeting," he told me. "Downstairs in the old suite."

So that's where they'd all gone.

"Marco is giving them twenty-four hours to decide," he added.

I nodded, but didn't ask any questions. They would decide what they would decide. It was frankly a relief that they even felt the need to talk about it.

I cleared my throat. "So, about the little guy—"

"I know of him," Rico assured me. "Augustine's suit fools the eyes, but nothing more."

And that, ladies and gentlemen, was exactly why vamp bodyguards were so damned amazing. Nothing got past them. I smiled gratefully and touched his arm. "Thanks."

He nodded soberly.

"Uh, I hate to interrupt," Saffy said. "But weren't you planning to yell at us or something?"

"I was planning to point out that there's cups here for you, too."

They looked at each other, then at me. And then they came over, because chocolate. Rico handed out the remaining mugs.

"You didn't make one for yourself?" I asked him, because that didn't seem fair.

"I don't like the chocolate," he told me.

"What?" I may have gasped.

He cocked his head at me curiously. "Why is it, whenever I say that around a woman, I get that response?"

"What response?"

"As if I had just blasphemed."

"Well, it *is* chocolate," I pointed out. "That's about as close to heaven as we get on earth."

Saffy snorted into her drink, and then choked. I patted her on the back, and she seemed to be okay. "Damn, I needed this," she told me.

"We were waiting up to see you," Rhea blurted. She hadn't touched her cup.

"Well, now you've seen me," I said. "And that's going to get cold. Better drink up."

She looked down and seemed surprised that she had a mug in her hands. She drank up. Saffy had already been belting back hers, and finished with a sigh. She put the mug back on the tray.

"Okay," she said. "Go ahead. I'm ready."

"Ready for what?" My head almost split open in another too wide yawn.

"For whatever you're going to say."

I regarded her sleepily. "I wasn't going to say anything. Except that it would be nice if you didn't trash the audience hall. We haven't even had a chance to use it yet."

"What did I tell you?" Rico asked her.

Saffy put her hands up. "Hey, preaching to the choir, okay? This wasn't my idea."

"What wasn't your idea?" I asked, and she rolled her eyes.

"Ask her," she said, looking at Rhea.

"You okay?" I asked Rhea, and she nodded sharply.

No, in other words.

Great.

"Give us a minute?" I asked the other two.

"Come, you can help me clean up," Rico told Saffy.

"All right, but I get the spray sink!"

"Not if you are going to shoot me with the little hose again."

Saffy grinned. "Then you better catch me!"

She took off, using enhanced speed, with Rico on her heels. I drank cocoa, because it was good, and wondered why we didn't have any chairs in here. The only one was the aforementioned throne, into which the consul had put all of her thwarted designer energy, and it was hideous.

"I don't think she gets that chairs don't actually have to be gilded," I observed, before Rhea cut me off.

"I will leave tomorrow," she told me in a rush, her face red. "I understand, and I—I will leave tomorrow."

She started out, and I grabbed her arm.

It probably wasn't a good sign that I almost missed.

"I'm really tired," I said, stating the obvious. "And I have this thing I have to do tomorrow. Could you give me the condensed version?"

She just stared at me.

"Like, now?" I suggested.

"I—but you—but I—" She stopped and tried again. "But you *saw*—"

"Saw what?" I was trying for patience, but didn't think I was doing so great. I yawned again; I couldn't help it.

Rhea looked like she'd been slapped. Or maybe I was reading it wrong. I didn't know.

But then she blurted out a torrent of words that I didn't get half of, but that seemed to boil down to: the covens sprang a trap, but if she'd been able to shift like a proper acolyte, she could have gotten her and Saffy out of there before it got bad, but she couldn't because she was trash, so they'd had to stay, and the covens hadn't let them leave, and they'd kept goading and goading until Rhea snapped, because she was trash, so the two girls had fallen into their trap and almost gotten me killed or started a war, because she was trash.

Or something like that.

"And you were beating up poor Saffy because?" I asked.

"I—I wasn't. I just—" She stopped herself before another tirade started, and swallowed. "If I can't shift," she said carefully, "I should at least improve my combat skills, so that I don't get caught like that again."

"Why not just learn to shift?" I asked, and immediately regretted it when Rhea burst into tears.

Well, shit, I thought.

She ran off through the door before I could say anything or even try to reassure her. After a second, I started to follow, because obviously, and almost ran into a very grumpy-looking Hilde coming in the door. She had an old blue silk bathrobe crossed over her ample bosom, some kind of frilly cap over her curls, and an absolute scowl on her face.

"Bed!" she proclaimed, with all the panache of a town crier announcing the birth of a king.

It had been right in my face, so I shied back a bit. "Wh-what?"

"Bed!"

"Are you . . . talking to me?" I actually looked behind me.

And then turned around to find myself almost nose to nose with a red-faced chief acolyte. "BED!"

"I don't think that's how you're supposed to address your Pythia," I told her.

"That is exactly how I am supposed to address her when she has once again exhausted herself to the point of falling on her face! You were supposed to be back hours ago! Do you think it helps the court to have our chief defender running herself ragged? What if there was an attack, hm? What if we needed your support? Could you do that now?"

"Well, I think—"

"No! No, you could not. So, again I say, go to bed!"

"But Rhea—"

"Can wait. That young lady has a lot to learn, and she will. Oh, yes, she will."

The expression on Hilde's face was . . . kind of frightening.

I was suddenly glad that Rhea had escaped.

"I needed to talk to you anyway," I told her. "I agreed to do an errand tomorrow and—"

The next thing I knew, I was standing in my darkened room with my mouth open but nobody to talk to. I was about to turn around, march out, and find Hilde. And explain that you didn't just go around shifting your Pythia!

But then I saw my bed.

And, somehow, I ended up facedown among all the

velvet, just miles and miles of it, still in my clothes but who cared because BED.

I'll deal with it tomorrow, I told myself wearily. I'll deal with everything tomorrow. Tomorrow simply has to be better than today.

Right?

# Chapter Thirty-nine

Tomorrow was not better, although it started out that way. Tami woke me up with the breakfast of the gods, and I don't mean just perfectly cooked bacon, fruit in a leaded crystal cup, and coffee that tasted—and probably was—freshly ground. But also—

"What are *those*?" I asked, blinking sleep out of my eyes.

"Pancakes."

I blinked at them some more, and then poked them with a fork. But I poked carefully. Because the cake on top, the only one I could see out of a fat stack, was not the usual golden brown. Or, rather, it was in places, but in other spots it was . . .

"Rafe," I said, looking up at her.

Tami nodded. "He arrived this morning. Said something about being useless until they fix the mess, whatever that means, and—" She caught my arm. "Where are you going?"

"To see him!" We'd hardly had any time to talk before.

"Wait."

"What's wrong?" I looked around, but didn't see anything out of place. Just the door to the bedroom standing slightly open, and through the gap . . .

"Who is that?" I asked, because there were raised voices filtering down the hall.

"Uninvited guests," Tami warned me. "Get dressed and shift to the butler's pantry. I'll make sure it's clear."

I sighed. But I did as instructed, dragging on a tee and some jeans, running a comb through my bedhead.

Before grabbing my too-pretty-to-eat breakfast and shifting out.

The butler's pantry was deserted, as promised, although there was more almost-shouting filtering in through the louvered doors. I peered out of the ones leading to the main part of the apartment, but couldn't see much. Except for a bunch of leather coats, swaying in a nonexistent breeze, and crowding the small salon with the half-moon couches.

Well, crap.

I backed away and exited through the other door, into the kitchen. Where, sure enough, Rafe was holding court dressed in a huge apron and a chef's hat, and wielding several squeeze bottles of various-colored pancake batter. More bottles, of every possible shade, were scattered across the countertop beside the stove, where he was frying up masterpiece after masterpiece, none of which were long for this world.

"Bird!" a little towheaded tot ordered, and arguably the world's greatest artist paused to set down the bottles and jiggle the pan.

"Are you certain?" he asked somberly. "You would not wish a flower like your friend? Or a little cat? Or perhaps—"

"No! Bird!" she insisted, jumping up and trying to see into the pan. But she was nowhere near tall enough, and Rafe didn't pick her up, for fear, I guessed, that the grease would splatter. But he did expertly flip the pancake a moment later and slide it onto a plate.

Which he then presented to the child with a grin.

"Bird!" she said happily, clapping her hands at the exquisite bluebird that resided in the middle of the nicely browned cake, its wings outstretched as if about to take flight.

Marco had gotten pretty good at making smiley faces, Pikachu, and Mickey Mouse. Along with various bug-eyed monsters that resulted when one of the aforementioned designs went wrong and he quickly added some horns or fangs to pretend that that was what he'd been going for all along. But they weren't in the same ballpark as Rafe's. Hell, they weren't in the same *universe*.

"Marco's gonna have to up his game," I said, staring at the kitchen island. Where a bunch of kids were perched on stools, chowing down on priceless art.

"Marco's busy with your guests," Tami said, pulling up another stool for me and putting a place mat down.

"Do I want to know?" I asked her.

"War mages," Raphael informed me, glancing over his shoulder with a frown. He had the same fondness for the Circle as most vamps—maybe even less, after having served at Tony's for so many years. "They said the Lord Protector sent them for your errand?"

Everybody looked at me.

I paused with a piece of bacon halfway to my mouth and blinked back at them. "What?"

"For your protection," Tami said, looking at me accusingly. "Where are you going that you need protection?"

"Nowhere with them."

"Considering what she gets up to on a shopping trip, do you really want to know?" Roy asked, coming in.

He had another group of tots with him, all of whom had orders for the chef. I took the opportunity that the distraction provided to chow down, although it was hard to bite into even fluffy, still warm pancakes when they had a gorgeous basket of flowers embedded into them, the braided handle perfectly rendered, the small petals and leaves each looking as dewy and fresh as if just picked from a garden. Or a yawning feline on the next cake down, stretching in a patch of sunlight, radiating warmth and contentment. Or a girl on the one at the bottom, with flyaway curls and a mischievous grin, peeking around a door frame, her little toes peering out at the world from under the trailing hem of an old-fashioned nightgown.

It was me when I was about the age of some of the younger initiates. Rafe grinned as he saw me notice, and flipped another cake. "You don't look that different now," he said, taking in the bare toes under my robe.

"How long can you stay?" I asked, hoping he was going to say forever.

"A week or so at least," he promised. "There is little point in embellishment at the moment."

No, I guessed not.

"Why? What happened?" Tami asked, glancing between the two of us.

Rafe looked at me.

"Could I have some more bacon?" I asked, swallowing, because feeding people always got Tami distracted.

Only not this time.

"Cassie—"

And then Marco came in. "You done?" he asked, eyeing my plate.

"Why?"

"We got problems."

I sighed and shoved down another bite. "Then I guess I'm done."

"Here," Tami said, looking exasperated. And plopped a bunch of crispy bacon onto my beautiful portrait before wrapping it up like a burrito. "At least finish your breakfast!"

I happily took it along, greasy and dripping with syrup as it was. If people didn't like it, they could damned well lump it. Especially those people, I thought, making my way into the living room, where the cluster of huge war mages had gotten company of their own.

A lot of it.

"Don't curse her!" Eugenie bellowed, as I emerged from the hall and into a standoff between a bunch of unhappy magical police and an even larger group of their least favorite enemies in the world.

I ducked instinctively, clutching my burrito, but no energy bolts were to be seen. Or weapons, either, for that matter, although the atmosphere was thick enough to warrant them. Just a ton of witches, some of them familiar, some not, and none of them looking happy.

What else is new? I thought, and licked some syrup off my hand, where it was attempting to run down my arm.

"At least give me a moment to explain before you attack!" Evelyn said. To me, I guessed, judging by the fact that she was looking this way.

I glanced around and saw that there were a few vamps behind me, backing me up. Only one of them was Roy, who was casually sucking on a latte; one was Emilio, who was blinking sleep out of his eyes and had the terminal case of bedhead that only us curly-haired types really understand; and the last was Marco. And, okay, Marco had those massive arms crossed over the equally massive chest and was looking fairly fierce, but he in no way appeared to be in attack mode.

I looked back at Evelyn and swallowed pancake. "What?"

She stared at me for a moment, and finally seemed to take in the rumpled bathrobe, the messy curls, and the naked toes. And the syrupy snack that I was still working on, because I hadn't brought enough napkins. I inhaled a bit more while she made a mental adjustment.

"Did we get you out of bed?" she finally asked.

"Out of the kitchen. I was eating breakfast." I looked around at everybody, a number of whom were staring at my food. "You want some?"

The witches glanced at each other.

"I could eat," one of them offered.

And so we all went back to the kitchen.

The war mages followed and clustered near the door, muttering among themselves. But the witches went right on up to Raphael and peered curiously into his pan. And then stared in wonder as he began crafting them perfectly rendered pancake portraits of themselves, using three pans and vampire speed to expedite the process.

"You missed your calling," I told him softly, putting a hand on his shoulder so I could whisper in his ear. "You should have been a chef."

He laughed. "Perhaps I will take up a new profession. After so long, it may be time."

"Lady Cassandra?" one of the mages said, and I looked up.

"You want some breakfast?" I asked.

The man—an older, gray-haired mage with skin like burnished bronze—scowled at me. I didn't take offense; they always looked like that. "No. We want to talk to you."

"As do we!" Evelyn said, bouncing up from a stool with jam on her chin. She gestured at the witches clustered around Rafe, some of whom were suspiciously young-looking and appeared as wide-eyed and charmed as the initiates.

"I'll be back," I promised, eyeing up the girls. "Finish your meal."

She looked like she wanted to argue, because Evelyn always wanted to argue, but Zara put a hand on her arm and pulled her back down. The impressive-looking woman I'd first met at the train station, and who had afterward been part of the attack at the consul's, was standing behind them, looking awkward and out of place. I'd noticed her outside—she was hard to miss—but she didn't seem remotely menacing at the moment. Or all that impressive. More small and chagrined and deflated, with even the electric mass of her hair hanging dispiritedly around her face.

She also wasn't eating, which was a shame, considering that you didn't get a meal like this every day.

She saw me looking at her, and her face fell some more. "I—I wanted to apologize—" she began.

"Eat first, apologize after," I told her, and looked at Tami, who had just come back in with more stools, borrowed from the bar, by the look of them.

"Juice or coffee?" Tami asked, shoving one of the stools behind the impressive woman's knees.

"Uh. What . . . what kind of juice?"

Which was a mistake, because we only had about fifty. Good; that ought to hold her for a while, I thought. Tami started rattling them off, while I stepped outside with the mages.

"Cassie!" Marco called from the living room, before they could get a word in.

"Sorry," I told them, and hurried across the lounge, stuffing down the rest of my breakfast.

"Is it always like this around here?" I heard one of the mages ask.

"No, you caught us before the daily crazy starts," I said, and then wondered if I'd lied. Because Rico was striding across the living room, which wasn't a surprise. And had Rhea thrown over one well-muscled shoulder, which was. Especially considering some of the things that were coming out of her mouth.

One of the war mages reacted, but I put an arm in front of him. "You draw weapons in my house, you never see the inside of it again," I warned.

"But that's the Lord Protector's daughter!"

Looked like word had gotten around.

"And she's fine. Aren't you fine?" I asked Rhea, who had just been carted into the lounge.

"I'll be fine when he puts me down!" she snapped, red-faced and furious.

"I will put you down when you are back in your room," Rico told her easily.

"You will put her down now!" the belligerent young war mage said.

"Stay out of this!" Rhea snarled.

The older war mage sized things up. "Stay out of it," he told the younger man. And then he looked at me. "I suppose you need to deal with this?"

"Yeah. There's coffee in the kitchen, if you don't hex anyone."

His mouth twisted. "We'll try to refrain."

They went back inside and I turned around—and found only Marco there. "Where'd they go?"

He sighed. "To her room?"

"What happened?"

"I don't know any more than you. Didn't even know she'd gone." He eyed the suitcase that Rico had dropped in the middle of the floor when he'd decided he needed two hands to control Rhea's wiggles. "Is she leaving us?"

I scowled. "Hell if I know!"

I grabbed the case and went stomping past the half-moon couches. And then down the hallway that led to the bedrooms. And discovered that, sure enough, Rhea was back in her room, with Rico leaning against the door frame, temporarily trapping her there.

"Move or I'll move you!" she told him, furious.

"Without this?" Rico twirled a wand between his fingers adroitly.

"Where did you get that?"

"When I was a boy, I used to be . . . what is the English phrase? Glue-y fingered?"

"Sticky fingered! And you had no right to take that!"

"And you had no right to sneak out in the middle of the night without so much as a word to anyone," he shot back. "Including your Pythia."

"I told her!" Rhea thundered. "I said—"

"I heard what you said," Rico interrupted. Because of course he had. He'd been in the kitchen last night when Rhea and I had had our abortive conversation. Which, with vampire hearing, was practically the same as being in the room. But I guessed Rhea hadn't remembered that.

Because she suddenly burst into tears. But, weirdly enough, her voice still sounded furious. I couldn't see her, being out of sight of the doorway, but her tone was eloquent when she half yelled, half sobbed: "I'm *useless*! Don't you understand? I've always been *useless*!"

She said some other stuff, but it was muffled by something that was probably her head being pressed against a strong, manly chest. And, you know, maybe this wasn't the best moment to interrupt after all. I quietly set the suitcase down by the wall and tiptoed away.

Only to find myself confronted by another one, this time in Fred's hands, as he snuck out of his door down the hall.

He saw me at almost the same moment that I saw him, and his face went through a number of contortions before settling on panic. He suddenly broke and ran, scampering for the front door like all the hounds of hell were after him. And vamps scamper fast.

But so do shifting Pythias.

"Not a chance," I said, appearing in front of him as he reached for the door handle.

That resulted in me getting poked in the stomach before he snatched his hand back with a curse, but I was past caring at this point. Goddamn it! Couldn't life give me one peaceful morning before the shit show started? Like, just once?

"Cassie—"

"Don't 'Cassie' me!" I snapped. "Take that case back to your room, right freaking now, or I swear—"

"What's the point?" he demanded. "I know you know—"

"You're damned right I know! And we're going to have it out—"

"You said we could leave!"

"Everybody but *you*. You don't get to just slink away somewhere without—"

"I wasn't slinking!" he told me indignantly.

I glared at him.

His cheeks started burning. Fred was the only vamp I knew of who blushed. "I was sort of slinking," he admitted.

The door opened behind me, and I almost fell through. "Cassie?" That was Pritkin.

Normally, I'd have had a few things to say to him, too, considering everything. But the huge wave of relief at seeing him back safely was fighting with my righteous indignation. Not that I *could* see him, since something huge and pillowy and white was pushing its way through the door instead.

It looked like an overstuffed comforter, only fluffier.

"Try this on," he told me, from somewhere behind it.

"What?"

"Cassie?" That was Augustine, coming in from the halls in a huff, a beautifully quilted bathrobe falling off one bony shoulder and his hair standing out everywhere.

"What?" I said, exasperated.

"Somebody said there are witches here?"

"Yeah. They're in the kitchen—"

"What? What are they doing there?"

"Having breakfast—"

"Having—are you *insane*?" he practically shrieked, running up to me. "You know what we have in the—"

I jerked him down by the front of the bathrobe and clapped a hand over his mouth. "Shut. Up."

"Cassie?" That was Tami.

*"What?"*

"Don't take that tone with me," she said, hands on slim hips. "Why didn't you tell me we're about to have eight more mouths to feed?"

"What?"

"Not to mention beds to come up with, when we only have four extra rooms right now!"

"What are you talking about?"

"Cassie?" That was Rico, towing a tear-streaked Rhea into the room behind him.

"I'm talking about the new initiates," Tami said, her face thunderous. "We don't have staff for the ones we already have, and you're accepting new ones? How in the hell—"

"Hold that thought," I told her, then grabbed Rhea and shifted us to my room, where the silence charms had better be working, damn it!

And then a thought occurred, and I shifted back just in time to slam the door on Fred again. "You stay until I say!" I told him. And then I looked at Marco. "He stays!"

"He's not going anywhere," Marco said, and Fred sighed and sagged against the wall.

"Cassie—" Tami said.

"In a minute!"

I shifted back to Rhea, who was standing in the middle of my bedroom, looking nonplussed. "Did you mean it?" I asked her.

"Mean . . . what?" she asked, starting slightly, because I guess she hadn't seen me flash back in.

"That you wanted to help me?"

"What?"

"The other day!" I grabbed her by the arms and shook her a little. "Did you mean it?"

"I—yes. Yes, of course I did. But I can't—"

"You damned well can!" I exploded, and then told myself to calm down. It was too early to be freaking out. I didn't usually get this panicked until at least early afternoon.

"Lady," Rhea said, looking concerned. Because despite her own distress, her natural compassion was taking over. "What is it?"

I laughed. "Oh, nothing. Except that a bunch of witches, including one who tried to kill me last night, just showed up, and now they want to give me some girls—"

"What?"

"—that we don't have room for, so Tami's pissed off, but we can't refuse them or we'll never get this chance again—"

"No, no, of course we can't."

"—not to mention that some war mages are trying to muscle in on an errand that they'll only make worse, because they make everything worse—"

"I . . . they are?"

"—and Pritkin's back, which is good, because he's the one I really need for my errand, only I can't leave because Augustine is hiding a little . . . creature . . . in his workroom that he stole from the witches—"

"He's doing what?"

"—and if they find out, not only will we not get the girls, we'll probably piss them off again, and I can't deal with that right now!" I shook her some more. And then I stopped, because she was starting to look dizzy. "Listen," I said, trying for calm. "I don't pretend to understand everything you're going through, okay? I really don't. Your mom just died, and then you almost died, and I'm a terrible Pythia for not realizing how bad you were hurting and not taking some time to—"

"No!" She looked appalled. "No, this has nothing to do with—"

"—talk to you more and try to help you figure things out. But I suck at that and I didn't know what to say, and I was afraid I'd just make everything worse. So I didn't do enough and I'm sorry for that, I'm really, really sorry! And I'm not saying that just because I need you right now, although I do—"

"You . . . you need me?"

"—and I don't give a damn if you never learn to shift! I need you for plenty of other things, for *this*." I waved an arm around crazily, to indicate the general madness of my life. "And I need you now. Can you help me? Can you deal with this while I go do what I need to do?"

She just stared at me for a second, as if trying to catch up, which, yeah. I knew that feeling. But then her shoulders went back and some of the tragedy left her face. Because Rhea had a spine of pure titanium under all that sweetness, and she was never better than when helping others.

Including a clueless Pythia with far too much on her plate.

"Leave everything to me," she said, and then she hugged me. "Do your duty. I've got this."

# Chapter Forty

Several hours later, I was pretty sure that Rhea had gotten the better deal.

"Holy shit!" I breathed, my heart hammering, my mitten-covered hands clutching freezing stone.

It wasn't the view that had me gasping, despite being worth it. As far as the eye could see in all directions stretched clear blue sky, tall, snowcapped peaks, and air— a lot of it. Crystal clear and so cold that it hurt the lungs I couldn't seem to fill properly.

It felt like being on top of the world—and that was looking ahead. I didn't glance behind me, because if I had, I'd have seen a dizzying drop down a colossal mountain face, like looking back from the top of Everest. I hadn't had to climb all that way, although shifting hadn't been much less taxing, under the circumstances. But it wasn't exertion that had left me breathless, either.

No, that was due to what was moving in the narrow pass miles ahead, across the width of a deep valley, where the piece of sky visible between two huge crags was rapidly getting smaller.

"What *are* they?" I whispered, watching humongous creatures breaking off pieces of stone the size of 747s and throwing them into the gap.

"Manlikans."

"What?"

Familiar, icy green eyes turned from a pair of binoculars to look at me. The other war mages that had come to the suite had been a stopgap, because Pritkin was AWOL when Jonas first tried to reach him. But he'd been happy enough to make the substitution.

I wasn't the only one who'd thought that a part fey would be vastly better for this mission.

Not that Jonas was happy to have us here at all, but even he agreed that there was no better way to spy on our enemies. With the precautions the Svarestri had taken, nobody else could get anywhere near our current location. But my abilities bypassed all those, and unlike the other war mages, Pritkin's magic worked just fine in Faerie.

Not that we were using it at the moment. No, our current camo wasn't a spell but rather a couple of huge, puffy suits that blended in with the snow and had enough insulation to cut through the biting cold. Pritkin had paired his with a close-fitting cap of the same color, which left his face a shocking oval of peach, a vivid thumbprint against the sky, that looked surprised and then vaguely amused at my question.

Which was unfair, considering that I was looking at a moving mountain range!

The creatures in the distance were huge, dark gray, and craggy—what the snow hadn't covered, at least—and vaguely man-shaped, if men were hundreds of feet tall. And had beards of massive icicles hanging down almost to their waists. And small forests of trees growing out of their rocky skulls.

They looked like they'd been formed from the same dark stone as the surrounding mountains, except that mountains stay put, at least earth mountains do. Crazy-ass fey mountains, on the other hand, seemed to like to take a stroll, admiring the view, only with what, I had no idea, because they had nothing to see with. Just deep pits in the rock that gave me the creeps, and that was before I noticed one with a fir tree sticking out of its "eye."

Unlike the copse on its head, which was growing upward in a way that eerily resembled Pritkin's usual spiky hairstyle, this tree poked straight out. It made the creature look like it had been struck through the head by a giant arrow, although that didn't seem to be bothering it any. No more than did the small thatched-roof hut perched on one massive shoulder, which was moving rhythmically up and down with its strides. Or the campfire burning cheerfully in front of the hut, gleaming brightly against all that ice and serving as a hand warmer for a much smaller man.

Not that he *was* small. Like most members of the light fey, he probably topped seven feet, maybe by a lot. And that was without the tall white plume on his close-fitting, black helmet. But at this distance, and compared to his massive ride, he looked tiny.

"They all have riders," Pritkin whispered. "Someone to direct the magic that creates them, binds them together, and controls their actions."

"But what *are* they?"

"A fey construct. You know the fey can manipulate the elements?"

I nodded.

"Well, when they need something done that their physical bodies can't manage, they form servants out of their favorite element to do the work for them. And Aeslinn's element—"

"Is earth." Or whatever you called it here, because earth was far behind us now, back through the portal hidden in the trees that hugged the bottom of the slopes.

It had been cut long ago by Caedmon to spy on his rival, but hadn't been used in centuries. The Svarestri fortress it was supposed to watch had been buried in a landslide, so there'd been no real point. Not until Aeslinn destroyed all the other ways in here, forcing Caedmon to dig it out of mothballs.

The old portal was going to form the staging point for our army's invasion of Faerie, assuming that our current scouting trip worked out. And assuming that the pass the fort had once guarded, before the landslide, could be re-opened. And assuming that the massive things in the distance weren't doing what I thought they were.

Pritkin pulled his binoculars off his neck and passed them over, and I discovered that the manlikans were even more fascinating close up. One had a glittering slash of what appeared to be gold ore across its face, like war paint but cut into the stone. Another had the fossilized bones of some huge creature woven in and out of the rock on its shoulder and back, like some strange tribal tattoo.

And a third had a frozen waterfall spewing out of a gap in the rock where its mouth ought to be, making it look like it was perpetually in the process of losing its lunch.

It was disturbingly funny, like there'd been some kind of contest to see who could create the weirdest ride. As if the fey who had called forth these giants from the surrounding cliffs had a sense of humor, although I doubted it. I'd never seen the Svarestri—Aeslinn's silver-haired warriors—so much as crack a smile.

Of course, they were usually trying to kill me whenever we met, so I guess that might have had something to do with it.

"The riders are the only real vulnerability," Pritkin continued softly. "An external mind for the brainless creation. If you ever have to fight one, don't go for the creature itself; go for the one controlling it."

"I don't intend to fight one," I told him fervently.

"Don't think you'd win?"

I turned to look at him incredulously. *"No?"*

He laughed, and this time, he didn't bother to lower his voice.

"Shh!" I hissed, and tried to get a mitten over his mouth.

He caught my wrist, then just stayed there for a moment, regarding me thoughtfully. Before turning my hand over, tugging down the flap on my glove, and pressing a kiss to the strip of skin he'd revealed. My whole body suddenly went warm.

"You're in a good mood," I said, trying for jovial. But it came out sounding more like Marilyn Monroe visiting a Kennedy. I decided to blame it on the weather.

Only that doesn't work so well when you're dating an incubus.

Green eyes flashed hot in the cold-reddened face, almost as much as the lips still pressed to my pulse. I swear I could feel the heat radiating all the way up my arm. And into other places, I thought, squirming, as liquid warmth spilled through me.

My breath caught, my body tightened, and the grin on my partner's face expanded. "Your cheeks are red," he informed me.

"It's cold." I tried moving back a few feet, to keep a safe distance between us, if there was such a thing anymore, but he came with me. In a sinuous movement entirely unlike the man I knew, whose motions were precise, calculated, and efficient. Pritkin moved like a soldier, which is what he was, what he'd been for almost a century, not like . . . not like *that*.

"Your lips are, too." His head lowered, but stopped just short of the area in question.

"It's very cold," I whispered.

"It is." His breath was warm against my face. "You could catch your death."

That's what I'm afraid of, I thought, slightly hysterically. Because a mountaintop in Faerie with murderous . . . things . . . all around and our only lifeline the thin tether of my power, streaming through the portal far below, was not the place for this—whatever this was.

And I guess Pritkin realized that, too, because he pulled back after a moment, ducking his head and looking rueful. "Sorry. I'm having some . . . issues."

"Issues?"

"Not your fault." He took back the binoculars. "And I'm in a relieved mood," he added, answering my former observation.

I guessed that made sense, considering what he and Adra had found on their scouting trip. Because it seemed that we'd been getting our panties in a bunch for nothing. All the Ancient Horrors had been present and accounted for; even better, there were no signs of tampering with the wards that kept them that way.

And they weren't happy about it.

Their "incarceration" didn't sound so bad to me, being little different than what had been done to Pritkin when he was exiled to earth. They could roam around a cluster of prison worlds, in environments friendly to whatever form they usually manifested; they just couldn't leave. But while Pritkin had been fine with that arrangement, the Ancient Horrors didn't feel the same way.

He'd described them as seething against their bonds and scheming to get out, those that had mind enough to do so. While others raged and savaged each other and bellowed like animals—or monsters. It seemed they'd taken after their godly ancestors in more than just power, because they treated the peaceful life like it was genuine torture. If they couldn't terrorize and murder and subjugate, what the hell was the point?

But they weren't out, and they weren't going to be, with Adra and the council beefing up security and adding layers on top of layers to their wards.

I still had ninety-nine problems, but those bitches weren't one.

The damned pass ahead of us, on the other hand . . .

"So there's three ranges of mountains?" I asked Pritkin.

He nodded, staring through the binoculars again. "Arranged in concentric circles. The fey always say that Aeslinn doesn't need walls around his castle; the terrain made them for him."

"Or he made the terrain," I said, because his command over his element seemed kind of extreme.

But Pritkin shook his head. "He doesn't have that kind of power, although the gods he worships may have, at one point. Legend says they built his castle for themselves, when they first discovered this world, using it as a command center for their conquest of Faerie."

"And no portals," I muttered, watching the manlikans fill in our only way forward.

"For portals you need ley lines, and none are close enough." Pritkin hiked a thumb at the one far behind us now. "That's connected to the nearest line, but even it requires a powerful locus to function. It was never found because it was thought to be too far away for a stable gate."

Great.

I felt so much better now.

"So Aeslinn is forcing us to approach him the old-fashioned way," I summarized. "And blocking the passes to make it harder."

"And the worst of it is, he doesn't have to hold us forever. Just long enough for our time advantage to run out. Then he and his allies can carry out more attacks on earth, and maybe even in the hells—"

"Is that what Adra thinks they're doing?"

Pritkin shrugged. "He thinks it's a possibility. The attack on Hong Kong involved a group of disaffected demons who didn't like the new alliance. They didn't like the gods, either," he added, forestalling the question on my lips. "But they did fear them. They thought if they joined their side now, perhaps they'd get consideration when the inevitable victory took place. And if there's one such group, there are probably others—"

"Nice to know that everybody is so confident in our chances."

"—and once the time streams balance back out, we'll be stretched too thin to commit to a full-on assault."

"And we won't get another shot for a decade," I said, remembering what Caedmon had said.

Pritkin nodded. "We're going to need to push forward our invasion."

I managed to avoid rolling my eyes at him, but it was close. "Have you seen our army? They're cooks and musicians. They're not ready—"

"They will have to be." It was grim. "This is our best chance to win the war quickly and save countless lives. Knock out Aeslinn, and there won't be anyone to shelter our enemies. We'll hunt them down, wipe them out, and then let the bastard gods rage on the other side of the barrier. Your mother's spell has held for thousands of years; there's no reason to think it won't hold for thousands more."

I frowned, because that wasn't strictly true. "Mother said the gods got cocky while they were here, and grew too numerous," I reminded him. "She said there's not enough food where they are anymore—"

"Then let them starve! Or let them slaughter each other the way they slaughtered us!"

I looked at him in surprise, because that had sounded strangely vicious. I was usually the emotional one, with him being Mr. Cool-Headed—or pretending to be. His real feelings peeked through occasionally, but he usually kept a pretty tight lid on it.

But not today. Today, the green eyes were hot and the skin was flushed under the slight tan the Vegas sun had given him. And I didn't think that was all down to the cold.

"But they're not trying to do that," I pointed out. "They're trying to come back—"

"Yes, to destroy our people! Or distort them into hideous things to fight their bloody wars for them!"

"—and willing to take chances that they weren't before—"

"Let them destroy their *own* worlds—"

I grabbed his arm, because he wasn't listening to me. "Pritkin, they're desperate. They did it to themselves, but they're facing extinction—"

"Good! Maybe they'll cannibalize each other and save us the trouble!"

I blinked at him, slightly shocked. "My mother was one of them," I reminded him.

Green eyes blazed into mine. "You are nothing like your mother!"

"That's funny. Everyone else keeps trying to tell me the opposite lately."

"Then they're fools!"

"Are they?" I searched his face.

It was strange; knowing who my mother was hadn't changed my attitude toward the gods one iota. But the fact that Pritkin had some of their blood, too . . . weirdly enough, that did. It made me wonder about them for the first time.

"I still know so little about her," I told him. "About any of them. I've been fighting them for months, but I still don't know them."

"Just as well."

"Is it?"

I glanced at the oddly funny manlikans again. They made me wonder if I knew the Svarestri, either. Were they all like their crazy king, or were there some of them who didn't want this war any more than we did? And if they felt that way . . .

Did some of the gods feel the same?

"This all has to end sometime," I reminded him. "They aren't going to stop coming; we know that. So what's the end game? They all die or we do?"

"Or we prevent them from coming in. There's no other solution, Cassie!"

I frowned. "How do we know that, when we haven't even looked for one? People have wars all the time, but they don't end in annihilation. They make treaties, they compromise—"

"Yes! *People* do. People like you, who have compassion and a kind heart and want to do the right thing. Not the gods!"

"But that's—"

"No! Listen to me!" A strong hand gripped my shoulder. "I know what they are; how they think. I've seen the spawn they left behind. The things they designed— deliberately designed—to use against us! They would view your compassion only as weakness—"

"So you want them all dead, then."

"If that keeps them the hell out of here! As long as you're safe, I could give a damn!"

Hard lips came down on mine, and this time, there was no slow-building sweetness. It was liquid fire that spilled through me, running down every vein, stroking deep inside where no hand could reach. And, suddenly, I could have cared less that we were on a cliff's edge, teetering over top of the world, and not even our own.

But I did care about something else.

*"Pritkin!"*

"I know. Give me a moment," he said, struggling a little with the snowsuit.

"No! Not that!"

"What?" He blinked at me, the green eyes looking almost drugged.

"That!" I whispered, and physically turned his head toward what was coming around the side of the mountain.

"Bloody hell," he breathed, and flung himself on top of me.

# Chapter Forty-one

I was about to protest—not the *time*—when I noticed: the vivid arc of the sky had just dimmed and the mountains had blurred, as if covered by some kind of—

"Shield?" I whispered.

"Camouflage," Pritkin said, as my eyes finally managed to focus on what looked like a soap bubble stretching all around us. It was more or less transparent, except for the bits of snow catching on the surface. But I guess that wasn't true from the other side.

Because the giant sentinel coming our way didn't see us.

Not that it probably could have anyway, I thought, staring at the strangest creation I'd seen yet.

This manlikan was even jazzier than the one with the gold war paint, with a head that looked like a giant geode had exploded. One side was crusty and dirty, with clods of earth clinging precariously to the pitted "flesh," as if a tumor had eaten half the face. But the other half was breathtakingly beautiful, with chiseled features and crystalline spikes of what looked to be pure amethyst that caught the sunlight in dazzling profusion.

Everything from deep purple to palest violet speared out in all directions, with the largest being a massive column that had to be four stories tall. It was so dark in color at the base that it was almost black, before going through every possible shade of purple as it rose upward, until it finished almost clear at the tip, showing a distorted mountain scape beyond. And it was so heavy that the creature's "head" was permanently drawn slightly to one side.

For a moment I just stared. Faerie was the most beautiful hell I'd ever seen. And then I spotted something else, half-hidden among the crystalline forest. Something that looked a lot like a tent.

Maybe because it was, I realized, noticing the leather strips tied between two of the smaller spikes and holding up a patched and weathered hide.

One that a fey soldier had just come out of.

His black armor gleaming in the sunlight, his silver hair flying in the wind, he looked like something straight out of Tolkien, a vision of knightly splendor from a forgotten age.

Until he crouched awkwardly in front of a firepit with his knees around his ears and began trying to coax a spark to life.

"Shh," Pritkin whispered, entirely unnecessarily at this point.

The fey looked up, maybe coincidentally or maybe because their hearing isn't just a myth. But Pritkin's camo held. It helped that there were plenty of other sounds: the wind, whistling through chasms in the mountains; the distant call of some kind of hawk, far overhead; the rhythmic *crash, crash, crash* of stones as big as skyscrapers being thrown into the pass.

And the chittering of small things inside the bag I'd dropped when we arrived, who were obviously tired of waiting to be let out.

Pritkin and I both froze.

The bag was an oversize backpack, made of double-stitched nylon and sturdy, but not sturdy enough. A loud *scritch, scratch, scritch* carried clearly in the cold mountain air as something inside fought to get out, and fought hard. A second later, I saw a dark nail poke through the material, looking like a prehistoric talon.

Shit!

*Can you shut them up?* I mouthed at Pritkin.

He shook his head and glanced at the bubble. Not without popping the camo. And it was the only thing keeping us hidden, because the damned mountain obviously meant to come right past us!

Our saving grace was that the backpack was dark gray,

too, and almost matched the stone it was lying on. It had also become dusted with snow, furthering the resemblance to the natural surroundings. If they'd just *shut up*, I thought, there was no reason for them to be seen.

They weren't shutting up. They were also writhing around now, rolling this way and that, making the sack look like it was having convulsions as they fought to widen the hole they'd made. Probably because the fey had decided to prepare himself a little snack.

It looked like he and his ride were on guard duty, covering the perimeter of the huge construction zone, where he was supposed to keep a watch for nefarious types like us. But the other manlikans were busy at the pass and not paying him any attention. And our location, as luck would have it, was about as far from them as his circuit allowed.

Time for breakfast, then.

And time for us to get out of here, only we couldn't. We weren't finished yet! And it wasn't like there was anybody else to take our place.

Tristram, the creepy, dragon-hide-wearing mage from the consul's, was Caedmon's usual spy in the area. The king had employed him for years, because of plausible deniability if he got caught, which was why he'd been sitting with the fey instead of the mages during the war council. Part fey himself, he had disdained the human world as Pritkin had the demon, preferring his father's family, who happened to be part of a lower-level house aligned with Caedmon's court.

Despite his less-than-fey-like appearance, Tristram had inherited their stealth abilities, as well as a good bit of fey magic and an elongated life. He'd spent the last few centuries prowling around these mountains, learning every nook and cranny, every tiny, supposedly impenetrable pass and cave, and ingratiating himself with the locals down the slopes. He'd become known as a bolder-than-average trader who offered food in exchange for fey medicine, amulets, and hides.

The Svarestri knew of him, although not of his alliance with their enemy, and disdained him as they did all half-breeds. But their food situation was precarious enough that they let him operate anyway, viewing him as repugnant but harmless. Or, at least, they had up until the war.

Now, all trade had been suspended, and everyone who wasn't completely trusted had been banished from Svarestri lands or forcibly moved farther in. And that included everybody in the nearest towns, where Tristram had based his operation. Getting caught here now meant an immediate death sentence—assuming that Aeslinn's new, ramped-up security force didn't kill you first!

Not that this one seemed too interested in trying.

The fey soldier had stuck some strips of animal flesh on the end of a spear and was using it like a spit to roast his food. It smelled delicious, and I guess I wasn't the only one who thought so. Because the writhing had just gotten faster.

I saw Pritkin mouth something profane and felt his body tense. The great, crystalline head was almost on a level with us now, and he was preparing to jump the fey. Probably to keep him from sounding the horn that resided conveniently on a loop of hide by the tent flap.

And that . . . wasn't good. Not just because the fey had a few million pounds of backup. But because we had a payload to deliver, one that would almost certainly be discovered if the damned guard went missing!

I grabbed Pritkin's biceps, beginning a furious, if silent, struggle. And tried to decipher some mouthed words I couldn't make out but didn't need to. If the idiots in the pack didn't quiet down, right freaking now, we were screwed, because the mountain wasn't coming anymore; it was *here*.

Which is why I froze the little ankle-biting assholes, before they could attempt to mug a fey.

As usual, time stoppage was a *bitch*, even a small one. Which is why it felt like somebody had just punched me in the gut. But on the plus side, the little creatures had frozen in place as if trapped in a nonexistent block of ice.

Not that it mattered.

Because the walking mountain suddenly wasn't.

I don't know if it was the swirl of unfamiliar magic, or the sounds the creatures had been making, or what, but the massive sentry suddenly shuddered to a halt, almost on top of us. The snow flooded purple as daylight cascaded through semi-precious stone, and I contemplated having a heart attack. The manlikan's massive head had paused almost even with our ledge, with it and its rider practically close enough to touch.

He was close enough that I could feel the occasional warmth from his fire when the wind blew just right. Close enough that I could see his handsome, expressionless face as he scanned the area, gray eyes narrowed and bright and searching. Close enough that he almost landed on top of us when he put down his spear, grabbed his horn, and jumped—

Straight onto the snow beside our bubble.

Our camo rippled from the impact, and a little snow sifted off the top, which would have made me catch my breath if I'd had any, because he had to have seen that!

But he hadn't.

Maybe because he was focused on something else.

Pritkin realized it the same time I did. I saw his eyes follow the direction the fey was headed, the same one where a small, frozen creature had been caught, half in and half out of the bag, its knobby ass in the air and one tiny arm reaching for the breakfast it wasn't going to get. Because, in a second, it was going to be dead.

Like us, I thought, my heart hammering from lack of oxygen, my vision starting to gray out.

Or maybe that was due to something else. Because the missing snow on top of our bubble was suddenly replaced. It rapidly grew thicker, to the point that I could hardly see the guard anymore. A storm that had in no way been threatening broke overhead, sending translucent white veils dancing across the mountaintop and causing Pritkin to let out a stifled grunt.

I looked up to find him red-faced and straining, a hand extended as far as the bubble would allow, his eyes closed in what looked like pain.

And then half a ton of snow dumped directly onto the fey's head.

He went down, cursing, and almost slid off the ledge. He got up, flailed around for a second on the slippery ground, searching for purchase he didn't find. And then went down again when a strong gust of snow-laden wind slapped him in the face. That happened a few more times before he cursed and went running, his feet crunching on the new-fallen snow until he leapt the gap—

And natural light flooded back across the mountain-top as the huge creature filtering the sun slowly moved away.

For a moment, I just lay there wondering why things were still hazy, before I remembered. And took a deep breath, which Pritkin must have thought I meant to use to scream, because his hand came down before I finished. I thrashed around for a moment, finally got free, and gasped in enough air to right the mad Tilt-A-Whirl I seemed to have ended up on.

And realized that someone was shaking me.

"Why didn't you just freeze the guard?" Pritkin demanded.

I stared at him for a moment in disbelief, and then I started hitting him. I doubt he felt it through all the insulation, but I didn't care. Son of a bitch mother—

He grabbed my wrist. "What is wrong with you?"

"Nothing!" I hit him some more with my other hand until he grabbed that one, too.

"Try again."

I glared at him. "I shouldn't have to!"

He just looked at me.

"A boyfriend would have asked me how I am!" I told him furiously. Because it was true. I was pretty sure it was true. And because I didn't know what we were to each other anymore, and it pissed me off!

We used to be friends, and now we were obviously more than that, but how much I didn't know. Or if we were more than that, or if that was just my human side assuming things Pritkin had never verified, never even alluded to, because maybe this was friendship for an incubus. Especially one who had just gotten his power back and was having "issues," as he put it!

Well, maybe I was having issues, too! Because one minute, there we were in a passionate embrace, practically melting the snow off the mountainside, and the next, he was lecturing me like it was our first mission together and I didn't know anything! Like he hadn't listened to me about Adra when I pointed out that maybe running off with a guy who'd recently killed you wasn't the best plan. Or about the gods when I said, hey, you know what, maybe we ought to find out some more about the people we're fighting. Or anything else!

I knew it was fear and spent adrenaline making me freak out, but it wasn't *just* that. I'd been complaining that I never saw Pritkin, that we'd spent the last two weeks mostly apart. But now that we were together, I didn't know how this was supposed to work.

I'd had exactly one relationship before, with a master vampire who was more like a force of nature. Mircea had just swept in and handled everything. We'd rarely discussed our relationship at all.

I'd just somehow ended up in a luxury hotel suite surrounded by his guys, with a credit card I hadn't asked for and didn't use because it felt weird, sitting around waiting for his call. Like one of the many mistresses he'd had through the years, but not like anybody permanent. Not like a *wife*.

Because he already had one of those, and nobody was allowed to take her place.

So I'd never really had a chance to find out how a normal relationship worked.

But I didn't think this was it!

"I'm your partner, not your boyfriend, a word I hate in any—" Pritkin paused, and his head tilted. "Wait. Am I?"

"How the hell would I know?" I demanded, in a vicious whisper, because that thing was still too close. "When do we ever talk? About *anything*? Caleb's always there, or Tami's coming by with some more goddamned soup, or you're running off half-dead to do some crazy errand for Jonas, or we're both about to die!" I gestured around. "Even at the top of the world, something is always trying to kill us!"

Pritkin just looked at me some more, an odd expression on his face. I jerked away, waving my arms like a madwoman to dissipate the camo bubble. Outside, the sun was glaringly bright, but the snow was still coming down fast and hard. We needed to get this done.

I stomped over to the little bastards in the bag. They were called spriggans, and there were three of them, small, round, bumpy creatures that could hunch down and give decent impressions of rocks when they wanted. Which was why they were here.

Human tech didn't work so well in Faerie, especially if you want it to beam info back to earth, so the spriggans were a work-around. They'd long been used by the dark fey as spies on their enemies. Put one or more where you wanted, and have a *vargr*—a sort of fey seer—peer through their eyes and tell you what was going on.

Of course, *vargrs* could do that with birds, too, but they were being shot down left and right by the Svarestri whenever they got too close. Besides, birds gave a brief snapshot of a scene before wheeling off again, and we needed constant eyes on the ground—or, more appropriately, the pass—to make sure our work crews didn't get a surprise. Hence, the asshole contingent.

Luckily, Pritkin and I didn't have to worry about their attitude problems. We just had to get the living cameras into place, along with some supplies, without anybody noticing. And then get ourselves out.

Which was going to be the hard part, I thought, glancing back down the mountain. We had to get back to the portal after this was done, a feat that would have daunted Edmund freaking Hillary, except for the Pythian ability to shift through space. It wasn't as impressive as time manipulation, but it was a hell of a lot easier.

At least, it was when I hadn't already done a spatial shift and a time stoppage practically back to back! And even a brief time bubble was expensive, powerwise. I needed to refuel.

"Do you have any granola—" I asked, starting to turn, before something caught my eye.

Because it didn't look like Pritkin had conjured up a snowstorm after all. He'd conjured up a *wind*storm, which had picked up snow from one part of the mountain and dumped it on another. Including the snow that had been covering something sprawled beneath a nearby boulder.

Something wearing a dragon-hide coat.

It was bright green and shimmering softly under the brilliant sun, like a spill of emeralds. But it didn't feel like them. It felt like sharp-edged silk, something almost liquid it was so fine, running through my fingers like water when I tugged on it, trying to see—

Oh God.

I stumbled back a step, because the head . . . wasn't there. A ragged, blackened stump of a neck and a frozen bloody pool were all that was left. Until I spotted the missing piece a yard or so off, wedged between some rocks.

It hadn't decomposed, being so high up. But it looked like it had been pecked at by birds or gnawed on by animals—maybe both. The eyes were gone—thankfully—and so was a lot of the soft tissue.

But the cracked and blackened teeth were still the same.

I stared into that frozen rictus, and a wave of dizziness hit me. Because that . . . was impossible. The remains looked like they had been here for days, maybe weeks, before the snow covered them up. But I'd been talking to Tristram just last night, and in a place that checked people for glamouries before they came in. He *couldn't* have been anyone else—

Unless that someone else was a nine-hundred-year-old mage with the equivalent of a master's powers. I'd even thought it myself: what if Jonathan had developed new abilities over all those years? Like being able to morph his looks without the need for glamouries?

It would explain how he'd been able to elude both the Circle and senate for so long, and how I could have been talking to him last night when—

When he'd suggested coming up here. When he'd sworn that he couldn't get past Aeslinn's security to spy on the pass. When he'd insisted that he needed me and my power to do it instead—

Holy *shit*.

I jumped back to my feet and spun around, a warning on my lips.

Only to find myself face-to-face with someone, but it wasn't Jonathan.

It wasn't Pritkin, either. He was where I'd left him, with an out-flung arm and a half-open mouth, caught in the middle of a spell. One he'd never had a chance to finish because somebody had frozen him, like I'd done to the little creatures in the bag.

Probably the dark-haired woman standing in front of me.

"Hi!" Jo said brightly, and stabbed me.

# Chapter Forty-two

The only thing that saved me was my Michelin Man jacket, stuffed with a hundred ducks' worth of down, and the matching padded overalls I was wearing underneath. I guess Jo hadn't been expecting that. Like I hadn't expected to feel the blade pierce my flesh, a sharp, burning pain; or to see my white suit flood bright red; or to smell my own blood on the air as the world tilted from shock—

And then I was reaching for my power and pushing *back* against time, although it felt like moving a mountain, like moving the whole world. Because this *wasn't* my world, and every action in Faerie took ten times the strength. And that was without a knife sticking out of my ribs!

But I wasn't dying here, not at anyone's hands, and especially not *hers*.

I felt it when my power surged around me, when time slowed and then stopped, leaving the vicious satisfaction frozen on Jo's face. The narrowed eyes glittered; the dark hair flowed out like a frozen banner behind her; the lips snarled, baring teeth almost as sharp as a vampire's. But that wasn't what had me staring.

What had me staring was that she looked exactly the same as always.

Jo was a necromancer, whose freed spirit jumped bodies with ease, and so death for her was a little different than for most people. But I hadn't expected to see her like *this*, like nothing had ever happened. Stupid, stupid!

Spirits manifest bodies in Faerie, as I knew from some of Billy Joe's adventures. I should have expected her to end up here, sooner or later, where my power couldn't track her. Especially since she'd been working with the goddamned Svarestri!

Like I should have expected her to pull herself out of my spell within seconds, because she was an adept, too.

There was no transition, as I'd seen with the few others who had the power to break through a time stoppage. No time to see the thick, black eyelashes flutter, or the chest rise and fall as she drew in a breath. No time for anything.

One second she was frozen, and the next I was battling for my life with a blade still stuck an inch into my flesh.

Until I used one of the moves Pritkin had showed me and twisted out of her grip, cutting myself in the process, since the knife stayed stationary. But it was a flesh wound, burning and stinging and bleeding enough to stain my suit, even through all the padding, but not mortal. And I was too busy throwing Jo to the ground and kicking her upside the jaw to care.

The sharp ice cleats on the bottom of my boot sliced open three gouges across that pretty face, but she didn't react except to tackle me again as I lunged for Pritkin. I needed to get a hand on him to pull him out of her spell, but that wasn't going to be easy. She didn't try to freeze me, probably because she couldn't, having just done the same thing to him. But she could grab my legs and send me crashing to the ground.

So I smashed her in the face with my cleats some more, causing her to cry out and let go, and allowing me to scramble ahead for a couple of yards while staring behind me—

Before having to dodge to the side, to avoid the knife quivering out of the rock where my torso had just been.

I rolled over, kicked her in the stomach as she sprang at me, heard her scream—

And then she was gone, as suddenly as she'd appeared.

I lay in the snow for a second, breathless and staring. Then I scrambled for Pritkin and jerked him out of the remnants of her spell. The one he'd almost finished breaking himself, which had me doing a double take. Jo must have realized he was almost free; that's why she ran.

But where? And to do what? I stared around, because

Jo just. Didn't. Quit. It was her most memorable attribute.

Well, except for the hate.

*"Are you all right?"*

I realized that Pritkin was yelling at me. I swiped a sleeve across my face; my nose was running and I was breathing hard. And my side felt like—

I looked down.

Like someone had fucking stabbed me.

"It isn't that bad," I told Pritkin, who was shaking me. And then cursing, and looking around.

"Jo," I said. And saw his eyes widen, because I'd told him about her during some of our abortive visits.

Or perhaps that look was down to something else, I thought, following his line of vision. And catching sight of what was barreling at us through the clear blue sky like a gigantic missile. Only it wasn't a missile. Or a manlikan. Or anything else I could possibly have expected.

*"What the fu—"* Pritkin yelled.

And was cut off when I shifted us, trying to get out of the way of the latest impossible thing to threaten our lives. But it was coming too fast and I was still dizzy, and then it didn't matter anyway. Because we were standing in the aisle of an old-fashioned steam train.

That's what I'd seen screaming toward us through the skies, as crazy as that sounds, and I guess I hadn't been hallucinating. Or, if I was, my brain was still working overtime, showing me a crowd in Gibson Girl outfits with high collars and long skirts, or three-piece suits with top hats and pipes. The latter of which were falling out of mouths that had opened in shock, because it didn't look like they understood what the hell had just happened, either.

Neither did I; I just knew we were about to—

"Augghhhhhhhh!" The entire car screamed as one when the train hit the ground and plowed through a couple hundred feet of snow, and then kept on going. Because we weren't on a level; we were on a small, tip-tilted plateau at the top of a mountain that dwarfed most on earth, and now we were—

"Shiiiiiiiiiiiit!" I screamed, and grabbed Pritkin.

I had a split second to see the world tilt, to see the sky skew around us, to see the ridiculously steep and rocky slope going down, down, down slide by outside a window—

And then we were falling. Or, to be more precise, we were rolling, because antique steam trains are not designed to ski down Everest! The train car started rotating, and people started tumbling—like the guy with a copy of the morning *Times* still firmly wedged under his arm and a pair of small spectacles perched on his nose, who flattened me to the floor.

He didn't stay there long, because we were rolling constantly now as the train really got into it, throwing people around, breaking windows, and slamming me in the face with someone's boot and someone else's umbrella.

Which is why I didn't understand it when our ride suddenly smoothed out.

I fought my way free of some petticoats, shoved aside somebody's little yappy dog, and looked up to find Pritkin standing over me. His arms were outstretched, his face was agonized, and despite the weather, he was sweating bullets. Which made no sense, because he wasn't *doing* anything.

Except for that, I thought, as I stumbled to my feet. And looked out a window. And saw us, the whole long train of us, *skiing down Everest*.

I scrambled closer to get a better view, crawling over people who didn't object, because they were staring at the same thing. It took me a second to figure out what was going on, because of all the snow and icy bits being flung up at the broken windows, hitting me in the face. But after a moment, I caught a glimpse of something familiar—namely the distinctive blue of Pritkin's shields.

They were underneath us, forming a pad that I guess was taking the brunt of the beating and banging of who knew how many tons of iron slamming its way down a mountain. The result was a magical shock absorber for us, and a stroke for him, because he clearly wasn't going to be doing this much longer. I didn't know how he was doing it *now*, or how Jo had grabbed a train out of time and flung it through the air at us, which was way above her pay grade—hell, it was above *mine*—or how this was happening in Faerie, where our power wasn't even supposed to work!

And then it got worse.

"What is *that*?" a woman beside me screamed, clutching a crying baby. And staring out of the window at the geode-headed manlikan, which was matching our pace down the mountain and now carrying two riders.

And a couple of rocks.

Only no, not rocks. They were boulders the size of large buildings, which came crashing toward us a second later, because I guess we weren't dying fast enough. One hit something that caused it to bounce over top of us, but the other—

Slammed into a bolt of power that Pritkin threw out the window, shattering it into a million pieces that peppered the train like bullets, startling the stunned crowd and starting the screaming again.

Or maybe that was the rolling, which had also started up again, because Pritkin's shields had just cut out.

I grabbed him as we went over. "Handle the train!" I yelled. "I'll handle them!"

Only it didn't look like he'd heard me.

He was clutching me to his chest, trying to shield me, when I needed him to be shielding the train, goddamn it!

Then we hit a patch of ice and momentarily stopped rolling, and started sliding out of control. As the train slung around, I recognized the second rider as Jo, her dark hair flying, her hand clutching a fey spear that I assumed was meant for me. Because no way was she letting me walk away from this.

We had far too much history for that.

I shoved my hand into a pocket of my shirt, pulled out a little bottle, and flicked off the cork with a thumb. The contents smelled rancid enough that they caused a nearby man to rear back in alarm, in spite of everything. But to me, they were sweet as candy.

Okay, bitch, I thought. Want to play? Let's fucking play.

And I belted back a whole bottle of the Tears of Apollo.

It hit like a train wreck itself, watering my eyes and etching my throat like acid all the way down. I barely noticed. Because right on the heels of the pain was power, a sudden, eye-opening, vein-expanding, world-altering rush of it, tingling out from my core to my fingertips, and just in time.

Because the manlikan had found another rock, and this one was the biggest yet, looking like a small mountain itself. Pritkin's lips had been working as he muttered a spell, probably trying to get the pad back, but at that he cut off. And prepared to launch another bolt, which probably wouldn't work because of the rock's size, and wasn't needed anyway!

"No!" I shook him. "You handle the *train*! I'll take *them*!"

And I know he heard me this time, since I was practically screaming in his face, but he wasn't letting go, and he wasn't shielding, because he thought the rock was a priority. Which it was—until I shifted it out of the air as it came screaming for us and popped it just behind the manlikan's head instead. Which it nailed a second later, right in the skull.

The massive geode shattered, sending pretty shards flying everywhere, like a crystal firework. I didn't see what happened to the fey rider, but Jo was a different story. Because she was suddenly here, vanishing off the manlikan's shoulder and appearing behind Pritkin, spear raised—

Only to have it crumble to pieces in her hand, the sharp metal point clanging against the floorboards as I aged the wooden shaft to powder.

Pritkin's eyes widened; I guess he hadn't seen me duel before. Things changed while you were gone, I didn't say, because I didn't have time. That move would have bought me a few seconds from someone else, but not from Jo. She threw out her other hand, not missing a beat, and I barely managed to counter.

Leaving two time spells meeting and fighting each other in midair.

I'd seen that snarl of boiling colors before, and it never ended well. Best-case scenario, they'd ricochet off each other and age whatever they encountered out of existence. Worst-case—

They did that, I thought, seeing bubbles start to form where the two spells met, like the foam on a glass of beer. Ones that were about to fly off in every direction and age tiny holes through everyone and everything in the damned train car. And *screw* that!

I threw a spell with my other hand—not something I'm particularly good at—but it connected. Just not like I'd planned. I'd meant to shift just Jo, but I guess we were linked by the time spells, because I ended up going, too.

Out onto the roof, where the wind blew us both off our feet and almost off the train!

But the time bubbles sailed over our heads and into the void, which was good. And I almost followed them, sliding backward half a carriage length before my stomach caught the end of the car, which was bad. Then Jo blew into me, sending us both into the gap and down onto the tiny platform that connected the carriages. And, okay, that was worse.

Because her knee in my wound knocked the air out of me, while her hands tried their best to push my head into the wheels, which were still churning away for some reason!

Probably because the engine was still running, I realized, watching a plume of dark gray smoke stream by overhead, framing the wild, manic face of the woman above me. Jo . . . did not look remotely sane, with a Joker-worthy grin splitting her face halfway open. "Isn't this fun?" she screamed.

And kept on screaming as I aged the life out of her, my hand clenched around her throat, my voice screaming along with hers. Because the trauma of having to do this twice in two days was almost worse than the power drain. But I kept it up, even as her eyes bulged, as her skin drew up like a desiccated mummy's, as her clothes rotted off. Yet the sinewy arms kept trying to force my head under the wheels, which were getting closer and closer, to the point that I couldn't tell what was her scream, what was mine, and what was the damned train's!

Until she exploded, papery bits of flesh and sinew flying everywhere, like a fleshy bomb.

And before I could figure out if that had been because

of the time spell or another reason, another reason was looking down at me.

"Come on!" Pritkin yelled, thrusting out a hand. I grabbed it, and he pulled me back into the car, slamming the door behind us and holding me against his chest. "Brace for it!"

Brace for what? I thought, staring around in confusion.

But I didn't get a chance to ask. Because the next second, the winter wonderland streaming by outside the windows was replaced by something else. We'd just torn through the portal, I realized, shredding its power on either side with our bulk. And were riding the midnight express through Dante's, the glittering, clanging, colorful casino I called home.

No, I thought, staring around.

Wait.

The train didn't wait.

We hit the back wall of the casino's main drag, bounced off, and then kept on bouncing as train car piled on top of train car, cushioned somewhat by Pritkin's spell, but the best shields in the world won't fully absorb the impact of thousands of pounds of iron hitting at top speed. It seemed to go on forever—how many damned cars were there?—before finally settling down into a jumbled wreck of billowing steam, splintered wood, and people who weren't even screaming anymore but just clinging to whatever they could find, looking shell-shocked.

At least, those in our car were. I could hear other screams from outside, but dimly. I wasn't sure if that was because people were caught beneath the wreckage, muffling the sound, or because of what felt like every warning siren ever going off inside my head.

Pritkin had me in a death grip, but I wriggled free, climbed over a seat, and pushed my head out of a missing window.

It didn't help.

I couldn't see past the smoke.

I also couldn't exit through the doors at either end of the car, which looked like they'd been welded to the carriage by the impact.

"Move back," Pritkin told me, coming up alongside.

And the next thing I knew, there was a new door in the side of the car, where a section had been blown out and flung who-knew-where. I didn't care. I was scrambling through it and out into a jumbled-up mess of black iron and shattered glass and drifting smoke—

And an area of clear floor up ahead that I shifted onto in a crouch, only to stare around in horror.

Smoke was billowing everywhere, and the scattered coals from the engine had started fires here and there, whenever they encountered something flammable. But the cars looked mostly intact, and there were stupefied faces starting to peek out of the mostly missing windows. I didn't know how Pritkin had done it, but he'd held the shield long enough to make the disaster at least survivable.

But not *right*, I thought, looking around at a faux Old West town filled with shops and cafés, souvenir stands, and yard-long beers. And a taco-selling donkey cart that shouldn't be here—none of this should—because it had all been a casualty of the war!

Before I could figure out what was going on, I was pushed to the side by hotel security, who had arrived in force and were trying to hold back crowds of screaming tourists and get to the others who were scattered across the ground. Because they hadn't had shielding, had they? The drag looked like a battlefield—again—which is what I guessed it was, but I couldn't seem to concentrate on it. I couldn't seem to concentrate on anything.

Until I spotted a used paper cup in the mess by an overturned trash can.

People were jostling, security was yelling, and—somewhere—Pritkin was calling my name. I barely heard. Because I'd zeroed in on that cup like a spriggan on a meat spear, and nothing was keeping me from fighting my way through the crowd and grabbing it.

And then just standing there in the midst of the huge, unruly mob, being jostled this way and that while an alarm bell rang inside my head. Which went up a couple hundred decibels when I turned the cup over and read the name printed in cheerful, leaping flames on the side:

"Welcome to Diablo's Hotel and Casino. Have a devilish good time!"

I staggered back and abruptly sat down.

Oh, I thought.

Holy shit.

# Chapter Forty-three

Four hours later, I hit a wall.

Or, to be more accurate, I hit two.

I'd just shifted into the old Pythian Court in London with a couple more displaced train passengers. Getting everybody back where they belonged was stage one in repairing the timeline, but it was easier said than done. A lot easier.

I'd already decided that this was going to be my last trip of the day, even though I'd barely made a dent in the several hundred people the train had been carrying. But the leaps had been getting harder and harder, with this last one feeling like I was wading through cold molasses. I groaned with effort when we finally pushed past the last sticky filaments holding us back—

And popped into one of the parlors on the ground floor of the old Georgian mansion the court had once called home.

It was a small, cramped room where supplicants usually kicked their heels waiting for the current Pythia to see them. And since she had more visitors than she wanted, she hadn't bothered to make it too pleasant: the dark, heavy furniture looked uncomfortable, and the fussy velvet drapes left it gloomy, even when it wasn't night. But it had been working well enough as a landing pad.

At least, it had until now.

Something was wrong.

I staggered into a wall, one covered in beige wallpaper with tasteful burgundy ribbons, and also into one featuring unpainted drywall and food splatters above a plastic garbage can. My eyes kept trying to cross because I was seeing both at the same time and couldn't seem to stop. Just as I couldn't stop my legs from collapsing underneath me.

In my body, I hit the floor; in my head, I saw another Cassie. I had no idea what was happening, only that she seemed to have been left behind when I shifted, peeling off me like I suddenly had a twin. A very confused one.

But after a moment of standing in the middle of the drag, looking as blank as I felt, she moved toward one of the cafés. It was mostly intact, having just been clipped by the carnage. As a result, although the servers had been sent home or pressed into service elsewhere, the emergency crews had been helping themselves to refreshments all afternoon.

While I was transitioning here, the other Cassie had followed suit, slipping behind the counter and into the kitchen, only to find that all the coffeepots were empty. Since there were about a thousand people trying to clean up the mess that one vengeful adept had made, she'd decided to start some more. But that wasn't what had happened.

She ended up on the floor, too, coffee grounds scattered around her, the pot clutched in one hand that didn't seem to want to let it go. I watched her smash it again and again into the wall, until there was glass everywhere and her hand and arm were cut and bleeding, but she still didn't stop. A garden of bloody fist prints bloomed like roses on the drywall, her feet made garbage angels in the trash after she kicked over the can, and—and—and—

And now we were both convulsing, her in that other time and me in this one, my back arching like it would break before slamming itself against the hardwood floor.

The two train passengers I'd brought with me just stood there, staring straight ahead, their glassy eyes making them look like mannequins. They'd been mind-wiped by members of the War Mage Corps, which had been helping with the cleanup, and that left people pretty zoned out for a while. So they weren't going to be calling for help.

And neither was I. My teeth were clenched hard

enough to hurt, but something had started foaming out of my mouth onto the floor, like I'd been chewing on soap. I stared at it in horror, and not just because of me.

But because that other Cassie had started to choke.

I was on my back, too, but with my head rolled to one side; she was staring straight upward, at the stained tiles in the kitchen ceiling that were never changed, because no guests were supposed to be back there. One was missing, giving the whole lineup a gap-toothed smile, like the universe was laughing at us. Like Jo, I thought, seeing her hateful face again.

But she wasn't here! She was dead! Finally, completely!

Like I was about to be, I thought, despite the Pythian Court being a working anthill of people.

They were coming and going not twenty feet away, passing quickly across the large entryway that the parlor opened onto. I could see them past the male passenger's legs: war mages with grim looks on their faces, tracking muddy footprints across the marble floor; acolytes rushing about, the hems of their long white dresses damp from the snow that swirled in every time the door was opened; dull-faced castaways standing around, looking blank, waiting to be led gently away; and Gertie—

Gertie.

My brain skidded to a halt. The current Pythia had stopped in the middle of the hall, her motherly shape more motherly than usual due to the corset she wasn't wearing, because I'd gotten her out of bed. That had been hours ago, when I'd shifted here to ask for help, because the passengers were her people and because I desperately needed it. Like I desperately needed her to look at me now.

But she wasn't. The parlor was dark, with just enough light filtering in from the entryway to see by. There was no reason for anyone to look over here, no reason at all, except for the small movements of my leg, spasming against the female passenger's skirt. And I didn't know what I could do to draw attention—

Now that I was choking, too.

My leg began kicking harder, but just the one. The left was as rigid as if taped to a board, but the right was determined to make up for it, battering the woman's skirts viciously. I tried to move slightly, so that my kicks would hit her shin instead of all that material. If she woke up, even just to scream at me, it should be enough.

She didn't wake up.

The glassy-eyed stare never wavered, the slack jaw never firmed, the body never moved. Maybe because *I* couldn't, at least not at will. I kept kicking the damned skirt instead of her, violently enough to send it swaying—

Into a table full of tchotchkes.

I stared at them, my panicked brain finally clutching onto an idea. She was an elderly woman wearing a big, old-fashioned bustle on the back of her dress, the kind that had been out of style for a while even in this era. And it felt like there was some sort of solid framework under there, not just a bunch of material, which made it considerably heavier than the skirt. I watched, my heart in my throat, as the bustle slowly took on a life of its own, the continued movement having a cumulative effect. It swayed back and forth, back and forth, *back and forth*—

Until the wildly swinging undergarment finally followed the path of the skirt and slammed into the little table. It had a round marble slab above a slender wooden base and had already been top-heavy. Now it fell to the side, sending the knickknacks it supported scattering widely—

Right onto the overstuffed cushions of a sofa.

I stared at them in disbelief. The room contained a hardwood floor, a bunch of heavy wooden furniture, and a glass-fronted cabinet. Most of the ornaments were glass, too, and should have made a racket loud enough to wake the dead. But, somehow, they'd landed in the one spot sure to muffle it all.

Meanwhile, the room was darkening, and not because of the storm outside. My eyesight was failing, although part of that was likely due to the tears of mingled rage and dismay leaking down my face. I'd come so far, overcome so many odds, from hateful acolytes to vengeful gods, and now I was going to die to a time accident and a goddamned *sofa*?

But try as I might, I couldn't break out of the seizure,

or whatever was happening to me. I couldn't move at all, other than for spasms I couldn't control. I couldn't do *anything*.

But someone else could.

I could just see well enough to make out the slender wrist and bitten nails of the woman who bent over and plucked a round glass paperweight from between the sofa cushions. It was faintly green, with a lot of captured bubbles, and looked heavy. I knew that because she held it right in front of my face.

"I could let you die here," Jo said softly. "Just sit down and watch you drown. But what would be the point in that?"

I stared at her, certain I was imagining things. I'd just seen that same smiling face be eaten away by age and rot. Seen papery skin tear off and stream away, along with clumps of solid gray hair. Seen teeth through a hole in her cheek and her skull through dead, empty eye sockets.

Yet here she was, dark hair sleek and shining, green eyes bright and mischievous, red lips grinning at the expression on my face.

"You should feel special," she whispered. "You're the only one to ever beat me. But the game's not over yet, is it?"

She tossed the paperweight up and down, up and down, laughing softly at something that only her demented brain could understand. Then she stopped and sat the glass ball on the boards of the floor in front of me. Less than a foot away, but impossible to reach.

"I'm not just going to win, Pythia," she told me. "I'm going to *crush you*. You're going to see everything you love turn to ashes before the end, and when you do, *remember it was me*."

She gave the paperweight a sudden, violent shove and disappeared. I watched it bump, bump, bump across the floor, alternatively obscured and revealed by the woman's still swinging skirt. I saw it hit Gertie's ankle, heard her curse, saw her eyes jerk up to meet mine. But I barely noticed.

I was too busy mentally screaming.

* * *

"It's called Chimera," Gertie said, while I sat in the midst of a mountain of blankets, clutching a large mug of tea. The storm was lashing outside, screaming like a whole army of banshees, but I could barely hear it in here. The room was warm, with a large fireplace splashing light and heat everywhere the blankets around me were thick and cozy, and the tea was almost hot enough to scald my tongue.

None of it helped.

I was still freezing.

"It has a name?" That was Pritkin. He was sitting on the edge of my sofa, across from Gertie, who was ensconced in a large, overstuffed wing chair by the fire.

She looked a lot like her sister Hilde, although with far more questionable taste. At the moment, she was wearing a crimson satin dressing gown that gleamed richly in the firelight, the same color as the cherries that littered half the furnishings in here. I swear the woman had a fetish.

"Oh, yes, indeed."

"Then it wasn't an accident?"

Gertie started to say something, then stopped and looked at me for some reason. "I'm not sure what it was," she said, and sipped her own tea.

We were in her private sitting room, following a harrowing few minutes in the parlor, which had quickly filled up with acolytes, war mages, and servants, all jostling the two displaced passengers, who were still blissfully oblivious to it all. Including when Gertie did something that jerked the two Cassies back together. I didn't understand what, because reintegration with my other half hadn't helped with the convulsions.

It had taken Pritkin for that.

He'd been coordinating with the Circle on both ends of the time stream, first in Vegas, to help the hotel's security contain the problem, and later here, to work with the Edwardian Circle to locate a substitute train. Once I retrieved all the passengers, Gertie and her acolytes were going to put it back on the track moments after Jo jerked the other one away, thus repairing the timeline. Which is why he'd been on hand to spell me to release my jaw, and to force a potion down my throat that stopped the seizure.

It hadn't stopped the terrible cold, which I'd noticed after I was no longer fighting for my life, and which was still tearing through me at odd intervals, jerking my hands violently enough to send tea sloshing onto my woolen cocoon.

Like that, I thought, trying to take a sip and getting more on me than in me, while Pritkin scowled at Gertie.

It was his I-don't-understand scowl, not one of his more fearsome varieties, but it made the green eyes flash and caused the wet crown of spikes he called hair to perk up a bit more. He'd shed the jacket of his snow suit, leaving him in a long-sleeved shirt that hugged his muscles and would have been sexy if not paired with Michelin Man pants. The fact that they were connected to suspenders, making him Farmer Michelin Man, didn't help.

But Pritkin rarely noticed what he wore, and his personality—especially tonight—was forceful enough that nobody else did, either.

"What do you mean, you don't *know*?" he demanded. "If this thing has a name, then you must be familiar with it and what it does. Is it a common mistake? Because if so—"

"It isn't a mistake."

"I beg your pardon?"

Gertie glanced at me again. I gave her dead eyes back. I wasn't sure what she wanted, but I was certain I didn't have it.

"It's a technique taught to advanced acolytes for emergency use," she explained, after a pause. "It allows one adept to operate in multiple timelines, or in more than one place in a single timeline. It splits the soul—"

"What?"

"—into two or more pieces—"

"*What?*"

"—each of which can act independently. The Pythian power provides them with bodies by—"

"Wait. *Wait.*" Pritkin was glaring, and this time, it was one of the nastier ones. "You split her *soul*?"

Gertie raised an eyebrow at the tone, which wasn't one usually used with Pythias. But that was as much of a reaction as he got. Most people found Pritkin in a mood to be intimidating, but if I'd felt better, I'd have told him to save it.

Nothing intimidated Gertie.

"I didn't do anything, young man," she said, with perfect equanimity. "Cassie did."

"You just said it wasn't a mistake!"

"It wasn't. Or, rather, the technique is not a mistake. Her deploying it probably was, or perhaps the power was attempting to help her." Gertie's shrewd brown eyes found mine again and regarded me steadily. "Can you think of any reason why that might be?"

"Jo." I didn't elaborate, because I'd filled her in on what had happened when I first arrived. "I thought she had a body because she was in Faerie, but that wasn't it."

Gertie nodded. "Too restrictive. It would trap her there."

"While I'm here on earth." Along with everyone I loved. I glanced at Pritkin. If she hurt him—

But of course she was going to hurt him. Or, at least, she was going to try. She'd seen us together in Wales, where I'd finally caught up with his dispossessed spirit. She knew what he meant to me.

Which put him at the top of her list.

I glanced around the room, eyes narrowed, breath coming faster, as if expecting her to walk out of a wall. She didn't, but it didn't help much. I could almost feel her watching me.

Or Jonathan. Because no way weren't they working together. He'd killed Tristram in order to take his place at the senate meeting, got me on that mountaintop, and then sent his little attack dog after me. But for what?

Because that hadn't felt like an attempted kidnapping to me. Maybe Dorina was wrong, and he didn't care about my power. Or maybe he and his allies were on a different page. They wanted me dead, he wanted me captured, and Jo . . .

Jo just wanted to play.

"The power likely used Chimera to alert you to the

fact that the rogue was doing the same," Gertie told me. "And could therefore follow you beyond the confines of Faerie."

"She said she was going to hurt everyone I loved," I said, my voice harsh. "She said she was going to beat me—"

"At what? If she meant finishing what she started in Wales, that makes little sense. If she somehow obtained enough power to knock several hundred people out of the timeline, she could have shifted a god through the barrier and ended this immediately!"

I shook my head. I wasn't sure how Jo had done what she did, but I did know one thing. "She doesn't want the gods back, not now. She was never a true believer like Aeslinn. She didn't care about them one way or the other, except as a way of getting revenge on the magical community she felt had wronged her. But I doubt she even cares about that anymore."

"Death does tend to change one's priorities," Gertie agreed.

"And bringing the gods back would end her little game."

"What game?" Pritkin demanded, looking angry. Probably because he wasn't understanding half of this— not a usual circumstance for him. When it came to magic, it was usually the other way around, with me running to catch up while he explained things. But I knew ghosts— which is essentially what Jo was now, no matter how many substitute bodies she made for herself—better than anything.

"Jo isn't human anymore," I told him. "She's a vengeful ghost who wants to beat me, to show that I just got lucky last time and that she really is the best after all. And she won't rest until she does—"

"But beat you at what?" Gertie repeated, like a terrier with a bone.

"I don't know. She's tied up with Jonathan, this crazy dark mage high up in the Black Circle. He's working to help them in the war, but he's also running his own game—"

I stopped, because I didn't need any more drama tonight, which is what we'd have if Pritkin found out that Jonathan was after my power.

"I don't know what he wants," I repeated. "But he may be where she got all that extra energy. He's high up in the Black Circle leadership; he could get her whatever she needs."

"Life magic, to extend her stamina and allow her to access more of the Pythian power," Gertie said, frowning.

"Something that will drive her mad!" Pritkin said.

"She's already mad," I pointed out. "Hell, she's already dead—twice now. She won't care what the cost is, as long as she defeats me."

"But the Black Circle would," Pritkin argued. "Their leadership isn't like the rank and file; they would have been caught years ago if so! They are shrewd, calculating, and extremely jealous of their magical stores. They would not give away mass amounts of power for no purpose."

Which is why Jonathan wants mine, I thought. What had she promised him? Give me what I need and I'll get you your very own demigod, one you can drain over and over? That I could see. She'd tell him anything to get what she needed to take me on.

But what had he, in turn, promised his Circle?

Because I didn't think it was me. His allies wouldn't take the risk of having me get free, as Louis-Cesare had. I hadn't been willing to risk it with Lizzie, and she could channel far less power—and wasn't Artemis's daughter. No way would they let him keep me as one of his pets.

If so, he wouldn't have had to pal up with a nutcase like Jo.

No, he was running his own game, but he had to be giving them something, or promising them something. Something big. Pritkin was right; they wouldn't give him carte blanche otherwise, and they wouldn't do it for long. Father had run his con on the Black Circle's leadership for a while, but even he—who did have genuine ghosts in his service, just not the army of them that he'd promised— had eventually had to flee.

What was Jonathan working on?

"This is speculation," Pritkin said. "Can we discuss more pressing matters?"

"Such as?" Gertie inquired pleasantly.

"Such as Chimera! You can't go around splitting souls! It opens you up to possession, to disintegration, to something gaining access to your power—and in this case, possibly the Pythian power as well—and draining you dry!" He turned from Gertie to glare at me. "A whole soul has a certain amount of protection, but damage can allow inroads even with shields, which you don't have in any case!"

"I didn't do it on purpose—"

"Exactly my point," he interrupted. "We still have the majority of the passengers to ferry back. What if your power decides to 'help' you again?"

"It won't."

"And if you're wrong? You don't know what it might do. That damned spell almost killed you!"

"Pritkin, just drop it, all right?"

He didn't drop it.

"Not to mention," he added, turning on Gertie, who had been giving me the evil eye the whole time, "that a technique so dangerous to the user is hardly what I would call helpful! There was clearly something wrong with the 'body' the Pythian power somehow formed—something you never explained, by the way—which affected Cassie's real one as well! We have to find out—"

"Three things," Gertie said, abruptly putting her cup down and standing up, and thereby forcing Pritkin to his feet as well. "First, the Pythian power came from the gods originally, energy beings who form themselves bodies whenever they wish to interact on the physical plane and reabsorb them when they are finished. The power can do the same for a Pythia, although with a caveat: it cannot duplicate a soul—"

"So you *rip it apart*?"

"Shh," she told him, taking his arm and walking him toward the door. "Second, the soul isn't ripped apart, it is pulled into two pieces, as if you grasped a balloon in the middle, causing it to bulge at both ends. Its integrity remains; it is simply somewhat divided now, you understand?"

"Yes, but—"

"Good. Now, both of these pieces are still tethered together, and are connected to each other across time. That tether is what I used to pull the two parts of Cassie back into one, by the way. The technique is not harmful, but it is dangerous in combat, as a halved soul has half the power. Now, if you will excuse me," Gertie said, as they paused by the door, "it is getting very late, and I need my sleep, or what little is left of it."

"Wait." Pritkin looked confused, maybe because I hadn't gotten up yet. "You said three."

"What?"

"You said three things. You've only discussed two."

"So I have," Gertie agreed, and closed the door in his face.

# Chapter Forty-four

There was, of course, an immediate scuffle from the hall, probably involving the two hulking war mages that Gertie had guarding the door. I started to get up, because I knew how that was likely to go, and we didn't need any more enemies. But she raised a hand.

"Is there a problem?"

"He tends to be . . . overly protective," I told her.

"Ah. Thank you for telling me." The scuffling sounds abruptly stopped.

I stared from her to the door, then I ran over and flung it open. One of the war mages was looking perplexed, maybe because Pritkin was nowhere to be seen. The other was plastered to the wall by some weird, white, sticky filaments and cussing up a storm.

I shut the door again and whirled on Gertie.

"Where did you send him?"

"To the depot," she said, referring to the converted train station that the Circle had set up as temporary housing, because even the Pythian Court couldn't hold so many people. "He's fine, if somewhat chilly. I believe he forgot his . . . coat?" She looked with distaste at the snow suit jacket lying on the back of the sofa.

Like she could talk.

"Damn it, Gertie! You can't just—"

"I can, though," she demurred. "It's my court, at least for now. And we need to chat."

"About what?"

"I think you know." She sat back down and picked up her tea, taking a sip, taking her time. The fire played over her curls, picking out the gray roots under all the lavender, which I assumed was some kind of hair dye gone wrong. Or maybe she liked it that way.

Gertie had always been a rebel.

I'd first met her on the hunt for Pritkin. One of the stops his wildly careening soul had made on its journey back through time had been on her turf. I hadn't managed to catch up with it there, but I and the demon lord I'd had with me—Rosier, who was supposed to apply the counterspell—had nonetheless set off all kinds of alarms.

I hadn't expected that, having previously traveled across many Pythias' territories and been ignored. Rosier, however, made a huge difference, since apparently dragging powerful demons across time is a no-no. And while we narrowly escaped dealing with Gertie at the time, a later stop in old Amsterdam had been a different story.

Because, instead of just leaving us for another Pythia to deal with, she'd *followed us through time.* Even though we weren't in her era anymore. Even though we'd only been there very briefly. Even though we hadn't even caused any problems while there.

But Gertie wasn't having it.

Thereafter had followed a crazy chase across time, with me after Pritkin and Gertie after me, and damned if she hadn't been a colossal pain in the ass every step of the way!

It didn't look like things had changed any.

"How much did you take?" she asked, looking at me over the top of her cup.

I didn't answer.

"You know," she told me genially, "I always like it better when I talk anyway, so I'm going to talk. And you're going to listen," she added, as I started for the door again. "If you want my help."

I glared at her, but it wasn't like I had a choice.

I sat back down.

The fire popped and hissed. Gertie stared at it thoughtfully. I pulled a blanket back around me, because I was literally freezing.

"I assumed you were an adept, a rogue heir perhaps, when I first met you," she said. "You have an instinctive grasp of the power like nothing I've ever seen. But I also assumed you were no Pythia, because of your obvious lack of any kind of support."

"I have support," I muttered.

"Then where is it? What happened to your court, Pythia?"

I'd been fighting with the damned blankets, but at that I jerked my head up.

"Oh, don't look so surprised," Gertie said, seeing my face. "I'm not a dullard. Did you think it escaped my notice that the only person I've seen returning passengers is you?"

She looked at me expectantly.

I gave her one of Pritkin's patented scowls back. "You know I can't talk about that."

Pythias who met up in the course of their duties weren't supposed to talk at all, especially about the future, in case something was mentioned that changed it. It was a rule I'd once railed against, but had eventually come to accept, after seeing how dangerous even a small time change could be. Little things could grow into huge ones, as Gertie ought to know.

It was her successor who had taught it to me.

So why was she pressing for even more than I'd already had to tell her?

"Rules," she told me, "are guidelines for normal practice. This is a little beyond normal, wouldn't you say?"

How the hell would I know? I thought resentfully. I didn't do normal. I did nail-biting anxiety, constant self-doubt, and terror. *That* was normal for me.

But good luck explaining that to Gertie, who had probably never doubted herself in her entire life. She'd been in her element all night, barking orders, striding about, and organizing the shit out of everyone. Including the huge, dripping-with-weapons war mages who made up her bodyguard, and who scared the crap out of most people who met them.

Except for Gertie, who had been using them like errand boys without a second thought.

*That's* a Pythia, I'd thought, watching a couple hundred people running around, snapping to attention at her every word, including a whole phalanx of white-robed young women. And these weren't the kids that were all that was left of the Pythian Court in my day, but a bunch of late teens to twentyish young women, each of whom had had more training and probably understood more about the Pythian power than I did.

I'd watched them in awe the few times I'd had a chance to take a break, gulping water or tea from the shadows as they swept about, looking elegant in their Pythian finery. I'd always thought the white lace, high-necked, long-sleeved dresses the court used to wear to be a little ridiculous, not to mention restrictive, in case you needed to fight. But now—

They just looked elegant, as did the acolytes' perfectly upswept hair, their tasteful earrings that glittered under the great chandeliers, and their serene and confident movements. They'd been popping in and out with the passengers I'd brought back, whom they were ferrying to the train depot. Or reappearing from errands they'd run, stepping out of thin air in between one step and another, easily dodging the war mages and servants running around.

It had been breathtaking, eye-opening, and envy inducing, all at the same time. *This* was what the Pythian Court was supposed to be: a well-run machine capable of handling any problems, any challenges, with ease. This was what it always had been, for thousands of years.

Until me.

God, no wonder Jo had been laughing! She wouldn't have dared to go up against a court like this! But mine . . . I'd never realized how truly vulnerable it was until today. With only a half-trained Pythia and a couple of acolytes, one of whom was little more than an initiate and couldn't even shift yet, and another who should have been enjoying a well-earned retirement. And a bunch of children who were basically sitting ducks because I couldn't protect them, not alone, not from all these new enemies that kept jumping out of the—

"You see my problem," Gertie said, interrupting my thoughts. "I'm faced with a talented young Pythia, but who has little training and less help. And with quite a few challenges before her. Including a rogue acolyte—from another court, perhaps? Trying to undo Artemis' spell and bring back the old gods?"

"You're not supposed to know about that," I said, annoyed, despite the fact that her memory being intact was one of the reasons I'd been able to persuade her to help me. "You said all of you would mind-wipe each other after what happened in Wales. You said—"

"Did I?"

"Damn it, Gertie! Do the others remember as well?"

Because that . . . would be bad. The big showdown in Wales that Jo and her allies had engineered had required an army to stop it. Specifically, an army of Pythias. It had broken every rule in the book, bringing what had looked like the entire line of Pythias together to try to channel enough power to literally take on a god.

And since that god was Ares, it hadn't even worked. But it *had* bought time, with the Pythian power leashing and then holding him back from fully entering this world, long enough for us to pull out a win by the skin of our teeth. But goddamn, it had been close! I'd been grateful for the other Pythias then.

I was feeling less so now.

"If even one of them changes her mind about something because of what they saw—"

Gertie cut me off. "The others were mind-wiped, as agreed. I was the last, and was supposed to have had one of my acolytes handle it."

"But you didn't."

"I thought you might need help. It seems I was right."

It was said so calmly, and so insufferably, that for a moment, I just looked at her. And then I got up to leave, fighting a bit with the blankets first. Which is how she caught me before I hit the door, her hand surprisingly strong on my arm.

Or maybe I was just that weak.

"How much did you take?" she demanded again.

"None of your business!"

"You know it kills, yes? In high doses?"

I stopped with my hand on the doorknob.

"It didn't kill me."

"It almost did." Her voice had gone flat and lost its warmth. "That seizure you had wasn't caused by Chimera, which you somehow did correctly. It was caused by this."

She held a bottle up to the light.

It was small, triangular, and, unlike every other potion I'd ever encountered, it lacked a label. Because it was made for only one person—me. Or whoever was Pythia at the time.

The Tears of Apollo glinted in the firelight, looking like liquid gold through the bottle's amber glass. It was greenish-yellow outside it, with tiny herbs that floated in the solution, like Roy's favorite drink. I knew that because the residue was still clinging to my shirt from the foamy saliva that had dripped from my mouth during the seizure. And because I could still taste it on my tongue, bitter and metallic harsh, something no tea could wash away.

But I licked my lips and reached for it anyway, unthinking, almost mesmerized—

Only to have it jerked back.

"I don't think so."

My eyes flew up to meet Gertie's, and I felt myself flush. "I didn't have a choice," I told her. "Jo surprised us in Faerie. If I hadn't used it—"

"And all the other times?"

"What other times?"

She just looked at me. It got uncomfortable surprisingly fast. "I didn't have a choice then, either. You were chasing me all over Wales!"

"And you haven't taken any since then? Yet you just happened to have an entire bottle on you in Faerie?"

I'd walked off, back toward my blankets, because Gertie's fire was complete shit. I almost couldn't feel it at all. But at her words I spun around. "You have no idea what I've been dealing with! No idea!"

"Then tell me." She leaned back against the door.

I laughed, and it was bitter. Because sure. "And screw up the timeline even more than it already is?"

"I have a selective memory. And if anything preys on me too badly, I'll take that mindwipe I dodged in Wales."

I stared at her, but she sounded sincere. A Pythia actually wanting to hear my story? It was absurd. When I'd gone back in time trying to get some training from her successor, she'd shot me in the butt!

But Agnes had been a straitlaced stickler—about most things, I thought, thinking of Rhea. Whereas Gertie . . . hell. I was better at following the rules than she was! She'd been the one to grab all those Pythias out of the timeline to help hunt my punk ass down. And, somehow, she'd managed to talk them into it, even her predecessor, Lydia, who made Agnes look like a freewheeling hippie chick. And that was *before* they knew about Ares.

I didn't know how she'd done it.

Or maybe I did, I thought, feeling the power of those eyes on me.

"It doesn't matter," I told her, after a moment. "You wouldn't understand."

"Try me."

And, somehow, before I realized what was happening, I was back on the sofa with a new mug of tea, and Gertie was sitting beside me. Only I didn't want tea. I wanted a rest, a break, a few days away from the constant pressure. I wanted—

What she'd just sat on the table, the little bottle shining in the firelight, that made all that go away. That made me feel invincible, like this impossible job was easy and that nothing in the world or out of it could hurt me. The Tears of Apollo made me feel like my mother, who had bestrode the world like a colossus, but had failed to pass on most of her godly attributes.

So far, the only one I'd noticed was the ability to open the gates between worlds, allowing me to shift from earth to the hell regions—even the ones I wasn't supposed to be visiting—and back again. Mother had used the gift to hunt there, picking off powerful demon lords and absorbing their energy, and thus feeding her own. The Great Huntress, they'd called her, in awe and terror as their armies broke and ran before her. It was a name that had echoed through time so loudly that even the humans knew it. And built her a great temple that had once been among the wonders of the world, after her hunts made her more powerful than any other god.

Maybe more than all of them, because she'd thrown them out, hadn't she? Exiling the entire pantheon and slamming the door behind them, the door in question being the barrier she had erected, which was still protecting us to this day.

But even a goddess isn't invincible, and the battle had taken most of her power, so much so that she could no longer hunt the demons that had once fed her without becoming prey herself. So she'd faded, over thousands of years, unable to feed in any meaningful way, until she became so weak that a fat crime boss of a vampire had been able to do what entire demon armies had not, and take her out. But not before the goddess famed for her virginity did what nobody had expected: she had me.

And what had I done with that legacy? So far, I'd used my single talent to help rescue Pritkin from his father's court after he broke his parole and got dragged back to hell. And that . . . was about it. If there were any other godly attributes lurking inside me, they were lurking pretty damned deep.

And that wasn't enough. *I* wasn't enough. My eyes found the little bottle again.

Not without help.

"My predecessor was strong, with a large, capable court," I told Gertie. "On the surface, everything seemed fine. But she was fighting a war without even realizing it. The gods had determined to come back, starting with Apollo, because he had the ability to whisper to her acolytes through the Pythian power—"

"Because it was once his," Gertie said.

I drank tea and nodded. I didn't want it, but it warmed me inside, like clutching the mug kept my hands from shaking. "It didn't serve him any longer, but he could still use it as a conduit. He eventually turned the Pythian heir, who poisoned her mistress and tried to seize control of the court. Only the power went to me instead—"

"A random girl?"

"Not . . . exactly." I thought about trying to explain my

background, decided it would wreck the hell out of any credibility I had, and vetoed it. "My mother was the previous heir, who'd run away to get married," I said instead, because it was true.

Mother, in desperation, her power almost depleted, had finally gone to the only source of godly energy left in the world: the well of it that had been gifted by Apollo to his seers at Delphi all those centuries ago, and was still in use by the Pythian Court. She had glamoured herself and been taken in as an initiate, quickly rising through the ranks. She'd eventually been named the heir, something which she hadn't wanted, out of fear that it would draw the attention of the Spartoi, some demigod sons of Ares that he'd left behind.

They'd been hunting her ever since the great battle that had exiled their father, and they'd particularly been watching the court. They knew she'd show up eventually, and it hadn't taken them long to realize who the new heir actually was. They'd come after her, intent on avenging their father and forcing down the barrier holding him and the other gods back, but she'd eluded them with the help of my bumbling, kind of crazy, but occasionally brilliant father. Only to end up being killed by Fat Tony, some years later.

Life . . . was weird.

"I inherited some of her abilities," I added. "And the power came to me."

"And the girl? The rogue heir?"

"She died."

"Good." Gertie was emphatic. "And the rest of the court?" Because, yeah, there should have been plenty of other people to help me, shouldn't there?

"Some of the fey, specifically Aeslinn, king of the Svarestri, are working with the gods," I told her. "He wants to bring them back because his people basically ruled Faerie when the gods were here. They've fallen in stature since then, and they're salty about it."

Gertie looked confused.

"They don't like it," I translated, because my slang was a century too early. "They told the other acolytes that Ares would be back soon, one way or the other, and would kill them all unless they helped. So they started trying to get that"—I pointed to the Tears—"and shift him through the barrier."

"And what happened to them?"

I didn't say anything.

I didn't kill Myra, the former heir, although you could argue that I helped. But the acolytes were a different story. I saw them now, pretty girls with hate-filled faces, pushed by their families to excel, to be the next Pythia, to gain their clans wealth and status and power. They'd been ripe for Apollo's offer: be the one to bring me through and rule at my side for eternity.

It had started an all-out war that left one of them dead at another's hands, and one imprisoned by the Circle. But I'd had to kill the rest. I still saw them in my dreams sometimes, nightmare visions that left me sitting up in bed, panting and wanting to scream.

I guessed I'd dream about Lizzie now, too.

There was no mirror in sight, so I don't know what was on my face, but I felt Gertie's arm go around my shoulder in a motherly embrace. "It has been difficult, hasn't it?"

I didn't trust myself to speak; I only nodded.

"And now you've dealt with the old acolytes, except for Jo. But that's left you with what? A court full of little girls and half-trained initiates?"

I nodded again.

"And you've been compensating by using this?"

She picked up the little bottle, and for a moment, I thought she was going to relent, that she was actually going to give it to me.

But then it went in the pocket of her dressing gown, and she looked at me sternly. "I understand the temptation. Likely not as well as you, but we've all felt it. It makes you feel indomitable, able to take on the world— for a while. But it exerts a terrible price."

"So does dying!" I snarled, because she still didn't get it. "I told you—I don't have a choice!"

"Oh, but you do, dear girl. Most emphatically."

"What?" I looked at her in confusion.

"I've broken a dozen rules in the last little while; why not one more?" She pulled me to my feet. "Your problem isn't a lack of power, Cassie. It's the opposite. You've been using raw power to compensate for a lack of technique. We're going to fix that."

*"How?"* I stared at her. "Don't you think I've *tried*?"

"Yes, but I haven't."

"And what does that mean?"

Her head tilted, like a curious bird. "Why, it means I'm going to train you, of course."

# Chapter Forty-five

There was a claw-footed bathtub in my bedroom. It was just sitting there, in between the bed and the door, getting in the way. But I'd never been so happy to see anything in my life.

I filled that sucker almost to the brim with water so hot it would make a sauna envious and climbed in. It was the weirdest sensation. I knew it was hot; the amount of steam coming off the surface, which had already fogged up the full-length mirror on the side of a wardrobe, was enough to show that. But it didn't feel that way.

Or, rather, it did, but it didn't matter. The cold refused to budge. To the point that I was sitting there with my skin rosy and about to slough off, yet I was shivering and shaking like I was in the middle of the storm outside.

Even worse, I'd forgotten about my wound, which a kind medic had bandaged up for me that morning but which was now stinging like a bitch. But it was just going to have to deal with it, because I wasn't getting out. Not until I warmed up, if I ever did.

The soggy bandage had partly peeled off, so I finished pulling it away and examined my stiches. I couldn't see them too well. Electric lights were everywhere downstairs, but the reno hadn't yet extended up here. The only light was a kerosene lantern on the bedside table that the initiate who'd led me up here had brought. It made the water look almost black, with little yellow-tipped waves. I couldn't see much past it, and finally gave up.

It didn't feel like I was bleeding to death.

I lay back against the porcelain and shut my eyes, letting waves of shivers run through me. I didn't understand what was going on. It wasn't withdrawal; there hadn't been time for that. And besides, I knew exactly what that felt like.

In the aftermath of the whole thing in Wales, I'd had nausea, trembling, muscle aches, and a whole host of other symptoms, none of which I'd understood. I just thought I'd caught a sixth-century case of the flu. Until I took a hit of the Tears, because I had things to do and I felt so damned bad.

And, suddenly, I didn't anymore.

It hadn't been hard to figure out after that. But breaking the habit had been a lot more difficult. Not because I liked having to use a crutch, but because there just wasn't enough of me to go around these days. And now . . .

God, now.

I opened my eyes to watch the lamplight flicker on the ceiling, but I wasn't seeing it. I was seeing Jo. I'd never seen anyone wield so much power, not even my mother. And that was while using Chimera, a spell that should have halved her ability to channel the Pythian energy!

It was like she'd died, but instead of becoming a ghost, she'd become a god. It should have taken a few dozen Pythias to manage what she'd done with apparent ease. And then had enough strength left to almost kill me!

Even with the Black Circle's help, I didn't know how she'd managed it. I had a huge amount of power, too, but my weak human body could only channel so much of it. The same limitation should have been on her even if she'd conjured herself up a new one, yet it didn't look that way.

I was thankful for Gertie's offer, but I didn't think any amount of training would allow me to overcome *that*.

And neither did Jo.

Whatever she said, she wanted me dead. She just wanted to enjoy it first. But if she thought there was any chance she was going to lose . . .

I'd be dead already.

Although I felt kind of like it anyway, like a damned frozen corpse, because the water wasn't helping. My skin had flushed red enough that it was visible even in the low lighting, but the ice at my center hadn't budged. I was *freezing*, and I didn't know why.

I finally sat up in the bath, my arms wrapped around myself, my teeth chattering. I was so cold I *hurt*, a bone-deep ache that had me wanting to tear at my skin in order to reach it, to make it stop. It was so bad that I found myself sobbing after a while, and feeling ridiculous but not caring. I finally decided to hell with it; the court had to have a healer on call, and I clearly needed one. Even if it came with another lecture from Gertie.

I started trying to crawl out of the bath, but my muscles were spasming and ignoring my commands, and the porcelain side of the tub suddenly seemed a mile high. All my thrashing did was send a wave of soapy water over the edge, hitting the hardwood floor and leaking toward the door. The one I couldn't reach.

But I didn't have to. Because someone was already pounding on it, something I hadn't noticed in my distress, and when I made some sort of incoherent noise it burst open. Pritkin was standing there, silhouetted by the light leaking up the nearby stairs, his hair and the long coat he'd found somewhere dusted with snow, his face furious.

Until he saw me.

I couldn't even say "help," although I tried. But nothing came out except for a vague whimper. It would have been embarrassing another time, but I was way past caring. I held an arm out to him, sudsy and shaking and—

And then he was there, kneeling by the side of the tub.

He was cold, but not like the burning, horrible ache that was eating me alive. He was human-warm under all the snow, maybe more so than usual because he was breathing hard, as if he'd run all the way back here. And when his hand took mine, I felt a little of that terrible ice fade away.

But not most of it. I cried out, desperate for something, and I didn't even know what it was. What was *wrong* with me?

Pritkin was saying something, but I could no longer concentrate well enough to understand him. I only knew that he got up to leave, probably to get help, and I panicked and grabbed on to his sleeve. And then something strange happened—stranger than anything on this very weird day.

Because *someone else* turned to look back at me.

It was Pritkin's face, but not his eyes. These were greener, brighter, almost incandescent. They were also familiar.

I'd seen them once before, on that battlefield in Wales. Ares had been trying to rip open the sky, the wind had been howling and sparks had been flying, and two great armies had been clashing together in the distance. Yet the most riveting thing to me had been those same eyes.

Pritkin's incubus nature, long starved and half-dead, had peered out of his face for the first time in more than a century. And it had been looking at me. I stared back at it now, wondering if it remembered what had followed, how we'd come together in desperation, just wanting to feel something at the end of the world, and instead had ended up saving it.

Because the power we'd generated that night from the incubus feedback loop had been so great that neither of us could contain it. Pritkin's incubus had been so starved, and thus so empty, that it had been able to hold far more of the Pythian power than it normally could. And had therefore been able to send back so much more, after its nature magnified what I'd given, that it had almost torn me apart. But instead, it had torn the fabric between worlds, when I used it to let the ghost of Apollo loose onto the battlefield.

But that had only been possible because Pritkin had gone without sex for a century. I didn't think we'd make nearly so much power this time, but I didn't care if we did. I didn't care about anything but filling that terrible ache inside me, the one I finally recognized not as cold but as *hunger*. I was starving, and he was the only one who could give me what I needed.

But he didn't want to.

I didn't understand why, but it was in the set of his shoulders and biceps, rock hard and resisting my attempts to pull him closer. It was in the white-knuckled grip of his fingers on the side of the tub, in the protruding tendons of his neck, in the stubborn set of his jaw. I knew Pritkin; I knew he didn't want this for some reason I didn't understand.

But someone else did.

He finished turning back around, and his head dipped down, to find the cheek I'd just turned to him, because I didn't understand this. I just knew Pritkin didn't want it, so neither did I—right up until his mouth touched my skin. Since I'd turned my head, it was nothing more than a chaste kiss on the cheek, the kind you'd give a friend or a relative, just nothing at all. But it didn't feel that way.

His lips were chapped and a little cold. There was melted snow on his face, and the scent of winter—cold air, coal fires, and damp wool—hung about him. His hair was hard and scratchy, like inverted icicles, spearing up everywhere. But it was the eyes—it was always the eyes—that gripped me when I turned into the kiss. So close, so very close, and so alien—

Only not. Because the creature gazing out at me was part of Pritkin, too, no matter how much he hated his demon side. Clear green eyes stared back into mine, not like emeralds this time but like glass, as if I could look through and see his soul. And maybe I could, but if so, his soul wanted the same thing I did. He was *hungry*.

When our lips touched, it was as if a firework exploded, only that's too tame. It was more like a bomb went off. There was none of the playful teasing of the mountaintop, none of the normal human hunger of our night at Dante's. This was a desperate coming together of two aching souls that could only find aid and comfort in each other.

And comfort there was. Pritkin shed his clothes while we tried to eat each other alive, and the next moment he was crawling into the tub alongside me. And that changed everything.

Suddenly, the water wasn't hot, it was scalding. Suddenly, I wasn't starving, I was ravenous. Suddenly, the room was alight with magic, maybe his, maybe mine, I didn't know. But I could see it everywhere.

The lamplight felt solid and real, like the beams were caressing my skin. The water sloshing about me was silk, sliding sensuously along my body. Even the dust motes in the air had power, hovering around us like sparks off a bonfire—

And then I was back there again, in that tent on the battlefield, because yes, he knew; yes, he remembered. That other part of Pritkin knew what we'd done together, knew what we could do again. And he was grateful— God, so grateful. I saw it in his eyes, felt it in his kiss when his lips caught mine again. Felt all those long years of waiting, the desperate need to fulfill his true potential but always denied, denied, denied.

The little sips of power he'd obtained through the years, from this or that random encounter, had barely been enough to sustain him. And most of that he'd given back in service of his master, boosting his power, sharpening his senses, widening his focus. But it had never mattered, it had never been enough to prove himself. Never close to enough—

And then came that terrible night a century ago, with the master's wife.

I didn't know how we were communicating, if it was mind to mind or soul to soul, but I felt it, just as he had. Abrupt, sudden, unexpected joy. He was feeding! He was finally being allowed to feed! Not in little bits and pieces but fully, completely, for the first time ever. It caused a rush of joy so bright, so overwhelming, that it blinded him to what was happening—and to what he was doing. He didn't understand until the beautiful power abruptly cut out, until he looked about in confusion and loss . . . and slowly, in mounting horror, realized what they held in their arms.

No! No, he couldn't have done that! He recoiled, even as his master roared in pain and grief. He hid, deep inside, terrified, appalled, sickened by the realization that he'd destroyed his master's one chance for happiness, and his only chance to ever again feel that wondrous power in his veins.

He'd never be let out now. He saw that with perfect clarity. He'd never live, never thrive, never be allowed to do his only duty, because if he'd been hated before, it was nothing to this! Nothing to the scorn and self-loathing his master felt, that he felt, because they really were one, no matter how much he'd come to think of them as separate beings.

There was no actual divide, but there may as well have been, because the two halves of his nature would never meet after this. He knew that with a certainty he'd never had before. And that one, tiny spark of hope he'd cultivated through all the long years died.

What was there to hope for, to live for, now? He was like a vestigial organ, there but unwanted, unused, a relic from another age. And he *deserved* it.

He felt that with burning shame, knew it had all been his fault. He'd carried the guilt close to his heart, knowing that his penance was just and right. That he didn't deserve to taste that flood of life-giving energy, that he should be boarded up, forgotten, left in a cell of his own pain to slowly starve.

And so it had been, day after day, week after week, year after long, lonely year. No respite, no hope, no slight reprieves like in the past, because his master was completely celibate now. There was nothing to feed from, nothing at all, and he had felt life slipping away from him, a slow, steady *drip, drip, drip* as whatever power he'd once had faded into nothingness.

He was waiting to die.

But then something unbelievable happened. He had been virtually comatose for so long that rousing himself seemed impossible as well as futile. He hadn't wakened fully in years; hadn't even opened his eyes to look around. What was the point? There was nothing there.

Only, suddenly, there was. Something had jolted him out of his slumber like a bolt of lightning. Or what it was—a bolt of pure energy, incubus energy, *life* energy. He'd stared around, confused and groggy, not comprehending what was happening. Even when it hit again, harder this time, hard enough to crack the walls of the prison he'd made for himself and to send them blasting away into nothingness.

Leaving him huddled there in the darkness, all alone, stunned and frightened and unsure what to do.

Until another bolt hit, blowing open his eyes, leaving him looking at—

He wasn't sure.

A woman, yes, but not human; not human at all.

He didn't see her with the eyes of a man, because he wasn't one. He saw her as others of his kind had once seen her mother—a glowing being of pure light, of pure life—only she wasn't threatening him. She wasn't trying to hurt him. She was . . . she was . . .

No! It was a trick! She couldn't be offering herself to him—why to *him*?

Incubi respected power, and he had none, had never had any. And he was so small, so shriveled, so completely powerless now that his own people wouldn't have even bothered to cannibalize him, had they been able to get past his master's formidable defenses, for what would be the point?

He had nothing to give.

But it was irresistible, the lure of all that power. It would have been to any of his kind, but to him it was completely overwhelming. He knew he had no right to it, knew how furious his master was going to be if he so much as tried to touch it. But no power within him meant no power to resist, and it drew him out of the depths like a moth to a flame.

And if, like the moth, it cost him everything, he didn't care. If he died, he didn't care. Let it be a trick, let it be a nightmare, for what nightmare could be worse than what he'd already lived? Just let him *feed* . . .

And she had. To his amazement, she had. There had been no hesitation, no holding back. The power was simply there, fully and freely given, all he could ever want and more, so much more, than he could ever hold.

He'd been tentative at first, just taking a little bit, a dainty sip at that vast ocean, afraid that it would overwhelm him. And it had, but not in the way he'd feared. Instead of more pain, the price of long disuse, he felt . . . fire. Not the kind that burned but the kind that energized, flowing like a river of sparkling life through his veins.

He felt himself opening back up, the long-disused, almost calcified pieces of himself filling out, plumping up. His vision brightened, and she came more into focus, a flurry of sparks flying behind her, her blond hair floating out on currents of her own making, her eyes blue flame. She was the most beautiful sight he'd ever seen—

And then it was like a match thrown on a gasoline-soaked bonfire. His hunger reawakened, his true nature surged to the surface, his claws came out and then sheathed again, because he didn't want to hurt her, no, no, never hurt her! But he couldn't, he found, because she was drinking him down, too.

As fast as he could absorb that river of energy, as fast as it bloomed and blossomed within him, his gift turning it into so much more than he'd been given, she was taking it back. She was pulling it out of him, but he didn't care. Because as soon as one wave retreated, another came to replace it, a never-ending stream, because how do you drink the *ocean*?

You can't drain her, he'd thought, the realization hitting him hard. You can't *hurt* her! And that meant—

He felt his eyes blow wide, his mental state rocked to its core, his reality tilt and whirl and break off to fall into the void. And then he didn't feel anything, at least nothing he would ever be able to describe. Because, for the first time in his existence, he did what he was meant to do, and opened wide the floodgates of his power, taking everything she could give and more, until he was overwhelmed with it, until he was laughing hysterically, half out of his mind, or perhaps all the way out, because what was *this*?

Fire tore through him, power overwhelmed him, he felt himself do something else he had never been able to before—and grow. And with size and power came something else: rage at the creature trying to hurt her, to kill them both. He turned with a roar on the god tearing his way into this world, not in fear but in challenge, because right then, he felt like he could take on the world.

But she was ahead of him.

He sent back all that he could, one last time, which was nowhere near all that he'd managed to absorb. But it was enough. They'd won, a god had died, and he had basked in more energy than he'd ever known existed. It had invigorated him ever since, allowing him to do his job properly for the first time, and give his master more strength, more endurance, more raw power than he'd ever had to work with before.

Together, they'd been a force to be reckoned with. Together, they'd been unstoppable. But now he was hungry once more, and she was here.

Time to feed.

# Chapter Forty-six

But Pritkin had two halves to his nature, and one of them was not on board. *"No."*

It was low-voiced, but harsh enough to pull me out of the fog. The visions or whatever his other side had been sending shattered, and I clung to him, our bodies slick and intertwined, the warm water sloshing around us. And somehow I managed to focus on his face.

The eyes were green, but not incandescent. The jaw was tight, but not in anger. It was his implacable face, the one with enough strength to turn what should have been average features—too large nose, too thin lips, eyebrows too blond for his skin—handsome.

I tried to focus. It was really difficult. "Why?" I finally managed to ask.

"I *can't.*"

It wasn't true. I could feel how much it wasn't. I frowned, and slid against him again, and watched his eyes close as if in pain.

And then, without his gaze on me, I noticed something else about that face. It was drawn and tired-looking, almost haggard; the small crow's feet were deeper and more pronounced; and there were dark circles under the eyes, as if he hadn't slept for a week. He looked exhausted, and he shouldn't be. He'd been fine when confronting Gertie; tired, yes, but not to the point of exhaustion. And even when he'd burst in here, he'd just looked a little winded . . .

"What's wrong?" I asked, smoothing a finger along one of his eyebrows, dislodging a drop of water that had been trembling there. "What is it?"

Pritkin didn't say anything.

But then, he didn't have to. Because I could feel a change in me, too. A few moments ago, I'd been freezing, unable to get warm even in almost scalding water. There'd been a block of ice at my center, radiating shivers outward with every breath. But now . . .

Now limbs that had been painful and cramped were supple and moved freely. The pounding ache in my head and neck was gone, as if it had never been. And instead of freezing cold, I was warm, almost languid, like I'd been basking in the sun for hours.

Pritkin had given me some of his power—a lot of it—but he hadn't taken anything back.

"Take it back," I told him now, because that's how the feedback loop worked. Power from me into him, where his incubus nature could magnify it, feed from it, and then pour an equal or greater amount back into me. The incubus royal line were the only ones with that ability, which was why Rosier had been desperate to have a child.

But Pritkin wasn't feeding.

He could, I knew he could, and his incubus was definitely on my side. I could feel it now, no longer talking but begging with his whole body. We slid together, soap-slick skin against soap-slick skin, and God, it was good! I didn't know how he was holding back; I barely was! And then he kissed me and I thought—*finally*.

But there was no power behind it.

I almost heard his incubus whimper; it was so close, and so hungry. It had given him all it could, ever since the battle in Wales, assuming that the days of fasting were over, that there would be nothing but feasts from here on in. But this was no feast, and I couldn't force the issue; I didn't want to. I just wanted *him*.

There was no way for me to initiate demon sex, and I wasn't mentally up to a long conversation tonight about why he should. But there was one thing I could do to wipe that look of sadness and exhaustion and defeat off his face. Oh, yes, there is, I thought, and slid my arms around his neck, deepening the kiss.

I tasted his surprise, felt his arms go rigid around me, heard the sound he made deep in his throat. But he didn't push me away. Which is why I broke the kiss, panting for breath, and stared into his eyes before climbing on top of him.

That didn't last long. He spun me in the water, sending another wave over the side—Sorry, Gertie, I thought—and pushed me back against the end of the tub.

That was better, I thought.

That was perfect.

Right before I saw his face.

"We're not doing this tonight."

For a second, I thought I'd heard wrong. "What? No, I didn't mean the other thing—"

"We're not doing anything tonight!"

I frowned. "Why not?"

"Why not?" He looked at me like I'd lost my mind. "Cassie, you have a wound in your side with twenty stitches in it! Not to mention that you almost died a few hours ago! You're in no condition—"

"Let me be the judge of that."

I tried to kiss him again, but he pulled away. "You're in no condition to judge anything! Nobody is under an incubus' influence! You're going to bed." And before I could argue, he was climbing out of the tub, giving me a glimpse of a god-tier physique gilded by lamplight, picking out the golden hair on his chest and thighs, and the muscles moving as he turned, bent over, and plucked me out of the tub as if I weighed nothing.

It felt good to be in his arms, but not good enough. Not nearly enough! Pritkin and I had had so little time to ourselves since my declaration on the battlefield, when I'd finally admitted I loved him. Everyone always needed us for something, and it was hard to find even a moment when we could be alone.

And doing so in the future wasn't likely to be any easier, and not just because of Mircea. But because the whole reason I was having so much trouble bridging the gap between supernatural communities was that the Pythias were supposed to be neutral, only we hadn't been. Not for a long time.

The Circle guarded the Pythias, but their presence involved more than that. They also influenced them, and everybody knew it. How could you go to a Pythia expecting a fair ruling on some argument if the group you were arguing with was standing right there at her side, glowering at you? It had been a problem for centuries, but things had started to get really hinky under Agnes.

She and Jonas had tried to keep their affair secret; as far as I knew, he'd never admitted it to anyone until after she had died, and to damned few then. But it had nonetheless been known by the leaders of the supernatural world. And any credibility she'd had went out the window with it.

I *knew* that, and yet I'd fallen for a war mage, too.

And the damned man didn't *get it*. Times like this, far away from prying eyes, far into the past where no one knew us and no one cared . . . might be our best chance to be together. Yet here he was, patting me dry and putting me down in crisp, cold sheets before toweling off himself. As if preparing to get dressed and go to whatever room they'd assigned him.

Which is what happened every night!

But not this one.

Pritkin turned back to me, probably to kiss me good night, and I used one of his own tricks to tumble him into bed instead.

The green eyes narrowed. "We've had this conversation—"

"We haven't had any conversation! You talked; I listened. That's not a conversation."

"And you want to have one now?"

No, I want to bang your brains out, I thought, but didn't say, because the dense man's hands had come up to my hips to steady me, distracting me. But that was all they were doing. I was naked, still warm and moist from the bath, and sitting on top of evidence that he wasn't nearly as disinterested as he appeared. Yet what was he doing?

Offering a conversation.

Fine.

Two could play it that way.

"All right," I said, and grabbed the discarded towel. "So, talk."

"We need to have a discussion about a number of things, including what just happened in here. But that can wait until—what are you doing?" he demanded as I began patting down his pecs, which were still quite damp. He hadn't done a very good job of toweling off.

"I don't want my bed wet," I said innocently.

"Then let me get out of it."

"I thought you wanted to talk?"

"No." A hand gripped my wrist, because I'd started patting farther down. Only it was less like patting and more like stroking. "*You* wanted to talk. I want to sleep."

"You don't want to sleep," I said, and wiggled farther down, so I could pat at other things.

"Cassie—"

"We never get this chance!" I told him, suddenly furious. "Jonas has you running all over the world, almost getting killed before you even get over almost being killed the last time! This is not the way to have a relationship!"

"Is that what we're having?" he asked, suddenly intense.

"We are now," I told him, and grabbed evidence of that, which was right in front of my face.

Pritkin stared at me down the length of his body as I ran a thumb over the top of him. And watched the reaction from that one small gesture ripple through his whole frame. Oh, yes, he wants this, I thought, no matter what he says.

He wanted it badly.

And then I licked him.

Only, no, not licked. Stroked with my tongue, slowly, sensually, delighting in the half groan, half curse I pulled out of him. And then, before he could argue—and he was definitely about to argue—I fogged his brain by taking the whole slick, delicious head in my mouth, rolling my tongue all around it, and starting to suck. Hard.

I guess he hadn't expected that, because it tore another sound out of him, and this one was definitely a curse.

I ignored him and gripped the long, thick shaft, starting to massage it while teasing the little slit at the end with my tongue, during which he writhed and cursed and told me, very unconvincingly, to stop. I would have laughed at that, if I hadn't had my mouth full. And when he somehow managed to get enough brainpower together to tell me, very sternly, that this was over, I did laugh around him.

And then I grabbed something a little lower down.

Finally, I had his full attention. Pritkin stared at me, and it was no longer the impatient release-me-woman glare of a moment ago, but more a who-are-you and shit-I'm-in-trouble-now bewilderment. And yes, I thought, squeezing a bit and seeing his eyes pop; yes, you are.

The problem with Pritkin, I thought, as I went to work, one hand fondling the velvety globes, one massaging the silken shaft, and my tongue doing the rest of the work, was that he'd mostly missed the last month or so. And it had been a hell of a month. First, having to find out where Rosier had taken him, then having to break him out of hell—a phrase I'd never really thought to hear myself utter—and then, when I finally managed to get him in front of the demon council, to get their damned, unfair sentence lifted, what did they do instead?

They cursed him out of existence!

I sucked harder in remembered anger, and Pritkin let out a howl. I hope the rooms are soundproofed, I thought, and then remembered the storm, banshee wailing outside. Oh, that was all right, then.

And then came that long, frustrating, seemingly-never-ending chase back through time, with Gertie hounding me and Rosier bitching at me and Pritkin staying always, always, just out of reach! It was enough to send a woman crazy, only I hadn't gone crazy, possibly because I was already there. What it had done instead was to expand my skill set, because the power teaches the Pythia, or so Agnes had said because she didn't want to train me. But what she forgot to mention was that it did so only when it thought you needed a new ability—which was usually in the middle of a crisis when you were scared out of your mind!

It had been a brutal apprenticeship, but it had worked, to a degree. I didn't fool myself that I was at Gertie's level, but I had learned a lot. I'd been forced to. And not all of that had been about the Pythian power.

Pritkin bucked underneath me, and judging from his

face, I wasn't sure if that was out of pleasure or pain, or a combination of both. I took my mouth off him long enough to ask, "Do you want me to stop?"

"Stop and I'll scream," he gritted out.

"You'll scream anyway," I promised, and went back to work.

This last month without him had been hard, harder than anything I'd ever gone through in my life. And, considering my life, that was saying something. There were so many times that I'd thought: this is it. You've fought a good fight, but you're not going to get past this. Nobody could get past this.

Yet, somehow, I had. Somehow, I'd found depths within me that I'd never even suspected existed. I was used to doubting myself; how could I not, growing up with Fat Tony, who never missed a chance to tell me how worthless I was, how stupid, how I wouldn't last a day outside of his scummy court, off in the real world that was supposedly so much worse? And, in fairness, it *had* been worse, especially lately, but it had been better, too.

Because I wasn't worthless. I wasn't stupid. I wasn't any of the things he'd always said and that I'd half believed without even realizing it.

I'd started to understand that, in fits and starts, this past summer, as I somehow stayed alive and kept others alive, despite some really long odds against us. But it hadn't been until the search for Pritkin that I really grasped how much I'd changed. With few allies and a ton of enemies, with a ticking clock constantly in my ears, and with the god that personified war trying to come back and doing a damned good job of it, causing conflict everywhere I turned, yet I just. Kept. Going.

Maybe Jo and I had something in common after all, I thought, as Pritkin writhed and bucked and grabbed my head, trying to let me know what was coming.

As if I didn't already know, I thought, swallowing him down, and finally hearing that scream I'd promised myself.

It was lost in the storm outside, in the swirl of power around the bed, in the glow of satisfaction that suffused me along with his essence, because I'd *earned* this. All those terrifying days and sleepless nights, all the times I'd been so exhausted I couldn't see straight, and muddy and bloody and scared almost literally to death, had been worth it. Because I'd *won*.

He spilled into my mouth, finally erasing the horrid taste of that potion, and I swallowed him down, staring into his eyes as I did so, and then licking up every drop.

I earned this, I thought again; I'd earned *him*, and however many obstacles stood in our way, I wasn't giving him up. I'd find a way, just as I'd found all the others. I would, because—

There was a knock at the door.

I looked at Pritkin, who was lying there, dazed and drunk on the power we'd made together, even with just regular old sex. Which never seemed so regular with him. "You gonna get that?" I asked.

He looked blankly at me.

Guess not.

My body humming happily, I got up, grabbed a robe that somebody had thoughtfully left draped over a chair, and opened the door.

And heard a gasp from the young acolyte standing behind two hulking war mages. I glanced behind me. Damn; I'd forgotten about the coverlet, leaving Pritkin drugged out and sprawled on the bed in what was obviously a sexually satisfied stupor.

The war mages, who had looked menacing and dangerous a second ago, sized up the situation pretty fast. The younger of them blushed. The older raised an eyebrow at me.

"I suppose there's no emergency?"

"Not so much."

He nodded and tugged on his buddy's sleeve. "We have other things to do."

The two men moved off, leaving the girl—a blonde who was drinking in the sight of my boyfriend before I blocked the view—behind. "Is—is there anything you need?" she asked, like she hadn't just pimped on us to the war mages.

"Yes. Mage Pri—the mage will need some clothes and toiletries. We both will. You can send them up to this room—*tomorrow*."

She nodded, tried to see past the hanging, voluminous sleeve of my robe again, failed, and curtsied. I closed the door on her before she finished and rejoined Pritkin on the bed, who had managed to throw the coverlet over his lap, at least. I pulled it up and climbed underneath, after shedding the robe I didn't need, because the room was now borderline hot. Or maybe that was me.

I snuggled close, and a strong arm went around me. We had a thousand things to talk about, to work out and to work through, but we didn't say another word. Sleep was pulling at me hard, and there'd be time for that tomorrow. There'd be time for everything.

I'd make sure of it.

# Chapter Forty-seven

A bolt of spell fire tore through the big room, and almost tore through me. But I shifted at the last second, leaving it to detonate against the wall, and reappeared behind my assailant. I spun, grabbed her long dark hair as a handle, and pulled out a knife.

Only to see Lizzie's face suddenly in place of hers, causing me to let go and stagger back.

"Concentrate," Gertie's voice boomed. "This is no time to lose focus."

I'm not losing focus, I thought savagely, and shifted, as half a dozen more dangers converged on me.

"Human weapons have their uses," Gertie's voice was saying, as I reappeared, panting, behind a column. "As do magical ones. Specifically, they are good for saving your strength, since they cost very little power to deploy."

Another brunette threw a magical snare at me, but I shifted it out of the air and behind her, and the lariat-looking device grabbed hold of her torso and wrapped her up like a mummy. She could have shifted out of the trap, but it took her by surprise. Leaving me plenty of time to stab my dagger into her chest, only I didn't.

I told myself that it was because two more adepts had just targeted me, but their spells flew through the air where I'd just been, not on the ground where I'd just hit. I'd slammed myself down beside the bound girl, who, like me, looked completely freaked out by all this. Her eyes were huge as she stared at the dagger in my hand, which was shaking along with it. I said a bad word and threw the damned thing away, then shifted the mummy girl into the two adepts springing for us through the air.

And, okay, this was *not* how I'd assumed the Pythian Court did their training sessions! I understood the concept of live fire training. Human armed forces used it all the time, because otherwise, soldiers might freak out the first time they had real ammo coming at them. But this was *insane*.

Seriously, what the hell? I thought, as the force of my shift sent the bound girl flying sideways into the two acolytes, blowing them off their feet and into the warded will-kill-you-if-you-touch-it barrier, because this arena of horrors wasn't bad enough on its own.

They hit, the ward flashed, and their bodies burst into a haze of ash. I could feel it on my skin, taste it on my tongue, gagged on it as it caught in my throat. I tried to avoid losing my lunch, which thankfully I hadn't eaten much of anyway, and mostly succeeded.

Mostly. "Guns, knives, and magical snares allow you to dispose of or trap an opponent without using up your reserve of strength," Gertie's voice continued, as if nothing had happened. "But they can also give away your position and thus leave you vulnerable for a moment—and a moment is all it takes."

No shit, I thought, and then screamed as a bunch of fiery arrows flew at my head. I didn't see who'd sent them; didn't care. I just threw a time bubble that aged the wood to nothing, using up all their fuel. Which left little puffs of fire going off all around me, like silent fireworks. It was disorienting, but not as much as the spell that hit me right afterward.

Goddamn it!

The ballroom, where we were having our little afternoon in hell, suddenly tilted wildly. I was standing on the ground, or to be more precise, I was crouching behind a sofa, but that's not what it felt like. It felt like I'd just gotten shoved out of a 747 cruising at 35,000 feet, without a parachute.

I screamed again, but not because of the spell. But because I knew what was coming. Jo had already acquainted me with what it felt like to get stabbed in the chest, and I could really do without a repeat. Or being electrocuted by the barrier. Or being garroted by the big acolyte, who

I'd been told was only sixteen but who could have line-backed for any pro football team. Hell, she was bigger than some of the war mages, and she loved her little bit of string.

I loved keeping my head on my body, so I wasn't real thrilled to see her heading my way.

"The Pythian power is inexhaustible. You are not," Gertie intoned, because that was all I needed. "Reserve your strength at all costs; it may be what saves your life."

No, what would save my life is getting out of here, I thought viciously. But since that wasn't possible, I shifted to the grand piano, which looked like a Picasso drawing, thanks to my wonky head. Or maybe that was the angle, because my shifting abilities had also been screwed up by the disorienting spell, and I was a little off target.

Like maybe twelve feet in the air off, before I dropped like a stone to smash into the delicate wooden bench seat. I hit the ground in the midst of a pile of carved wooden shards, one of which had stabbed my calf—thank you, Gertie! And all of which I shifted blindly, not being able to tell what was happening, just that a large blur was headed for me at a run.

My vision cleared a moment later, I didn't know why. And then I did, when the blur resolved itself into five aco-lytes who had been running and were now sliding across the marble floor on rivers of their own blood. Because I'd just shifted the equivalency of a couple dozen wooden stakes *into* their bodies.

They slid at me, their eyes going glassy, their hands still outreached, while the spell one of them had used on me died along with the caster.

I didn't scream this time; I didn't make any sound at all. One of the girls slid straight into me, and all I could do was to scramble back, my nose running, my eyes water-ing, and vile-tasting stomach acid dribbling down my chin. She was the blonde from the previous night, the nosy one with the pretty curtsy.

Never learned how to curtsy properly, I thought dazedly, although my governess had tried her best to teach me. The same one who had ended up in pieces scat-tered all over the floor after Tony finished with her. Like my parents, who'd been blown apart in a car bomb he had set. Like Pritkin, getting cursed by the demon council, halfway through a leap, his body crashing lifeless to the floor—

I screamed, holding my head, as picture after picture out of my past flew at me, hammered at me, beat on me. It was so much like my dreams, like the nightmares that sent me sitting bolt upright in bed, sweat slicking my skin, or the visions that had paralyzed me in panic attacks for years, that it took me a moment to realize that it was another spell. One I didn't know how to throw off, because my knowledge of regular magic was close to zero.

That was another legacy from Tony, who had forbidden any of the crap mages he employed to even try to teach me. He was afraid I'd use any spells I learned against him—and he was probably right—so I'd remained ignorant. And after I ran away, I had to avoid the magical community at all costs, knowing that he was looking for me there.

So, no, I couldn't shake this latest bit of hell. Fortunately, I didn't have to. I'd lived with this shit, with these memories, every day of my life. If they were going to destroy me, they'd have done it already.

Which is why, after the blonde's body disappeared along with the others, I got back to my feet, wiped a hand across my lips, and faced off with my last opponent: Agnes, the current heir.

I hadn't expected to see her here. I hadn't seen her at all last night, despite the number of trips I'd made in and out with the passengers. I'd assumed that Gertie was purposefully keeping her away, not wanting to have to mind-wipe her again. I wasn't sure how many times you could do that before somebody went loopy, and if Agnes went loopy, I died, considering that it was her warning that Tony's men were closing in that would one day save my life.

But here she was anyway. And quickly proving why she was the heir. Unlike the others, the petite brunette with the wide blue eyes hadn't attacked me. She'd stayed on the sidelines, watching, waiting . . . for what, I didn't know. Maybe to see how I fought? Because she'd fought the others, many times apparently, since this kill-o-rama seemed to be a monthly event. But she hadn't fought me.

Until now.

I pushed sweat-damp hair out of my eyes and wondered how to approach this. Agnes was too close to the barrier for me to shift behind her, unless I wanted to end up crispy-fried. But she was also out in the open, not near any possible sources of cover, for her or for me. There wouldn't be any sneaking up on Agnes.

So what gave her an advantage? Because I knew that face; knew those expressions. And she clearly thought she had one. But what the hell—

And then two more Agneses walked out from different parts of the ballroom, one from behind another pillar, and one rising like the freaking undead from behind a table. Only she wasn't undead. She was—

"Chimera," Gertie's voice boomed helpfully, "is one way to have the best of both worlds. Allowing a hybrid of magical, human, and Pythian powers to be employed simultaneously."

As if on cue, one of the copies pulled out a gun; one spilled a golden whip out of her hand, or maybe that was a snare—I couldn't tell from here; and Agnes herself raised a hand, a time bubble forming around it.

"You have got to be *shitting me!*" I said, stumbling backward a few steps.

They weren't shitting me.

I stared at them, caught flat-footed, because we were *already* in Chimera. That's how they did their bloody testing rounds without actually killing each other. I could see past the barrier, to where the whole group of us, including the acolytes I'd already killed, were clustered around Gertie, watching and learning.

Although what they were learning from me, I didn't know, because this was bullshit!

"This is bullshit!" I heard my own voice call, from beside Gertie. "She doesn't know how to do Chimera!"

"Then she should learn," Gertie said calmly, and we both cursed.

And, for a second, I lost control, seeing things through my other half's eyes. Giving me a dizzying view of Agnes' back, and my terrified face—dead white skin, head of wild blond curls, puke- and blood-stained dress. And desperate eyes, because I didn't know how to deal with this. And because Agnes had just let loose.

She sent everything at me at once, from all three directions, so I did likewise. There was no time to think, no time to plan, not even time to scream myself hoarse some more. No time for anything except throwing everything I had left into a time bubble that I didn't send in any specific direction, just *out*.

And out it went.

"Oh, shit," I heard the other Cassie say, but I didn't see anything, because I was huddled in a ball, afraid to look, and more afraid to die, because if that hadn't worked, I was a sitting duck. I didn't have any energy left to defend myself with; barely had enough to stay conscious. And while this was supposedly a duplicate body I was in, it didn't feel that way.

Which meant that dying was probably going to hurt like a bitch.

Only . . . I didn't die.

I didn't do anything but hunker there as the girls screamed, as Gertie cursed, and as something fell with a clatter, loud enough to jolt me out of my terror, metal on stone.

I finally looked up, peeking out from between my crossed arms, and—

"Oh."

The crash had been one of the big curtain rods that had been holding up a huge swath of rich, burgundy velvet. It, or maybe the bolts holding it into the wall, had decayed enough to fail, as a couple centuries or more hit it all at once. Likewise, the once shining marble floor was now cracked and stained and had grass growing up through it, and vines were climbing the walls on fast forward, eating through crumbling plaster and shedding piles of leaves that sprouted, grew big, and then shriveled and fell, all in seconds, causing them to pile up in large drifts.

Like what I assumed were Agnes' bones, which had made three small piles approximately where her doppelgangers had been standing.

I stared at them and swallowed, feeling ill. And then flinched when the piano caved in, in a cacophony of yellowed ivory keys. I glanced overhead, worried about the chandeliers, but they seemed okay, just cobwebbed and dust encrusted, like something out of a haunted mansion. None looked like they were about to fall on me.

Unlike Gertie.

She was glaring at me from beside the door, where she and a bunch of wide-eyed girls were clustered in the same little knot. Or maybe in a somewhat tighter one than before, because she was shielding them from the effects of my spell, I wasn't sure how. Until I noticed: she'd thrown a time spell, too, one running counter clockwise to mine, youthening instead of aging.

And stirring up a whole lot of little bubbles along the borderline where the two spells met.

"Oh, holy sh—" I began, right before they exploded outward, peppering the entire ballroom with tiny holes—in the walls, in the ceiling, in every painting and piece of furniture. And in me.

My vision skewed and showed me that other viewpoint again, quickly enough for me to watch daylight stream in a hundred tiny spotlights through my duplicate body, which somehow stayed on its feet for a second. Before collapsing on the floor, not even twitching, while the room literally fell apart around me. Walls crumbled into rubble, half the ceiling caved in, a chimney fell through the now-Swiss-cheese-looking roof and exploded on the destroyed marble, sending a spray of bricks everywhere.

I barely noticed. I was too busy staring at my fallen body, still visible in the middle of a small lake of red, and wondering how many people get to see themselves die. And why I never seemed to get used to it.

And then I lost my remaining lunch, all over the pretty ring of intact marble under our feet.

"It doesn't count as a win if you perish in the attempt," Gertie snapped, and swept out.

I guess class was over.

*Bang! Bang! Bang!*

I almost jumped out of my skin when somebody started

trying to hammer their way through my door. I'd finished changing into a less bloody dress, or was trying to. But the current fashions assumed the presence of a maid, which I didn't have, or a boyfriend, who wasn't here, because Pritkin was off at the depot. Leaving me fighting with a back full of tiny buttons when the door was attacked.

I jerked one of the little fabric-covered things off in surprise, frowned at it, and made my way over to the door.

Three war mages were standing on the other side, along with Gertie and Agnes. Oh, I thought. And then the mages were pushing past me and starting to toss the room.

Literally.

Pillows and blankets went flying, drawers were flung open and upended, and one guy almost disappeared inside the wardrobe. "What—" I began, before I was physically jerked out of the room.

"Where is it?" Gertie demanded.

I stared from her to the guys and back again, because I had no idea what she was talking about. "Where is what?"

"Don't give me that!"

Gertie was looking more pissed than I'd seen her since, well, since a few of our adventures in Wales. Her color was high, painting her cheeks a more natural hue under her rouge, and her brown eyes were snapping. She scowled at me for a moment more, while I looked in bewilderment back, then she nodded at Agnes.

"Do it."

"Do what? What are you—" Which is as far as I got before sweet, baby-faced Agnes, with her big blue eyes and proper updo, who looked like she ought to be auditioning for a brunette Alice in Wonderland, threw me into the next room and started stripping off my clothes.

Considering that they weren't completely on yet, it wasn't hard. Or it wouldn't have been, but I decided to protest. I didn't know much about Edwardian hospitality, but so far, I hadn't been enjoying my stay.

"Cut it out!" I snapped, and smacked her hand away.

Only to have her slap me across the face.

I stared at her in shock. "What—have you lost your *mind*?"

"Oh." Blue eyes opened wide as she wrestled me for my dress. "Did you expect to get away with it?"

"Get away with what?"

"You know very well!" she snapped, and spun me around, only to jerk the damned dress off my shoulders.

"The only thing I know is we're about to throw down," I said. "And if you'll recall, you lost last time!"

"Yes!" Her color was high, too, when I spun back around, and she didn't much resemble the serene Pythian heir anymore. Her hair was half-down around her face, and her lips were set on snarl. "That is easily done when your opponent cheats!"

"What?" I was not getting less confused here. "Which of them cheated?"

*"You did!"*

And she actually raised her hand again.

I caught her arm midway to my face. I was not a particularly imposing figure, with my dress sagging around my hips and my blood-stained bra, because I was damned if I was wearing a corset. But I wasn't going to take this, whatever this was.

"I didn't cheat!" I told her flatly.

Agnes said a very bad word.

My eyes widened, and I was about to make a smart remark, when I had to catch *the other hand*.

This. Bitch.

I looked over at Gertie. "If you don't want your acolyte sent to Siberia—"

"And how would you do that, hm?" she demanded, finally coming in the door. She'd waited in the hall to say something to the mages, who I guess had finished tearing my room apart. I'd have been more annoyed, but it was mostly her stuff anyway. If she wanted to trash her own guest room, fine by me.

But this shit had to stop.

"How would I do . . . what, exactly? Shift?"

"Yes!" She looked at Agnes. "Are you capable of shifting right now?"

And Agnes literally growled at me. "No!"

I caught myself before I stepped back a few paces, because she was starting to terrify me a little. But I'd been raised at a vampire's court. I knew when to show fear and when not to, and this was definitely "not to" territory.

I straightened up.

"Do you have a point?" I asked Gertie, and tried to restore some dignity by getting the dress back on, but Agnes had torn one of the sleeve holes.

This. *Bitch*.

"Indeed, I do. You just put on quite a performance down there, one that should take my entire court some days to undo. After, that is, we finish cleaning up your last debacle—"

I frowned at her. Because that had been her choice. She'd used a spell on the castaways that she'd hit me with a time or two, one that returned people to their point of origin in the timeline. It had jerked the lost souls back to where they belonged, but was apparently exhausting, maybe because of the numbers we were dealing with. But I hadn't asked her to do it. Quite the contrary, in fact.

"You *told* me to train—"

"—so the least you could do is tell the truth."

"About *what*?" I stared at her in exasperation. "Make some sense!"

"All right, how's this? There is no way—*no way*—that you were able to defeat my entire group of acolytes, including my heir—"

Agnes growled again.

"—if you didn't have help. So *where is it*?"

And, finally, I got a clue.

"If you're talking about the Tears, I don't have any. I took the last—"

"Liar!" That, of course, was Agnes.

"—on the train," I persisted. "I had a bottle; I used a bottle—"

"She lies!" Agnes yelled.

"You know," I told her, "we heard you the first ti—" And I had to stop to *grab her arm again*. "You slap me," I told her seriously, "one more time—"

"You see? You see?" Agnes was literally hopping mad. I'd never known that actually described a real thing before, but she simply couldn't stand still. "If she's willing to duel me, after all that—"

"I do see, and I want an explanation," Gertie said, looking at me. "I am willing to help you, but not if you continue to lie to me. The Tears is a weapon, and a dangerous one. I will not have it misused under my roof."

"I haven't lied!"

"Then explain how, if you took no potion—if, as you say, you do not even possess any—you did *that*." She gestured at the stairs leading down to the foyer and the ballroom.

Or what was left of it.

I looked at her a moment and licked my lips. I could explain, but if she didn't take it well, I'd be out of a trainer almost before we started. Not that that sounded so bad, after this afternoon, but I had Jo to think about. She'd always said she wasn't a great duelist, but she probably knew all kinds of tricks I didn't, and she'd somehow come up with a crap ton of extra power. Not to mention that Jo lied.

I needed Gertie, but I honestly didn't know what to tell her, when the truth would sound like the biggest lie of all.

"Well?" she demanded.

"All right," I said. "I'll tell you."

# Chapter Forty-eight

Several hours later, there was another knock on my door.

"What?" I demanded crabbily.

Pritkin stuck his head in. And then cocked it, curiously. "What are you doing?" he asked.

"Freezing," I said, because it was true.

I had what might be every blanket in the house piled on top of me, to the point that I wasn't sure I could have gotten up to answer the door even if I'd felt like it. It was like "The Princess and the Pea," only in reverse. I was the pea. A disgruntled and grumpy little pea who just wanted to be left alone.

Of course, that didn't happen.

"Did you enjoy your training session?" he asked, coming in. And then looked slightly alarmed when I wheezed out a laugh. And then did it some more, and some more, until I was in danger of suffocating under all those blankets.

He started pulling them off, until I stopped him, because this place was freaking freezing. I was surprised there weren't icicles hanging off the water heater, which did exactly bubkis. I didn't know why the whole court hadn't died of pneumonia.

"I take that as a no," Pritkin said, and sat down on the edge of the bed.

I laughed some more, because it was either that or cry, and I'd cried enough. "Yeah," I finally said. "That's a no."

"You want to talk about it?"

I almost said no, because I always said no, at least lately. I hadn't had anyone I could confide in through all the craziness of the last month. Only, no, that wasn't true.

I hadn't had anyone I could confide in *completely*, some-one who wouldn't try to use anything he learned against me, or get freaked out and start worrying obsessively about what I told her, or start trying to fight my battles for me, even when they were ones I had to win myself.

After Pritkin left, I'd had people I could confide in about some things, but no one I could talk to about every-thing, and I'd missed that fiercely. It had taught me things, forced me to learn to pick my way through the minefield of the battle with Ares on my own, made me more resil-ient. But it had been damned lonely, and there'd been plenty of nights—

God! So many nights hugging my pillow, my eyes wet, anxiety clawing at my breast for sleepless hour after sleepless hour, because what if I was *wrong*? What if I made the wrong decision, did the wrong thing, out of ig-norance of the magical world, or of the cultures of the different groups, or of all the politics I didn't understand yet? There were so many things that went into a right decision, and so many ways it could go wrong. But after Pritkin was taken, I'd had no one to talk it all out with, no one to lay the options on the table with clinical efficiency and let me see things clearly.

And now he was back.

He was back and we were alone and oh my God, I could *talk*!

So I did. It spilled out in half-incoherent sentences, the words almost falling over themselves because I didn't have to weigh each one, didn't have to leave it trembling on my tongue while I ran down all the reasons why I couldn't say that to this person, because to this person, I could say anything. And while his jaw got tighter and tighter as he listened, he didn't try to interrupt me.

"It's not that I don't get it," I said, long minutes later. I'd sat up against the headboard, the blankets around the legs I'd pulled up to my chin, but my toes sticking out. "The Pythian Court faces some next-level shit some-times, and despite being time travelers, you don't always get do-overs—"

"Like yesterday," Pritkin said, speaking for the first time.

I nodded. "My power isn't reliable in Faerie. If I went back to try to keep Jo from changing time, I might end up changing it worse, and getting all those people on that train killed. Or like on the search for you. I'd love to pop back to Wales and *finish this*. But the way things played out, Ares got dead. What if, by killing her—permanently this time—I changed that? So I get why the court is like it is. I *do*."

"But you don't like it."

"God, no!" I thought back to those little girls clustered around Gertie. Her entire court hadn't been in the ring, just the acolytes. And some of the younger initiates hadn't even been in the room. But some of them had.

There'd been one girl, maybe fourteen or so, the same age I was when I ran away from Tony the first time. I remembered how scared I'd been then, how my heart had seemed to hammer in my ears constantly, how I almost never slept, not for days, so sure that he or his men were right behind me. How I'd stopped even looking in the mirrors in the bus stations and fast-food places where I briefly stopped, because I didn't like my expression.

The same one I'd seen on her face today.

She hadn't wanted to be there; she hadn't found it exciting. Some of the others had, their eyes shining, their fists clenching at their sides, so wanting to be in there! I could get that, too. Women in this period didn't have a lot of chances at power, and the idea could be intoxicating for some. But for others . . .

Whatever happened to being a kid? Playing with freaking dolls, or coloring books, or whatever they played with here? What ever happened to not shouldering the cares of the whole world before you'd figured out how to ride a bike?

"No," I told Pritkin now. "I don't like it."

"Then do your court differently. Every Pythia's court is different, some radically so. Your court can be whatever you want—"

"Pritkin! I don't *have* a court!"

I threw off the blankets, even though it was cold, because it was cold underneath them, too. I'd taken off the ruined dress, and had been napping in what they called a "chemise," which was less Victoria's Secret and more Granny's Closet. I had to remember not to trip over the flounce as I paced around.

"I don't have a court," I repeated. "I have a bunch of little girls I can't protect—"

"Little girls? Like the ones I saw the other night?"

I ran a hand through my hair. "Yes, the initiates are all that's left, with an average age of maybe eight. Some of them are barely walking yet! They take them from their families early, plop them into court, and don't care if it brutalizes the hell out of them—"

I stopped talking, my throat tight, but kept pacing.

"Some of the Corps' training techniques would likely shock you as well," Pritkin told me quietly. "Not to the degree of killing living, physical bodies—although I strongly suspect that has more to do with not having them to spare than with squeamishness. But, of course, the men and women who take part volunteer—"

"And they are *men and women*," I said savagely. "They're not children!"

"The concern is that if powerful clairvoyants are left with their families, they may come under the influence of those who would misuse their gifts. As that vampire did yours."

I nodded miserably, because he had a point. Tony had used what he learned from my visions to profit off of all kinds of things, from natural disasters to stock market drops to underworld wars. And he'd hurt plenty of people along the way.

I wouldn't wish that on the girls, either, and the court did keep them safe from that kind of thing until they grew up. And a mature clairvoyant in charge of her skills is a damned hard person to manipulate. It also gave them training on how to control their gift, so that it didn't torment them the way it had me, with visions coming hard and fast, sometimes one after the other, until there were days when I'd crawled under my bed, trying to get away from them, biting my lip to keep from screaming myself hoarse, because I knew that would alert Tony to the fact that I'd Seen something.

"Before the current rules, powerful magical families

used their clairvoyants against each other," Pritkin told me. "The court existed, but until the high middle ages, there was no requirement for families to surrender their daughters to it. Most felt that it was an honor, but some held them back, hoping to give their clan an advantage."

Like the covens still did, I thought.

"The court does some good," I admitted, although that was hard to do today. "I just wish—"

I cut myself off. It didn't matter what I wished. And I didn't even know what that was, anyway!

But Pritkin, who had been reclining on the bed, sat up. "What do you wish?"

I shook my head. "I don't know. And it doesn't matter now. We're at war. They're not going to change anything just because I want it."

"Who is 'they'?"

I'd gone back to pacing and was facing away from him, over by the door, but at that I turned around. "What?"

"Who is 'they'?" he repeated.

"I—the Circle, for one—"

"The Circle doesn't control the Pythia."

"Well, Jonas thinks he does! At least, he acts that way most of the time."

Pritkin shrugged. "He can act however he likes. As can anyone else. But the fact remains that there is no 'they' when it comes to the Pythian Court. There is only you. So, what do you want, Cassie?"

I stopped pacing, and for the first time, I thought about it. Not about what I had, which was a mess, but what I'd *like*. "Girls would still come to the court," I said slowly. "To protect them and give them basic instruction in how to control their gifts. Doing anything else would leave them open to predators of all kinds."

"And?" Pritkin prompted, after a moment.

But I shook my head. "There is no 'and.' That's it. That's all I want."

He frowned. "They have to be able to protect themselves—"

"*I* have to protect them! That's my job! Their job is running and playing and learning and just *being*."

"Ideally, yes. But you know that's not how the world works, especially now."

"That's how the Corps works," I pointed out. "You just said so. Magically gifted children don't join the Corps. They grow up, then make that decision. The initiates should have the same chance. And when they're older, it would be their choice if they took advanced training or not. Not their parents', not the Circle's, not anybody else's. Theirs.

"*That's* what I want."

And it was. I just hadn't realized it until now.

"All right," Pritkin said. "How do you get there?"

I almost laughed, although not with humor. "Good question."

"You do have an acolyte, though, do you not?" Pritkin asked, his forehead wrinkling. "Ms. von Brandt?"

"She's also almost two hundred years old," I reminded him. "Every time you use the Pythian power, it takes a toll. It's not so bad when you're young, but she's not, whether she realizes it or not. Every time she shifts, I'm afraid she's going to have a heart attack—"

"But that's her decision, isn't it?" he murmured.

"—and Rhea can't even shift at all—"

"Rhea?"

"The dark-haired girl you saw the other night." God, I forgot how much he'd missed out on! "The one paired off with Rico in the eating contest?"

"Ah."

"She joined the court while you were away. I've been trying to teach her; Hilde has, too. But it hasn't been working. Maybe that's why they do it this way, I don't know."

Imminent death provided a hell of an incentive.

"Perhaps she doesn't have the skill," he pointed out. "Not all do. Most, in fact—"

"Oh, she's got the skill, and then some. Considering who her parents are—"

I broke off suddenly, faintly horrified.

"What is it?" he asked, and glanced around the room, the green eyes missing nothing.

I sat in a chair in front of the dressing table, biting my lip and staring at him.

"Cassie?"

I could tell I was starting to worry him, but damn, how could I have forgotten about *that*?

"If you don't say something—" he began, but I shook my head.

"No, it's fine. I just forgot you don't know."

"Know *what*?"

And now the old Pritkin was resurfacing. He'd been deliberately calm while I had my little freak-out, but now the familiar scowl was coming back. Probably because he'd had a lot to absorb these past few weeks, and he was afraid another earth-shattering bit of information was headed his way.

"Relax," I told him. "It's just . . ." I stopped, not knowing quite how to phrase it. "Rhea is . . . well, you know how Jonas and Agnes were having an affair?"

For a moment, Pritkin just looked at me, as if he were waiting for the punch line. Only that *was* the punch line, which I guess he figured out. Because a corner of his mouth started twitching. And then the other decided to get in on the act. And suddenly he was laughing.

No, he was *laughing*, full-on belly-deep guffaws that had him falling back onto the bed and rolling around on the sheets. And now I was the one staring worriedly. And looking around the room, because I was halfway afraid somebody had snuck in and cursed him or something.

Pritkin didn't *laugh*. Hardly ever, about anything, and certainly not until his face was red and tears had started to leak out of the corners of his eyes. But he was now. I knew that because I'd climbed onto the bed, seriously concerned, and planted my hands on either side of him so I could look into his face.

He could barely breathe.

"I'm not joking!" I told him.

He tried to gasp out something, failed, and started beating the bed with a fist.

"What is wrong with you?" I pushed his shoulder. It didn't help, and then he dragged me down beside him, one arm around me, my head cradled on his still laughing chest.

I gave up and just let him get it all out. It took some time. I guess he'd kind of had that pent up for a while.

"Every time, *every time*, I think I have the world figured out, it proves me wrong," he finally gasped. "Perhaps I should stop trying."

"Works for me," I told him.

"So Jonas has a daughter," he mused, staring up at the ceiling. "And kept it hidden all this time."

"He didn't know," I corrected. "Not until recently."

"He didn't *know*?" Pritkin looked like he didn't understand how that worked.

"Agnes didn't tell him," I explained.

"Why not? Why would she—" He stopped, probably at the expression on my face.

Because I wasn't laughing.

I rolled over onto his chest. "We should be enjoying this while we can," I told him soberly. "The moments in between, as Tami calls them. Once we get back—"

Green eyes met mine frankly. "What happens when we get back?"

"I don't know. It's one of about a thousand things I don't know right now."

Pritkin's face grew thoughtful, but I didn't add anything. He didn't need me to connect the dots. He never had.

"You're saying people will think you're controlled by the Circle if we're together. That is why Lady Phemonoe hid her relationship . . . and her child?"

I shook my head. "There was more to it than that. She feared that Jonas would jump at the chance to have his daughter as Pythia. He did everything he could to influence the office through their affair."

I remembered the passionate, fiery girl I'd seen today, and the closed-off, overly careful woman I'd met in later years. She'd learned not to trust people, to the point that she'd never even considered believing me when I showed up for training. Maybe because she couldn't even trust her own lover.

I thought uncomfortably of Mircea. That had been our problem, among others. I still loved him, probably always would, but I couldn't trust him. And how could you have a relationship like that?

Of course, love covered a multitude of sins. At least, I

guessed Agnes had thought so. Because she and Jonas had been together right up until her death, yet she'd never told him about Rhea. Never breathed a word.

"She wanted to protect her," I said. "From him, and from what I saw today. I always wondered why she never let Rhea be trained. Now I know."

"And you?" Pritkin asked. "What do you want?"

It caught me off guard, I don't know why. He was never anything but direct. But I didn't hesitate.

Because on this, I'd had plenty of time to think.

"I want what she never had. No skulking in corners. No lying. No hiding everything about who I am—and who I love."

Green eyes blazed into mine, but he didn't move a muscle. Because yeah. It wasn't that simple.

"I know, okay?" I told him. "I understand the dangers, especially with the never-ending war! We need everyone on our side; I can't be seen to be playing favorites—and I won't be! I think Jonas understands that now."

"And the others? The vampires?"

I sighed. There were so many people to be considered—about my damned love life! "I don't know, but I can't live a lie. Not forever. I had to tell Gertie one today, just to stay here, because I didn't know what she'd do if I told her the truth—"

"The truth?"

"About what happened in training. She didn't understand why I was able to do that. I had to tell her I took a potion."

"But you didn't?" He leaned forward, suddenly intense.

"No, I ran out. But you gave me some power last night, so I had extra juice I wasn't expecting. That's all."

"That's all," he repeated, looking a little weird. A succession of expressions crossed his face, too fast for me to follow. But he didn't look like a guy who'd just been told "I love you"—for the second time!

"What is it?" I asked.

"Cassie," he paused, and looked like a guy who was choosing his words carefully. "Before you decide anything, you need to know—" He stopped again when he took my hand, and then looked up at me in surprise. "You're freezing."

"I told you so."

"I didn't think you were serious!"

"It's the damned weather. And that," I said, nodding at the water heater. "They need to get it working."

"It *is* working. It must be ninety degrees in here."

"Just because you're from the frozen north—"

"I'm from Britain."

"Like I said. And I haven't eaten."

"At all?"

I scowled. That had sounded more like the annoyed trainer than the concerned boyfriend. And you know, in my head, this whole moment had been a lot more romantic!

"I got up too late for breakfast, and lunch doesn't count if you lose most of it."

"You have to eat!"

I'd been in the process of pulling a blanket back up to my chin, but at that I stopped. "You have food?"

I checked him out. He was in one of those buttoned-up, three-piece suits they liked here—plain brown, but it fit like a glove, hugging broad shoulders and muscular thighs. Which I'd have appreciated more right now if he'd been holding a sandwich.

"I don't have it on me!"

I pulled the blanket up again.

He pulled it down. "But I know a place; if you don't want to eat here, that is. They're serving dinner in a few moments; I was sent up to fetch you."

I made a face. Dining with a table full of people I'd just killed, and who thought I'd done it by cheating my ass off. Sounded like fun. My stomach grumbled.

I didn't want to move, but I didn't want him to leave, either. Besides, anything he brought back through this weather would be stone-cold by the time it got here. "Is the food good?" I asked suspiciously.

"Best in the city."

My mouth started to water.

"And you haven't even heard what's for dessert."

# Chapter Forty-nine

Dessert better be pretty damned epic, I thought grimly, after getting dressed and slogging through slushy, snow-filled streets. To be fair, the buildings blocked most of the wind, but every so often a cross breeze, which was more like a cross gale, would hit and I honestly thought I might turn to ice. Which would have been fine, except we weren't on our way to a cozy restaurant with a roaring fire, where I might have been able to thaw out.

"A *pharmacy*?" I said, not bothering to keep the disbelief out of my voice.

"Pharmacies had lunch counters in the US not so long ago," Pritkin informed me as we hurried down a darkened alley. "And Rothgay's is known for its food."

My stomach grumbled unhappily. It did not seem impressed by this knowledge. It wanted steak, not some dime-store sandwich. Or roast beef—didn't the Brits do good roast beef? Or fish and chips or Irish stew or meat pies—God, I could really go for a meat pie right now! Or anything served in an old-world pub with leather booths and pints filled with frothy beer that was almost like a meal itself.

My stomach grumbled again, louder this time.

"It was a holdover from the Middle Ages," Pritkin continued. "When apothecaries sold candy and cakes—"

Wish modern docs prescribed those, I thought enviously.

"—due to being the main source for sugar and spices, many of which were also used in medicines."

"That's great, but—"

"In fact, apothecaries were originally part of the Company of Grocers, which itself belonged to the Guild of Pepperers, and sold wine as well as sweets. But in the early seventeenth century, they broke away and established the Worshipful Society of Apothecaries, which still exists today."

I narrowed my eyes. I was starting to suspect that I was being teased. "Pritkin—"

"However, in the magical community, the association between food and medicine—or potions—has remained strong."

I was about to put my foot down—damn it, I was *starving*—when he threw open a door at the end of the alley, and—

"Oh!" I just stood there for a moment, staring. You know that scene in *The Wizard of Oz* when Dorothy goes from a black-and-white farmhouse to Technicolor Munchkinland? It was like that. Only with *food*.

I stepped through the door into a world of bright marble and gleaming countertops and bustling, happy shoppers and a rotating centerpiece sculpture three stories high that seemed to be made out of candy, not to mention case after glass-fronted case full of—

"Would mademoiselle like a canapé?" A tall brunet in a green apron paused to offer me a shiny silver tray. It was full of some kind of mushroom tarts that were *oh my God wonderful*.

I was about to grab another six when Pritkin dragged me away, past a long case stuffed with stuffed things: figs and eggs and peppers and tomatoes, all bursting with goodness and ready to eat. And then another with seafood: clams and calamari and salmon served about eighty different ways, including intriguing little roll-ups that looked like they had cream cheese in them. And then past another case with all sorts of meats and sausages, and one with a couple hundred cheeses, and then half a dozen with pastries, an explosion of colorful glazed and sugared and honeyed—

"Dinner first," Pritkin said sternly, and pulled me away again.

"We're not already there?" I asked, staring around. And realized that we'd barely covered a tiny bit of the huge room, with its gleaming marble floor and walls plastered with blackboards behind the counters, listing the day's specials, and shelving crammed full of all kinds of things in baskets and jars, and an absolute mass of curved windows above it all that gave the room a giant greenhouse effect. It kind of reminded me of some of the church roofs in Russia, only transparent and rising up several more stories to show the darkly clouded skies outside.

*They* looked familiar, at least. Grumbly and laced with lightning, and dark enough that I was pretty sure I would have noticed a massive cathedral of food rising above the streets on the way here. How did they hide all this?

"This is magical London; we just came in through a side door," Pritkin said, helping not at all. "Look, they'll make you a sandwich with whatever you like," he added, as we finally stopped in front of a polished wood and glass counter.

And, okay, yeah. Sandwiches were starting to sound better all the time, I thought, my eyes going huge at the selection. I finally settled on thick-cut ham with a honey glaze, sliced chicken piled high, three kinds of cheese, some spicy Italian sausage, even spicier brown mustard, mayo, boiled eggs, sliced tomatoes, and pickled asparagus, because when I asked for pickles they asked what kind and had only about a hundred different ones to choose from.

Seriously, they pickled everything. Plain old cucumbers were apparently passé. But they gave me a sample, and these were garlicky and good, and—

"Oh, oh! Can I have some of the bacon? The thick kind with the pepper?"

The guy making the sandwich cocked a bushy white eyebrow at me, probably because the big, torpedo-shaped roll with the generous dusting of black poppy seeds he was holding was already straining at the seams. I looked back at him hopefully. He made it work.

And then, of course, it was just a matter of picking out the right potato salad, which took a while because, again, they had maybe twenty kinds.

I finally settled for one with tiny whole potatoes in a vinaigrette, and Pritkin got the same—and nothing else.

"You aren't hungry?" I asked him.

"I'm going to eat half of yours."

I actually pulled the tray away. "You are not!"

"If you eat all that, you won't want dessert."

I glanced at the nearest case of mouthwatering goodies. Including glazed fruit tarts piled so high that I had no idea how you'd eat them. Or wobbly little jellies in a rainbow of colors that quivered whenever the case was opened. Or an array of French creations in gold cups that almost looked too pretty to eat.

Almost.

And some cream puffs that I swear were the size of my head.

Damn, I needed one of those!

"A third of my sandwich," I said grudgingly, and Pritkin laughed.

The guy behind the counter started for some reason, like somebody had pinched him, and stared at him in shock. "Put it on my tab, would you, Bertie?"

The man nodded, and Pritkin and I moved away, him taking the tray because it had gotten heavy with food and the two beers in glass steins we'd also ordered. "You know him?" I asked, glancing back to where the man was still staring after us, looking like he wanted to cross himself.

"I was assigned to London for a while, doing training for the Corps. The center is just around the corner."

Guessed that explained why there were so many war mages in here. Most of whom were also staring at us as we walked past. "They know you?"

"I trained half of them."

"Yet they're not coming over to say hello?"

Pritkin snorted. "No."

We found a table. It was in another big white room full of them, which ramped up the greenhouse effect by also including scattered pots of herbs. It was connected to the food hall, but without any doors. They just sort of flowed together. There were some French doors on the opposite wall, flung open to show a round sort of hub, this one with a shiny wood floor. Multiple rooms appeared to branch off it—the apothecary stuff, I guessed—with lots of shoppers coming and going.

"After my—after Ruth died, I went looking for my father," Pritkin said. "When I came back, I was . . . upset. Some of them encountered me before I calmed down."

"Oh."

Probably explained why several of them had moved to keep us in sight and thrown their coats back to free up their weapons. Pritkin ignored them and put the tray down, filling the table with our humongous sandwich. It was a true monster, now that I got a good look at it. But damn, was it good!

I ate half, I don't know how. But I was ravenously hungry and stuffed it in. I even managed some of the potato salad. But my cream puff—

Damn, there was just no way.

"We'll get takeaway," Pritkin promised.

I brightened.

"Cassie—" he began. And then cut off, scowling.

I looked about in confusion and noticed one of the war mages approaching the table. Another one appeared to be trying to stop him, but he looked determined. I blinked at him.

He was tall, with a bulldog face that hadn't completely gone jowly, but only because its owner hadn't yet run to fat. But he looked like he was headed that way. Like he looked to be spoiling for a fight.

"You should be careful with him," he blurted out before he'd even reached our table.

"Excuse me?" I answered, because he'd been talking to me, although he was staring down Pritkin. Who hadn't moved, although that didn't mean anything. Something the other mages seemed to know, because more were converging on us.

"The last woman he was with up and disappeared," the man said, still not looking at me. "Never seen again. Wouldn't want that to happen to you."

"Kind of you," I said dryly. "Now go away."

That finally got me a glance, at least.

"I'm going to have to check you for curses," he said, and raised a hand—

Only to have Pritkin grab his wrist before anyone could blink.

"You don't touch her."

"I told you so!" the man said, his voice slightly higher. "Didn't I tell you? He's got her under a compulsion!"

"So they can come here to eat?" Another—slightly smarter—mage asked. "You're making a scene, Harry—"

"Not as much as I'm about to if you don't get your filthy hand off me!" he told Pritkin.

"Let him go," I told Pritkin, who glanced at me, then released him abruptly enough that the man staggered and almost fell, because he'd been pulling away.

"Demonic scum!" he said, and whirled—on the other side of the city, because I wasn't in the mood.

Pritkin blinked, because I guess he hadn't expected that. One of the other mages swore, and several others came running over. Because it didn't look like they had, either.

"Pythian acolyte," Pritkin said quickly. "She shifted him, nothing more."

"And why are you eating with one of them?" a dark-haired mage demanded, like it was any of his business.

"I haven't seen you before," a guy with slicked-back blond hair said, glaring at me.

"And that's my problem how?"

He scowled. "I'm going to need you to come with me."

"Thomas!" the slightly smarter mage said, sounding exasperated. "You're as bad as Harry. Let them eat in peace."

"I'll let them eat—as soon as we've verified the situation with Lady Herophile—"

"Cassie," Pritkin said, seeing my face. Which had probably been getting redder, considering my mood. I'd had a day, and these assholes weren't making it better.

"Let me help you with that," I said, and shifted the blond straight to Gertie.

And then Pritkin was on his feet, at the same moment that weapons were drawn by the half a dozen assholes who were left.

I kept my seat. "Spatial shifts are easy," I told them. "I can do this all day. And you can explain yourselves to Gertie in person. She's already in a mood, so have fun with that."

"You can't go around shifting war mages!" the brunet snapped.

"I can when they start it by assaulting my dining companion—for being my dining companion," I said, and ate a potato at him.

The man started to answer, but the smart one grabbed his arm. "She's right. You want to verify, you call the Lady and ask her. This is over."

The brunet glared some more—I guess the hotheaded blond was his friend—and shrugged off the smart guy's hand. But he went back to his table, after straightening his lapels at us, like some tough guy out of a movie. As if to say that he was only doing this because he felt like it.

I felt like adding him to Jowly's swim around the Thames, but Pritkin put a hand on my arm. "Don't."

I didn't. Mainly because I didn't want to interrupt my happy food haze any more than I already had. The rest of them left, but nobody apologized, not even the smart one.

Maybe he wasn't so smart after all.

"Let's go get a coffee," Pritkin said, eyeing me.

"Not a chance." I wouldn't give them the satisfaction of thinking they'd run us off. "Let them be the ones to leave."

"They're merely concerned for you."

"They shouldn't be!"

"Shouldn't they?"

I'd been glaring at the guys, but at that, I turned to look at him. "What?"

A silence shield snapped shut around the table, probably because the asshole contingent was trying to spy, judging by their expressions when the sound cut out.

"They have a point," Pritkin told me.

I frowned. "What point? They treated you like some kind of monster!"

"Cassie." The green eyes were sober. "I *am* some kind of monster."

I started to give the response that deserved when he stopped me.

"Adramelech said you know what I am, what my father's experiments made of me."

And goddamn it, Adra! I sighed and leaned back

against my chair. "That's what this is about? I should have made him promise to let me tell you."

Pritkin stared at me. "How can you be this blasé? You know—"

"What I know is that it doesn't change anything."

"It changes everything!"

"How? You're still the same person you've always been. The same as last week and the week before that, and all the other weeks before you knew—"

"That I was designed to be a killer, just like the Ancient Horrors?"

"Bullshit!"

"That is what Adramelech thinks," he persisted. "What the council were trying to prevent when they cursed me."

"I know," I said, covering his hand with mine, because he was clearly taking this hard. "Adra said as much—"

"You *know*?"

I nodded.

Pritkin frowned. "What do you know?"

"That the council freaked out. The genetically designed super soldier and the demigoddess scared the crap out of them. They found out that we were involved, were afraid that you'd increase my power more than they could handle, and killed you to deprive me of my 'battery.' Adra admitted it when you were off getting your weapons, and it *doesn't change anything*—"

"How can you say that?"

"Because I told him the truth." I leaned over the table and lowered my voice, despite the silence shield. And so that Pritkin's body blocked the damned war mages from reading my lips. "We can generate the power of a god between us—for a moment, maybe enough for a single spell. But we can't hold on to it. It would burn us up if we tried—"

"Cassie—"

"—which means they were wrong. We're not a threat—"

"We're not a threat *yet*," Pritkin said grimly, and something about the way he emphasized it stopped me.

"Meaning what?"

He let go of my hand and sat back, crossing his arms over his chest, closing himself off. "You already know the answer to that. You saw what lies within me last night, the monster I live with—"

I burst out laughing. I couldn't help it. He stared at me some more.

"I'm sorry," I told him. And I was, because Pritkin clearly didn't find this remotely funny. "But you can't seriously equate that poor little starved thing with—"

He suddenly lunged at me over the table, fast enough to pull several of the watching war mages back to their feet. Pritkin didn't even notice. "That poor little thing is the hybrid of a demon lord and a fey with godly antecedents!" he hissed. "It is what the gods were trying to create, but failed to manage—"

"I know that—"

"No, you *don't*," he insisted, his face flushed and angry. "No more than they did! Nobody thinks about the incubi! The gods likely never even considered my father's people when doing their experiments, and why should they? They were looking for power, some already uncommonly strong creatures that they could make even more so. Not the notoriously weak incubi.

"But that is the chief power of my father's people—*we mix with anything.* That is why other demons pay my father whatever he asks for a night with him—his power doesn't just magnify that of some of the demon races; it magnifies *all* of them. He is the universal solvent, the power stream that will blend with and enhance any other it touches, the very thing the gods needed but never found.

"But somebody else did."

"Rosier," I said, but thinking of the beautiful, mercurial, powerful woman who had been Pritkin's mother.

He nodded. "By accident, at least I'm fairly sure, but does it matter? And if that poor little starved thing you feel so sorry for becomes less starved—"

"That's why you didn't want to do it last night?" I asked, suddenly understanding. "You said—"

"That you were injured, which you were—and still are—and I didn't want to make it worse. And demon sex is nothing if not . . . intense. But I also worried about what continued exposure to that kind of power might do—to both of us!"

"Why?" I challenged. "You never explored that part of yourself, never even tried. How do you know—"

"Thankfully!"

"—that you wouldn't like the results? You don't know what might lie ahead—"

"And I don't want to know! And neither should you!"

I looked at him steadily. "You don't scare me, Pritkin. And you never will."

"But I should!" He saw my expression and swore. "Cassie, the council isn't as worried about what we *are*, as much as about what we might *become*. The gods tried a number of different experiments through the centuries, from the dark fey in Faerie to the vampires and weres on earth—"

"What?"

He nodded absently, as if that was somehow old news. Which it definitely wasn't! "That's what the demons believe caused mutated humans on earth—more godly tinkering. But it didn't work, not the way they'd hoped, because those creatures were far less mutable than they needed. But demons—most of them—are spirits like the gods, and spirits are notoriously—"

"Wait a minute. Go back," I said, feeling the usual need to run to keep up with what Pritkin was saying.

But he wasn't going back.

"—*changeable*. Like my spirit is, courtesy of my father's abilities. And, thanks to your mother . . . like yours."

# Chapter Fifty

"Wait, what now?" I said, but I didn't get an answer that time. Or if I did, I couldn't hear it. Because those strange sirens had just gone off in my head again, like on the train when time had just been seriously messed up. But nothing unusual was happening here.

Until I looked up and froze, stock-still.

What the *hell*?

My brain couldn't seem to get a grip on what I was seeing, to the point that it felt like my eyes were trying to cross. The skies were the same as before: blue-black and angry, with an occasional thread of silver lightning in the distance. No moon or stars, which had been drowned out by the ambient light from the city, or hidden by the heavy cloud cover. Everything was perfectly normal.

Except for the huge wedge of orange-red boiling away in the middle of it.

It looked like someone had decided to patch the heavens, but got the color wrong. It looked like someone had cut a piece out of a movie and glued in another movie. It looked more like a hellmouth than an actual hellmouth, because there were flames leaping, and black smoke billowing, and—

And the whole thing spearing straight down on top of the restaurant.

I shifted the table of belligerent mages, along with me and Pritkin, to the area with the wooden floor, because that was about as far as I could take so many. And because I didn't know what would happen when that thing hit down. A second later, with a mage's foot in my face, I found out.

There was no sound when it happened, no shuddering thud or massive explosion, no anything. Half of the formerly pristine atrium was just suddenly on fire, bisected almost exactly in two, along lines where the great wedge had come to rest. The part closest to the café was a glowing orange conflagration so hot that I thought my face was going to peel off. The other, where I'd put us down, was cold as a freezer from the frigid air coming in the big front doors all night. There was even a dusting of snow across what looked like the Rothgay's logo set into the floor, although it was hard to see details because of all the people suddenly trampling us trying to get out of the doors—

And the damned mages trying to curse the hell out of Pritkin!

I'd have shifted them away, but then the overhead lights went out.

Maybe, I realized, because the huge patch of glass above us was about to—

*Shit!*

I shifted us again, right before the smoke-blackened roof—which looked like it had been burning for hours—fell in. And there was sound *this* time. A cracking, tinkling, crashing cacophony of it, and massively leaping flames, because of all the new oxygen that had just been let in.

But not because anything had hit the floor. I landed along with the knot of struggling men on the icy cobblestones of the street outside at the same moment that the roof should have come down, killing the crowd attempting to follow us. Instead, what looked like a couple tons of glass and iron had hit the shield Pritkin had thrown up and was somehow still maintaining, although for how long I didn't know.

Because the damned mages were still trying to fight him!

I shifted them out; I didn't have a choice. Although it felt like it ripped my guts out to do it. I hadn't had a chance to recover from the last couple of days yet, and shifting multiple people was a *bitch*.

And it was insult to injury in this case, since we really

could have used their help. Because the shoppers weren't wasting any time. They fled, mothers with kids in hand, their frantic faces painted by flame; old people hobbling— but hobbling fast—with the help of canes; tall men ducking under the new low ceiling, their eyes huge as they stared at what was hovering in the air just above them; and everyone with the capacity popping out shields of their own. They filled the small space above their heads like multicolored soap bubbles, looking ridiculously flimsy next to Pritkin's solid blue wall, and rubbing together as the crowd elbowed and jostled and fought and fell, all trying to fit through the big double doors at once.

Only where they were going, I wasn't sure.

Because I'd just looked up again.

And then just stood there for a moment, staring like an idiot, because the wedge . . . wasn't alone.

The entire sky was full of the things, hanging in the air like bright jewels. They weren't all wedge shaped, but looked more like someone had taken a hammer to a massive pane of glass and scattered the pieces across the sky. Or maybe a window, because they seemed to show different places inside their surfaces.

The orange-red ones were the brightest, like firelit rubies, casting leaping shadows onto the frightened faces of the crowd. They were also shedding flurries of sparks, not constantly but in fits and starts, like they were being carried by a breeze I couldn't feel right now. And, in one case, an entire plank, like off the side of a house, came spinning into the night and then lay in the street, burning.

There were also some ugly yellowish ones, with a haze inside that was leaking out, wrapping them in dirty cocoons. And a group that appeared to show a cheerful blue sky, like a bright spring day, strangely eerie under the circumstances. And still more that roiled with dark gray clouds, massive bursts of lightning, and powerful gusts of wind that sent debris flying down onto the crowd, many of whom were standing around, staring up in wonder—

"Cassie!" Pritkin gritted out, bringing me back down to earth. I realized that the people streaming out of the inferno were too panicked to grasp that he was the one shielding them. Because they kept running into him, threatening his concentration.

And if it went, his shield did, too.

I got in front to attempt some crowd control, feeling the heat on my skin and the suddenly dry air in my lungs, and watching the dark silhouettes of people against all that light, trying to fit through one door, because the other was being consumed by flames. It should have kept my attention, and it did—helping people up who fell down the incongruously still icy steps and sending them to the right, because the left side of the street was a dead end. But even so, I kept stealing glimpses at the sky.

And realized that there was one more version of the strange phenomena that I hadn't noticed at first, because it blended so well with the night. It seemed to show a cityscape, only I couldn't see details, because there were no streetlights or house lights anywhere. It was so dark that all I could see was the brilliant arc of the Milky Way stretching overhead, coldly beautiful against the night. And a few moonbeams limning a mass of tightly packed buildings that were otherwise blanketed in darkness; I didn't know why.

And then I found out why.

Because something came flying out of the surface, but it wasn't a plank.

A bomb hit a building down the street, which detonated in a roar of shattering wood and flying brick. Pritkin cursed—I couldn't hear him, I couldn't hear anything over the sound of the explosion—but I saw his lips move as I jerked my head around. He didn't have that option, having to remain concentrated on the apothecary, but he somehow managed to jerk his shield over us as well.

And just in time.

I was left staring at a hail of burning bits shooting into the pale blue ward, like a thousand daggers stabbing for our hearts. And for those of the crowd, I realized a second later, *who he was also protecting.* He'd somehow managed to throw his shields all the way across the street, putting up a barrier between the explosion and the mass of now screaming and fleeing people.

It shocked me, even after what I'd seen him do on the

train, because shields don't work like that. Even war mage shields don't. Not surprisingly, the section protecting the street was much thinner than the one in the atrium, looking like a sheet fluttering in a breeze because of how far it had to stretch. Also not surprisingly, it was getting shredded.

But shredded isn't down, and it was somehow holding. And acting like a fisherman's net, something that also has a lot of holes but manages to trap plenty of fish. Or bricks and burning roof tiles and larger pieces of wood in this instance.

But some of the smaller stuff made it through, although it had been slowed way down. Which meant that the flimsy shields of the regular Joes and Janes in the crowd could handle the impact—at least for those who had them. But some didn't, being too frightened to hold concentration, because they weren't trained for this!

I saw a middle-aged woman shriek and fall as something slammed into her leg. I saw an old man's body bow outward as he took shrapnel in the back. I saw a small child get splattered by her father's blood when he was hit in the shoulder, causing him to drop her in the middle of the street. And then panic and run away, leaving her standing there, screaming—

Until I shifted her into my arms.

I clutched the crying child and stared at the burning street in horror. But also in dawning realization. I didn't know what this was, but I bet I knew who was behind it.

"Jo!" I yelled at Pritkin, but wasn't sure he heard.

I barely did. The blast was echoing in my ears like a hundred kettledrums, while he looked like he had on the train, with the cords on his neck standing out and straining, broken blood vessels in his eyes, and his face flushed bright red. Although that may have been the hellish light from the burning building and burning skies and burning street. The whole damned place was burning!

And then, just when I thought things were as bad as they were going to get, one of the pretty blue shapes started to descend, and it was dropping something, too.

I stared up in disbelief as it began spewing forth a crowd of pale bodies. And since it was still three or four stories off the ground, they slammed down on the pavement with meaty-sounding splats, in a jumble of broken limbs, cracked skulls, and ruptured torsos. Where they lay seemingly unfazed.

Probably because they already looked like corpses.

There were huge black lumps on their skin, blood and pus on their faces, and they were naked and filthy and all tangled up, like they'd been in some kind of communal grave. A young woman caught my eye, tinged a sickly greenish hue, as if mold had already started to grow on her body. She had a baby clutched to her breast, and looked like a Madonna from a funerary monument, beautiful and marble-cold. I stared at her, at the fall of matted dark hair, at the sweet face that couldn't have been more than sixteen, at the long lashes shading the youthful curve of her cheek—

That suddenly opened, revealing a cavity crawling with maggots.

Pritkin cursed and stumbled back, almost losing his grip on the shield, as the whole pile started moving. The dead baby mewled and tried to suck; limbs writhed like pale snakes, attempting to detangle, and the corpse of a dog began silently barking. It was beyond horrible—

But not dangerous—except to my sanity.

"She's trying to scare us!" I yelled at Pritkin, because the street was suddenly filled with screams, ones I could barely hear because the sound of the explosion was still echoing in my ears. "No necromancer can animate more than two or three zombies at a time! I don't care how powerful she is!"

"Then explain that!" he said, as a dozen of the creatures leapt for us all at once, clawing and biting and digging at the shields he'd just pulled tighter around us.

*"Fuck!"*

I stumbled back, despite the fact that they couldn't reach me, then shifted them into another group leaping for some of the shoppers. And I do mean *into*. I didn't mean to do it, but I was freaking out and hurrying, and there were a lot of them, and—

And that, I thought, doubled over in pain from multiple shifts in close succession, yet still staring. At what looked like a human rat king, with the bodies of one group spearing those of the other, in a huge, meaty mess that had the shoppers retching and slipping on decomposing entrails, even while the bloody, filthy mass of limbs kept on squirming and reaching out, trying to drag them down—

"Jo!" I screamed, staring at the skies. "You want me? Come after *me!*"

But there was no answer. Unless you counted the other two blue diamonds suddenly starting to descend. And that was while bodies were still spilling from the first, and now jumping for people in midair.

Pritkin stared at them, but there was nothing he could do without dropping his shield, and people continued to stream out of the massive apothecary. Strange as it seemed, all of this had happened in maybe a minute or two, with no opportunity for those on the upper levels to even reach the street. So I did the only thing I could think of, and threw a bubble of slow time over the surface of the nearest blue hell.

But while it didn't stop the flow of bodies, it did slow them way, way down, leaving something that looked like a modern sculpture hanging in the air as they leisurely descended in a waterfall of flesh, their bodies sickly pale under the dirt, their faces savage against the night. I stared up at it in disbelief, clutching the sobbing child and feeling dizzy.

And not just because I had a new entry in the impossible-shit list in my brain. But because they'd touch down eventually, and when they did, they'd join the others now spilling out of the other two diamonds and running in all directions. And I couldn't slow them all!

"Focus their attention on us," Pritkin gritted out.

"What?"

"Don't let them scatter! They'll slaughter the whole street!"

And, okay, he had a point, but what the hell was I supposed to—

"Damn it, Cassie! Do it now!"

So I did it now, shifting the drifts of flaming debris piled along the sides of the street into the bodies. And I shifted a lot. For a second there, it looked like a couple of armies had lined up to shoot volleys of fiery arrows at each other. There wasn't a corpse that wasn't riddled with pieces of flaming wood, and some looked like fiery porcupines.

But these corpses weren't the brittle, desiccated kind that might have gone up like kindling. They were damp, even soggy in some instances, and burned slowly, if at all. So all I'd done was to piss them off.

Way off.

I was nauseous from the power drain and seriously considering losing my dinner, but I nonetheless noticed when the whole street suddenly stopped, like somebody had barked out an order I couldn't hear. And turned as one, their jaws working as if biting the air, and the milky or missing eyes somehow focusing. On us.

And then they leapt, all at once, which . . . yeah. That might not have been the best plan after all. Because, sure, it had saved the crowd—for the moment, anyway. But who was going to save us?

And I guess Pritkin agreed, because his eyes had just blown wide.

"Shift out!" he ordered, right before the whole damned street slammed into his shields, scrabbling and clawing and trying to bite.

"Like hell!"

"Goddamn it, Cassie! Do as I say!"

"One of these days, you're going to learn that that doesn't work," I snapped. "Might as well be today."

Pritkin cursed, which got him nowhere. If I shifted out, he was coming with me. But if he went, so did the street, because he was a one-man army, and was literally the only thing holding it together right now.

But he wasn't going to be doing it for long.

His shields, once so solid that they'd resembled blue ice, were bucking like a storm on the high seas under the onslaught. And that was a problem for more than just us. It sent the heavy glass and iron pieces sloshing around over the crowd's heads back in the atrium, to the point that even I could see that they weren't going to last. And no way could I shift that much!

But I didn't have to.

There'd been a time in this job when I'd run around like a headless chicken, reacting more than thinking, because stuff like streets filled with fiery zombies tended to fuck with your head. But I'd had a four-month apprenticeship in hell—sometimes literally—and I was harder to rattle now. So I pulled my power around me, trying to scrape together enough for a shift—back in time.

I didn't need much, just an hour or so, maybe even less. Just enough to give us some goddamned warning! And allow us to get forces in place to handle this, whatever the hell this was!

I *had* the power. I could feel it, shuddering at my fingertips, cascading through my body, shivering down my spine. Easily enough for a short jump to warn the court, to get Gertie involved, to—

To do nothing, because I went nowhere.

I tried again and then again, panic rising in my throat, magic swirling around me. But the result was the same: I couldn't shift. I didn't understand it—I'd been shifting things all night! But when I tried this time, something felt off, something felt *weird*, although that word really failed to describe the skin-crawling sense of wrongness that sent my body shuddering every time I tried, because— because I didn't know why! I didn't know what this was!

"Shift, goddamn you!" Pritkin yelled, but I barely heard.

Because if I couldn't shift, I couldn't save him— I couldn't save any of us! We were going to die, the timeline was going to be permanently fucked, the world was going to spiral into who knew what kind of hell, and for what? Some dead bitch's sense of entitlement?

I realized I was screaming and cursing Jo's name, over and over. And this time, over the cries of the crowd, over the detonation of faraway bombs, over the sound of fire eating up the street, I swear I could hear her laughing. Because she knew we couldn't handle this. Not alone. It would take an army—

And then an army arrived.

Suddenly, all the green shutters on the second floor of the great pharmacy slammed open, almost at once. And a group of aproned employees stepped out onto the balconies, fists full of tiny potion bottles, the kind the world paid a premium price for. Because Rothgay's was the best in the business, the Cadillac of potion sellers, the place where even war mages shopped when they couldn't be bothered to brew their own.

As evidenced when a hail of death rained down onto the street.

Dozens of tiny bottles hit the cobblestones, sending up waves of brittle blue flames that turned anything they touched into powder. Hundreds of bodies puffed away all at once, creating a cloud of pale ash so thick that, for a moment, it looked like a sandstorm on the other side of the barrier. The cremated remains slammed into Pritkin's shields harmlessly, but there was another group of attackers right behind them, scrabbling and tearing at the thinning blue walls, as if nothing had happened.

That wave went up in flames, too, and part of a third, the rest of which were caught by a sticky black substance that looked like tar but flowed upward from shattered vials on the ground. It climbed the rotting bodies in seconds, surging along their torsos and over their heads, blinding them. And then abruptly jerked them down.

They were left stuck to the road in a writhing pool of sticky black, yet still reaching for the heavens, like something trying to emerge from the primordial ooze. It was horrible, mind-bending, macabre. And lucky.

Very lucky. Because the blind eyes and reaching limbs tripped up the fourth wave of the assault, not knowing what they were grabbing. They dragged them down, and the black ooze covered them, too. Some completely, while others were only trapped by a foot or a leg.

But they were going nowhere.

Unlike the throng surging around them, or using the backs of the fallen like stepping-stones in a river, not caring how much damage they caused as long as they reached their objective: us.

And plenty of them managed it. Because the remaining blue diamonds were almost at street level now, and were vomiting up an army of the dead. Ones that hadn't been damaged in the fall like the others, but were fresh and fast and deadly. And while Rothgay's people were doing their best, there was no way to contain them all.

It was something the potion sellers seemed to have figured out, because they'd resorted to protecting the area nearest to their shop, providing a narrow escape route for the remaining customers.

It appeared to be working.

But it also left us standing alone.

The area inside Pritkin's shields had shrunk as he drew them tighter and tighter to save power. They were barely three feet from his body now, and didn't look like water anymore. They were more like rubber, stretching inward in the shape of hands and elbows and knees, and the ghostly faces pressed against the surface on all sides, their mouths open, their teeth bared and biting. They were going to eat us alive, I thought, clutching the little girl. They were going to—

And then Pritkin's head jerked around, I didn't know why. I couldn't see anything but death. But then I heard it, faintly over the screams from the street, the still echoing drumbeats of the explosion, and the little girl's sobs: the sound of boots hitting stone—hundreds of them.

And I realized: the real army had just arrived.

War mages flooded the scene like a brown leather river, more than I'd ever seen in one place before. They knocked away the monsters, ripped straight through them with spells I didn't know and couldn't name, surged up the street. A dozen took over shielding the main hall of the apothecary, just as Pritkin's great shield failed. While the rivers of leather and pale flesh met and clashed up the road, with so many spells being thrown that I was all but blinded by the light.

# Chapter Fifty-one

For a moment, I just stood there, being battered by the army of leather coats swarming all around us, watching pale bodies rain from the sky, while fire, both human and magical, lit up the night. It had started to snow again, lightly, barely a dusting across the scene. But it was enough to smear the colors across my vision, turning the battle into something almost pretty for a moment— And then Pritkin was jerking me back, over to the scant protection of a portico.

He was yelling but I couldn't hear him over the battle raging all around us. Until he made a savage gesture and my ears popped. "—out of here! Get back to court!"

"I can't—"

"You can and you will! Or I'll drag you there myself!" His eyes were wild.

"You don't understand. I *couldn't* go, even if I wanted to. I can't shift!"

"What?"

"There's something wrong with my power—"

"You've been shifting for the last—" he began furiously, and then paused, I guess because he wasn't sure how long this had all been going on, either.

Time gets distorted in battle, hurrying up or slowing down in weird ways that have nothing to do with the Pythian abilities and everything to do with terror. Or, in Pritkin's case, exhaustion, because he'd just channeled as much magic as an entire squad in what was probably literally a couple of minutes. I'd seen it, and I still didn't quite believe it.

"You've been shifting!" he finished, and I nodded.

"Yes, but I can't now, I don't know—" It was my turn to stop, but not because of the confusion of battle. But because a frantic woman had just run up and snatched the child out of my arms, screaming and hitting at me.

Since the little girl immediately went to her, grabbing her around the neck in a death grip, I was pretty sure this was mama. And that she was going to get them both killed, because she was already trying to run off. And war mages or no, this place was not safe!

As indicated when Pritkin somehow summoned even more power and blasted a couple of running corpses to pieces, but not before they got close enough to smatter us all.

That wasn't his fault: one of the strange, gaseous shapes had just hit down in the middle of the battle, spreading a thick, yellowish haze everywhere. It extended out even this far, although it was thinner here. But it was still bad enough to make it hard to identify friend from foe at any range.

But the woman didn't understand that. Frankly, she looked unable to understand much of anything at the moment. She was crying and screaming and hysterically pulling at the hands I'd put on her arm, to keep her from running away. Because she was in no shape to make good decisions!

Or to listen to me. I got clocked upside the chin, hard enough to break my hold and to send me staggering back. While she started to run—

Straight into the path of five or six of those horrible things. I yelled a warning she ignored or didn't hear, then shifted both her and her child. To the Pythian Court instead of somewhere closer, because I could barely concentrate, being too busy screaming at a power loss I couldn't afford.

But it worked: the woman and girl popped out, and Pritkin nailed the leaping creatures, then turned on me with a snarl. "I thought you couldn't shift!"

I stared at him, and belatedly realized what I'd done. "I don't—I couldn't—a minute ago—"

"Well you obviously can now!" He looked down at his nice brown suit with disgust, I guess because it didn't contain nearly enough weapons for his liking. Although it contained enough. A couple of knives, a bunch of potion vials, and a handgun all jumped out and began establishing a perimeter around us. The handgun was not remotely period appropriate, but judging by his expression, Pritkin had reached fuck-it mode a while ago.

Something that did not change when he looked back at me, fury written in every line of his body. "Go! Home!"

"Fuck! You!"

And, okay, that got me a blink, at least. "This is Pythian business," I told him, while I had an opening.

"Then let the Pythia damned well handle it! This is Lady Herophile's problem—"

"Not if it's Jo who caused it! She's my responsibility—"

He grabbed me on my side, right over my wound, because he was a *bastard*. "You're wounded, exhausted, and frightened out of your mind. You're no good to anyone like this!"

I struck his hand away, gasping. "That's not your call!"

"I'm making it mine." It was grim.

"This is *Jo*!" I said, livid. "This is more my problem than yours. If anyone goes to hide back at court, it should be *you*!"

Pritkin gave me a level stare out of eyes like chips of green ice. "I forgot how pigheaded you can be."

"And I forgot what an asshole you can be! But we're stuck—" I broke off and shifted a little vial out of the air and then halfway down the street, because it had been sneaking up on me. "Goddamn it, Pritkin! Stop trying to roofie me!"

He didn't even bother to deny it. "I'm not letting you die in this—"

"I'm not planning on it, you—"

Hard hands grabbed my shoulders. "You don't understand! You don't die!"

And, for what might have been the first time ever, I looked up into that familiar face and wasn't sure I could reason with him. Because he looked more than a little crazed. The features were pale and strained, and the eyes—

Were a revelation.

"You never said it," I whispered, my voice filled with wonder.

"What?"

"You never said 'I love you'—until now."

He looked at me as if I'd lost my mind. "Of course I love you, you complete idiot!" And he pulled me against him.

I laughed, I couldn't help it, and it was louder and went on longer than it might have elsewhere, because it was tinged with an edge of madness. And then I kissed him, because the world was insane and I didn't care anymore. And, for a surreal moment, he kissed me back.

And then he thrust me away in order to kill a couple of zombies, and didn't that say everything about our love life, I thought, staring at them.

Until Pritkin jerked me back into the doorway.

His eyes kept scanning the street, looking for threats, but his throat was working. "You don't understand," he said again.

"Then explain it to me. Explain that this is not about my competence—or your view of it. Because you haven't been around. You haven't seen—"

"It's not about your damned competence!"

"Then what is it?"

He glanced at me, a quick gleam in the night, and then looked back at the street. "We need to get out of here."

Goddamn it!

Why did I keep picking men I needed a crowbar to get anything out of?

"This is *Jo*," I told him again. "I have to—"

"You don't know that!"

I grabbed him, his biceps rock hard under my hands. "Pritkin! Look around you! Who else could do this?"

For a second, he just stared at me, anger, fear, and frustration so massive that he might have just invented a new emotion all warring on his face. But that prodigious intellect won out instead. I saw him glance at the strange jewels gleaming in the sky, and then at one of the blue-black variety that was slowly descending across the street.

Only it didn't look like a jewel from this angle. It looked like a dark shadow had fallen on a row of houses, snuffing out the lights, deepening the night, and ignoring the slurry of colors from the fight down the road as if they didn't exist. It also changed little details, I noticed, watching flowerpots vanish, a mail slot appear in a door, and a banister railing change from stone to cast iron as the darkness fell.

Because we were looking at the same street, I realized, just in a different *time*.

And, finally, something clicked.

And I guess it did for Pritkin, too. "The Blitz," he said blankly, as an air raid siren blared out of the shadow, followed by brilliant bursts of light that tore across the darkened sky above the houses, lighting up his face.

I nodded. My Victorian nanny had told me stories of the bombing of London, back during World War II; I'd just never thought to see it for myself. Much less to potentially die in it!

"And if that's the Blitz, that's the Great Fire," he added, glancing at one of the boiling orange shapes, which had just crashed into a building at the end of the street, causing it to go up like a torch.

"The what?"

"In 1666, it destroyed most of the city." He stared around at the other shapes, stunned disbelief on his face.

"The plague," I added, watching the never-ending fall of bodies. "She must be animating the corpses—"

"How?" Hard hands gripped me. "She's a bloody acolyte!"

"She's a ghost of an acolyte," I corrected, thinking back to something I'd learned on the search for him. "And ghosts aren't like humans—or demons. There's no upper limit on how much power they can absorb. That's why the ghost of Apollo was such a threat to Ares—he could have drunk him down, all of him, because they don't get full—"

The street whited out.

For an instant, I didn't know what had happened, because my hearing had just cut out, too. It was only a second or two, but it felt like forever, and then I was staring at a wash of dirt and cobblestones pelting Pritkin's shields. One that just went on and on.

.

I shifted us to the flat roof of a nearby building. It was no safer—nothing was safe now—but it got us off the street. What was left of it.

There was a big smoking crater where we'd just been, which is probably why Pritkin staggered and went down to one knee. Because, yeah. Everyone has their limits, and it looked like he'd just reached his.

I knelt and held him while he heaved and shuddered and gripped me like he thought—well, like he thought we'd both almost died, which we had. We couldn't handle this, I thought again, this playground of horrors that Jo had somehow conjured up. And there's only one way to stop a spell you don't understand.

But Pritkin already knew that; he just couldn't face it.

"When I was lost," he said hoarsely, after a moment, "I didn't know what was happening to me. Adramelech's spell was . . . shocking, disorienting. I fell, for what felt like years, not knowing where I was, or even who. But every once in a while I would surface, like a drowning man clawing at the air, and every time that happened—*every* time—it was because of you."

"I . . . don't understand."

"You were my lodestone, the only thing I saw that made sense. I didn't know who you were for a long time, but you were *important*. You were the only thing that was. And now you want me to let you—"

"I'll be all right," I whispered, because there was something in my throat. But it came out so low that I wasn't sure he'd heard. Until the green eyes were blazing into mine, furious—and terrified.

And I realized that the fear I'd seen cross his face before hadn't been for him.

It had been for me.

"You won't," he told me flatly. "You've seen what she can do, how much power she can channel. You're already tired; what do you think you're going to do against *that*?"

"I don't know, but I have to try. If—"

And then I got cut off—*again*—by a commotion from below.

We'd ended up near the roofline, overlooking the front of the house, where a young war mage had just run up to the gate protecting a small garden area. He tried to get in, but either the gate was locked or he was too panicked to figure out how it worked. He finally grabbed on to it and shook it, screaming, until Pritkin barked out an order.

The man—or boy, because he looked about sixteen—started and stared upward. For a moment, his face froze in a look of pure shock. And then it crumpled in a combination of terror and relief and shame and hope, with the latter finally winning out.

"Sir! Sir! What do we do?"

"Stay there until I tell you!" Pritkin snapped, which seemed a little harsh to me. But the boy abruptly straightened up and even managed a salute. But Pritkin didn't see the snappy response, having already turned back to me.

"I have to go," I told him.

But he wasn't listening—and he wasn't letting go. His hands were clamped on my arms, and he knew—he *knew*—it was hard as hell to shift that way and not take him with me. But he couldn't help me with this.

"She's sending every curse London ever suffered at once!" I told him desperately. "She'll kill thousands of people—and destroy the timeline!"

"Yes, she will." Gertie said, stepping out of the night. She did it as seamlessly and gracefully as her acolytes had back at court—all of them seemed to be with her.

I'd never been so happy to see anybody in my life.

"I can't shift in time," I told her quickly. "I don't know why. But if you can send me back, we can catch Jo before she has a chance to do anything—"

"She's already done it," Gertie said briskly. "Shredding the timeline this way has made temporal shifting impossible until it's fixed."

I stared at her. "What?"

"You can't go back in time until you kill her!" Agnes said, looking at me in disgust. "You did this! You destroy everything you touch! Who the *hell* was stupid enough to make you Pythia?"

You were, I didn't say—not because I was being diplomatic. But because Gertie was talking again. "She put a lot of thought and planning into this for mere revenge—-why?"

I shook my head. "I don't know. I don't even know what's going on!"

Agnes snorted.

"Do you remember the light I used in Amsterdam, to search for you?" Gertie asked.

I nodded. It had been dark as pitch, because seventeenth-century cities didn't have streetlights. But Gertie had opened up what I'd thought had been a portal to another time, one with a sunny day that followed her around like a puppy, and was better than any searchlight. It was one of those times that had shown me just how lacking my training had been.

"It is called Shards," she told me now. "It is supposed to be used as a window on another time, to check on a problem in one era while you are dealing with one in another. But this Johanna has distorted it into a weapon."

"One that's unraveling the time stream as we speak!" Agnes said. "I'll go after her!"

"You'll do no such thing," Gertie said sharply.

"Why the hell can't you all go?" Pritkin demanded. He was usually more polite to Pythias, deferential even, but he'd obviously had enough.

She looked at me, and I explained. "If she dies, if any of them do, it'll screw up the timeline even more than Jo is doing. That's why Pythias clean up their own messes. Jo is my problem."

I tried to move back, to give myself room to shift, but Pritkin wasn't having it. He held on, fighting me, I didn't know why. I gave up and pulled him a little way off.

"Jo intended to trap me here," I said, before he could say anything. "But it works both ways. She can't run—"

"She doesn't want to run. She wants to kill you!"

"Which is why I have to face her. Pritkin, *there's nobody else who can*."

A hundred expressions chased themselves over his face, before he finally settled on grim determination. "Listen to me. I didn't get a chance to finish telling you what I had to say in the café—"

"It can wait—"

"It can't!" The green eyes burned. "You don't see it, but I do—everyone does. You're changing, becoming more like your mother. And yes, I know what I said before, about her kind! But there are advantages to your heritage as well as the rest, one of which is in how they *feed*."

"Pritkin—"

He gripped my shoulders. "If you could feed from me last night, you can feed from Johanna! Get close, get her distracted, and take her down the way your mother did a thousand demon lords—"

"I'm not my mother!" I whispered. "I can't hold that much power—you know that!"

"Then take what you can and use it against her. Don't let her direct the fight—keep her on the defensive. Remember what I've taught you."

I nodded.

"You can *do* this. You may not have had their training, but you've had mine! You're better in a fight than she is, you're stronger where it counts, you're—"

He broke off and pulled me into his arms. The kiss was burning, fiery, explosive—almost as much as the street around us. Maybe more. Because I felt power flooding into me, a torrent of it, because he wasn't holding anything back. And he kept it up until I broke it off, staggering a little and pushing him away, afraid he'd give me too much, afraid he'd give me everything.

"Stay alive!" he told me hoarsely, and I nodded.

"You, too." But he'd already turned away, I guess so he wouldn't see me go, and was already issuing commands to the crowd of young men assembling at the gate. And, unlike the others, these mages didn't look afraid of him. They looked desperate and grateful and, in a few cases, hero-worshipping, because most of them appeared to be trainees, probably from the nearby center, and there was finally someone to take control.

Like I had to do now.

Jo, I thought, reaching for my power, feeling it tingling around me, flooding through me, coursing down to my fingertips. Take me to her.

And the street winked out.

# Chapter Fifty-two

There was nothing but a yellowish haze everywhere I looked, and the air was thick and heavy in my lungs. Even worse, it burned in my nose, my throat; every mucus membrane I had felt like it was on fire in seconds. It was like breathing acid.

And to top it all off, I couldn't see a damned thing.

"They call it the Great Smog," Jo's voice came from somewhere nearby. It was full of laughter, and sounded clear; she could breathe, at least.

And she could fight.

A second later, a burst of spell fire came boiling through the air, barely missing me. And only because clawing anxiety is really good for the reflexes. I felt the static electricity of a spell raising the hair on my arms and flung myself to the side just in time to see a streak of red crash into something that sent brick-like shards everywhere.

They peppered my body, but not for long. I'd already shifted before most of them hit me, although shifting when you can't see is . . . not optimal. I fell into open air, then crashed down onto something soft and spongy. Mud, with bits of grass in it. A park? Somebody's front lawn? I didn't know.

And I didn't have time to find out. Spell bolts slammed down all around me, throwing mud and burning grass into the air and lighting up the smog, but not dispelling it. Forcing me to shift blind again, and this time, I wasn't so lucky. I hit down hard, stumbling into what felt like an iron fence, and smacked my head into a post. The world went swimmy for a second, and I cursed myself.

So much for taking the offense!

Because Jo might not be much of a duelist, but she knew how to give herself an advantage. My lungs were burning, I couldn't see, and already I was injured.

This is going well, I thought, struggling to breathe and fumbling around the edge of the fence.

I was definitely in a park, and a waterlogged one at that, judging by the way my feet sank into the earth. That put paid to moving fast, but I couldn't keep shifting. Pritkin was right; I *was* tired, and I wasn't a ghost with a huge energy store to draw from.

I finished this soon, or not at all.

Another spell came sizzling past, hit the fence I was now on the other side of, and ran down it like red lightning. It kept glowing from the heat even after the spell's magic was used up, the iron dripping down the posts like wax off a spent candle, the whole casting red shadows on the smog. Then Jo's voice came again, in a singsong lilt that would have been creepy under any circumstances but right now was just macabre.

"Ten thousand people died, a hundred thousand were hospitalized. All from burning too much coal and having a stagnant weather pattern. Crazy, huh?"

Yeah, like you, I thought, and tried to shift her to me.

But the voice was echoing, maybe off of surrounding buildings, maybe through whatever shield she was using to be able to breathe, I didn't know. But I couldn't get a lock. Still, she must have felt something, because she laughed.

"No, no, no, not so easy. Have some fun with it!"

And the next thing I knew, reality was tilting, the world was shattering, and I was falling—

Into a cyclone—or at least that's what it felt like. The yellow haze had abruptly changed into a storm-tossed night, although the rain-laced wind was so harsh it didn't make much difference. All I could see was a lot of gray. And the chimney I'd just slammed into.

I staggered back, almost fell off a roof, and went to my knees scrabbling at soaked wooden roof tiles. And not finding purchase, because it felt like I'd landed in a hurricane, with the winds trying their best to drag me into the night. Until a hand reached out from behind the tower of bricks and jerked me forward—

Into Hilde's gigantic bosom.

"Get down!" she yelled, and threw us both flat on the rooftop, right before the chimney exploded.

But this time, I didn't get beaten up any further. Because the flying stone just puffed away, aged to dust in an instant. And the remains were scattered by the violent winds almost before I realized what was happening.

"Time shield," Hilde said, puffing, as she crawled back to the peak of the roof, I guess to try to see over it.

"What are you *doing* here?" I said, because it was surreal. She was creeping around the roof like a ninja—only ninjas didn't wear support hose! Or have a bunch of similarly unlikely commandos with her.

Because two old women and three middle-aged ones were arranged around the roofline, why, I had no idea. Until I noticed: one of the older gals had stuffed herself into a too-small, high-necked, white lace dress that looked terribly familiar. Oh, no, I thought.

No, please.

"I saw you duel," the tiny, rotund woman told me, rheumy eyes bright. "So many years ago now. Well, so many for me. You were the best I ever saw—"

"You never saw me," Hilde said, crawling back down to join us.

"No, you'd already left the court by then," the tiny old woman agreed, like we were having a pleasant conversation over tea.

"No," I told Hilde, before she could say anything. "No, get them out of here!"

"You said to bring them round for an interview—"

"This isn't a goddamned interview! They're going to get themselves killed!"

"They are if you don't give them their power back," she agreed.

"I can handle this! I don't need—"

"Then I suppose you can tell me what spell Johanna is using?"

"Shards!" I snapped, mentally thanking Gertie.

"And how to break it?"

I glared at her. "I don't need to know that! I just need to kill her!"

"Yes, you do. And the longer it takes, the more the timeline suffers. How long until we can't repair it at all? How long before a world falls because you don't work well with others?"

"Now, now, that's not fair," tiny grandma said, patting my hand. "Don't listen to her. She tends to get excitable when she's nervous."

I stared at her. And then I transferred the look to Hilde, who was already puffing up. "I'm not nervous!"

She also wasn't wrong, I thought, as a hail of spell bolts streamed toward us, causing me to hit the roof again. They were blown off course by the howling wind—fortunately. Because they'd looked like the kind a war mage might throw: thick and sturdy and unlikely to be stopped by any shield I might throw up!

Not that I could afford the power drain, anyway. Pritkin had given me what he could, but both of us had been bottomed out. Would that be enough for Jo?

At a guess, no, I thought, as several more chimneys exploded.

The winds snatched the bricks and sent them streaming off into the wind, like they were odd-shaped leaves. The women must have been shielding or we'd have been blown off ourselves by now. So they had some magic, at least. But damn it! I didn't need any more people to die for me!

Or to betray me, not that that was a big concern right now.

Jo was perfectly able to kick my butt all on her own.

"It's hard, I know," tiny grandma said. "I never could have done your job, not that it would have gone to me. My mother is a mage, but my father was human. I age faster as a result, and could never have borne such power. But I can support you, in the burden you must bear. If you will let me?"

I looked around at all of them, these women who didn't have to be here, who probably had comfortable lives back home and didn't have to help me. But who inexplicably wanted to anyway. I didn't know what to say.

But I guess my face must have been enough, because Hilde nodded briskly. "Good, that's done, then."

Which is how I ended up with a posse.

Which was lucky, all things considered. Because a lightning strike scattered the women's shield a moment later, and a savage gust blew me off the roof and onto another. Where I clung to a weathervane and tried not to look down while attempting to regain my footing.

I failed. But not because of my two left feet. But because Jo was gleefully sprinting across the rooftops, like she was immune to lightning, while throwing bolts of her own.

I stared at her, in the brief glimpses the lightning offered: the crazed face twisted by hate and fiendish glee, the wet blond hair almost glowing under the strobe-like lightning, the lithe form ignoring the pelting rain and the sharply pitched roofs and the wind that lashed and blew like a wild thing, trying to pluck our tiny bodies up and send them spinning off into the darkness.

None of which she seemed to notice.

When you've already died a couple of times now, I guess it just doesn't have the same effect.

And then the roof I was on exploded.

It took me a moment to realize that I hadn't gone with it, because somebody had shifted me back at the last second. Hilde, I thought, grabbing her ample form. "You have to say it!" she yelled, shaking me.

"Say what?"

"You have to give their power back!"

"Is there a ritual?" I screamed, and then screamed again as lightning flashed right above us.

But somebody must have had some coven training, because it was all redirected—at Jo. She disappeared off the top of the building where she'd paused one second too long, and the laughter abruptly stopped. I wasn't sure if that was because she'd shifted or because she'd been fried, but I *really* hoped it was the latter.

"It doesn't matter!" Hilde shook me. "The power knows what you mean. Just *say it*!"

"You're hired!" I yelled, just before I was jerked onto another rooftop, where soaked wooden tiles cascaded under my scrambling feet.

A body landed heavily beside me, a knife blade flashed and came down, burying itself in wood, and I shifted to the next roof, screaming—

And then pushed a crumbling chimney down onto the woman who had followed on my heels.

Jo cursed and shot a spell, but the bricks hit her arm, and it went awry. I fell off the roof anyway, because the damned thing was pitched at a freaking sixty-degree angle, but somebody's spell grabbed me out of thin air and shifted me—somewhere. I couldn't tell with rain blinding me and thunder deafening me and something tugging at my mind, something I'd seen, something strange. Only who the hell could think in this?

And it didn't get any better. What followed was a surreal game of hide-and-seek played out across the rooftops of London in a storm for the history books, and maybe it was in them, I didn't know. All I knew was running and leaping and thanking God they built houses almost on top of each other whenever the hell this was, and falling and scrambling and feeling spell bolts hit down all around me, crashing through chimneys and punching through roofs, and that was with my posse deflecting most of them off into the storm.

I could see them now, in glimpses, those courageous, insane women, popping up on rooftops here and there, limned by lightning, throwing spells at Jo that she dodged as easily as she did the bolts stabbing down from above every few seconds, because the very heavens seemed to hate us!

At least they hated me. Because a forest of lightning—not blasts this time but threads—surrounded me suddenly, like a cage. It caused me to have to stop on a dime, to keep from plowing straight into them—

Unlike some pursuers that I hadn't even noticed until now.

"You have got to be *shitting me*!" I screamed as a group of pale bodies sprang at me out of the night, only to be roasted on the bars of my cage. I shifted out, the

smell of cooking meat in my nostrils, to a nearby roof.
And looked back—

Only to see what had to be thousands of bodies swarming through the narrow streets, surging up the sides of
buildings and crawling over rooftops in ways that human
bodies just don't. I guessed they were staying low to avoid
the winds and hugging the roofs to keep from being
blown off them, but that's not what it looked like. It
looked like I was being followed by an army of pale,
human-sized spiders, something that, despite everything,
had me almost frozen in horror for a second.

And then the real lightning storm started.

Because the heavens all but cracked open, and what
had to be a thousand deadly silver threads slammed
down, blasting through the ranks of the dead, incinerat-
ing half of them where they stood or crawled, and blowing
many of the rest back through the air, away from me.

And I guess Jo didn't like that. Because a second later,
she shattered this shard, too, like she had the last, when I
went from smog to hurricane. And now where was I?

All I knew was that I fell into the middle of a darkened
street from what had to be four stories up. It should have
broken every bone in my body, but somebody got a shield
underneath me at the last second. One that I bounced on
a couple of times before falling off into the road—a very
different one.

It was bone-dry, under a cloudless night sky. It was
paved, with streetlights on the corners, only they weren't
lit. It was also eerily silent, with my labored breaths
sounding loud in the night.

That and the fact that there were no lights in the windows, or lighted signs over shops, or any form of illumination at all other than the nearly full moon overhead, was
enough to tell me where I was.

And when.

But if the bombers were coming, they weren't here yet.
And the streets of wartime London were as deserted as
they ever got—for a moment. Until the swarm came, boiling over buildings and around corners on every side: hundreds, thousands, and then what might have been tens of
thousands of them, I didn't know. Just that they were

everywhere, including at both ends of the street, cutting me off. And when I tried to shift for the fiftieth time today, I went nowhere.

She'd been wearing me out, I realized, the ozone smell of lightning and depleated power in my nose.

Even with all her power, she'd been worried, and Jo wasn't like the other acolytes I'd faced. She didn't overestimate her abilities or underestimate mine. She got backup—a crap ton of it—and still took the time to tire me out to the brink of exhaustion before she was finally ready to end this.

I guess I should be flattered, I thought, as she appeared at the end of the street.

And then someone tried to shift me away.

I could feel the tug of magic, pulling on me; just as I could feel another, far stronger stream slap it down. Over the next moment, I experienced the sensation of almost shifting again, and again, and again, as more of my acolytes located me. There was a second when I swear I could see spectral versions of myself leaping into the sky, in all different directions, like petals on a flower—

Before slamming back into place, hard, because Jo was done playing.

But my acolytes weren't, only I don't think "play" was the right word. Not when the hordes of bodies leaping toward me suddenly paused in midair. And then began moving a whole lot slower. They surrounded us, clawing and reaching but barely moving, forming a stadium of flesh, ghostly pale against the night—

And, suddenly, I understood one thing, at least.

"That was my father's idea!" I yelled at Jo, who had paused to admire her handiwork, I guess. Or to fit in one last gloat.

"I know an old friend of his," she agreed, walking slowly toward me. "And there were so many ghosts in the Badlands, so desperate for another chance—"

"You couldn't have fed this many!" I raged.

"I didn't feed them," she said casually. "The Black Circle did. I made the same deal that your dad worked out with them, only I didn't lie. He promised them a ghostly army; I delivered. Just with a twist."

Yeah, a big one. Facing a ghost army would be bad enough, but Jo had borrowed another idea from dear old dad. She'd stuffed her ghostly corps into real human bodies, combining the two types of necromancy into one.

Only that still didn't make sense.

"You can't control this many! No necromancer could!"

"I don't control them. I don't have to. They follow the orders of whoever rings the dinner bell."

"Meaning what?"

"That if they don't follow orders, they don't get any more life magic, and they slowly fade away. Unlike humans, ghosts don't bite the hand that feeds them."

And no, they didn't. Like Billy Joe, asleep in my necklace, still worn out from almost draining himself in our fight at the consul's. He was loyal, but he couldn't help me here. No more than my acolytes could.

I stared around at her ghost army, clad in the rotting flesh of the plague-riddled bodies she'd dug up, and felt my stomach drop. They were going to break over us in a minute, and there was nothing I could do. Nothing! Ideas cascaded in my frenzied brain, but none of them stuck, except for one.

The one I didn't know how to do!

"Wait!" I said, as she raised a hand.

"Oh," she said politely. "Is this where we pause so I can tell you all my dastardly plans? Sorry, Pythia. I'm not in the mood tonight."

"Why? Who am I going to tell?" I asked desperately, and she laughed.

"You? No one at all. But your acolytes might. I'll go after them, once you are dead, but there's always a chance I might miss one. And that would be a shame."

"Wait!" I said again, trying to come up with another question; anything to buy a little time. Although that didn't seem like a great strategy when we were about to be swamped anyway. I glanced up at the leaping creatures who were about to close over our heads, and then past them, to where the moon shone serenely down, the light as pure and clear as it always was.

Mother's symbol; but she couldn't help me now, either. And I shouldn't need it! Damn it, why couldn't I *think*?

"You gave me a good chase, I'll give you that," Jo said, sounding almost sympathetic for once. "But you're out of acolytes, Pythia, and out of time."

She raised a hand again.

"Not entirely out of acolytes," someone said, which would have been weird enough, because there were only the two of us here.

But it sounded like it came from Jo's throat.

And then she stepped into a moonbeam, and I completely lost the thread, with my brain going from careening out of control to stopping dead.

Because that . . . wasn't Jo.

# Chapter Fifty-three

*"Lizzie?"* For a moment, I didn't believe my eyes. I'd killed her; I *knew* I had. But it was absolutely her: the same blond hair, still frizzy despite the rain; the same small, slightly myopic blue eyes; the same pretty, if slightly pinched, face.

Until she started laughing.

But not at me.

"Really? *Really?* Lizzie the Loser is going to come riding to the rescue?"

It was Jo's voice, but it was coming from Lizzie's lips. And I finally realized what had been bothering me earlier. A flash of that terrible lightning in the last shard had lit up a shining head of hair—blond hair. Jo was a brunette.

Only maybe not anymore.

And then a different voice came out of the same mouth, higher pitched, breathier, and angry. Lizzie's voice. "Don't call me that!"

"Why not?" Jo asked. "Everybody else did. Lizzie the Loser, Lizzie the Layabout, Lizzie the Lummox—"

"Shut up!"

"Do you remember how they laughed at you? All the other acolytes? Far worse than me. I think they were scared of me. But you—"

"Cut it out!"

"Or what? You'll make me? You forget who is in charge here."

I just stood there, my head spinning. Because a woman who shouldn't be alive was *standing in the road, arguing with herself.* I didn't get it.

Until she helped me out. "Chimera!" Lizzie's voice snapped, and then there were two.

Just as in my vision, on the floor of Gertie's cramped little waiting room, the single body split into what looked like identical twins. Right down to the waterlogged gray Edwardian outfit they were both wearing. It looked heavy as hell, which might explain why Lizzie #2 was taking off her jacket and throwing it aside.

Or maybe there was a different reason.

"Oh, you're going to fight me now?" Jo asked mockingly, out of Lizzie #1's mouth.

"You think I can't?"

"Yeah. I think you can't." It was dry. "Don't be a fool—"

"Don't call me that!"

"Then stop acting like it! You have a reward waiting for you, just as soon as this is done—"

"Yeah," Lizzie #2 said. "Sure thing. Like you promised last time, when you told me I'd be Pythia! That I'd make my family proud. God, I *was* a fool then!"

And a mass of power suddenly went boiling through the air at Jo.

She countered it, barely in time, and I hit the dirt. The time wave flew overhead and ate a hole in the surrounding wall of bodies big enough to drive a car through. Unfortunately, it was three stories up.

Not that it made a difference. Getting away wasn't the plan. Killing Jo was the plan.

Only Lizzie was doing better at that than I was.

"You got me into this!" she yelled at her doppelganger. "You told me we had no choice!"

"We didn't—"

"Liar! I ended up in jail and you—you ran off to Faerie and forgot all about me. Until you realized you needed a body the Pythian power couldn't trace!"

Another blast, and this time, it almost connected. Instead, Jo dodged to the side, some instinct saving her at the last moment, and the blast aged a patch of road to rubble. She threw a bolt back, but Lizzie countered and the shot went wild. But it gave Jo time to jump back to her feet, and the two started circling each other.

Meanwhile, I began to get a clue.

Jo had needed a body for this fight. Otherwise, she would just be a huge column of energy—her own and all that she'd acquired from her Black Circle friends. Which is not a great idea when dealing with a bunch of hungry ghosts.

But she hadn't wanted to conjure one through Chimera, because Lizzie was right—the Pythian power was looking for her. And while it wasn't a human and might not understand the concept of "jail," it certainly understood "rogue." It would throw me at her wherever she was in history as soon as she showed her face.

So she showed it Lizzie's instead.

I'd even considered the idea myself: one of my reasons for executing Lizzie had been so she couldn't be used by Jo. I just hadn't realized: she already had been. Jo must have cast Chimera or Lizzie sometime in the last two weeks, allowing for the creation of two Lizzies: one to stay in that cell and die, and one for Jo to shift out of there and then possess, giving her the perfect camouflage.

It was pretty smart, because no one realized how much power Jo had. As a human, she'd been limited to an acolyte's abilities, which would leave her at a significant disadvantage next to a Pythia. And as a ghost . . . well, I'd thought she'd go begging for power, like most ghosts did. Not feasting on the Black Circle's vast stores.

But she had, and as a ghost she didn't have a limit. She could absorb as much as they'd allow, and they'd apparently allowed a lot. Giving her the strength to freeze time in that cell, liberate Lizzie, and not have the Circle's guards be any the wiser. Just like she'd probably stepped out of her body tonight to cast Shards, before calling in her ghost troops.

But by dragging Lizzie into this, she'd also done something else. She'd given up some of her power to her twin. A fact she was currently regretting.

"I helped you," Jo snapped. "And this is how you repay me?"

"Helped me?" Lizzie sneered. "You only broke me out because you needed a body! You never cared about me—"

"Cared?" Jo's face flushed dark enough that I could

see it, even in the terrible lighting. "What, did you think we were besties? Was I supposed to make you a friendship bracelet or some shit? We made a deal—"

"A terrible deal!"

"—one that got you out of *prison*—"

"I was only in prison because I believed you! I trusted you!"

"—and I saved your fucking life! And now you're going to fight me for *her*?" She flung out an arm. "She *killed* you!"

They both looked at me.

I felt a little dizzy.

"She showed me more compassion than I ever got from you, or anybody, ever!" the real Lizzie snapped. And then she laughed. "Doesn't that say everything about my life? The woman who killed me was the kindest I ever knew! It hurt her to do it, while you go around killing people left and right, because you don't care about anybody but yourself! You *bitch*!"

This time, the two women's spells met overhead, a glistening, gleaming arc of power, like a clear rainbow. Until the deadly foam started to boil along the edges. A second later the surrounding bodies had a few thousand extra holes in them, allowing tiny beams of moonlight to spear down through the ruined flesh. And to give me flashbacks to the training salle at Gertie's.

I started furiously checking myself, but I was all right. I guessed the two Lizzies were, too, because they were back to sniping at each other. I stayed down, hugging the ground, hoping they'd forget about me, and stretched out a hand.

And remained like that for a moment, trying to follow Pritkin's advice and feeling like an idiot, because nothing was happening!

Masters could draw blood particles, and therefore power, through the air, as easily as biting someone. But I was no master—or incubus, either. And that was the problem, I realized. Both creatures had a conduit into someone else's power: blood or sex, it didn't matter, as long as you had an in.

I didn't.

Pritkin hadn't realized: I may have drawn power from

him last night, but it had been through the conduit he'd opened between us—or that his starving incubus had. I didn't have that ability, and without it, Jo could have all the magic in the world, but I couldn't touch it.

I needed a plan B.

I started poking Billy.

"Drugged half out of your mind, for weeks, is a great way to get some damned perspective," Lizzie was saying. "I realized that all you ever cared about was yourself—and helping that creepy-ass mage to finish making his stupid golems—"

"Shut up!" Jo growled.

"—that's what they're planning, you know," Lizzie told me, causing me to freeze halfway to my feet. "Distracting you so they can stuff a bunch of ancient demons in some big fey rock things. I don't know what you call them—"

"Manlikans," I said, my eyes blowing wide.

"Yeah, that's it. They plan to trap your army in a valley and then turn those things loose to slaughter them all—"

"Shut up or I'll make you shut up!" Jo snapped.

"Then make me," Lizzie said, and fired off a bolt of slow time that Jo shattered in seconds, before sending back some kind of spell that—

"Lizzie!" I screamed, but it was too late. Her head had just been sheared completely off her body. It rolled like a kicked soccer ball into the wall of slowly moving corpses, the dead eyes fixed and staring, the headless corpse collapsing onto the dirt. Jo turned to me, a snarl on her lips.

"Chimera," she said, in Lizzie's voice.

And then there were two.

I burst out laughing, a hysterical giggle, and stumbled back a step. Even Jo seemed taken aback. I guess she'd forgotten: she was in Lizzie's body. If one half of the Chimera spell died, the soul merely snapped back into the other. Like I had done after my duplicate was killed in Gertie's training salle.

The new Lizzie smiled at me, like nothing surprising had happened. And I guess, for her, it hadn't. If Agnes had used Gertie's style of training for her court, this was probably old hat to them. The only difference was that they were working without a net this time.

I was working to keep down my dinner.

"Jonathan found this book, right?" Lizzie said. "In that fey king's library. It was a copy of some old scroll from the age of the gods, giving the names of their children—*all* their children. The fey had never paid it much attention, but he realized: he had a complete list of the monsters the demons call Ancient Horrors.

"And if you have the name of something, you can summon it."

"Holy shit," I said, and she nodded, but not at me. She was keeping an eye on Jo, who was pacing like a caged animal. Probably trying to figure out what to do now.

Or maybe, like me, she was starting to wonder if she'd underestimated Lizzie. Because intentionally or not, she'd created the perfect trap: if Jo stayed in her body, she limited her power to what a human could channel—specifically the human she was now facing, because they were twins. But if she came out of it, to use the full scope of her power, her ghost friends would fall on her like the ravening horde they were.

Dinner bell or no dinner bell, no ghost could resist a feast like that.

I glanced upward, at the surreal wave slowly breaking over us, and when I looked back down, Lizzie was watching me.

Way underestimated, I thought, as she kept talking.

"He came up with a plan to summon the Ancient Horrors, which would get them past the barriers the demon council had put up to contain them, then place them under a compulsion using fey magic, which they don't know. Then hey, presto! A force tailor-made to fight the army you've been creating.

"In fact, it might have been what gave creepy mage his next big idea. 'Cause demons can't really fight in Faerie. Sure, he could turn them loose to terrorize earth and keep you guys busy, but you might still invade. One of his early test subjects, from a Horror whose name was already known, was sent to disrupt the invasion force, but you lot took it down—"

"Kulullû," I said, as Billy poked a sleepy head out of his necklace.

And cursed vividly.

But he'd learned a few things since last time, and I didn't have to tell him to slip inside my skin. I just had to tell him what I wanted, and feel his shock and then agreement before he shot out of me again. Off on an errand that I wasn't sure even he could do.

"Yeah, that was it," Lizzie agreed, her eyes flickering slightly as she watched him go. But she did nothing to draw Jo's attention, whose eyes never left her face. "So they came up with the idea to put them in the manlikans, to make huge golems out of them. Then your demon army would be met by their demon army—and they had bigger demons."

A lot bigger, I thought sickly.

"So everything was great, except for one small problem: creepy mage couldn't open the book!"

"It was guarded by an Ancient Horror," I said, thinking of the gaseous cloud that had shredded the fey forces in the shopping mall. And then went on to terrorize the Shadowland.

Lizzie nodded. "Yeah, a pretty nasty one. The mage didn't think he could take it, but he couldn't read the book until it was out of the way. So they thought, you know what? Maybe a goddess could open it. So creepy mage disguises himself as this shop owner—"

So evil Santa really was evil, I thought.

"—and gets the book to you. They hoped you'd open it there and then, and fight the demon while they made off with the book. But instead—"

"I took it to the covens," I said, remembering.

"Yeah, it was awesome. You take it to some hidden fey enclave that nobody can find, and then you leave it there! And while they're looking for it, you go tell the demons all about it—who of course send one of their people to retrieve it. And get this—this is the best part. The demon they sent thought, you know what? Why take this thing to the council and get a pat on the head when I could take it to Aeslinn instead? So he did! Creepy mage was *furious*."

"But . . . wasn't that what he wanted to have happen?" I asked, confused.

She laughed. "Hell, no. Jonathan had delusions of

grandeur. After all, if he had an invincible army, what did he need with the fey? Or the Black Circle? Or anyone?"

"He was a fool," Jo suddenly snapped. "Thought he was going to rule Faerie and use all its magic for himself—"

"Better than what you planned," Lizzie said. "She's crazy," she told me. "I didn't know it for sure until we shared body space. But thoughts leak over—"

"I'm not crazy!" Jo snapped. "I thought you of all people would understand. Look how you were treated—"

"Which makes me hate my family, not want to blow up the timeline!" Lizzie snapped back. She looked at me, and her face subtly changed. And her voice, when she spoke, was softer. "Shards, if misused, will destroy everything. She basically took pieces of the timeline and threw them at another piece of the timeline. It's all unraveling."

"I know."

"So you have a plan?"

"I have . . . kind of a plan."

"Good. That's more than I do," she said. And stabbed Jo.

It shocked me, because that wasn't what I'd meant at all. It looked like it shocked Jo, too, because everybody was right: she was a lousy dueler. Specifically, she'd forgotten Gertie's rule about not disdaining plain old human weapons.

They can surprise you.

Jo looked damned surprised.

For a split second, that is, before the pretty face went slack and she rose up out of the dying woman, a column of silver-gold energy as bright as the sun and as tall as an office building. She boiled right through Lizzie, turning her to ash in an instant, before I could even scream. Before whirling around again, this time toward me.

And then it got worse.

Because another familiar voice rang out, down the empty street. One that had my heart seizing in my chest. Hilde, I thought. You didn't.

But she must have, because a section of the wall of bodies was suddenly blown out. And in the smoking remains, among the charred and burning flesh, stood a slender figure in a white lace dress. "Touch her and die."

"Rhea!" I screamed. "No!"

But it was too late. Jo turned on a dime, either because of the anguish in my voice or because, from her perspective, I was all but done for anyway, just awaiting the coup de grace. But she didn't know what this new threat was, what she could do.

But I did, and it wouldn't be enough.

Jo surged back down the street and I threw out a hand, desperately trying to throw a spell I knew I didn't have the power for.

And I was right.

But someone else did. Someone who must have gotten Billy's message after all, and cast a spell he shouldn't have known, because it had been outlawed for five hundred years. But he was Pritkin, so of course he did.

*Nodo D'Amore*, I thought, as a huge pulse of power slammed into me, enough to knock me off my feet. Because I might not have the power to drain Jo, but the Prince of the Incubi certainly did. And right now, his power was mine.

I tightened my grip, and power surged up my arm. It felt the way it had once in the ghost realm known as the Badlands, when I'd been reclaiming some of my strength from a bunch of thieving ghosts. That had been my power; this was not. But this would do.

I got back to my feet and *pulled*.

Jo hadn't noticed the first little sip, which had barely been a drop in the vast ocean of her power, but she noticed that one. The great head turned around again, with a horrible sound that shuddered through my body and vibrated the road underneath my feet. And then she came flying back at me.

And, suddenly, I understood how mother had fought all those demons. The coil of power around my left arm fed me, while leaving my right free to throw spell after spell, draining Jo of her power even while attacking her. I also understood why mother had enjoyed it.

Euphoria spilled through me from the rush of more power than I'd ever felt in my life. The pretty facade of a nearby house crumbled into a pile of ancient bricks as a huge patch of road churned and broke and cracked down the middle, as a hundred leaping bodies disintegrated into a cloud of powder and a rattle of falling bones. And I laughed and laughed and laughed, understanding at last how all those dark mages got addicted. This was the best feeling ever!

And, unlike the mages, I wouldn't pay a price for it, because Pritkin was made to absorb multiple forms of energy. Incubi were the universal solvent! I could do this all night!

But the world couldn't, I realized, as reality shivered around us. And while I could fight Jo now, I couldn't beat her. I didn't have any place to store all that power. I could use it, letting it flow through me, expending it on spell after spell as soon as I got it. But I couldn't drain her, not in time.

And it wouldn't do any good to duel until time itself fell apart!

She didn't have to overcome me to win, I realized. She just had to stall me. And she was doing a damned good job, because, as I kept telling everybody, I wasn't my mother.

Fortunately, I didn't have to be.

I threw a final spell, deflected the response, then stumbled, letting Jo think she had an advantage. She dove; I held position, letting her get as close as I could, to the point that all I could see was a glittering wall of white. Then I shifted—to Rhea.

I grabbed my courageous, idiotic, suicidal acolyte and shifted again, this time to the rooftop where the other acolytes had congregated, I guess to maintain their slow time spell.

It looked like it was wearing on them—good.

"Drop it," I gasped.

"What?" Hilde stared at me, apparently having trouble keeping up.

"Drop it, drop the spell, do it, do it now!"

They dropped the spell, finally releasing Jo's huge ghost army.

Who promptly rang the dinner bell, one last time.

# Epilogue

"Now, this is what I call a party!" Billy Joe yelled.

He'd somehow talked Hilde and poor, gullible Emilio into using Chimera to conjure him up a temporary body— I strongly suspected by playing up his part in saving the world. As a result, he was currently a curly-haired vamp clone, who'd been belting back margaritas for the past hour. He was, he had informed me gleefully, intending to get very, very drunk.

I wondered how long it would take him to figure out that vamps are basically immune to alcohol.

But at least he was enjoying himself. I just wished I could say the same. But the kitchen was so crowded that I could barely move, and so loud that I couldn't hear myself think. There were eight blenders all going full blast, and the sound of crushing ice drowned out pretty much everything else.

I tried to ask Tami a question, but found a tray of glasses shoved into my chest before I could.

She looked a little crazed, maybe because this was the first party we'd had in the new digs. It was supposed to be a simple housewarming/glad-we're-all-still-alive kind of thing, but the guest list had gotten a little out of hand. Which was why she was in the kitchen, supervising the guys, who had sleeves rolled up and aprons on and were valiantly trying to make enough drinks and hors d'oeuvres to go around.

"Go!" she yelled, pushing me at the door. "Circulate!"

I went.

I didn't think the guy I was looking for was in there anyway.

The rest of the suite was just as crowded. I made my

way over to where Mircea, Marlowe, and the consul were
standing, off to one side of the huge living room. The
consul was one of the chief reasons we were so jam-
packed, since +1 wasn't a concept she understood. It was
more like +200, but at least she'd opted for a killer LBD
instead of the usual slithering sheath.

Baby steps.

"Refill?" I bellowed, because the older initiates had
taken over the stereo and appeared to be techno fans.

The sound abruptly cut out, probably because Marlowe had just thrown a little device on the ground. It created a bubble of peace, an oasis of tranquility in all the
noise. I breathed a sigh of relief.

"Thank you," Mircea said. "But I have not finished
this one yet. It has an . . . unusual . . . flavor."

I checked out his glass. "It's chocolate. Fred was ex-
perimenting."

"About Fred," Marlowe began, trying to look charming.

"Don't even."

The charm evaporated. "He's my best man!"

"Something you should have thought about before you
sent him to spy on me."

I should have figured it out before Mircea told me, as
part of his new honesty offensive. Marlowe had been bug-
ging my rooms—and sometimes my person—practically
since I got this job, but Pritkin had been finding and removing the spells. So Marlowe had gotten sneaky and
sent a physical spy instead.

And he'd sent a good one.

*I found Fred on the terrace, the night after Jo almost
destroyed everything, smoking a cigarette. On anyone
else, the red embers would have cast an ominous light
over his face, making him appear a little sinister. But
Fred was just Fred.*

*"People always expect James Bond, you know?"
he said, as I joined him. "But he wouldn't work at all."*

*No, I guessed not. But the bumbling, food-
obsessed, crappy dresser, who most people found immediately forgettable, would. It was why he was so
good at his job—well, that and the fact that he was*

*one of the rare vamps who could alter their auras at will, to look like they belonged to any family they chose.*

"For what it's worth, I'm sorry," he said, and looked it. "I know it doesn't make a difference, but I wanted you to know that."

"You seem awfully tenderhearted for a spy," I pointed out.

He shook his head. "Not normally. Most of the people I go after . . . but you're not like that. And this place—" He glanced around, and in the darkness, his eyes looked liquid. "It's funny, I can look like I fit in anywhere, but this is the first place in a long time that I actually . . ." He blinked suddenly, and looked away. "Well. I'm sorry, is all."

"So, you'll be going back with Santiago, then? And the others?" Because, while most of my guys were now actually my guys, some had voted otherwise. I'd be sorry to lose them, but Fred . . . Fred hurt. He hurt a lot.

He'd been looking out over the city, but now he turned to blink at me several times. "What?"

"I asked if you'd be going back with the others, or if you'd decided to stay."

It was a simple enough question, but Fred seemed to be having trouble with it. His face kept gyrating around, like he was having some kind of stroke, and then he turned away again. Before abruptly spinning back around and throwing out his hands, sloshing most of the whiskey in his highball onto a nearby bush.

"What?"

"I asked—"

"I know what you asked! You can't be serious! I betrayed you!"

"You did your job. I understand—"

A flurry of more gyrations, both facially and arm-wise, cut me off. "Don't understand! Rant at me! Rave! I deserve it! I've been beating myself up over it for weeks, ever since I overheard that conversation between you and Rian. I'd been piecing things together for a while, but I wasn't sure—not until then.

*Not until you mentioned Arthurian freaking Britain! Then I knew, I knew who Mage Pritkin really was, and what did I do?"*

"Your job," I repeated, because I'd had time to process this. And to realize that Fred was like the rest of us, bumbling around, just trying to figure out what was the right thing to do, and getting it wrong half the time. Like I'd gotten it wrong with Lizzie.

"I executed somebody," I told him. "I didn't want to, I put it off for weeks, agonized over it. But in the end, I did it, thinking it was my duty, that I didn't have a choice. I was wrong, too."

Fred didn't ask any questions. He probably didn't need to. There were plenty of people who knew the story now.

"She was better than I thought her to be," I told him. "Better than anybody did. I thought she was stupid and venal and faithless, and sometimes she was. But she could also be smart and generous and loyal, but I didn't see that until the end, and I got it wrong, Fred. I got it so fucking wrong!"

"You couldn't have known."

"I could. She even told me she'd die an acolyte, but I didn't understand what she meant. She'd already decided what to do then; she knew what Jo was planning, knew what was on the line. But she was in a Chimera spell with her and couldn't be sure what might leak over. So she couldn't tell me, and I didn't see—"

"Cassie—"

"Until it was too late. And I can't even go back and save her! Time was so snarled up there, and everything had to go perfectly—one mistake and I don't know what would be left. Probably nothing! And Lizzie knew that, too. She knew what Jo was like, better than anyone, so she did what she had to do.

"She died an acolyte."

And somehow, I ended up in his arms, and he ended up holding me, and stroking my hair and whispering soothing things that shouldn't have helped, because I didn't deserve them, but that somehow did anyway.

Marlowe could bite me.

"You don't understand," Marlowe was saying now. "I can't simply replace him. His gift—"

"Is his own, to do with as he likes!"

"It damned well isn't!" The dark eyes flashed. "I need—"

He was cut off, to my surprise, by the consul. She'd been looking with distaste at our latest hors d'oeuvres selection, which appeared to be Vienna sausages on a stick with a cheese cube, because I guess we'd reached back-of-the-pantry status. But at that she looked up.

"The Pythia saved your life recently, when your temper got the better of you. The vampire is hers."

She walked off without another word, probably because Caedmon had just come in with a huge coterie of glittering fey, who looked far more interesting than us and our lousy appetizers. Leaving Marlowe behind—for a second. Until he stormed off after her.

"Thanks," I told the real Emilio, who was still holding the tray. "We're good."

"I think we have some pimento cheese left," he offered.

"Yeah, and there's some old olive loaf in the back of the fridge. Maybe Tami could do something with that."

He shook his head. "That went out twenty minutes ago."

He moved off.

Leaving me alone with Mircea, and the small device he pulled out of his coat. It looked like a cellphone, discreet and easily misjudged. Like the man holding it.

*Strangely colored fingers of fire leapt for the heavens, glittering overhead. Mircea and I, on the other hand, were swathed in shadow, on the edge of the forest. Or at least, this version of us was. The other was us up ahead, on the rise of ground behind the consul's house, the burning couture turning our bodies into silhouettes against the flames.*

*"You could kill him," I said, watching the dragon-coated mage climb the hill at the consul's side.*

*We'd flashed back to the night Jonathan had come here in order to spy on the senate's plans and to set me up. Because if he couldn't drain Faerie as he'd hoped, he'd drain me instead. Only he couldn't if somebody drained him first.*

*Like the master vampire at my side.*

*"You could do it right now," I repeated, even though I knew he wouldn't. And that it would disrupt the damned timeline anyway, so we couldn't. But a girl could dream.*

*The bastard had hurt so many people, disrupted so many lives. And that was just by loosing Jo on us! God knew what he was planning next.*

*But Mircea had another idea.*

*"My daughter will kill him, when this is done," he murmured. "You have my word on that. But in the meantime, he can be . . . useful."*

*"And the golems he made? You're just going to leave them there?"*

*"We know where they are, but our enemies do not know that we know. They will stay on patrol, day after day, waiting for an army that will never come."*

*"But we could go back, destroy that book at least—"*

*"And prevent them from ever being made, yes. But the names are still out there, known to some in the demon lands. Harder to assemble that way, but still possible. And our enemies now have demon allies."*

*I remembered the little thing in the tank in Adra's office. Kulullû, Kulullû was all it had been able to say. But that would be enough.*

*We watched the foursome talk, and then the mage walk away, back toward the house. Mircea started after him, but I caught his arm. "If he notices—"*

*"He won't."*

And I guess he hadn't. Because the tiny charm Mircea had managed to plant on him was doing its thing, as indicated in the cellphone-looking device he held. But it was more than just a tracking spell. It was a locus—one that would allow us to open a portal into lands where that was supposed to be impossible.

And bring through an army the fey would never expect.

"This could end it," Mircea murmured, his eyes going

to the strange creature Augustine had been protecting. His small, lumpy head was almost invisible, being surrounded protectively by a group of coven leaders—the ones not aligned with Jonathan. That included the impressive-looking woman I'd met at the train station and the girl with the antlers in her hair.

They'd been reluctant participants in the attack at the consul's, although not out of bigotry or hate. But because they were afraid that I'd guessed their great secret. The little lumpy guy wasn't, as Augustine had thought, an overworked sweatshop employee. He was one of the original fey, the oldest of all the races, the ones the gods had never had a chance to tinker with because they'd never known they existed.

His kind had fled to earth at the first sign of trouble, afraid that the arrival of the gods meant the end of fey culture, which they were determined to preserve. They'd partnered with the covens ever since, teaching them their magic, crafting their armor and weapons, and sharing with them their one very special gift: the ability to bend ley lines.

Not to a ridiculous extent, and not by the application of great amounts of magic. But by simply coaxing them from their beds, slowly tugging them a little here or a little there. Until they went somewhere they had never been before, allowing the covens to create things like an enclave in the desert, far from where any ley line was supposed to be.

And for us to reach the locus that Jonathan was unwittingly providing, straight into the heart of Aeslinn's kingdom.

"It could," I agreed, as Caedmon swept past the consul and everybody else, zeroing in on the tiny creature.

At which point we were gifted with the sight of the towering king of the fey, glowing bright against the dim light of the room, dressed in velvets and jewels and a golden circlet on his brow, stumble and almost fall in shock, because he'd been told but hadn't believed it.

He went down on one knee in front of the wizened little thing in the Augustine T-shirt. And, for a moment, I thought he was going to cry. I guess the tiny old guy did, too. Because when Caedmon bowed the glowing blond head, the wizened old fey patted him awkwardly on one shoulder.

"Cassie," Mircea began, and this time, his voice was different. The smooth operator of a second ago was gone, along with the honeyed tones of the man I knew. There was a new urgency in the voice, an impatience that I was starting to think of as symbolic of the new man—or maybe the old reborn. Mircea the Bold was returning.

"I'll take you back," I told him. "I'll take you to Elena."

There was silence for a long moment. I was still watching the fey, all of whom were now bowing, half of them looking like they'd seen a ghost—or a myth. But when it dragged on too long, I glanced at Mircea.

And if I'd had any doubts, there it was, written all over his face.

Yeah, he still loved her, whether he knew it or not.

"I'm not promising anything," I added, because I knew him. "I won't change time for you. But we'll take a look and see what's feasible."

I started to leave, but he caught my arm, almost making me spill my tray of drinks. *"Why?"*

Because I love you and don't want to have to kill you, I didn't say, although it was true. But so was something else. "I know what it is to lose someone—and to get him back. If I can give you that, I will."

This time, he let me go.

*Fires burning on all sides, shards of time exploding in the sky, raining down strange shadows that dissipated before they hit the ground, war mages everywhere. Some were staring at the heavens in confusion. Some were trying to pull me away to join the mind-wiped masses now sequestered in safe zones. And some were watching in awe as Gertie and what looked like a hundred acolytes appeared and disappeared, their pale dresses bright against the night as they stepped confidently in and out of the renewed timeline, quickly putting the street back together.*

But the one person I most wanted to see was no-where in sight.

I finally found him inside the ruined pharmacy, cursing at a doctor, while nine war mages attempted to hold him onto a stretcher he clearly didn't need. Something made obvious when half of them abruptly went flying. And then he saw me.

And suddenly Pritkin quieted down, as if he hadn't just been throwing people around the room and roaring. "Like a damned lion!" the doc muttered, finally managing to get a sling on what looked like a badly broken arm.

"My lion," I whispered, hugging him.

And I shifted.

Ready to find
your next great read?

Let us help.

**Visit prh.com/nextread**